MY
FATHER
SITS
IN
THE
DARK

and other selected stories

Books by Jerome Weidman

MY FATHER SITS IN THE DARK

AND OTHER SELECTED STORIES

Jerome Weidman

RANDOM HOUSE
New York

First Printing
Copyright © 1961 by Jerome Weidman
All rights reserved.

Published simultaneously in New York by Random House, Inc.,
and in Toronto, Canada, by Random House of Canada, Limited.

Library of Congress Catalog Card Number: 61-8955

The author and publishers of MY FATHER SITS IN THE DARK and OTHER
SELECTED STORIES are grateful to the editors of the following periodicals:

Story Magazine, The New Yorker, Mademoiselle, The American Mercury,
Good Housekeeping, Harper's Magazine, Decision, Cosmopolitan,
Woman's Home Companion, Today's Woman.

Manufactured in the United States of America
by The Colonial Press Inc.
Designed by Betty Crumley

TO WOLCOTT GIBBS

1902-1958

Introduction

BY JEROME WEIDMAN

There are, in the lives of most people, bad years and good years. For the author of these notes 1932 was both.

On January first of that year, a dismal day in any year for even the most optimistic of citizens, I found myself trapped by an impulse that several decades of more crowded living have led me to believe is sufficiently widespread almost to justify the use of the word universal: I took stock of my life. It was neither a lengthy process nor a cheering one.

My worldly goods consisted of the clothes on my back and a few scraps of furniture that littered—even now I find it impossible to think of these objects as "decorating"—the Bronx tenement flat I shared with my parents. I had a job, which was of course more than could be said for far too many people in 1932, but it brought me no joy and only the most approximate equivalent of what is known, rarely with strict accuracy, as a living.

A firm of certified public accountants on Seventh Avenue, needing an office boy, a junior auditor, and a stenographer, but being unable in those depressed days to afford three employees, had resorted to the simple solution of advertising for someone who could, and was willing to, perform the duties of all three. I knew nothing about auditing, but with the help of a couple of books borrowed from the public library I had taught myself to use a typewriter and write an approximation of Pitman shorthand, and then as now the talents needed to empty wastepaper baskets and carry cardboard containers of coffee were not beyond any reasonably able-bodied male. A certain amount of desperate rather than skillful lying about my totally nonexistent knowledge of accountancy filled, at least temporarily, the major gap in the advertised requirements. To resort, for purely historical purposes, to one of the great clichés of the period: P.S. I got the job.

The salary was twelve dollars a week. Of these, six went to my mother—off the top, as they say in the theatre—for my board and keep. With the other six I managed to buy my clothes, pay for my lunches, and underwrite my simple, perhaps I should say primitive, social life. Who, as Mr. Gershwin had just with lyrical brilliance asked a reeling world, could ask for anything more?

The answer, on January 1, 1932, was depressingly simple: I could.

Life, which I was being told daily on the radio can be beautiful, was all too apparently hideous. Other men were flying the Atlantic with ping-pong balls stuffed into the wings of their planes; girls with nothing more than ice skates and cute figures were winning gold medals at the Olympic games in Lake Placid; a physicist named Harold C. Urey up at Columbia was discovering something called deuterium; and a group of energetic promoters were putting the finishing touches to an office building at the corner of Thirty-fourth Street and Fifth Avenue that rose somewhat improbably one hundred and two stories into a sky that was clearly smiling everywhere on men with dreams in spite of the fact that Great Britain had just abandoned the gold standard and half the counties in Kansas were declaring a moratorium on taxes in a desperate attempt to save the state's farmers from bankruptcy.

Everybody, or so it seemed, was doing something and getting somewhere. What was I doing? Emptying wastebaskets for my inferiors and running hot coffee from Liggett's for my masters. Where was I going? Nowhere. The galling fact had to be faced: my life was not only a failure; it was over. Why, as the embittered heroines in all those Warner Bros. movies to which I was then addicted used to say in the penultimate scene before the hero broke in the door, why prolong the agony?

There was only one way out. Better men than I had taken it. At long last I could understand why. When the moment of truth came, Socrates had not hesitated. The least I could do—God knew, in my long and utterly wasted lifetime, I had never done much more than the least—was emulate my betters. I was nineteen.

The next day, while distributing the ten o'clock containers of coffee to the girls in the office steno pool, an odd thing happened.

The fact that I was still around the next day was not due to the fact that I did not want to slight any of the traditions attached to my decision and, as a result, had postponed action until I could locate somebody named Asclepius to whom I owed a cock, but rather to a trait in my character of which I am not particularly proud: a tendency toward prudence.

All my life I have admired the rash and the impetuous, those romantic leapers-to-their-feet who never ask the whys and wherefores, or indeed the precise location of the fire to which, usually with somebody else's hose or bucket, they rush off as soon as—not infrequently before—the alarm is sounded. My embarrassing inclination is to ask nervously not only where the fire is, but also whether the alleged conflagration might not conceivably be nothing more than the fine glow in somebody's intoxicated eye.

It was this kind of nervous self-questioning that prevented me from acting at once on the decision I had reached the day before when the year 1932 had begun and my life had ended. I had no answers to my questions. Not, that is, until I started distributing those ten o'clock containers of coffee on the morning of January second.

As I handed them around, I became aware that one girl was recounting for the others an incident she had witnessed less than forty-eight hours earlier when, in the company of an admirer, she had helped welcome the arrival of the New Year in a crowded Brooklyn hotel dining room at, as she put it, "four and a half bucks a head." Perhaps because, like most people who are about to depart this life, my senses were more alert to matters I had never before paid much attention to, I found myself becoming quite excited by a combination of two curious facts: the girl who was talking seemed totally unaware that the incident she was describing was basically unpleasant, and she did not seem to grasp that the other girls were not really listening to her account of it.

The most interesting aspect of the experience, however, was that I was not puzzled by my excitement. It seemed perfectly natural because it stemmed from a sudden knowledge—where the knowledge came from I could not say, and at the moment I did not care —that I could fix what was wrong with that girl's performance. I knew—deep down in whatever physical or mental recesses harbor my deepest convictions I was all at once absolutely certain—that I could take this unpleasant, yet attractive because it was well formed, incident and make it seem so attractive that those disinterested girls would become interested in it.

I did not know then what I was to learn through tedious experience later, namely, that the incident struck me as well formed because it was that great rarity, a casually overheard fragment that has a beginning, a middle, and an end. In short, it was not an incident at all. It was a story.

I carried my excitement into the back room, where, at a small desk between the ceiling-high metal bins of ledgers, I was paid, after the wastebaskets were emptied and the containers of coffee distributed, to perform my secretarial duties. Writing in shorthand, so that anybody, especially my boss, coming through the room would have no reason to suspect I was engaged in anything other than the company's affairs, I managed, perhaps because most of the words I used were not mine but the girl's, to set the incident down on paper in a little less than an hour.

The remainder of the day was an agony of waiting: I could write the story under the eyes of my boss, but I could not type it until he and all the other employees had gone home.

It was almost seven-thirty when I sat down at my typewriter. People who had jobs in 1932 suffered from a tendency to put in more hours than they were paid for, in the hope that, as the depression deepened and staffs were cut, their devotion to duty would be remembered and help move them lower on the inevitable list of those to be fired. This fear, with which like everybody else in that office I had for so long lived, vanished as I transcribed my Pitman squiggles into typewritten words. When the transcription was finished, I held in my hand what, after almost three decades, still seems to me, an admittedly prejudiced commentator, one of the more satisfying things the human animal can produce: a finished story.

I was so satisfied that I almost resented considering the question that at once presented itself: What was I going to do with it?

The more obvious answers, some profane and all obvious, did nothing to diminish my feeling of excitement. I had done something, I was convinced, that merited the plaudits of the multitude. The only problem was how to make the multitude aware of what I had done. At nineteen all problems are not only large—how to commit suicide in a manner worthy of Socrates; how to attract the attention of the entire world—but also soluble.

The solution to this one was supplied, somewhat surprisingly, by my boss, a compulsive reader who, it occurred to me years later, might just conceivably have been a perceptive critic. "Here, you can throw this out," he said to me irritably one afternoon as he handed over the copy of *Look Homeward, Angel* he had sent me out to buy the day before because he had read a glowing reference to it in one of the innumerable magazines to which he subscribed as industriously and pointlessly as other men subscribe to profanity. "Throw it out?" I said in horror. "You mean you don't *like* this book?" My boss made a short, sharp gesture of annoyance as he said, "For God's sake, I was writing compositions in that kind of English when I was in high school." What, I asked myself with contempt dripping from each unspoken word, what could you expect from a Philistine who felt I was worth only twelve dollars a week?

Quite a lot, I discovered twenty minutes later as I shuffled through the unread, in most cases still unwrapped, magazines that were stacked like cordwood on the table in his office, in the hope of finding one that might be interested in the story I had just typed. All, however, were so forbiddingly impressive in one way or another— they had been founded by people like Benjamin Franklin, or edited by names that sounded as though they were printed in Latin around the edges of coins, or were read by millions—that I could not quite see any of them as the proper frame for my four-page, beautifully typed but still merely four-page, manuscript.

I was about to give up when, near the bottom of the pile, I found something that looked promising. It was clearly not a magazine and yet, even though it was even more clearly a four-page newspaper, it did not look like any newspaper I had ever seen. The front page, I discovered with interest, was devoted to two short stories, both almost exactly the same length as the one I had just written. I carried it back to my desk, copied the address under the masthead onto an envelope, helped myself to the proper postage from the office stamp box, dropped the envelope down the mail chute, and on the subway ride home I calculated that, allowing one day for the envelope to reach 55 Fifth Avenue, one day for the manuscript to be read, and one day for the reply to reach me, the entire transaction should take three days.

I was wrong. Two days later, in my Bronx mailbox, I found a note that ended with the typewritten words: "The Editors." Above this appeared a single sentence: "We like your short story and are accepting it for publication in the *American Spectator*."

Aside from my miscalculation about the length of time that would elapse before I heard from the magazine, I saw nothing at all unusual about the entire transaction. As I said, I was nineteen.

I was also in the grip of an emotion I did not quite understand. I worked on it without success all the way downtown in the subway and for most of the morning. Toward noon I had it. I looked up the *American Spectator* in the phone book, called the number, and asked the girl who answered if her employers paid for the contributions to their publication. They certainly did, she said, and wanted to know why I had asked. I told her. She urged me to hold on for a few moments while she looked something up. When she came back on the phone she uttered nine words that changed my life as suddenly and irrevocably as the eruption of Krakatoa changed the geography of the Sunda strait.

"Your check for ten dollars will be mailed today."

I stepped out of that phone booth with a feeling that I am convinced was not unlike the feeling with which Dreyfus stepped out of his Devil's Island cell when word came that the hideous farce was over at last. Wrapped in my new and exhilarating sense of freedom, I did not walk into the office of my boss, punch him in the nose, and walk out. I am, as I have already reported, a prudent man. Even in 1932, when body and soul could be kept in fairly close contact on six dollars a week, a check for ten was not the wealth of the Indies.

It was, however, something infinitely more important, something I sensed on that extraordinary day that writers, painters, sculptors, creative people of every kind must have been discovering for more years than I could imagine, namely, that the artist is the only truly free man. With his imagination and his hands—in my case with the help of a pencil and a pad of paper—he breaks the gyves that bind his less fortunate brethren to the treadmill of dreary breadwinning. He is not, of course, free from the necessity of earning that bread. But it is the manner of the earning that sets him apart. Perhaps only a young man would grasp this at once, in a blinding moment of discovery, like Saul on the road to Tarsus. I grasped it so clearly that, even though I was still blinded as I left that phone booth, I nonetheless saw clearly that while others less fortunate would have to continue to do the bidding of those in authority who could withhold or limit the amount of their daily bread, I would not. I had just joined a select company. My waste-basket-emptying days were over. Or at least numbered.

I returned to my desk in the back office and, after a brief interval of thought, set down in my Pitman squiggles another story. That night, after running it through the typewriter, I sent the manuscript off to the *American Spectator*. I did this every day for a week, toward the end of which I began to be troubled by the fact that "The Editors," who had been so prompt with their reply to my first offering, had been silent for seven—no, eight! Then nine! And ten! And eleven!—full days.

On the twelfth, unable to continue living with the suspense—or the five additional manuscripts I had accumulated but decided not to send until I had some news of what was happening to the seven I had, since my initial triumph, mailed down to 55 Fifth Avenue— I decided to write and ask what was happening. Having reached this decision, I did not quite know how to act on it. How did one address a letter to a publication the editors of which, according to their masthead and stationery, were George Jean Nathan, Ernest Boyd, Sherwood Anderson, James Branch Cabell, and Eugene O'Neill?

To single one out might be considered a slight by all the others. "Gentlemen" or even "Dear Sirs" seemed cold and unfriendly from a man they had, less than a fortnight before, plucked from the galleys. While I was struggling with the problem, my second letter from the *American Spectator* arrived. It began, a trifle coldly I naturally thought, "Dear Sir." It ended with those now familiar typed two words, "The Editors," which seemed to me, however, because of the paragraph above them, as warm as flowing lava:

"We like all seven of your stories, and to prove it we are buying three, but we must point out that we are a four-page, once-a-month publication. If we ran everything you sent us, there would be very little room, in fact none, for other material, and since we started the *American Spectator* more or less as a forum for our own ideas, this would not only vitiate our original intent but it would also make us resentful of you, and we like your work too much to allow that to happen. We are taking the liberty, therefore, of turning over the four stories we cannot use to the editors of other magazines with whom we are friendly and in whose literary judgment we have sufficient confidence to make us feel that they will buy these stories. If they don't, do not be angry with us. Also, since we will be running your stories several months apart, and we now own four, we hope you won't mind our suggesting that you don't send us any more stories for at least two years."

I did mind, but I followed the suggestion of "The Editors" for a couple of reasons. First, by the time the two years were behind me, the four stories my distinguished but to me unknown friends at the *American Spectator* had sent on to *their* friends had been sold, along with a dozen others, and second, sadly, the *American Spectator* was no longer in business.

I use the word "business" advisedly. It underscores the point these notes are intended to make.

Years after the events described above, when I came to know—much too briefly and never, to my regret, very well—the man to whom this volume is dedicated, I told him late one afternoon over a drink how he had come to buy—he was one of the friendly editors to whom "The Editors" of the *American Spectator* had sent my surplus—the first of my stories to appear in his magazine. He took a thoughtful sip—few of the people who were fortunate enough to know him better than I did realized, I find, how thoughtful a man he was—and said:

"There is abroad in the land a lamentable tendency to confuse failure with quality. The notion that because nobody will buy it, it must be great, is as foolish as the belief that a rookie who can't find the plate is obviously major league material. I'm sure the history of publishing is full of stories about great manuscripts that editors were too stupid to buy. I'm equally sure the word 'full' is an outrageous exaggeration. Human beings make mistakes, and editors are human beings. It's been my experience that, by and large, material that merits publication manages somehow to get published. The boys in the ivory towers are probably doing worthwhile work, but I think it's worthwhile only to themselves, the way an aspirin is worthwhile to a man with a headache. It isn't really art. It's therapy. Therapy for the man in the ivory tower, I mean. It's foolish, even inhuman, to be against that kind of therapy, but it's equally foolish, and to me even more inhuman, to try to foist the treatment on the healthy. What the man up there in the ivory tower produces is worthwhile only when it has value to the man down in the street. When that happens, I take off my hat to him up there, and while I may think he's a little foolish to live in such an odd place when he could afford to come down and enjoy the fun of the rest of the human race, it's a matter of *de gustibus*, and I respect his right to choose his own digs. I ask in return that he respect my right to insist that, if you'll bear with the pun, clarity is all. Comprehensibility is more important than euphony, although if you can achieve both you're doing a better job. Obfuscation, I have found, is the refuge of the second-rater, and life is too short to waste time on second-raters. Always write as well as you can, without ever forgetting how important it is to keep trying to write better than you can, but never forget that writing is a form of communication, probably the noblest form ever invented by the human animal, and for God's sake don't ever stop battling us to pay you higher prices for what you write."

I never did, even though I was then too young to understand all of what he said. Years later, when he was dead, I suddenly grasped, from another man's words, what he had meant.

I had attended the opening night of a play that moved me deeply. So deeply that, when a week later I read in my morning paper that the play had closed, I wrote a note to the playwright, who was a total stranger, telling him not only what I thought of his play but also of a public that could turn its back on so worthy a piece of work. His reply was for me as great a revelation as that moment in the phone booth in 1932 when I learned I was a free man.

"Thank you for your very nice note," he wrote. "I'm glad you liked my play. So did I. Unfortunately, it is not enough for just the two of us to like it."

It has never been enough for me.

Contents

xix

M Y
FATHER
SITS
IN
THE
DARK

and other selected stories

—And Everything Nice

Then she heard the faint whirr and the short, sharp click, and she found herself holding her breath. Because now she knew she was awake, and all at once she was more afraid than she could remember ever having been in all her life.

She did not know how long she had been lying there, not daring to move for fear of waking her husband, who slept restlessly beside her. He was a light sleeper, lighter even than her mother, who would awaken at the first faint hiss from the radiator when the steam came up in the early winter mornings. Her slightest movement would have been enough, and she did not want him to wake up, because if he did, she would have to tell him. It had been easy to fool herself, to keep her eyes closed and remain rigid, pretending that she was asleep.

But now there was no more chance to pretend. She had little more than a few seconds, at most a minute. She was positive about that. Then the alarm would go off and not only would she have to open her eyes and move about, but Harry would wake up, too, and she would have to begin to talk.

Those two little noises, the slight hum of a released spring and the faint slap of one small bit of metal on another, were the warning signals. She knew that clock. For more than seven years it had helped to get her to the office on time. She had learned long ago to gauge those few moments between the time it made those small preparatory noises, like clearing its throat, and the time the bell finally rang, exactly at a quarter after sev—

The alarm went off with a blast that was startling in the small bedroom. Her tense body heaved violently, and the breath she had been unconsciously holding came through her lips in a sharp hiss. She lay there, quivering with terror, listening to the squeaking of the bed and the hideous jangle of the bell.

II

"Gosh," Mildred said for the third time. "This is *gorgeous*. I really don't know how to thank you girls."

She was at her desk, taking out pieces of ruby-red glassware from a huge box in front of her and putting them back again. The others were grouped around her.

"I'm glad you like it," Miss Miller said, smiling. "That certainly is a load off our minds. You wouldn't believe it, the trouble we had trying to figure out what to get you. We even thought of giving you the cash, so you could get yourself whatever you wanted, but we knew a small amount like that would be like a drop in the bucket to you and Harry."

"Oh, go on," Mildred laughed. "What do you think he is, a millionaire?"

"He must be close *to* it, from what you tell us about him. Why don't you have him come up here? Call him up and tell him to call for you tonight. Come on, Mildred, we're dying to see him."

"Not tonight," she said. "He's cleaning things up at his office before we go away. And then, we've got those theater tickets for tonight. But honest, girls," she added brightly, "it's wonderful of you to give me this. I mean it. I'll never forget you and how nice you all were."

"Oh, no, you won't!" Miss Miller laughed. "I'll bet as soon as you come back from your honeymoon, and start fixing your home, and spend your time shopping and all that, you won't even remember there ever was such a thing as an office."

"And we won't blame you either," another girl said, stretching her arms wide and pretending to yawn. "Imagine waking up in the mornings and not having to get up to go to work! Oh, boy, Mildred, you don't know how lucky you are!"

Mildred smiled but did not answer. Suddenly there was a long buzz followed by two short ones.

"It's for you, Mildred," Miss Miller said. "J.T. wants you."

She went in without knocking, as was the custom when he buzzed for somebody. He looked up with a smile from behind his desk and waved his hand toward a chair at one side. "Come in, Mildred," he said. "Have a chair."

When she was seated he reached out and said, "Congratulations. I hope you're getting as good a bargain as he is."

"Thanks, Mr. T.," she said, taking his hand and feeling her face grow red. "I—I think I am."

"That's fine," he said, and was quiet for a few moments while he played with a small envelope he held in his hand. Finally he said, "Have you thought over what I spoke to you about the other day?"

Mildred nodded and said, "Yes."

"Same answer?"

She nodded again, keeping her eyes fixed on her hands.

"Well," he said, with a long sigh, "I'm really sorry, Mildred. You've been with us so long, and your work has always been so satisfactory, that we've sort of grown to depend on you. We're going to miss you a lot."

"You're awfully kind, Mr. T.," she said, "and I'd like to stay. But I can't."

He started to make a gesture with the envelope, but stopped, as though struck by an afterthought. "By the way," he said, "if it's just a matter of a few dollars extra, why, we think enough of you not to quibble. Just say the word, and the raise is yours."

"Thanks a lot, Mr. T.," she said, "but it's not that. It's just that my intended—my husband—he doesn't want me to continue working after we're married."

"Old-fashioned, eh?" he laughed. "Woman's place is in the home and all that?"

"Well, not exactly," she said with a smile. "But something like it, I guess. He says if he couldn't support a wife, he wouldn't get married in the first place. He doesn't want me to work at all after we're married."

"All right, then," he said, sighing again. "I really ought to be angry with him. He's just about knocking the bottom out of my office force."

She felt her face and neck grow warm again, but she said nothing.

"Here's a little something to remember us by," he said, pushing the small envelope toward her. "I hope you're very happy."

"Thanks a lot, Mr. T.," she said, taking the envelope and standing up. "You've been so nice to me, I really hate to leave."

"I wish you weren't," he said. "But I guess it can't be helped."

At the door she turned and made a slight movement with the envelope. "Thanks again, Mr. T."

In the outer office the girls crowded around her with questions.

"What did he say, Mildred? What did he say?"

"Nothing," she laughed. "He just asked me again not to leave, and wished me luck. That's all."

"Did he give you anything? What did he give you?"

She hesitated a moment, clutching the small envelope tightly in her hand. But then she remembered that she had not seen the check inside. J.T. might have been angry with her, and not as generous as he usually was. The check might be for a small amount.

"Nothing," she said.

"Nothing?" they echoed in amazement.

"Well, not exactly," she said, and smiled. "He said I should go out and buy myself anything I wanted and just charge it to him."

"Gee," they breathed. "You certainly are a lucky one, Mildred."

They were still discussing the things she might get, when J.T. rang for Miss Miller. She came out of his office a few minutes before five, with her notebook and some papers.

"You want to do me a favor, Mildred?" she said, holding up the papers. "I've got half a book full of notes, and this report. And J.T. wants it all out tonight. You want to make a copy of the report while I transcribe my notes? It won't take you long. It's only a short one. Two pages. Otherwise I'll never get out tonight."

She did not have to leave early. Even if she left after six o'clock she would still have plenty of time. And she liked Miss Miller and wanted to help her with the report. But she couldn't stay, not after what she had told the girls during the day, and the arrangements she had made with herself.

"Gee," she said, "I'm awfully sorry. You know I'd do it gladly.

But Harry's got those tickets for a show and we're going out to dinner first. I've got to rush home in a few minutes to get washed and dressed and ready on time."

"Oh, sure," Miss Miller said, pleasantly enough. "I forgot you told us. You go right ahead, Mildred, and forget it. I'll get one of the other girls to help me."

In the subway she tried to read her paper, but her mind refused to follow her eyes along the lines of print. She kept thinking of the few short days that were left, and she found herself becoming panic stricken.

She sat up very straight, arching her back against the curve of the seat, and told herself sternly to stop being a fool. There was no sense in losing her head. She wasn't a baby. After all, there couldn't be much she had forgotten, considering the months of careful shopping she had just completed. She would check her list. She knew it by heart. Slowly, and then more quickly, because she knew exactly what she had bought, she ticked off each item mentally. By the time the train came to her station, she had decided that the only thing she had left out was a sachet for the handkerchief box, and in the house, before she sat down to eat, she made a note in the small book she carried in her purse to buy the sachet the very next day.

After supper she yawned and said, "I think I'll take a nap, ma. Wake me up about eight."

Her mother looked up from the dishes. "Isn't Harry coming over tonight?"

"Yes," she said; "about nine."

"So late?" her mother said. "You're going out so late!"

"No," she said. "We're not going out. I guess we'll just sit around and talk. You know."

By a quarter to nine she was carefully arranged in the living room, reading a magazine under the lamp and in the chair that faced the door, so that when Harry walked in he would see her as she wanted him to.

It still lacked a few minutes of nine when the bell rang.

"Hello, hon," he said, coming into the room.

"Hello, Harry," she said, lifting her face for his kiss; then, "You're early."

He sat down on the sofa, facing her. "I know. We took most of the inventory, except for a few odds and ends, so I said I had a date and the other fellows they said, sure, go ahead, we'll finish it up without you. Otherwise I'd never've made it."

"That was nice of them. They're a nice bunch to work with, aren't they?" she said, smiling a little.

"You bet. Nicest bunch of fellows you ever want to meet. You know," he said with a laugh, "it's the funniest thing you ever saw. They're taking up a collection now for the gift they're going to give us. I'm not supposed to know anything about it, but honest, even if I was blind and deaf, I'd know about it. What a bunch," he said, shaking his head and laughing again.

"I wonder what they'll get us?" she said.

"I don't know, but it'll be something nice. I'll bet you on that, all right."

"You know," she said, "I wish they'd make it cash. We could use that better than anything."

It was quiet for a few moments. Then he said, "Come on over here, hon. What do you want to sit way over there for?"

She crossed the room and sat next to him on the sofa. He put his arm around her and she dropped her head on his shoulder. They stared at the lamp for several minutes.

"Happy?" he asked.

"Uh-huh."

"Not sorry about anything?"

"What for?" she asked.

"You know. I mean about having to work for a while yet, till I begin to make more, and—"

She sat up straight and faced him. "Listen, Harry, are we going all over that again?"

"No, no," he said quickly, trying to draw her head back to his shoulder. "I just wanted to—"

But she refused to put her head down again, and continued to look directly at him.

"I wish you'd get this through your head, Harry, once and for all," she said. "I'm marrying you because I *love* you, and not for anything else. Just because you're not making enough money yet doesn't make any difference to me." She spoke quickly but carefully, as though she knew so well what she was going to say next that she was a little afraid the words might come out in the wrong order if she did not watch them. "I've got a good job and I don't mind working also, until you begin to make enough for two. We've talked it over at least eight dozen times if we've talked it over once. I thought it was all settled and over with. Why do you have to keep on—"

"All right, hon, all right," he said soothingly and with a smile, forcing his arm around her. "I'm sorry I said anything. I just wanted to—"

"Well, then, let's forget it," she said, dropping her head back on his shoulder.

"Love me?" he asked softly.

"What do *you* think?" she said, smiling back, and kissed him.

III

Long before the bell stopped ringing she could feel Harry beginning to move. It wouldn't be long now, she knew. And a few minutes wouldn't make any difference. But she kept her eyes tightly closed and her shoulder hunched away from him, pretending to be asleep.

She did not answer when he called to her softly, and he got out of bed and went about his dressing. In a few minutes he came back and shook her gently, saying, "Wake up, hon. It's late."

For a while she allowed herself to be rocked by his hand. Then, after what she considered to be a proper interval, she opened her eyes wide and stared up at him.

"Come on, you sleepy-head," he laughed. "It's almost eight. We'll both have to hurry."

But she made no move to get up.

"Come on," he said, laughing again. "You don't want to be late for work the first day after your honeymoon. You'll get enough kidding without that."

He leaned on the bed, one hand resting on either side of her, and dropped his smiling face toward her, his lips pursed for a kiss. But she drew away from him slightly and sat up, resting on her elbow.

"Harry," she said, "I can't go to work today." She had a moment of fear. It didn't sound right. The tremor she had been mentally rehearsing had not come out so smoothly as she had hoped.

His face stopped moving toward her. The lips relaxed, the smile disappeared, and a worried look took its place.

"What's wrong, hon?" he asked anxiously. "You sick or something?"

For a moment she hesitated. Then she shook off the feeling of fright and began to speak carefully. "No," she said. "I feel all right. But I can't go back there. They fired me the day before we went away. They said they don't believe in keeping married women. I didn't want to tell you before because I didn't want to spoil our honeymoon."

The worried look had left his face, and now it was blank. She reached her arms up around his neck and tilted her face for a kiss. But he pushed himself up from the bed, away from her, and her arms slid down onto the covers.

"I'm sorry, Harry," she said quickly. "It would only have spoiled our trip if I told you before. But it's nothing," she added brightly. "I can get another job easy. I know lots of people in the business."

"That's all right," he said.

He turned away and, seizing his hat, made quickly for the door.

"Harry!" she cried suddenly, fearfully. *"Harry!"*

But he did not turn back. She heard the hurried stamp of his feet going through the kitchen and the foyer. Then the outer door slammed hard, and all that remained was a faint hum from the vibrating window and a slight swaying of the curtain.

My Aunt from Twelfth Street

When I was a child, the strangest thing to me about my Aunt Tessie from Twelfth Street was that she lived on Fifteenth Street. I liked her and she liked me, but I was not permitted to visit her very often because the rest of our family always considered her something of a renegade. She was a large woman, with a quick laugh, a generous purse, and a small tailor shop that her husband had left in her hands when he died, and she baked the largest and best sugar-covered cookies that I have ever eaten. But these virtues were impressive only to me. It was hard for my mother and father and our other relatives to forget that she did not live, by choice, among us.

We were Galicians and lived, quite properly, on East Fourth Street. Sixth Street was almost exclusively Hungarian, Fifth Street was full of Litvaks, Seventh and Eighth Streets were reserved for Russians, and so on. Nobody lived on Twelfth Street.

We all knew Aunt Tessie's explanation for not living with her own people—she said furnished rooms had been cheaper on Twelfth Street than in any other place in the city when she landed in America—but it was disregarded. The difference in rent between Twelfth and Fourth Streets was not enough to excuse such a lapse in nationalistic loyalty. Therefore, in our family she was always referred to, with an uncomplimentary twist of the lips, as Tessie from Twelfth Street.

. Later, when she married the small tailor on Fifteenth Street and moved three blocks uptown to live in a tiny apartment behind the

shop, she was still called that. Even after her husband died, Aunt
Tessie showed no signs of capitulation. "You know Tessie," my father
said with a shrug. "You say black, she says white. As long as she
knows you want her to move to Fourth Street, where she belongs,
she'll spend her life on Fifteenth Street, there, with the Italians and
the Irish. That's Tessie from Twelfth Street for you."

It was hard to understand her loyalty to Fifteenth Street. From
the few glimpses that I had had of her section of it, between Avenue
A and First Avenue, the family accusation of stubbornness seemed
justified. In fact, the street was so cold and dreary-looking, so
shabby and lifeless, that I still don't know why I liked to go there.
Fourth Street, where we lived, between Avenue D and Lewis, was
no Coney Island, but at least it was cheerful and friendly, with
plenty of movement and noise, if nothing else. But on Fifteenth
Street the houses were dirty and old; no children played in the gutter; nobody yelled or laughed; no groups stood on the sidewalks and
gossiped. Fifteenth Street was dead. But I liked it and never seemed
to be able to visit it often enough.

Just after my tenth birthday, however, I was treated to what I considered a windfall. My mother, I was told, was about to "go away for a
while." This puzzling phrase was delivered with a benevolent smile
and later, in translation, proved to mean the addition of a baby sister to the household. The problem of getting rid of me for a few
days became a choice between a Fourth Street neighbor and a Fifteenth Street aunt. Finally, and with reluctance, my parents decided
on the latter.

Arrangements were made several weeks in advance, and one hot
July evening my father delivered me at the small tailor shop with
final instructions to be a good boy.

"Don't worry so much," Aunt Tessie told my father. "We're people here the same as you are on Fourth Street, not wild animals. I'll
take care of him."

She started me off with a handful of her huge cookies and told me
I could stand near the window of the shop and look out into the
street while she prepared dinner.

"Can I go outside and sit on the stoop, Aunt Tess?" I asked.

"No," she said. "We'll be ready to eat soon. You can stand by the
window and look out."

I was puzzled by her refusal. It was too hot to be indoors. But I couldn't disobey her, so I went to the front window and looked out into Fifteenth Street as I munched cookies. There wasn't much to see. The intense July heat had driven more people than usual out into the street, but they seemed curiously listless and disinterested. Occasionally an automobile drove through and once an ice wagon went by, but they did not stop. The only change that the heat seemed to have made in Fifteenth Street was that all the windows were open. I could tell by the way the curtains fluttered in and out whenever a faint breeze found its way into the block. On Fourth Street you could tell when a window was open because someone was almost always framed in it, leaning on a small pillow and usually yelling into the street or to a neighbor a floor or two above or below. But nobody leaned out of the windows on Fifteenth Street. The heat and the inactivity were depressing. I began to wonder why I had looked forward to this visit and by the time my aunt called me to dinner I was wishing I was back on Fourth Street.

After dinner I asked my aunt if I could go outside.

"No," she said.

"But it's so hot, Aunt Tess!" I protested.

"Well," she said, hesitating; then, "All right. Wait till I finish the dishes and I'll go out with you."

When she was ready we carried two folding chairs out onto the stoop and I helped her set them up. She settled herself with her knitting in one of them and I took the other. The dinner hour was apparently over for most of the block, because a surprising number of people were sitting on the stoops of the houses, the men in shirt-sleeves and the women in house dresses, fanning themselves with folded newspapers. There was only one sign of activity on the block. A car was parked at the curb directly across the street from us. A handsome young man, with a tight, dark face and beautifully combed hair, was sitting in the front seat, leaning on the door and talking to three girls who stood on the sidewalk beside the car. The girls were quite pretty, or, rather, they seemed so without hats and in their light summer dresses. And the young man must have been very witty, because every few minutes they would all throw back their heads and laugh loudly at something he had said. Nobody on the block was paying any attention to them. I glanced quickly at my aunt once or twice. But she was engrossed in her knitting. She didn't seem to hear the loud laughter or see the bright little group on the other side of the street. I turned back to watch them.

Just as the sun was disappearing behind the "L" on First Avenue, another young man turned the corner and came down the block. He was carrying his hat and his hair was as thick and handsome and perfectly combed as that of the young man in the car. In fact, he looked almost exactly like the first young man, except that he seemed a little older and he wasn't smiling. He walked up to the car with an insolent swagger and put his foot on the running board and leaned his elbow on the door. The young man in the car smiled up at him and said something and everybody laughed. They talked for another minute or so and then the girls joined in a farewell burst of laughter and walked away, waving once or twice, leaving the two young men with the gleaming hair alone together.

They talked earnestly for a while in friendly fashion. Occasionally the first young man, still seated in the car, would shake his head vigorously or smile. Finally he got out of the car and the two of them started to walk off together toward First Avenue. The first young man continued to shake his head as the other talked and a few times a snatch of his quick laughter came back to me on my aunt's stoop.

Then, suddenly, as I watched them, an amazing thing happened. The second young man pulled something from his pocket, pointed it quickly at the first young man, and there was the single snapping crack of a gun. The first young man jerked himself erect, as though someone had taken him by surprise and poked him sharply in the small of the back, and then he crumpled quickly and fell into the gutter. The murderer ran the few steps to First Avenue, turned the corner, and disappeared.

"Aunt Tess!" I cried, jumping up.

In an instant the motionless block was full of a quivering, voiceless activity. Every stoop was bobbing with silent, swiftly moving people. Nobody yelled; nobody screamed; nobody ran toward the young man in the gutter. My aunt clutched my arm. "Come on," she said sharply. "But Aunt Tess!" "Come on," she repeated, and dragged me toward the door. Windows were being slammed shut all along the block. Both sidewalks were empty and in a moment every stoop was cleared. As my aunt pulled me through the door I had a last glimpse of Fifteenth Street. Except for the crumpled young man in the gutter, it was deserted and quiet.

My aunt hurried into the kitchen, dropped her knitting, and ran back into the store, where I was standing at the window.

"Get away from there," my aunt said.

She pushed me aside roughly and I watched her in amazement as she closed the windows and hauled down the long green shades.

"Aunt Tess, what—?"

"Keep quiet," she said.

She seized my arm again and dragged me into the kitchen, pushed me into a chair beside the kitchen table, and sat down at the other side, facing me. Then she picked up her knitting and began to work quickly. With all the windows shut, the heat was almost unbearable in the small room. The sweat gathered on my forehead and I could feel a thin trickle of it begin to work its way down my spine.

"Aunt Tess," I said, "what—?"

"Don't talk so much," she said.

Her voice was hard and frightened. She had never spoken like that to me before. She continued to knit determinedly, scowling at her nervously working fingers, without looking up and without wiping the sweat from her face.

"But Aunt Tess," I cried, "what happened? They—"

"Shut up," she said.

Not a sound came through to us from the street outside. The sweat was running into my eyes.

"It's hot in here!" I cried. "What—?"

My aunt did not look at me. "Just shut up!" she said.

The Bottom of the Mountain

"Will you have one with us, sir?" The second lieutenant was not drunk but he was not completely sober, either. He looked very young, a boy of twenty-one or twenty-two at the most. There was an airborne flash on the shoulder of his unpressed American uniform that told Crayne, who had never seen him before, almost as much about the boy's recent movements as a less carefully trained observer could have learned from reading all the papers in the boy's pockets. "It's real chartreuse, sir," he said.

He was holding a tall, dark green, dusty bottle as though it were an infant fresh from the delivery room. The girl with him looked even younger. She was very pretty in a shy, almost frightened, breathless, British way. She was quite sober. Crayne would have taken the long end of a reasonable bet that she had never consumed anything stronger than an occasional glass of sherry in the presence of her family, say at Christmas. She and the lieutenant had stopped at Crayne's table, probably because the lieutenant had noticed Crayne's rather obviously American clothes. The British are admirably open-minded about many things, but they have not yet seen the virtues of the shirt with the button-down collar.

"That's very nice of you," Crayne said. "But I'm drinking scotch."

"It's real chartreuse, sir," the lieutenant said. There was a hint of pride in his smile. "I brought it over from Normandy this morning."

D-Day was not so many weeks old that the boy's pride could be considered unjustified or his simple statement unthrilling.

"Thanks," Crayne said. "I'll stick to my scotch."

The boy looked hurt. The girl squeezed his hand reassuringly as they walked back to their own table. Crayne had a moment of anger with himself. It wasn't much to do for an American kid several thousand miles from his home in Iowa or Oregon in the middle of one of the most exciting periods of a great war. Why had he refused to take a drink? The fact that he disliked chartreuse and casual drunks was not the answer. Crayne finished his scotch in a gulp. Apparently it was not as easy as he told himself it was to be facing your thirty-ninth birthday in civilian clothes among kids who wore khaki as though tweeds and double-breasted worsteds had never even been invented.

"Bring me another one of these," Crayne said to the waiter. "Double, please."

The waiter brought the drink. Crayne put the young lieutenant out of his mind. He was not here for fun, even though it was supposed to look that way to the casual observer. Crayne went back to the job of watching the thinning crowd from his side table.

The small downstairs ballroom of the Crescent Hotel in London was not small and it was not downstairs. There were sixty feet of polished dance floor between the ballroom entrance and the bandstand, and diners able to afford the cover charge could reach the ballroom only by climbing a short, ornate flight of stairs from the hotel lobby. It was called the small downstairs ballroom to distinguish it from the larger restaurant at the other side of the lobby, facing the Strand, where the food was the same but the house charge was lower because diners in it could not dance between courses to the expensive rhythms of Cedric Hummert's orchestra. All of London, or rather those parts of it that could pay the price, had been dancing to his music for twenty years. When somebody rang you up and asked you to be in "the Small Downstairs at nine," you didn't have to say, "The small downstairs where?" It meant the Crescent in the Strand. And when you went to the Crescent in the Strand it was not for the food or the drink. You went for Cedric Hummert's music.

"Time, sir," the waiter said. "We're closing the bar. Will you have another, sir?"

Crayne looked at his watch. For the purpose of learning what time it was, the gesture was unnecessary. Since he had taken on this special work for the Colonel, Crayne had acquired a number of interesting skills. One of them was to know always, without having to look at a timepiece, exactly what the hour was. Another was never to indicate unnecessarily, so that an innocent bystander might be impressed into directing his attention toward Crayne, that he possessed these skills.

"Thanks, no," Crayne said. "Bring me my check, please."

The war, which had kept Crayne away from Broadway for nearly three years, had created, or perhaps only awakened, in him a concealed but stubborn patriotism that expressed itself even in small things. Most Americans, after two weeks in London, learned to ask for their bills in restaurants. Crayne, after more than a year, still asked for his check.

"There you are, sir," the waiter said. Crayne picked up his change and pushed a coin back across the table cloth. "Thank you, sir."

Crayne stood up, gave the room a final glance, and moved toward the door. So far as the information the Colonel wanted was concerned, the evening had been a failure. But Crayne was glad to be going. For almost an hour the two small electric signs, in the center of the mirrored panels that flanked the orchestra, had been lighted. Crayne didn't think he was more afraid of the raids than most people in London. It was simply that he did not like to be in the small downstairs ballroom of the Crescent when they were coming over. The room had been done in peacetime by a world-famous decorator who was then in his Oriental Period. There were so many priceless drapes and tapestries on the walls that no sound from outside penetrated to dilute the dance music. Crayne, who had weathered Jap shells and sniper bullets in New Guinea as well as the next man, was all right in London so long as he could hear the sirens. There was something unsettling about being warned that death was overhead by two unobtrusive bits of neon tubing that flashed, discreetly and silently, the almost innocent word "Alert." When he reached the door and put his hand into his pocket for the coat room tab, Crayne realized that he had been jumpy for almost an hour.

"Will you wear it, sir?"

"I'll carry it. Thanks."

Crayne threw the coat over his arm and turned for a last look through the doorway. Very few people were left in the Crescent's small downstairs ballroom. It was late. Three or four couples were still on the dance floor. The waiters were stripping tables of empty glasses and crumpled napkins. The band was playing with the soft finality that meant the next number would be "God Save the King." A young American officer, holding the hand of the girl beside him, stood at the foot of the bandstand, talking to the conductor. Cedric Hummert leaned far down from the platform to hear better. Hummert grinned and nodded and straightened up. The young officer turned. It was the boy with the airborne flash and the dusty bottle.

"Would you take this back for a moment?" Crayne handed his coat to the cloakroom attendant. "Some friends I want to say good night to."

He walked back into the room and sat down as the band broke into "Night and Day." When the lieutenant and the girl reached the table they stopped and looked at Crayne in surprise. He stood up.

"I've changed my mind about that drink," Crayne said. "May I?"

The surprise in the boy's face turned to pleasure.

"You bet, sir." He took an empty glass from the next table, set it beside the two in front of him, and filled all three from the dusty bottle. Crayne pulled out a chair for the girl and they sat down. "To our side, sir," the boy said.

"To our side," Crayne said. "And to our Allies."

"To our side," the girl said. "And to *our* Allies."

Crayne noticed that she touched the glass to her lips but did not drink. He didn't blame her. The stuff was vile. "It isn't much to do for one's country in time of war," the Colonel had said when, months before, he urged Crayne to take on his curious assignment. It wasn't, and Crayne had taken it on. It had not occurred to him then that drinking bad chartreuse would be a part of the odd duties that nobody in all the world, except the Colonel and Crayne, knew Crayne was performing. The orchestra slid into the second verse. Under the table the lieutenant and the girl were holding hands. The band stopped.

"Great tune," the boy said. "I asked Mr. Hummert to play it for us."

"It's terribly sweet of him," the girl said. "He's such a nice man."

"Yes," Crayne said. "Very."

The boy waved toward the band and Hummert grinned and waved back. The orchestra stood up to play "God Save the King" and Crayne and the lieutenant and the girl rose. When it was over, the musicians snapped off the lights over their music stands and began to pack their instruments. Hummert jumped down from the platform and lighted a cigarette as he came across the deserted dance floor toward them.

"I asked him to have a drink with us," the boy said. He moved forward a step and took Hummert's extended hand. "Thank you, sir," he said. "That was really swell."

"Glad you liked it," Hummert said. "Hello, Crayne."

"Oh," the boy said. "You know each other?"

"Know each other?" Hummert laughed as he pulled over a chair and sat down. The laugh was like his clothes and his manner: very good, very smooth, the best that money and careful study could produce, yet a little too full, just a shade too flashy. "I've known Crayne for donkey's years, long before he got to be a big-shot Broadway columnist. Why, I knew Crayne when he was just a cub reporter around the big street." He nudged Crayne and laughed again. The lieutenant looked at Crayne with quick interest. "I'm just a New York boy myself," Hummert said. He wasn't. He came from Mapleton, Ohio, but, after twenty years in London, he pretended, perhaps after two decades of self-deception he even believed, that he was a native New Yorker. Most people mistook him for an Englishman. Hummert did not correct them unless someone like Crayne, who knew he was not, happened to be present. "We're old, old friends," Hummert said. "Aren't we?"

"Yes," Crayne said. "Old friends."

They weren't. Crayne had heard about the older man only vaguely in his cub reporter days, when Hummert was just beginning to be known around Broadway. His name was Charles Hummert in those days. Twenty years later, when Crayne came to London as a war correspondent, Hummert had looked him up. He looked up all the American newspapermen. It was not something you could hold against him. Orchestra leaders were like that. They lived on publicity. It was part of their business to be friendly with the press. Three years had gone by, however, since it had been Crayne's business to be friendly with orchestra leaders. He wanted no part of them. During those first months in London he had not returned Hummert's enthusiastic overtures. He didn't know why he disliked Hummert, but the feeling was strong enough to cause him to stay away from the Crescent's small downstairs ballroom. His obvious coolness had apparently not been noticed by the older man. Whenever Hummert saw Crayne he continued to treat him like an old school chum. Crayne had been annoyed by this attitude. But since the Colonel had assigned him to this job, Crayne regretted his earlier coolness. The chances of his coming up with what the Colonel wanted depended almost entirely on Hummert's belief that he and Crayne were really close friends. Crayne was not sure that he would succeed. He had sufficient self-confidence to believe he possessed a few of the qualities that had caused the Colonel to ask Crayne to work for him, but Crayne felt certain he was not a good enough actor for that.

"Are you an American, sir?" the lieutenant said.

Hummert laughed at the surprise in the boy's voice and he slapped him on the back.

"I'll tell the cockeyed world," he said. "American as apple pie."

He wasn't. There was something wrong about him. Even his slang was dated and false. From the core of his recently aroused and unsuspected patriotism, Crayne wondered if that was why he disliked Hummert. That, plus the fact that Hummert was a naturalized Englishman.

"You'll have another drink, then, sir," the lieutenant said.

"You bet your life I will," Hummert said.

The boy tipped the chartreuse bottle. It was empty. The boy blushed.

"Never mind," Hummert said. "We'll have one on me. For old time's sake, eh, Crayne?" He snapped his fingers at a waiter who was stacking chairs. "How about a quick round for me and my friends, Victor?"

"I'm sorry, sir. The bar is closed, sir."

"To hell with that," Hummert said and his voice echoed loudly in the empty ballroom. "Just tell them it's for me."

"I'll try, sir."

"Step on it, Victor. My friends are thirsty." Hummert laughed. "They always say that," he said to Crayne and the lieutenant and the English girl. "That's the British for you. You've got to know them to get anything out of them. Me, I know them like a book. Inside out. I'm one of them. I've got them in the palm of my hand."

The waiter came back across the ballroom. Most of the lights were out now.

"I'm sorry, Mr. Hummert. The steward's locked up and gone off, sir."

"That's a hell of a way to treat me and my friends," Hummert said. "What's all his rush?"

"There's an alert on, sir. Been on for a couple of hours, sir. I imagine he was anxious to see how things were at home, sir."

Hummert scowled and looked quickly at the lieutenant and then at the girl. Crayne's reaction was divided between his purely personal pleasure in the blustering band leader's embarrassment, and his swift professional awareness that the unprofitable evening had suddenly and unexpectedly taken a turn that might lead to what the Colonel wanted.

"Tell you what," Hummert said. "How about everybody coming over to my place for a couple? I've got plenty of liquor in the house. All kinds. Everything you want. What do you say?"

Crayne crushed out his freshly lighted cigarette, moving his hands to relieve the inner tension. It had taken an effort to restrain himself from making the obvious suggestion.

"That's awfully nice of you," Crayne said. "But it's very late and I don't think we'd want to disturb your family."

"You won't be disturbing them," Hummert said. "The wife and kids are in the country. Sent them down two weeks ago, when these bloody things started coming over. Come on. I'd like you all to see my place, anyway. I've got some interesting things to show you."

"Well," Crayne said and he looked at the lieutenant and the young girl with the awkward, worried hesitation of a man desperately anxious to avoid an imposition. Perhaps he was a better actor than he thought. "If it's all right with these youngsters," he said. During his few months in the Colonel's strange business that was now his business, too, Crayne had learned that, while you could only rarely shape the events with which you had to work, it was always possible to take correct advantage of them when they shaped themselves for you. "I certainly could use a drink," he said.

There were only five or six people in the bus queue on the north side of the Edgeware Road when Crayne came down the street. It was midafternoon, too early for the shoppers and office workers to be going home to Willesden and Maida Vale. The sun, which had finally broken through the overhanging mist, glinted brightly on the barbed wire and the anti-aircraft guns in Hyde Park.

Crayne walked past the queue, turned left, crossed the road, and stopped to buy a paper from the newsboy in front of the Cumberland Hotel. Crayne turned left again, into Old Quebec Street, walked around the block, and came out once more into the Edgeware Road. A bus, perhaps two, had apparently stopped for passengers while Crayne was circling the block. The length and the character of the queue had changed. Now the line included several women with shopping bags, a couple of British R.E.M.E. corporals, half a dozen schoolboys excitedly discussing a movie they had just seen, and an American officer with a white mustache.

Crayne took his place at the end of the queue and read his paper as he waited. A Number Sixteen bus came along and stopped. The schoolboys and the R.E.M.E. corporals jumped in. The bus roared away. Several women joined the queue behind Crayne. A few minutes later a Number Eight bus swept around Marble Arch and stopped in front of the queue. Crayne got on behind the women with shopping bags and the American officer. A few of the women found seats downstairs. Four of them, the American officer, and Crayne climbed to the top deck. Several people were scattered about on the seats upstairs. The women with the shopping bags settled themselves up front. The last seat in the rear, a double one next to the stairs, was empty. Crayne took it. The bus lurched sharply. The American officer staggered, clutched at a strap, missed, and dropped into the vacant space next to Crayne. He smiled apologetically.

"Sorry," he said.

"Quite all right, sir," Crayne said. Sitting like that, side by side in the rear seat next to the stairs, there was nobody behind or on either side of them. All the people on the top deck of the Number

Eight bus were in front of them. The clippie came upstairs and rapped her ticket rack on the rail. Crayne took a shilling from his pocket. "Two fivepenny tickets, please."

"Where to, sir?" the clippie said.

"The Gaumont cinema," Crayne said. "Kilburn High Road."

"That's right, sir." Americans in London were no longer a novelty. Americans in London who knew the bus fares still were. "Two fives, sir."

She took the coin, punched a couple of tickets, dug two coppers out of the leather wallet at her side, and gave the tickets and the change to Crayne.

"Thank you," he said. The clippie moved on down the aisle toward the other passengers. Crayne said, "We're after the wrong man, sir."

"We can always be mistaken," the Colonel said. "We frequently are." He might have been discussing the weather. Because of the chattering passengers up front and the noise of the bus motor, his voice, like Crayne's, carried only far enough to be heard by the man sitting beside him. "We can't close our files on him, though, until we're certain."

"I think you can close them," Crayne said. "I'm certain, sir."

"Why?"

Crayne turned slightly to look at the handsome, white-haired man beside him. He had first met the Intelligence officer six months before. Then as now the Colonel seemed to know everything about him. Crayne, whose business for years before the war had made it necessary for him to know or know about everybody, had never even heard of the Colonel until the older man sent for him. During the six months that had gone by, Crayne had grown to like the older man. It was a liking based solely on his respect for the Colonel's ability. Crayne had nothing else to go on. Their meetings were infrequent. They were arranged by telephone, and held in odd places, to discuss a new assignment for Crayne or to hear Crayne's report on a current job. Nobody, not even the members of the Colonel's own organization, was aware that Crayne was in any way connected with their work. The Colonel never talked about personal matters. Neither did Crayne. His private life was his own business. The Colonel obviously felt the same way about his own private life. Consequently, Crayne knew almost nothing about his chief as a person. There were times, such as now, when this made their business relationship a difficult one for Crayne. He was certain that the Cedric Hummert case was closed. He was not certain that the reasons for his certainty would be accepted by the Colonel.

"I finally got to his house," Crayne said. "Last night."

"Alone?"

"No," Crayne said. "With a second lieutenant just back from Normandy and his girl. Hummert picked them up in the Small Downstairs. I happened to be with them. He asked me to go along."

The Colonel stroked his mustache lightly and looked out the bus window at the shabby houses of the Edgeware Road. By this small gesture, which Crayne had come to recognize, he knew that the Colonel's interest had been aroused. It was Hummert's practice of taking young American officers to his flat late at night, after the Crescent's small downstairs ballroom closed, and feeding them more liquor than was good for them, that had aroused the suspicions of the Colonel's organization. For a couple of months before D-Day, and during the weeks that followed, there had been a number of small security leaks in London. Bits of information that were not individually important, but which in combination might have been, had filtered through to the enemy. Several of these leaks had been traced back to the small downstairs ballroom of the Crescent. It had been a popular place with the American officers who had been stockpiled in London for the invasion and, after D-Day, with the men who came back from France on missions or on leave.

The Colonel had no real evidence to go on. Merely a hunch. But in this work hunches were often as important as evidence. The Colonel felt there was something peculiar about an American band leader who had left his own country, settled in London, and remained there for twenty years without going back even once for a visit. The Colonel was not given to dramatic statements but it looked, he said, as though Hummert had renounced his native land. The reason did not matter, although it would have been interesting, probably even helpful, to know it. Such men made good enemy agents. There were now in the Colonel's employ a number of Germans who had renounced Germany at one time or another for a variety of reasons. It would have been dangerous sentimentality to think it impossible that an American who had renounced America could not be in the employ of the Germans. There was no room for sentimentality in the Colonel's business. He had assigned Crayne, whose background made him a good choice for this type of job, to the Hummert case.

"How did it go?" the Colonel said.

"Very well," Crayne said. "There was a hell of a raid on."

As he spoke, the sirens went. The bus had just rolled out of the Edgeware Road into Maida Vale. For a moment the women with shopping bags at the front of the bus stopped talking. Crayne stopped, too. Then, in a few seconds, the hum of conversation resumed. There were always a few minutes between the alert and the first robots. It was silly to waste them. They might be your last.

Crayne told the Colonel about his three hours in Hummert's house with the young lieutenant and the girl. He spoke clearly, without emphasis, using as few words as possible, the way he wrote his reports when the Colonel could not get away to see him in person, but his ears were alert for the droning sounds that might be coming toward them at any moment. There was not much to tell. Hummert had spent most of the time showing them his possessions: the piano that had once belonged to the King of Rumania, the set of Swinburne with the poet's autograph on each flyleaf, the liquor cabinet that was a present from someone related by marriage to the royal family, the portrait of his wife by a member of the Royal Academy, the rug that had come from the floor of a bankrupt duke's castle. The young lieutenant, and even the English girl with him, had been impressed.

While Hummert showed and described his treasures, Crayne gradually remembered all that he had known and forgotten about the orchestra leader in those early days on Broadway. It was not much. Hummert had never been a really big name on the big street. He had been just another young man with a band that worked fairly regularly and was paid fairly well. One day he had disappeared. A few questions were asked about him, but not many. Charles Hummert was not missed. Soon he was forgotten. Bigger names and better talents had disappeared from Broadway in Crayne's time with even less fuss. The memory of Broadway is no longer than the memory of any other street in the world. To Crayne it had seemed odd to be re-

membering all that during the small hours of the night, in the midst
of an air raid, in another country, during a war. Odder still was the
feeling of embarrassment that came over Crayne as he watched and
listened to Hummert. At four in the morning the lieutenant and his
girl and Crayne said good night and left Hummert's house. Crayne
put the youngsters into a taxi, walked through the blackout to
his own flat, and lay awake until dawn thinking the thing out. By the
time he pulled the sleep mask over his eyes and took a Nembutol
capsule and rolled his face away from the morning sun to get some
rest, Crayne was sure he had the problem solved.

"I see," the Colonel said.

The all clear sounded. The part of Crayne's mind that had been
in the skies overhead came back to the top deck of the Number Eight
bus. The heavy vehicle swayed into the left fork at the top of Maida
Vale, swinging the passengers to one side, and pressed the silver
eagle on the Colonel's shoulder against Crayne's tweed coat. The
bus stopped. The Colonel sat up straight. A couple of women got
off. The bus started again.

"I may have it figured wrong," Crayne said. "I don't think so, sir."

The Colonel did not answer. He stared out the window at the
queues in front of the fish and vegetable hucksters' carts on the Kilburn High Road. He seemed absorbed in the teeming scene. It was the
absorption of a tourist seeing a foreign land for the first time. Crayne
wanted to tell him irritably that there was nothing remarkable in
the sight of housewives buying haddock and potatoes from push
carts. The same thing happened every week day on Second Avenue
in New York. Crayne was irritable because he felt silly. It was his job
to get information. He had performed that job well on previous assignments. On this one he had come up, not with information, but
with a theory. It had been an embarrassing theory to explain, in an
undertone on top of a bus, to a man about whom he knew nothing
except that he was hardheaded and appeared to understand and
want to deal only in facts. It seemed, all at once, a little like telling
a bunch of roughnecks playing poker in the city room about your
secret passion for Shakespeare's sonnets. It was annoying to see that
his theory was not even interesting enough to distract the Colonel's
attention from a street of fish and vegetable peddlers.

"Of course, all this is based on only one visit to his home," Crayne said. "Hummert could hardly be expected to try to get information out of an army officer while I was present. He wouldn't have invited me to come along if he'd wanted to do that. Just the same I don't think he's the man we're looking for." Crayne regretted that his irritation was coming through in his voice. "I think the files on Hummert should be closed."

The bus stopped. Several people from the top deck got off. A quarter of a mile up the road, three more stops on their fivepenny tickets, were the tall gilded minarets of the Gaumont cinema. The bus started with a lurch.

"I think I'll get off at the next stop," the Colonel said. He stood up and pushed the bell button. "I must get back to my office." He smiled suddenly, a broad, friendly grin that caused a neat, straight gap to appear down the middle of his white mustache. "I'll buy your theory," he said. The bus began to slow down. The Colonel took one of the bus tickets out of Crayne's hand, stepped over to the stairs, and turned back for a moment. "I'm going to close my files on Hummert," he said.

The phone rang on the desk at the other side of the office. Crayne did not get up to answer it. He was trying to finish a dispatch. There had been two heavy raids that morning and his secretary, an English girl who had been blitzed out of three different dwellings in four years, had rushed off to Putney to see if she would have a place in which to sleep that night. The phone continued to ring. Crayne remained at the typewriter. His paper in New York did not know about his work for the Colonel. He could offer no explanation if he fell behind in his coverage of the London news. Crayne saw to it that he did not fall behind. The phone rang shrilly on his secretary's desk. He stood up, finally, and went across the room.

"Hello?" It was a woman's voice. British. "Mr. Crayne, please."

"Speaking."

"Oh." The voice sounded upset. "This is Mrs. Hummert. I don't think we've met. Mrs. Cedric Hummert?"

That explained the voice. It matched the cold, rather silly portrait Crayne had seen over Hummert's fireplace three nights before.

"Yes," Crayne said. "How do you do?"

"I know this is frightfully rude, but could you come around to our flat right away?"

"I'm afraid not. I'm busy at the moment."

"Please, Mr. Crayne. Couldn't you possibly? It's frightfully important, really."

"I'm sorry. I can't right now."

"Please, Mr. Crayne."

The flat, impersonal, superior cadence had not changed, but there was a small, almost desperate increase in pitch. It was enough to cut through Crayne's divided attention. His mind left the dispatch in the typewriter at the other side of the room. His own voice did not change, but now he was paying complete attention.

"What's wrong?" he said.

"Our flat's been hit. This morning's raid. The first one. My husband is asking for you, Mr. Crayne."

"For me?" Crayne was not pleased with the surprise in his voice. "Why me?"

"Yes. I don't know. He keeps calling your name."

"Is he badly hurt?"

"Yes, rather. They rang me in the country at noon. I came up by the first train. It was a stroke of luck that I managed to locate your phone number and find you in. He wants you, Mr. Crayne. Do say you'll come."

"I'll be right over."

"Thank you so much. We're at Westminster Gardens. If you'll just ask any taxi driver?"

"I know Westminster Gardens."

In the taxi Crayne could not decide whether he was more annoyed by the tone of Mrs. Hummert's voice, which had indicated clearly that she thought he lacked the intelligence to find Westminster Gardens without detailed instructions, or by her husband's upsetting summons. The files on Hummert were closed. The Colonel had ended the case the day before because Crayne had convinced him on top of the Number Eight bus that they were after the wrong man. Why should Hummert send for Crayne now? Crayne was not one of his friends. Hummert did not know about Crayne's work for the Colonel. He could not possibly know that he had been under suspicion.

Crayne sat up straight on the taxi seat. There *was* a way by which Hummert could have known he was under suspicion. It was the only way: if Hummert was guilty.

The taxi stopped. The street in which Westminister Gardens stood was roped off. Crayne paid the driver, walked up to the policeman on guard, and showed his press card.

"Right, sir." The policeman lifted the rope. Crayne ducked under. "You'll have to use the side entrance. I'm afraid the front has been knocked out, sir."

It occurred to Crayne again, as it had occurred to him three nights before when he came here for the first time with the young lieutenant and his girl, that Westminster Gardens was just the sort of place an American orchestra leader who had gone completely British would choose to live in. It was an expensive, gaudy, modernistic block of flats, with vast sheets of seamless glass instead of window panes, and too many oddly cut mirrors and curiously shaped pieces of onyx and metal tubing in the lobby.

The robot had landed in the street, fifty yards or so beyond the entrance. The blast had knocked out the front of Westminster Gardens and sliced away sections of the smaller blocks of flats on either side. Several small houses across the road were completely leveled. It was impossible to tell whether there had been three or four in the row that was now a flat, smoking ruin. A number of ARP men with *Heavy Rescue* patches on their sleeves were working in the rubble. The pavement was almost hidden under a treacherous layer of powdered glass. The air was sharp with the hard, thin, penetrating smell of high explosive mixed with charred wood and fine mortar dust. Crayne picked his way through the debris to the side entrance. He showed his card to another policeman at the door.

"You'll have to walk, sir. The lift's gone. Back stairs are over there, sir, to your left."

Crayne walked up three flights. The back of the large structure was still standing, but most of the seamless glass on the court was gone. The acrid odors of the street poured in with the draft. The door of the Hummert flat was ajar. The blast had sprung the hinges. Crayne pushed the pearl button on the jamb. He was not surprised to hear the buzzer sound inside. Blast damage was unpredictable. It could wreck a roomful of bronze statues and leave intact a delicate vase on a spindly table in the middle of the chamber. The door was opened by a smartly dressed woman of about forty with a hard, lined face and marcelled blonde hair.

"You're Mr. Crayne?"

"Yes."

"I'm Mrs. Hummert. It's frightfully kind of you to come. This is Dr. Farquarson."

Crayne shook hands with a middle-aged man who wore striped trousers and a wing collar. Mrs. Hummert and the doctor looked at Crayne expectantly, as though they had been waiting for him to arrive with information of great importance. Crayne had come to get information, not to give it. He glanced about as though unaware of the awkward pause. They were standing in the foyer. He could look into the kitchen and the dining room because the doors of these rooms had been torn from their hinges. The beautiful Hummert flat was a mess.

"Mr. Hummert keeps calling your name," the doctor said. "Mrs. Hummert and I were wondering if you know why?"

"I have no idea. Do you want me to ask him?"

Dr. Farquarson and Mrs. Hummert looked at each other.

"I'm afraid it's impossible to question him," Dr. Farquarson said. "Mr. Hummert's condition is quite grave."

"That's too bad," Crayne said. "Is there anything I can do?"

Mrs. Hummert and the doctor exchanged another glance. She nodded slightly.

"If you will come this way," Dr. Farquarson said. "I must ask you not to excite him. He has lost a considerable amount of blood. He is very weak."

"Of course."

Crayne moved toward the bedroom door and stopped. Dr. Farquarson had moved toward the door of the living room.

"The bedrooms are almost completely gone," Mrs. Hummert said. "That's why Cedric was injured. He was asleep when the bomb landed. He always sleeps late because he seldom finishes at the Crescent before one or two in the morning. They found him a couple of hours later and rang me up in the country. I left the children in the country. We've put him in the drawing room. It's the one room that wasn't hit so badly. It faces the court, you see."

Crayne did not like her any better than he had liked her voice on the telephone or her portrait by a member of the Royal Academy, but he admired her self-control. It would have been difficult for a stranger, certainly for an American stranger, to know that Mrs. Hummert was talking about her own husband.

"We must be very quiet," Dr. Farquarson said. "He must not be disturbed."

Crayne nodded. The doctor opened the door. Crayne stared into the room which, when he had seen it three nights before, had been so carefully and laboriously arranged that it had resembled a room in a museum rather than part of a man's home. The piano that had belonged to the King of Rumania was cracked wide open, like a child's toy that has been dropped to the pavement from a great height. The priceless autographed set of Swinburne was torn to bits, the pages scattered like confetti around the room. The liquor cabinet that had been a present from a member of the royal family was recognizable only because the twisted nickel fittings gleamed through the pile of shattered ebony and mother of pearl. The portrait of Mrs. Hummert by the Royal Academician lay on the floor, the frame broken, the canvas slashed in several places as though with a knife. The seamless glass windows had apparently been open at the time of the explosion. The glass had been spared. The windows were now closed and the curtains, which had also been inexplicably overlooked by the freak blast, were partly drawn. Hummert, his head propped up on two pillows, lay motionless in a large bed that had been moved into the middle of the ruined room.

"He's asleep," Dr. Farquarson said quietly. "I gave him a sedative an hour ago."

Crayne nodded. He did not speak. He was shocked by Hummert's appearance. The band leader had changed more completely than the room. His head was bandaged and his left arm, bound in splints, lay stiff and straight at his side. His right fist was tightly clenched. His eyes were closed. He trembled slightly, as though with cold. His heavy, irregular breathing was painful to hear. Most amazing was the fact that Hummert seemed to have shrunk since Crayne had seen him three days before. The large, blustering band leader now looked small and frail under the thin covers. His ruddy face was white and drawn. The weight and the life had been drained from him. All that remained of Cedric Hummert was a bundle of bones in a loose sack of skin. His head rolled an inch or two on the pillow and he opened his eyes.

"Crayne," he said hoarsely. "Get Crayne."

The effort to force the words out left him weaker. His chest started to heave more rapidly. Crayne stepped over to the bed.

"Here I am," he said.

A gleam of recognition sparked for a moment in Hummert's eyes. His parched lips cracked apart in a horrible approximation of a smile and then, as his glance caught Dr. Farquarson and Mrs. Hummert, the smile stopped.

"Alone," he said. "Want talk Crayne alone."

Crayne turned to the others. Mrs. Hummert's hard, lined face was pinched, not with the suspicion that Crayne was prepared for and would have understood, but with a sort of angry, childish petulance, as though a puzzle on which she had been working for some time had been snatched from her grasp at the moment when she felt she was about to solve it. Dr. Farquarson looked disturbed.

"I won't upset him," Crayne said. He did not want any witnesses to what Hummert was about to tell him. "Of course, if you'd rather I didn't?"

The doctor hesitated for another moment or two and then, with a gesture of finality and firmness that surprised Crayne, he took Mrs. Hummert's arm and led her to the door. She stopped and looked across her shoulder. Crayne made a reassuring movement with his hand and they went out and closed the door softly. Crayne turned back to the man on the bed. Hummert's eyes were closed.

"We're alone now," Crayne said. "What did you want to tell me?"

The band leader did not answer. Crayne bent over the bed. Hummert's breathing was weaker. His right fist pulsed up and down, as though he were trying to make it shrink by kneading the fingers into his palm. Crayne pulled over a chair and sat down beside the bed.

"Take it easy," he said. "I won't go away."

Crayne wanted a cigarette badly, but he had neglected to ask the doctor if it was all right to smoke. He was finding it difficult to suppress a mounting feeling of excitement. The Colonel had closed the files on Hummert because of Crayne's analysis of the few facts he had remembered about the band leader. It was true that Crayne would look foolish if Hummert, knowing he was about to die, had sent for Crayne in order to make a complete confession. But Crayne knew that, in this work he had undertaken voluntarily, personal discomfort was of little consequence. Only one thing was important now: to correct a mistake he had caused the Colonel to make.

"Whenever you're ready," Crayne said. "I'll wait."

He watched the man whose life was slipping away before his eyes and wondered where his analysis had gone wrong. Crayne had seen it all clearly three nights before as he watched and listened to Hummert exhibit his treasures to the young lieutenant and the girl. Hummert was like most of the men Crayne had known on and around Broadway. He had wanted success. More than anything in the world, he had desired fame and money, the simple, difficult things for which most men lusted. And like most men, his ambition had been larger than his talent. Hummert never really reached Broadway in the full meaning of that phrase. The competition was too strong. His ability was too small. He reached the fringes of fame and money. He touched the edge of success. He never really held it firmly in his grasp. Success was the pinnacle of a tall, tall mountain. He had struggled and climbed. He had come close, but never close enough. He knew finally that, like most men, he would never reach the top. But Hummert differed from most men in one respect: he faced the reality that if he remained on Broadway he would never have what he wanted. He made what must have seemed at the time a wise decision. He left Broadway. He came to London.

In the British capital the competition was not so great. Here, in London, the mere fact that he was an American was an asset. The talent that had not been big enough for Broadway was big enough for the West End. In London Hummert got what in his own country had been denied him. In London he achieved fame, earned money, became a success. In London he reached the top of the mountain. The air was sweet. It was as he had always dreamed it would be. It was difficult to give it up, to come down from the mountain to the less heady air of home. Hummert stayed on. And the longer he stayed, the more difficult it was to go back. He set about the task of making it impossible for himself to go back. He changed his name from Charles to Cedric. He married an English girl. He sent his children to British schools. He lost touch deliberately with his relatives in America. He cultivated a British accent. And finally he became a naturalized British subject. Twenty years had gone by. They were good years. It was a good life. There was nothing wrong with it. He was happy. He was respected. He was successful. He had everything he had ever wanted. Everything except the one thing he had always had but no longer possessed: his own country.

"I want you to take a look at this liquor cabinet." Crayne could hear Hummert's voice again as he showed his possessions to the young lieutenant. "It was presented to me by a member of the royal family. Here, let me show you this piano. It used to belong to the King of Rumania."

There had been a pathetic and revealing eagerness in Hummert's voice. For all his hearty British manner, his Savile Row clothes, his fabulous possessions, he had looked and sounded like a small boy explaining how, in spite of his black eye and bloody nose, he had really won the fight from which he had just come home in tatters. Long before he left Hummert's flat at four o'clock that morning, Crayne knew that the band leader did not take young American officers from the small downstairs ballroom of the Crescent to his house and fill them with liquor to pry military secrets for the enemy.

The war, the air raids, the young men in uniform from his own country, all of these things in combination had shaken Hummert's belief in the decision he had made twenty years ago. He was too old to have his belief shaken. It had been with him too long. He was forty-seven. When the robots started coming over, he sent his wife and children to the country. He had to remain in London. Not only because of his work. He was an Englishman now. Englishmen did not run away from bombs. He was alone much of the time. His loneliness had nothing to do with the many people by whom he was surrounded constantly in his work. He had done a good job on himself in twenty years, but it was not perfect. The British knew he was an American, and the Americans thought he was British. He was comfortable with neither. He began to entertain young American officers at his house. To ingratiate himself with them, perhaps to capture their sympathy, he told them he was a native New Yorker. No doubt it was pleasant for them, as it had clearly been pleasant for the young lieutenant three nights before. For Hummert this entertaining was more than pleasant. For Hummert it had become a necessity. The admiration of the young men for his possessions was reassuring. The roomful of treasures was the symbol, the price he had received for giving up his country. Hummert needed reassurance. It was important to be told, over and over again, that the bargain was worth it. It was necessary for him to believe now that what he had done twenty years ago was right.

That was how Crayne had figured it. That was the basis on which the Colonel had closed Hummert's file. Where had the analysis gone wrong?

"Want you do me a favor."

Crayne leaned over the bed. He was about to find out. Hummert's eyes were open. They were curiously alive in that shrunken, inert body.

"What do you want?" Crayne said, trying not to sound eager. He was not completely successful. The confession would clear up the case for the Colonel. It would not answer the question that kept drilling in the back of Crayne's mind: why had Hummert chosen him? Why not his wife? Or Dr. Farquarson? Why had Hummert sent for an American newspaperman who had never taken any pains to conceal his dislike for the band leader? "Tell me when you're ready," Crayne said. "I'll be here."

Hummert closed his eyes and rolled his head weakly from side to side on the pillow. He was telling Crayne without words to wait. He was gathering together whatever was left in him for a final effort. Crayne waited. His glance slid across the room toward the door. He did not want the doctor or Mrs. Hummert to interrupt. Crayne's eyes, coming back to the man on the bed, skipped across the fragments of the shattered room. It was all worthless now, of course. But it had been quite a price. Crayne had known men in his time who had sold more of themselves for less. It was not his business to judge. It was his business to pay close attention and hear clearly what Hummert had to say. He would have to repeat it without error to the Colonel.

"Want you take this."

Hummert tried to lift his hand from the bed, but he lacked the strength. He opened his clenched fist. On the moist palm lay a crumpled wad of paper. Crayne took it and spread it open. It was a tiny brochure, dated 1923, describing the Mapleton Hills Cemetery located on the outskirts of Mapleton, Ohio. Crayne looked at the man on the bed. Hummert's dry lips were moving. Crayne leaned down.

"Family owns plot," Hummert said, forcing the words out one at a time, with painstaking care, like a man trying to make himself understood across a great distance. "Please send cable." His body arched upward in a final, convulsive spurt of strength and Crayne slipped his arm under the thin shoulders. "Cremate," Hummert said. "Send ashes Mapleton. Family will pay. Bury ashes home. Not here. Home."

The stiffness went out of him, from all of his body and all at once. It was as though Crayne had been holding one of those inflated rubber figures with which children play on the beach and suddenly, without warning, all the air had escaped. Crayne lowered the limp body to the bed and straightened up. The Colonel's files would not have to be reopened. Charles Hummert had started his journey back home.

Briefing Period

There are many ways to classify the members of the human race, and in his forty-seven fairly active years as a farm-machinery engineer Kerr had heard most of them; but the one he liked best was his own: there are people who need alarm clocks, and there are people who don't. Kerr, a modest man who would have been stunned by the accusation of vanity on almost any ground, was nevertheless proud of the fact that he belonged in the latter group. He was awake when the phone rang. He always was.

"Seven o'clock, sir," the girl at the switchboard said. "You left a call for seven, sir."

"Thanks," Kerr said. "My watch says five to."

"I beg your pardon?" the girl said, her voice swaying with sudden surprise. "Well, I may be a little early," she said, allowing a note of irritation to break through the impersonal surface of her professional manner. "Anyway, this is your seven-o'clock call."

There was a sharp click in the earpiece, indicating that the telephone company's injunction against yanking plugs out of switchboards had been violated, and as Kerr put his phone back on the table beside his bed, he wondered what had made him say what he had said.

After nearly four months in Room 4216, he knew almost every employee of the Admiral Hotel by sight and most of them by name, but he never had met the girl who was on the switchboard from midnight to eight in the morning. Kerr, a man of regular habits, was always in bed before she came on duty at night. And as he always used up an hour and a half from the moment he received his completely unnecessary seven-o'clock call every morning until the moment he was ready to face the world, the girl always was gone by the time he went into the lobby.

The sudden realization of this omission, the consciousness of this gap in what his highly developed sense of neatness had converted into a well-ordered existence, caused Kerr to frown thoughtfully at the ceiling of Room 4216. Then, aware that the thought was time-consuming and upsetting his schedule, he kicked back the covers and got out of bed.

"To hell with it," he said irritably. "I'll be leaving here in a day or two, anyway."

Getting out of the bed in Room 4216 once was a simple process, requiring little thought and involving no danger. That was in the days before Philip Kerr of Portland, Oregon, checked in. Since his arrival, the process of getting out of the bed in Room 4216 had become, if not precisely complicated, certainly one to which you had to give all your attention. Not even Kerr, who was responsible for the change, could do it with his mind on other matters.

The Admiral Hotel, which stood on a slight hill just north of Capitol Plaza in Washington, D. C., was what is known in the chaste phrases of motoring guides as a medium-priced hostelry and in the more vigorous language employed by drummers and other habitual travelers as a flea bag. Neither definition was strictly accurate. Room 4216 was one of the Admiral's four-dollar, or better, rooms. This distinction was not due to its size, which was eight feet by fourteen, the dimensions of the hotel's lower-priced chambers; nor was the price due to 4216's private bath, with which the Admiral's three-dollar, and even some of its two-dollar, rooms also were equipped. Room 4216 was priced at four dollars per day because it was on the quiet side of the hotel.

The windows of the Admiral's cheaper rooms looked out on Union Station. This made those two-dollar and three-dollar cubicles perfectly adequate for hanging up clothes or mixing a drink, but somewhat less than satisfactory for restful slumber; every night the trolley cars of the nation's capital gathered in the Plaza between the hotel's front entrance and the marble portals of the railroad station and, from midnight until dawn and to the accompaniment of clanging bells and the maniacal cries of invisible spectators, proceeded to shatter themselves into tiny pieces of grinding metal. The single window of Room 4216, on the other hand, looked out on the Capitol Dome, and the noises made in this majestic structure, even when both houses of the national legislature remained in session far into the night, did not carry to the Admiral Hotel.

Kerr, a family man of twenty years' standing, liked his eight hours' sleep. After his first night in the Admiral, which was spent in one of the hotel's two-dollar rooms, he had asked to be transferred to a room on the quiet side. Even though the price of Room 4216 took a substantial bite out of the six dollar per diem the government allowed him while he was in Washington, where he was undergoing a briefing period in preparation for the mission to China he had agreed to perform for IARA, Kerr figured it was worth it. There is nothing like a good night's sleep to prepare you for the strenuous daily round. And as long as you have to suffer through the foolish business of a briefing period before leaving for overseas to do the kind of job you have spent your whole life doing without any briefing periods, you might as well be comfortable. It was Kerr's passion for comfort that had converted the process of getting out of the bed in Room 4216 of the Admiral Hotel from an inconsequential moment in the day's routine to an activity that required, at the very least, some concentration and a good deal of nimble footwork.

Still scowling over the puzzling impulse that had caused him to speak sharply to the unknown switchboard operator, Kerr put his feet down cautiously into the nest of shoes lined up in the narrow space that separated the bed from the dresser, and his bare toes found his bedroom slippers. When Kerr arrived at the Admiral, his luggage included only two pairs of shoes, because he had been warned, by the Processing Division of IARA, that he would have to travel light. He now had seven, one pair for each day of the week and each pair stretched on trees. Kerr reached to the dresser and flipped the switch of the electric percolator, which he had purchased in Garfinckel's after his second week at the Admiral and which he washed and filled with fresh grounds every night before going to bed. The percolator stood between the small cluster of bottles that was Kerr's liquor cabinet and the tastefully grouped array of tiny cheese-spread jars and biscuit boxes that made up his snack bar. Kerr always had canapés with his drink before dinner when he was at home in Portland, and he saw no reason why this pleasant custom should be discarded merely because he was camping out in a medium-priced hostelry, or flea bag, some two thousand miles from home.

Stooping low to avoid the extension cord by which the percolator drew its power from the multiple socket he had installed in the ceiling light, Kerr came erect in front of the illustrated calendar he had received as a Christmas greeting from the Congress Hand Laundry on H Street. Laundry facilities were still difficult to arrange in the nation's capital, even though the war was over, but Kerr was fussy about his linen, and after a couple of weeks' experience with the Admiral's version of laundry service, he had found what he wanted in the Congress Hand Laundry on H Street. The calendar was fastened to the wall between Kerr's tie rack, a folding affair made of leather and aluminum, and the framed pictures of his wife and two children. Next to the pictures was a row of hooks he had bought in the five-and-ten on I Street. These hooks held the brush with which Kerr scrubbed his coffee percolator, a whisk broom, a corkscrew, a can opener, a pickle fork, a dish towel, and a pencil with a ring in its top. Kerr took down the pencil and carefully X'd out the number sixteen on the calendar. Today was the seventeenth. Even though the telegram from the Chief of the Farm Machinery Division of the International Agricultural Rehabilitation Administration, of IARA, which had summoned Kerr to Washington, had stated that his briefing period would last no more than three or four days, a week at most, Kerr had just spent his one hundred and thirteenth night in the Admiral Hotel.

Stepping across the carton of soap flakes on the floor at the head of the bed, Kerr reached to the short clothesline he had rigged up between the curtain rod on the window frame and the slats of the transom over the bathroom door. His socks, which he washed every night, were dry. Swinging his hip adroitly to avoid the sharp corner of the upended trunk, Kerr stepped into the bathroom. Forty minutes later—Kerr had a tough beard and a tender skin, and shaving was a complicated ritual with him—he stepped back onto the handkerchief-size square of uncluttered floor space in the middle of

Room 4216. Keeping his feet firmly planted, moving only his hands and arms, Kerr plucked from the various drawers of the dresser and shelves of the upended trunk, which he kept slightly ajar for this purpose, the items of apparel he had decided the night before were to grace his person on this, the seventeenth day of the month.

By the time he was dressed, the coffee was ready. He liked his first cup of the day strong. He switched off the percolator, and from the glass shelf he had fixed to the wall over his bed, he took down his cup, saucer, and spoon. Sitting on the bed, which brought him into the correct position facing the upended trunk that also served as his desk, he read the long letter he had written the night before.

In the upper right-hand corner the top sheet bore the number 113. Every night, before he washed his socks and filled his percolator and decided what he would wear the following day, Kerr wrote a detailed account of the day's happenings to his wife in Portland. He numbered these letters, so that if by some accident in delivery she should receive one or more out of sequence, she could arrange and read them in proper order. This was important to Kerr. It was through these letters that, as the mysterious movements or lack of them of Washington officialdom gradually and imperceptibly had lengthened his stay in the nation's capital, Kerr had made known to his wife his desire for more shoes, his winter overcoat, extra underwear, and other items. It would have offended Kerr's sense of neatness to receive, for example, his long underwear before he received his overcoat, because he had requested the overcoat first. Mrs. Kerr, who after two decades of marriage knew her husband's habits thoroughly, had not made this mistake. The parcels had arrived and continued to arrive in Washington in the same sequence as the letters Kerr had written and continued to write to his home in Portland.

Satisfied with letter number 113, Kerr sealed it in one of the five hundred envelopes he had had addressed, before he left Portland, on the multigraph machine in the offices of his own firm, from which he had taken a year's leave of absence to go to China for IARA. He rinsed his cup and saucer and spoon, dried them on the dish towel, and turned to the last chore he performed every

morning before he left Room 4216: the task of filling his briefcase
with the things he would need that day.

Kerr had received the briefcase from his wife as a Christmas present. In accordance with the agreement they had made shortly after
they were married, this Christmas present, like the nineteen that
had preceded it, was not a surprise. Kerr had specified, all the way
back in letter number 28, what he wanted, and Mrs. Kerr had met his
specifications: the briefcase had an expanding pocket that enabled
it to open to the size of an overnight bag.

Kerr snapped the catch, closed the straps, took his hat, and left
Room 4216. For the one hundred and fourteenth time he stepped
out of the elevator at precisely eight-thirty and skirted the potted
rubber plant near the brass spittoon as he crossed the lobby to the
desk.

"Morning, Mr. Kerr," Charley said. "How are you this morning,
sir?"

Charley was an elderly Irishman without teeth, who had worked
in better places and said so. Suffused in a mildly alcoholic glow that
did not seem to interfere with his efficiency, Charley presided over
the Admiral's desk from eight in the morning to six in the evening.
As these were the hours during which Kerr was out of the hotel and
the time of day during which he suspected he would receive his call,
if it ever did come, from the IARA Processing Division, instructing
him to report to Bolling Field to board the plane that would take
him to China, Kerr had made an arrangement with Charley during
his first week in Washington to provide for this event. In the pocket
of his soiled alpaca coat the elderly Irishman had at all times a copy
of Kerr's daily itinerary, complete with telephone numbers. Whenever Kerr planned to deviate from his schedule, he asked Charley for
the itinerary before he left the hotel in the morning and marked the
deviation on the typewritten sheet. In theory at least, therefore,
Charley could reach Kerr by phone at any hour of the day. This system never yet had been put to the test, of course, and Kerr had some
misgivings about its efficacy; but it was the best he could devise and,
as a sort of anchor to windward, he prayed that when the big moment finally did come, he would be either in the IARA offices or
at the hotel to receive the call himself.

"I'm fine, thanks," Kerr said. "Anything for me?"

"The usual," Charley said, handing Kerr the air-mail envelope that contained Mrs. Kerr's daily letter. "No packages today, Mr. Kerr. But they got waffles and bacon in the Coffee Shoppe this morning to make up for it."

"Thanks," Kerr said. "I think I'll give myself a treat and eat on linen this morning."

Charley's naked gums appeared in the middle of his cackling laugh, and Kerr forced a small smile. It was a standing joke between them. The Admiral Coffee Shoppe's club breakfast, which was much better than its rooms, cost forty-five cents, but it was served on linoleum-topped tables with paper napkins. Across the street, in the Union Station restaurant, the same breakfast cost fifty cents and was served on real tablecloths with real napkins. Every now and then Kerr, homesick for the tidy little breakfast nook in his house in Portland, would decide to splurge an extra nickel on breakfast for the privilege of eating, as he and Charley put it, on linen.

"Think you'll be getting off soon?" Charley said.

"Any day now," Kerr said. He had been saying this, along with all the other words that had just passed between him and Charley, every morning for almost four months. "Here," he said, opening the expanding briefcase and pulling out the wrapped pint of rye that was Charley's semiweekly fee for keeping Kerr's itinerary in his pocket. "Don't use it up during working hours."

"Thanks, Mr. Kerr," Charley said, slipping the bottle under the desk. "Never touch it during the day, you know," he said with a sly grin. "Same schedule today, Mr. Kerr?"

"Same schedule," Kerr said.

"No changes?" Charley said.

"No changes," Kerr said, fastening the straps of the briefcase. "Well," he said. "See you at five-thirty."

"Five-thirty," Charley said. "Yes, sir."

The shortest distance between the Admiral's front entrance and the Union Station restaurant was diagonally across the Plaza, but Kerr always went the longer way around, down I Street along the perimeter of the square. He liked to take one thing at a time, and the first thing was always the station itself. He crossed the waiting room to the shoeshine stand, pleased as always by the sense of belonging, the solid feeling that the vast chamber, full of people scurrying back and forth with luggage and tickets and crying children, was part of what in four months he had come to think of as his home.

The bootblack Kerr patronized every morning was free. "Good-morning, Mr. Kerr," the bootblack said, reminding Kerr, as he was reminded every day at 8:40 A.M., that he was probably the only person in the large crowd swirling around them who was known to the bootblack by name. "Light today?"

"Yes, please, Joe," Kerr said. He had a theory that tan shoes aged better if light polish was used on them one day and dark polish the next. During his second week in Washington, back in November, when he and the bootblack had reached the Mr. Kerr-Joe stage, he had made this theory known to the bootblack, who agreed it was a sound one. Since then Joe had kept track of Kerr's shoes and, when Kerr wore his tans, the correct polish. "Watch the back on this left one, will you, Joe?" Kerr said. "Right here, just over the heel. I nicked it the other day on a taxi door."

"You bet, sir," Joe answered. "Them taxis sure are murder, aren't they?"

While the bootblack worked, Kerr read the letter from his wife. It was like the one hundred and twelve letters that had preceded it, and yet, because it came from the place, the thing, the person—in his mind they were all intertwined—that Kerr valued most in all the world, namely, his home, he read it with as much interest as he had read the first: the children were fine and asked for him a dozen times every day; the rainy season was hanging on a bit longer than usual this year, but everybody expected it to clear before long; the roses in the west bed were coming up much better after the extra-careful mulching they had received in December; it didn't seem as though the government were really anxious to help the Chinese with their farm machinery or they would have done something about getting him out of Washington and on his way to do the job they had hired him for long before this; the sweater he had asked for in letter number 110 was on its way by parcel post insured; while she hated the thought of his being all the way out there at the other side of the world among people who apparently never had heard of

orange juice and fresh vegetables and ate nothing but rice, she did
wish the government would get a move on and send him off, because the sooner he got to China the sooner he would be back home
in Portland; yes, she had checked with his secretary at the office and
the insurance on the car was paid up for two years; the moment he
was out of the country he was to remember to start taking his vita-
min tablets.

"There you are, sir," the bootblack said.

"Thanks," Kerr said, folding the letter and slipping it into his
pocket as he climbed down from the chair. "There *you* are, Joe."

"Thanks," Joe said, taking the coins. "Think you'll be getting off
soon, Mr. Kerr?"

"Any day now," Kerr said. "See you tomorrow, Joe."

He crossed the bustling, noisy waiting room, stopped to discuss
the weather for a moment with the man at the newsstand, where he
picked up his newspaper, and went into the restaurant. The girl in
the black dress, holding the armful of menus at the velvet rope between the brass posts, smiled at him, and Kerr smiled back. She
signaled to a waitress at the back of the room, unhooked the velvet
rope, and Kerr passed through.

"I sure thought you were in China by this time," the waitress said
as she pulled out the small round table so he could slip into the
circular pew upholstered in red leather, where he always sat when
he ate on linen. "Where you been keeping yourself, Mr. Kerr?"

"Oh, around and about," Kerr said, glancing at the other people
in the large room, the unfortunate itinerants to whom this was just
another railway-station restaurant. To Kerr it was a private dining
room, the part of the home he had built for himself in Washington
to which he went when he wanted to dine in style. "How have you
been, Iris?"

"I can't complain," Iris said, and proceeded to demonstrate, while
Kerr looked at the menu, that she was underestimating her ability
in this direction.

The special on the menu was waffles and bacon. Apparently all
the coffee shoppes in the nation's capital had signed a pact to serve
this dish that morning. Kerr, about to order it, suddenly had a recur-
ring twinge of the vague discomfort with which he had awakened,
and he became aware that Iris was talking to him.

"So I said okay, you're the manager of this coffee shoppe," she said. "If that's the way you want to run it, okay, that's the way you want to run it. I'll serve mint jelly with the leg of lamb whether they ask for it or not, only don't go blaming me if we run out, and then, when some poor customer comes along that really wants the stuff, you know, I gotta say sorry, we're all out. What'll it be, Mr. Kerr?"

"Prunes and poached eggs," Kerr said.

"We got waffles and bacon on the special this morning," Iris said. "They're real good, too, Mr. Kerr."

"No, I'll take the prunes and poached eggs," Kerr said, unfolding his newspaper to conceal his unexplained annoyance. "And coffee with, please, Iris."

"As if I'd forget," Iris said reproachfully as she scribbled the order on her pad. "Think you'll be getting off soon, Mr. Kerr?"

"Any day now," Kerr said.

The Pershing Building, which housed the Washington staff of IARA, was on Independence Avenue, three blocks north of the Senate Office Building. The quickest way to reach it by foot from Union Station was to leave the railroad terminal by its north entrance and cut diagonally across Capitol Plaza, but here, too, Kerr preferred the long way around. He had several stops to make before he checked into the IARA offices. Dislodging bits of prune and poached egg from his teeth with the quill pick wrapped in tissue paper that Iris always brought him with his change after he ate on linen, and carrying his expanded briefcase, Kerr went all the way through Union Station, left by the south entrance, and crossed the taxi ramp to the sidewalk in front of the post office.

"Good-morning, Mr. Kerr," said the Negro beggar crouched on his tiny platform near the hydrant. "Lovely morning, sir."

"Yes, it is nice," Kerr said, dropping his daily dime into the hat in front of the platform. "How are you this morning, Milton?"

"Very well, sir," the beggar said with a grin. "Thank you, sir."

Kerr was proud of the fact that, shortly after he struck up his acquaintance with Milton in November, the cheerful little man had told him that, in all his thirty-five years on this spot in the nation's capital, Kerr was the second person who had spoken to him and the only person who ever had asked his name.

"Getting a little warmer, isn't it?" Kerr said.

"Maybe just a little," Milton said. "But we'll have plenty more cold days before that old sun really begins to shine, sir."

"They won't bother you, Milton," Kerr said with a smile. "Will they?"

"No, sir, Mr. Kerr, them cold days sure won't bother me," Milton said, his grin growing broader. Kerr had promised Milton that, when the call from the Processing Division of IARA finally came through, he would give his overcoat, which he had owned since before the war, anyway, to Milton as a farewell present. "Think you'll be getting off soon, sir?"

"Any day now," Kerr said. "See you tomorrow, Milton."

"You bet, sir," Milton said. "See you tomorrow."

Kerr climbed the steps of the post office and went to the parcel-post window. He opened his briefcase and took out the package he had wrapped and addressed the night before.

"Good-morning, Mr. Kerr," the clerk said and, as he put the parcel on his scale, "Two today, eh?"

"Well, I thought I might as well get rid of them a little faster," Kerr said. "Time's getting short."

In letter number 76 Mrs. Kerr had reported that it was almost impossible to buy soap flakes in Portland. Kerr had spent three afternoons, during which he was somewhat nervous because there was no way to mark these unscheduled movements on the typed itinerary in Charley's pocket and he was therefore out of touch with the IARA Processing Division, combing the grocery stores of the nation's capital. Finally, in a wholesaler's warehouse near Silver Springs, he had located and purchased a case of forty-eight one-pound packages of soap flakes and had brought the case in a taxi to the Admiral Hotel. Every morning since then he had mailed one package to Portland. The night before, taking inventory before he went to bed, Kerr had discovered that he had twelve packages left. In an inexplicable, and for him quite unusual, burst of impatience, Kerr had wrapped two packages instead of one. He wondered now, as the post-office clerk stamped the parcel, whether it was this deviation from his normal routine that could be responsible for the odd feeling of discomfort that had been with him since he woke up at five minutes to seven.

"Thirteen cents, Mr. Kerr," the clerk said. "How do you mean, time's getting short? Think you'll be leaving soon?"

"Any day now," Kerr said, pushing the coins across the counter.

"We'll sure hate to lose your business," the clerk said with a grin. "See you tomorrow, Mr. Kerr?"

"You bet," Kerr said. "See you tomorrow."

He left the post office by the west entrance, circled the rear of the Admiral Hotel, and walked the four blocks along H Street to the Congress Hand Laundry.

Harry Cairn, the proprietor, was working on the marking machine when Kerr came in. "Hi, Phil," Mr. Cairn said. "I was just talking about you."

"Hi, Harry," Kerr said. "Good or bad?"

As soon as he had become aware, back in November, of the laundry situation in the nation's capital, Kerr had set himself to the task of licking it. This had involved raising his relationship with the laundryman of his choice above the level of mere business. The campaign had consumed a good deal of Kerr's time and many bottles of far from inexpensive rye; but to a man as fussy about his shirts as Kerr, the time and the money had been well spent. He had grown to like Harry Cairn. In fact, Kerr thought of him now as one of his best and oldest friends.

"What do *you* think?" Cairn said. "I had the missus on the phone a little while ago, and she says when am I going to see you. I looked at the clock up there and I said: 'Dixie, it is now twenty-seven minutes after nine, and it is Wednesday. Phil will be in here with his loaded briefcase in exactly eighteen minutes.'" The proprietor of the Congress Hand Laundry grinned as he nodded toward the clock. "A quarter to ten, right on the button," he said. "How's that for timing?"

"You ought to be running the IARA," Kerr said, putting his briefcase on the counter and loosening the straps. "They could use a little efficiency. What did Dixie want?"

"She wants to know can you come to dinner tonight. She's just put her hands on a ham, don't ask me how, and she says she doesn't want to waste the whole thing on a lug like me. How about it, Phil?"

"Thanks, Harry. I'd like that," Kerr said, pulling his soiled shirts from the briefcase. "Why don't you stop by at the hotel about six to pick me up, and we can have a drink before we drive out to your house?"

"That's a deal," Harry Cairn said, counting the soiled shirts. "Only five?" he said.

"I've got a couple more," Kerr said. "But I thought maybe I'd better not have them all in the laundry at the same time. Just in case."

"Why?" Cairn said. "Expect to be getting off soon, Phil?"

"Any day now," Kerr said. "Well, I'll be on my way, Harry."

"Right," Cairn said. "See you at six."

During the war the Pershing Building, which had been built toward the close of the Coolidge administration as an annex for the overflowing staffs of several government bureaus, had been turned over to a number of war agencies created for the duration of the emergency. After V-J Day, when these temporary agencies were disbanded and the International Agricultural Relief Administration was organized, the postwar agency moved in. The highly charged war atmosphere, which had included armed guards at all the doors and numbered identification badges for all employes and visitors, had disappeared long ago, but the partitions remained. The Pershing Building, which from the outside looked like a Greek temple made of marble and sandstone, bore a distinct resemblance on the inside to a closely packed series of rabbit warrens.

Kerr, carrying his now completely collapsed briefcase, entered the Pershing Building at ten o'clock. In the cubicle on the third floor presided over by Miss Ames, the IARA attendance clerk, he signed the attendance record and smoked a cigarette while Miss Ames told him what she thought of the weather, the boss, the habits of Washington taxi drivers, and the House Appropriations Committee, which was holding up the IARA budget for some damn-fool reason. This monologue, which did not help dispel Kerr's feeling of vague discomfort, required nothing from him but his presence. It was the same every morning, and it always disposed of the first ten minutes of his day in the Pershing Building.

"Well," Kerr said as he punched out his cigarette in Miss Ames' ashtray, "I guess I'd better be getting on to Finance."

In the IARA's Finance Division, eleven doors from the attendance-record room, Kerr smoked a second cigarette with Miss Carwell,

who said, nope, the check for his last month's per diem voucher had
not yet come through, although there was no occasion for him to
worry, since everybody in town knew that the General Accounting
Office was way behind on all disbursements because they were waiting to see what the House Appropriations Committee would do to
the IARA budget, but they'd be putting on some extra help to catch
up as soon as the Appropriations Committee passed the IARA
budget, which, according to all the rumors, would be this afternoon,
so he'd probably be getting his money in a day or two.

"Well," Kerr said as he punched out his cigarette in Miss Carwell's
ashtray, "I guess I'd better be getting on to Processing."

The IARA's Processing Division was on the fourth floor, a fact
that Miss Oppenheimer, who was Chief of the Division, found a
source of ceaseless annoyance, because the Pershing Building's es-
calators did not go beyond the third floor. Kerr smoked a third cigarette while Miss Oppenheimer told him how she would construct the
government's office buildings if the job were put in her hands and
advised him that, while his passport and transportation had not yet
come through, she had every reason to believe these documents,
for which Kerr had now been waiting one hundred and thirteen days,
would be along momentarily, as soon as the House Appropriations Committee passed the IARA budget that afternoon.

"Well," Kerr said as he punched out his cigarette in Miss Oppenheimer's ashtray, "I guess I'd better be getting on to the Briefing
Room."

The Briefing Room, a large chamber on the second floor, in
which during the war the executives of several war agencies used to
gather for their directive meetings, now in peacetime performed
for the IARA approximately the same function that the word miscellaneous performs for a traveling salesman's expense account: anything that could not be fitted in elsewhere was thrown into it. There
were stacks of files on the floor waiting to be sorted; tied bundles
of books nobody found time to open; miscellaneous chairs and
smoking stands that might someday be needed to furnish the offices
of divisions and sections that had not yet been created; cartons of
stationery of defunct war agencies that ultimately would be cut up
to make scratch pads; and the IARA field representatives who were

awaiting passports and transportation to their assignments overseas.

When Kerr first arrived in Washington, there were seven other
men, specialists in various branches of agriculture, who had been
hired in different parts of the country, summoned to Washington,
and dumped into the Briefing Room on the second floor of the
Pershing Building to wait for passports and transportation. One by
one these men had gone off, to Greece and Bulgaria and India and
Poland, until Kerr was the sole survivor. The agency was very active,
and new men were being recruited all the time, so there was always
the chance that at any moment new faces would appear in the Briefing Room; but for the time being, Kerr was—in fact, for the past
three weeks he had been—the only occupant.

Now he put his briefcase on the large conference table in the middle of the room, sat down in a high-backed chair, put his feet on the
briefcase, and took from his pocket the traveling manicure set his
partner in Portland had given him as a farewell present. There were
other things to do in the Briefing Room, of course. There were
books on Chinese soil erosion to be read, and there were pamphlets
on various kinds of farm machinery to be studied; but during his
first few weeks in the Briefing Room, Kerr had learned all he wanted
to know about Chinese soil erosion, and during two decades as a
farm-machinery engineer, he had learned all there was to know
about tractors and manure spreaders and combines and automatic
balers. So, like all the other field representatives who had preceded
him, every morning when Kerr reached the Briefing Room, he
worked on his fingernails.

By a quarter to twelve he had done as much to them as he could
without causing himself serious injury and he was beginning to
feel hungry. Kerr put away the manicure set, took his hat and briefcase, and went out. He walked up Independence Avenue to the
People's Drugstore, where he lunched every day, and slipped onto
his regular stool at the far end of the counter. The soda clerk waved
to him and, as this was Wednesday, made him a ham and cheese
on rye and put the milk shake on the malted machine before he
came down the fountain.

"Morning, Mr. Kerr," he said, setting down the sandwich. "We got some chicken salad today, but confidentially it's mostly veal, and anyway, this being Wednesday, I thought you'd want your regular."

"That's right, Nick," Kerr said. "Thanks." It occurred to him that probably today he would have preferred chicken salad, even if it was mostly veal; but he decided, as he took his first bite, that there was no point in succumbing further to the unreasonable, annoying discomfort that already had caused him to send two packages of soap flakes to Portland instead of one and, before this curious day was over, might cause him to do other foolish things. The soda clerk went down the fountain to the malted machine and came back with the silver container.

"How's it going?" he said, pouring the milk shake. "Think you'll be getting off soon, Mr. Kerr?"

"Any day now," Kerr said. "Thanks, Nick."

By the time he had finished his sandwich, the luncheon crowd, which he managed to beat to his favorite stool by leaving the Briefing Room every day at a quarter to twelve, was streaming into the drugstore. Kerr took his check, and at the cashier's counter he bought a vacuum-packed tin of peanuts. His snack bar on the dresser of Room 4216 was running low, and he wanted something for Harry Cairn to nibble while they were having their drink at six before going on to the laundryman's home for dinner. Kerr put the can of peanuts into his briefcase, and near the door of the drugstore he stopped to glance at the notices thumbtacked to the Barter Bulletin Board on the wall over the machine that for a penny told your fortune along with your weight.

The management of the drugstore had installed the Barter Bulletin Board as a convenience for its customers during the war, when it was almost impossible to purchase certain commodities. The device had proved so popular that, even though the war was over and it was now easier to buy things, the management had allowed the Barter Bulletin Board to remain. Kerr noticed that the woman who wanted to swap her set of Thackeray for a two-slice electric toaster had not yet met with success, that the Wellesley girl who worked for the Department of Agriculture and was looking for a roommate who had gone to the same college was still living alone, and that the man who for almost a month had been willing to dispose of his well-behaved Persian cat had at last found a home for his pet. A new notice tacked to the bottom of the board caught Kerr's eye:

"Portable combination radio and record player, good condition, willing to swap or sell. B. F. Kiefer, 2314 A Cathedral Avenue. Don't call before 5:00 P.M."

Kerr read the card again, and as he stood there, the small sense of discomfort with which he had awakened that morning, the odd little feeling that something was askew, seemed to click back into place in his mind. He had come to Washington to spend a few days, a week at most, before going to China. The few days, the week at most, had stretched to almost four months. In that time, bit by bit, almost unconsciously, the habits of a lifetime had asserted themselves. Bit by bit, almost unconsciously, out of a second-rate hotel room and the fragment of a strange city that surrounded it, he had made a home for himself. Or rather as he saw now, he had made almost a home, because it wasn't much of a home these days that didn't have a radio and a phonograph. It was the missing piece, the finishing touch, the thing he had been needing without knowing that he had needed anything. Kerr pulled out the thumbtack, put the card in his pocket, and walked back to the Pershing Building, his stomach churning with excitement.

He made his second regular daily tour of the offices, smoked his second string of cigarettes with Miss Ames and Miss Carwell and Miss Oppenheimer, and heard them say for the second time that day, nope, no news yet; but he wasn't really listening to them. He was rearranging in his mind the complicated furnishings of the Admiral Hotel's room 4216, trying to find the best location for the "portable combination radio and record player, good condition, willing to swap or sell," which he had not yet seen and which, according to the card in his pocket, he was forbidden to see until five o'clock. It was only a few minutes after one when Kerr got back to the Briefing Room. As a rule, he spent the afternoon reading the newspapers, but because in his excitement he had forgotten to buy the afternoon papers on his way back to the Pershing Building, there was nothing for him to do during the next few hours except dig deeper into the literature on Chinese soil erosion. Kerr was in no mood to face this alternative. He spent an hour or so sketching floor plans of his hotel room, shifting the bed and the dresser and the trunk and the clothesline and the glass shelf and the row of hooks in the wall, trying to decide on the perfect setting for the piece of furniture that would make his home complete.

Suddenly Kerr looked up from the conference table, his face creased in a startled frown. Suppose the combination radio and record player was gone? It couldn't be, of course. The card was new. It had not been on the Barter Bulletin Board the day before. Anybody who was interested would have taken it down, and Kerr had the card in his pocket. It might have been read, though, by someone who didn't know the procedure, someone who could have copied the name and address and gone off to swap or buy the coveted object. In that case, however, wouldn't the former owner have stopped at the drugstore to remove the card from the board? You would think so, but you couldn't be sure. Kerr well knew that most people did not have his neat habits. He also knew that he couldn't remain in the IARA Briefing Room much longer in his present frame of mind. He looked at his watch. Twenty after three. He took the card from his pocket and looked at the address. Cathedral Avenue was in the third alphabet. It probably would take a half-hour by taxi. That meant he would be there a few minutes before four, and the card said, "Don't call before 5:00 P.M." The owner might not be there. Or the owner might be annoyed by the premature visit, and the annoyance might be reflected in the sales price. It didn't matter. Kerr had to take the risk.

"Twenty-three fourteen A Cathedral," the taxi driver said a half-hour later. "That's sixty cents, sir."

Kerr paid him and got out. He was standing in front of a small, red-brick apartment house. He took a deep breath, straightened his tie, tucked the briefcase under his arm, and went up the walk. There was a panel of six letter boxes in the foyer. The card in the slot under the box marked "2B" said "B. F. Kiefer." Kerr pressed the button and stepped back, as though taking up his stance for a long wait, but almost immediately there was a series of answering clicks. He opened the hall door.

"Yes?" a woman's voice called down the stair well. "Who is it?"

"I've come about your portable radio and record changer," Kerr called back. "That card you had on the board in the People's Drugstore."

"Oh, yes," the voice said, and Kerr's heart leaped with relief. The voice was friendly. "Won't you come up, please?"

Kerr went up and at the top of the second landing was met by an attractive woman with blonde hair and a pretty smile. She was wearing a pink suit with a dark blouse, and Kerr, whose methodical mind was trained to make calculations and assessments almost automatically, guessed that she was in her late twenties.

"I'm sorry to barge in on you this way," he said. "The card said not to call before five, I mean. But I didn't want anybody to get ahead of me."

"That's quite all right," she said. "You see, I work at night and don't usually get to bed before nine or ten in the morning, but I've been up since three o'clock. Won't you come in?" She led the way into her apartment. "My name is Kiefer, but I suppose you know that from the card. May I take those?"

"Why, yes, thanks," Kerr said, handing her his hat and briefcase. "Thanks very much."

She put them on a small table near the door, and Kerr, looking around the living room, noted with approval that it was tastefully furnished and well kept.

"There it is," she said, pointing to a leather box on the window sill. "I don't know if it's what you had in mind, but it's in rather good condition, and I'm anxious to get rid of it. I've just bought this large one, you see." She tapped a mahogany cabinet near the sofa. "And the apartment is so small that anything extra, even something as small as this, gets in the way."

"It looks grand," Kerr said. "May I try it, Mrs. Kiefer?"

"*Miss* Kiefer," she said, smiling again. "Please do."

They tried it, and it was plain, after a few twirls of the knobs and several bars from a couple of Tommy Dorsey records, that Miss Kiefer had told the truth when she had said the machine was in good condition.

"I'm afraid I don't have anything to offer as a swap," Kerr said. "I live out West, and I'm just staying here in Washington at a hotel for a while, so if you don't mind taking cash—"

"Not at all," Miss Kiefer said. "Would twenty dollars be too much? It cost thirty-five when it was new, but that was several years ago."

"If you don't think you're cheating yourself," Kerr said. "Frankly, I thought it would be more."

"No, twenty seems fair enough," Miss Kiefer said.

"Will a check do?" Kerr said. "I don't have that much cash on me."

"A check will be fine," Miss Keifer said.

"It's on a Portland, Oregon, bank," Kerr said, pulling out his checkbook and fountain pen. "But if you'll call the Admiral Hotel —that's where I'm staying—they'll vouch for it, I'm sure."

"Did you say the Admiral?" Miss Kiefer said.

"Yes," Kerr said. "Why?"

Miss Kiefer started to laugh. "That's where I work," she said.

Kerr stared at her for a long moment, and then, for the second time that day, something seemed to click back into place in his mind. "On the switchboard?" he said. "From midnight to eight?"

"Why, yes," Miss Kiefer said in surprise. "How did you know? And why are you laughing?"

"Because I think I owe you an apology," Kerr said. "I'm afraid I spoke sharply to you this morning when you gave me my seven-o'clock call."

Miss Kiefer's laugh, which Kerr noticed was even prettier than her smile, tinkled gaily through the small, attractive living room. "You're in 4216!" she said. "Your watch said five minutes to."

"That's right," Kerr said. "I didn't mean to speak sharply. It's just that I'm—well, you'll think it's silly."

"I'm sure I won't," Miss Kiefer said. "Look, since we're practically old friends—I mean, we've been talking to each other on the phone for months, now, and you've just bought my radio—you must have a drink. Will you?"

While she was in the kitchen mixing the drinks, Kerr stood in the doorway and told her about his own special way of classifying the members of the human race, and when she brought the glasses into the living room and he said he was rather proud of the fact that he belonged to the group that didn't need alarm clocks, Miss Kiefer said it might interest him to know that she belonged to the same group, although she confessed she never had thought of such an ingenious way to classify people, and she apologized for the fact that there was nothing in the cupboard to make canapés to go with the drinks.

"Working nights the way I do," she said, "I don't get much chance to shop."

"May I?" Kerr said, crossing the room to his briefcase and pulling out the can of peanuts he had bought to go with Harry Cairn's drink. "How about these?"

Miss Kiefer was delighted, and when Kerr explained how he happened to have a can of peanuts in his briefcase, she was positively ecstatic. Thus encouraged, Kerr told her more about his life in Washington during the past one hundred and fourteen days, a subject Miss Kiefer seemed to find fascinating.

When they had finished their drink, she offered to make another, but Kerr suggested that the day was too pleasant for staying indoors —by then, the sun was shining almost as brilliantly as if it were summer—and perhaps she would like to go for a stroll. She agreed immediately that this was an excellent idea, and told him there was a charming little church in the neighborhood that he perhaps might like to see.

Together they walked down the stairs and out of the red-brick apartment house.

They sauntered slowly for two or three blocks, Miss Kiefer directing at the corners and Kerr talking to her, now quite eagerly, about his one hundred and fourteen days in Washington.

The little church he found to be as charming as she had promised it would be. After they had walked all around it, and even investigated its quiet interior, they sat down to rest on the stone base of the surrounding fence. Kerr was glad to rest—and to set down the combination radio and phonograph, which he had carried from her apartment and which had grown very heavy. Miss Kiefer had insisted on carrying his briefcase. She still seemed to find his conversation fascinating, and urged him to talk further about himself.

While they were sitting there—Kerr talking eagerly and Miss Kiefer listening with flatteringly rapt attention—there was a brief diversion. A barrel-organ man and his trained monkey approached. Kerr would not have thought they existed anywhere these modern days—especially in Washington—and their presence added momentarily to the brightness of the sunshine, and to the brightness of Miss Kiefer's really delightful smile.

They sat there for, perhaps, half an hour, and when Miss Kiefer finally looked at her watch and said, oh, dear, she had a date at the hairdresser's, Kerr felt a twinge of disappointment that was new to him. He was not, ordinarily, a garrulous man. An enraptured audience was a fresh experience. It occurred to him that he hadn't had such a good time since he'd arrived in Washington and, made courageous perhaps by the drink, he said that he felt he had to seal his apology for speaking sharply to her on the phone that morning, as well as pay her back for the drink and conversation, so would she have dinner with him?

"I'd love to, but I can't," Miss Kiefer said, with so much obvious regret that for a moment Kerr felt a glow of warmth that more properly should have been the result of her acceptance. "This date is for a permanent, and you know what that means. I'll be at the hairdresser's until ten or later, and I'm due at the Admiral switchboard at midnight."

"Well, then, some other time," Kerr said. "Will you have dinner with me tomorrow night?"

"I'd be delighted," Miss Kiefer said, smiling her charming smile. "But remember, it will really be breakfast for me."

All the way back to the Admiral in the taxi, holding the combination radio and phonograph on his knees, Kerr felt the way he had felt when, after finishing his ham and cheese on rye in the People's Drugstore, he discovered the little card on the Barter Bulletin Board. The missing piece, the finishing touch, the thing he had been needing to complete the home he had built for himself around a second-rate hotel room in a strange city had been found at last, and it wasn't what he had thought it was when he first looked at the card on the board. A combination radio and phonograph doesn't make a home complete. All the furniture in the world can't take the place of the thing that really makes a home. There was a quality of maturity, of ripeness, about Miss Kiefer that set her apart from all the girls Kerr had met in the IARA offices, and occasionally lunched with. Miss Ames and Miss Carwell and Miss Oppenheimer and their friends were nice enough girls, but they were girls, and their appeal was behind Kerr, a family man of settled habits in his late forties. Miss Kiefer, however, was a woman.

"You said the Admiral, didn't you?"

Kerr looked up quickly. The taxi had stopped in front of the hotel.

"That's right," he said, getting out. "Sorry, driver. I was thinking of something else."

He hurried through the lobby and into the elevator. As he opened the door of Room 4216, the phone started to ring. Kerr, ducking the clothesline and stepping carefully across the neatly cluttered carpet toward the phone, paused to set the combination radio and phonograph on the bed. He sat down beside it, and as he picked up the telephone, the last floor plan he had sketched in the Briefing Room that afternoon came into his mind. He had been right. It was the best of the lot. The leather box would fit on the glass shelf over his bed. The coffee cup and saucer and spoon could go on the dresser, between the percolator and the snack bar.

"Hello," Kerr said.

"Mr. Kerr?" It was Charley, and Kerr could tell, from the sound of the desk clerk's voice, that his advice against consuming the pint of rye during working hours had again been disregarded. "That you, Mr. Kerr?"

"Yes," Kerr answered. "What's up, Charley?"

"I thought I saw you come in," Charley said. "But you didn't stop at the desk, the way you always do, so I thought I'd better call and—"

"I was carrying a heavy bundle," Kerr said, surprised and then annoyed by the reminder of this unconscious variation from his routine. "What's the matter, Charley?"

"I been trying to reach you since three-thirty," Charley said. "But you wasn't at any of the places on the list, and you said this morning same schedule for today, no changes, so I didn't know what to do except wait till you came back at five-thirty, the way you always do, but holy smoke, Mr. Kerr, you're late. It's a quarter to six now, and you know I go off at six."

"I'm sorry," Kerr said impatiently. "I got stuck. What's on your mind, Charley?"

"Your office called at three-thirty," Charley said. "A Miss Oppen-

heimer, Processing Division, she said, and she said it was important."

Kerr's wandering thoughts came away from the floor plan and the
combination radio and phonograph and gathered together in a sudden, tight knot that made his head ache. The call for which he had
waited one hundred and fourteen days had come at last. "My passport?" he said. "The transportation? They've come through?"

"I guess so," Charley said, his alcoholic voice quivering with the
excitement of revelation. "This Miss Oppenheimer, she said it was
important, and you should—"

"What else did she say?" Kerr said. "No, wait. Get her for me,
Charley. Republic 7500. Extension 82546. Get her on the phone for
me."

"She ain't in the office any more," Charley said. "It's a quarter to
six, Mr. Kerr. She said if you didn't come back by five, I should have
you call her at her home. She gave me the number. She said—"

"All right, all right, all right," Kerr said with sudden anger. "Get
her for me, will you? Stop yammering, and get her for me."

"Yes, sir," Charley said. "Just hold on, Mr. Kerr."

Kerr held on; as his glance swung around Room 4216, the anger
churned up from his stomach, spreading through his body. They
couldn't do this to him. They couldn't tear a man away from his
home like this, without warning. There was too much to do. There
were the hooks to be taken out of the wall, the clothesline to be
dismantled, the contents of the liquor cabinet and snack bar to be
disposed of, ten packages of soap flakes still to be wrapped and sent
to Portland. There were the overcoat to be delivered to Milton, the
glass shelf over the bed to be taken down, his shirts in the Congress
Hand Laundry to be retrieved, the trunk to be packed, and—his
swinging glance catching the combination radio and phonograph
on the bed beside him—there was his dinner date with Miss Kiefer
tomorrow night. The thought of Miss Kiefer brought Kerr's fury
at the IARA to such a pitch that his ear, against which he was pressing the receiver, began to sting. Damn them, they couldn't uproot a
man from his home at a moment's notice, as though he were a va-
grant, without possessions or responsibilities. They didn't have the
right. It wasn't neat. It wasn't fair.

"Here's your call, Mr. Kerr," Charley said. "Go ahead."

"Hello." It was Miss Oppenheimer's efficient voice. "Mr. Kerr?"

"Yes," Kerr said savagely. "Now, look, Miss Oppenheimer. The IARA has kept me hanging around Washington for four months through no fault of mine. For one hundred and fourteen days I've been patient, I haven't complained, but I'm damned if I'm going to let myself be shoved into a plane for China just like that, without any warning or chance—"

"I'm afraid you're not going to China," Miss Oppenheimer said. "By plane or any other way. The House Appropriations Committee took up the IARA budget this afternoon, Mr. Kerr, and they slashed it in half. The Director called a meeting at once in the basement auditorium, and I ran down to the Briefing Room to get you, but you weren't there. I called your hotel, but you weren't there, either. I'm terribly sorry, Mr. Kerr, but we're not sending out any more field representatives. We don't have the money."

"Oh," Kerr said as the anger drained out of him, and then, "You mean I'm fired?"

"Well, not exactly," Miss Oppenheimer said. "Except that I suppose you are. The Director ordered me to advise all field representatives waiting in Washington and other parts of the country that they will be relieved from duty at once. We don't have the money to send you to China, Mr. Kerr. You can go home now."

"Home?" Kerr said.

"Back to your own business in Portland, I mean," Miss Oppenheimer said, and her briskly efficient voice seemed to unbend slightly. "The Director has asked me to say that it was very patriotic of you to volunteer your services, and we're all sorry that you won't get a chance to go to China, but I suppose in a way it's quite a relief to you, isn't it?"

"Well," Kerr said.

"I mean, I thought you'd be pleased by the chance to get back to your home and your family." Miss Oppenheimer took up the slack in her voice. "If you'll come into the office tomorrow morning, I'll give you your ticket," she said. "I have a reservation for you on the four-o'clock plane for Portland."

A long moment went by before Kerr realized he was holding a dead phone. He replaced it on the hook and, without thinking, reached for his cigarettes. His hand touched the leather box on the bed. He turned and stared at the combination radio and phonograph while he lighted a cigarette. There was a knock on the door.

"Yes?" Kerr said automatically.

The door opened, and the proprietor of the Congress Hand Laundry walked into Room 4216. "Hi," Harry Cairn said. "Six o'clock on the button. How's that for timing? Where's that drink you promised me?"

"Why," Kerr said, like a man coming awake after a bad night, "why, help yourself, Harry." He nodded to the small cluster of bottles next to the percolator on the dresser. "I won't have time to join you," he said. "I'm afraid I won't even be able to help you eat that ham Dixie managed to put her hands on."

"Why not?" Harry Cairn said and then, his voice lifting with sudden comprehension, "You got your call?" he said "Phil, you're leaving at last?"

"That's right," Kerr said. "I'm leaving at last."

"Boy, oh, boy. Off to China," Harry Cairn said, picking up a bottle from the dresser and reaching for a glass. "You lucky son of a gun."

"No, not to China," Kerr said.

But the rest of Harry Cairn's statement was true. He was lucky, all right. Miss Kiefer had a quality of ripeness, of maturity. Kerr, who had been married for twenty years, knew it was a quality that had a tendency to cling. You couldn't get rid of it so easily as you could get rid of an old overcoat or the contents of a snack bar or ten boxes of soap flakes. If another twenty-four hours had gone by, if he had been held over in Washington long enough to keep the dinner date that was really breakfast to Miss Kiefer, he might have had to begin classifying the members of the human race into two entirely new groups: the people who know where their homes are and the people who don't. If the one hundred and fourteen days had become one hundred and fifteen, there was a good chance that Kerr would have had to stop being proud of the group to which he belonged.

"Here," he said, pushing the combination radio and phonograph toward Harry Cairn. "Here's a little farewell present I got for you and Dixie. When my shirts are ready, you can send them by parcel post. Better insure them, just to be on the safe side. I'm in a hurry, Harry, and I've got to travel light."

"Gosh, thanks, Phil," said the proprietor of the Congress Hand Laundry. "But where the devil are you going, if not to China?"

"I'm going to a better place," Kerr said as he looked around the cluttered room, at the hooks in the wall, the overcoat, the soap flakes in the carton, and he punched out his cigarette as he pushed himself up from the bed with a decisive shove. There were many things to be done before he climbed into that four-o'clock plane tomorrow, and he didn't want to leave any of them undone. It wasn't neat.

"I'm going home," Kerr said cheerfully.

Chutzbah

The people on our block never had any doubts about Marcel Cohen's ultimate success in life. Dr. Cohen's son was considered an unusual child. First, because he was "a doctor's son," and second, because of his name—Marcel.

As far as all of us on Fourth Street, from Avenue D to the East River, were concerned, the name was a new one. It was considered bad taste to call children anything but Harry or Julius or Aaron. But a doctor was permitted a certain amount of freedom from convention. Doctors were different. They had gone to college and were, as a rule, American-born, and had telephones and, occasionally, automobiles.

Until he graduated from public school, Marcel was not permitted to play on the street with the other children. Mrs. Cohen explained to the women in Deutsch's Bakery or Greenberg's Butcher Shop that this was not because he was too good for the other boys. It was simply that Marcel was an unusual child. The mothers of the block thought the explanation adequate.

After the *bar mitzvah* ceremony that marked his thirteenth birthday, however, Marcel was allowed to mingle with the other boys, and he became better known.

He read a great deal, and in the years of his seclusion he had accumulated an unusual collection of Frank Merriwells and Nick Carters and other paper-covered books. Every boy on the block devoured books of this nature, and when news of Marcel's collection leaked out, he was besieged with requests for them. At first he said his mother would not allow him to lend them. Shortly afterward, however, he let it be known that she had granted him permission to sell them.

He charged three cents a copy, and bought them back for a penny after his customers finished reading them. A boy could read a Merriwell in one or, at most, two days. Marcel had enough to go around for six months, until every boy on the block had read the entire collection, at two cents a copy. Then he disposed of them all at two cents apiece.

The mothers of the block thought Marcel was a good influence on their sons. He kept them off the streets a little. He was the first one to start a stamp collection. He sent for stamps on approval and sold them to the boys, making a little commission on the side. Many times he would show his friends a stamp in his album, say what he had paid for it, and substantiate his statement by showing them the price in Scott's. Then someone would offer to buy it and Marcel would let it go reluctantly. Later, after they found that Scott's listed an ordinary U. S. two-cent stamp at five cents, it was felt that Marcel had been overcharging them by using catalogue prices, but nothing came of it. Marcel could talk very convincingly.

His face was clean-cut and honest-looking, more so than those of his companions, and his clothes were always new and neat, of the department-store type, which in itself was enough to set him apart. All the other clothes on the block came from the *storkes* on Avenue A and Stanton Street. Mrs. Cohen was the only woman on the block who shopped in department stores.

Among his friends, he soon established a reputation for nerve. He avoided fights and "raids," claiming that he had a weak heart, but he did things the other boys were afraid to do, or, rather, never thought of doing.

If a boy had a nickel and wanted to buy candy, Marcel would offer to do it for him, guaranteeing him more for his money. He would go into the candy store and wait until the woman's back was turned. Then, deft as lightning, he would snatch something from the counter and jam it into his coat pocket. When the proprietress turned around, he would be waiting quietly for change or to be served. He looked so honest and clean-cut and incapable of wrongdoing.

From his father's books, particularly from the pictures in them, he gleaned an early, if somewhat sketchy, knowledge of the facts of life. Resting on a stoop or in an empty hallway after a game of Kick the Can and Hiding, or Leevio, he spread his information among his friends. Talking in his low, convincing voice, his handsome face set in seriousness, he repeated what he had read and seen, simplifying and enlarging. He taught them to sing bawdy songs, and even added occasional lyrics. But of all this the parents of the block knew nothing.

Every boy on the block was a practitioner of the art of hitching on the backs of wagons, but Marcel improved even on that. He introduced the practice of hitching on trucks. There was excitement in this. Getting off a moving truck was a difficult feat in our neighborhood, because there were no traffic lights then, but Marcel was adept at it.

Dr. Cohen pointed with pride to his son, and told patients to feed their children as he fed his. Regular meals, the Doctor insisted (and believed), were responsible for his son's rapid growth. No eating in between meals, no fancy foods, and, above all, no delicatessen. But Marcel was already leading expeditions as far west as Astor Place for long red weenies, with plenty of sauerkraut and mustard, at a nickel each. Frequently, one of his companions, unable to finish his hot dog because of a recent meal, would throw part of it away. Marcel soon stopped this. All leftovers and unfinished parts were turned over to him. He ate all day, even shamelessly asking for remains of lunches in school. The Doctor, watching him down his evening meal, and noting his ruddy cheeks, plump body, and close approach to six feet in height, complimented himself on the excellence of his theory about regular meals.

Marcel's self-assurance was amazing. He lied with an ease and grace that was disarming. While in high school, he was caught operating a "pick-board," a gambling device that cost fifteen cents and yielded three dollars in profit. The school disciplinarian sent for the Doctor. Marcel stared at them innocently for a while. Then he broke down and confessed: he didn't even know what he had been doing. A strange boy had approached him in the lunchroom and asked him to hold the "pick-board" while he got some lunch. He went into details about time and the color of the stranger's hair. He

walked out of the disciplinarian's office, his name officially unblem-
ished, pledged to aid in the discovery of the true culprit.

Shortly before he graduated from high school, the Doctor had
a serious talk with him.

"Son," the Doctor said, being very American and modern, "what
do you want to do when you grow up? What do you want to be?"

Marcel was probably the only boy in the neighborhood who had
ever been thus spoken to.

"Anything at all, Pa. Anything you say." Marcel creaked into a
more comfortable position on the most expensive sofa on the block.

The Doctor looked sternly down at his son. "Well, what do you
like? What are you good at?" He couldn't help but sound a bit exasperated.

"Everything. Anything," Marcel said.

The Doctor suggested medicine, not very enthusiastically. "O.K.,"
Marcel said. Or maybe law? "O.K.," Marcel said. Teach? "Yeah,
O.K." Well, *what?*

"Oh, anything, Pa. I can do anything." Marcel was getting tired
of this.

"Well, *what?*"

"Oh—say medicine. No, wait." Marcel remembered his father's
stories of the hard years he had spent in study. He felt so comfortable now. "How about pharmacy? That's like medicine, isn't it?
It won't take me so long and I could be earning money soon."

"All right, son, if that's your decision. If you feel you'd be good
at it."

"Yeah. I'm good at anything."

The Doctor went to give the news to his wife, feeling that he had
stirred his son from his lethargy. Marcel went to sleep.

His pharmacy studies kept him busy only part of the day. He
looked around for a job to fill the spare hours. An advertisement
asking for young men to sell X-ray supplies to doctors and hospitals caught his fancy. He went around to see what he could do.
They were not particular about the men they hired (it was on a
commission basis), but they asked for a deposit on the samples
they supplied to their salesmen. Marcel soon talked them out of this
notion.

In a few weeks he was earning so much money that he begrudged the few hours he had to spend in school every day. His success as a salesman amazed everybody but himself.

"I knew I'd be good at it," he told his father.

X-ray materials were supposed to be difficult to sell. Marcel didn't think so. He bluffed his way into the offices of hospital purchasing agents and kidded nurses of private doctors into placing their orders with him. But he remained in school, paying his own tuition until he graduated.

A year after he passed his examinations, while working in a drugstore on Seventh Avenue, he talked his grandfather into a non-interest-bearing loan and bought his own store on the West Side. The store had been losing steadily for three years when he took it over, but within fifteen months he had repaid his grandfather, and he owned it free and clear.

One day a man came in and asked for a bottle of expensive perfume. Marcel didn't have it in stock, but he had a dummy bottle in the showcase. He wrapped the bottle neatly and sold it. As soon as the customer left, he telephoned his jobber for a bottle of the perfume and sent his porter to fetch it immediately. Shortly afterward the customer returned with the dummy bottle. Marcel apologized profusely for the "accident," gave the man the bottle just received from the jobber, and returned the dummy to the showcase.

One day he arrived at the conclusion that his fountain was not profitable enough. He was paying too much for the "makings." In a week he had organized a druggists' association. He had no difficulty because there were no membership fees or dues. It was merely a collective buying organization, with Marcel as its spokesman.

He spoke to his milkman. "What am I paying you for milk?"

"Ten cents."

"How many druggists on the West Side buy from you?"

"Twenty-three."

"Well, if you had a hundred, all buying from you, would you sell for eight cents?"

"Nope. Can't be done."

"O.K.," Marcel said, turning away. "Don't deliver here any more after today. And," he added, "that goes for twenty of your other twenty-two customers."

"Ah, gee, Doc, now listen. Don't be like that. I tell ya—"

After the two-cent reduction in milk, Marcel turned to the baker, the ice-cream company, and the syrup manufacturer. It wasn't long before his fountain was running at a profit more to his liking.

During the prohibition era, he wasn't supposed to sell liquor save on a doctor's prescription, but he carried several impressively labeled, although cheap, brands. As his customers disliked the bother and difficulty of securing a doctor's prescription, here was a source of revenue that insisted upon being tapped. For the privilege of printing his own name in one corner, Marcel supplied several of the neighboring doctors with all the prescription pads they needed, and as each order of pads came from the printer, he took one or two for himself, and sent the rest to the doctor. In this way he had quite a variety to choose from, and when one of his many steady customers came into the store for supplies, Marcel scribbled something illegible on one of the pads, passed the bottle across the counter, and filed the "prescription" away.

With repeal, the slot-machine racket began to receive considerable attention from City Hall, but it paid a split of fifty per cent on all takings, and Marcel was loath to let his machines go. So he moved them behind the prescription panel and catered to a discriminating clientele. He was one of the few who continued to defray expenses in this easy manner throughout the reform period.

The store was on the West Side, and it was a long trip home to his father's house, late at night, after closing. Very frequently, particularly on Saturdays, because his clerk was off on Sunday and he had to open the store early himself, he slept in the neighborhood. But hotels are expensive, and not very private. Marcel soon arranged with the superintendent of a neighboring apartment house for the use of a furnished apartment while its tenant was out of town. In return, Marcel supplied him with medical supplies and third-rate whiskey. It was a convenient arrangement, in more ways than one.

All his escapades, everything that happened to him, he related to his father. They would sit in the waiting-room, smoking cigars that Marcel brought from the store.

"So when the real tenant, you know, when he came home unexpectedly and he found me there, in the apartment, what do you think I said?" Marcel would ask with a grin.

"That the superintendent let you in?" the Doctor would suggest gleefully.

"No-o-*oh!*" Marcel's voice would be tolerantly reproachful. "Naturally, I didn't want to get the *super* in Dutch. I told him, I said, I was a new tenant and I must've gone to the wrong apartment by mistake. Naturally, the super backed me up."

The Doctor never failed to laugh heartily. Some boy, this son of his. What a head! What brains! What nerve!

The stories were too good to be kept secret. The Doctor repeated them to the neighbors of the block, adopting his son's method of presentation, asking for a solution before overwhelming his listeners with the climax.

They laughed, too, sincerely and appreciatively. They remembered Marcel as a boy and were glad to hear that he had "turned out all right." A doctor was entitled to have an unusual son.

Even among themselves, when the Doctor was absent, they spoke highly of Marcel. They reminded each other of their prophecies, made years before, when he was a boy.

"A *finer jung!*" they would say. "He's all right, that boy. He's got *chutzbah!*"

The Clean Slate

It was not the headache that bothered her, even though Irene could tell that soon it would be worse than a headache. Nor was it the fact that Irene could not understand why she should have one. It was not even the annoying look of sympathy on Seraphina's good-natured face as she listened to her mistress' instructions for the day. What bothered Irene was that she should have allowed herself, on this of all days, to wake up in anything less than the absolute pink of condition.

"Have you got all that straight, Seraphina?"

"Yes, Mrs. Creel," the stout, middle-aged Italian woman said. "I understand."

Irene wondered irritably if she did. Holly Trait, when she found Seraphina for her soon after Irene arrived from New York, had insisted Seraphina was the best all around servant in Rome. After almost a year, during which Seraphina had not only done all the cooking and kept the apartment spotless but had also taken complete charge of the children, Irene saw no reason to alter Holly's excellent reference. There were times, however, and this morning was one of them, when Irene wished that the motherly Italian woman, who was all heart, was also just a little quicker at grasping simple instructions.

"I think perhaps you'd better repeat the whole thing back to me," Irene said, trying to keep the impatience out of her voice. After all, the fact that she had a splitting headache at eleven o'clock in the morning of this day when so much depended on her physical appearance, was not Seraphina's fault. "Just to make sure you've got it right."

Seraphina nodded eagerly, the way she did when the children asked her to join in one of their games. The reason she was probably so good with Connie, aged five, and Petey, aged six, Irene thought as she tried to remember where she had left the aspirin bottle, was that Seraphina, for all her fifty odd years, was still something of a child herself.

"Today, this afternoon, three o'clock, when the lessons they are finished, Seraphina does not go to the school, as she does every day to bring home the bambinos," she said. "Today, this afternoon, three o'clock, when the lessons they are finished, it is Mrs. Creel who will go to the school to meet small Peter and small Constance, because today is a very special day."

That was the word, all right. Special.

"Yes," Irene said, closing her eyes slightly against the dull throbbing ache in her temples, and trying not to sound hurried. The trick with a headache like this one was to nail it fast with aspirin, before it got away into something worse. But Irene did not want to upset Seraphina. It was important on this very important day that everything go smoothly. "And while I'm taking the children from school out to the airport to meet Mr. Creel's plane," she said to Seraphina, "you'll be shopping and arranging flowers and cooking and doing whatever you have to do to make tonight's dinner special enough to match this special day."

Seraphina bobbed her head.

"I will do," she said, and then the annoying look of sympathy reappeared as she asked, "The signora does not feel good?"

"Nonsense," Irene said sharply. "I feel wonderful. What ever made you think—?"

The tinkling of the telephone bell saved her from completing the question she neither wanted to ask nor have answered. If she looked the way she felt, the thing to do was not discuss it with Seraphina. The thing to do was swallow some aspirin fast and go back to bed for a couple of hours so that, by the time she drove out to Ciampino with the children at three o'clock, she would look the way for more than a week she had been reminding herself night and day she *had* to look when Frank stepped out of that plane from New

York. Irene moved across the living room toward the telephone near the window through which, if you twisted your neck hard to the left, you could get a fairly respectable view of an attractive slice of the Borghese Gardens. She picked up the phone.

"Hello?"

"Hi, sweetie," Holly Trait's high-pitched, slightly nasal voice said. "How do you feel?"

It was the question Holly asked every morning.

"Fine," Irene said, because that was the reply she made every morning. "How do *you* feel?"

"Just great," said Holly. "Which makes me as bad a liar as you are." She giggled. "Actually I feel the way Pocahontas would have felt if, while she was trying to save Captain John Smith's life, some bad-tempered Indian had run a knife around the top of her skull and lifted her scalp exactly one half inch from its normal resting place."

In spite of the throbbing in her temples, Irene smiled. Holly Trait didn't have any money, and if her failure to make a dent in Hollywood and on Broadway was any yardstick, she didn't have much talent as an actress, either. But she certainly had a gift for vivid verbal imagery. She and Irene had met and become friends during Irene's first week in Rome, and since Holly called her every morning, and the conversation always started in exactly the same way, it meant that the bouncy little blonde from Poughkeepsie, who had come to Rome three years ago to find a career in television films—or so Holly said, anyway—had managed to describe her hangover graphically more than three hundred times, without once repeating herself.

"That's exactly the way *I* feel," Irene said. "Except that I can't figure out why."

"I can fill that gap for you, sweetie," Holly said dryly. "You laid the groundwork for it at the Vitibellis' last night."

"The Vitibellis'?" Irene said.

"Sweetie," Holly said through another giggle. "Don't tell me you don't remember being at the Vitibellis' last night?"

Irene didn't tell her because, for several awful moments, Irene was incapable of speech. Once again, without warning, she had been plunged into the now familiar terror, the recurrent fear that had touched her for the first time two years ago in New York, on

Irene said more calmly. "I won't be able to have a drink with you and Mr. Peccarari this afternoon."

"But sweetie, why not?"

"I'm going out to the airport with the children at three," Irene said, wishing she'd had the courage to ask Seraphina to find the aspirin and bring it to her. The throbbing pain was becoming unbearable. "Frank gets in from New York this afternoon."

"Oh!" Holly said. The single syllable, and the moment of silence that followed, were eloquent. In the excitement of meeting Mr. Peccarari, whoever he was, Holly had obviously forgotten temporarily how special this day was for Irene. "Jeepers," Holly said. "That's right." There was another pause, and then she said, hopefully, "Maybe, sweetie, after you and Frank get back to the apartment from the airport, maybe you could sneak away for a little while? After all, the plane gets in at four, and this date with Mr. Peccarari is at five, which would give you a whole hour with Frank, and he'll be so crazy to see the kids, he probably won't mind being alone with them in the apartment for an hour or so while you run over to the Hassler to meet me and this Peccarari guy, and—"

"No, I'm sorry," Irene said as firmly as the pain in her head would allow. "You know how important this visit of Frank's is. Everything depends on it. I can't take a chance on his getting any wrong impressions his first day here. You go meet this Mr. Peccarari if you want to, Holly. I'm not leaving Frank for a minute. Not only today, but for the entire week he's going to be here in Rome."

"Sure, sweetie," Holly said slowly, making no effort to conceal the disappointment in her voice. "I guess you're right."

"I'll speak to you in the morning," Irene said. "I've got to hurry, have my bath now."

She hung up, and she did hurry, but not toward her bath. Irene hurried to the bedroom, and then to the medicine cabinet in the bathroom, and then back to the dresser drawers in the bedroom, and then out to the foyer for the pill box in the purse she had dropped when she came in last night, but the frantic hunt proved fruitless: the pill box, like the medicine bottles in the bathroom cabinet and the bedroom dresser drawers, was empty; there was no aspirin in the apartment. There certainly wasn't any within reach.

"Seraphina!" Irene called as she came back across the foyer into the dining room, aware that the rage in her voice was directed at herself, because the pain in her head was now unbearable, and her knees felt weak, and she was on the verge of tears. "Seraphina, for heaven's sake, where the devil did you put the—?"

The swinging door from the kitchen groaned open.

"Signora?" Seraphina said in a frightened voice. "Signora, you are sick?"

"No, I'm *not* sick! And will you please get that damned look off your face? All I need is a—"

Irene's voice stopped. That wasn't what she needed. Not any more. This headache was now beyond aspirin. Irene made a tremendous effort and, in spite of the pain, she managed a small smile.

"I'm sorry, Seraphina," she said quietly. "Please pay no attention to me. You can go back to the kitchen." But Seraphina did not move. Not immediately, anyway. And it became necessary for Irene to say more sharply, "I said you can go back to the kitchen, Seraphina!"

This time she did, her large, shapeless body moving backwards, her simple, innocent face creased by a troubled frown. Before the swinging door had groaned shut, Irene had stepped swiftly across the room, to the silver tray on the sideboard, and even though her hands shook badly, she managed to pour the stiff shot of whiskey without spilling a drop, and she drank it off without pausing to set the bottle down. She was pouring a second shot when, unexpectedly, without warning, the sound of the bottle rattling against the rim of the glass tripped a trigger of memory.

Irene looked up, startled, into the mirror over the sideboard, wondering what it was her mind was trying to disgorge, and then she saw the reflection of the swinging door at the other side of the room, and the dreadful picture came back.

It came back so fast, roaring at her like a wave rolling up a beach, that it seemed to carry Irene with it, hurling her backward in time and space, from this moment in her apartment overlooking the Borghese Gardens in Rome, back to the morning that was just a little more than a year old, the morning in the apartment overlooking Central Park into which Frank and Irene Creel had moved the week after he became the youngest and brightest vice president at

Shenton & Shaw, the oldest and biggest advertising agency on Madison Avenue.

It was still early, not quite ten o'clock, so that Frank had not yet left for the office. But it had been a bad night. Really bad. One of the worst Irene had gone through since that frightening morning after her twenty-third birthday party when she realized she had blacked out for the first time. It had happened often enough since then to blunt the edge of that initial terror, but on this morning all Irene could remember of the night before was an argument with a man on the sidewalk in front of the Stork Club while Frank was paying the taxi driver who had brought them there from the theatre. Irene couldn't remember who the man was, or how the argument had started, or where she went after the Stork Club, or whether Frank had gone with her. All she knew was that this was one morning when she couldn't wait until Frank left the apartment for the office.

As soon as he disappeared into the bathroom, she slipped out of bed, hurried across to her dressing table, opened the bottom drawer, pawed about under the neatly folded nightgowns, and pulled out the bottle. She had gulped down the first stiff shot, and she was pouring the second, when the sound of the bottle rattling against the rim of the glass caused her to glance up nervously, into the dressing table mirror, and then she saw Frank.

He was standing at the other side of the room, in the bathroom doorway, holding the empty aspirin bottle, the irritated and still unuttered comment on its emptiness forgotten as he stared across the bedroom.

In the long, long moment of silence, even as she struggled desperately to summon up plausible answers to the questions Frank had not yet had a chance to ask, Irene was grateful for that first stiff shot she had managed to get down before she was caught. Already, even before Frank started across the bedroom toward her, the whiskey had begun its healing work.

Frank stopped in front of her, and he took the bottle from Irene's hand, and he looked at it for another long moment, as though he were trying to memorize the words on the label, before he looked up at his wife.

"How long has this been going on?" he said.

"You're a fine one to talk!" Irene snapped. "If you haven't got a hangover of your own from here to here, what are you doing with the aspirin bottle first thing in the morning?"

"Aspirin bottles first thing in the morning are bad enough," Frank said. He tapped the whiskey bottle. "How long have you been dipping into this kind before breakfast?"

"Don't you give me that holier-than-thou tone of voice! Just because I happen to take a drink before breakfast for the first time in my life, that doesn't mean you have the right to—"

Frank leaned over, shoved aside the nightgowns in the dressing table drawer, and pulled out the other bottle.

"First time in your life?" he said. Irene didn't answer. Frank held the bottle out to her. "I asked a question," he said. "How long has this been going on?"

"None of your business!"

"Anything is my business that starts kicking holes in my job," Frank said.

"What are you talking about?"

"Your little performance last night on the sidewalk in front of the Stork Club."

"That drunk!" Irene said.

"That drunk was not only cold sober," Frank said. "He happened to be T. B. Jarvis of Jarvis Razor, Shenton & Shaw's biggest client and my special account."

"Oh," Irene said.

"Yes, oh," Frank said. "It was bad enough calling him names on the sidewalk in front of the Stork, but two hours later, when we ran into him again at the St. Regis—"

"At the St. Regis?"

As soon as the words were out, Irene realized they were a mistake. But it was too late. Frank was staring at her in a funny way.

"You really don't remember," he said quietly. "Do you?"

"Of course I remember!" Irene said. "It's just that—"

Her voice stopped. So did her anger. It wasn't accomplishing anything. She could tell from the look in Frank's eyes.

"I've suspected it for over a year," he said. "Ever since your twenty-third birthday party."

Irene's heart leaped as though she had been punched.

"Suspected what?"

"That the drinking has been getting away from you," Frank said. "That you can't handle it. That you've been blacking out. I haven't said anything because I'm not a teetotaler myself, and also because it hasn't really done any harm." Frank looked down at the bottle he had pulled from under the nightgowns in the dressing table drawer. "But now—"

"It's not as bad as you think," Irene said quickly. "No man would be childish enough to take his account away from an agency just because—"

"I wasn't thinking of T. B. Jarvis," Frank said. He turned to glance across the bedroom, toward the door that led to the nursery. "I was thinking of Petey and Connie."

"There's nothing wrong with them!"

"Not yet," Frank said, and he seemed to know that the quick anger leaping in her eyes and to her lips would spend itself, because he merely waited. When it became obvious that she had no reply, Frank said, very quietly, "What's happened to us, baby?"

Irene didn't know, even though she remained in the apartment all day, trying to work out an answer. From the moment Frank left for the office she sat slumped in a chair near the window, staring out at Central Park, hearing the sounds of the household around her, the clatter of the cook in the kitchen, the hum of the vacuum cleaner, the voices of the children, the clucking words of the nurse, the slamming of doors as they came and went. All day Irene sat there, listening to the bits and pieces of the life she and Frank had fashioned between them, picking them apart, rearranging them, trying to put the pieces together into an answer to Frank's question, but it wasn't any good.

It was like a jig-saw puzzle from which the picture had been stripped away. She had all the pieces, she could see them clearly, but there were no clues to tell her how to fit them together.

Irene could see herself and Frank in Battle Creek High School, and then at the State University. She could hear her mother saying she certainly didn't believe in long engagements, not as a general rule, and if a boy and girl were in love, why, they should get married, that's all, but didn't Irene think it would be wise to wait just a *little* while, at least until Frank got a job? She could see Frank's face, the day he came up the walk to the porch where Irene was sitting with her mother, shelling peas, and she could hear his voice as he told her about Butler & Gottschalk, and how much they were paying him to start.

Irene could see the church on Farragut Avenue, and she could hear the voice of Reverend Brewer, and she could see the way the lump in Frank's throat moved when he looked into her eyes and said, very quietly, "I do!" Irene could see the one-room cabin on the lake in Minnesota where they had spent their honeymoon, and the small frame house on Truesdale Road where they lived until Petey was born. She could see the roses Frank brought her the day Butler & Gottschalk promoted him to copy chief, and the bottle of champagne they ordered in Feberwalter's the night the offer came through from Shenton & Shaw.

Irene could see the face of the stewardess in the plane that had carried them to New York, and the stoop of the brownstone on Barrow Street in which they had lived until Connie was born. She could see the apartment on Park Avenue in which she had gone to her first cocktail party, and the walkup on East Forty-Eighth in which, now that Frank had brought the Renshaw account into the office and had been suitably rewarded by a salary boost, she had given her first sit down dinner party for which the help had not been hired just for the evening.

Irene could see the faces of all the men she had danced with during her first visit to the Stork, and the dress she had worn to her first Rodgers & Hammerstein opening, and the decorator who had recommended the chartreuse carpeting for the living room of this apartment after Frank had been made a vice president.

Sitting at the window, staring out at Central Park, Irene could see the pieces, and each piece as she looked back on it still retained its special glow, the touch of brightness that had made it memorable. But there was something wrong with the memory, just as there was something wrong with the glow. It provided no illumination.

It did not help to explain what had happened along the way between Battle Creek High School, when she and Frank had been seventeen, and this chartreuse carpeted living room, now that she and

Frank were twenty-five. It provided no answer to the question Frank had asked before he left for the office: "What's happened to us, baby?"

"I don't know," Irene said to him when Frank came back from the office that night. "But I know this," she added in a low voice. "I don't want any more of it to happen."

"Neither do I," Frank said.

"I don't want you to think I'm blaming anybody," Irene said. "I'm not trying to duck the responsibility. But I've been sitting here all day, trying to figure it out, and the nearest I can come to an answer is that it's not us. It's not just you and me. It's the life we lead."

"Other people lead that life," Frank said. "This town is full of advertising executives. Cocktail parties and dinner dates and martinis at lunch and night clubs in between are part of our jobs. It's a rat race, sure. But I can't stop doing what I have to do to make a living."

"You don't have to stop," Irene said. "The drinking hasn't gotten away from you. You can handle it." She paused. "I can't."

Frank stared at her for several silent moments.

"I've got a solution," he said finally.

"What's that?" Irene said.

"None of this happened until we hit New York," Frank said. "Let's get out of New York."

"And go back to Battle Creek?"

"No, of course not," he said. "We couldn't afford to do that. But why can't we give up this apartment and buy a house in the country and move out to the grass and trees? I wouldn't mind commuting. Lots of guys do it. It would be healthier for the kids, and you'd be—"

Irene shook her head.

"No, I wouldn't," she said. "I know a dozen girls who have moved to the country thinking they're escaping the New York rat race. All they do is carry the rat race with them. Any place that's within commuting distance of New York is just an extension of it. All those girls are staying up just as late and drinking just as much on all that grass as they drank on Fifty-Second Street. And a lot of them are seeing even less of their children because they have to keep dashing into New York to go with their husbands to the parties the

husbands can't stay away from if they want to hold onto their jobs."
Irene shook her head again. "Moving to the country and turning
you into a commuter is no solution," she said. "I'd only be kidding
myself if I did that."

"What do you want to do?" Frank said.

"Wipe the slate clean," Irene said quietly. "I want to start all over
again."

Frank looked puzzled.

"Where?" he said. "How?"

"I want to go some place far away," Irene said. "Some place where
they never heard of a Madison Avenue advertising executive's wife
and where nobody knows me. I want to take the children with me,
and settle down for a while, and give myself a chance to get to know
them, and give the children a chance to get to know me."

"For how long?" Frank said.

"Until I stop being what I've become here in New York,"
Irene said. "Until I get back to being what I used to be in Battle
Creek."

"But what about me?" Frank said.

"It's you I'm thinking of," Irene had said quietly. "It's for you
I want to wipe the slate clean."

She had meant it. She had meant every word of it. That was why,
soon after she arrived in Rome and she met Holly Trait and Seraphina had been established in the apartment and Peter and Connie
were set in the American school to which all the embassy people sent
their children, Irene had decided to try for a career in TV films.

It wasn't that she needed the money. The allowance Frank had
agreed to provide for the trial period of one year was enough to keep
her and the children comfortably. But the mere fact that it *was* an
allowance troubled Irene. If you were going to wipe a slate clean,
then you ought to do it with a damp cloth for which you had paid
with your own money. She wanted to do something she hadn't really
been doing since Battle Creek. She wanted to stand on her own
feet.

Besides, soon after she met Holly and Holly started introducing
her to Holly's friends, it occurred to Irene that one of the things that
had been wrong with her life in New York was that she didn't have
anything to keep her busy. Servants had taken care of the apart-

ment and nurses had taken care of the children. No wonder there had been all that time for boozy three hour lunches and cocktail parties and night clubs.

Here in Rome, however, if she had any sort of luck, and Holly had assured her that a girl with her looks should have no trouble at all finding as much work as she wanted to do, Irene would not only find a career that would give some meaning to her days, but she would earn enough money, if not completely to support herself and the children, then at least to enable her to tell Frank to reduce the amount of her allowance.

The fact that it hadn't quite worked out that way, the fact that after a full year in Rome she had not yet earned a single penny, did not change the fact that she had tried and was still trying. It was true that American TV films were being shot on every street corner in Rome, but it was equally true that most of them were pilot films that were being shot on shoestrings. The producers couldn't afford to pay very much even for established actresses, so they could hardly be expected to pay anything to people like Irene. If she had not actually earned any money, however, she had accumulated a good deal of experience, and this in time would pay off. Because it had served one of the purposes for which she had come to Rome: she had learned how to stand on her own feet.

Irene was certain Frank would see that. And the certainty made her feel a good deal better about this crucial day than she had felt when she woke up.

In fact, as she turned from the sideboard in the dining room toward the tinkling of the telephone bell in the living room, Irene realized that her headache was gone. She did not realize, however, until she reached the window from which you could catch a glimpse of the Borghese Gardens, that she had carried the bottle and the glass in with her. Before touching the phone, just to be on the safe side because she knew from experience how tricky these headaches could be and how important it was to nail one in its tracks so it couldn't return, Irene poured herself a second shot and swallowed it quickly. Then she picked up the instrument.

"Hello?" she said.

"Hello, sweetie, it's me again," Holly Trait said. "Are you feeling any better?"

"Much," Irene said. "Why?"

"Because I called Mr. Peccarari—"

"Who?"

"Mr. Peccarari," Holly said impatiently. "That film man, the tall one with the red mustache that we met last night with the Vitibellis."

"Oh, him," Irene said. "What about him?"

"I called him up and told him you wouldn't be able to have a drink with us at the Hassler at five because your husband was coming in from New York on the four o'clock plane, and he said okay, how about switching the date to lunch at one o'clock, and I said I'd call you up and ask."

"Lunch?" Irene said.

"Why not?" Holly said. "You don't have any other date, and you've got to eat somewhere, and this guy, honestly, sweetie, he's absolutely loaded, and he's got a whole string of films planned—fifty-two of them, Vittorio Vitibelli said last night—and he's taken a kind of shine to you, and he said he was pretty sure he could work us both into his program, but he wants to have a talk with both of us first, and oh, God, sweetie, do I have to draw maps for you?"

"No, of course not," Irene said irritably. "I just wish it wasn't today, that's all."

"But what *difference* does it make?" Holly said. "You don't have anything to do between now and the time Frank's plane comes in, and besides, for what you want to discuss with Frank, you'll be in a much better position to get what you want if you can say to Frank you've got a job lined up from a guy like this Peccarari, so why not—?"

Why not, indeed? After all, now that the headache was gone, there was no necessity for going back to bed until plane time.

"All right," Irene said. "But only on one condition."

"What is it?"

"That it's clearly understood I can break away at two-thirty, because before I go out to the airport I've got to go over to the school and pick up the kids."

"Okay, sweetie, I'll tell that to Peccarari," Holly said. "Capriccio's at one?"

"Capriccio's at one," Irene said.

As soon as she got there, her last doubts fell away. They always did when Irene came into Capriccio's. It was so much like the Stork and "21" in New York that it made her feel at home.

Irene nodded and smiled as the hat check girl waved a greeting across the shoulder of the Mexican bullfighter who had come to Rome to play Count Rostov in Cinecitta's production of *War and Peace*. Irene said hello as she crossed the foyer to Felice Baker, who was at a small side table with the American magazine editor to whom, Felice had told Irene the night before at the *Sundown* opening, she was trying to sell the idea of sending her to Moscow to do a series of candid camera shots of the Russian people at work and play. And Irene blew a kiss to Vittorio Vitibelli, who was standing on the top step just outside the entrance to the bar with the British playwright in the Italian adaptation of whose last three plays Vittorio and his wife Sylvana had appeared on the Roman stage but whose name Irene could never remember.

"You look lovely, darling," Vittorio said as she passed, and he dropped his famous eyelid in a wicked wink. "Quite an achievement after last night. Holly is waiting for you in the bar."

She was doing it, Irene saw as soon as she stepped down into the bar, in a manner that Holly herself identified as The Full Treatment.

"Sweetie!" she cried as soon as she saw Irene. "This is the most heavenly man!" Holly put her hand on his arm, which was resting on the bar. And she batted her eyelids at him as though he were not merely a reasonably attractive heavy-set male of middle years with a red mustache but an incandescent bulb of such overpowering brightness that the human eye could not contemplate it without shrinking. And in the voice of a starved and shivering urchin begging alms on a wintry street corner, Holly said, "Please, Mr. Peccarari, do tell Irene what you just told me about Garbo!"

Mr. Peccarari—who was clearly endowed heavily with one of Italy's great natural resources: charm—bowed over Irene's hand, brushed her knuckles with his mustache, signaled to the bartender, and told Irene what he had just told Holly about Garbo. This proved to be a highly improbable account of a contractual arrangement, allegedly completed the day before, by which the great Swedish movie star had agreed to return to the screen under Mr. Peccarari's banner in a series of half hour TV films devoted to the lives of history's great mistresses, all to be shot on the streets of Rome.

The waiter came back with three Bloody Marys, two of which Mr. Peccarari distributed to his female guests in a manner that compared favorably with newsreel shots Irene had seen of the Archbishop of Canterbury placing the crown upon the head of his sovereign at the coronation of Queen Elizabeth.

"Well," Irene said, hesitating as she took the glass, because she remembered the two healing shots of whiskey she had downed before leaving the apartment, and then she figured oh, well, there was no point in being stuffy as long as she remembered to be careful. "Just this one drink," she said. "I've got to leave at two-thirty."

"I know," Mr. Peccarari said through his charming smile. "Miss Trait has told me."

Holly had quite obviously also told him that neither of Mr. Peccarari's two luncheon guests would be insulted if he could manage to find parts for them in one or more of the films he was on the verge of producing. At any rate, Mr. Peccarari soon made it plain that in several of the stories, particularly the ones dealing with Sir Walter Raleigh, Leif Ericson, and John Cabot, all of whose careers had touched the shores of North America, he would need a couple of American actresses to support Garbo. After the second Bloody Mary it became even plainer that, while he had not yet reached any final decision, Mr. Peccarari had no violent objections at this stage to considering for these supporting roles none other than his two charming luncheon guests.

"I won't speak for myself," said Holly with a modest smile, "but I can tell you this: Irene would be just great in the Walter Raleigh story."

In view of this generous comment, it seemed only fair to Irene to point out to Mr. Peccarari that, while she might seem prejudiced, since Holly was her friend, she was stating no less than the simple truth when she said Mr. Peccarari could hunt all over Rome, and indeed throughout Italy, without finding an actress who could do half the job Holly Trait could do in the Cabot story.

"I am sure of it," Mr. Peccarari said through his charming smile, and he signaled to the bartender. "Let us have just one more of these, and then we will eat."

But they didn't, because by the time they finished the third round of Bloody Marys, the contractual arrangement Mr. Peccarari claimed he had completed with Garbo did not seem improbable at all. In fact, it seemed a damned shame to Irene that a man with so much ability, a man who had succeeded where every producer in the world had for years failed—namely, getting the great Swedish star's name on the dotted line—and a man who had the intelligence to see practically at a glance what so many other producers had thus far been blind to—namely, the talent that Irene and Holly so obviously possessed—it seemed a shame to Irene that such a man should be prevented from carrying out his great design merely because he was having some silly trouble with his financing, and she said so.

Several times. In tones so indignant that they attracted the attention of two men further down the bar. These, to everybody's astonishment, turned out to be none other than Mr. Peccarari's own partners, the two men with whom Mr. Peccarari had wandered into *Nino's* the night before while Irene and Holly were having supper with the Bakers after the *Sundown* opening. This chance meeting naturally called for another round of Bloody Marys, during the course of which one of Mr. Peccarari's partners tried to reassure both Holly and Irene, who were now quite worried that the whole project, not to mention the roles they had been offered in it, was doomed to die a-borning because Mr. Peccarari might not be able to raise the money with which to get it under way.

"Nonsense," said this partner, who looked so much like the other one that Irene couldn't tell them apart. "There is nothing to worry about," he said, speaking with almost, but not quite, as much charm as Mr. Peccarari. "As you Americans say, there are more ways than one to skin a cat. If we cannot raise the money here in Rome because our Italian compatriots are too blind to see a gold mine when it is offered to them, we will raise it elsewhere, from people with courage and foresight. In New York, for example, a city I know intimately, there are hundreds of people who would leap at the opportunity to—" He paused, and his face brightened, as though he had been struck by a sudden thought. "Your husband, for example, madame," he said to Irene. "Did you say last night at the Vitibellis' that Mr. Creel is the president of Shenton & Shaw?"

"Did I?" Irene said.

"Of course you did, sweetie," Holly said with a warning frown.

"That's right," Irene said at once. "I did." She giggled. "I mean he *is*."

Mr. Peccarari and his two partners giggled with her, and then all five of them burst into loud peals of laughter, and Mr. Peccarari signaled the bartender again. They were all bent in a huddle over the bar, on which Mr. Peccarari with a swizzle stick was scratching the breakdown of production costs on the pilot film for the series which would be shot with the money to be put up by Frank Creel, when somebody tapped Irene on the shoulder. She looked up. It was Vittorio Vitibelli. He had apparently come across from the table at which he was lunching with the British playwright because Vittorio was carrying his napkin.

"Darling, I don't mean to interrupt," he said. "But didn't you say last night that you were meeting the four o'clock plane from New York?"

Irene looked at him with annoyance. Why couldn't some people mind their own business? Here she was, after almost a full year of trying, on the verge of landing a big part in an important pilot film, and while she was talking to the producer and his partners, a busybody like Vittorio Vitibelli had to come along and interrupt!

"Thanks," Irene said coldly. "I'm perfectly capable of keeping track of my own—"

Her voice stopped. Her glance, swinging away from Vittorio and back to Mr. Peccarari, had paused on the clock over the bar. It showed twenty minutes to four. At once Irene's annoyance shifted from Vittorio Vitibelli to herself. It was at least a half hour by taxi out to Ciampino, maybe longer, so that even if she left this minute, she was bound to be late, and one of the few things Frank could be really sticky about was tardiness. It wouldn't surprise her one bit if he should be annoyed enough by her being late to refuse to put up the money for Mr. Peccarari's pilot film, and thus deprive Irene of her first real chance to show what she could do professionally. If that happened, Irene thought angrily, she would have nobody to blame but herself. Holly must have been thinking more or less the same thing, because all at once she snapped her fingers.

"I know what let's do!" Holly said. "Let's *all* go out to meet Frank's plane! We'll be a little late, but you can tell him you wanted to make it a real welcoming committee, sweetie, and it took a little time to get the gang together!"

"Splendid!" said Mr. Peccarari. "Let us go!"

"But we just ordered a fresh round of Bloody Marys!" Irene said.

"Let's take them with us!" Holly said.

They did, holding their glasses aloft like torches as they paraded out of Capriccio's and up the street to the Via Veneto, where they found a cab. It was an old one, and the jump seats were broken, but this didn't matter because Irene sat on Mr. Peccarari's lap and Holly sat on the lap of one of his partners.

For a while, as they raced along toward Ciampino, the other partner kept insisting that they stop the cab so he could pick up a girl to sit on *his* lap. But Holly poured part of her Bloody Mary into his collar, thus calming him down somewhat, and reminded him that this was no time to fool around with chippies off the street, because they were all embarked on a serious mission, a mission that would affect all their futures.

"When Irene left New York," Holly explained to Mr. Peccarari and his partners between sips at her Bloody Mary, "Frank said she could have a year in Rome. He would support her for that length of time, Frank said, and then he would come over and get her and take her back to New York. A couple of months ago, though, Irene decided a year wasn't long enough. She didn't write and tell this to Frank, because she knew he'd say no right away if she asked him to stay longer. But she figured if she didn't say a word, if she just waited until he arrived, and he saw how wonderful she looks—" Holly paused, and she tipped her head to one side, beaming with alcoholic admiration at her friend, and she said, "Irene *does* look wonderful, doesn't she?"

"Absolutely marvellous," said Mr. Peccarari, beaming in the same direction as he gave Irene an affectionate little pat and moved her into a more comfortable position on his lap. "She looks lovely."

"As soon as Frank sees her," Holly continued, "Irene and I figure he'll realize right away that living in Rome is wonderful for her, and so when she tells him she wants to stay another year, Frank will just have to say yes, that's all."

Holly took a long pull at her drink. The cab swerved and she emitted a small, involuntary, guttural sound.

"Oop," Holly said. "Sorry." She giggled and burped again and took another swallow. "Anyway, that's been the plan for the past couple of months," Holly said. "But now—"

She paused, and she beamed first at Mr. Peccarari and then at the partner on whose lap she was sitting.

"Now that we've got this new thing," Holly said. "Now that we've decided to let Frank put up the money for the pilot film for this series in which Irene and I are going to be co-starred with Garbo—"

Holly paused again, and even though her attempt at an eloquent shrug was spoiled somewhat because the cab, swerving this time in the opposite direction, poured part of Mr. Peccarari's drink down *her* neck, she managed to enunciate clearly enough.

"So you can see that this very important day in Irene's life has now become a very important day in *all* our lives." Holly reached across and she tweaked the cheek of the Peccarari partner on whose lap nobody was sitting. "It certainly is no time to risk making a bad impression on Frank by stopping to pick up chippies off the street just because your knees are cold," she said. "Especially since we're late already."

But the plane was late, too. So that when they got to Ciampino there was time for another Bloody Mary, which they had out on the terrace overlooking the landing field, where quite a few people were waiting. When the plane finally did come in, and the disembarking platform was rolled against its huge silver side, and the door opened, and the passengers started coming out in single file, Irene suddenly found she had stopped listening to the small, charming sounds Mr. Peccarari had been murmuring through his red mustache into her ear.

All at once, for no reason she could figure out, it was as though a warning bell had been sounded, and Irene found herself waiting, all the muscles in her stomach drawing together slowly in a tense, hard knot. Then Frank came through the door of the plane, carrying a large square package and stooping slightly, because of his height. He straightened up on the platform, and he paused for a moment on the top step to squint against the sun toward the terrace railing at the far side of the landing field where friends and relatives were watching the disembarking passengers, and then Irene knew why her stomach had tightened and what it was she had been waiting for.

It was as though the curtain of alcoholic haze, which had begun to
build up with the two healing shots of whiskey in the apartment and
had slowly grown thicker with the accumulation of Bloody Marys
at Capriccio's, had suddenly been slashed so that, through the narrow slit, Irene could get a clear glimpse of her husband. Seeing Frank
standing there, so tall and straight and clean-looking in the afternoon sunlight, she remembered all at once, with a sense of shock
that was almost physically painful, how much she loved him, and
how much she had missed him, and then she had a moment of rage
and self-loathing for allowing herself to be drunk at this moment,
but it did not last long. The slit in the curtain had closed.

"I'll bet that's him!" Holly squealed. "I've never seen him, but I'll
bet that's him! The tall, good-looking one carrying the package!"

She was right, but she continued to squeal, while passports were
examined by immigration officers, and luggage was routed through
the customs shed, and Irene was finally allowed to run across toward
Frank. He met her halfway, and dragged her into his arms with an impatient, almost harsh pull so that the package he was carrying dug
painfully into her back, but Irene didn't say a word. She couldn't.
He was holding her too tight. Then he released her, and he pushed
her away, and he held her at arm's length, and he grinned.

"Hi, baby," Frank murmured. "It's been a long time."

Irene swallowed hard, trying to think of something to say, but
just then Holly came up with Mr. Peccarari and his two partners,
and Irene didn't have to think about what she had to say. She just
introduced Holly, and Holly introduced Mr. Peccarari, and Mr. Peccarari introduced his two partners, and then they were all talking at
once, telling Frank about Garbo and the pilot film and the role in it
that was being reserved for Irene and what a wonderful investment
TV films were for a man like Frank because it allowed him to avoid
the high tax brackets and take a capital gains instead. Frank smiled
and listened politely, but all the time they were talking at him they
seemed to be doing something complicated with his hands, and
after making a determined effort, Irene managed to bring him into
focus and she saw what he was doing. Frank was undoing the
wrappings of the package.

"Okay," he said finally, holding up a great big doll in a pink dress
and a brand new yellow catcher's mitt. He looked around impatiently,

with eager expectation, across the heads of the chattering Holly and the charming Mr. Peccarari and his grinning partners, and Frank Creel said to his wife, "Where are the kids?"

The innocent syllables, so lovingly uttered, might have been a savage blow across her face. Once again, as Irene stood there in the customs shed at Ciampino, she was reminded of that dreadful morning following her twenty-third birthday party when she had realized for the first time in her life that she had blacked out. Except that this time, in addition to the terror, there were the despairing words, drilling relentlessly through the alcoholic haze that blanketed her mind: *How could I have allowed this to happen? How could I have forgotten Petey and Connie?*

Perhaps because she was not personally involved, or perhaps because she carried her liquor better, it was Holly Trait who recovered first.

"They're waiting for their daddy," she said brightly. "At the apartment!"

All the way back to the apartment in the taxi, through the terror that fought with the alcohol for possession of her senses, Irene prayed that Holly was right. *The children,* she kept saying to herself over and over again as though the words were a talisman, *the children, oh, God, please, do anything You want with me, I deserve any punishment, but please, God, please, don't let anything happen to Petey and Connie!*

"Signora!" Seraphina said happily through her enormous smile when she opened the door, and then, disregarding Holly Trait and Mr. Peccarari and his two partners, the motherly Italian woman turned the smile on Frank. Bowing slightly, Seraphina said, "Signor Creel, welcome to Rome!" Then she seemed to become aware of the doll and the catcher's mitt in Frank's hands, and the smile disappeared. Seraphina's voice rose with sudden concern. "Where are the bambinos?"

"The *who?*" Frank said sharply and apparently without thought, because a moment later he obviously didn't need an answer. Not to that particular question. A moment later he had stopped being a polite visitor. A moment later, his face tight, the doll and the catcher's mitt discarded on the table in the foyer, his voice flat and hard, Frank said, "Where are the children?"

"I don't know!" Seraphina said in a frightened voice. "Every day, three o'clock, after the lessons, I go to the school to meet them! But today, today the signora said no, today Mrs. Creel said it is special, today the signora told me—!"

She turned appealingly to Irene, who was trying desperately once more to cut through the alcoholic haze, pawing for a rent in the fog through which the insane confusion by which she was surrounded could be viewed with some sort of clarity. But it was not easy. She couldn't seem to make her mind work. All she could do was repeat the prayer, over and over again. *Please God, please, not the children, not Petey and Connie!* She scarcely saw Holly, whose presence Irene had forgotten, step forward and put her hand on Frank's arm.

"It's just a little misunderstanding," Holly said in her high-pitched, nasal voice, and she gave Frank the seductive smile that was the cornerstone of her Full Treatment. "There's nothing to worry about," Holly said. "The kids are probably—"

With a short, sharp, seemingly effortless movement of his arm, as though he were brushing away a fly, Frank sent the drunken little blonde from Poughkeepsie reeling to the other side of the foyer.

"The school," he said to Irene in his flat, hard voice. "What's the telephone number of the school?"

The question seemed to come from far away, and then everything in the foyer—the table, the walls, the people—everything seemed to be jumping crazily from side to side. When she realized what was happening, when she understood that Frank was trying to shake her sober, Irene wanted to cry out. But she couldn't seem to make her tongue work, either. She could hear, though. With surprising clarity.

"It is here, signor!" she heard Seraphina's voice saying. "In this book, Mr. Creel!"

Frank snatched the book, and he picked up the phone, and he had rapped out the number and told the operator to hurry, before he apparently realized he was not making himself understood.

"Here, you better do this," he said, thrusting the phone at Seraphina. "Quick!"

Seraphina took the phone and told the operator in Italian what she wanted and then she waited, while Irene, breathing heavily, trying fiercely to lift herself out of drunkenness by a sheer effort of will,

could feel the tension in the crowded foyer mounting slowly and
steadily, like flood waters in a cellar. *Please, God,* she prayed, holding onto the words that were the only oasis of sanity in the whirling
web by which she was surrounded, *please, God, not Petey and
Connie!* Finally Seraphina made a small, gasping sound in her throat,
and holding the phone, she turned with wide, terror-stricken eyes
to Frank.

"There is no answer, signor!" she said. "The school, it is closed!"

"Is it far from here?"

"Perhaps a mile, signor."

"Do Petey and Connie know the way?"

"Si, signor. Every morning for a year I take them, every afternoon
I bring them back. They know the way."

"Then even if they started walking home alone," Frank said, looking at his wrist watch. "It's now a quarter after five. They'd have
been here long ago?"

"Si, signor."

Frank rubbed the side of his jaw hard, two swift strokes, one up
and one down, and then he turned back to Seraphina.

"How do you call the cops in this town?"

"Signor?"

"The cops! The police! How do you—?" He shook his head. "No,
wait!" He picked up the phone and shoved it back at Seraphina.
"Get me the American Embassy!" She did, and then Frank snatched
the phone back. "Look," he said into the mouthpiece, "I don't
know if I'm calling the right people, but this is an emergency, and I
don't know anybody else to call. Can you connect me with somebody
who—?" His voice stopped, and there was a pause while the connection was made, and then Frank said, "Hello? My name is Frank
Creel. Listen." He recited the facts swiftly and then, in answer to a
question at the other end, he read off the telephone number on the
instrument. "I'd like to come along and— Oh. But couldn't I help
you—? Oh. I see. All right," he said through a scowl, "I'll wait here
for your call. Thanks."

He hung up, and with his clenched fist he made the two hard rubbing motions along the edge of his jaw, once up and once down, and
then he turned to look at Irene. She was slumped in a chair near the
window through which, if you twisted your neck hard, you could

catch a glimpse of the Borghese Gardens. But not now. Not at this hour of the evening. Not in all this rain that had suddenly begun to come down so hard. And not while you were praying. Irene made another effort. There was something she had to add. *Dear God,* she said, *take me instead. Don't let anything happen to Petey and Connie, and you can have me instead. I'm no good, anyway. Please, God, take me instead of the children.* She could feel the hysteria bubbling inside her, like the lid of a simmering pot, cutting through the alcohol, giving the numb prayer new meaning. *If anything happens to Petey and Connie,* she decided, *I'll kill myself.* The decision seemed to help. At any rate, she was able to turn and meet Frank's glance.

"I know," she said in a thick, hopeless voice. She sounded as though she were talking through a mouthful of food. "I know what you want to say."

"No you don't," Frank said quietly. "You don't have any idea what I want to say."

Perhaps not. But she had a pretty good idea what he was thinking. In Frank's place, if their positions had been reversed, she would have been thinking the same thing. Assuming that she was capable of thought, that is. Which at the moment she wasn't. Not with what was beginning to happen inside her head. Soon, very soon, Irene knew, it would be worse than a headache. But there was nothing she could do to stop it. Because she knew, too, that there was no aspirin in the house. It was the one thing she remembered clearly. There was no aspirin in the house.

"Frank," she said. "I want to say something."

"I don't want to hear it."

"You must," Irene said. "Because in a little while, very soon, I won't be able to say anything. My head is very bad, Frank, and it's getting worse. There's something I have to say while I can still say it." She paused and drew a deep breath. "If anything happens to Petey and Connie," Irene said, and even in her own ears her voice now seemed to be coming from an incredible distance, "I want you to know whose fault it is."

"I know whose fault it is," Frank said.

"No you don't," Irene said. "You can't know."

But it was terribly important that he should. And she was the only one who could tell him. There was nobody else from whom Frank would ever learn the truth, because nobody else knew it as clearly as Irene did: *it was Holly Trait's fault!*

If she had not met Holly Trait, if a year ago during her very first week in Rome, Irene had not run into this girl who was so exactly like all those other girls with whom Irene had done all her running around and drinking in New York, if there had been no Holly Trait in Rome to befriend Irene Creel when she arrived and introduce her to the Vitibellis and the Bakers and the rest of the crowd at Capriccio's, none of this would have happened. If it were not for meeting Holly Trait, Irene's whole year in Rome would have been different. If there had been no Holly Trait to lead her astray, Irene Creel would not be sitting here now, listening to the hammer strokes in her own head, waiting for a dreaded telephone call that might—

"Hello?"

Her heart leaped as she turned from the window and looked up. It was Frank, talking into the phone. Irene forced her mind to push its last tentacles of awareness through the pain in her head. She had not heard the ringing of the bell. She had to hear the rest.

"Yes, this is Mr. Creel," Frank said, and he paused to listen, holding the phone with two hands, as though it were a weight that required all his strength to support. "I see," he said finally. If there was any expression in his voice, Irene could not read it. "How long?" Frank said. "I see." There was another pause, and then he said, "Thank you."

He hung up slowly, and Frank Creel turned to his wife.

"Connie and Petey are all right," he said. Irene sagged back in the chair as the tears of relief began to burn down her cheeks. "When you didn't show up this afternoon at the school the way you promised," Frank said, "the kids decided to go out to the airport on their own." He swallowed hard, but the expression on Frank's face did not change as he said, "It seems they didn't want to miss meeting their daddy's plane." Frank paused again. "So they started to walk to Ciampino. They didn't have any idea where it is, of course, or how long it would take, but they kept on walking. By the time it started to get dark, and a policeman who saw them thought there was something peculiar about a couple of kids their age in American clothes wandering around all alone in the rain, they'd been soaking wet for a couple of hours. The cop took them to a hospital, where they were put to bed. That's where this man I just talked to at the Embassy located them when he started a telephone check of all the police stations and hospitals in town. He says there's nothing wrong with them, except maybe a couple of bad head colds, and if I come down to the Embassy right away, he'll go over to the hospital with me to pick them up."

"Thank God!" Irene said in a whimper. "Thank God!"

"That's right, thank God," Frank said quietly. "We were lucky this time."

He started for the foyer where Seraphina, who had heard the explanation from the doorway, was eagerly holding out his hat.

"I will go with the signor to the hospital?" she said pleadingly. "Please?"

"All right," Frank said. "Get your coat."

She hurried away and Frank, turning back to wait, stopped with the hat halfway to his head.

"Oh, now, don't run away!" Holly Trait said petulantly as she appeared with a glass in the doorway from the dining room and leaned drunkenly against the jamb. "Seraphina can go get the kids by herself," Holly said. "She takes care of them all the time, anyway, and besides, we have things to talk about!"

"Yes, important things!" said Mr. Peccarari, appearing beside Holly with a drink of his own. "We have not yet had the opportunity to present you with a breakdown of the costs for our pilot film," he said, smiling with alcoholic graciousness as he made room for his two partners, who came weaving out of the dining room carrying drinks and scraps of paper. "Here, let us show you how we propose to make you rich, Mr. Creel!" Mr. Peccarari took the slips of paper from his partners, and the charming smile rose to new heights of incandescence as he came toward Frank. "Surely, at a time like this, Mr. Creel, you are not going to allow a small children's escapade to interfere with your wife's future?" He thrust the papers at Frank and said, "May I suggest—?"

He never finished the suggestion. Frank Creel's fist caught the words at their source. Mr. Peccarari, with an astonished grunt, fell back into the arms of his partners. To receive him, they were forced to drop their drinks, which caused Holly Trait to scream and run toward the foyer, where Seraphina had just appeared in her coat.

The motherly Italian woman stared in amazement as Signor Creel, firmly grasping the collar of a Peccarari partner in each hand, dragged the two charming but oddly helpless men across the room. Seraphina stepped aside quickly. Frank thrust the two TV film impressarios out into the hall, came back for Mr. Peccarari, and shoved him after his colleagues. Holly Trait, who had preceded her friends under her own power, now poked her head back into the apartment to hurl a drunken insult at the man who was, at least technically, her host. This proved to be a mistake.

Frank, just straightening up from the disposition of Mr. Peccarari, seized the drunken little blonde from Poughkeepsie by the shoulders, spun her around, and sent her on the way to join her producers by placing his foot vigorously against what is, in any country, an extremely popular target.

"Now that we've got the garbage out of here," Frank said to Seraphina, "I guess we can go get the children."

"Si, signor!"

Frank clapped the hat on his head and turned back to Irene.

"We may not be so lucky next time," he said grimly. "So I'm fixing things to make sure there won't be a next time," Frank said. "You can start packing their stuff now," he said. "I'm taking the kids back to New York with me on the first plane tomorrow."

For several moments after the door slammed shut behind him, the words meant nothing. They were like so many stones dropped into a pool. Very soon, however, in the space of time that it took Irene to get from the chair near the window in the living room to the silver tray on the sideboard in the dining room, the words started to come back to the surface. After the second shot, when the sharpest edge of the pain in her head had already been blunted and she was pouring the drink that Irene knew from experience would rout it completely, the full meaning of what Frank had said struck her. Irene's hand shook. The neck of the bottle rattled against the glass.

"Back?" she said aloud, in a frightened voice, to her reflection in the mirror over the sideboard. "To New York?"

But she *couldn't* go back!

Going back meant admitting to herself that the year had been wasted. That her failure was not Holly's fault but her own. That what had happened to her after she left Battle Creek was not the result of the life she and Frank had led in New York, but was due to some weakness within herself that she had brought from Battle Creek to New York and had then carried with her from New York to Rome. Going back meant confessing that no matter where she went, because the flaw would always go with her, she would always find a Holly Trait to make friends with.

"No," Irene said firmly to her reflection in the mirror. "I'm not going back."

She poured the third shot, looked carefully at the level in the glass, added another half inch of whiskey, drank it off, and waited. She did not have to wait long. In a matter of moments, or so it seemed, the solution came to her. It was so simple that Irene wondered why it had not occurred to her at once.

"I won't say a word tonight," she said craftily to her reflection in the mirror. "I'll wait until tomorrow, when he's all calmed down."

Then, casually, across the breakfast table, or perhaps later in the morning, when they were walking with the children in the Borghese Gardens, she would tell Frank what she had really known from the very beginning, a year ago, the moment she set foot in this city, but had lacked the courage to write and tell him then.

"Rome isn't any good," she would say with the sort of complete and disarming candor that Frank had always respected in her. "It's the wrong place. It's full of too many of the same kind of people we used to know in New York."

Pouring herself another drink, Irene chose her next words with care.

"The thing to do is start all over again," she said. "As though this past year hadn't happened. In some place that's *really* different. Some place where they never heard of the New York rat race, where I can settle down quietly for a while with the children, and relax and give myself a chance to get to know them, and give the children a chance to get to know me. Some place like Madrid, perhaps. Or London. Or even Paris."

The place didn't matter. As long as she got a chance to wipe the slate clean.

Death in the Family

On Wednesday of the week before Easter my cousin Laura was taken sick suddenly and was rushed to the hospital. Her appendix had burst and the doctor said she had peritonitis. My mother and father were both very much upset, because Laura was their favorite niece. My father kept a small dry-goods shop in Brooklyn, and the week before Easter was the busiest of the year, but early Thursday morning, before the store became crowded, my mother hurried to the hospital. She was not permitted to see Laura. Visiting hours, they told her, were from seven to nine in the evening, which was out of the question for all of us. The store had to be kept open until ten.

Friday morning my mother tried again, but she met with the same answer. She explained the situation to the girl in the reception room at the hospital and pleaded with her, but it didn't help. Patients, the girl said, could not be disturbed during the day. If they let my mother see Laura, they'd have to let everybody have visitors. They couldn't make exceptions. However, the girl did call the doctor on the inter-hospital phone and then told Mother that there was a "fair chance" that my cousin Laura would recover.

Mother came home in a state of nervous excitement, and my father, who had been waiting anxiously for news, lost his temper and shouted at her, saying she shouldn't have let them put her off like that. My mother started to cry, and he ran out to the drugstore on the corner and called the hospital. There was no change in my cousin Laura's condition, they told him.

Business was very brisk during the afternoon, but my father and mother were so worried about Laura that when I came home from school my father told me to stay in the store and went off to the hospital. We had a hard time handling the customers, because I didn't know as much about the stock as my mother did and she was too distracted to pay much attention to what she was doing. At five o'clock my father returned, more worried than ever, and almost beside himself with anger. They hadn't let him go up to see Laura.

By seven o'clock the store was jammed and my father couldn't really spare me, but he had to know about Laura, so he sent me to the hospital to visit her, with instructions to stay as long as possible, but not too long, and then rush home.

I reached the hospital at twenty to eight and went up to the girl at a desk in the reception room. I asked her where I could find my cousin. The girl hunted through a small card index in front of her and asked me to spell the second name, which I did, and then she shuffled a thin batch of cards that had been stuck loosely into one corner of the desk pad. Finally she looked up, holding one card in her hand.

"Harrison?" she asked.

"Yes," I said.

She looked at me curiously.

"You her brother?"

"No," I said. "I'm her cousin. I'd like to go up and—"

"Well, I'm sorry," the girl said, pushing the card back into the corner of the desk pad. "She died at seven-fourteen tonight. No one can go up except the immediate family. Sorry."

"Harrison?" I said. "*Laura* Harrison?"

"Yes," she said in a softer voice. "Seven-fourteen. Sorry."

I turned away from the desk. My only emotion was bewilderment. I didn't know Laura very well, but I had been sent to bring news of her improved condition, and here she was, dead. It was like being sent to the bakery for bread and coming back with fly paper.

All the way home on the trolley car I tried to think of what to do.

It wasn't so much that I was upset about Laura; in my fourteen years I had never known her very well. But I was worried about my father and mother. They were crazy about Laura and they were expecting me to say she was feeling better. I couldn't tell them she was dead. It would be too much of a shock.

As soon as I came into the store, my mother cried, "How is she? How does she look?"

"They wouldn't let me see her," I said. "They told me she was feeling a little worse."

"Worse?" My father looked startled. "When was this? What time?"

"A little before eight, I guess."

He glanced at his watch and, forgetting the customers around him, pushed me to the door.

"It's a quarter to nine now," he said. "Run to the drugstore and call up. Find out how she is."

I went to the drugstore and bought a package of gum, chewed a piece until all the flavor was gone, and then walked back to our store.

"Well?" my mother asked anxiously.

"Not so good," I said without looking at her.

"What do you mean, not so good?" my father shouted. "Talk so a person can understand you. What did they say?"

"They said she wasn't feeling so good." I went behind the counter and waited on a couple of customers. My mother and father went on selling dry goods, but their minds were in the hospital on Clarkson Street. Ten minutes later my father hurried over to me.

"Go and call up again," he said. "Find out how she is. Quick!"

I went out to the drugstore once more. Mr. Metzger, the proprietor, looked at me curiously when I came in.

"Hello!" he said. "Falling in love with my place, or something?"

"Pack of gum," I said.

He laughed when he handed it to me and took my nickel.

"You know what to do with gum, don't you?" he said. "You don't swallow it right away. You chew it for a while."

I laughed a little, too, embarrassed.

"I know," I said, and put the gum in my pocket and went out. The store wasn't very crowded when I got back.

"What did they say?" my mother and father asked together.

"She's getting worse," I said.

They stared at me for a moment. Then my father threw down the box of underwear he was holding and went for his hat.

"Business or no business," he said, with more fright in his voice than anger, "I'm going down to the hospital now!"

My mother started to follow him.

"There's no sense in going," I said quickly. "They won't let you in. It's after nine. No more visitors. They told me that on the phone."

He put his hat back slowly on the clothes tree and returned to the counter. We all worked for a few minutes. There were no sounds in the store except the rustle of paper and a customer's occasional question about size or price.

"I'm going out to call up," my father said suddenly.

"I'll go," I said, and before he could reply I was past him and out in the street. I didn't want to go to the drugstore again, but this time I knew my father was watching me through the front window, and I couldn't help myself.

Mr. Metzger looked at me in amazement when I came in.

"Could you let me have a couple of nickels?" I said.

"Sure," he said. "Why not? You're getting to be one of my steadiest customers."

I put a dime on the counter and he gave me two nickels. Then I went into a phone booth. I could see him staring at me through the glass door, so I dropped a coin into the slot, held the receiver to my ear, and tried to figure out what to tell them when I came back. Suddenly there was a click at the other end of the wire and the operator said, "Number, please." I jumped and hung up without speaking. Then I went out and walked back. There was only one customer in the store when I came in.

"She's pretty bad," I said.

The customer, a stout woman with a faint mustache, looked at me in a puzzled way, and then she turned to discuss her purchase with my mother. While it was being wrapped, my father spoke quietly from the other end of the counter.

"You better go out and call again," he said.

This time, when I came to the drugstore, I didn't look at Mr. Metzger. Instead I walked into the phone booth, dropped the other nickel in the slot, and held the receiver away from my ear. When I had counted ten, I hung up.

"Hey!" Mr. Metzger called after me as I walked out. "What's the matter? Something's wrong maybe?"

"No," I said, without turning back.

There were no customers in the shop when I came in. My mother and father were putting the stock in order for the night. My mother had a bolt of cloth in her hands. She held it in mid-air, half-way to the shelf she had been reaching for. My father was straightening a box of shirts. I closed the door very gently behind me. For a moment there was silence while they looked at me. I could tell that they already knew what I was going to say.

"She's—she's dead," I said finally.

The tissue paper rustled a little as my father closed the shirt box. My mother finished putting the bolt of cloth on the shelf and sat down heavily on the stool behind the counter. A single large tear hesitated on her cheekbone for a second and then went bouncing down her face quickly.

I wasn't worried about them any more. I knew now that they would be all right.

A Dime a Throw

"It's not so bad, really," the woman in the dirndl said. "It might even be fun."

"You can stop trying to sell it to me," her husband said. "I'm here. Period."

They stood just inside the wooden gate near the parking lot and looked at the crowd. The fairgrounds were in a vacant field to the left of the state highway, less than a quarter of a mile from the little summer town of Inniggsville.

"There's no point in being sore. Losing your temper." The woman in the dirndl did not turn her head to look at her husband. She spoke through a small smile of eager interest as she stared at the colored lights and the moving people. But there was an edge to her voice. "It wouldn't have looked nice if we hadn't come. We're summer visitors. The natives would have noticed it."

"Leave out the Emily Post angle," the man said, also keeping his eyes on the fairgrounds as he spoke. "For my money, the natives know what they can do."

"As long as you're here you might try looking as though you enjoyed it."

"Don't count on it," the man said.

He lit a cigar and they walked into the crowd side by side. The fairgrounds were laid out in the form of a square. To the right and left of the entrance gate stretched two lines of tents and flimsy booths. At the far end, facing the entrance gate, a merry-go-round and a Ferris wheel made the fourth side of the square. The space enclosed was jammed with men, women, and children from the farms and summer places for miles around. Between their heads and the evening sky hung strings of colored lights, stretched across from booth to booth. Above the laughter and the shouting and the voices of the barkers the music from the merry-go-round banged away. The woman in the dirndl smiled every now and then at someone in the crowd. Once in a while her husband followed her smile with a short nod. They stopped in front of a booth where an old man with a sad face was playing checkers with all comers at five cents a game.

"Look at that," the woman said. "He's playing four, seven, nine, ten, eleven—he's playing eleven people at once!"

"I'm looking," the man said. "How long do we have to stay here?"

"For heaven's sake. We can't just come and run. It wouldn't look nice."

They walked on, past a Bingo game, a penny-pitching contest, and a tent in which you could win a carton of cigarettes or a sack of sugar by knocking down a pyramid of blocks with three baseballs. When they reached the shooting gallery, the man stopped short. He stood with his cigar poised in the air halfway to his mouth and watched. His wife glanced at him in surprise and then she smiled.

"Why don't you try a round?" she said. "You used to be able to snuff out the candles four out of—"

She stopped and turned to follow her husband's gaze. He was not watching the shooting gallery. He was looking beyond it at a booth in which blankets were being offered as prizes at ten cents a chance. The front of the booth was a counter covered with black oilcloth, which was blocked out into numbered squares. A wheel marked with the same numerals was fastened on the wall to the left of the counter. The players put their dimes on the numbered squares and the barker spun the wheel. At the top a little leather indicator rattled as the pins of the wheel whirled by, making a sound similar to that of a pencil being drawn swiftly along a picket fence. When the wheel stopped, the barker looked to see where the leather indicator had come to rest and called out the winning number.

"Step right up, folks," the barker chanted. "A dime a throw, folks. Win a one-hundred-per-cent pure-wool blanket for only ten cents. Come on, folks. Step right up. A dime a throw."

Directly in front of the counter, facing the barker across the black oilcloth, stood an old woman. She was short and fat and dirty, and the hem of her cheap gingham house dress was ragged. Her feet were stuck into a pair of shapeless men's shoes that had no laces or tongues. Her scraggly gray hair hung over her face and down the back of her neck. With her left hand she clutched to her bosom a patent-leather purse that was flaking away at the edges. With her right hand she kept pushing the hair out of her eyes. She watched the wheel, the numbered squares, and the barker with a tight, concentrated eagerness, as though she were trying to memorize his words. Her head shook and her lips quivered with the intensity of her effort.

"Isn't that Mrs. Ratchek?" the woman in the dirndl said. "And isn't that her granddaughter Marie?"

"Yes," her husband said, without turning his head. "I want to see this."

Next to the old woman stood a thin little girl in a faded dress that was even more ragged and dirty than her grandmother's. Her bare toes were curled rigidly into the flattened turf. She clutched the old woman's dress with one hand and moved her head in tiny jerks, watching the wheel, the barker, and her grandmother with wide, almost frightened eyes.

"Come on, folks," the barker sang. "Win a blanket for only a dime. Step right up and carry it away, folks. A pure-wool blanket. Only a dime a throw."

A small crowd had gathered behind the old woman and the little girl. The old woman took a dime from her purse, moving her hands very carefully, as though the coin were fragile, and peered down at the oilcloth counter. She hesitated, put the dime on a number, took it off, put it on another number, mumbled something to herself, shifted the dime again. She seemed to be in great agony. Finally she made her choice. As soon as she took her fingers away from the dime, her agitation increased. She couldn't seem to wait for the barker to spin the wheel. She looked up at him, her face a mixture of pleading and anger and suffering, and urged him with small, impatient gestures to start the game. The barker tried to coax more players to the oilcloth counter. He was not very successful. The crowd seemed more interested in the old woman and the little girl. At last three or four people came forward and put down their dimes. The barker's voice rose triumphantly, like that of an auctioneer who has received a higher bid after a long period of inactivity, but he couldn't pull any more players out of the crowd.

"O.K., folks," he said. "Here it goes."

He spun the wheel. Everybody watched. The old woman's head stopped quivering. The little girl's face froze solid. The leather indicator clicked busily. The wheel slowed down and stopped.

"Sixty-nine," the barker sang. "Anybody got sixty-nine?" He looked down at the numbered squares on the oilcloth counter. "Nope, nobody. Sorry, folks." He swept the few dimes together and dropped them into the pocket of his leather apron. "If all the numbers are covered, there's a winner every time. Come on, folks. Step right up. You may be the lucky one. Win a pure-wool blanket for only ten cents."

The old woman's body sagged. The little girl tugged at her skirt, but the old lady opened the battered patent-leather purse, took out another dime, and began hunting for a number on the counter. The barker pretended not to see her. He looked over her head as he harangued the crowd. The desperation with which she was playing the game seemed to make him uncomfortable.

"My God," the woman in the dirndl whispered. "She can't afford this. We've all been giving her money for food. All the summer visitors. Only this morning I went out into the kitchen and saw Marie at the back door begging the cook to give her a—"

"Let it go," her husband said, without turning his head. "This is her own business."

"But she can't afford it! They're starving. They're practically public charges in Inniggsville. If it weren't for the food and the little money the summer visitors give them, why, they'd—"

"This is her own business. Period."

The woman in the dirndl bit her lip. Her husband drew steadily on his cigar. They watched Mrs. Ratchek repeat the same performance four more times. Each time she lost she seemed to grow more desperate, and the look on the little girl's face deepened to terror.

"The old girl must want that blanket pretty bad," someone in the crowd said. "She's been at it over an hour now."

Finally, after the woman in the dirndl and her husband had seen Mrs. Ratchek put down six dimes, a middle-aged man in a panama hat won a blanket.

"There it goes," the barker chanted, as he handed the blanket to the winner. "I told you so, folks. The more numbers are covered, the better chance of winning. If every number is covered, there's a winner every time. Come on, folks. Step up and win your blanket. A dime a throw."

Mrs. Ratchek and the little girl watched the man in the panama hat walk away with the blanket. There was no envy in their eyes. They just watched him. Then the old woman turned back, opened her battered purse, and clawed around in the bottom for a dime. The little girl tugged her grandmother's dress again, but Mrs. Ratchek shook her off.

"This is ridiculous," the woman in the dirndl said. "She can't afford this and she needs that money for food and—"

"I told you to let it go," her husband said. "This is her business."

His wife gave him an angry look, turned sharply, and hurried after the man in the panama hat. She stopped him and they talked for a few moments. The man in the panama hat seemed surprised and then embarrassed. Finally he nodded and handed over the blanket. The woman in the dirndl gave him some money and came back to the booth.

"Listen," her husband said. "I told you to stay out of this."

She paid no attention to him. She strode up to the old woman in front of the booth.

"Here, Mrs. Ratchek," she said. "Here's a blanket. You'll never win one that way. Take this and—"

The old woman peered at her through a scowl of annoyance, her hand still groping inside the patent-leather purse. Then she seemed to realize the meaning of the offer. The annoyance on her face turned to anger. She snatched the blanket and threw it on the ground.

"Get away from me," she said harshly. "Don't you go telling me what to do. Everybody always telling me what to do. You get away from me."

The woman in the dirndl stared at Mrs. Ratchek. She put her hand up to her cheek, as if it had been slapped, and her face grew red. The little girl released her grandmother and swooped down on the blanket.

"Grandma, look!" she cried in a high, excited voice. "We got the blanket! Grandma, look! We got the blanket!"

Mrs. Ratchek turned angrily and slapped the blanket from the little girl's hand.

"You leave me be," she snarled. "All of you. Always telling me what to do. You leave me alone."

The little girl started to cry. The barker sucked his teeth and looked uncomfortable. The crowd was so silent that the music from the merry-go-round in the distance seemed to blare out with a tremendous roar. The woman in the dirndl caught her breath in a gasp, turned on her heel, and hurried away. Her husband dropped his cigar and followed.

"I told you not to mess in there," he said quietly, almost gently. "It's her business."

His wife looked at him once out of the corner of her eye, but did not answer. She continued to push her way through the crowd. He walked along after her. When they reached the booth where the old man with the sad face was playing checkers, the woman in the dirndl stopped, opened her purse, and examined her face in a pocket mirror. She did a few small things to it with lipstick and powder. Her husband lit a fresh cigar.

"What do you say?" he said. "Go?"

"No," she said, and she snapped the compact shut. "The natives would talk."

He examined the end of his cigar to make sure it was burning evenly, then followed his wife. They walked slowly past the Bingo game, the penny-pitching contest, and the booth where you could win a sack of sugar by knocking down a pyramid of blocks with three baseballs. At the far end of the fairgrounds, near the merry-go-round, a small crowd had gathered. The woman in the dirndl and her husband stopped to look.

"Well!" she said in a startled voice. "Did you ever?"

In the middle of the crowd stood Mrs. Ratchek. The little girl with the wide eyes was still clutching her grandmother's dress. Mrs.

Ratchek was holding the blanket she had hurled to the ground twice a few minutes before.

"Feel it," Mrs. Ratchek said in a proud, excited voice. "Feel how soft it is. A hundred-per-cent pure wool. It's worth ten dollars easy. Maybe more. And I won it with only sixty cents. Honest. The sixth dime." Her hands quivered with her happiness. Her head shook. "Feel it," she said. "Feel how soft it is. And I won it for only sixty cents."

The people in the crowd felt the blanket good-naturedly and congratulated the old lady. Some of them stroked the little girl's head.

"After insulting me like that," the woman in the dirndl said. "In front of all those people."

Her lips grew thin and she took a step forward toward the crowd. Her husband jammed the cigar into his mouth and grabbed her wrist.

"Let it go," he said in a low voice. "Just let her alone."

His wife looked at him in the same way she had looked at Mrs. Ratchek earlier in the evening, as though her face had been slapped. Then her eyes dropped to his hand on her wrist.

"She insulted me in front of all those people!" she said, her voice rising uncontrollably. "She's lying to them and saying she won the—"

"Never mind," her husband said quietly, like a teacher explaining to a child a problem he knew it could not possibly grasp. "Just let her alone."

"But why? Why? She's telling them she—"

"I said never mind," her husband said. "Just let her alone."

Dumb Kid

He was bent down, behind the counter on which the cash register stood, when he heard the door open. For a moment he remained there, his back bent, his hands on the shoe boxes he had been arranging, wondering who it might be.

It couldn't be Mr. Lazarus. It was only a little after eight, and Mr. Lazarus never came in before nine-thirty. "Myself, I'm here in the morning half-past nine, ten," he had said. "You got plenty time to open up around nine. It's a business neighborhood. Nobody buys shoes early in the morning when they're rushing to get to work on time."

But Dave opened the store at eight. He wanted to show Mr. Lazarus that he wasn't lazy. In that hour he could straighten up the stock room in the back and run the vacuum cleaner over the rug and arrange all the boxes that had been left over from the day before.

Maybe it was a customer. That would be fine! Not only would he have the store all arranged and ready for business when the boss came in, but he'd actually have a sale on the register, too! He hoped it *was* a customer.

The door slammed shut and he straightened up.

A girl in a bright-colored dress, without a hat, was standing in the doorway.

"Oh!" she exclaimed, and then smiled. "You scared me. You're not hiding, are you?"

114

"N-no," he stammered, and felt his face grow warm. "I—I was just straightening things up a little."

She smiled again and came further into the store. He watched her face, fascinated by the way she smiled, her teeth slightly parted and gleaming behind soft red lips. She looked around quickly and then back at him.

"It's pretty early, isn't it?" she said.

"It is, a little," he started to say, then remembered that she might be a customer. "But we're open for business," he added brightly.

She seemed not to hear him, moving her head around, looking into every corner of the store. The smile had gone out of her face, but her mouth was still open, as though she had forgotten to close it when she stopped smiling. Her hair was blonde and a little out of place because she wasn't wearing a hat, but he thought that somehow it seemed right that way. It made her look vague and soft, as though he were not looking at her directly, but only seeing her reflection in a body of water.

Suddenly she turned back to him, and the pleasant smile was on her face again. "I want to get a pair of shoes," she said in a friendly voice.

A customer!

"Certainly!" he said, smiling back at her and coming out briskly from behind the counter. "Won't you have a seat?"

She sat down, crossing her legs, and drew her skirt down over her knees.

He slipped onto a stool in front of her and reached for her shoe. "Let's just take a look at the size," he said, trying to sound like Mr. Lazarus.

She raised her foot a little toward him, and he slid the shoe off gently. There was a small hole in her stocking over the big toe. He could feel himself blushing and he looked at her quickly, but she did not seem to be embarrassed. She swung her leg gently while he looked inside the shoe.

"Five and a half," he said and stood up. "Anything special you wanted to see? I mean, an opera pump, an oxford—?"

She frowned slightly and looked undecided. "Oh—I don't know," she said. "Let's see something to match my dress."

He went to the shelves and pulled out a box. Suede, with a single strap and a neat buckle. No—a little too conservative for a young girl like that. Maybe, though. She looked quiet and reserved. She might want a conservative shoe. He took down another box. The same, but with a patent leather bow. A little more dressy. That ought to be about right. He turned around with both boxes. She was looking at him and their eyes met. She smiled. He blushed and looked away.

"I don't know if this is what you want," he said, coming toward her and avoiding her eyes. "But let's just try it on to see if the size is right."

"Oh, no!" she cried, releasing a peal of tinkly laughter, when he held the shoe out to her. "I want something a little more—well, *you* know, something a little—"

"Oh, sure!" he said quickly. "I just wanted you to look at it, that's all." What a fool he was! A young, pretty girl—and him showing her a dead-looking shoe like that! "How about this one?" He held up the shoe with the patent leather bow.

She looked at it dubiously, the full red lips pouting.

"Just slip it on for the size," he said hurriedly. Gosh, he hoped he didn't lose a customer just because he was too dumb to bring out the kind of shoe she wanted! "Just try it on, and if it fits I'll show you some real nice stuff. Just try it on," he urged.

She held out the foot with the torn stocking and he felt his face grow warm again as he slid the shoe onto it. He kept his eyes on the shoe and swore at himself for being nervous. She must think he was a dumb kid who didn't know what it was all about!

"How is it?" he asked, patting the sides of the shoe.

"It *feels* okay," she said, "but—"

"All right," he said, reaching for the shoe again. "Now that we know the *size* is right, I'll show you something you'll like."

She wriggled her toes as he slipped the shoe off and he almost dropped the shoe. She smiled at him and he turned away quickly to hide his embarrassment. What the devil was wrong with him?

If he didn't pull himself together, she'd be sure to get disgusted and walk out. And not only wouldn't he have a *sale* on the register when Mr. Lazarus came in, but he wouldn't even have the store cleaned up!

"Say!" he heard her laugh behind him. "All I'm getting is *one* pair."

He looked at the boxes he had been unconsciously pulling down from the shelves and smiled foolishly.

"I was just—" he began.

"Here, wait a minute," she said kindly. "Let's see what you've got." She stood up and walked toward him, moving unevenly because she was wearing only one shoe.

"You take them down," she said, "and I'll look at them. All right?"

"All right," he said, relieved, and began to pull out boxes. She stood at his side, their shoulders touching, facing the wide wall of closely packed shoe boxes. He pulled out a box, opened it, held it in front of her. She looked at it quizzically for a moment, then shook her head and said, "No." Or she would smile and nod and say, "Maybe this one," and put the opened box aside. After a time she said, "Whew! This ought to be enough. Now let's see."

Both of them surveyed the litter of boxes and covers and tissue paper.

"Gee," she said, looking up at him with a smile of apology, "I certainly messed up the place for you, didn't I?"

"That's all right," he laughed happily. "As long as you get something you like." He meant it, too, he assured himself, a little surprised, and wasn't just saying it because she was a customer.

She picked up several boxes and hobbled back to her seat. "You want to bring the others?" she asked over her shoulder, smiling at him.

"You bet," he said and carried across the store the rest of the boxes she had set apart.

He wanted to help her try them on, but she was working too quickly, taking shoes from the boxes, slipping them on, kicking them off, trying on new ones. He sat on the stool in front of her and watched her turn the half-dozen pairs of shoes into a hopeless jumble of boxes and covers and paper. For a moment he thought of the work he'd have, straightening them all out again. He glanced at the clock. It was twenty to nine. He'd never be able to get the store arranged before Mr. Lazarus came in. But that didn't matter. He'd have a sale on the register!

And, anyway, for a girl like that, so neat looking and soft and
pretty, a girl that—that—he couldn't think of a word to describe
the warm glow that spread through him when he looked at her—
for a girl like that he'd clean up *any* mess. Even if she *didn't* buy!
But no. She wasn't just looking. She really meant to buy. He could
tell by the serious way in which she looked at the shoes she slipped
on, matching them against the color of her dress.

He stole a glance at her. Their eyes met again and he blushed.

"Say," she said, smiling at him, "which of these two do you like
best?"

She was holding her foot straight out, looking at the shoe on it,
with her head cocked to one side. In her hand she held up another
one.

"Oh, I don't know," he said, pretending to examine both of them
closely. The one on her foot was neat and simple. He thought it
looked well on her. The one in her hand had a large ribbon on the
instep. It was a little too—too—well, not just exactly right for a
nice, quiet-looking girl like that. "Of course, it's all a matter of
taste," he said in Mr. Lazarus' best manner. "But, personally, I prefer the—"

"I like *this* one better," she said with sudden decision.

She kicked off the shoe on her foot and slipped on the one she
had been holding. She gave the large ribbon an adjusting pat and
stuck her leg straight out, twisting her head and wriggling her foot
back and forth at the end of the leg to get a better view.

"Yes," she said finally, "I think that looks about the best of the
bunch. Don't you?"

"*I* think so," he said, looking at the shoe critically. Funny how it
didn't look so good when she held it in her hand, but the minute
she put it on it seemed perfect, as though it had been made for her.
"It looks fine on you, all right."

"Good," she said. "I'll take them."

"Shall I wrap them up, or will you wear them?" he asked, trying
to hide the excitement in his voice. He had made a sale!

"I'll wear them," she said quickly, and slipped on the second shoe.

He stood up, a little out of breath, but smiling and victorious.
"That'll be three ninety-five," he said.

She looked at him for a moment and then said quietly, "I haven't got any money."

He gasped stupidly, the sound escaping from him as though he had been violently struck. His mouth hung open and he stared at her in amazement, without comprehension.

"Come on, come on," she said, and her voice was suddenly hard. "Snap out of it!"

He continued to stare at her, openmouthed, trying to bring back into focus the soft face, the gleaming teeth, the full, smiling lips.

She stood up and faced him with a cold, calculating half-grin.

"Well?" she said, and cast a meaningful glance toward the curtained doorway of the stockroom in the rear of the store.

"Oh!" he said, as though he had suddenly remembered something, and stepped back, away from her. He shook his head quickly. "Oh, no," he said.

"Oh, well," she said with a tired shrug, twisting her lips into thin angry lines, and sat down. She lifted one leg across her knee to get nearer to the shoe and began to undo the large ribbon bow.

For another moment he stared at her, then he said quickly, "It's all right—you don't have to take them off."

At once her face brightened into a pinched, knowing smile and she looked up at him. But he took several steps away from her. She shrugged again and re-tied the ribbon hurriedly. Then she stood up and walked toward the door with a faint swagger, looking back at him derisively over her shoulder.

He continued to stare at the door for a few moments after it had closed. His eyes were still unblinking with a look of astonished disbelief as he took his thin wallet from his hip pocket and counted out four dollar bills.

The bell of the cash register shook him from his trance.

"Gee whiz," he exclaimed, softly, as he dropped the bills in and took out a nickel.

Dummy Run

"You hear what I hear, Clyde?" The fat man in the sheepskin coat shifted his heavy boots on the sill of the stove and looked up from his newspaper. "My ears, maybe, or is that another batch?"

The young man at the desk raised his eyes from his book and listened attentively. From the street outside came the dry, crunching sound of heavy footsteps approaching on the snow.

"I'll tell them," Clyde said in a low voice as he stood up. "Too bad they have to come all this way for nothing on a night like this."

He glanced toward the door and then across the wooden railing that divided into two sections the single room of the small frame building which served as immigration depot for the crews of ships loading or unloading in this Canadian port or anchored in its harbor while waiting orders to join convoys. The door from the street opened into the office section of the room, which contained the small stove and the desk, a couple of extra chairs, and, near the door, a long, waist-high wooden counter. The other and larger part of the room, dimly lit and very cold, was an improvised waiting room with wooden benches running along its bare walls. About twenty seamen —American, British, Canadian—were asleep or dozing on the benches; each of them wore a pink slip tucked in the ribbon of his hat. They had come ashore that morning or the day before on twelve- to twenty-four-hour passes and were now waiting for the harbor launch to take them back to their ships. Clyde saw that none of them had been roused by the approaching footsteps. He walked to the counter. The door opened and he dipped his head slightly to avoid the rush of wind and swirl of snow that came hurtling into the room.

"Close it, Clyde," the fat man said irritably from the depths of his sheepskin collar. "Tell them to close that damned thing."

The door slammed shut. Six men and a woman had come in. They stamped the snow from their boots and stood in an awkward group, blinking helplessly in the weak yellow light.

"Good evening," Clyde said pleasantly. "Terrible night, isn't it?"

The newcomers nodded very quickly, as though they had been reprimanded for some unconscious act of impoliteness. Five of the men were young—under thirty. They wore heavy blue mackinaws and blue pancake hats. A line of gold print, the characters strange and foreign, ran around the bands of their hats. The sixth man was older, perhaps forty or forty-five, with a strong, lean face and very broad shoulders. He wore a thick brown overcoat and an officer's cap without insignia. The woman was completely muffled in an old raccoon coat with a huge collar that stood up around her head and hid her face. They looked as though they had just come from a shopping expedition. The five young sailors were carrying clusters of small parcels, paper sacks with packages of toothpaste and shaving cream sticking out of their tops, a string bag full of oranges, and cartons of cigarettes. The woman had a large, unwrapped box of face tissues under one arm and, clutched tightly in a mittened hand, a bouquet of gaudy artificial flowers whose stems were wrapped in the glazed tan paper peculiar to five-and-ten-cent stores. The older man carried no parcels. Clyde's greeting seemed to puzzle and embarrass them. The five young sailors and the woman looked expectantly at the older man. He took off one glove, stepped up to the counter, and held out seven pink slips of paper. They had obviously been torn from the same pad as the slips that the sleeping men in the larger section of the room were wearing in their hats.

"Tell them to scram," the fat man in the sheepskin coat said behind Clyde. "There's no boats going out tonight."

"I know what to tell them, Coombes." Clyde spoke without turning, and his high voice shook with faint annoyance, but he smiled across the counter at the older man in the officer's cap. "I'm sorry about these," Clyde said, and tapped the pink slips in the man's hand. "We can't send you out to your ship tonight. A lot of ice has formed in the harbor and a lot more has drifted down from Bedford Basin. The launch can't get through it tonight in the dark. I suggest you try to find some accommodations here in town for the night, and tomorrow morning, at eight-thirty, we'll send you all out to your ships. We should be able to get through the ice or around it in daylight. We can't try it tonight."

The older man laid the pink slips on the counter and pointed to them with a large forefinger. It was plain that he hadn't understood Clyde's explanation.

"They're a bunch of Poles from that freighter came in last night," Coombes said from his place at the stove. "That's the captain or the first mate or something with his wife and those five young guys are his gun crew. They came through on the morning launch when Drew was on duty and he gave them twelve-hour passes. They don't talk English. Tell them to beat it till tomorrow morning eight-thirty."

"How can I tell them if they don't understand English?" Clyde said in an exasperated tone. "I wish you'd let me do this in my own—"

Coombes dropped his heavy boots from the ledge of the stove with a bang that rattled the kettle steaming on top. He stood up and walked over to the wooden railing that divided the room.

"Hey!" he called loudly. "Any of you men speak Polish?" The seamen asleep or dozing on the benches stirred. Several looked up and squinted at Coombes. "Polish," he said, his voice rising. "Any of you men speak Polish? Any of you understand it?" The men looked at one another and back at Coombes. Nobody answered. Coombes took the pipe from his mouth and spat across the rail in disgust. He walked back to his chair beside the stove and sat down. "No Polish. Nobody understands them and they don't understand us. Just tell them to beat it. Do it in sign language. Anything. Get them out of here."

"I'm afraid we cannot send you out tonight," Clyde said, spacing his words and enunciating with care, as though he were talking to a deaf man. "There is ice in the harbor. Do you understand? Ice? Ice in harbor? *No boats tonight.*"

The middle-aged Pole turned and spoke sharply to the group behind him. The five young sailors shifted their parcels and dug into their blue mackinaws. The woman put the bouquet of artificial flowers in her other hand and opened her fur coat to reach an inner pocket. The huge collar fell away from her face and the bulky coat dropped open, revealing an attractive, slender woman in her early thirties. She and the five young sailors handed small, square booklets to the older man. He bounced them on the wooden counter to make an even pile and pushed it across toward Clyde.

"No, no," Clyde said. "We don't want your passports. We saw your passports when you came through in the morning, when you went ashore, when our Mr. Drew gave you these twelve-hour passes." He smiled quickly, a friendly, strained grimace. "Nothing wrong with your passports." He waved his hand across the railing toward the men on the benches. "Nobody's going back tonight. These men are all staying over tonight, too." He pushed the passports back across the counter and then, remembering, began again to space his words and raise his voice. "You find place sleep tonight. Hotel or rooming house. Come back in morning." He stopped. The older man was staring at him, the lean, strong face expressionless except for his eyebrows, which were rising slowly. "You can all stay here if you like. On benches like the other men. But I think—" Clyde stopped again and all of his thin face grew as red as the tip of his thin nose. "The lady with you. I think it's too cold for her to sit up all night in there. I don't think it would be—" His uneven voice petered out.

"Lay off the lady stuff," Coombes said drily. "That's his wife and these Poles get jealous easy. He'll take a sock at you."

Clyde looked with embarrassment at the Pole; apparently the older man had not understood. He put the passports in his pocket, his face still blank. With a deliberate, dignified gesture he pointed to a line of print on one of the pink slips: "Your launch will leave Bedford Wharf at——." "10:30 P.M." was penciled in the blank space. Then he pointed up at the old alarm clock hanging from a nail in the wall. The clock showed twenty-five minutes after ten.

"I know," Clyde said patiently, his high voice becoming more ragged. "Ordinarily we would have a launch going out at ten-thirty. But tonight we—" He stopped, struck by an idea. He took one of the pink slips, crossed out "10:30 P.M.," and wrote in "8:30 A.M." above it. "You see?" he said eagerly, tapping the slip with his pencil and leaning far forward across the counter as though he hoped to cross the barrier of language by bringing himself physically closer to

the other man. "Not tonight. Not ten-thirty. Tomorrow morning.
Tomorrow morning eight-thirty. Time is changed. Because of ice.
Ice in harbor. Too dangerous. No boat tonight. No—" He stopped
again and pointed desperately to the figures "8:30 A.M." on the pink
slip. There was no sign of understanding from the impassive Pole.
Clyde drew a deep breath and waved his hand toward the men in
the other section of the room. "It's not only you. All these men—
they're not going at ten-thirty tonight. All waiting for tomorrow.
You better try to find a place to stay for the night. You can use the
phone here to call a hotel. I'll help you if you want." Like a teacher
explaining a problem with diagrams on a blackboard, he pointed to
the box phone on the wall, flanked by a large Canadian Pacific calendar and a newspaper picture of Winston Churchill. "Find hotel,"
he said. "Or rooming house. And then tomorrow—"

The sound of laughter, low but derisive, came across the rail from
the other section of the room. "How's about cutting out the jokes
so we can sleep," one of the American sailors called. "If there was a
room anywhere in this town, you think we'd be sitting up all night
in this icebox?"

Clyde tugged hopelessly at the folds of the woollen muffler
around his neck. The middle-aged Pole looked without expression
across the railing at the men sprawled on the benches, shifted his
glance to Clyde, to Coombes beside the stove, and then back to
Clyde. Slowly he pulled off his other glove, unbuttoned his thick
brown overcoat, dipped into an inside pocket, and pulled out a fat
wallet. He slid open the zipper fastener and, very deliberately, began
to count out a pile of bank notes on the counter. Clyde stared
blankly.

"Well, I'll be a son of a gun," Coombes said. Clyde turned, his
face puzzled. "He don't believe us," Coombes said slowly, getting
up. "He thinks we're not sending them back because they're Poles or
something." He pulled the pipe from his mouth and came up to the
counter. "He wants to pay us for sending the launch out."

"We can't do that." Clyde swung back to face the Pole. "It's
not a question of money. You're entitled to the launch trip free. It's
the ice. Ice in harbor. No boat because of ice. *Ice. No boat. Dangerous.*"

The Pole drew several more bank notes from his wallet and added them to the pile. His face was still blank, but there was a suggestion of contempt in the movement of his wrist as he flicked the money over.

"Who says we can't?" Coombes' bilious face was creased with cold anger. He spoke to Clyde but he kept his glance on the Pole. "We can't send the launch because it might get banged around. Sure. But if this wise guy is willing to put up the dough for any damage. O.K." He grinned unpleasantly as he pulled the sheepskin collar up higher around his ears and buttoned it across his chin. "Stamp up those passes. I'll take them out."

"Listen, Coombes. That's—"

"Stamp them up," Coombes said, his cold glance fixed on the Pole. "I'll take them out, the wise guy."

Clyde hesitated, then picked up the rubber stamp, punched it down on an ink pad, and began hitting the pink slips. He stamped six and stopped.

"I'm not going to stamp the woman's," he said. "The men, all right, if they insist. But I'm not going to stamp the woman's."

"Stop being a damn fool," Coombes snapped. "It's their funeral. They're asking for it."

"I don't care," Clyde said stubbornly. His voice quivered. "The men, all right, if they insist. But not the woman. It's too cold and it might be dangerous. I'm not going to—" Coombes snatched angrily at the rubber stamp. Clyde swung it out of reach. "No," the younger man said in a shaking voice. "If you stamp the woman's, if you take the woman, I'll report you, Coombes. The others, all right. They're insisting. But not the woman."

Coombes glared at him. "All right," he said finally. He came around from behind the counter and poked his finger at the five sailors and the middle-aged man. "You and you and you and you three. Not the woman. Come on." The middle-aged Pole said something sharply. Coombes shook his head. "I don't know what you're saying, brother, but if it's about the woman, no soap. Here." He thrust the pink slips at the six men. "You coming or not?"

The Pole turned to Clyde and spoke again, a stream of short, sharp words.

"No," Clyde said, his face white. "I'm sorry. It's too cold and it might be dangerous. I won't let the lady run the risk."

All the control seemed to go out of the Pole's face. He hit the counter with his big fist and spoke angrily, in a furious roar. The upper part of Clyde's body bent backward, away from the angry man, but the front button of his jacket still touched the edge of the wooden counter. He shoved the seventh pink slip behind his back and shook his head again.

"No," he said. "I'm sorry. She can't go. It's too dangerous."

The Pole drew a deep breath, turned to the five young men, and spoke in a low voice. The young men nodded. The middle-aged Pole placed his own pink slip on top of the bank notes, moving his wrist with the small, contemptuous gesture.

"O.K., he's staying behind, too," Coombes said brusquely. "Come on, you guys." He pushed through the swinging gate in the wooden railing. The five young Poles followed him across the room toward another door, which led to the dock. There was a flurry of movement among the men on the benches. "Don't get excited," Coombes said to them. "This is only a dummy run. There's no launch in the harbor can get through that ice tonight, but these birds are willing to pay for taking a chance. Relax, you guys. You got till eight-thirty tomorrow morning."

He pulled open the door, ducked his head into the wind and the snow, and the five young men followed him out onto the dock. The men on the benches sank back. In the other section of the room the young woman and the Pole remained erect, staring at the closed door. From the dock outside came the sputter of a motor. The sound became a roar, rose higher and higher, and began to fade. Soon it was gone and the only sound in the room was the gentle hissing of the kettle on the stove. Clyde's hand shook as he brought it out from behind his back to place the woman's pink slip next to the rubber stamp.

"Would you care to come in here?" he said awkwardly, with a gesture toward the stove. "The lady, she might be warmer near the stove? In here? Warmer for the lady?"

The middle-aged man gave him a long glance, full of hatred and contempt, stalked to the benches, and sat down on a vacant seat. The young woman followed timidly, clutching the box of face tissues and the bouquet of artificial flowers, and sat down next to the man. She placed the box on the seat beside her but still held the artificial flowers. The other men in the room stared at them curiously for a while, then relaxed into their former postures. The Pole and the young woman sat erect and stared straight ahead, across the heads of the reclining men. Clyde sat down at the desk and picked up his book. During the hour that followed he did not turn a single page.

At last, muffled by the snow and the wind, came the purring roar of the motor. The men who were not asleep sat up straight. Clyde put down his book. The middle-aged Pole and the young woman turned their heads slightly. The purring roar grew louder and then it stopped. Clyde looked at the alarm clock. It showed twenty minutes to midnight. Feet tramped heavily across the snow-covered dock. The door opened and Coombes came in, followed by the five young sailors. Everybody watched as they crossed the room. Coombes walked with a firm, fast, purposeful stride, slapping fresh snow from his coat. The young Poles moved more slowly, uncertainly. They all looked tired and very cold. Coombes snatched the pile of bank notes from the counter, pushed through the wooden gate, and strode to the bench where the Polish officer and his wife were sitting.

"Here." Coombes dropped the money contemptuously into the man's lap. "We don't want your dough."

He shoved his way back through the gate, went behind the counter, and flung himself into the chair beside the stove.

"What happened?" Clyde said. "Did you—"

"What did you expect to happen?" Coombes barked the words as he filled his pipe, tamping the tobacco in with fierce thrusts of his thumb. "We couldn't get through. The ice is too damn thick and you can't see where the hell you're going in all that damn snow." He jerked his head toward the other section of the room, where the five young sailors were talking rapidly to the older man, explaining in Polish what had happened. "We used up a little gas, but at least we'll have some peace around here. Damn near froze their ears off, but now they can tell that wise guy when I say a launch can't get through, it can't get through." He lit his pipe, taking huge, angry sucks on the stem, and buried his head in the newspaper.

Almost immediately the door from the street opened and a man wearing a heavy coat sweater and a peaked cap came in. "Hello, Clyde," he said, brushing the snow from his sweater as he walked behind the counter. "Hello, Coombes."

Coombes grunted without raising his head from the newspaper. "Hello, Drew," Clyde said. "You're early."

"The hell I am." The newcomer blocked out half of Winston Churchill's face by hanging his peaked cap on one of the nails that held the picture to the wall. "That alarm clock is slow. It's after midnight. You been off duty five minutes already, Clyde, only you don't know it." He laughed, walked over to the counter, glanced idly at the papers there, and looked across to the benches. "This whole bunch waiting for the eight-thirty?"

"Yes," Clyde said. He stood up, took his neatly folded overcoat from the back of his chair, and slipped into it. "Their passes are all stamped. All except one." He finished buttoning his coat, picked up the unstamped pink slip from the counter, and marked it with the rubber stamp. "Those seven over there," he said in a low voice, keeping his glance on the man who was relieving him, "they're Poles. They don't understand English. You might make the lady a cup of tea later if you get a chance." He nodded toward the kettle on the stove. "She'll be pretty cold by morning."

"Sure," Drew said cheerfully. "I remember them going through this morning." He looked across the railing at the woman and winked at Clyde. "Not bad, huh?"

"You, too?" Coombes said from behind the newspaper. "Why don't you two guys keep your mind on your work?"

"What's up?" Drew said with a sly grin. "Clyde been—?"

"Quit it," Clyde said, his face bright red. "It's just she'll probably be cold and it's a long wait till eight-thirty." He walked out from behind the counter, pushed through the wooden gate, and stopped in front of the group of Poles. His hand shook as he put the pink slip on the middle-aged man's lap. "This is the pass for the lady." He spoke slowly and clearly, his voice quivering, like a convicted prisoner who knows the jury will not believe him but makes his final, hopeless protest of innocence for the record. He looked directly at the man and carefully avoided looking at the woman. "You'll all get through to your ship in the morning, when it's light. I hope the wait isn't too uncomfortable for you. Good night."

He swung around abruptly, pushed through the gate, and pulled his coat collar up around his narrow head as he walked stiffly toward the door, like a man who knows he may be shot in the back but is determined not to give way to his terror by turning or running.

"So long," Drew said. "See you tomorrow."

"So long," Clyde said, pulling the door open. "Good night, Coombes."

"Good night," Coombes grunted from behind the newspaper. "Close that damn door, will you? It's—"

He stopped and lowered the newspaper. Clyde was hesitating at the door. The middle-aged Pole had jumped up. Everybody watched as he took the young woman by the hand and helped her to her feet. He led her through the swinging gate, toward the door, his lean face expressionless. The young woman walked trustingly beside him. Clyde stood there, his hand on the knob of the open door, his head bent slightly against the wind and the snow that poured in and seemed to freeze him in his tracks. His frightened face grew white and he stepped back slightly when the Pole reached him, as though he expected to be struck. The Pole stopped and bowed stiffly. He took the bouquet of artificial flowers from the young woman and held it out. Clyde stared at the older man, at the flowers, at the young woman, and then back at the man. The Pole bowed again and held the flowers out further. The young woman curt-seyed. Drew started to laugh. Clyde flushed scarlet.

"It's for you," Drew said. "He's making you a present."

Clyde reached out hesitantly, his hand shaking, and took the flowers. His fingers slipped on the glazed tan paper and he almost dropped them.

"Thank you," he mumbled. Then he cleared his throat and spoke louder. "Thank you very much."

The Pole bowed once more and said something in his own language. The young woman nodded gravely. Clyde stared at the flowers, which he held gingerly, as though he expected them to explode, and then his thin, scared face broke into a small smile of gratitude and understanding. He bowed stiffly, awkwardly, to the Pole. He whipped off his old felt hat and bowed to the young woman. Both of them bowed to him.

"Listen," Coombes called. "You going to close that damn door or you going to let the—" The door slammed shut and Clyde was gone. For a few moments the sound of his steps on the snow could be heard and then it faded out in the windy night. The Pole and the young woman walked back to their bench. The kettle hissed gently in the silent room. "What do you say, Drew?" Coombes said from behind his newspaper. "You going to make that lady that cup of tea now?"

An Easy One

"What's the capital of Louisiana?" the boy asked.

"Louisiana?" his mother said. "Let's see, now. New Orleans?"

"No," the boy said, laughing. "Baton Rouge."

"Why, of course," his mother said, laughing with him. "Baton Rouge. Go ahead. Ask me more."

"All right. What's the capital of Illinois?"

"Chicago," the mother said promptly.

"No," the boy cried, squealing with delight. "Springfield. Everybody makes that mistake. Everybody says Chicago."

"Oh, dear, that's true," the mother said with a hint of annoyance in her voice. "Springfield. What else?"

"I better give you an easy one. What's the capital of Florida?"

"Oh, I know that," the mother said. "Tallahassee."

"That's right. But that's an easy one. What's the capital of—wait." The boy looked up at the ceiling of the car. "I know! What's the capital of Washington?"

"Seattle."

"No, it isn't! It's Olympia!"

The boy clasped his hands gleefully between his knees and bent over to enjoy his laughter. His mother smiled, her face a mixture of pride and mild irritation, as she put out her hand protectingly to prevent him from toppling out of his chair. The roadbed was not particularly smooth and the train rocked and jounced so hard that all the furniture in the lounge car rattled. It made the lamps shake

and caused the lights streaking by in the night outside to shiver
wildly. The boy straightened up, his face split wide in a happy grin,
and the mother took her hand away.

"I better ask you another easy one," he said. "What's the capital
of Maryland?"

"Sh-h-h," his mother said, still smiling, but with a trace of sharp-
ness. "Not so loud, David dear. You'll disturb the other people in
the car."

She glanced about with an expression of apprehension that was
delicate and yet at the same time curiously exaggerated. There were
three men in the car, sitting widely spaced. They were smoking and
holding magazines bound in leather covers on which the name of
the publication was printed in small gold letters. The three men
were not reading, because the boy was talking so loudly that their
attention was practically forced in his direction. They watched with
small, genial smiles. It was almost a very pleasant sight, and it was
difficult to say why it was not utterly charming.

The boy, who appeared to be about nine or ten years old, though
small for his age, was dressed as if he were younger. He wore a blue
cheviot suit with short trousers that left his knees bare. A stiff white
Eton collar spread out on his narrow shoulders and was pulled snugly
about his throat with a dull-red tie on which the crest and the initials
of a private school were embroidered in yellow silk. His blond hair, a
shade or two darker than his mother's, had obviously been combed
just before dinner. It was still damp, but the forelock, which had
dried more quickly than the rest, was tousled. His legs, which did not
quite touch the floor of the car, swung back and forth happily. He
seemed completely unaware of the three men in the car.

His mother, however, knew they were watching. She was young
and pretty, at least from a distance of several feet, at which the little,
hard lines at the corners of her mouth were invisible. She wore long,
black, artificial eyelashes, and when she laughed she threw back her
head so her beautiful white teeth showed clearly and the tip of her
conical, saucy hat brushed the window behind her. She wore a
silver-fox cape and a tweed suit with a tight skirt. Her handsome
legs were crossed at the ankles, one high-heeled shoe locked behind
the other, and she maintained her balance in the shaking chair with

one toe pressed firmly into the dull-green carpet. She gave the three men in the car a little self-conscious smile that was supposed to convey embarrassed apology, and almost did. The boy saw the smile and looked apprehensively toward the men. His mother opened her large, square, black suède purse, took out a cigarette, and struck a match.

"Just a little more softly, David, please, dear," she said as she blew a neat stream of smoke up at the ceiling. "You mustn't disturb the other people."

"Yes, Mother," the boy said in a low voice. "I'm sorry." Then, grinning again and louder than ever, he asked, "What's the capital of California?"

"Oh, dear, let me see now. Los Angeles? No, no—wait. Wait, I have it. San Francisco!"

"No!" the boy squealed. "Sacramento!"

He had forgotten the men entirely and, clasping his hands between his knees with delight, let his laughter rock him in the chair. His mother laughed too, much more moderately, and glanced around the car. Two of the men smiled and then, embarrassed, buried their heads in their magazines. The third man, who was sitting obliquely across the car about ten feet away, laughed out loud. He looked at the mother and their eyes met.

"He's—uh—he's quite a boy," the man said experimentally. "Isn't he?"

"Yeh-hess," the mother said, laughing through the word as she broke it into two syllables. "But I'm afraid he's disturbing everybody, showing off his geography this way."

"Not at all," the man said, squirming into a more comfortable position in his chair and dropping the leather-covered magazine flat on his lap. "It's a pleasure to listen to him."

The boy pretended he didn't hear them. He scowled at the flickering lights that whisked by in the night outside, as though he were thinking hard, but out of the corners of his eyes he was watching the man who had spoken to his mother.

"All right," the child said suddenly, his voice pitched high to attract his mother's attention. "I have one. I have one. An easy one this time. What's the capital of Nevada?"

His mother looked down at him. She took a few seconds to concentrate, doing it very prettily, one forefinger poking a dimple in her cheek.

"What's the capital of—" she began. "Oh, yes. Nevada. The capital of Nevada. Reno?"

"No," the boy giggled. "Carson City."

"Oh, now, David, that's not fair," she said sharply, pouting through a cloud of cigarette smoke. "You're studying them in school now and I haven't been to school in years." She smiled across the boy's head at the man. "You shouldn't ask such hard ones," she said, softening her voice to a prettily maternal tone of mild reproof and fanning her long, dark eyelashes up and down. "It's been years since Mother studied the capitals, you know."

The man who had dropped his magazine now threw back his head and laughed boldly, a series of short, hacking bellows. He hesitated for a moment, and looked down the car speculatively. Then he stood up, tossed the magazine onto his chair, and walked over to the mother and the boy. He was a tall, clean-looking man with a slightly flushed face and smooth black hair parted in the middle. He hiked up the trousers of his tweed suit at the knees and stooped down in front of the boy until their heads were at the same level.

"Suppose I ask you one or two capitals, son," he said in a deep, throaty voice. He smiled questioningly at the mother, as though he were feeling his way in unknown terrain, and said, "May I?" She smiled back, fanning her eyelashes again, and nodded. The man grinned quickly and turned back to the boy. "What's the capital of New Hampshire, son?" His voice sounded confident, even faintly triumphant. The boy didn't answer. His little legs stopped swinging and he drew back slightly in the chair. "Don't be frightened, son," the man said cheerfully. "Your mother said I could ask you. What's the capital of New Hampshire?"

The boy didn't answer. He turned to look at his mother, his small face pinched with sudden anger at this interloper who was breaking in on their game. His mother was watching the man.

"Go on, David," she urged. "Tell the nice gentleman what's the capital of New Hampshire."

The boy blinked at her in silence and his grip on the arms of the chair tightened.

"Sure, come on," the man coaxed. "Be a good fella, David. Tell me. What's the capital of New Hampshire? You know it. That's an easy one. What's the capital of New Hampshire?"

"I don't know," the boy said shortly.

"Why, David!" his mother said. "What nonsense!"

"Come on," the man coaxed. "What's the capital of New Hampshire?"

"I don't know," the boy said sullènly. "I told you I don't know."

The speeding train took a curve without slowing down, and the man, poised on the balls of his feet like a catcher in back of home plate, was thrown off balance.

"Woops!" the man said as he lurched to one side. The mother said, "Oh!" and put out her hand to prevent him from falling. He caught himself on the edge of the empty chair next to hers and, with the same movement, heaved himself into it. The woman was now sitting in the middle, between her small son and the big, clean-looking man. "Boy!" the man said, laughing. "That was close, wasn't it?"

"I'm so sorry," the mother said. "You might have—"

"Nothing at all," the man said, laughing more loudly. "But that calls for a drink. Will you join me?"

"Why, yes," she said, with a small expression of surprised delight. "Thank you so much."

The man reached behind him and pressed a buzzer. When the porter came, the man looked inquiringly at the woman.

"Scotch-and-soda?" he asked. The woman nodded. "Two," he said to the porter. Then he leaned across the woman, placing his hand on the arm of her chair, and spoke to the boy. "What about you, David?" he said jovially. "A lemonade?"

The boy didn't answer. His chin was sunk so hard into his stiff white Eton collar that it seemed to be cutting deeply into the flesh of his neck.

"David," his mother said in a voice that contained enough sudden irritation to cause the boy to jump slightly. "The gentleman is talking to you!"

"No," the boy said in a gruff voice.

"No, what?" his mother asked sharply.

"No, thank you," he said, scowling.

"David doesn't seem to want to play any more, does he?" the man said affably, still leaning forward so his head was directly in front of the woman, almost touching her silver-fox cape. "He won't tell me the capital of New Hampshire and he won't have a lemonade."

"Yes, he is acting sullen, isn't he?" the woman said carelessly. "I can't understand what's got into him."

The train lurched again and the man's head swung with it. His cheek brushed the woman's silver-fox cape. He sat up quickly and looked frightened, as though he had destroyed by unnecessary haste a small and fragile edifice that had taken much time and patience to build.

"Sorry," he said.

"Quite all right," the woman said, smiling easily. The frightened look disappeared from the man's face. A slow, steady, confident grin took its place. The boy's lower lip started to quiver. He sank his upper teeth into the flesh to hold it steady. "This roadbed is rather rough, isn't it?" the woman said.

"Terrible," the man said. He turned to the waiting porter. "Two scotch-and-sodas, please."

"Yes, suh," the porter said. He bowed and went away.

The man and the woman turned toward each other and began to chat animatedly. She told him she was a widow, that she lived in New York, that she had taken her son out of school for a short visit to her mother in Salt Lake City, that they were now on their way back to New York. The man smiled at her as she talked, looking straight into her face, nodding his head to the rhythm of her words, and crossing and uncrossing his legs many times. When she finished he cleared his throat and told her he was in the oil business, that he lived in Chicago, that he made frequent business trips to New York, that he usually flew but had missed his plane and had taken the train instead, that this was the first time he had ever been glad he had missed a plane. They both laughed at this, quite hard, as if it were something that got funnier and funnier the more they thought about it. The boy watched them in silence, his lower lip still clamped in his teeth, his small hands gripping hard at the arms of the shaking chair, his eyes pinched with something that might have been resignation but had enough tenseness in it to look like fright, as though he were poised for a blow that he knew he could not dodge. The porter came back with the drinks, his shining black face broken into a neutral smile as he swayed his way expertly through the car, keeping the glasses level on the small tray in spite of the jarring of the train.

"There we are," the man said, uncrossing his legs and turning away from the woman toward the porter. "That looks good, doesn't it?"

"It certainly does," she said.

The porter pulled over a large smoking stand with a wide metal pan surrounding the ash tray in the middle. The woman crushed out her cigarette while the porter set the glasses down on the metal pan. They rattled noisily with the movement of the train. While the man hunted in his pocket for money, the porter stood with his hands clasped behind him, smiling good-naturedly at the silent boy.

"Did you say a lemonade for the boy, suh?" he asked politely. "Ah wasn't sure—"

"Why, yes," the man said, as though he had suddenly remembered something. "I wanted him to have one. What do you say, David? A lemonade?"

The boy didn't answer.

"The cat seems to have gotten his tongue," the woman said through a scowl of exasperation. "He doesn't seem to know how to talk any more. David, the gentleman asked you a question!"

"I don't want any," the boy said rudely. "I don't want his old lemonade."

The man seemed startled by the boy's vehemence. The mother's face contracted into an expression of anger that brought out the deep, hard creases at the corners of her mouth. The porter saw what was about to happen and spoke before the mother could.

"Ah heard him say the capitals of all those states," he said in a friendly, helpful voice. "Ah wonder if he knows the capital of mah state, Alabama?"

"Sure he does," the man said heartily as he handed the money to the porter. "That's an easy one. What's the capital of Alabama, David?"

"I don't know," the boy muttered.

He stared with hatred straight at the man. His little back was arched stiffly.

"Now, David, you stop this nonsense at once," his mother said

sharply. "You do know. You've been asked a question and I want
you to answer. What's the capital of Alabama?"

The boy's head jerked around until he was staring directly at his
mother. But he did not speak.

"David!" his mother snapped. "I told you to—"

"Ah guess he's tahd," the porter said apologetically. He seemed terribly embarrassed by the curiously tense situation his innocent question had created. "Ah guess he's—"

"He is *not* tired," the woman said angrily. "He's just being sullen
for some ridiculous reason. David, you answer, do you hear? What
is the capital of Alabama?"

The boy's lower lip quivered noticeably in spite of the grip he had
on it with his teeth. Still he did not speak.

"Let's forget it," the man said, no longer making any pretense of
geniality. He was definitely annoyed. He picked up his drink and
took a long pull.

"Very well," the woman said grimly. "If you're going to act like
that, David, you can't stay here." She turned to the porter. "Will you
please take him to our section and see that he goes to bed at once?"

"Yes, Ma'am," the porter said. He was not smiling now. He looked
vaguely frightened. "Yes, Ma'am."

"Go ahead, David," the woman ordered sharply. "Go to bed at
once."

The boy's rigid body relaxed, as though the blow against which
he had been steeling himself had finally landed. He slipped off the
chair, the jacket of his blue cheviot suit bunching up around his
hips and his short pants sliding up and away from his naked knees.
He put his little hand in the porter's outstretched big one. For a moment he stood there, staring at his mother. There was no longer any
doubt about the look on his small, pale face. As the woman picked
up her drink and smilingly touched glasses with the big, pink-faced
man, the boy looked at her with eyes in which resigned despair and
blind terror were evenly mixed. The porter led him through the
lounge car, steadying him against the sway of the pounding train.
Behind them the man and the woman were laughing and talking and
clinking the ice in their glasses. At the end of the car the porter
pulled open the heavy metal door. He leaned over the boy solici-
tously to help him across the threshold.

"Ah'm surprised at you," he said in a soft, gentle, chiding voice. "A smaht boy lahk you not knowing the capital of Alabama."

The boy's teeth came away from his lower lip. He screwed his face into a tight scowl to prevent it from quivering and looked down at the floor of the car.

"Sure I know," he said in a listless, uneven voice that was almost a whisper. "It's Montgomery."

Everybody and His Brother

"Who?" Pearson said. "No, I don't," he said, and then he listened, his head tipped to one side, cradling the phone between his shoulder and his ear, while his eyes ran along the lines of the neatly typed letter on top of the pile in front of him and, for the first time in three and a half years, he wondered idly why government typewriters were equipped with blue ribbons. "Oh," Pearson said, and his left hand came up fast to keep the phone against his ear as he straightened in the chair. "Sure, yes, of course," he said. "Give me a couple of minutes to sign these letters, Miss Mead. Then you bring him in when you come for them."

He put down the phone and took one of the two pens from the brown and black onyx base with the small brass plaque that said "To Raymond B. Pearson From The Staff V-E Day May 8, 1945." Pearson started to read the top letter, stopped as though he had suddenly remembered something important, raised his head, and looked around the room.

It was a rectangular room, about twenty-five feet long by fifteen feet wide, with the large, glass-topped desk at the far end. The single window was behind the desk. At the other end of the room, near the door, there was a heavy library table on which were piled neat stacks of FCC reports, copies of the Congressional Record, and a set of thick looseleaf Prentice-Hall Tax Service binders. On the wall above the table, facing the window and the desk, hung a large production chart framed in black wood. A heavy line zigzagged boldly up the face of the chart, from a point in the lower left-hand corner marked "Dec. 7, 1941" in red, to a point near the upper right-hand corner marked, also in red, "May 8, 1945." The rest of the line, which was dotted and drawn with lighter ink, disappeared under the frame at the top of the chart. To the right of the desk, fastened to the wall with scotch tape, was a reproduction of the Atlantic Charter. Under it, also fastened with scotch tape, was a glossy print of a group of men with briefcases photographed standing around a jeep in which Franklin Delano Roosevelt sat in front of a C-54 on an airstrip with palm trees in the background. Pearson, looking at least twenty years younger than anybody else in the picture, and three or four years younger than his actual age, which was thirty-six, was at the extreme right, blinking against the sunlight reflected from the windshield. On the floor of the office, which was several shades darker than the pale gray walls, there was a wine-colored carpet with one ragged edge. The carpet seemed too small for the room. A low-slung red leather chair with brass nail heads stood next to the desk. It matched the chair behind the desk except that Pearson's chair swivelled and had a higher back. On the desk, flanking the onyx fountain-pen set, were two imitation mahogany trays, one marked *In* and the other *Out*. A black DDT bomb was holding down the papers in the *Out* tray. All the furniture in the room had small stencil code numbers stamped in yellow on the edges.

It was an impressive room by war agency standards, but a person who didn't know much about those standards, a person accustomed to private business offices, for example, or a naval officer who had never been inside a war agency office, might not have thought it was impressive. Pearson stopped scowling, put the pen between his teeth, turned around, and adjusted the Venetian blind so that the morning sun fell more brightly into the room. Through the slats the Capitol dome and the square bulk of the House Office Building could be seen a quarter of a mile away. The phone rang again.

"Yes?" Pearson said around the fountain pen. "All right, yes." He took the pen out of his mouth. "I'm ready now, Miss Mead."

He signed the letters quickly, without reading them, and he was pushing the pen back into the desk set when the door opened and Miss Mead came in with the young man in naval uniform.

"Mr. Pearson," she said. "This is Lieutenant Lomas."

"How are you, Lieutenant?" Pearson said, coming out from behind the desk with his hand outstretched. "My God," he said, thinking how much wiser he would be if he were not saying it, "you look like a Christmas tree."

Lieutenant Lomas looked startled, glanced down at the ribbons on his chest, and then, as he took Pearson's hand, a slow pink flush of embarrassment came through his tan. He was a tall, good-looking young man of about thirty, with black hair and square white teeth, who looked so well in uniform that it was difficult to imagine him wearing anything else.

"Oh, hell," he said. "You know how it is, sir. Every time you stop at a place to take on water they slap another area ribbon on you. I'm very glad to meet you, sir."

"I'm glad to meet you, too," Pearson said. He nodded to the letters on his desk. "All right, Miss Mead."

She picked up the letters, walked back to the door, and stood there for a moment, holding it open and looking at Lieutenant Lomas. The two lines of neat black lettering on the ground glass of the open door that said "Raymond B. Pearson, Chief, Hard Fuels Branch" were just over her head. Lieutenant Lomas became aware of her glance and turned. Miss Mead smiled and stepped quickly out of the room and pulled the door shut.

"Miss Mead is partial to the navy," Pearson said. "Her brother is somewhere with Halsey. Sit down, Lieutenant. When did you get in? How is Clyde?"

"Thank you, sir." Lieutenant Lomas waited politely, until Pearson got back into his own chair behind the desk, before he dropped into the red chair next to it. "Clyde's fine," he said. "Just dandy. About two hours ago," Lieutenant Lomas said. "Few minutes before nine."

"All the way from Guam?" Pearson said.

"Yes, sir," Lieutenant Lomas said with a grin. "All the way from Guam. You sure move fast these days, once you get going. It's damned nice of you to see me like this, sir, just walking in on you, without an appointment or anything."

"Don't be silly," Pearson said. "Any friend of Clyde's is welcome to anything I've got, certainly my time, and I think the war effort can spare a few minutes of that for a friend of Clyde's. We grew up together. Everything all right with him?"

"Yes, he told me you grew up together," Lieutenant Lomas said. "Everything's fine with him. He'd like to get home for a while, everybody does after two years, and I guess he will, pretty soon, although those things are never definite, but aside from that he's great. He's been promoted, you know."

"Lieutenant commander?" Pearson said, his voice rising. "When?"

"Yes, sir, lieutenant commander," Lieutenant Lomas said. "It came through about two weeks ago. No, wait, let's see. I left Guam Thursday and today's Monday, that's four days, and it happened just a week before I left. Eleven days ago."

"That's wonderful," Pearson said, and then, because it didn't sound quite right, he said, "That really is terrific. Eleven days. I guess that's why we haven't heard yet. I imagine it'll be in his next letter, except he's so damned modest."

"He sure is," Lieutenant Lomas said. "A real swell guy, sir."

"Tell me more about the old son of a gun," Pearson said. "No, wait." He picked up the phone. "I'll call my wife and you come to dinner tonight. We're in Arlington, but I'll drive you out and see that you get a taxi back. She'll want to hear, too. She's known Clyde since we were both kids."

"No, I'm sorry," Lieutenant Lomas said, half rising in the chair. "I wish I could, sir, and it's damned nice of you to ask me, but I'm afraid I can't make it. I've got a seat on the one o'clock plane to New York. My family's up there. I won't be in Washington but another two hours."

"That's a shame," Pearson said, and then, into the phone, "Never mind, Miss Mead." He dropped the phone back onto the hook. "Mrs. Pearson will be disappointed. Well, you tell me and I'll tell her. By the way, what's the one on the left, with the blue and white in the middle?"

Lieutenant Lomas looked down at his chest and then he started to fumble awkwardly in his pocket.

"Philippines Liberation," he said, pulling out a pack of cigarettes. "Will you have one, sir?"

"Thanks, I don't smoke," Pearson said. "But you go ahead."

Lieutenant Lomas twisted his head to get his eye away from the smoke as he blew out the match, and his glance stopped on the glossy print under the Atlantic Charter. Pearson began to feel a little better.

"Is that you, sir?" Lieutenant Lomas said. "On the right, near the windshield?"

"Yes," Pearson said. "I was with him at Casablanca in January of '43."

Lieutenant Lomas leaned over to examine the picture more closely. "He sure was a wonderful guy, sir," he said. "Wasn't he?"

"A wonderful guy and a great man," Pearson said, and he could feel himself growing tense with anticipation but, from the speed with which Lieutenant Lomas' glance swung around the room, it was clear that neither the chart on the wall at the far end, nor the reversed black lettering on the ground glass of the door, held any significance for him. His glance stopped on the ragged edge of the carpet on the floor and he started to rub the two gold stripes on his sleeve absently. "Well," Pearson said, "I guess there isn't really much more to tell, is there? Except that he's well and doing fine and been promoted."

"Yes, sir, that's about all, really," Lieutenant Lomas said, looking up from the carpet. "Clyde's well and he's doing fine and he's been promoted."

"I know how it is," Pearson said, beginning to rub the sleeve of his tweed coat. "Every time I go over on a trip, people here in Washington always give me a long list of friends and relatives to look up, and I always do, even though it means running yourself ragged, but when I get back all I can really tell them is their friends and relatives are well, and doing fine and, once in a while, that they've been promoted. They're always disappointed and want to hear more, but there never seems to be any more to tell. I was almost glad when I had to turn down the trip to Yalta and send my assistant, because we had a big battle coming up on the Hill and I had to be here for the hearings." Pearson waited a moment, but Lieutenant Lomas had either never heard of Yalta, or he was not listening. He was drumming his fingers on the brass nail heads of his chair and looking for an ash tray. "Here," Pearson said, wishing he had not talked so much and wishing he did not feel the way he felt, as he pulled an ash tray out of his desk drawer and pushed it forward. "Not being a smoker myself, I always forget that other people use them."

"Thank you, sir," Lieutenant Lomas said. He punched out his cigarette and lit a fresh one. "Yes, that's how it is, I guess," he said.

"Well, now, Lieutenant," Pearson said, making a final effort, knowing it was foolish to feel the way he felt. "Is there anything I can do for you during the two hours you've got here in Washington?"

Lieutenant Lomas looked up from his examination of the end of his cigarette. "As a matter of fact, sir, there is," he said. "But I'm sort of embarrassed to ask."

"Nonsense," Pearson said. He stopped rubbing his tweed sleeve and he sat up straighter. "Anything I can do, it will be a pleasure to do it, I assure you."

Sitting far forward in the low chair, his elbows on his knees, and scowling down at the cigarette which he twirled between the fingers of both hands as though it were a swizzle stick, Lieutenant Lomas explained what he wanted. His wife's brother, a kid of twenty, was a corporal in the army. They knew he was in China but they were not sure just where in China. He had been there for a year and a half and had written home regularly, but, several months ago, his letters had stopped. Two parcels that his sister, Lieutenant Lomas' wife, had sent him months ago had been returned last week without any explanation, and only yesterday a batch of her most recent letters had come back. Lieutenant Lomas' wife had not written her husband about this because she didn't want to worry him but, an hour or so before, when he got off the plane here in Washington, he had called her long distance from the airport to say he had a seat on the one o'clock plane and would be in New York that night, and she had told him about the problem and asked if he could try, during his few hours in Washington, to get some information about her brother. She and the rest of the family were worried sick. They had written to the War Department several times, but the replies had not been very helpful or reassuring. All the War Department would say was that the corporal was not listed as injured or missing. The War Department would not, or could not, explain why the boy had stopped writing or why his letters and parcels were being returned.

"I haven't seen the kid for two years," Lieutenant Lomas said. "Before I went overseas. He wasn't quite eighteen then, and he wasn't in the army yet, but he was kind of a wild one, I guess. Sort of irresponsible and reckless, the way kids that age are, you know, and frankly my wife is afraid that he may have got himself into some kind of jam." Lieutenant Lomas raised his head from the cigarette, dusted the long ash carefully into the ash tray, and smiled apologetically. "Frankly, sir, I thought of you right away, not only because Clyde had told me to look you up, and I was coming to see you anyway, to give you his regards and all, but also because Clyde has told me a lot about you and how much weight you pull in this town. I know it's a hell of a thing to ask a man you've just met to do for you, but I just can't think of anything else. I don't know anybody in Washington."

Pearson made a small gesture with his forefinger, as though he were rubbing away the mist on a train window so he could look out to read the sign on a station platform, and he smiled back at Lieutenant Lomas. There was genuine pleasure in the smile. For the first time since the younger man, and he couldn't be so very much younger, had come into the room, Pearson felt like himself again.

"Don't apologize," he said, picking up the phone. "I'm delighted to be able to help." He was telling the truth. "Miss Mead," he said into the mouthpiece. "Get me General Wheeler at the Pentagon, will you? I'll hold on. It's important."

He tipped his head to one side, tucking the instrument into the bend of his shoulder, and he watched Lieutenant Lomas' forehead begin to crease.

"Is that General Wheeler you're calling, sir?"

Pearson nodded and hoped, as he put his free hand over the mouthpiece, that the small, exultant skip of his heart was not reflected in his face.

"The General and I work very closely," he said. "We were at Casablanca together and actually, although this is off the record, of course, I briefed him for Yalta when I found I couldn't get away myself. We're very good friends. He just sent this thing over to me this morning." Pearson reached across the desk and lifted the DDT bomb from the papers in the *Out* tray. "We've been having some trouble with mosquitoes at our house out in Arlington, and you can't buy this stuff commercially, you know." Pearson bounced the black metal container in his hand several times and set it back in the *Out* tray. "Yes, that's all right, Miss Mead," he said into the mouthpiece. "I'll hold on. It's important." Pearson put the mouthpiece back against his chest. "Too bad you can't stay overnight," he said. "The General and Mrs. Wheeler are coming to dinner."

"I guess Clyde wasn't kidding when he said you were big stuff in this town," Lieutenant Lomas said with a grin. "Wait till I write him about this."

"What's that?" Pearson said into the phone. "Oh. Well, look. Will you leave word for the General to call me as soon as he gets back to his office? It's important. Yes." Pearson hung up. "He's at a meeting, but they expect him back within the hour. I'll tell you what, Lieutenant." Pearson pulled a pad from his drawer and took one of the pens from the onyx set and held them out to Lieutenant Lomas. "Why don't you put the kid's name and serial number and his APO down on this pad, and write your own address in New York under it, and when the General calls me back I'll get the dope from him and send you a wire or write you a note. You'll be in New York for a while, won't you?"

"Yes," Lieutenant Lomas said, taking the pen and the pad. "I've got thirty days."

"Well, fine, then," Pearson said. "You'll get this tomorrow or the day after, at the latest."

"That's damned swell of you, sir," Lieutenant Lomas said. Pearson made the motion in the air with his forefinger again. The lieutenant put the pad on his knee and hunched himself over it to write. Pearson noticed how much smaller the lieutenant was than he had looked leaning back in the low-slung chair. Even the uniform, which had seemed so smart and well cut when he was standing up, was now bunched up around his chest and the collar stood away from his neck. "There it is, sir," Lieutenant Lomas said, standing up and putting the pad and the pen on the desk. "That other name, that's my mother-in-law. We gave up our apartment when I went in, and my wife's been staying with her."

"Right," Pearson said, glancing at the pad as he pressed the buzzer under the ledge of his desk and stood up. "Don't you worry about this any more, Lieutenant. I'll see that you get the information."

"I don't know how to thank you, sir," Lieutenant Lomas said. "My wife and her family will be very grateful to you. I know I am, right now."

"Not at all," Pearson said, and he smiled as he put out his hand. "It's been great fun meeting you, Lieutenant. Good luck, and if you write to Clyde, give him my regards."

"I sure will, sir," Lieutenant Lomas said, shaking Pearson's hand. "And thanks again."

The door opened and Miss Mead came in.

"Oh, Miss Mead," Pearson said. "After General Wheeler calls me, will you be sure to remind me to wire or write to Lieutenant Lomas in New York?"

"I certainly will," Miss Mead said.

Pearson nodded and waved, and Lieutenant Lomas waved back as he went to the door. Miss Mead held it open for him and, when he reached her, she smiled.

"I beg your pardon," Miss Mead said. "But could you tell me what that one is? I've seen it several times before, but I never found out what it's for."

"This?" Lieutenant Lomas said, looking down at his chest. "Oh, heck, that's just the Presidential Citation. Everybody and his brother has that. So long, sir," he said, across his shoulder. "And thanks again."

Pearson didn't answer. The smile slid from his face as they went out, and he sat down abruptly in the red leather chair with the high back and the brass nail heads. Pearson took his lower lip in his teeth and he swivelled himself around and he stared out through the slats of the Venetian blind at the Capitol dome, trying hard to bring back the good feeling, to erase the sudden irritation by cutting from his mind the few moments after Miss Mead had come in, fighting with himself to leave only what had been there before she opened her big mouth, but he couldn't do it. He wasn't that good. When the phone rang he reached for it and brought it to his ear without turning.

"Yes?" Pearson said.

"General Wheeler returning your call," Miss Mead said.

"I'm not in," Pearson said, letting just enough of his irritation come through in his voice so she would know it was meant for her and not for the General. "The call wasn't important," he said. "Just thank him for sending over the DDT and tell him I'll talk to him tonight."

Examination

"The doctor will be here very soon," the nurse-receptionist said. "In just a few minutes."

Wayne looked at his wristwatch, which showed twenty-eight minutes after seven. "But he told me on the phone yesterday—he said seven-thirty!"

"I know." The receptionist smiled peculiarly and for a moment Wayne thought she was going to scream. Then he saw that her smile was intended to cover a yawn. "Dr. Manck called me a little while ago and said he knew about the appointment with you. He didn't forget, but he got delayed. He asked you to please wait. He won't be very late, he said." The smile won out over the yawn and she looked more cheerful as she blinked away a faint film of tears. "Will you have a seat, please?"

"Thanks."

Wayne stepped out of the small foyer, in which her desk stood, into the empty waiting room and sat down in one of the overstuffed chairs. As soon as he took the weight off his feet he felt the tiredness in his knees that told him he had been up too late the night before. The receptionist picked up her fountain pen and dipped her head into the circle of yellow light from the desk lamp. She suppressed a new yawn delicately, with her fingertips against her lips. Wayne caught the yawn from her. He turned in the chair to look out the window at the early-morning grayness of Seventy-third Street and the small wedge of Central Park visible at the end of the block.

Then he turned back to the room, glanced at the prints on the walls, and picked up a magazine from the small table near his elbow. The receptionist rose from her chair, but Wayne reached up over his head and switched on the lamp himself. The receptionist smiled as she sank back and he smiled, too.

"I guess I ought to apologize," he said, "making you come down to the office so early."

"That's all right, Mr. Wade. I come—"

"Wayne."

"I'm sorry. 'N, e'?"

"That's right."

"Mr. *Wayne*. I come in early like this quite often. Dr. Manck has a great many patients with important government jobs—war positions, you know. They're always going down to Washington these days or rushing off to catch planes and things, so they have to come early."

"Really?" Wayne said, losing part of the feeling of importance the early-morning appointment had given him. He glanced at his wristwatch again: twenty-five minutes to eight. "How prompt a man is Dr. Manck?"

"Oh, he's *very* prompt," the receptionist said. She looked down at her wristwatch. "A few minutes perhaps this morning, but no more."

Wayne nodded and opened the magazine. His regular doctor, Harry Holdridge, was a friend of his. Harry would have seen him in the evening or on Sunday, when Wayne wasn't so rushed for time. Or he might even have filled in the form and signed it without going through the formality of a physical examination. They had been friends since childhood and he knew that Wayne was in excellent physical shape. But Harry was somewhere in the Pacific now. He had a commission in the Navy, and Wayne had made this appointment with Dr. Manck, whom he had never seen, because Harry Holdridge had turned his practice over to Dr. Manck when he left. As Wayne read, he kept touching the top of his head, where the hair was getting thin.

"That window bothering you?" the receptionist said. "If it's a draft I could close it."

Wayne glanced up from the magazine. "What?" He saw the receptionist looking at the window beside his chair. It was raised two or three inches. "Oh," he said, "no. No, thanks." He dropped his hand hastily from the top of his head. "It's perfectly all right."

"I always like to open it a little in the morning. It's so sort of stuffy when you come in early like this."

"Sure," Wayne said, looking at his wristwatch pointedly. It was now a quarter to eight. He was due at the Army Air Forces Intelligence office at nine. Unless Dr. Manck showed up soon, there wouldn't be enough time for a physical examination, he'd have to leave, and the whole point of this early-morning appointment would be wasted. "The window doesn't bother me. But I'm worried about—"

"He'll be here any minute now," the receptionist said. "Dr. Manck is very prompt."

At eight o'clock the door opened with a bang, and a tall young man in a shapeless blue overcoat came in.

"Hi, Miss Perrin," he said cheerfully. He took off the coat, tossed his hat onto her desk, and looked across her shoulder at the mail in front of her, all in a single complicated whirl of activity. "What's new?"

"Good morning, Dr. Manck," she said, then, nodding toward the waiting room, "Mr. Wayne is here."

Dr. Manck grinned and beckoned to Wayne with his hand. "Sorry to keep you waiting, Wayne. I had to drop over to the hospital. Hurry call. Come on in and we'll have you out of here in no time." He pulled open the door to the examination room at the other side of the foyer, and, as Wayne reached him, stuck out his hand. Wayne took it. "Glad to know you," Dr. Manck said, kicking the door of the examination room shut behind him. "Sit down. Make yourself comfortable." He slipped out of his jacket and took down a white coat from a hook on the door. "Had a letter from Harry yesterday."

"You did?" Wayne said. "From where?"

"Postmarked San Diego," Dr. Manck said, punching his arms into the sleeves of the white coat. "Didn't say much. He's not allowed to. Just he's going to sea soon and he expected to be seeing action in a little while and he'd write if he could, but not to expect much mail, and I should take care of his patients." Dr. Manck laughed. "Great guy, Harry."

"He certainly is. Swell guy."

Wayne, who was twenty-nine, the same age as Harry Holdridge, was surprised to see that Dr. Manck was also about that old. He didn't know why, but when Harry had told him he was turning his practice over to Dr. Manck, Wayne had assumed that Manck was an older man. It was the phrase "turning over," he supposed, which sounded like something out of a bad but well-intended war poem—turning over the reins of the home front to age while youth went off to battle. Dr. Manck, with his boyishly cheerful face, his loose-limbed stride, and his unruly crop of thick blond hair, looked even younger than Wayne. "O.K.," he said as he hauled the white coat, stiff with laundry starch, down in the back. "Where does it hurt?"

"No, no. There's nothing wrong with me," Wayne said. He pulled a folded sheet of paper out of his breast pocket. "It's just I have to get this thing signed by a doctor, saying I'm in good physical shape."

"Oh," Dr. Manck said. He stopped grinning, took the paper, and scowled at it for several moments, longer than was necessary to learn what it was. "What's this for?"

"Air Forces," Wayne said. "I don't come under the regular Army rules, Army doctors, and all that, because it's something special."

"How do you mean, special?"

"I'm not supposed to talk about it," Wayne said apologetically. "I'm going abroad for them on a special thing and they want me to—"

"Going to one of the fighting fronts?"

"I don't want to sound important," Wayne said with embarrassment, because it *did* sound important. "But no kidding, I'm not supposed to talk about it."

"Spy stuff, eh?" Dr. Manck gave a curious little laugh that caused Wayne to look at him in surprise.

"My God, no. It's just that they, well, they—" Wayne stopped. "I'm not supposed to talk about it," he said helplessly. "They instructed me not to."

"All right," Dr. Manck said. "Take your clothes off." He bent over a small basin, turned on the tap, and started to wash his hands. Wayne took off his coat, loosened his tie, and unbuttoned his shirt. "Take them all off," Dr. Manck said, glancing at him over his shoulder. "Strip."

"All of them?" Wayne said, his voice rising. "Everything?"

"The blank calls for a complete physical examination."

"But I'm all right. I'm in good shape. I don't need—"

"That's what I'm supposed to attest to," Dr. Manck said. He snatched a small towel from a pile on the glass shelf over the sink. "Take off everything."

"I mean you've got my records from Harry's office, haven't you?" Wayne said. "He used to check me over regularly. He gave me a complete physical only a couple of months ago, before he got his commission. I don't think you have to—"

"If you want me to sign that blank, Wayne, I'll have to give you the complete physical examination it calls for," Dr. Manck said curtly. "Dr. Holdridge's records are Dr. Holdridge's records, not mine. He's not signing this blank. I am. Shoes, too, please."

Wayne took off all his clothes, piled them neatly on a white enamelled chair, and turned back, naked, to face Dr. Manck. "O.K.?" he said with a hint of sarcasm in his voice. "This all right?"

"Your wristwatch, too," Dr. Manck said dryly. "And lie down on the table, please." Wayne took off his wristwatch and climbed up on the padded examination table. Dr. Manck put the Air Forces blank on top of a white metal cabinet next to the sterilizing machine and pulled a silver pencil from his vest pocket. "I'll fill these things in lightly in pencil as we go and then Miss Perrin can type over my pencil notations later and I'll sign."

"That'll be fine."

"We'll see," Dr. Manck said, making no effort to conceal his own sarcasm. He wound the band of the blood-pressure meter around Wayne's arm. "Drink much?"

"Not very. Just a—"

"I've heard that before," Dr. Manck said, watching the gauge as he pumped the bulb. The air hissed slowly out of the band. "Lot of you young guys who say you don't drink much are just one step away from apoplexy." He pumped up the band again, pressing the bulb gently, and looked at the gauge as the air escaped. Then he removed the band from Wayne's arm and stepped over to the white cabinet to make a note on the blank with his silver pencil.

"How's my blood pressure?" Wayne asked from the examination table. "High? Low?"

"It's all right," Dr. Manck said. He sounded disappointed. "Sit up, please." Wayne sat up. Dr. Manck placed a stethoscope against his chest and listened intently. "Cough, please." Wayne coughed. "Breathe deeply." Wayne breathed deeply. "Slowly, now, please." Wayne breathed slowly. "All right. That's enough."

Dr. Manck stepped over to the white cabinet again and frowned as he made a note on the blank.

"How's the heart?" Wayne asked. "Hear any loose bearings?"

"You needn't get cocky. We'll find something wrong. All you guys who come in and tell doctors you're in fine shape, there's nothing wrong with you, you're in wonderful physical—stay on the table, please. Lie back."

Wayne dropped back on the examination table. He had an odd feeling of mixed anxiety and elation. The physical examination, which he had resented because he felt it was unnecessary and because he was in a hurry, had turned into a contest between him and Dr. Manck. Wayne felt the way he used to feel in high school when, as sophomore swimming champion, he was about to swim against a boy he knew he could beat. He felt excited because he was on the threshold of another victory and yet slightly worried because, until the race was over, there was always the chance that he would lose.

"The teeth are all right," he said. "I wound up with the dentist yesterday."

"I'll look for myself, if you don't mind," Dr. Manck said. "Open, please."

As each item on the blank was filled in, Wayne's spirits rose higher and the look of annoyance on Dr. Manck's face grew deeper. Wayne had a moment of doubt when Dr. Manck wet the soles of his feet to take an impression of his footprints; he didn't remember ever having been tested for flat feet, but apparently they were all right, too, because Dr. Manck made the note on the blank with a small, angry flourish. Finally, when Wayne was standing on the scales and Manck was adjusting the crossbar on his head to measure his height, the young doctor's face broke into a smile.

"All right," he said. "You can get dressed now."

"What's so funny?" Wayne asked cheerfully as he pulled on his clothes. "Find I've got cancer or something?"

Dr. Manck's smile spread, but it wasn't friendly. There was a curiously deliberate expression on his face. He looked almost as though he were sighting a gun. He waited a moment, running his hand slowly through his own thick, blond hair, and then he said, "You're all right, but you haven't got very much on that scalp of yours, have you?"

With an effort, Wayne managed to check the involuntary movement of his hand to the top of his head, where the scalp showed. His fingers fumbled at the buttons of his shirt and he could feel his face grow hot. He finished dressing hurriedly, tied his shoelaces, knotted his tie, and buttoned his coat.

"If you'll give this to Miss Perrin on your way out—" Dr. Manck said, holding out the blank. "I've signed it at the bottom. She'll type in the entries I've made in pencil."

Wayne took the blank and went out.

Miss Perrin raised her head from the circle of yellow light thrown by the desk lamp and smiled. "Everything all right?"

"Yes, great," Wayne said. He explained about the pencilled notes and asked her to mail the blank to his home after she had finished typing them in. "Send my bill with it, too, will you, please?"

"Oh, Dr. Manck doesn't bill his patients till the end of the month, Mr. Wayne. There's no rush."

"There might be," Wayne said sarcastically, reaching for the outer door. "A man with a perfect scalp, a head of hair like his—the Army'll be wanting him any minute now. I don't see how they could have passed him up so far and still expect to win the war."

Miss Perrin giggled as she rolled the blank into her typewriter. "Not him," she said. "Dr. Manck tried to enlist the same time as Dr. Holdridge. He has a bum heart."

"Oh," Wayne said with his hand on the knob. He glanced at the closed door of the examination room and had a sudden impulse to go back. He wanted to say something to Dr. Manck—tell the poor guy that he was sorry. But there wasn't time. He saw by his wristwatch that it was a quarter to nine. If he took a taxi he could just make his appointment at the Air Forces Intelligence office.

"I'll tell you what," he said awkwardly as he pulled open the door. "There's no rush on that bill. Send it to me at the end of the month, when you send out the others, in the regular way."

The Explorers

It was a warm day, too warm for that time of year, and the lake in the park had a couple of dozen rowboats on it. The freshly painted benches had been brought out on the asphalt apron between the boathouse and the water. Here and there people sat on them, reading newspapers or straining their faces to the sun, their eyes closed, trying to catch a bit of sunburn to carry home proudly. The weather was of the sort that, had it come on a Sunday, would have permitted the newspapers to report record-breaking crowds in the park. But it was an ordinary Wednesday morning and there weren't any crowds.

Just that handful of unexciting people, spread about as though by arrangement, one to a bench. They seemed to have no interest in one another beyond a sharp glance or two when a newcomer arrived and began to hunt for a seat. Nobody chose a bench with someone on it already, even though the man or woman might be sitting all the way over at one end. Everybody wanted a bench to himself.

The boathouse was a gray imitation-stone affair, with a huge clock on it that faced the lake so that the people who had rented boats and were out on the water would know when their time was up. The benches were arranged in front of it in two rows. This left a lane down the middle, four or five feet wide, that led from the cashier's window of the boathouse to the water's edge, where the boats were tied.

The three young men came down this lane at a curious gait, walking a shade faster than the ordinary bench hunter and yet too slowly to indicate any other purpose. They were very well dressed, much better dressed than most of the people on the benches. But their coats were taken in a trifle too much at the waist and the brims of their hats snapped a bit too sharply. They advanced to the water's edge and looked at the lake.

They did it as though somebody had told them recently that a lake was a fascinating thing but they didn't believe it and had come to look for themselves. They didn't seem to be impressed. Their faces, which had started out with identical looks of faint incredulity, were soon reflecting definite contempt. After a few moments they turned their backs on the lake abruptly and lit cigarettes. All three of them. They smoked slowly, inhaling huge quantities of smoke, and sent their eyes over the people on the benches. They were quick little eyes that moved in darts. For a while they saw nothing, apparently, that merited changing the expression on their faces, which continued to reflect their uncomplimentary opinion of the lake. Then the roving eyes stopped on the last bench to the left.

A young girl, a pretty girl, was sitting in the exact center of the bench, reading the *Times*. She, too, seemed to be much better dressed than the other people on the benches. She held the *Times*, which was folded lengthwise down the middle, in her left hand and her left elbow rested on the back of the bench. This brought her shoulders at almost right angles to the bench. Sitting like that, with her legs crossed and her right hand resting in her lap and touching the bottom of the *Times* lightly, she made a very attractive picture.

The three young men at the water's edge looked at her for a moment. Then the one in the middle nudged the other two and winked. He was carrying a copy of the *Daily News* folded under one arm. He dropped his cigarette and walked up the lane swiftly. The others followed and they all stopped next to the girl's bench. The first young man leaned toward the girl and held out his folded newspaper.

"Pardon me, Miss," he said, "but you through with that paper? I'm through with this one. I figured you give me the *Times*, I give you the *News?*"

The girl looked up quickly, startled and confused. But somehow she didn't seem to be startled or confused enough. Her elbow, for instance, which appeared to be perched so precariously on the back of the bench, didn't slip from its resting place, even though she had jumped visibly. She looked up at the young man for a moment and then swung herself forward on the bench and buried her eyes in the paper. The young man looked at his two friends. His face was expressionless.

"You think it's possible she don't read the *News?*" he said aloud. "Only the *Times?*"

"You ask me?" one of the others said. "Ask her."

"A nice girl like that reading only the *Times?*" The young man with the folded paper shook his head as though he couldn't quite believe that. "She doesn't read the *Tribune,* she doesn't read the *Mirror,* she doesn't read the *Daily Worker*—all right, a thing like that I could understand. But the *News?*" He leaned toward the girl again. "Pardon me, Miss. You got a grudge against the *News?*"

The girl's face took on a look of exaggerated disdain, but she did not raise her head from the *Times.*

"That's how life is," one of the other young men said. They all spoke alike, in loud, clear voices, as though they were accustomed to addressing slightly deaf people. "A pretty girl like that, she's got nice clothes, so three gorillas come along and bother her. She didn't have such nice clothes, she didn't look so pretty, so no three gorillas wouldn't bother her." He shook his head sorrowfully.

"It's not a question of bothering," the first young man said. "A pretty girl like that, she don't read the *News,* that's something must be looked into. You can't leave things like that without looking into it."

"You wanna look into it, Flassy?" the second young man asked.

"We *must* look into it, Lou," said Flassy.

He sat down quickly, about two feet to the right of the girl. At the same time Lou sat down at her left, the same distance away. The third young man took up his post in back of the bench, about two feet behind her, so that she was completely surrounded. For a moment, while this was happening, the girl looked genuinely frightened. Then she recovered, turned a page of the *Times* defiantly, and continued reading. She continued looking at the paper, anyway.

"We gotta study this calmly," Flassy said.

"Calmly, I don't care," said Lou, on the left. "Intelligently we gotta study it."

"All right," the one in the rear said. "But let's study it."

They talked across the girl and over her head. They leaned toward each other and peered closely at the paper she was holding. But they were scrupulously careful not to touch her or even brush her clothes. They never touched her once.

"Books maybe," Flassy said. The girl was looking at the book page of the paper. "Ask her she likes books."

"That's an idea." Lou leaned toward the girl. "You like books, Miss?"

The girl read on stonily.

"Tell her I read a book once," Flassy said. "Very good, too."

"I don't think she likes us, Flassy," Lou said.

"No, no. That's too hasty. It's only books she don't like." Flassy peered at the paper in the girl's hands. It was open at the theatrical page. "I know what she likes. She likes Ethel Barrymore. Ask her."

Lou leaned toward the girl. "There's a rumor going around you like Ethel Barrymore. You like Ethel Barrymore, Miss?"

The girl turned the page calmly. She had recovered from her original surprise.

"She don't like Ethel Barrymore," Lou said.

"John, maybe. Ask her she likes John."

"Pardon me, Miss. You like John? John Barrymore?"

No answer.

"She don't like John, either."

"Maybe because he's married. *You* ask her this time, Gus," said Lou to the man in the rear.

Gus leaned forward to look down on the girl. "You don't like John because he's married, Miss?" he asked.

Flassy nudged his arm. "Tell her we can fix that," he said.

"Miss, you don't like John because he's married, we can fix that," said Gus. "You want us to fix that?"

The girl turned a page carefully.

"Maybe we wouldn't have to fix that," Lou said. "You know John."

"That's right. The way John is, maybe by this time we won't have to fix that," said Flassy.

Gus shook his head. "I'm afraid it's not John, fellas."

"Who then? Bob?"

"Bob? Yeah, well, maybe. It could be Bob."

"Bob who? Which Bob?" asked Flassy.

Lou seemed surprised. "That's a question to ask? A pretty girl like this, a pretty girl with sucha nice clothes, which Bob would it be? Use your head."

"All right with my head. But it could be two Bobs. It could be Taylor. It could be Montgomery."

Gus shook his head at him. "Flassy," he said, "you surprise me. Honest. A girl like this you say Taylor? With a girl like this Taylor hasn't got a chance. A Chinaman's chance. This is a Montgomery girl, Flassy."

Flassy shrugged. "Maybe," he said. "I could be wrong. I was wrong once. But how I could be wrong with a girl like this, I don't know. Montgomery? Better ask her."

Lou leaned over. "Pardon me, Miss. There is an argument here. We decided with you it's a Bob. But question: Are you a Taylor or a Montgomery? Which?"

The girl turned another page and rustled the paper into comfortable reading position.

"You know what I think, fellas?" Gus said. He was looking across her shoulder at the paper.

"What?"

"I think we're getting no place very fast."

Flassy looked shocked. "I can't believe that," he said. "That's impossible. Why should you say a thing like that?"

Lou pointed at the paper. "She's reading the editorials," he said.

Flassy was impressed. "Editorials," he said. He shook his head. "I'll admit it looks bad. Editorials. My God!"

He turned to look out across the benches toward the lake. A small Negro boy of seven or eight was walking idly down the lane toward the water.

"Hey!" Flassy called. "Hey, Joe Louis!"

The small boy turned quickly.

"C'm 'ere, kid," Flassy said. He motioned toward the bench with his hand. "Something I wanna ask you."

The boy came up shyly. He seemed a little frightened, but not much. He was wearing a half-sleeved light-blue jumper that fastened to the top of his short pants with large white buttons. His knees were bare and looked startlingly thin and fragile.

"Yes, suh?" he said timidly.

"You wanna make a nickel?" Flassy asked.

"Yes, suh," the boy said eagerly.

"Find out first he's got working papers," Gus said.

"Flassy wants him only for a small job," Lou said. "For what Flassy wants him, he don't need no working papers."

"That's right," Flassy said. "What I want you for, it'll take a minute. Easiest nickel you ever made, Joe Louis."

"I don't think his name is Joe Louis," Gus said.

The girl rustled the paper as she turned a page.

"Better work fast, Flassy," Lou said. "She's getting impatient."

"A pretty girl like that," Gus said, "she's got a right to be impatient." He leaned toward the girl. "You go ahead and be impatient, Miss. You got a right."

The girl's lip curled slightly as she read through the *Times* obituaries.

"I'm working fast as I can," Flassy said. "This is a delicate situation. Has to be handled with kid gloves. I gotta work through a third party. I gotta work through Joe Louis here."

"I still don't think his name is Joe Louis," Gus said.

"Better get his right name, Flassy," said Lou. "Always get the right name."

Flassy turned back to the small boy. "What's your right name, Joe Louis?"

"Johnson," the boy said.

"Johnson?" Gus said, looking at the sky. "Johnson? Johnson? Johnson? Never heard that name before."

"The first name," Lou said. "Get the first name, Flassy."

"What's your first name, Johnson?"

"Martin, suh," the small boy said.

"Martin Johnson?"

"Yes, suh."

"That's an explorer," Flassy said. "Martin Johnson is an explorer."

"No," Gus said. "He goes to Africa with a camera. He takes pictures."

"But he goes to Africa. No?"

"Sure."

"Then he's an explorer. Anybody goes to Africa, he's an explorer."

"He's no explorer. He's married," said Gus.

"Him, too? Everybody's married. It's the new thing."

"Not Martin Johnson," Lou said. "He got killed in an airplane crash."

"That's right," said Flassy. "My God. First he was married. Now he's dead. My God."

"You gotta work fast here, Flassy."

"That's right." Flassy spoke to the small boy. "Here's what I want you to do, Johnson. You see this very pretty girl here?" He nodded toward the girl beside him, and the small boy looked at her.

"Yes, suh," he said, but the eagerness for the promised nickel was gone from his voice. It sounded troubled and his eyes began to look vaguely frightened again.

"You go up to this here pretty girl," Flassy said, "and you ask her why she don't like us. That's all. Just you say to her, 'Miss, why don't you like these three very handsome gentlemen?' For that you get a nickel. Think you can handle the job, Johnson?"

The small boy mumbled something in a scared voice and began to back away. Flassy's hand shot out and clamped down on the boy's wrist.

"Johnson," he said, "you shock me. You yellow, Johnson?"

"Flassy," Gus said, "you're color-blind. He's not yellow. He's—"

"Quiet," Flassy said. "I'm handling this."

"O.K.," Gus said. "Handle it."

Flassy turned to the boy again and pulled on his arm slowly until he was back where he had been.

"Johnson," he said, "three friends ask you to do them a favor. Three of the best friends you ever had, Johnson. A little thing they ask you to do, and they want to give you a nickel to do it. You going to turn them down, Johnson?"

The terror in the small boy's eyes spread to the rest of his face and to his body. He strained away from Flassy and tried to free his hand, but the hold on his wrist did not relax.

"He's not talking," Lou said.

"He'll talk," Flassy said. He drew the small, frightened boy to him and held him between his knees. Then he lowered his face to look into the boy's eyes. "Johnson," he said, "I am very much annoyed. I am disturbed. I am disappointed. I am all these things. But mostly I am annoyed. The way things are going, Johnson, I may even get sore. I hate to get sore, because it makes my collar wilt. It is not gentlemanly. Johnson, don't make my collar wilt. Now, once more." He held up his forefinger in front of the terrified boy. "You will go up to this very pretty young girl here and you will say, 'Miss, why don't you like these three gentlemen?' That's all. For that you will get a nickel. O.K., Johnson?"

The girl didn't raise her head from the paper, but her eyes were watching the scene. The small Negro boy's chin began to quiver. The girl bit her lip and dropped her eyes to the paper again.

"Johnson isn't talking," Gus said.

"True," Flassy said. "Johnson isn't talking." He sighed and pulled a small leather notebook from his pocket. He flipped it open and held up his hand. "Pencil," he said. Gus took out a pencil and put it into the upraised hand. Flassy lowered the pencil to the notebook. "Johnson," he said, "what are you doing in the park this time of day? Why aren't you in school?"

The small boy scowled and dug his fist into his eye.

"I—I—" he began.

"Too bad, Johnson," Flassy said. "Hooky. I thought so." He sighed again. "You know who I am, Johnson?"

"Tell him, Flassy," Lou said.

"I will," Flassy said. "I'm a truant officer, Johnson."

The small boy started to cry violently. His shoulders shook with his sobs and the tears rolled down his face like water from a dripping faucet. Flassy pushed him a little further away, but still held him clamped between his knees.

"Careful of the suit, Johnson," he said. He dug the pencil into the paper of the notebook. "Martin Johnson," he said as he wrote, "I asked you a simple favor, but you wouldn't do it." He shook his head sadly. "Too bad, Johnson. Now I must report you. What class, Johnson?"

"Two B," the boy said through his tears.

Flassy wrote.

"Teacher's name?" he asked.

"M— M— Miss Goldberg," the boy said, sobbing.

"Miss Goldberg?" Flassy said. He looked up at the other young men. "You hear that? Playing hooky from Miss Goldberg!"

"One of the nicest teachers I ever saw," Gus said.

"Playing hooky from Miss Goldberg," Lou said. "My God!"

Flassy shook his head.

"This is bad, Johnson. Bad." He started to write the name, and stopped. "You got one more chance, Johnson. You talk to this pretty girl here like I asked you, you do what I tell you, I won't report you. What do you say, Johnson?"

The small boy stopped crying for a moment and looked at the girl, sniffing. Then he was off again, blubbering wildly, his thin little body shaking, and hiding his face in the bend of his elbow.

"Tchk! Tchk! Tchk!" Flassy said, beginning to write. "I'm afraid it's curtains, Johnson. This is too—"

Suddenly the girl smacked the *Times* onto her lap angrily.

"Oh, why don't you let the boy alone!" she snapped. "You—you —you great big overgrown—"

The three young men stared at her and then at each other in pleased surprise.

"Say!" Gus said. "She's talking!"

"I told you let me handle this," Flassy said. He swung himself around to face the girl and the pressure of his knees was released. The small boy darted out and began to run. Flassy reached for him quickly, but missed. "C'm 'ere, you dirty little—"

"I'll get him," Gus said.

"Never mind," Flassy said. "We don't need him any more. Let him go. We saved a nickel. We got her talking."

The girl rustled the paper in her lap and glared at him. She was breathing quickly and her lips were pressed thin.

"A poor little kid like that," she said.

"Girlie," Flassy said, "a girl with eyes like yours, you shouldn't never—"

Lou reached over and touched Flassy's knee. He pointed to the clock on the boathouse. "Flassy," he said, "it's late. We better get going. Johnny'll be waiting."

All three of them looked at the clock.

"That's right," Flassy said.

He stood up at once and the three of them walked away briskly. They buttoned their tight coats and adjusted their hats as they went, but they did not look back at the girl on the bench.

Eyewitness

"You sit here," Major Pennon said. He pulled a straight-backed chair away from the wall and set it next to his desk. "That all right?"

"Yes, sir," Cotter said. "Sure. Any place."

"And then we can put Mrs. Maywood—well, let me see." The Major took his lower lip between thumb and forefinger as he looked thoughtfully around the small, bare office. One wall was covered by that week's Army Service Forces Newsmap, there was an insignia chart on the wall facing it, and the glass panel of the door from the corridor was hidden by an enlarged photograph of three B-17's in flight. "I guess near the window, don't you think?"

"I guess so, sir," Cotter said. "Yes."

Major Pennon pulled another chair away from the wall and set it in the stream of sunlight that poured in from Fifth Avenue.

"It's not very comfortable, I guess, but it seemed a little better than taking her to a restaurant or a bar or something." The Major was pinching his lower lip again. "I don't want it to seem too impersonal and sort of cold, but a restaurant or a bar—you know, it makes it look like a party or something. Sort of bad taste, don't you think?"

"Yes, sir," Cotter said. "This looks fine, sir."

"Good." Major Pennon smiled suddenly, with relief, and touched Cotter's shoulder. "You sit down, then, and I'll go out and get her."

"Yes, sir."

Cotter remained standing while the Major crossed the room

briskly. At the door, Major Pennon paused, his hand on the knob, and gave the small office a final, hasty glance, like a hostess surveying her dining room before going up to dress for dinner. He nodded, tapped his tie into more precise position in the V of his tunic lapels, and went out. Cotter drew a deep breath, exhaled through his open mouth, and turned to look out the window.

He had heard in London that there was a ban on pleasure driving in New York and the London Sunday papers were full of feature articles on how the face of Manhattan had changed because there were so many uniforms on the streets, but Fifth Avenue looked just about the same as it had always looked in the late-afternoon sun from a seventeenth-story window. Cotter's forehead creased as he thought of what he was going to say, tried to figure out how he was going to begin, and he wished to God it was an hour later, or even twenty minutes later, because no matter how he began, or what he said, it couldn't possibly take longer than that, and all he wanted was to get it over with. Cotter didn't blame Mrs. Maywood for wanting to come all the way from Ohio to see him, or Major Pennon for asking him to talk to her, but he just didn't see what there was to tell her. She knew all there was to know. She knew everything he knew.

A girl in a bright-green hat stepped off the curb in front of St. Patrick's and Cotter's eyes followed with interest her darting progress, among the taxis and buses, clear across the Avenue. The door behind him opened and he turned quickly.

"This is Sergeant Cotter," Major Pennon said. "Mrs. Maywood, Sergeant."

"How do you do?" Mrs. Maywood said. "It sure is swell of you to let me come and see you like this, Sergeant. I certainly appreciate it, I really do."

Cotter nodded awkwardly as Major Pennon helped her into the chair by the window. Mrs. Maywood looked just about as Cotter had expected and probably about the same as she had always looked. There was nothing tragic or unusual about her appearance. She was short and stout, a woman of about forty, with a pleasant, broad face and a slightly unpleasant voice. She wore a black suit with a neat white collar and a small black hat with a brim that was a trifle too saucy. The cloth coat she held folded on her lap showed the label of a Cleveland department store.

"I think, if you don't mind now, I'll leave you two alone." Major Pennon smiled kindly. "Is that all right?"

"Yes, I think so," Mrs. Maywood said. "Thank you, Major."

"Yes, sir," Cotter said, even though he had a moment of annoyance. He had not counted on being left alone with Mrs. Maywood. "Sure."

"I'll be back in a little while. In the meantime, if there's anything you want, if you want me for anything, just open the door and speak to the adjutant. He'll get me. All right?"

Mrs. Maywood and Cotter nodded and the Major went out. The door, swinging shut, sent a draft across the room and for a moment the only sound in the small office was the faint crackling of the Newsmap on the wall.

"I want to thank you again for letting me come to see you," Mrs. Maywood said. "It was really nice of you to take all the trouble."

"That's all right," Cotter said. "I live right here in New York and I'm on sick leave. It's no trouble, really." Mrs. Maywood smiled politely, but it was plain that her mind was on other matters. She was looking down at her coat, tracing the stitching of the department-store label with a stubby forefinger. "How long are you staying here?" Cotter asked. "I mean in New York."

"Until tomorrow," Mrs. Maywood said. "I came on just to have this talk with you and then I've got to go back. I left the children over at my mother's house. She's wonderful with them. They love her and all that, but you know how it is, especially now." She stopped and looked up. "Tell me how it happened, Mr. Cotter. Sergeant Cotter."

"Well." Cotter took a deep breath. "There isn't much to tell, I'm afraid."

"You were with him, weren't you?"

"Yes. We were together. I was—well, you know what happened."

"Please tell me the whole thing, Sergeant Cotter. The way it happened. Everything."

"Well, sure. Of course," Cotter said. It was not her eagerness that embarrassed him. He could understand her wanting to know in detail, to know more than was contained in the War Department's formal notification, more than he himself had put into the letter that Major Pennon had sent her. What embarrassed Cotter was the fact that there just wasn't any more to tell. He had told it all in his letter. There were no further details. "You see, I was sent down to London from the aerodrome where I was stationed to pick up a truck and drive it back. I don't know why. Those things happen all the time in the Army." Cotter spoke slowly, keeping his eyes on the photograph of the B-17's on the door, trying to enlarge the shamefully trivial incident with irrelevancies about himself. "I got the truck all right, but it was too late to drive back that night because of the blackout, you know, so the lieutenant said I could have the night off there in London and drive back in the morning. I got myself a room at the Red Cross and had my dinner there and played some cards with a few of the men there. Pinochle. Then we went out to a pub—that's what they call a bar over there—for a couple of beers." Cotter stole a glance at Mrs. Maywood. She was leaning forward over her folded coat, her inexpertly rouged lips parted, listening eagerly, like a child hearing an old bedtime story told by a stranger, hoping that perhaps this time the familiar ending would be different. Cotter's face grew hot and he looked away. "There were quite a few American soldiers in the place and when I left a bunch of them were going out. I didn't know any of them—just met them in the pub, you see—and I found myself walking along in the blackout beside one guy—one man. I couldn't even see his face, it was so dark. It turned out later he was your husband."

Now that he was into it, now that he was reconstructing the scene for Mrs. Maywood, Cotter could see the whole thing clearly, could almost smell the odor of weak beer that came from the stranger in khaki walking along beside him in the blackout toward Hyde Park Corner. Suddenly the siren went, and Cotter could hear again the derisive laughter from the soldiers ahead of them down the street and the ribald comment by the man at his side. Cotter was chuckling at the man's remark when he heard an astonished gasp, followed by a sickening thud. Cotter stopped and spoke to the man. There was no answer. The man had simply vanished. Cotter called out nervously. The soldiers down the street came back.

One of them had a flashlight. He flashed it and they found that the man who had been walking beside Cotter had fallen down an areaway.

"We got him out and found a doctor right away, but it was too late. Fractured skull. He was dead by the time the doctor got there." Cotter paused and glanced at Mrs. Maywood. She was sitting back in the straight-backed, uncomfortable chair, staring at Cotter with disappointment. The story had not come out differently. The ending was the same. Cotter dropped his eyes. "A couple of months later, I received a letter from Major Pennon. He said you'd asked for details, and I wrote him that letter he sent on to you. About three months after that, I was shipped home. Last week Major Pennon got in touch with me and said you were coming to New York and, well, that's all there's to it, I'm afraid."

Mrs. Maywood shifted in her chair and leaned forward. She shook her head very quickly, as though she were brushing away an expected objection.

"That's what Major Pennon told me," she said impatiently. "And that's what you said in your letter. But there must be more. It's very important. Please tell me, Sergeant."

"I wish I could," Cotter said. "But that's all there is, really. There's no more to tell."

"Please, Sergeant Cotter." Her plain, broad face was suddenly creased into lines of anguished pleading. "There must be more. Please try to remember. It's so important."

"Well," Cotter said slowly. "Let me think a moment." He stared across her black hat, with its saucy brim, at the insignia chart on the wall, scowling hard and chewing his lower lip, pretending to be in deep thought and fighting back the exasperation that was rising in him. There was no more to tell. Why did she keep nagging him? It was a silly, a stupid, even a slightly sordid way to die in a war, falling down an areaway and cracking your skull on your way home from a saloon during a blackout. It made Cotter uncomfortable just to think about it. Six months after the event, how could Mrs. Maywood stand talking about it, begging for more details? Cotter supposed he could tell her how her husband had looked when they got him to the Army hospital, a middle-aged, lifeless man, his lips parted in an expression of hurt surprise, as though the shock of death had come like an unexpected insult from an old and trusted friend. The only other thing Cotter remembered was the dead man's hands. They were very white and seemed curiously small, like the hands of a doll, and the fingers were spread wide, as though at the moment of death their owner had been holding them out for a manicure. Cotter supposed he could tell her that, and in his exasperation he was tempted to do so, but he shoved the impulse back and shook his head. "No, I'm sorry, Mrs. Maywood. I've told you everything I can remember. I can't think of anything else."

"What about shooting?" she said. "Wasn't there any shooting going on?"

"Shooting?" Cotter looked at her in puzzlement. "What do you mean, shooting?"

"You said the siren went, there was an air raid. There must have been shooting."

"Oh, that." Cotter shook his head. "No. You see, they came over regularly, and the siren used to go all the time, every time they were reported on the way, but they were usually stopped before they got to London. This was long after the blitz, you know, and the British had air superiority. Every once in a while a plane or two would get through, and then the barrage would go up or a bomb would come down, but very seldom. The siren didn't mean anything."

Mrs. Maywood shook her head, dismissing the explanation.

"There must have been shooting," she said. "Please try to remember." Cotter opened his mouth to say no again, but she wagged her hand quickly to silence him. "You must remember," she said angrily. "What am I going to tell the children? What am I going to tell my parents, the neighbors? I've got to go home tomorrow. The other men who were with you when it happened, Major Pennon says they can't be traced. You're the only one who was there, the only one I can talk to. You're the only one who can say it. Please help me, Sergeant. Please try to remember. Please."

"Well," Cotter said, feeling in his throat the slight, painful constriction he had felt during his first air raid. He looked down at his hands until the tightness eased a little. "Now that I think of it, there was quite a bit of shooting."

"There was?"

"Yes, quite a bit." Cotter continued to look at his hands so he would not have to see her leaning eagerly toward him. "A couple of them must have got through, more than a couple, probably, because the anti-aircraft batteries opened up with everything they had. It was a mess, as I remember. The papers said the next day it was the heaviest raid on London since the blitz. Many people were killed, a great many."

The door opened, sending a draft through the room that caused the Army Service Forces Newsmap to rustle on the wall, and Major Pennon entered.

"Well," he said, "everything all right?"

Cotter stood up and Mrs. Maywood began to gather her coat and purse.

"Oh, yes, Major," she said, blinking her eyes rapidly through a cheerful smile. "Everything is fine now."

Gallantry in Action

"Look, Dad, this one here, with the blue band in the middle and the wide gold stripes on both sides," the small boy said in his high-pitched, eager voice. "That's the Air Medal." He stood up on his toes and pointed to the ribbon over the second lieutenant's pocket. "For meritorious achievement," he recited, stumbling slightly over the long words, "while participating in aerial flight."

"Bobby, stop." The middle-aged man smiled at the young officer and pulled the boy back gently to his side. "That's not very nice, you know, pointing."

The lieutenant, his shoulder bumping back and forth on the foyer wall at the end of the dining car, looked up from his magazine. He grinned good-naturedly at the boy, nodded to the father, and returned to his reading. About a dozen people, most of them service men, were jammed into the foyer, waiting for seats in the crowded diner. They looked down with amusement at the boy. He was small and thin, about ten or eleven years old, with a narrow, intense face and thick-lensed glasses sitting a bit crookedly on his snub nose. His face and hands were freshly tanned and his dark hair was closely cropped. The lapels of his expensive camel's hair jacket were covered with army and navy insignia, including two sets of a captain's silver bars. He sucked nervously on the gold brace across his upper teeth as he peered about at the uniforms around him.

"The Purple Heart, Dad, look," he said, leaning far over to point at the ribbon on a sergeant's tunic. "All purple with the narrow white stripes at the ends." He tugged at his father's hand. "For wounds received in action against an enemy or as a direct result of an act of the enemy," he recited. "The Purple Heart."

The sergeant grinned self-consciously, dropped his freshly lighted cigarette, and ground it out with his toe. The soldiers around him laughed in a friendly way and peered into the dining car, where a second group of people could be seen waiting at the other end.

"Bobby, don't. It's not nice to point." The father hauled the boy back to his side. He was a heavy man in the late forties, with a strong, pleasant face, and an air of authority that made his somewhat awkward affection for the boy seem oddly attractive. None of the men in the foyer looked directly at the boy or his father, yet all were watching them with obvious pleasure. The father smiled at the soldiers around him as he drew contentedly on his excellent cigar. "He knows all the insignia, every decoration, every ribbon," he explained, speaking to the entire group but to no one person in particular. His rich, well-modulated voice contained a note of pride as well as apology. "The colors, what it's for, how it should be worn and when, everything. Memorized them from a book, every one of them."

The steward came bustling down the aisle between the tables, ducked under the tray a waiter was holding aloft, and bobbed up in front of the group in the foyer. His forehead was damp with perspiration.

"Two singles," he said, breathing hard, fanning himself with a batch of menus, and smiling automatically. "Two singles, please?" Nobody moved for several moments. Finally a couple of soldiers squeezed through the group. They looked about questioningly, at the waiting men, and then at each other. "Two, thank you," the steward said impatiently, backing away. "This way, please." The soldiers followed him self-consciously into the dining car. "A few more minutes, gentlemen, please," he called back to the people in the foyer. "Just a few more minutes, please."

"Few more minutes," a captain said. "That's pretty good. We've been waiting damn close to an hour now."

"And there's a gang big as this one up the other end," the first lieutenant next to him said. "What do you say we say the hell with it, Don? By the time we get seats, there won't be any food left, anyway."

"You're probably right," the captain said, turning around. He was a young man, very handsome in his tailored uniform, with blond hair clipped in a crew cut. "We lay over in Cleveland for twenty minutes or so to change engines, I hear. We'll be able to get a sandwich or something in the station. Let's go."

The enlisted men pressed back against the walls to make room. The small boy's face brightened. He pulled his father's hand as though it were a bell rope and he pointed up at the young captain's chest.

"Look, Dad," he said. "The Silver Star. Just like Marvin."

"Now, Bobby, please," his father said, trying to pull him out of the way. "I told you that's not nice."

"It *is* the Silver Star, Dad," the boy said. "The red stripe in the middle, and then the white on either side, with the blue outside that. I know it, Dad." The glasses started to slip down his tiny nose and he pushed them back excitedly. "For gallantry in action," he recited. "Just like Marvin."

"I'm sorry, Captain," the father said. "He's a little excited. His brother's got the Silver Star, too. My oldest boy."

"That's all right," the captain said. He smiled and rubbed his hand through the boy's closely cropped hair. The gesture swung the boy's attention from the decoration to the man. He blushed through his tan and stepped away quickly. "What outfit's your brother with, son?"

The boy, suddenly speechless with awe and embarrassment, dropped his eyes and hid behind his father.

"Eighth Air Force," the middle-aged man said. "Somewhere in England."

"He is?" The captain's eyes spread with interest. "That's our outfit, too." He nodded toward the first lieutenant at his side. "Mine and Hap's, here."

"Really?" the father said. "The Eighth?" The captain nodded. "Well, now, that's quite something, isn't it?" The middle-aged man looked into the crowded dining car and then he turned back to the two young officers. He took the cigar from his mouth and snapped his fingers. "I've got an idea," he said. "Come with me a minute, gentlemen, will you?"

He led the way through the group jammed in the foyer, across the platform between the dining car and the Pullman beyond, and he pushed the door shut behind the two young officers and his son.

"What's up?" the captain said. "Anything wrong?"

"Not a thing," the middle-aged man said with a smile. "But I couldn't help hearing what you and the lieutenant said. About the chances of getting any dinner out there, I mean, and it gave me an idea. Bobby and I, we've been waiting almost an hour, too, and it doesn't look very hopeful. Here's what I thought." He raised his voice a bit to make himself heard above the clacking of the train wheels. "We've got a drawing room all to ourselves at the end of this car, Bobby and I, and I've got a couple of bottles of good scotch in my bag. How about you and your friend, the lieutenant, here, how about having a few drinks in comfort while I take a crack at bribing our porter to bring us something to eat in our drawing room? Sandwiches or something, whatever he can get out of the galley, there, before the food runs out? How does that sound?"

"Why, it sounds swell to me, thanks," the captain said. "Hap?"

"You bet," the lieutenant said. "Thank you, sir."

"Then it's settled," the man said cheerfully. "Bobby, you take these gentlemen to our drawing room while I round up the ice and some glasses. All right?" The boy nodded eagerly. "Go right along, gentlemen. I'll join you in a moment."

The boy turned and walked down the shaking car, steadying himself against the berths on either side. His small back was arched with excitement and he breathed rapidly, his mouth open, as he peered ahead through his thick glasses. At the end of the car the boy pushed in the heavy drawing room door and held it open with both hands, standing aside shyly for the captain and the lieutenant to enter.

"After you, Bobby," the captain said. The boy blushed and shook his head, clutching the door knob hard. The captain laughed and ran his hand through the boy's hair again. "Okay, Hap," he said to the lieutenant. "Bobby after us."

They went in and sat down on the settee. The berths were closed and the table was set up between the facing seats. Four beautiful pigskin bags were stacked on the floor against the wall. The boy went to the top one, opened it, and pulled out a bottle of scotch.

"That's the stuff to give the troops," the lieutenant said. "Right, Bobby?"

"Yes, sir," the boy said and his voice cracked with happiness. He cleared his throat and set the bottle on the table and then he stood there awkwardly, blushing and trying to get rid of his hands. "My father will be here in a minute," he said. "Would you care to have a drink before he comes back? There are paper cups in the bathroom."

He was halfway across the room before the captain stopped him by placing his foot up against the door.

"No, we'll wait," the captain said, leaning back on the couch and lighting a cigarette. "Where did you get the sun tan?"

"In California, sir," the boy said. The ease with which the lounging young men talked seemed to relax him. "I have been staying with my uncle for my health," he said, speaking neatly and precisely, as though he were reciting a lesson for a teacher. "My father came out two weeks ago to take me home to New York." He stopped, as though he had come to the end of his recitation, and he sucked the brace on his teeth. Suddenly he drew a deep breath, gathering his strength for a special effort, and he said, "What did you get the Silver Star for, sir?"

"Nothing very important," the captain said through his easy smile. "Where did you get the bars?"

The boy touched the two sets of captain's insignia on his lapels.

"They're my brother's, sir," he said. "He sent them to me in California. He said in his last letter he's going to send me his Silver Star, too."

The door opened and the middle-aged man came in, carrying a tray with glasses, ice, and soda. The lieutenant stood up.

"Here, let me take that, sir," he said. "No porters, eh?"

"Thanks," the man said. "On the table, I think, don't you? That's fine. No, I found one, all right, but I sent him after the food. He said he wasn't sure, but he thought he might be able to get us something if he got back to the galley fast enough. If not, we'll be pulling into Cleveland within the hour, he told me, and they'll put more stuff on board while they're changing engines. He'll try to get us something then. I made it worth his while." The middle-aged man laughed. "I see Bobby got the bottle out. Thanks, Bobby." He poured the drinks and handed them around. "You all right there, or would you prefer to sit at the table?"

"No, we're fine," the captain said. "Anyway, I am. You, Hap?"

"I'm fine," the lieutenant said. "Swell."

"Well, here's to a happy meeting," the middle-aged man said, holding his glass high. "To our side, to a speedy victory, and to the Eighth."

"Our side, a speedy victory, and the Eighth," the captain said.

"Our side, a speedy victory, and the Eighth," the lieutenant said. They drank. The lieutenant sighed and smacked his lips. "Boy, that's good," he said. "I didn't know there was scotch like this around any more."

"There isn't," the middle-aged man said. "My brother put a couple of bottles in my bag before we left California. He makes airplanes out there and he gets a case every now and then, don't ask me how." He laughed again and sat down at the table, turning sideways to face the young officers sprawled comfortably on the settee. "Bobby's been out visiting him for a while, getting his health back."

"Yes," the lieutenant said. "He told us."

"Here, sit down and be comfortable, Bobby, and take this," his father said. The boy slid into the seat at the other side of the table and took the glass of plain soda. "Feel all right?" his father said.

"Yes, Dad," the boy said. "Thank you."

He sipped the soda slowly as he watched and listened to the young officers and his father. As the train sped through the night, everybody in the drawing room on that particular Pullman was having a good time, but it was plain that the small boy, who didn't say a word, was having the best time of all. His father explained that he was in the silk business, that his plant had been converted completely to war production, that he felt guilty about taking the time off to go to California but he'd been worried about Bobby and, anyway, the moment he got back to New York he'd be in that office seven days a week for the duration to make up for it. The officers said they were back from England on a training mission, had wangled a ten-day leave, which they'd just spent with the captain's family in Chicago, and were now returning to their assignments in

New York. The young men drank steadily, two or three highballs to the middle-aged man's one, without much visible effect. They laughed and told funny anecdotes about their experiences with the British and in the air over Germany. Twice the subject of the young captain's Silver Star came up, and the small boy leaned far forward, but both times the captain dismissed it with a laugh and said Hap, who had been flying on his left wing, should have received the decoration. Hap grinned and said nuts and reached for the bowl of ice. It was empty.

"I'll get some more," the middle-aged man said, getting up. "You might open that other bottle while I'm out."

"Let me get the ice," the lieutenant said. "You went the first time."

"You're my guests," the middle-aged man said, pushing the lieutenant back onto the settee. "Besides, I want to find that porter and see about the food he promised."

"Bobby, here's to your father," the lieutenant said, raising his glass. "A swell host. Your health, Mr. —" He paused and blinked. "My God, we haven't even introduced ourselves," he said. "Here, sir." He put his hand on the captain's shoulder. "This is my pal, Don Babcock, and me, my name is Wilde, Hap Wilde."

"A very great pleasure, gentlemen," the middle-aged man said. "My name is Loewenstein, Frank Loewenstein. And this is my son Robert."

"Glad to know you, sir," the lieutenant said, smiling and touching his glass to Mr. Loewenstein's. "And you, too, Bobby."

The boy blushed with pleasure and touched his glass of soda to the lieutenant's highball.

"How do you spell that?" the captain said. "Your name?"

"L,o,e,w,e,n,s,t,e,i,n," Mr. Loewenstein said. "My oldest son's name is Marvin. You know him, perhaps?"

"No," Captain Babcock said. "I never heard of him."

"Well, I'll get the ice and see about the food," Mr. Loewenstein said. "Be back in a minute, gentlemen."

He went out. Captain Babcock looked around the drawing room, examining each corner as though he had not seen it before. His eyes came to rest, finally, on the four pigskin suitcases. He sat up on the settee, leaned over, and placed his highball on the top suitcase. The train lurched and the glass slid several inches, leaving a wet streak across the leather.

"Hey," Lieutenant Wilde said. "You're messing up that bag."

"It's only water," Captain Babcock said. "Doesn't stain." He sucked in his cheeks, pursed his lips, and narrowed his eyes, as though he was in deep thought. Lieutenant Wilde splashed some whiskey into his own glass and reached over to freshen the one on the suitcase, but Captain Babcock stopped him. "No more for me," he said. "I've had enough." He leaned forward, his elbows on his knees, and he smiled at the small boy. "You really want to hear how I got the Silver Star, Bobby?"

The boy's face grew crimson with pleasure.

"Yes, sir," he said.

"Val, I'll tal you," Captain Babcock said, and his handsome face contracted into a complicated grimace and he twisted his shoulders in what was apparently his version of a dialect comedian's routine. "In de whole skvodron dere vass oney fun plane vid a pilot a lootenint, und dot vass me."

Lieutenant Wilde stared at his friend in quick surprise and, after a short glance at the small boy, he said, "Hey, Don, look." Captain Babcock shook off the interruption with a wave of his hand and swung into an account of a flight over Germany that, from the details he described, could only end in disaster. It was a thrilling story, in spite of the odd manner in which the young captain had elected to tell it. The suspense mounted even though Captain Babcock was an embarrassingly bad performer. Lieutenant Wilde sat slumped down on the settee, behind his friend, and hugged his highball glass in both hands. He kept moving his head from the talking captain beside him to the listening boy at the table, and his lips were spread slightly, as though his gums hurt. The boy listened with his whole body. He stared straight at Captain Babcock, his eyes unblinking behind the thick glasses, and his tongue ran back and forth across the gold brace on his upper teeth. His small tanned hands were clasped tightly together in his lap, and his narrow shoulders were hunched forward in the camel's hair coat, as though he was cold. Occasionally, when the movement of the train swung his rigid little body off balance, he seemed to be shivering.

"So I gafe heem two boists vid da guns," Captain Babcock said, "und den I peeled off."

The door opened. Mr. Loewenstein came in, carrying a fresh bowl of ice and three bottles of soda. Captain Babcock didn't glance up. He continued talking. Mr. Loewenstein stopped in the doorway, holding the ice and the bottles. The boy, oblivious to everything but the story, did not seem to be aware of his father's presence. Lieutenant Wilde looked at the middle-aged man in the doorway, set down his glass, and started to get up, his hands outstretched for the bowl and the bottles. Mr. Loewenstein smiled and shook his head. The lieutenant sank back on the settee. Mr. Loewenstein remained standing, his hands full, and listened attentively while the cigar went cold in his mouth.

"De next ting I knew, de two Jerries dey vass boining und falling," Captain Babcock said, leaning back in conclusion. "Und me? I opened up de trottle vide, I headed for mine base, und ven I came down safe dey vent und dey giff me da Silver Star."

He grinned at the boy. There was a long moment of silence. The only sound in the drawing room was the rhythmic clack of the train wheels. Finally, the boy's intent, expressionless face cracked, like a piece of shatterproof glass on which a stone has been dropped, and tiny wrinkles of confusion spread from his mouth to his eyes. He unclasped his small hands and looked timidly around the room, at the grinning young captain, at the sober-faced lieutenant, at his father in the doorway, as though waiting for the word of explanation to something he knew he should have understood but which, because of his inexperience or stupidity, had escaped him.

"I'm sorry I missed the first part of that," Mr. Loewenstein said. "Judging from the end, it must be an exciting story."

He moved into the room, dropped his dead cigar into the waste basket, and dipped down to place the bowl and the bottles on the table. As he straightened up, he let his hand rest for a moment on his son's shoulder. The boy swung around to face him. His father smiled as he squeezed the camel's hair gently.

"I'll be glad to repeat it," Captain Babcock said. "It's no trouble."

"Will you?" Mr. Loewenstein said. "Thanks. But would you wait just a little while? I've got that porter started on the food, and I want to make sure it gets here. Have another drink. I won't be but a minute, and when I come back we can eat." He turned the smile down on his son and it seemed to change slightly. "Don't you be afraid, Bobby," he said. "I'll be right back."

He went out and walked down the car. At the far end he met a porter carrying a tray piled high with sandwiches.

"All set, sir," the porter said. "Turkey, ham, cheese, and a couple of tongue, on rye and white. I got a big pot of coffee coming along in a minute, too."

"That's fine," Mr. Loewenstein said. "Don't take it in yet, will you?" He drew the porter into the men's washroom, which was empty, and he pulled a five-dollar bill from his wallet. "How soon before we get into Cleveland?"

The porter shifted the tray to one hand and looked at his watch.

"About five minutes, sir. Maybe six or seven."

"All right," Mr. Loewenstein said. "Here's what I want you to do. Go back to my drawing room and leave these sandwiches for the two officers you'll find in there. Then tell the little boy, that's my son, tell him I want to see him. I'll wait for him in here. Then I want you to get our bags out of there. Four of them. My hat and coat, too. And bring them in here." He put the five-dollar bill into the porter's hand. "That all clear?"

"Yes, sir." The porter looked at the five-dollar bill and then at the tray of sandwiches. "But don't you want these?"

"No, they're for the officers," Mr. Loewenstein said. "My son and I, we'll get something to eat in Cleveland."

"In Cleveland?" the porter said. "Ain't you booked through to New York, sir?"

"I was, but I find my plans have changed and we'll have to lay over in Cleveland for one night." Mr. Loewenstein stared through the washroom window, at the night smashing by outside, and he fingered the side of his strong face delicately, like a man probing for an old, forgotten bruise that has unexpectedly become painful again. "And porter, a little later," he said without turning, "you won't forget to bring the officers their coffee, will you?"

Goodby Forever

She knew it was late because the kitchen had been getting steadily darker. But she did not turn on the light. Nor did she glance up from the ironing board to see the time. She did not want to waste the few moments it would take to cross the room to the switch or to look at the clock. It was enough to know that it was late, that the remaining hours were few, without adding the pain of computing how few they were. It was best to work as she was working, without thought, quickly, yet carefully, so the things would not look too much like they had been laundered at home.

"Ma! Oh, Ma!" His voice came from the other end of the flat.

"I'm coming, Victor," she called back.

She folded the ironing board and put it behind the door. Not until she had gathered the freshly-ironed clothes into her arms did she glance at the clock. It said six-thirty, and she felt relieved. It was late. Now she would have to work like mad to get things ready on time.

He was standing in front of the dresser, adjusting the knot in his tie, when she carried in the pile of laundry. She saw him watching her in the mirror as she carried the bundle across the room to the trunk and set it down. She wanted to pack them in for him. She wanted to make sure that they would not be crushed, that they would be arranged so that he could reach a handkerchief or a shirt without disturbing the rest of the trunk. But she knew how finicky he was, how he hated to have his things handled; she simply separated them into stacks on the closed trunk; the underwear, the socks, the shirts, the handkerchiefs, and then turned quickly to go. At the door she hesitated.

"I'm going down to the grocery for a few minutes, Victor," she said, looking past him as she talked. "I need a few more things for tonight."

He glanced at his wrist-watch. "Okay, Ma. But don't be late."

When she entered the grocery there were two women at the counter. She stood aside, waiting for the grocer to finish with them. But as soon as he saw her, he stopped waiting on the others and came forward.

"Hello, Mrs. Morris," he said. "I was going to send my boy up after you already. I thought you forgot to come down." He turned to the other customers, smiling broadly. "You'll have to excuse me a minute," he said. "Mrs. Morris comes first today. She's in a hurry. She's making a party for her son. No, Mrs. Morris?"

She nodded, but did not speak.

"So all right," he said, rubbing his hands, "what'll you have, Mrs. Morris?"

She handed the list to him and stood back.

"What kind of party?" one of the other women asked.

"A goodby party," the grocer said. "Mrs. Morris' Victor is going to Europe. To England. He's leaving tomorrow. No, Mrs. Morris?"

She nodded again.

"To England?" the woman asked.

"You mean to say you live on the block here and you didn't hear about it? He won a scholarship in college. There were over six thousand boys, older ones, too, but Mrs. Morris' Victor, he won it. So now they're sending him to college for a year in England. No, Mrs. Morris?"

"Yes," she said quietly.

"That boy's got a head," the grocer said admiringly. "Out of six thousand there, he was the one! And how old do you think he is altogether? I'll bet he isn't even eighteen yet. How old is Victor, Mrs. Morris?"

"Seventeen," she said.

"See?" the grocer said to the women. "I told you. He's a baby yet."

"A young boy like that, to go away for a whole year," one of the women said, shaking her head. "Aren't you afraid to let him go alone, Mrs. Morris?"

"What's there to be afraid of?" the grocer said. "It's only for a year. No, Mrs. Morris?"

"That's right. It's only for a year," she repeated.

He was waiting for her, holding the door open, when she got back.

"Gee whiz, Ma," he said, looking at his watch, "you better hurry. They'll be here soon."

"Don't worry, Victor," she said. "I'll have the things ready."

She carried the package of groceries into the kitchen, and then hurried back for a last look at the living room. He stood in the doorway, smoothing down the points of his collar with thumb and forefinger, watching her adjust the candy dishes and fruit bowls and nuts.

"Okay, Ma, okay," he said irritably. "That stuff is all right. But how about the soda and the sandwiches?"

"I'm going to make them now," she said, without looking at him. "I want them to be fresh. I'll bring them in a little later, when your friends've been here a while."

She was in the kitchen, making sandwiches, when the doorbell began to ring and the door began to open and close. She could hear their voices, laughing and joking, as he let them in and guided them to the living room. She did not have time to distinguish the words. She was too busy doing the work that she had had plenty of time to do hours before. But as the noises at the other end of the flat grew louder she was glad she had left it for the last moment. It was almost easy to keep herself from thinking as long as she knew she had to work.

Later, when she carried in the first tray of glasses and bottled soda and sandwiches, they greeted her cordially. She smiled pleasantly when they said, "I guess you'll miss Victor, eh, Mrs. Morris?" But she did not reply, because this time she thought it best not to trust her voice. She merely smiled and hurried back to the kitchen to prepare fresh supplies.

She did not pause for a moment, and each time his voice called out, "How about some more sandwiches, Ma?" or "You got a couple of bottles of soda in there, Ma?" she had a tray ready to carry in.

Gradually his calls for refreshments grew less frequent. Soon they stopped altogether. She sat at the kitchen table, with nothing to do, staring dully at the tray of freshly-made sandwiches, no longer able to fight off the thoughts that her feverish activity had helped her to avoid all day.

After a time she couldn't bear to sit still any longer. She got up and walked toward the living room, carrying the heaped tray. Near the door she paused for a moment, remembering to set her face in a smile.

The voice of one of his friends rose above the rest and reached her where she stood in the foyer.

"But that's nothing," the voice said. "You just wait till you get to *Paris*, Vic. The dames I hear they got *there*—oh, boy!"

There was a roar of laughter that drowned out her son's reply, but it died down quickly as she stepped across the threshold into their midst.

She put the tray down carefully and set the plates of sandwiches on the table. Then, just as carefully, she collected the empty plates and glasses and bottles.

She picked up the tray of used dishes and started to walk out of the room. She could feel them watching her, smiling pleasantly, holding their words until she would be gone. But she did not smile back, or even look at them. She was afraid that if she raised her head they would all see how the dull fear that had been in her heart all day suddenly had become a terror that she could no longer hide.

The Great Healer

The car was parked at the right of the entrance to the office building. It wasn't exactly near the hydrant, but there was not so much
distance between them that a policeman with a grouch wouldn't
have felt justified in making a few acidulous remarks about parking
regulations. The same was true of the space between the front
bumper and the automobile parked just ahead. It looked wide enough
for a person to walk through, but actually it wasn't. The stenog-
raphers and office boys and clerks who rushed out of the office building to get to the trolley in the middle of the gutter, or the subway
kiosk across the street, found this out. Crossing in front of the car
would have brought them a split second closer to home, or to the
trolley or subway train that was to take them home. But they
didn't know they couldn't cross in front of the car until they tried
it. The distance was deceptive. When they discovered their miscalculation they all did the same thing. They contracted their lips in a
pinched, irritated grimace, they hiked their fresh evening newspapers
up further under their arms, and they glared angrily at the woman in
the car as they hurried around to the rear, where there was plenty of
room for crossing.

The woman in the car didn't seem to notice the small annoyances
she was causing or the glares that resulted, although she should
have. The car was a convertible coupe and the top was down. It was
too cold to have the top down. She wore a mink coat with a collar
that bunched up warmly around her neck and hid her chin. Her purse

was open and lying on the steering wheel. The horn button kept it from slipping down into her lap. A small mirror on a narrow leather thong hung over the side of the purse. She twisted her head to right and left so she could see it from all angles in the tiny mirror as she dabbed her hair more precisely into place under her hat. There were faint streaks of gray in the hair, very faint streaks, that were quite handsome. From the way she kept poking at herself, it was hard to decide whether she was trying to hide these almost unnoticeable bits of gray or whether she was experimenting with more becoming arrangements. Anyway, she was completely absorbed in her work and she didn't notice the inconvenience she was causing the people who wanted to rush across the street on their way home from work.

A man came out of the office building and walked up to the car. The woman didn't see him until he twisted the handle of the door and pulled it open.

"Oh," she said. "Hello, John. Just a second. Let me close my bag or you'll break the mirror, as usual." She slipped the mirror into the purse, snapped it shut, and held up her right cheek. "You're late," she said as he kissed it. "I've been waiting—"

"You haven't been wasting time, though," he said as he got in beside her and pulled the door shut. "What you want to throw away money on hairdressers for? All you have to do is call for me five minutes earlier every night and bring along a curling iron."

"Now, now," she said as she turned on the ignition and released the brake. "None of that, now."

He looked behind them to see if there was room for her to back up.

"Okay, come ahead," he said. "Six more inches and you'd been sitting on that hydrant. How you get away with it, I don't know. If it was me that parked like that, I'd have a cop on my neck and a ticket before you could say—"

"I do it with my charm," she said, swinging the car out into the busy stream of traffic. "My womanly wiles. My fetching beauty." The light at the Fifth Avenue corner turned red. The traffic stopped. She turned to him with a smile as she pressed in the clutch and disengaged the gears. "The cop takes one look at my ravishing—" She stopped and the smile disappeared. "Where's your hat?"

"My hat?" His hand went to his tumbled, black hair. The wind was whipping it about. "Oh, God. Forgot it again. Oh, well."

"For heaven's sake, John, I've told you a hundred—" He nudged her and pointed ahead. The light had turned green. She kicked the clutch. When she swung the car around the corner into Fifth Avenue and shifted into high the gears rasped complainingly. "I don't think it's so damned funny, going around without a hat. I don't think it's—"

"I didn't say it was funny," he said. "I said I forgot it. Now you forget it. Let's not—"

"I will not forget it. It may be boyish and charming to you. Going around without a hat may be your idea of being youthful and collegiate and all that junk. But I don't think it's—"

"Oh, God. Now, Helen. I forgot it. Tomorrow I won't forget it. The day after tomorrow I won't forget it. From tomorrow on, until I reach a hundred and twenty years of age, I won't forget it. Satisfied? Now, for God's sake, let's shut up about it. It's only a hat."

She drove in silence for several blocks, with savage concentration, but with enough carelessness to earn a few angry horn toots from cars she passed too closely. She got the car across Fifty-fourth Street a second or so after the green light went out. A pedestrian who had started to cross jumped back to the curb and shouted something after them.

"Oh, nuts," she muttered. "Look where you're going."

"I think that's just what he was yelling after us," John said. "The way you're giving the car a shellacking, I hope the insurance is paid up."

"Oh, shut up."

"My, my, aren't we in a temper tonight?" he said mildly. "You didn't happen to have lunch with Alice, did you?"

"As a matter of fact, I did," she said acidly.

She turned the car into the Fifty-ninth Street entrance to Central Park. She passed so close to the policeman in the middle of the street that he turned to glare after her. But she hadn't really passed too close to him to earn more than the glare. And there was too much early evening traffic for him to spend too much time on what was only a technical violation.

"That's one member of New York's Finest who won't have to go

to the barber tonight," John said. "You passed him close enough
to—"

"Don't give me lessons in driving," she said. "If you don't mind,
I was driving a car when you were still studying logarithms."

"Yes, teacher," he said with mock humility. "Only I never studied
logarithms. Never got beyond plane geometry."

She raced the car along the winding arcs of road through the park.
It was quite dark now. The roadster's powerful headlights cut
through the night and picked out bits of rounded curb, park
benches, trees, the small red lights of a car ahead. For a while
neither spoke. The hum of the tires on the asphalt was the
only sound. It was soothing.

"Anything happen at the office?" she asked finally.

"Same old junk," he said. "Sent McPhail down to Special Sessions
to get an adjournment on the Palmer case because I had to be in
Commercial Frauds on something else, and the damn fool all but got
the case dismissed. Damn fool. Had to send young Steindler down
to straighten it out. Good kid, Steindler."

"He's not a kid. He's twenty-seven."

"Well, he's good, anyway. Best in the office. I think I'll give him a
raise in a month or so. The rest of those damn fools. Come out of
law school without the slightest conception of what the hell it's all
— Oh, nuts. I came out of law school myself once. What you do
today?"

"I told you," she said, sounding the horn as she passed a car.
"Lunch with Alice."

"That must've been fun. Like hell. What's the latest communiqué
from the Henderson battlefield?"

She didn't answer for a moment. She waited until she finished
passing another car.

"John," she said. "About Lou."

"What about Lou?"

"Is he running around?"

John turned quickly to look at her in astonishment. This caused
the current of air to strike his head from a new angle and sent his
hair tumbling wildly in another direction.

"My God, Helen," he said. "For God's sakes. What do you think
I am, a Pinkerton man? How would I know a thing like that?"

"Well, I just wanted to know, because Alice thinks so. She told me today at lunch."

"Alice is nuts. She thinks too damned much for her own good. I'm not signing any affidavits for Lou Henderson. But only because I'm not signing any affidavits for anybody about those things. That's their own business. Let Alice and Lou worry about it. You just stick to your driving and see that you don't rip any fenders off—"

"I think Alice is right this time."

She said it calmly, a trifle grimly. He looked at her again. The astonishment on his handsome face deepened.

"Helen, are you going nuts, too? That dizzy dame Alice. She doesn't know if she's alive half the time. How the hell can you say a thing like that? How can you say you think she's right this time?"

"Alice says he called up four times in the last two weeks said he can't come home for dinner he's working late. Every time she called back later in the evening he wasn't in the office. Every time he came home after one o'clock, once it was nearly three, she says, half-past two anyway. Said he was entertaining salesmen from out of town."

"Which he probably was. Alice is just wacky, that's all."

"Yesterday he told her he has to go out of town on a five day selling trip," Helen continued in the same implacable voice. "Lou Henderson hasn't gone on a selling trip in five years. Alice told me at lunch."

"My advice is you better stop eating lunch with that Alice Henderson. Join a reading group or a Browning Society or make an extra visit to the hairdresser or brush up on your mah-jongg. That Alice woman is dynamite. Her idea of evidence. My God. Lou entertains some salesmen and goes out of town to do some selling on his own, so he's playing around. My good God."

"I believe it," Helen said. She banged the horn button several times, hard. The car in front refused to slow down or pull over. She stepped on the gas and passed the car with a sharp whoosh. "It's only natural."

"What's only natural?"

"Alice is forty-eight and Lou is thirty-nine. They've been married ten years. It's only natural for him to start—"

"Now, Helen, for God's sakes—"

"—running around. It was all right when they were first married.

She was thirty-eight and he was twenty-nine. She didn't look her age and he always looked older than he was. Most of his hair was gone then already. And that long, thin face of his. It wasn't so bad then. But now—"

"Oh, my God. Do I have to sit and listen to—?"

"—Alice is beginning to look her age. She's getting fat and her hair is turning— She's losing her looks and her pep. It's only natural. I'd believe it of any man, and I'd certainly believe it of Lou Henderson. I never trusted him, anyway. Slimy little heel. It's only natural."

"You'd be doing me a real favor, Helen, if you'd concentrate less on what's natural for Alice and Lou Henderson and more on your driving. That last car almost—"

"There's nothing wrong with my driving," she said savagely. "I think Alice is right. I think Lou is—"

"I don't care if she's right or wrong or if Lou is or isn't. It's none of my damn business and it's none of yours. Now, for God's sakes, let's quit this—"

A sharp whistle sounded behind them. She kicked the brake and the clutch. The car slid jumpily to a stop. They looked back. A policeman was walking toward them.

"Where do you think you're going?" the policeman asked when he reached them. "What's all the—?"

"I'm sorry, officer," Helen said. "We were—"

"Pull over to the curb."

She maneuvered the car to the park side of the wide street. The policeman walked along, pulling off his glove as he went.

"We were just—" she began again.

"Never mind what you were just. See that light up there? It's got colors. It's not there for decoration. Red means stop. Lemme see your license."

She opened her purse, fished around inside with her gloved hand, and came up with a small, leather folder. The policeman opened it and read it.

"Yeah. Hirr. Well. Okay. Now, you look, Mrs. Brewster. Those lights, they—"

"I think I can explain, officer," John said. "We were—"

"You just keep out of this, sonny," the cop said with a sarcastic wave of his hand. "I'm talking to mama, here."

John's face went white and then, very quickly, bright red.

"The car is registered in my name," he said coldly. "I happen to be Mr. Brewster."

"Oh," the cop said. He looked at the man's hatless head with its tousled hair and youthful face, then at the woman's gray-streaked hair, so becomingly arranged under her hat, and at her throat. The high collar of the mink coat had fallen away. She stared back at him calmly and bunched the collar smoothly up around her throat again until her chin was buried in the fur. "Oh, I see," the cop said. He wet his lower lip with his tongue, then shoved the small leather folder back at her. "Okay," he said. The sarcasm was gone from his voice. "Let it go this time. But remember those lights. Red? Stop. Understand? Go ahead this time."

He walked away. Helen put the leather folder back in her purse and started the car. They drove all the way up to Ninety-sixth Street without speaking. There she turned the car to the left and stopped in front of an apartment building.

"Listen," John said. "Listen, Helen." ·

"Yes?"

"Let's not talk about it," he said. "For God's sakes, forget Alice and let's not talk about it. We've still got eight years."

The Half-Promised Land

One of Capri's great charms is its size. Or so I thought when my wife and I first arrived. The compactness of the island appealed to me at once. I like neat places. I enjoy the feeling, whether I am in my own workroom or in a foreign hotel, that everything around me is in its place, within easy reach, and readily accessible.

On the third day of our visit, when I came back to the hotel with the sandals and other tourist trinkets for which I had spent the afternoon shopping, I began to wonder if Capri was not, perhaps, just a trifle too compact.

"Pio has been asking for you," my wife said.

I was not surprised, but I was beginning to feel a bit hounded: Pio had been asking for me ever since we arrived.

"What does he want?"

"He didn't say," my wife said. "But I suppose you can guess."

I certainly could. People who live with an obsession are fairly predictable. They also have a capacity for making other people, those who do not share their obsession, feel inadequate.

"I suppose I'd better go down and see him," I said uncomfortably. "Do you want to come along?"

"I'll join you in a little while," my wife said. Then, apparently stabbed by a twinge of guilt for what looked like desertion, she added, "Why don't you just tell him that you're not the Secretary of State?"

"I've tried that, several times, but it doesn't do any good," I said.

"The trouble is that Pio thinks all Americans are touched by God."

It was not difficult to understand how the thought had taken root in his mind, once you knew his background. Pio had started filling it in for me a half-hour after we disembarked from the small steamer that had brought us from Sorrento.

The Hotel Semiramis, which commands a magnificent view of the Bay of Naples, was almost empty when we checked in. The tourist season had been over for a month. When my wife and I, on the day of our arrival, came into the bar for a drink before dinner, the only other occupants of the large, somewhat gloomy room were a German couple and the barman.

"Good evening," he said with a bow. "Would you perhaps care for a really good dry martini?"

We said we would and, after the first sip, my wife and I exchanged a look of pleased surprise.

"Where," she asked the barman, "did you learn to make a martini as good as this?"

"In Montana," he said. "Where I learned also to speak English."

My wife and I uttered the appropriate expressions of astonishment, and the barman introduced himself as Pio. He was a good-looking man of about fifty, not very tall but well-built, with a dignified and rather sad face that brightened amazingly when he smiled. He gave me the impression of great strength and, because I have always assumed since I read James Oliver Curwood as a boy that the two qualities go together, I took it for granted he was reticent. As a result, even though I wanted to ask Pio what he had been doing in Montana, I was hesitant about putting the question to him. My hesitation proved unnecessary. Pio did not wait for the question.

"Before I went to Montana," he said, "I was a sailor."

It was during the days as a sailor that he had been seized by the obsession that ruled his life. Pio did not call it an obsession. He merely recited the facts.

Pio was born in Naples. His family was very poor. At sixteen he went to sea as a steward. He was not quite seventeen when his ship steamed into New York harbor one sunny April day and he had his first glimpse of the new world. It was enough. From that moment, until my wife and I met him almost thirty years later in the Hotel Semiramis, Pio had only one desire: to live in America.

"But legitimate," he added firmly. "I want to be a citizen."

The importance of this point had been driven home to him almost at once. The day after his love affair with the United States began, almost thirty years ago, Pio jumped ship. He made his way to the home of a distant cousin who lived in Brooklyn. The cousin, an older man who had come to America many years before, explained the facts of life to Pio.

"He told me about the immigration laws and quotas," Pio said. "He told me as soon as the captain of my ship found out I was missing, he would have to report to the immigration people, and then the police would begin to look for me. He told me even if it took them many years to find me, when they did they would deport me. The only way to come to live in America, my cousin said, was the legitimate way, under the immigration quota. Only in that way could a man become a citizen. That night I left my cousin's house, and I went back to my ship."

For sixteen years, while he sailed the seven seas to earn his living, Pio never stopped trying to enter the United States as a legal immigrant. The quota always barred his path. Pio did not despair. In his heart, which he had given to America at first sight, he knew that some day his great dream would come true. It took a war, however, to justify his confidence.

The day that Mussolini brought Italy into the conflict, Pio's ship happened to be at Panama, waiting to enter the canal. The ship was seized at once, and the crew was sent to an internment camp for enemy aliens in Montana.

There were members of that crew who resented this imprisonment. Pio was not one of them. His passion for America was so great, he had lived for so long with the dream of a promised land, that it did not occur to him to resent the fact that the piece on which he had finally been allowed to set foot was surrounded by barbed wire.

His view was restricted, but Pio liked what he saw. He liked it even better when, apparently because of his cheery smile, he was ordered out from behind the barbed wire to serve as barman in the understaffed officers' club.

"There it was I learned to make a dry martini," he said. "And there it was that General Hershey destroyed my hopes."

"General Hershey?" I said. "What did he have to do with it?"

"He was the Director of your American Selective Service," Pio said. "After Italy was knocked out of the war, General Hershey announced that Italian internees in the United States who enlisted in the American Army would be eligible for citizenship. I hurried quickly to enlist."

Pio paused. His sad face brightened. He seemed to have forgotten our presence. He was staring across our heads, toward the silent German couple at the far side of the gloomy room, but I knew Pio was not seeing them, either. He was staring back into the past, to the time when General Hershey had almost made Pio's dream come true, to the moment when, for a fleeting instant, the unattainable had at last seemed to be within his grasp. Then the smile vanished. Pio brought his glance back to us.

"I was not quick enough," he said quietly. "General Hershey made another announcement. The United States Army did not need more men, he said. Internees were not wanted. When the war ended, I was sent back to Italy. Will you have another?"

My wife and I had another, but we did not enjoy the second martini as much as the first. The trouble was Pio's eyes. Looking into them, you could not help seeing that to this simple man you were one of the anointed. Suddenly, with a small feeling of guilt, you were forced to wonder if you deserved what you had been taking so casually for granted ever since it had been handed to you at birth: the right to call yourself an American.

"From the end of the war until today," Pio said, "I have not stopped trying for a single moment to return to America." He shrugged, and continued, "Always, however, it is the same problem: the quota."

"Well," I said awkwardly, as I lifted my glass to his health, "I hope you make it some day."

"Thank you," Pio said, and his wonderful smile seemed to light up the gloomy room. "I know I will."

In view of the stubborn facts that had thus far stood in his way, I found the quiet certainty in his voice distressing. It did not seem right that any man, wanting anything as much as Pio had for thirty years wanted to become an American, should be barred from it by something so impersonal and inflexible as a quota. Neither did it seem right, however, for a man of fifty to pretend those stubborn facts did not exist. Pio must have read my thoughts.

"A quota is like a stone wall," he said. "A man cannot go through it. But a man can always go around a stone wall."

A tall, slender youngster came in, carrying a wooden bucket full of chopped ice. He carried the bucket behind the bar. Pio dipped down, lifted the chromium lid of a chest, and held it open while the boy poured the ice into the chest. There was something about the way Pio did it, adding a touch of affectionate concern to the casual act, that made me take a second look at the boy. He was very handsome, with a long, delicate face that had something of Pio's sadness in it. He seemed to be about nineteen or twenty. He straightened up with the empty bucket. Pio dropped the chromium lid into place, and put his arm around the boy's shoulders.

"This is my son," he said. "Valerio."

My wife and I nodded and smiled and murmured greetings. The boy blushed furiously, bobbed his head, said, "How do you do?" in heavily accented but intelligible English, and almost ran out of the bar with his bucket.

Pio watched him go with a smile.

"Valerio is very shy," he said. "But he will get me around that stone wall."

"How?" I said, turning back to the barman.

"I learned in America other things besides how to make a good dry martini," Pio said. "I learned what American girls like. I think my son Valerio has it." He sent another glance toward the door through which the boy had disappeared. "He is good-looking, is he not?"

"Very," my wife said. "He looks like his father."

Pio smiled and bowed.

"Thank you, Madame," he said, and then his face became grave. "Valerio has more than good looks. He has brains. He wants to become a doctor. I encourage him. He is about to enter medical school. In four years, with his diploma and his good looks, Valerio will be ready."

"For what?" I said.

"To marry an American girl."

"Oh," I said.

Pio nodded.

"It is the only way around the stone wall," he said. "Many American girls come here to Capri in the tourist season. Valerio will choose one and marry her. After she goes home to America, she will send for him. There are no quotas for husbands of American girls. Then, after Valerio becomes an American citizen, he will send for me. There are no quotas for the fathers of American citizens, either," Pio smiled. "It is simple, is it not?"

"Yes," I said.

I did not add that I thought it was a trifle too simple. The chain of events Pio had sketched sounded fine—until you examined it for a moment. The examination revealed that it was not a chain at all. It was merely a string of suppositions, a flimsy structure built of wishful thinking, a grab bag of hopes. There was no certainty that Valerio would win a diploma. If he did, there was no certainty that it would win him an American wife. If it did, there was no certainty that she would want to help bring Pio to America. The only certainty, in fact, seemed to be that Pio's obsession had made him a trifle unrealistic.

And yet, as you looked at this quiet, dignified, self-possessed man, something of his confidence seemed to reach out and touch you. The string of suppositions seemed to become more than that. The flimsy structure built of wishful thinking took on solidity. The bits and pieces in the grab bag of hopes became an unbreakable chain. What held them together was Pio's faith.

"The important thing is never to despair," he said. "One must have patience."

There was at least one other requirement, but my wife and I did not discover it that night. The next day, when we returned to the hotel after a visit to Axel Munthe's villa at Anacapri, I found in my box a note from the barman.

"I hope you will be able to stop in the bar this afternoon," he wrote. "It is very important that I see you. I come on duty at four-thirty. Thank you. Gratefully, Pio."

Four-thirty is much too early for cocktails. In our family, anyway. My wife, therefore, suggested that I go down to the bar alone, and she would join me later. It was not, apparently, too early for the German couple. They were sitting at the same table they had occupied the day before. They were, aside from Pio, the only people in the room. The barman's handsome, dignified face brightened when he saw me.

"You are very kind to be so prompt," he said, and then, with an anxious glance at the door, "and Madame?"

"She'll be along in a little while," I said. "I thought I'd better come down at once because you said in your note what you wanted to see me about was important."

"It is, yes," Pio said. He looked across my head at the silent German couple, and then he dropped his voice. "Are you acquainted with the Potomac River?"

I could feel my forehead crease with puzzlement.

"The Potomac River?"

"Yes," Pio said. "In America? The Potomac River? You are acquainted with it?"

"I don't think I understand what you mean," I said slowly. "I know *about* the Potomac. I mean I know where it is, and I know roughly how it flows, but—"

"Could you tell me if, in the Potomac River, there are salmon?"

I was aware, as I stared at the barman, that I was more than astonished. I was also a little suspicious. It occurred to me that this sad-faced man, who had aroused my sympathy the day before, might now be pulling my leg.

"No," I said with a slight edge in my voice, "I don't think there are salmon in the Potomac."

"You are certain?" Pio asked anxiously.

"Fairly certain," I said. "If there were, I think I would have heard about it."

Pio scowled. My answer, quite obviously, was not the one he had hoped for.

"But—" he began in a troubled voice. Then he shrugged as though, in a lifetime of disappointments, this new one was hardly unbearable. "Thank you very much," Pio said quietly. "And now may I make you a dry martini?"

He did, and when my wife came into the bar he made me another, but he did not again raise the subject of the Potomac. Not then, anyway.

The next morning my wife and I took the funicular down to the

Marina Grande and hired a motorboat to take us to the Blue Grotto. When we got back to the hotel at noon, a man approached our cab as we stepped out. He had obviously been waiting for us. He was wearing a shiny but neatly brushed blue suit instead of his white barman's coat, and so I did not recognize Pio until he smiled.

"Excuse me," he said, and then I noticed that the smile seemed forced. The quiet confidence that had impressed me on our first night in the Hotel Semiramis had vanished. Something had obviously gone wrong. Pio looked upset. He said, "May I take perhaps a half hour of your time?"

"Both of us?" I said.

"Well—" Pio said with obvious discomfort.

"You run along," my wife said promptly. "I want to go up to the room and change for lunch, anyway. I'll wait for you here."

Pio bowed gratefully. My wife went up the steps and disappeared into the hotel. I turned to the barman.

"What can I do for you?"

"If you will be so kind," Pio said. "Come."

He led me into an alley that ran alongside the Hotel Semiramis. We emerged, at the back of the building, in a small square built out to the very edge of a cliff that dropped several hundred feet to the bay below. From this square, curving and twisting down like a welt raised by the lash of a whip, ran a narrow footpath that had been hewn out of the solid rock. It was quite steep, paved with small round cobblestones, and guarded on the bay side by a stone wall.

Walking down this path behind Pio was a little like descending a ladder while facing in the wrong direction. I found myself leaning backwards as I walked and, every now and then, feeling behind me for the rungs. After a few minutes, we came to another alley. It branched off at right angles from the cobbled footpath. I noticed, as we turned into the alley, that it was marked by a stone sign: "Via Mulo."

Perhaps a hundred feet down the Via Mulo, Pio stopped in front of a black iron gate set between two crumbling gate posts. On the gate hung a small, battered sign: "Villa Augusto." Pio opened the gate. I followed him into a tangled, overgrown garden with weeds that towered over our heads. We went along a cracked stone walk,

and up to a dirty old door that sagged on its hinges. Pio knocked.
The door was opened at once by a toothless old woman wearing a
filthy pink wrapper and a green eye shade. Pio said something to
her in rapid Italian. She squinted at me, bobbed her head, and
turned.

"All right," she said in English. "Bring him along."

Pio and I followed her into a shabby little room that was obviously used for some sort of consultations. There was a square table
in the middle, surrounded by straight-backed chairs. The walls were
hung with phrenologist's charts, horoscopes, and diagrams that were
meaningless to me but which, to judge by the greasy fingermarks that
covered them, received a good deal of use.

The old woman sat down at the table. Pio took the chair facing
her and indicated, with a small, polite bow, that I was to take the
chair between them. I did. The old woman folded her hands on the
table in front of her and stared at her cracked, black-rimmed fingernails.

"You say there are no salmon in the Potomac River?" she said.

For several startled moments, I did not realize she had addressed
me. When I did, I sat up straighter in my chair.

"Yes," I said. "I mean no, not to my knowledge."

She unclasped her hands, rubbed her nose with a forearm, adjusted the green eye shade, and turned to Pio.

"Tell me again how it was," she said. "Slowly, please."

Pio leaned forward anxiously.

"I was flying through the air with a sword," he said, speaking with
great care, as though he were dictating to a stenographer. "Suddenly I saw a river beneath me. I flew down to identify it, and saw
a sign that said it was the Potomac. A moment later I saw a great
silver salmon swimming in the river. I swooped down and speared
the salmon with my sword. Then I woke up."

It suddenly dawned on me where I was and what was happening.
The toothless old woman was evidently a dream interpreter. She
turned back to me.

"You heard him," she said. "Do you still say there are no salmon
in the Potomac?"

I looked at Pio. He was watching me hopefully, almost implor-
ingly. I did not know what the problem was. I did know that I wanted

to help him. I did not see, however, how I could do this until he told
me precisely what sort of help he wanted.

"Look," I said. "I'm not an authority on these matters. Fish and
rivers are a little out of my line. All I can do is tell you what—"

"Answer the question," the old woman said irritably. "Are there,
or are there not, salmon in the Potomac River?"

"To the best of my knowledge," I said patiently, "definitely not."

"I'm sorry," the old woman snapped, pushing back her chair.
She stood up and made a gesture of dismissal to Pio. "There's
nothing I can do for you."

She stalked out of the room. I looked at Pio with a feeling of discomfort. I had obviously failed him. I couldn't, however, quite imagine how.

He stood up slowly, his face fixed in a troubled scowl, one hand
stroking the side of his jaw gently, as though he were probing for
an elusive pain. I followed him in silence, out of the Villa Augusto,
across the tangled garden, and back along the Via Mulo to the cobbled path. I waited until we had started the upward climb before I
cleared my throat noisily.

"I don't seem to have been of much assistance to you," I said. "I'm
sorry."

Pio's shoulders moved in a small, hopeless shrug.

"It cannot be helped," he said. "You are an American. You know
better than we do if there are salmon in the Potomac River."

"Perhaps I could be more helpful if I knew more about what you're
trying to do."

"What I have been trying to do for thirty years," Pio said quietly.
"Move around the stone wall of the quota."

Twenty minutes later, in our hotel room, as I explained the situation to my wife, I realized I was really trying to get it straight in my
own mind.

"It's a matter of half a million lira, or about eight hundred dollars," I said. "Pio must have it for the first payment of Valerio's tuition in medical school. It's due on Monday, and the only way a
man like Pio can put his hands on half a million lira is to win it
in the national lottery. The drawing takes place on Saturday, and
today being Thursday, that gives Pio two days to buy his ticket. He
can't do that, however, until he figures out the tip he received in this

dream he had about the salmon in the Potomac. Pio feels it's the key to the winning number. That's why he asked me about it yesterday, and that's why he took me to the dream interpreter just now. Unfortunately, I don't seem to have—" I paused, and gave my wife a sharp glance. "What's wrong?"

She was staring at me with a small, troubled frown.

"Don't you find it a little frightening?"

"What?" I said.

"Pio's faith."

"Yes," I said.

I also found it a trifle incredible. He apparently believed firmly that if he did not get his dream interpreted properly, he would not win the lottery, which meant he would not have the money to pay for Valerio's medical school tuition, which meant the boy would not be able to marry an American girl, which meant Valerio would not be able to go to America and become an American citizen, which meant he would not be able to send for his father, which meant Pio was right back where, when he fell in love with America thirty years ago, he had started from: facing the stone wall called a quota.

"Listen," I said, "are you enjoying your stay here on Capri?"

"Why do you ask?" my wife said.

"It's a pretty small place, and it seems to me we've just about seen everything there is to see," I said. "I was wondering why, instead of waiting until Sunday, we couldn't leave tomorrow? It would give us an extra couple of days in Rome."

My wife gave me a shrewd glance.

"It would also give me the feeling that we're running away," she said. "Pio's faith may be upsetting to contemplate, but it's hardly our responsibility. I wish I could help him, just as you do, but because you can't interpret a dream about a salmon in the Potomac, I don't see why we should try to leave Capri ahead of schedule. Besides," my wife added, "now that you've demonstrated your inadequacy as an interpreter of dreams, I have a feeling that Pio will stop bothering you."

She was wrong, of course, as I found out the next day, which was Friday, when I came back to the hotel from my shopping expedition and learned that Pio had been asking for me.

"I hope you do not think I am a nuisance," he said awkwardly when I came into the bar. "I do not, however, have much time left to buy my lottery ticket, and I wondered if perhaps you had since yesterday had any further thoughts about my dream?"

"No, I'm sorry," I said. "All I can say is what I've said before; to the best of my knowledge there are no salmon in the—"

I stopped. I had caught sight of my wife, who had promised to join me in a little while, hurrying into the bar. She is not an excitable person. Over a dozen years, however, I have learned to recognize certain symptoms. They are scarcely discernible to the untrained observer. To me they indicate clearly when my wife has reached a point approximately similar to that which caused Archimedes to start shouting in his tub. One of the symptoms is a total lack of awareness that I am alive.

"Pio," my wife said, disregarding me completely as she came up to the bar. "I think I've got it!"

He did not bother to ask what. To a man with an obsession, she could be talking about only one thing.

"Madame!" Pio said in a light little voice. "Madame, tell me, please!"

"I think you've been attacking the dream from the wrong angle!" my wife said. "It just came to me as I was combing my hair! I don't think it matters whether there are salmon in the Potomac or not! I think what matters is the Potomac! It flows through Washington, D. C. That's where the immigration laws were written! That's where the quota was born! And Washington is the capital of the United States! In other words, it's our number one city! Do you see what I mean? Number One! Do you understand what I'm trying to—?"

If he didn't, I don't think Pio would have seized her hand the way he did: with every intention, or so it seemed, of crushing it to a pulp.

"Madame!" he said in a choked voice. "Madame," he repeated, and the tears came to his eyes as he struggled with the phrasing of his gratitude. "Madame, this is what I have been waiting for! The first number! It is all I need! The number one! Madame, you have saved—!"

He couldn't finish the sentence. It was not, of course, necessary. He couldn't seem to get out of the bar fast enough, either. As a result, I had to mix our own martinis that night. It was a pleasure. By the next morning, the day the lottery drawing was to take place, this pleasure had been replaced by a feeling of uneasiness.

"I've just had a horrible thought," I said to my wife at breakfast. "Suppose the winning number does not begin with the digit one?"

"I've been having that horrible thought since late last night," my wife said morosely. She stared thoughtfully into her coffee cup for several moments. Then she said, "When do they draw these lottery numbers?"

"At noon, up in Rome," I said. "According to Pio, the winning numbers are announced on the radio at once, so that everybody in Italy knows about it in a few minutes. Why do you ask?"

"Well, Capri is a pretty small place, and it seems to me we've just about seen everything there is to see," she said casually. "I was wondering why, instead of waiting until tomorrow, we couldn't leave this morning? It would give us an extra day in Rome."

I stared at her. Like a good many married men, I find there are times when it suddenly occurs to me, with a feeling of complete astonishment, that I have been living with a genius.

"Wait here," I said, putting down my coffee cup, and pushing back my chair. "I'm going to find out at the desk about transportation."

There was, I learned, a steamer that came in at eleven from Naples and sailed back to Naples at eleven-thirty. At eleven o'clock, after settling my bill, I left with the hall porter of the Hotel Semiramis an envelope addressed to Pio. It contained a small sum of money and a note of thanks, in which I explained that we were sorry to leave Capri without saying good-by to him in person, but our plans had changed unexpectedly and so we could not wait until four-thirty when he came on duty, and I closed by saying that my wife and I both hoped his great dream would come true and some day we would meet him in America.

At eleven-fifteen my wife and I were standing on the *quai* at the Marina Grande, surrounded by our luggage, and wondering nervously how the steamer could leave for Naples at eleven-thirty if it had not yet arrived. A half-hour later, when this question had become academic, the steamer came gliding into the Marina Grande. Ten minutes after that, while passengers from Naples were still disembarking, I became aware that there had been a sudden cessation of activity among the porters who had been unloading the luggage. They were all gathering around a neat little Lancia which was parked near the foot of the *quai*.

"What's happening?" I said to my wife.

"There's a radio in that car," she said. "Unless I'm mistaken, they've started drawing those lottery numbers up in Rome."

She was not mistaken. As I joined the porters around the small Lancia, I could feel my heart begin to beat faster. I was well aware that we were running away, that we had arranged to leave Capri before the numbers were drawn because, if Pio lost, my wife and I did not want to have to face him. On the other hand, if he won, I knew I would be pleased by the role my wife had played in helping him to choose the winning number. It was with mixed emotions that, during the next twenty minutes, I listened to the excited voice coming from the Lancia dashboard. I did not understand the words, of course. But words were not necessary. Numbers are a universal language.

"Well, I guess that's that."

I turned quickly. It was my wife. I had not realized she had come up beside me.

"Yes," I said, "I guess it is."

Only the first six numbers had been drawn. But these were the only ones that carried substantial awards. A great many other numbers would be drawn before the next hour was finished. None would bring their lucky holders enough to pay for a year of tuition in a medical school. And none of the first six numbers began with the digit one. The small steamer's whistle blew a warning blast.

"I think we'd better get going," my wife said quietly. "The luggage is aboard already."

I nodded. We turned away from the crowd around the Lancia and moved down the *quai* to the gangplank. When we reached it, we both stopped short. Pio, wearing the shiny but neatly brushed blue suit, was waiting at the foot.

"I came early to the hotel because I wanted to be with you when the numbers were drawn," he said. "The hall porter said you were gone to the ship and he gave me your note. I came as quickly as I could."

I searched his face, then looked quickly at my wife. She, too, seemed to be puzzled by the question that was bothering me: if Pio knew what we knew, namely, that he had lost, why didn't he look defeated? I turned involuntarily toward the little Lancia. Pio touched my arm. I turned back.

"It is all right," he said quietly. "I heard the winning numbers from the ticket man in the funicular. He, too, has a radio."

"I'm sorry," my wife said. "I don't seem to be as good an interpreter of dreams as I thought."

Pio laughed. I stared at him in astonishment. Far from looking defeated, he looked positively jaunty.

"I disagree, Madame," he said with a small bow. "I think you are an extremely able interpreter of dreams."

"I don't see how you can say that," my wife said. "As a result of my advice, you won't be able to pay Valerio's tuition on Monday."

"I will pay it the following Monday," Pio said, and he laughed again. "Your interpretation was correct. What matters, you said, was the Potomac. Not the salmon in the Potomac. And not the city of Washington on the Potomac. Only the Potomac itself. And the Potomac begins with the letter P, which is the sixteenth letter in the alphabet. The number I should have chosen, therefore, should have begun, not with one, but with a one *and* a six!" Pio paused, and smiled. "A small error, of no consequence," he said. "Next week, when I buy my lottery ticket, I will select a number beginning with sixteen, and the Monday after that, thanks to you, Madame, I will pay Valerio's tuition."

I stared at him the way I had stared at him during our first night in the Semiramis bar, when we had first learned about his obsession and Pio had told us his plan to circumvent the stone wall that had, for thirty years, barred his path. Once again I asked myself if he really believed what he was saying. And once again, as I stared into his eyes, I was touched by the absolute certainty of his simple faith. They were the eyes of a man for whom there could be neither defeat nor doubt. He lived by an inner fire.

"In that case," my wife said as she put out her hand, "I suppose we'll be seeing you in America after all."

"I am certain of it," Pio said as he took her hand and bowed over it. "Thank you, Madame."

The whistle blew. Pio straightened up. I put out my hand.

"I'm still sorry we didn't get that dream interpreted correctly the first time," I said. "We've delayed you for a week."

For a moment, watching the extraordinary smile that set his face aglow as we shook hands, I wondered which of us—the man who had ever since birth possessed the right to call himself an American, or the man who had for three decades dreamed of acquiring that right —was one of the anointed.

"I have been on my way for thirty years," Pio said. "What does one more week matter?"

The Hole Card

Some people wake up slowly and wait for the delicious possibilities of the day to come thronging into their minds. These people are usually young.

Other people wake up abruptly and begin at once, with resignation or impatience, to plan their day, sorting out the chores they can delay no longer from the tasks that will have to wait until tomorrow. These people are usually old.

Mrs. Jessie Bulwer, who was neither, always woke up as though she had been kicked out of bed by a malicious prankster, her mind in wild disorder. This was due to a number of factors, the least important of which were two:

First, Mrs. Bulwer never knew, during those first disjointed moments of wakefulness, where she was. Second, the instrument that brought her from the fitful stupor that, in recent years, had served her as sleep, was always a jangling phone.

Mrs. Bulwer's groping hand found the source of the shattering sounds. After a short struggle with the bed clothes, she managed to bring the phone to her ear.

"Mrs. Bulwer?"

"What?" she said, and then she identified the voice. "Oh, Mr. Shoup," she said, and because voices like Mr. Shoup's were to Mrs. Bulwer inseparable from the places that gave them their special quality, Mrs. Bulwer knew where she was. The knowledge did not cheer her. She said, very cautiously, "Good morning, Mr. Shoup."

"Good afternoon, you mean," said the manager of the Hereford Arms. The edge in his voice made Mrs. Bulwer bridle with a tremor of indignation she knew she was not entitled to. If her luck had been better during the past month, nobody would dare talk to her that way. Least of all the desk clerk of a three-dollar flea-bag. "It's twelve-fifteen," Mr. Shoup said, and he added, with the childish sarcasm reserved by men like Mr. Shoup for women like Mrs. Bulwer when they are far enough behind in their bill, "I hope I didn't wake you up?"

"Of course not," said Mrs. Bulwer. Since her husband's death, fourteen years before, Mrs. Bulwer had lived only in hotels, and only in hotels of a certain type. She had learned the importance of never disagreeing with the managers of such hotels about anything, even when she was solvent. "I've been up for hours," she said with an attempt at asperity that was not completely unsuccessful. "Is there anything in my box?"

"Not a thing," Mr. Shoup said, and Mrs. Bulwer remembered, with a familiar stab of apprehension, that for at least a week and perhaps longer, she had been giving Mr. Shoup the routine about the insurance check she was expecting momentarily in the mails. Or was it the manager of the Stafford, over on West Seventy-ninth, where she had lived for six or seven weeks before coming here, on whom she had used the insurance-check story? The question was important.

Mrs. Bulwer shook her head sharply, a process supposed to help clear it, but it served only to make her somewhat dizzy. Dizzy or not, she remembered now that the insurance-check routine and the Stafford belonged together. Here, at the Hereford Arms, she had been using the pension-check story. The one about the monthly payments she had been receiving since Mr. Bulwer had died at Château-Thierry and how this last check had not arrived on time, but Shoup needn't worry, it would be along any day now. "There's not a thing in your box," Mr. Shoup said. "Not even the *Turfman*."

Mrs. Bulwer's eyes shot open. If the *Turfman* was not in her box, it meant that Alvin, who owned the newsstand at the corner of Seventy-second and Broadway, had failed to deliver it. Alvin stopped making deliveries only when a customer's credit reached the limit Alvin had set firmly for himself: five dollars. Well, she thought with a sigh, that settled the most important question of the day, anyway.

She couldn't possibly be solvent. Mrs. Bulwer, to whose way of life the *Turfman* was essential, would not allow herself to fall that far behind with Alvin unless she was really hard up. She had not realized it was as bad as all that. Now that she was almost fully awake, she knew precisely how bad it was. Down to the last penny. She pushed herself erect in the bed. There was nothing like knowing where you stood. Except a run of luck, of course.

"Well, I wouldn't worry if I were you, Mr. Shoup," she said into the phone. "My pension check will be along in the next mail, I'm sure."

"I'm not sure at all," Mr. Shoup said. "And I'm not worrying, either." Mrs. Bulwer had to admit the skepticism in the hotel manager's voice was justified. Mr. Clyde Bulwer, far from having laid down his boisterous life for his country at Château-Thierry, had died in a traffic accident on his way to Hialeah in 1934, leaving Mrs. Bulwer with a twelve-year-old daughter named Alice to support. Mr. Shoup said, "If there's anybody that should be doing any worrying, Mrs. Bulwer, it's you. You owe a total of—"

"Now, look here," Mrs. Bulwer said, her voice lofty. "I told you my pension check would be along any day now. I am not accustomed to being spoken to in this way."

"Neither am I," said Mr. Shoup. "I'll have to ask you to drop into my office on your way out."

"I'm afraid I've got too much to do today," Mrs. Bulwer said, and then added, in a tone tinged with conciliation, "However, I'll try."

Mr. Shoup said coldly, "I'll be expecting you in my office."

Mrs. Bulwer sighed as she replaced her phone on the small table beside her bed. The world, in which she had come down a good deal further since Clyde's death than she cared to admit, had certainly changed. The chivalry had gone out of it. Men didn't talk that way to women in Clyde's day. Not even when their luck was running in the wrong direction. Nobody's luck, good or bad, lasted forever. You'd think even a man like Mr. Shoup would understand that.

Mrs. Bulwer sat up painfully. No point in rooting about in the past for *if's*. That didn't pay any bills or pick you any winners. The important thing was to keep going.

Mrs. Bulwer knew what she needed. And fast, too. Her toes, probing over the side of the bed for the pink satin mules, stopped dead.

Something Mr. Shoup had said, coming back all at once into her mind, had caused the throbbing ache between her eyes to lurch warningly.

Mrs. Bulwer sat quite still and tried to think through the pain. Mr. Shoup had said it was twelve-fifteen. Before she could begin to wonder why this should strike her as significant, Mrs. Bulwer had raised an arm to look at her wrist watch. It was not there. Several moments went by before she remembered she had left the watch the day before with Dave, in the cigar store on Eighty-first Street, as collateral for the twenty dollars she had borrowed from him to get into the game at Irene Vorbst's place last night.

The memory of the cards she had drawn brought a grimace of distaste to Mrs. Bulwer's once pretty face, but it did not clear up the problem of why Mr. Shoup's announcement that it was twelve-fifteen should be bothering her. She closed her eyes and tried to think hard. There were days when Mrs. Bulwer was not awakened by a jangling telephone bell until three or four in the afternoon. So it couldn't be the hour that was significant. It was the day. She had something important to do today.

"Yes," she said aloud. "But what?"

Mrs. Bulwer looked around the tiny, crowded room, hunting among its disheveled contents for some clue. Her glance skipped across the pile of clothes she had dropped, as usual, on the floor when she had undressed to go to bed. Her eyes slid past the tumbled contents of her purse, which she always emptied on the dresser before she went to bed because Clyde had always believed firmly that the best way to insure a lucky tomorrow was to take from your pockets everything they had contained yesterday. Giving your luck an airing, Clyde used to call it. Mrs. Bulwer found no clues.

"Well," said Mrs. Bulwer, many of whose most enlightening conversations were held with herself, "it'll come back to you as soon as you've had your cobweb chaser, dearie."

She stood up, waded through the pile of clothes, reached the closet, opened it, and dipped down. She swept her hand through the tangled mess of soiled underwear, small suitcases, shoe trees, wire coat hangers, and old copies of the *Turfman*. Her nervous fingers found the bottle. A small shiver of anticipation and relief shook her. She carried the bottle into the bathroom, reached for the tum-

bler, and stopped. Her spirits took a sickening drop. The bottle was
empty.

She stared in disbelief. For a long, bad moment, Mrs. Bulwer
thought she would cry. It was too much for one person to bear. On
top of all her troubles, to have taken from her the one thing she
could still count on to help stiffen her for the struggle of the new
day—it was too much. It is possible she would have cried, but the
crashing of the telephone bell saved her.

"Jessie? Is that you, dearie?"

Mrs. Bulwer, recognizing the voice of Irene Vorbst, relaxed slightly.
"Of course it's me," she said. "Who'd you think?"

"I don't know what to think any more," said Mrs. Irene Vorbst.
Since this was a fairly accurate, if unintentional, statement of Mrs.
Bulwer's opinion of her friend's mental capacities, Mrs. Bulwer did
not contradict her.

"It seems like I can't hold onto things any more," Mrs. Vorbst said.
"Jessie, dear, you wouldn't happen to know what I did with my
compact, would you? The silver one with rubies?"

"Now, Irene," Mrs. Bulwer said. "How would I know a thing like
that?"

"I'm just asking," Mrs. Vorbst said. "I remember seeing it on the
bed last night just before the game broke up. There were all those
hats and coats and bags, and I could have dropped it in the wrong
bag or something. I'd hate to lose it. It's one of Lennie's things, you
know."

Mrs. Bulwer knew. Irene Vorbst's friends were all on intimate
terms with each of the things Irene's husband, Lennie, had given her
before he went to South America in 1938, on what was supposed
to be a six-week business trip, and never returned. Most of Irene
Vorbst's friends had, at one time or another, advanced small sums
to Irene on the strength of Lennie's "things."

"Could you just take a look, Jessie?"

"All right," Mrs. Bulwer said. "Hold the phone." She went to the
bureau, poked listlessly at the jumbled mass of keys, lipsticks, old
gin-rummy scores, cigarettes, change purse, scraps of paper with forgotten tips on horses scribbled on them, and she stopped. There,
somewhat incredibly, was Irene Vorbst's ruby-studded compact. It
was only after she had returned to the phone and said, "It's here,

Irene," that it occurred to her that if she had not spoken in such haste, she might have pulled herself out of the hole. If Dave, in the cigar store on Eighty-first Street, would give her twenty dollars on her stainless-steel wrist watch, he would undoubtedly advance a hundred, or even more, on this choicest of Lennie's "things." In justice to Mrs. Bulwer, it must be recorded that her mind recoiled instantly from the shocking thought. Mrs. Bulwer might be going through an unlucky period, but she had not come to *that.* "I'll hold it, Irene," she said. "I'll give it to you next time I see you."

"What do you mean, next time?" Mrs. Vorbst said. "Aren't you coming to the game tonight?"

"I can't say," Mrs. Bulwer said, although she could. She knew precisely how much money she had, and it was not enough. People like Mrs. Jessie Bulwer and Mrs. Irene Vorbst are fond of telling each other that few things could break up a friendship such as theirs. One of those few things, known clearly to both of them, is going into a tablestakes poker game with a bank roll of five dollars and twenty-five cents. "I'd like to come," Mrs. Bulwer said. "I don't know that I can make it, though."

"What a shame," Mrs. Irene Vorbst said. "I was hoping you'd get a chance to take back a little tonight. You're entitled to a break."

"You can say that again."

"Where you going today, Jessie?"

Mrs. Bulwer, her eyes squeezed tight, wished she knew. The dreadful feeling that something important was waiting to be done sat leadenly on her brain.

"I can't say. It's personal."

"Well, look," Mrs. Vorbst said. "How's about lunch, then? I'd like to get the compact back today, Jessie."

Mrs. Bulwer hesitated. Lunch with Irene Vorbst might interfere with this unidentified chore that was hanging over her. On the other hand, Irene would be so grateful for the return of the compact she would undoubtedly pay the check.

"All right," Mrs. Bulwer said. "Same place?"

"Same place, dearie. Same time?"

"All right," Mrs. Bulwer said.

She dropped the phone into its cradle, made another futile attempt to dredge up out of her reluctant memory what it refused to yield, then began to dress hurriedly. Even though it was a warm day, Mrs. Bulwer put on her silver-fox jacket. It was as important a part of her equipment as the *Turfman*. She was perspiring slightly when she came out of the elevator. Skirting the center of the lobby, she walked along in the shadow of the row of potted palms toward the door. As she reached for the knob, Mr. Shoup blocked her path. Mrs. Bulwer jumped.

"I hope I didn't frighten you," Mr. Shoup said. "I also hope you were on your way to my office, as you promised."

"I didn't promise anything of the sort," Mrs. Bulwer said, her spirits sagging. "I told you I was in a hurry. I said I would try."

"Try this, then," Mr. Shoup said, and he pulled a ledger card from his pocket. "You owe us—"

"I don't want to hear—"

"—one hundred and forty-seven dollars and eighty-five cents," Mr. Shoup said. "Either you clear up this bill by tomorrow morning, Mrs. Bulwer, or—"

Mr. Shoup's voice stopped. His hand dropped from the door. He made a small, ironical bow, and Mrs. Bulwer, her eyes filmed by tears of helpless rage, swept past him into the street. She walked blindly, fighting the degrading threat of futile tears, and turned into the cool and welcome gloom of Henry's Tavern, near the Seventy-first Street corner.

She climbed up onto a stool near the door, moving her lumpy body with a mincing grace that was almost comic. Henry, coming up along the bar toward her, did not laugh. He nodded, put a small glass in front of her, and filled it with rye.

The drink was gone before he had drawn the chaser. He set down the glass of water and glanced inquiringly at Mrs. Bulwer. She shook her head. One was all she needed at this time of the day.

Henry replaced the bottle on the shelf and leaned back, waiting. Mrs. Bulwer waited, too. In a few moments, the healing warmth helped Mrs. Bulwer to achieve the victory she would probably have won unassisted, for as Clyde used to say, she was made of the stuff of conquerors. Still, even if the forty-five-cent shot of rye cut her five-dollar-and-twenty-five-cent bank roll down to four-eighty, it was better to be on the safe side. Mrs. Bulwer knew she was not going to cry.

She glanced at herself in the mirror behind the rows of bottles. Her face looked puffy and pale, and there was an unsightly roll of flesh beneath her button chin, but you had to expect that when you were pushing fifty. A few weeks of strict dieting and staying on the wagon, which she planned to start that very day, or tomorrow at the latest, would take care of the double chin. Besides, even if she did say it herself, she looked a lot better than half the girls she knew. Not at all displeased by what the mirror showed her, Mrs. Bulwer turned and smiled at Henry.

"Good morning," he said. "What do you say?"

"Not much," Mrs. Bulwer said. "Maybe this is my day."

"Hope so," Henry said. He pulled the punchboard out from under the bar and set it by Mrs. Bulwer. "Hit it hard," he said. "The house owes you a winner."

"You can say that again," said Mrs. Bulwer.

She stared at the board for a long time, and then she had a sudden inspiration. The brilliance of the idea left her breathless. One hundred and forty-seven dollars and eighty-five cents, Mr. Shoup had said. Well, she would show him. With a sense of mounting excitement, Mrs. Bulwer took the small metal punch and began to count: she counted one space down, four across, seven down, eight across, and five down. One forty-seven eighty-five, the unwelcome numbers Mr. Shoup had flung in her face. Mrs. Bulwer looked up at Henry, her eyes bright.

"What's up?" Henry said. "Got a system?"

"Sort of," Mrs. Bulwer said. "Here goes." She sank the punch into the hole, caught the bit of folded paper that came out of the back of the board, and opened it. "Two cherries and a pear."

Henry leaned over, and together they read the legend at the top of the punchboard.

"Nope," Henry said. "Nothing. Close, though. One cherry and two pears pays five bucks. Another one?"

Mrs. Bulwer shook her head. She opened her purse and looked down into it to hide her disappointment. She had been so certain that her inspiration, a roundabout and ingenious way of getting back at Mr. Shoup, would bring her a winner.

"No time," she said. "Got a lot to do."

She put the price of her drink on the counter and added a quar-

ter for her try at the punchboard. Well, the day was still young. And
she had four dollars and fifty-five cents left. She slid off the stool,
and then she remembered the thing she could not forget: something
was waiting to be done.

"Lose something?"

Mrs. Bulwer glanced up at Henry.

"No," she said. "Just looking for a dime."

Mrs. Bulwer walked across to the phone booth. She went in and
dialed her daughter's apartment. Mrs. Bulwer did it without enthusiasm. Since Alice had become Mrs. Saunders Grove II, four years
ago, the strained relationship between mother and daughter had
almost ceased to be even that. It wasn't that Mrs. Bulwer begrudged
her daughter the Grove money, or the apartment on Fifth Avenue,
or Alice's access to the magnificent Grove house on East Seventy-
eighth Street. As a matter of fact, Mrs. Bulwer was proud of how
handsomely Alice had done for herself. It was simply that Mrs.
Bulwer could not understand how she and Clyde had ever managed
between them to spawn a child so prissy and stiff-necked. Alice felt
that the Ten Commandments were hopelessly inadequate because
they did not include a specific injunction against poker. The knowledge that her own daughter thought of her only with disapproval
was the cross Mrs. Bulwer bore through life. She seldom saw Alice
in person, talked with her on the phone more rarely, and never
thought about her daughter unless she was particularly worried, as
she was now. It was possible that Alice, who had a mind like an adding machine and was irritatingly efficient, might know what this
thing was that Mrs. Bulwer felt she should do but couldn't identify.

Automatically, as she listened to the ringing of the phone at the
other end, Mrs. Bulwer memorized the number on the instrument in
the booth of Henry's Tavern. Numbers played a large part in Mrs.
Bulwer's life. There was no answer at Alice's apartment. Mrs. Bulwer, puzzled but impatient, hung up. She retrieved her dime and
left the booth.

"Keep punching," Henry said as she walked to the door. "You
never know when they're out on their feet, just waiting to be
pushed over."

"You can say that again," said Mrs. Bulwer, and she gave Henry a grateful smile. She waved her hand jauntily and said, "Be seeing you."

Despite the heat, she felt better as she walked back to Seventy-second Street and headed toward Broadway. As she approached the corner newsstand, she could tell from the way Alvin started to knead his hands through the coins in the enormous pocket of his canvas apron, that he had seen her coming.

"Good morning," Mrs. Bulwer said briskly, and without hesitation, she opened her purse. "I'm afraid I've been so busy I forgot to catch up on what I owe you. How much, Alvin?"

The look of suspicion washed down from Alvin's huge face and disappeared into his several chins.

"Lemme just see, now, Mrs. Bulwer." Alvin pulled a small notebook from his hip pocket. "I didn't mean to stop deliveries without giving you no notice," he said apologetically. "It's just I'm in business like anybody else, you know. I got to—" He found the right page. "Five dollars even, Mrs. Bulwer. Like I said, I got to—"

"Naturally," Mrs. Bulwer said. "Here you are, Alvin. It was very thoughtless of me to neglect— Oh, dear." Consternation, or a reasonably good facsimile of it, flooded Mrs. Bulwer's perspiring face. "Can you beat that?" she said. "I forgot to stop in the bank and cash a check. I'll tell you what," she said, as a look of distrust assumed a fixed position on Alvin's face. "Here's a dollar on account. I'll stop in at the bank and pay you the rest later in the day. Meantime, I'll take a *Turfman*, please."

Alvin took the dollar, and without a word handed her a copy of the dope sheet. Well, Mrs. Bulwer thought, as she turned and stepped off the curb, that leaves three dollars and fifty-five cents. Not a fortune, by any means, but as long as you're not in the minus column, you still have as good a chance as the next—

"Hey!"

Mrs. Bulwer, her ears filled with the screaming of brakes, leaped back to the curb. The gears of the taxi that had almost run her down protested as the driver, shifting them savagely, leaned out the window.

"Why don't you look where you're going, you old bag?"

Mrs. Bulwer, her heart thumping wildly, adjusted her hat and the silver-fox jacket.

"Why don't you watch your language?" she said, and her mind recorded automatically the number on the taxi's license plate. "I have a good mind to report you to the police."

The driver made an obscene sound and drove away. Mrs. Bulwer, her face flushed with anger, glanced quickly at the people around her. Several men were grinning. A few women were watching her with a sort of vacant yet intense curiosity. Mrs. Bulwer tucked her purse and the *Turfman* more securely under her arm, stepped off the curb again, and headed uptown.

Holding her head high, she stepped into Leroy's Coffee Pot and took her customary stool. Leroy wiped his hands on his soiled apron and came up to her.

"'Morning," he said, pulling his record book out of the apron. "Gonna knock 'em dead today?"

"I'm going to try," Mrs. Bulwer said. She liked Leroy. He wasn't like some of those other boys who wrote numbers, here today to take your money but gone tomorrow if you should happen to hit. Leroy was a solid citizen. If your number came up, you always knew where to find Leroy for the pay-off. "Tell you what," Mrs. Bulwer said. "I'll eat first."

"Right," Leroy said. "The usual?" Mrs. Bulwer nodded. She watched excitedly as he drew her coffee. She had two choices. She had the number of the phone booth in Henry's Tavern, and she had the number of the license plate on the taxi that had almost run her down. The problem was which of the two to use, and she was going to let Leroy, without knowing it, decide that. Mrs. Bulwer's "usual" consisted of coffee and a toasted English muffin. The coffee would represent the telephone number, and the English muffin would stand for the number on the taxi license plate. Whichever touched the counter first would be the number that carried her money today.

"Getting kind of warm out," Leroy said, "isn't it?"

Mrs. Bulwer nodded, her eyes fixed intently on Leroy's hands. He came toward her, carrying the coffee and the English muffin. As he stopped in front of her, the door slammed open. Mrs. Bulwer's tense body jerked, and she whipped around. A man in a polo shirt and a snap-brim felt hat had come in. When Mrs. Bulwer turned back, the coffee and the English muffin were standing in front of her. It was impossible to tell which had touched the counter first.

"How about it?" Leroy said. "Make up your mind yet?"

Mrs. Bulwer, with a baleful glance at the intruder who had destroyed her ingenious hostage to fortune, nodded.

"Two today," she said, giving Leroy both numbers. "A quarter on each."

"Hedging, eh?" Leroy made a notation. "Well, I hope one of them comes in."

"You can say that again," Mrs. Bulwer said dully. She put a dollar on the counter. Leroy took out of it the fifty cents for her bets and the twenty cents for her breakfast. "It's about time something came in for me."

Mrs. Bulwer sipped her coffee, but the usually revivifying beverage didn't taste right. She was down to two dollars and eighty-five cents, and as she bit wearily into the first solid food she had touched since the sturgeon sandwich in Irene Vorbst's place at three in the morning, Mrs. Bulwer remembered again there was something she had to do today, something so terribly important it made the English muffin taste like cotton batting in her mouth.

She put it down, took a dime from her purse, and went into the phone booth at the back. She dialed Alice's number and waited. There was no answer. Still puzzled, and now a little worried, Mrs. Bulwer left the phone booth. Alice was seldom out at this hour. Mrs. Bulwer stood there, hesitating. This was obviously one of those days when nothing went right, when the best thing to do was to go back to bed. But people like Mrs. Bulwer had to keep going.

With a heavy sigh, Mrs. Bulwer opened the *Turfman*, folded it into a manageable square, and extracted a pencil stub from the matted contents of her purse.

"So long," Leroy called after her. "See you tomorrow."

Mrs. Bulwer nodded absently and walked out into the street. She started slowly uptown, working on the dope sheet as she went. By the time she reached Dave's cigar store on Eighty-first Street, she had decided.

She looked around nervously as she entered. There were no customers. Mrs. Bulwer felt this was the first break she'd had today.

Dave's cigar store was usually crowded with fast talkers, and Mrs. Bulwer did not feel equal to fast talk at the moment. She scarcely heard Dave's friendly greeting. She was too preoccupied with the knowledge, as she put her two dollars on the cigar showcase, that she had exactly eighty-five cents.

"Running Sentinel," Mrs. Bulwer said. "In the fourth, to show."

Dave took the money.

"That watch you left with me yesterday," he said casually. "Any chance you'll be wanting it back?"

"Not today," she said. "Why?"

"Had a customer for it this morning," Dave said. "Told him I couldn't sell it, of course, but I thought I'd ask."

"The watch is not for sale," Mrs. Bulwer said icily. "I'll be picking it up tomorrow. Or," she added, because the twenty dollars she needed to reclaim it seemed, all at once, a hopeless sum, "the day after."

"Whatever you say," Dave said. He lifted the watch out of a drawer and held it up. "It's a neat little number."

Mrs. Bulwer, looking at this piece of her property that she now had no right to wear, saw with amazement that it showed twenty-five minutes to three.

"Is that right?" she said. "The time?"

Dave pulled out his own watch.

"On the button," he said. "They'll be going to the post for the fourth any minute now. Why?"

"I'm late," she said. "Be good, now."

"I'll try," Dave said. "It's no way to get rich, though."

"Ha," said Mrs. Bulwer, with faint bitterness. "You can say that again."

She hurried over to Broadway, caught a downtown bus, and arrived at the Lung Choo Chinese-American Restaurant, on Forty-ninth Street just off Seventh Avenue, with a bank roll that consisted of exactly seventy-two cents. Even though it was already after three when Mrs. Bulwer walked in, Irene Vorbst had not yet arrived. Mrs. Bulwer nodded to the Chinese girl behind the cash desk. Except for half a dozen waiters eating their lunch at the large round table in the back, the place was empty. Mrs. Bulwer walked up to the bar. The girl left the cash desk and went behind the bar.

"A Manhattan, please," Mrs. Bulwer said. "No cherry." She drank it in two swallows. The effect was immediate and beneficent. So much so, that Mrs. Bulwer was tempted to order another, but it had always been one of Clyde's contentions that when you are making a touch, however indirect, it is wise to be discreet. His widow said, "Put it on our check."

She meant Irene Vorbst's check, of course, but there was no point in being specific about these things with someone who couldn't possibly be interested in the distinction. Mrs. Bulwer left the bar, stopped in front of the slot machines near the phone booths, and hesitated again. There were three machines: one took quarters, another dimes, and the third nickels. Mrs. Bulwer, who had two quarters, one dime, two nickels, and two pennies in her change purse, decided to let fate make the choice. Without looking, she put her hand into her purse, and drew out the first coin her fingers touched. It was a dime. She put the dime into the slot machine, pulled the lever, and waited. There was a tantalizing whir of well-oiled machinery, a dull thump as the revolving drums were caught by the steel trip, and a neat click as the drums settled into place. Then silence. Mrs. Bulwer's bank roll was down to sixty-two cents. Her spirits dropped to a proportionate extent. The door opened, and she turned.

"Hi, dearie," Mrs. Bulwer said, as she met Irene Vorbst at their usual booth. "You were late, so I penalized you by having a Manhattan while I waited. I hope you don't mind?"

"Of course not," said Irene, a reply that caused Mrs. Bulwer to look at her friend sharply. Irene, even though generous enough when she had it, was inclined to accompany the bits and pieces she relinquished with elaborate protests of imminent insolvency. It was not like her to overlook the point of Mrs. Bulwer's carefully phrased remark, which made it clear that Irene would have to pay for the drink. Mrs. Vorbst's next statement was even less like her. "I need a drink myself," she said in her nasal voice. "Would you like another?"

"Just to keep you company," Mrs. Bulwer said carelessly. "Thanks."

She watched Mrs. Vorbst furtively while the drinks came. Irene was clearly upset. Her face looked harried. She was so preoccupied she even neglected to enter her customary arguments about the food.

"Listen," Mrs. Bulwer said when the second drink had disappeared. "You look worried, dearie. Is anything wrong?"

"I don't know yet," Mrs. Vorbst said through her pinched scowl. "You remember that Mr. Serena at the game last night?"

Mrs. Bulwer, lifting a forkful of *moo goo gai pan* to her mouth, paused and closed her eyes. It was difficult, especially when you were losing, to remember all the people you played with. After a moment of concentration, a picture of Mr. Serena came into Mrs. Bulwer's mind. A small man of about fifty, with spats and black hair that looked oiled. One of the girls had brought him, although she couldn't remember which one.

"Yes," she said. "The girls called him Vic, I think. What about him?"

"I don't know," Mrs. Vorbst said. "Thyra brought him, I think, but I haven't been able to get Thyra on the phone to check. Anyway, he called me up a little while ago, and he said he'd left his wallet at my place last night. Made of alligator, he said it was, with his initials on it in gold and six hundred dollars in it, he said, and he asked me to look for it. I looked all over the place, but I couldn't find it, and when I came back on the phone and told him it wasn't there, you know what he said?"

"No," Mrs. Bulwer said. "What?"

"He said I shouldn't pull any of that funny stuff on him," Mrs. Vorbst said. "He said he'd be coming around to the game later tonight, and either I'd have his wallet with the six hundred dollars waiting for him, or else."

Mrs. Bulwer, staring at her friend with horror, was reminded that Mr. Shoup had used almost precisely the same words to her in the lobby of the Hereford Arms. What was happening to the world? It was getting so that an honest woman couldn't go through a day without being insulted by half the riffraff in town.

"Why, the dirty little—" The appropriate noun refused to take shape on Mrs. Bulwer's lips. She reached across and patted her friend's hand on the table. "I hope you told him where to get off."

"How could I?" Mrs. Vorbst said irritably. "He hung up. Besides, how do I know who he is? Or what his connections are? You know

what a thing like that can lead to." Mrs. Bulwer knew, but Irene
Vorbst didn't give her a chance to say so. Irene glanced at her wrist
watch, and then she put her napkin on the table and stood up. "I'm
going over to Thyra's place to wait for her. If she's the one that
brought him, she might be able to talk to him or advise me. I'm
scared of this thing, and I don't mind admitting it." She fished in
her purse, pulled out a bill, and said hopefully, "Would you like to
come over with me?"

"I'd love to," Mrs. Bulwer said, and she meant it, but she was
aware, even through the pleasant insulation of two Manhattans, that
time was running out. "I can't, though. There's something I've got
to do right away."

"Well, I'll call you and tell you what happens," Mrs. Vorbst said.
"If you don't get to the game, I mean." She put the bill on the table. "Pay this for me, dearie, will you? I've got to run."

She did, and Mrs. Bulwer, watching her friend's retreating figure,
began to compute feverishly the price of the three Manhattans and
the food in the hope that the total plus a tip, when taken out of
Irene's five-dollar bill, would leave her with a small windfall. She was
ashamed of the way her heart was thumping as she signaled for the
check. The check came to four dollars and fifty-five cents. The five-
dollar bill was just barely adequate.

Mrs. Bulwer heaved another of her weary sighs as she struggled to
her feet. There she was, in the middle of the afternoon on Forty-
ninth Street, with sixty-two cents in her purse. As she arranged the
silver-fox jacket about her ample figure, a thought struck Mrs. Bulwer: Irene had forgotten to ask for the ruby-studded compact.

Breathing heavily, Mrs. Bulwer walked to the phone booths in the
back, wedged herself into one, and dialed her daughter's number.
Again there was no answer. Mrs. Bulwer was genuinely worried.
It was not like her to make so many attempts to reach Alice on the
phone, but it was even more unlike Alice not to be home. Mrs. Bulwer put the dime back into the slot, started to dial another number,
then stopped. In places where you were not welcome, she had
learned, it was unwise to give advance notice of your coming.

Mrs. Bulwer left the restaurant, dragged her weary body over to
Fifth Avenue, and took the bus to Seventy-eighth Street. When

she reached the imposing house with the black wrought-iron gate, Mrs. Bulwer had forty-seven cents in her change purse, and her feet hurt so badly she winced as she climbed the stone steps. She pulled her hat down a little over her forehead, drew a deep breath, and rang the bell.

"Yes, madam?"

The butler's tone could have been merely impersonal, but there was no mistaking the glance that raked her from head to foot. Happily, Mrs. Bulwer was indifferent to butlers.

"Mrs. Grove, please," Mrs. Bulwer said. "Mrs. Saunders Grove."

"Who wishes to see her, madam?"

"Mrs. Clyde Bulwer. Her daughter-in-law's mother."

The butler hesitated, quite obviously torn between disbelief and duty, but the decision was taken out of his hands.

"Mother," a startled voice said behind him. "For heaven's sake."

The butler stepped aside and disappeared discreetly. Mrs. Bulwer stepped into a high-ceilinged hallway, gleaming with crystal and polished mahogany, to face her daughter.

"Alice," she said, "is anything wrong?"

"Wrong?" Alice said. "No, of course not. Why?"

"I've been trying to get you on the phone at your apartment all day, and there was no answer, so finally I—" Mrs. Bulwer stopped. Terror, cutting through the cadged Manhattans and the attempt to disregard the obvious fact her daughter did not find her presence welcome, hit Mrs. Bulwer with the impact of a physical blow. "Listen," she said. "Is there anything wrong with Sandy?"

"Sandy?" Alice said. "Of course not."

"Where is he?"

"Why," Alice said, and she threw a glance across her shoulder. "Why, he's upstairs, having his nap."

"What's he doing having his nap here?" Mrs. Bulwer demanded. "Instead of home, where he belongs?"

"Why," Alice said again. "Why," she said slowly and then, more quickly, "Mrs. Grove asked me to bring him over for lunch, so I did, and I thought, instead of taking him home and getting him overtired, I'd let him have his nap here before Nettie takes him to the park."

"You sure he's all right?"

"Of course he's all right," Alice said, her face creasing with quick annoyance. "I ought to know if my own son is all right or not. You don't have any right to imply—"

"I have as much right as some others I could mention," Mrs. Bulwer said with spirit. "I happen to be his grandmother."

"So you are."

Mrs. Bulwer and Alice turned toward the new voice. Mrs. Saunders Grove, whom Mrs. Bulwer had seen only three or four times since the wedding at which Alice had become Mrs. Saunders Grove II, was coming down the stairs.

"It's so good to see you again," Mrs. Grove said, as she reached the bottom of the stairs. "You mustn't keep your mother in the hall, dear," she said to Alice. "Won't you join me for tea, Mrs. Bulwer?"

"Thanks, but I can't," said Mrs. Bulwer. The sincerity in the invitation struck her as approximately equal to that in a bookie's condolences to a heavy loser. "I'm in a hurry," Mrs. Bulwer said. "It was just I was worried something might be wrong with Sandy, so I thought I'd drop in. Hope you don't mind."

"Mind?" Mrs. Grove said. "My dear, I'm delighted. Sandy is quite all right, I assure you."

"I don't suppose I could see him?" Mrs. Bulwer said. "Just for a second?"

"Not while he's asleep, I imagine," Mrs. Grove said. "However, that's a question for his mother to decide, I should think, don't you, Alice?"

Alice looked uncomfortably from her mother to her mother-in-law and then back to her mother.

"Well," she said, "I—"

"You don't have to bother," Mrs. Bulwer said. "As long as I know he's all right, I don't want to wake him up." With a gesture of exaggerated elegance, she pulled the silver-fox jacket about her. "Sorry to bother you," Mrs. Bulwer said. "I'll be on my way."

"Mother," Alice said. "Wait." She looked again at her mother-in-law. Mrs. Grove, with a slight smile and an even slighter inclination of her head, disappeared into what Mrs. Bulwer was now convinced was the drawing room. "Mother," Alice said in a low voice, "do you need money?"

Mrs. Bulwer stared at her daughter. You could tell, just by looking

at her right now, you could tell that Alice assumed the only reason
Mrs. Bulwer had come here was because she wanted money. This
did not make Mrs. Bulwer angry. It puzzled her. She just couldn't
get over it, and that was a fact.

"Of course I don't need money," Mrs. Bulwer said. "What ever
put that idea into your head, dearie?"

"Well," Alice said uncomfortably. "I just thought—" She gave her
mother a searching glance. It did something to her face, which was
quite pretty, really, if she'd only remember to let herself go a little
instead of always worrying about appearances and things. Alice's face
relaxed a little. "I don't have much with me," Alice said, dropping
her voice even lower. "If you're strapped, though, I could let you
have—"

"Now, now," Mrs. Bulwer said, and she smiled as she patted her
daughter's cheek. "Don't you be worrying about me. You just worry
about that Saunders Grove III. He's the only grandchild I've got,
you know." She pulled open the door. "Well, I've got to be running
along."

"Mother," Alice said. Mrs. Bulwer turned back. "Maybe some day
next week," Alice said, "when things ease up a little, maybe you
could come over to the apartment during the day and spend an hour
or so with him?"

"Why, I'd love that, dearie," Mrs. Bulwer said. "You ring me when
those things, whatever they are, ease up a little."

"Where are you?" Alice said. "At the Stafford?"

"No," Mrs. Bulwer said. "I'm at the Hereford Arms." The words,
evoking a sudden picture of Mr. Shoup, caused Mrs. Bulwer to stop
and turn again. "I'll tell you what, dearie," she said, forcing another smile. "Maybe you'd better let me ring you. You know how
I am," she said. "In and out all the time."

She walked away from the house toward Lexington Avenue, without hesitation. Whatever it was that had to be done today would
have to wait. At least for a while, anyway. She was so preoccupied
with the immediate problem that, when she bought a token at
the change booth and dropped it into the subway turnstile, it did
not occur to Mrs. Bulwer to note that she was down to thirty-two
cents. For the first time that day her mind was not on her financial

problems. Mrs. Bulwer's mind was in the brokerage offices of Grove, Cravath, Torrington, and Grove, on Forty-second Street. Her exhausted body was there soon after, and apparently it made a far from favorable impression on the receptionist, who said with considerable coolness that she would see if Mr. Grove was in to his mother-in-law. He was. Saunders Grove II came out into the reception room at once to fetch her.

"Jessie," he said, taking both her hands. "What a pleasant surprise. Come in."

His cheery young voice filled Mrs. Bulwer with reassurance. She liked her son-in-law, and she suspected he liked her, too, even though they saw each other only rarely. Mrs. Bulwer always had the feeling, when she was with Saunders Grove II, that she and he would have seen a good deal of each other if it had not been for his mother and for Alice. Mrs. Bulwer did not hold that against him, however. A man's loyalty belonged to his wife and to his mother, and the fact that Saunders Grove II understood that made Mrs. Bulwer like him even better. The best thing about him, though, was her conviction that Clyde would have liked him, too.

"Take that one," Saunders Grove II said, pushing Mrs. Bulwer gently into the huge chair beside the desk in his private office. "And now suppose you tell me why I haven't seen you for so long."

"Oh, you know," Mrs. Bulwer said. "I've been pretty busy."

"Doing all right?"

Mrs. Bulwer gave her son-in-law a quick glance. He was bent down, twisting a knob on the side of his desk.

"Why," Mrs. Bulwer said, "I'm doing fine."

"Glad to hear it," Saunders Grove II said. He straightened up, and the side of his desk slid open, revealing a small bar. "I've had a rugged day, and I need something," he said. "Join me, Jessie?"

Mrs. Bulwer gave him another quick glance. She had never known her son-in-law to drink before sundown. He was carefully measuring whisky into a glass.

"I don't mind if I do," Mrs. Bulwer said. "Thanks, dearie."

He gave her the glass and watched his hands intently while he poured his own drink. He was concentrating so hard he did not seem to notice how quickly Mrs. Bulwer emptied her glass. In fact, he appeared to have forgotten he had given it to her, because when his own drink was ready, he reached over absently, retrieved her glass, and refilled it.

"There's nothing like a shot," he said, leaning back, "to take the kinks out of the afternoon."

"You can say that again," said Mrs. Bulwer. The hastily gulped first drink, reviving the fire kindled by the shot in Henry's Tavern and fed by the two Manhattans in the Lung Choo Chinese-American Restaurant, enabled her to relax and sip her second drink slowly. "I came to find out something," Mrs. Bulwer said. "I'd like a straight answer. Is there anything wrong with Sandy?"

"Good Lord," Saunders Grove II said. "What makes you ask that?"

Mrs. Bulwer told him.

"I don't care that they were pretty obviously trying to get me out of the house," she said. "I don't like to go where I'm not wanted, and I know I'm not wanted in your mother's house. Your mother is one kind of woman, and I'm another kind," Mrs. Bulwer said. "I don't hold it against her that she disapproves of me, and I don't suppose she'd care if she knew I disapprove of her." Mrs. Bulwer finished her second drink and put the empty glass on her son-in-law's desk. He reached for the bottle and refilled her glass. "All I'm interested in is one thing," she said. "Is Sandy all right?"

"So far as I know," he said, "Sandy has never been better."

"Then they were just trying to get me out of the house?" Mrs. Bulwer said. "It isn't that something is wrong with Sandy and they don't want me to know it?"

"They were just trying to get you out of the house," Saunders Grove II said quietly. "There is absolutely nothing wrong with Sandy."

"Thanks," Mrs. Bulwer said. "That's all I wanted to know."

She stood up.

"What's your hurry?" her son-in-law said. "Stay a while and talk."

"I can't," Mrs. Bulwer said. "Too much to do."

"Well, don't waste good liquor," her son-in-law said. "You haven't finished your drink."

Mrs. Bulwer glanced at her glass with the surprise of a child discovering an overlooked present in the heel of a Christmas stocking.

"Why, that's a fact," she said, picking it up. "Well, happy days."

"Happy days," Saunders Grove II said. He set down his own glass and pulled out his wallet. "Jessie, I wonder if I could ask you to do me a favor?"

"Anything at all."

"I'm so busy I don't get a chance to place a bet any more," he said. He pulled three twenty-dollar bills from the wallet. "How about picking a good horse tomorrow and putting this on him for me?"

For a moment, Mrs. Bulwer had the same difficulty she had experienced earlier in the day when Mr. Shoup had trapped her in the lobby of the Hereford Arms. Her eyes filmed, but only for a moment.

"You know," she said, "I once knew a man like you. He was Alice's father." She reached over and touched his shoulder lightly. "Save your money," Mrs. Bulwer said. "It's a sucker's game, and maybe Alice and your mother are right. One in the family is enough."

It was not until she got to the street, and was able to see the clock over Grand Central, that Mrs. Bulwer regretted the fact her wrist watch was in the possession of Dave in the cigar store on Eighty-first Street. It was five minutes after five, and she had to get all the way back to Seventy-eighth and Fifth Avenue before five-thirty.

Nettie, the nurse, was standing at the curb with the stroller, waiting for the lights to change, when Mrs. Bulwer alighted from the bus. She ran up the street, her heart hammering and her feet pulsing with pain at each step. Nettie, seeing Mrs. Bulwer coming, looked nervously across her shoulder into the park, and then she turned to glance even more nervously down Seventy-eighth Street, toward the imposing house with the black wrought-iron gate. Nettie did not want Alice, for whom she worked, or Mrs. Saunders Grove, who had interviewed her for the job, to know that every afternoon, when she took Sandy to the park for an hour after his nap, Mrs. Bulwer came along to sit on a bench and play with the little boy.

"I'm sorry," she said to Mrs. Bulwer. "I can't stop. They said I have to be back in the house with him at five-thirty sharp today." Nettie took a firmer grip on the handle of the stroller. "It's not my fault you're late."

"I know," Mrs. Bulwer said, trying to catch her breath, smile at the little boy who was smiling up at her from the stroller, wipe the perspiration from her face, and placate Nettie. "I got stuck downtown," she gasped. "I came as fast as I could."

"Well, I'm sorry," Nettie said. "I got my orders."

"Wait," Mrs. Bulwer said. "Only a minute."

She knelt on the sidewalk and took Sandy's hands. The boy gurgled with delight, worked his hands free, reached over, and stroked his grandmother's perspiring face.

"Mrs. Bulwer," Nettie said sharply. "I'm sorry. Tomorrow, maybe, but not now. I can't be late. Mrs. Grove, the old one, she warned me very strict. The party begins—"

Mrs. Bulwer rose from her knees as though she had been kicked.

"What party?" Nettie, looking suddenly miserable, put her hand over her mouth. "What party?" Mrs. Bulwer asked again, but she did not have to wait for an answer. She knew. In a quick burst, she remembered. It was the thing that had been hanging over her all day, the nameless chore that had been drilling in her mind from the time Mr. Shoup and his jangling telephone bell had awakened her. The realization she had forgotten what it would never have occurred to her she could possibly forget froze Mrs. Bulwer with a fear she had never before experienced. Was her mind actually going? If after weeks of struggling to prepare for it, she could forget that today was Sandy's second birthday, what confidence could she possibly have in herself for tomorrow, and the day after, and the rest of her life? Maybe she was really slipping. Maybe she— "Listen," Mrs. Bulwer said. There was no time for fear. She seized Nettie's wrist. "Listen," she said angrily, "what's all this about a party? The way I understood it, the way it's been arranged for weeks, we were to meet at my daughter's apartment, just me and Mr. Grove and—"

Nettie, now frightened as well as miserable, wrenched her wrist free.

"They changed it," she said. "Mrs. Grove changed it. The old woman. It's a party. In the big house. With a lot of children, and their mothers. It's for six o'clock. I wasn't supposed to say—"

"All right," Mrs. Bulwer said. No wonder they had been upset by her unexpected visit. No wonder they had been anxious to get her out of the house. "You didn't say. Forget you saw me." She spoke as calmly as she could. So they were afraid to let their fancy friends see Sandy's grandmother, were they? She'd show them. "You better get over to the house," Mrs. Bulwer said. She dipped down, kissed the little boy, and let him hold her tight for a long moment. Then she stood up. "Happy birthday, Sandy," Mrs. Bulwer said, and to Nettie, "The light's with you. Better hurry."

Nettie nodded quickly and pushed the stroller from the curb. Mrs. Bulwer started uptown, walking as quickly as her aching feet would allow. She didn't have any time to spare, but if she moved fast, she'd have enough. She was slow to anger, an emotion that had always struck Mrs. Bulwer as being a trifle pointless, but as Clyde used to say, when Jessie gets ready to pitch, don't bother trying to catch; just take to the hills. The recollection caused Mrs. Bulwer to smile grimly, and then as she climbed into the Seventy-ninth Street crosstown bus and dropped her thirteen-cent fare into the box, she thought of something else, and the grim smile settled more deeply into the lines of her puffy face. She would not only show Mrs. Saunders Grove the sort of stuff Clyde Bulwer's widow was made of. She would give the demonstration in the very center of that fancy drawing room she had never yet been allowed to set foot in.

"That Running Sentinel," she said to Dave as she entered the cigar store, "how did he make out?"

"Nobody knows," Dave said. "I hear they got searching parties out for him. He hasn't come in yet. Those ten-to-one shots are sucker bait."

"You can say that again," said Mrs. Bulwer. "Dave, I've got a little business for you, and I'm in a hurry."

"Want to buy back the watch?"

"Not yet," Mrs. Bulwer said. "I'm still on the other end." She took off her silver-fox jacket and put it on the cigar counter. "How much?"

Dave kneaded his hands expertly through the fur, turned it over, noted the frayed lining, and pursed his lips.

"Forty dollars."

Mrs. Bulwer's perspiring face sagged. "Dave, have a heart," she said. "It cost two hundred and eighty when it was new."

"Sure," Dave said. "But when was it new?"

Mrs. Bulwer chewed her lower lip and thought fast. She was too old

a hand at these transactions not to know the precise value of hag-
gling. In a half hour, she might bring Dave up to forty-five or fifty,
but that was still almost a hundred dollars less than she needed, and
she couldn't afford to waste any more of the precious half hour. Six
o'clock was her deadline, and she had a lot of ground to cover before
then. With a sigh that was almost a shudder, Mrs. Bulwer opened
her purse.

"All right," she said, "I'll take the forty, and I've got something
else you'll be interested in, but I warn you in advance, I want a hundred on it or nothing." Mrs. Bulwer's fingers probed in the jumbled
contents of her purse for the choicest of all Lennie's "things." Irene
Vorbst would be sore when Mrs. Bulwer told her what she had done,
but it wasn't as though Mrs. Bulwer were selling the ruby-studded
compact in order to put the money on a horse or pay her hotel bill.
This was for something more important. This was for something
even Irene Vorbst would understand. If she didn't, well, as soon as
her luck changed, Mrs. Bulwer would get the compact back from
Dave and return it to Irene. It was just a loan, really. "It's a compact,"
she said. "It's got—"

Mrs. Bulwer's voice stopped as though it had been slammed
against a wall. Her fingers stopped, too, and then they began to
work frantically through the mess of keys and matches and bits of
paper.

"What's the matter?" Dave said. "Lose it?"

Mrs. Bulwer's probing fingers lay limp in her purse.

"I guess—" She closed her eyes and forced herself to think, to re-
trace her movements during the past hours. The first time she had
seen the silver compact that day was in her hotel room, when Irene
had called and asked her to look and see if she had it. Then she had
put it in her— Or had she? Mrs. Bulwer opened her eyes. "Dave,"
she said, turning to the door, "I'll have to—"

"How about the forty on this?"

He still held the silver-fox jacket.

"Yes, sure." Mrs. Bulwer snatched the money and crammed it into
her purse. "Thanks," she said. "I'll be right back."

With part of the proceeds from the loan on the jacket, she took a
taxi to the Hereford Arms.

"Wait for me," she told the driver. "I won't be long. I want to go right back to that cigar store on Eighty-first Street."

The lobby of the Hereford Arms was deserted. Mrs. Bulwer ran from the elevator to her room, and flung open the door. Her knees seemed to melt with relief. The first thing she saw was the compact, gleaming on the dresser.

Running forward to snatch the compact, she stumbled and lost her balance. She clutched at the dresser. The flimsy piece of furniture teetered, swung crazily to one side, and just before it righted itself, everything on it slid to the floor. Mrs. Bulwer, dipping down to pick up the compact, stopped. Lying beside it, in a nest of combs, hair brushes, perfume bottles, curlers, and face tissue, was an object she had never seen before.

Mrs. Bulwer picked it up and stared at it. Not with astonishment. The fact it was there was no more astonishing than the fact the compact had been there in the morning; all sorts of things got mixed up at the games in Irene Vorbst's place. Mrs. Bulwer stared at the object with awe. It was one thing to have the tide of your fortunes turn. It was an entirely different thing to have it turn with the force of a tidal wave.

Mrs. Bulwer, her face creased by a frown, stood in the center of the untidy hotel room and she closed her eyes. For once, this device failed her. She didn't know what to do. Desperately she ransacked her mental file of Clyde's aphorisms, but she could not find an appropriate one. Quite obviously, what was happening to her now for the first time in her life had never happened to Clyde, either. The phone rang. Slowly, cautiously, she picked it up.

It was the girl at the switchboard downstairs. "You got a taxi waiting?"

"Yes."

"Wants to know are you coming down."

"Why," Mrs. Bulwer said in a dazed voice, and then her brain seemed to thaw out, the way it did right after she swallowed her cobweb chaser when she got out of bed. "Yes," Mrs. Bulwer said. "I'm coming right down."

Mrs. Bulwer walked out of her room.

"Take me to Trilling's," she told the driver. "Fifth Avenue and Forty-seventh."

"Thought you wanted to go back to that cigar store on Eighty-first?"

"I've changed my mind," Mrs. Bulwer said. "Step on it, please. They close at six."

All the way downtown, she tried to keep the gears of her mind from meshing. She wanted to be able to act on her decision before she was deflected by conscience, or habit, or memory. She didn't want to lose her nerve.

"Here we are," the taxi driver said. "Trilling's."

A bell started to ring as Mrs. Bulwer came into the store. A man in a dark coat, with a white flower in his lapel, stepped into her path.

"I'm sorry, madam," he said. "We're closing for the day."

"I won't be long," Mrs. Bulwer said. "There's something I've got to pick up."

She hurried down the aisles of Teddy bears and Raggedy Ann dolls and clay-modeling sets to the electrical-toys section. A girl in a black dress was yawning luxuriously. Her mouth closed with a snap when she saw Mrs. Bulwer.

"Yes?" she said, politely. "Can I help you, madam?"

"Electric trains," Mrs. Bulwer said. "The big set. I picked it out a few weeks ago. I asked you to hold it."

"What name, please?" Mrs. Bulwer told her. The girl walked away, and the man in the dark coat followed her. The girl came back in a couple of minutes. "Yes," the girl said. "We still have them. Charge or cash?"

"Cash," Mrs. Bulwer said. "I want to take them with me."

"They're awfully heavy, madam."

"That's all right," Mrs. Bulwer said. "I want to take them with me."

The girl started to write the sales check. The man in the dark coat came out of the back, carrying a large, heavy box. He put it down on the counter with obvious relief.

"I'm afraid you'll need some help with this," he said. "Would you like me to get you a boy?"

Mrs. Bulwer had set her purse on the counter. She had taken from it the alligator wallet, with the gold initials V.S., that she had found on the floor of her hotel room. She was counting the crisp bills carefully. Mr. Victor Serena, who had talked so nastily to Irene Vorbst on the telephone, may not have been a gentleman, but he was not a liar, either. He had said six hundred dollars. The wallet contained six hundred and ten. Mrs. Bulwer tore her glance from the money. She looked up at the man in the dark coat.

"What?" she said, and then, "Oh, yes. Yes, thanks. If you'll just have a boy put the box in a taxi for me, I'll be all right."

The man nodded and walked away. As she pulled two of Mr. Victor Serena's hundred-dollar bills from the wallet, Mrs. Bulwer's hand shook slightly. She had never stolen anything in her life. No matter what Alice or Mrs. Saunders Grove might think, Mrs. Bulwer knew she was as good as they were. She didn't harm anybody. All she asked was to be left alone. She was at peace with herself. Anyway, she always had been, up to now.

"That's one forty-two fifty," the sales girl said.

She reached for the money. Mrs. Bulwer's hand, holding out the crisp bills, shook with sudden indecision. She didn't really have to do this. The forty Dave had given her on the silver-fox jacket, plus the hundred she was certain he would have given her on Irene Vorbst's compact, would have been almost adequate. A few words of explanation to Dave would have brought him up another five or even ten, enough to cover. Dave was a good egg. Dave would have understood, just as Mrs. Bulwer was certain Irene Vorbst would have.

"Oh, dear," the sales girl said. "I forgot the tax."

She bent back over her order book. Mrs. Bulwer's hand, holding Mr. Victor Serena's money, dropped to her side. The man in the dark coat came back, followed by a boy.

"I'll go get you a cab," the man said. "The boy will carry the package out for you."

Mrs. Bulwer nodded helplessly. In her moment of need, she waited for some reassuring word from Clyde to come back to her. Clyde would know this was something she couldn't beg people like Dave to help her with. Clyde would be the first to appreciate the fact that she couldn't let Mrs. Saunders Grove and Alice and their fancy friends poison the mind of a little boy against his grandmother. Yes, and against the grandfather he had never seen, as well. Clyde would understand the importance of not allowing Sandy to be told later, when he was no longer a little boy, that his grandmother had not been able to get to his second birthday party, or even send him a present, because she was an irresponsible old drunk and worse. Clyde would see clearly that if she had to walk into Mrs. Saunders Grove's drawing room with the knowledge the triumph had been bought with a handout, there was no point in walking in at all.

Mrs. Bulwer pleaded silently with the memory that had never failed her. This was something she had to do on her own. Even if doing it that way meant she would be making herself something less in Clyde's eyes than, for fourteen years, she had tried to be. Even if doing it that way made her a thief.

The reassuring word did not come. Heavily, aware she was making a break with all of the past she had treasured for so long, Mrs. Bulwer raised her hand and put Mr. Victor Serena's money on the counter.

"Let me see now," the sales girl said. "That's one forty-two fifty, plus four twenty-eight tax, makes it—" She drew a line on the sales slip and added the figures. "Makes it a total of one forty-six seventy-eight."

Mrs. Bulwer, staring dully at the sales slip, felt a sharp, familiar sensation in the back of her mind. She leaned forward, holding her breath, and stared harder. It was something about the last three figures on the sales check. Mrs. Bulwer closed her eyes.

"I beg your pardon," the sales girl said. "Is anything wrong?"

"No, no, of course not," Mrs. Bulwer said, her voice rising with excitement. "I just happened to remember something," she said, opening her eyes. Six-seven-eight, the last three figures on the sales check, was the address of the Brookley, Irene's place. And the bunch would be gathering there right now, this very minute, for the game. It was the sort of omen that couldn't be overlooked or attributed to dumb luck. That kind of luck, Clyde had believed, doesn't exist. You make your own luck, Clyde used to say, by reading your hole card right and using your brains to figure the percentages. Always provided, he used to add through his wonderful grin, you never forget that the best hole card in the world is your own hunch. "I just remembered I have another engagement and I won't be able to take this with me," Mrs. Bulwer said. The voice out of the past had not failed her, after all. "I wonder if you could have the boy take it up to this address on Seventy-eighth Street for me," she said. "I'll pay extra, of course. It's important that it get there right away."

"I'm sure we could do that, madam."

"Thanks a lot," Mrs. Bulwer said happily. There was no doubt this was her night. She could feel it in her bones. By the time Mr. Serena showed up at Irene's place at nine or ten, Mrs. Bulwer knew, she'd be so far ahead of the game she'd be able to replace what she had taken out of the wallet for Sandy's present and also tell Mr. Serena, since Irene was obviously too dumb or timid to say it herself, that people of his type were not wanted in a friendly game, and he could just take his hat along with his wallet and go someplace else. Mrs. Bulwer said, "I'd like to put a card in with it, please."

"Of course," the sales girl said. "Here you are, madam."

Mrs. Bulwer took the pen and the small square of pasteboard. "Happy birthday to Sandy," she wrote, "from Grandma in the park." She looked at the card for a long moment, and then with a small, delicious shiver of loyalty, she added, "and from Grandpa far away."

She looked up and handed the card to the sales girl.

"It's for my grandson," Mrs. Bulwer said proudly. "His second birthday, you know."

"I'd say he's a very lucky little boy," the sales girl said, "to have a grandmother like you."

Mrs. Bulwer, reaching up to adjust the silver-fox jacket that was not there, laughed: a short, throaty peal of confidence and triumph, a sound she had not uttered for so long she had almost forgotten how much Clyde used to love to hear it.

"You can say that again," Mrs. Bulwer said.

Home by Midnight

When the bus stopped in Bushkill at nine o'clock, it had begun to get quite dark. The driver, a tough-looking young man with a pleasant face and closely-cropped yellow hair, switched on the ceiling lights. No passengers got out, but seven or eight new ones got in and went stumbling along the narrow aisle until they succeeded in settling themselves. They all asked the same question as they climbed in, and they all got the same answer from the driver.

"Yes, ma'am," he said in his bored but sharp voice. "Yes, sir. Last bus going through. Be in New York by eleven o'clock."

When everybody was settled, the driver waved his hand to the man in the station and swung the bus out into the main street. In a few minutes they had left the town far behind and were drumming along steadily in the darkness. The passengers coughed and twitched, or closed their eyes and tried to sleep, or rustled newspapers and magazines. It was a dark murky night, and the countryside was flat and unpleasant. There was nothing to see, but several passengers stared out glumly at the monotonous landscape. There was a little self-conscious whispering every now and then, but nobody spoke aloud.

About a half-hour out of Bushkill the bus began to give off a series of strange knocking sounds at intervals that grew closer and closer until the noise became a steady rattle, like that made by drawing a pencil quickly along the top of a picket fence. Suddenly the bus lurched sharply, as though it had received a terrific kick. It skidded to the side of the road and the tires began to screech as the driver worked desperately over the steering wheel and the brakes. The passengers were thrown forward onto the edges of their seats and several women had their mouths open, as though they were screaming, but the noise of the tires drowned out everything else. In a moment the noises stopped and the bus shuddered to a halt at the side of the road. The screams stopped abruptly. Every pocket-watch in the bus was pulled out and every arm that bore a wrist-watch was raised. It was exactly 9:38.

"Now nobody please get excited," the driver said, getting up quickly. His voice had lost its undercurrent of boredom. "Something wrong with the motor, I guess. Keep your seats and please don't get excited."

At once everybody in the bus became excited and tried to get up. The driver opened the door and jumped out onto the road. A small fat man near the front said, "What the hell?" in a surprised voice and got out after him. The women passengers began to chatter noisily and several men, who succeeded in squeezing their way into the aisle, followed the fat man out of the bus. They gathered around the driver as he lifted the hood of the motor and peered into it with a flashlight. He held the light with one hand and poked about with the other, turning knobs, tracing slender feed pipes with his fingertips, wetting his forefinger in his mouth and touching it to a twisted mass of wires. Occasionally an automobile went shooting by, disappearing to the tune of a wailing note, like a gong that is struck and dies away, or the sound of a shell in a war movie. The stretch of road was very dark. A tall man behind the driver laughed and shivered slightly.

"My God," he said, "I hope we don't have to stay here all night."

The driver straightened up irritably and pushed his hat to the back of his head.

"For crying out loud," he said, "I can't work if you guys keep hanging over my—" He stopped and bit his lip. "I mean," he said more calmly, "if you'll please step back I'll be able to—"

"What do you want," the tall man who had spoken first asked with a grin, "more light or more air?" He laughed unpleasantly as he moved back a few feet and the others followed him. "Temperamental, these guys, ain't they?" he said, looking at the others.

Two or three of the passengers smiled awkwardly. The rest merely looked worried. The driver continued to work over the motor, but it was soon plain that he was getting nowhere.

At a quarter to ten almost every passenger was outside, pacing up and down on the road, and worrying out loud. Several of them, like the man who had spoken to the driver first, were sarcastic; but most of them, especially the women, were worried. How were they going to get home?

By ten o'clock it was clear that the driver didn't know what was wrong and his efforts were hopeless. The tall man who had spoken first walked forward and tapped the driver on the shoulder.

"Pardon me," he said sarcastically, "but what are the chances of getting to New York tonight?"

The driver straightened up quickly and snapped, "Can't you see I'm trying to—?" He stopped and wiped his mouth with the back of his hand. "I don't know," he said simply.

"Doesn't the company make provision for such emergencies?" the man continued bitingly. "It seems to me that when you carry thirty people in a bus and you promise to get them to a certain place by a certain time you ought to—"

"I don't make the rules, Mister," the driver said quietly. Now that he had decided to face the fact that he didn't know what was wrong with the bus, he had himself under control again. "I just drive the bus. If I can—"

"I've got to be in New York tonight," the tall man said hotly. "I bought a ticket with the understanding that I would—"

"No sense in getting excited about it," the driver said calmly. He said it as though it pleased him very much to talk to so excited a man. "That isn't going to get you to New York, Mister."

The driver walked out into the road with his flashlight. He stood there, swinging the beam around in a wide arc on the road until an approaching car was close. Then he jumped out of the way quickly. He did it several times and finally one car stopped. There were four people in it. The bus driver held the light on his face and his uniform for identification purposes, and then walked over and spoke to the driver of the car. The bus passengers, gathered on the road, could hear him plainly.

"My bus broke down with a load of passengers," he said, "and I wonder if you'd be good enough to take a message into the next town for me?"

"Sure," the man in the car said.

"Thanks," the bus driver said. He unpinned his shield from his shirt and handed it to the man in the car. "The next town is Port Jervis. If you'll just give that to the man in the bus station and tell him where you saw me, they'll send out another bus for us."

The driver walked back to the group of passengers.

"There's nothing to worry about, folks," he said. The ring of authority was back in his voice. "That message'll be in Port Jervis in less than a half hour and they'll have a bus started out to pick us up a few minutes after that."

"Oh, gee," a woman said, looking at her watch. "It's almost tenthirty now already. That means we won't get picked up till after eleven, the earliest. That means, my God, we won't get to New York till after one in the morning."

A murmur spread through the group of passengers and worked its way to the rear. One o'clock in the morning was no time to get home, especially when families and relatives were expecting you at eleven. They paced up and down nervously, smoking and talking, vilifying the bus company, framing the telegrams they would send home from Port Jervis explaining their lateness. Several of the more militant passengers insisted that the bus company should pay for the telegrams, and one or two talked of legal action, but most of them were simply worried about getting home. They said so over and over again, and nobody seemed to be bored by the repetition.

Suddenly a young man pushed his way through the group and addressed the driver. He was short and thin but complete-looking, like a doll, and he wore a green sweater. His very dark face looked frightened and as he talked rapidly he made short pecking motions with his head, like a pigeon walking. The driver listened to him for a few moments with a puzzled frown and then looked inquiringly at the people near him. They shook their heads and looked blank. Nobody understood the frightened young man. He let out a wail and clutched at the driver's arm as he started his rapid speech again.

"Say, what the hell are you talking about?" the driver asked.

The young man stopped talking and looked desperate. The short fat man, who had been the first to follow the driver out of the bus, stepped forward.

"He's talking Italian," the fat man said. "I understand Italian."

"All right, he's talking Italian," the driver said reasonably. "But what is he saying?"

"He says he must get back to New York by twelve o'clock."

The driver looked disgusted. He waved his hand.

"Does he think he's got something there?" he said. "Everybody here wants to get back to New York by twelve o'clock."

He started to turn away, but the desperate young man pounced on him and began to pour the stream of Italian at him again. The fat man translated: "He says he has his girl with him and her father only let them go out for the day and he said they have to get back by midnight. If they don't get back by midnight," the fat man said seriously, "her father will kill them both. Her father said so."

The driver stared at the fat man and then at the young Italian as though he didn't quite believe his ears. Then the people near him started to laugh and he laughed too.

"Tell him not to be a sap," the driver said with a grin. "Tell him he can send a telegram from Port Jervis just like everybody else."

The fat man spoke to the young man in Italian. The young man listened earnestly until he understood, and then he began to shake his head violently and plead with the driver. The people around them started to laugh again, but there was something pathetic about the young man's unintelligible desperation, and the laughter sounded wrong. They stopped it.

"Where's the girl?" someone asked.

The fat man translated. The young man pointed to the bus. Everybody moved to the side of the bus and looked in. A young girl in a crushed black silk dress and a ridiculous black hat was sitting near the front. She sat very straight, with her hands on a shabby little purse in her lap. Tears were rolling down her face and into the corners of her mouth. Every few seconds her slight, doll-like body shuddered with her sobs. She looked so miserable and frightened that everybody turned away.

"Gosh," a woman said, dropping her cigarette. "We have to do something about this."

Everybody looked at the driver. He took off his cap and wiped the sweatband with his hand. The tough look had left his face and now, as he scowled at his hat, he seemed perplexed and worried.

"Listen, Tony," he said to the young man. Then he caught himself and he turned to the fat man. "Listen. Tell him there's absolutely nothing we can do. Tell him I'm sorry, but there's nothing I can do. Tell him he'll just have to explain to the girl's old man that the bus broke down. Hell, this isn't the first time a bus broke down. Trains break down, too. Tell him he can— Sure, tell him he can call me for a witness to talk to the old man or something, any time he wants to. Tell him— Oh, hell, I'd like to do something for the kid, but what can I do?"

The fat man translated while the passengers crowded around anxiously and the young man listened patiently. When he understood what the driver had said, he became violent again. He shook his head and waved his hands and talked rapidly in Italian. He seemed ready to burst into tears himself.

"He says," the fat man said with great care, "it wouldn't do any good. He says he's been begging the girl's old man for weeks to let him take the girl to the country for a day and the old man finally said all right only if they're home by midnight. He says the girl's old man would never believe the bus broke down just on this one day. He says the girl's old man will kill them both if they don't get home by midnight."

The young man's passionate Italian, translated into the fat man's deliberate English, was almost terrifying, like a jury verdict in a murder trial. The exasperated driver scratched his yellow hair and glared at his hat. Finally, he opened his mouth to say something, but the young Italian interrupted with a glad cry. He flung himself on the fat man and hissed a dozen sentences in his ear. The fat man stroked the back of his head and turned to the driver and the group of passengers.

"He says," the fat man said, "it wouldn't do any good if you"— he nodded to the driver—"acted as a witness, but he says you gave him an idea. He says if we drew up a paper saying that the bus broke down and that's why he was late; he says if we drew that up and everybody here, all the passengers, signed it with their names and addresses, that might do the trick. He figures like that he'd have something to show her old man."

For a moment there was silence.

"Sure," a woman cried happily, "we could do that!"

A wave of relief swept across the group of passengers. The chattering and the laughter began again, on a slightly higher note. Even the driver grinned. People scurried around for pens and pencils. They discussed the phrasing of the affidavit in high-pitched voices. Everybody had a witty insertion to make and they were all received with hilarious approval. The young Italian hurried into the bus to tell the girl what was happening.

"Well, folks," the driver said with a laugh, "what do you say we begin writing?"

He started to tear a sheet from his small pocket-notebook. The tall man who had been sarcastic to him stepped forward. He was carrying a briefcase.

"Pardon me, driver," he said pleasantly, "but I think you'd better let me do the writing. I'm an attorney." He sat down on the running board of the bus and drew a pad of foolscap from his briefcase. While the driver held the flashlight on the paper, the tall man used the briefcase as a desk and wrote an affidavit. Then the passengers formed a line and trooped past him gaily, signing the paper. At least seven or eight of them made reference to John Hancock and the Declaration of Independence, but nobody seemed to mind. The driver signed last and added the name of the bus company and his shield number.

"Boy," he said with a grin, "that ought to hold even Mussolini."

The laughing group surrounded the driver as he handed the paper to the young Italian. He looked at it and seemed impressed. Then he turned to the fat man and held it out to him. The fat man took it and translated it into Italian. The young man's head nodded slowly as he listened and for a few moments there was almost a smile of relief on his face. Then it disappeared and he shook his head sadly.

"What's the matter?" the driver asked anxiously.

The fat man listened and then turned to the passengers. "He says, thanks, this will help, but only if he's not *too* late. He says if he's not home with the girl by a little after midnight at the latest, her old man will kill them both, affidavit or no affidavit."

The driver and the passengers looked at each other. The laughter had disappeared. They were anxious and dejected again. The driver scowled and went back to scratching his head. For a moment it was so quiet on the dark road that the girl's sobbing could be heard clearly from the bus.

"Say!" a woman cried suddenly, "why can't we—?"

The driver spoke and moved at the same time.

"Sure!" he said. "We could do the—"

The rest of his words were lost as he dashed out into the road. He stood there, swinging his flashlight in a circle. The others hesitated for a moment, then understood, and ran out to join him. They improvised torches out of folded newspapers and waved them over their heads. Several of the more enterprising gathered twigs and brush from the side of the road and built small fires. One woman found a bottle of nail polish in her purse. She poured it over a thick piece of wood, ignited it, and had a reddish-glowing torch. Those who could find nothing inflammable concentrated on making noise and yelling. Two women beat on the fenders of the bus with the handles of tennis rackets until the spray of chipped enamel that they raised drove them back.

In a few minutes the first car to come along the road squeaked to a stop. The torches stopped waving and the noises died down. The bus driver ran over and talked earnestly to the man behind the wheel.

"No good," the bus driver called to the passengers as the car drove on. "He's going to Newark."

The yelling and the torch-waving resumed. The women with the tennis rackets had started on the enamel of the motor hood when the eighth car stopped. It was all right. It was going to New York. The man behind the wheel grinned at the bus driver's story, and said, "Sure. Put them right in the back."

The little Italian and his girl were almost carried from the bus to the car. In the helplessness of their relief and gratitude they looked more like dolls than ever. The girl grinned through her tears and held on to her idiotic hat. The young man kissed the affidavit and waved it gratefully. The car started with a jerk and sent them tumbling back onto the rear seat. A cheer went up from the people in the road and the wheels of the New York car went whining away, not quite like a struck gong, because there had been no momentum to give it timbre, but in a few moments it did sound like a disappearing shell, a very weak shell, in a war movie.

The bus driver blew a long, whistling sigh and looked at his wrist-watch.

"It's a quarter to eleven now," he said. "The way that guy's going, and how important I told him it was they should get to New York in a hurry, they oughta be in the girl's house by—" he cocked his head and squinted— "by, oh, by a quarter arter twelve, the latest. They even got a good chance to get there by twelve. I'll bet they'll be home by twelve, easy."

The passengers in the road beamed at each other. Then, suddenly, the short fat man spoke up.

"Say!" he said in a surprised voice. "But what about us?"

The Horse That Could Whistle "Dixie"

The pony track at the zoo lay in a hollow between the Small Mammals and the Flying Cages. There was a charge for those who wanted to ride the ponies, but there was no charge for watching, so even the people who couldn't afford to pay for rides stopped to let the children look and give themselves a rest after the walk from the Boston Post Road entrance and the exhausting business of hauling their young through the Small Mammal House and past the shrieking birds in the Flying Cages. A long, smooth iron rail that was just the right height for leaning on enclosed the track. The track itself was a large oval about a hundred yards from tip to tip, with a bridle path that went all the way round, hugging the iron rail and circling a floral centerpiece. At one end of the oval stood a tiny brick structure which housed a refreshment stand and the ticket office. In front of the house, inside the oval, was a small paddock with a dozen hitching posts, and here the children clustered.

The ponies not in use were tethered to the hitching posts. They were handsome little animals with shaggy coats, long manes, and saddles that seemed to have been designed for the specific purpose of being called "cute," a word much used by the spectators around the track. All the ponies looked tired; their sides heaved and their twitching nostrils hung close to the gravel that covered the paddock. Each hitching post had a nameplate that read "Dopey," "Grumpy," "Dixie," "Josie," and so on, and each pony had an attendant, a boy of about sixteen, wearing khaki breeches, a brown

suede windbreaker, and a numbered metal badge. They all looked
bored stiff.

Tickets cost ten cents and were good for one ride on a pony's
back or in a small wickerwork cart intended for children who were
afraid to sit in a saddle. It didn't matter whether a child knew how
to ride or not—the boys in the suede windbreakers took care of that.
They pocketed the tickets handed them by the parent, hoisted the
child onto the pony, and walked along holding the child in place
until the trip around the track was completed. Most children
scorned the pony cart and wouldn't ride at all if they couldn't ride
in a saddle. One of the things that contributed to the boredom of
the boy attendants was the number of timid parents who were
constantly finding this out.

A fat man with a derby and an expensive cigar with a raveled end
leaned on the rail with both arms, chewing his cigar and watching
with deep interest the movement of the ponies and the disputes of
the parents and children. Between his legs, peering through the criss-
crossed wires of the fence, was a small boy in a dark-blue chinchilla
coat with brass buttons and several interesting approximations of
naval insignia. The boy was as fascinated by the ponies as his father
was, but they seemed to affect him in a different way. He jumped
around excitedly between his father's legs and moved from side to
side in short, ecstatic leaps. The man kept him within bounds with
gentle nudges of his knees. Occasionally, when the boy grew too
excited for the confines of his father's legs, the man would give
him a sharp poke with his knee that would knock the boy back
into prescribed territory. The man was enjoying himself too thoroughly to look down at his son when he did this.

Every time a parent with a ticket tried to urge a child into the
wickerwork cart, the fat man on the rail would begin to chuckle. He
knew what was going to happen. The child would rebel and insist
on riding in a saddle. If the fight grew good and loud, with the child
screaming while the embarrassed parent tried to quiet him, the fat
man would look delighted as he rattled his derby into a more comfortable position on his head and dusted ashes from the frayed end
of his cigar. He would glance to his right and his left at the people
who were leaning on the rail beside him, and say with an admir-

ing grin, "Them kids, damn it, they got more guts than their old man."

He said this seven or eight times, and for a while the people on the rail kept changing, so he always had a new audience. Finally, when he said it once more, he realized that the man on his left had been there for about ten minutes. This embarrassed the fat man and he turned quickly to the man on his right. He got as far as "Them kids, damn it, they got more guts" before he saw that the man on his right had also been there long enough to have heard this observation at least three times. The fat man scowled and plugged one corner of his mouth with the battered cigar. "Come on, Timmy," he said through the other corner. "How about a ride?"

The small boy between his legs didn't hear him. He had his hands twined tightly in the metal of the fence and he was hopping with joy because of what he was seeing. His father reached down, seized his hand, and yanked him free of the fence. The boy looked startled, but he didn't cry. He probably didn't have time to cry. He was trying desperately to recover his balance as his father hauled him along, his thin, naked legs, with black shoes and blue socks at the ends of them, twinkling up and down and his free arm sawing the air. The two disappeared into the structure that housed the ticket office. Several moments later they came out through the other end, inside the oval. The small boy had recovered his balance and the fat man had recovered his composure. But the boy had lost the expression of glee he had worn when he was outside peering in. Being so close to the ponies was different from looking at them through the wire fence. He walked warily behind his father, turning his small face to right and left in quick, short glances. His father led him to the hitching post labeled "Dixie." The attendant, who had been lounging against the pony's side, straightened up and looked alert.

"Ride, sir?"

"Whaddaya *think* I want?" the fat man said jovially as he handed him a ticket. "The horse should whistle me a tune?"

The attendant paid no attention to the witticism. He slipped the ticket into his pocket and reached down for the child. But the small boy seemed to become suddenly aware of his danger. He shied away. The attendant didn't even look surprised. His look of boredom merely deepened and he put more accuracy into his second clutch. He slipped his hands deftly under the child's arms and started to lift him. The boy released a bellow of fear and a series of violent kicks. The attendant set him down promptly. The fat man looked surprised.

"Timmy!" he said sternly. "What's the matter with you?" Then, to the bored attendant, "Go ahead, son. Put him on."

This time the bellowing and the kicking started before the attendant's hands reached the boy. If his father hadn't been holding on to him, Timmy would have been well on his way to the Flying Cages. He was really frightened.

"Looks like he's scared of the horse, Mister." The attendant pointed to the wickerwork cart nearby. "How about a ride around in that?"

The fat man flushed scarlet. "Who says he's scared?" he snapped, and his jowls quivered.

The startled attendant opened his eyes wide. "All I said, Mister, I said the kid looks—"

"Never mind how he looks," the fat man said angrily. "You guys, you're paid to drive them around. Nothing else. You got your ticket. Put him on and drive him around."

The attendant's face grew red, too, and he opened his mouth to say something. But he glanced about him first. The little scene had attracted the attention of the people outside the rail and the parents inside who were waiting for children to finish their rides. Everybody, including the other attendants, was looking on with interest.

"Yes, sir," the attendant said through tight lips. He reached for Timmy again, but the boy yelled with fright and hid himself behind his father, where he started to cry, his small body shaking and one fist burrowing into his eye. The attendant straightened up with a shrug. "Sorry, Mister, but I can't—"

"Hold the horse," the fat man ordered.

"What's that?" the attendant asked in a surprised voice.

"Tzimatter, can't you hear? I said hold the horse."

The attendant's lips grew tighter, but he reached over and took the pony's bridle with one hand and stroked its neck with the other. The fat man dipped down for his son. The boy, still crying with fright, dodged his father's grasp. One of the men leaning on the rail laughed. The fat man's red face seemed to swell with anger. He grabbed his son, swung him up in an arc, and brought him down with a thump in the saddle. The pony reared and the boy screamed with terror. He rocked dangerously for a moment, but the attendant stepped to his side and put one arm around him.

"Listen, Mister," the attendant said in a low voice, "if the kid's scared, there's no sense—"

"He's not scared," the fat man almost shouted. "Go ahead and give him his ride."

The attendant shrugged and unhitched the pony. Just as they started, the boy's inarticulate terror found voice.

"Pa!" he screamed. "Pa! Pa! Paaaaa!"

The attendant hesitated and looked back, but the fat man waved him on angrily. "Give him the ride, I said, didn't I?"

The pony, with the boy walking along beside it, moved off. The fat man watched it for a moment and then he glanced around. Several people leaning on the rail were watching the moving pony. Two or three men were watching him. He dropped his eyes and busied himself with trying to relight his cigar. This was a hopeless task because the end was too frayed, but he worked at it until he recovered his composure. Then he walked abruptly into the small house. When he came out again, the pony was rounding the bend at the far end of the track. The fat man went to the hitching post and waited. Anyone could see the boy's terror was still with him, but he had stopped screaming. He was clutching tightly at the attendant's arm and whimpering. His eyes were glued on the hitching post and it seemed as though he would be able to hold his small, tense body together just long enough to make it. As they reached the post and the attendant put his arms under the boy's shoulders to lift him off the pony, the fat man stepped forward.

"Take him around again," he said curtly, holding out a ticket. The attendant stared at him in amazement. The fat man poked the ticket under his nose angrily. "I said take him around again."

The attendant took the ticket, and as he put it in his pocket the small boy seemed to realize what was happening. He broke into a fit of screaming and kicking that caused the pony to hop about nervously.

"Listen, Mister," the attendant said as he tried to quiet the plunging pony and keep the screaming boy in the saddle, "the kid's scared stiff. Can't you see he don't want—"

"You got your ticket, didn't you?" the fat man said savagely. "Well, give him the ride you got paid for. And leave out the advice."

Once more the pony carried the terrified child around the track. By this time everybody leaning on the rail or standing inside was watching the fat man and his son, but nobody was laughing. There was nothing funny about the sound of the small boy's hysterical whimpering or the sight of the father's flushed, sullen face. When the pony completed the circuit and reached the hitching post, the fat man shoved another ticket forward.

"Take him around again," he said.

The attendant looked at him with an angry sneer on his face, but he took the ticket. The small boy's whimpering rose a note or two, but died down as the pony started on its third trip. The people on the rail looked at one another and made room for newcomers who were being attracted by the strange sight. By the time the pony reached the hitching post again, a small crowd had gathered.

"Once more," the fat man said grimly, holding out a ticket.

The attendant took it and looked pleadingly at the crowd. Several people were scowling in a tentative, puzzled way, but nobody moved forward to interrupt. There was something formidable about the fat man in the derby, whose jaw was set so fiercely that thick ridges of muscle showed through the heavy jowls. The pony started around again.

The people on the rail were now whispering to each other nervously. Even the bored attendants were gathered in an excited knot at one side of the paddock. The fat man paid no attention to them. He chewed his cigar with slow, grinding movements of his jaws and watched his son. As the pony approached the hitching post for the fourth time, the man moved forward. The small boy wasn't making a sound. His wide, tense eyes stared out of his head, which was sunk in the collar of his brass-buttoned chinchilla coat. With his hands still clutching desperately at the attendant's arm, he was now a whipped, silent mass of tear-stained, quivering fright. The fat man didn't have any more tickets.

"All right," he said. "Take him off."

The attendant lifted the boy from the saddle and set him down

on the ground. The child staggered, but he managed to remain upright. The insides of his naked knees were a bright, glowing pink
where they had been irritated by the movement of the saddle and
the pony's flanks and his own terrified efforts to grip the saddle.
The fat man took the boy's hand and marched him firmly toward
the gate in the wire fence. He kept the stub of his cigar tilted toward
the sky and he stared straight ahead as he walked. The people who
had been watching fell back before him. Just as he reached the gate,
a fussy little old lady in a black fur coat stepped out of the crowd.

"That boy's knees," she said in shrill, indignant tones. "Look
what you've done to that boy's knees! You ought to be ashamed of
yourself. You take that boy to a drugstore right away and have them
put—"

The fat man's free arm shot out. It faltered just before it reached
the little old lady and then it brushed her aside, gently but firmly.
The cigar stub jiggled up and down.

"Madam," the fat man said through his clenched teeth, "would
you mind minding your own damn business?"

Houdini

It was Sunday morning and the sun on the river was bright without too much heat, the crowd of hikers on the ferryboat noisy and large. The girls wore ribbons in their hair and when they stood against the rail of the boat the wind whipped at their slacks. The young men chewed the stems of pipes with initials cut into the bowls, and they carried shoe boxes full of lunch, which were fitted with tricky little arrangements of rope or string, so that they hung over the shoulder or on the chest like a nightclub cigarette girl's tray. Some of them played kazoos or harmonicas or ukuleles, and they all sang. They sang loudly and steadily, and at times it seemed that the whole boat was singing the same song.

There was also on board a troop of Boy Scouts, who were very busy chasing back and forth across the deck and through the lounge, shouting, shoving, tossing their bulging knapsacks around, and tripping each other. There were sixteen of them and they were making so much noise that they could easily have been mistaken for twice that number, but the other hikers didn't pay any attention to them. Neither did the three scoutmasters. They leaned against the rail and watched the girl hikers with deep interest. Two of the men were thin and dark haired, with small mustaches, and it was obvious they hadn't shaved that morning. The third scoutmaster was taller and much broader, with stiff, blond hair and a pink, clean-shaven face. As the boat began to bump its way into the ferry slip on the

Jersey side, he turned to the other two. "We better get them all to-gether, huh?" he said. "Before we get off the boat, I mean."

The two dark-haired scoutmasters shrugged. "Yeah, sure," one of them said. "Might as well. Go ahead."

The blond scoutmaster left the rail and moved across the crowded deck toward the Boy Scouts. As soon as they saw him coming, they surged toward him, laughing as they pulled at his uniform and dodged his good-natured shoves. When he ordered them into line, they did not obey promptly, but there was no disrespect in their voices or their actions and gradually they formed two columns. He kept them in some sort of order and joked with them as he marched them toward the front of the boat. When the two other scout-masters fell in behind, the joking and the horseplay stopped im-mediately and the boys became quiet and subdued. They called these scoutmasters Mr. Bowen and Mr. Fuller, very respectfully. They didn't speak to the blond scoutmaster at all when the other two were within earshot. When they weren't, the boys called him Johnny.

On the shore, outside the ferryhouse, Bowen and Fuller con-ducted a brief inspection of the boys and of their equipment, and then gave the order to march north.

"We always go north toward Alpine," Johnny said. "I promised the kids today we'd take them south."

"Who are you to go around promising?" Bowen demanded. "Ful-ler and me, we got something to say in this troop, too, you know. In case you're forgetting."

Johnny flushed and drew them aside.

"Sure you have," he said earnestly. "I didn't mean that. It's just that the kids pestered me at the last meeting we should go south and—well, as long as that's what the kids want, I don't see that it makes any difference where we—"

"It's a matter of discipline," Fuller said.

"You let them ride all over you roughshod," Bowen said, walk-ing toward the boys and speaking over his shoulder. "Come on. We're going north, up toward Alpine." The boys hesitated.

"You heard what he said," Fuller said, following Bowen. "North to Alpine. I said it, also. That makes it two to one."

The procession started slowly and in sullen silence. Johnny led the way, several yards in front of the first two boys. Bowen and Fuller brought up the rear, several yards behind the last boys. For a while they maintained that formation, walking along without speaking. Gradually, however, the first two boys quickened their pace to catch up with Johnny. The others followed and it was plain that he was glad to have them. In a few minutes they were all bouncing along noisily in a formless snarl, with the big blond head and the pink-faced grin sticking up in the middle. Bowen and Fuller maintained their distance in the rear. Once, while the formation was breaking, Bowen started to step forward. Fuller stopped him.

"Aah, what can you do?" he said in a low voice. "You can't teach him nothing about discipline. It takes brains. Of which he's got you know how much. Let him alone."

As they walked, Johnny kept the boys' minds off the heat and the weight of their knapsacks by testing them on the names of trees, cloud formations, and birds. He reached up to pluck leaves from overhanging branches and he called for volunteers to name them. When he pointed out a piece of rock at the river's edge that he wanted them to notice for its color, they raced to it and fought to bring it back to him. At two o'clock they left the river path and made camp in a cleared space in the woods. The incident at the ferryhouse had been forgotten.

The boys paired off to do their cooking and Johnny went from group to group supervising the fires and the meals. Nobody would begin to eat until Johnny had tasted the first bite of blackened steak and pronounced it done. Bowen and Fuller busied themselves with their own meal.

After lunch the boys wanted to go swimming. Fuller said they would have to wait a full hour before going into the water. Johnny agreed and filled in the time by teaching them tricks with knots. His fingers were broad and clumsy-looking, but they curled with surprising deftness in and out of the twists and loops of the rope. After he tied a knot he would open it and do it over again several times, very slowly, until the boys watching him could repeat it. Then he would go on to a new one. Bowen and Fuller stood on the outskirts of the group for a while.

"Lemme take a look at that rope," Fuller said finally. "I got a little trick here I'd like to show you."

"Sure." Johnny handed over the rope. It was a seven- or eight-foot length, of the kind that is used for clotheslines. Fuller took it and turned to Bowen. "Come on," he said, "we'll show the boys something."

"Right," Bowen said, turning around and clasping his hands behind him. He did it without hesitation, as though he knew what was expected of him. Fuller tied Bowen's wrists together, then had him lie on the ground while he tied his ankles. A short piece of rope was left dangling. Fuller twisted this through both knots and hauled on them hard. Bowen's bound ankles came up to touch his bound wrists behind his back. Fuller tucked in the loose end of rope and stood up. "O.K., boys," he said, dusting his hands. "Take a good look."

Johnny and the boys came close and inspected the knots. One boy reached out and tested them. They were solid and tight. Bowen grinned up at them from the ground and shook his head comically. "He's got meh, boys," he said. "He's got meh."

"All right," Fuller said, waving them back. "You satisfied the knots are O.K.? You satisfied it's on the level?" Everybody nodded. "O.K.," he said to Bowen. "Do your stuff."

Bowen twisted himself over on his back, so that the knots were hidden behind him. In a few moments he jumped up. His hands and legs were free and he was waving the rope. Johnny and the boys looked at him in astonishment. Bowen bowed elaborately, like a vaudeville performer, and walked up to Fuller. "Now you," he said.

"Right," Fuller said. When his wrists and ankles were tied together, he twisted over on his back exactly as Bowen had done. He writhed gently for a few moments and then jumped up, holding the rope in his hand and grinning. Bowen took the rope from him and turned to the puzzled group.

"What do you say? Anybody else want to try it?" The boys glanced at each other and at Johnny. Nobody spoke. "What do you say? Any volunteers?" Bowen looked directly at Johnny. "How about you? You're such a shark with the rope, teaching the kids knots and all, what do you say? Like to try it?"

Johnny smiled slowly. "Well, sure, I don't mind," he said. "It's just that—let me ask you. Those knots. They're all on the level?"

"What then?" Bowen said. "You just got through looking at them, didn't you?"

"Yeah, sure," Johnny said. "I tested them."

"Of course, if you're afraid," Bowen said, "why, just skip the whole business."

"I'm not afraid," Johnny said quickly. "I just wanted to know if—"

"Sure, Johnny, go ahead," one of the smaller boys cried suddenly. "You can do anything they can do! You can do it better!"

Bowen and Fuller swung around sharply. The boy who had spoken looked frightened. He backed away and tried to hide behind the others.

"All right," Johnny said. "I'll try that rope trick, too."

The sixteen boys crowded around Bowen, watching intently. He appeared to be doing the identical job he had done on Fuller and that Fuller had done on him. The only difference was that he worked more slowly over the knots this time. When he finished, Johnny was lying on the ground, his wrists and ankles trussed tightly behind his back. Bowen stepped away and dusted his hands. "O.K., Houdini," he said. "Go to it."

For several seconds Johnny lay still. Only his fingers moved. He couldn't reach all of the knots, and those he could reach didn't have the loose ends of the rope in them. The boys gathered closer.

"I'll give you a tip," Bowen said. "That's not the way."

"Hey, now, wait a minute," Fuller said. "No coaching from the sidelines, there."

"A little tip like that is coaching?" Bowen asked.

"It doesn't matter," Fuller said. "A great woodsman like Johnny, he doesn't need any tips. He knows leaves and clouds. He knows birds and rocks. He knows knots. He knows everything. If you and I can do it, he can do it, too."

"He can do it better," Bowen said.

"That's right," Fuller said. "I forgot. It's a cinch for Johnny. He's a regular Dan Beard."

Johnny twisted over on his shoulder. He was very red in the face and he started to smile half-heartedly.

"What's the matter?" Bowen asked. "You licked?"

Johnny dug his teeth into his lower lip and tugged at the knots. The veins on his forehead stuck out. Three or four of the boys turned and walked away. They looked at each other guiltily as they went, but they did not speak. Bowen suddenly sat down on the ground beside Johnny. "O.K.?" he said. "Had enough?"

Johnny's left cheek was touching the grass. He didn't raise it from the ground, but he could see the circle of shoes around him. And he could see the legs of the boys who were walking away. He shook his head.

"Well, well, well," Bowen said, falling back on his haunches. "On top of everything else, he's one of these strong, silent guys, too." He pulled out a package of cigarettes, took one, and passed the package to Fuller. "Something for your nerves?"

"Thanks," Fuller said; then, with a nod toward Johnny, "Maybe the smoke'll bother him?"

Bowen leaned down close to Johnny. "What do you say, Houdini? Should we take it off?"

Johnny didn't answer. He was breathing heavily and his blond hair was tumbled forward on his face. His lower lip was bleeding from the pressure of his teeth.

"If that's the way he wants it," Fuller said witn a shrug, "so all right, that's the way he wants it."

Bowen shook his head and scowled. Suddenly the expression on his face changed. He dropped his cigarette and leaned forward. "Come on, Johnny," he said. "Stop acting like a jackass." He reached over for the knots. "You'll never get out of that. It's a trick and you don't know how to work it. Lemme open the—"

Johnny writhed violently and swung himself out of Bowen's reach.

"Go on, let him alone," Fuller said, his voice full of disgust. "If he wantsa be stubborn about it, O.K., lettim be stubborn. Come on, we'll take the kids swimming. We'll—hey!" He jumped up and looked around. The boys had all disappeared. "Well, of all the— hey, the kids! They—"

Bowen stood up and dusted his breeches slowly. "Aah, they're all right. They're around somewhere. Don't worry about them." He leaned over Johnny and spoke quietly. "Listen, Johnny, cut it out, will you? A gag's a gag, but this is gone too far. I'm telling you it's a trick. You'll never make it unless—" He reached for the knots. Again Johnny moved away from him.

"If he wantsa do it, he thinks he's so smart he can do it, let him do it," Fuller said. "Let's go find those kids."

"With you in a second." Bowen took out his pocketknife, opened the blade, and placed it behind Johnny within reach of his hands. "Don't be a dope," he said in a low voice.

Johnny looked at him. Then deliberately he swung himself over and rolled away from the knife. He lay there, panting with the effort. Bowen stared at the knife and stooped to pick it up. But he stopped halfway, straightened without touching the knife, and walked toward Fuller.

"Come on," he said. "Let's find the kids."

When they returned with the boys an hour later, Johnny was lying in much the same position. The boys huddled together, looking at him.

"Break camp," Bowen snapped.

He bent down for his knife and cut the rope from Johnny's wrists and ankles. Johnny sat up and began to rub his hands, looking down at them with scowling concentration, as though he had never seen them before. The boys kept their heads carefully averted as they dismantled the fireplaces, scattered the ashes, and strapped on their packs.

"Get up to the road and wait for us," Bowen said.

Without a word they began to clamber hastily out of the clearing that had served them as a camp.

"You all right?" Bowen asked awkwardly when the boys were gone.

"Uh, yeah," Johnny said. "I'm all right."

"Then come on," Fuller said. "What do you say we go?"

Bowen and Fuller climbed through the gap in the bushes that the boys had taken. Johnny got up slowly and followed. It was late, almost five o'clock, and the heat had gone out of the sun. On the path, which was crowded with noisy hikers going to the ferry, the sixteen boys stood in a silent, ragged group. Bowen and Fuller walked out of the bushes and approached the boys. Johnny came last and stood a bit to one side, rubbing his wrists. The boys watched him furtively.

All the confidence was gone from their eyes and all the affection.

"O.K., Johnny," Bowen said. "Let's get started."

Johnny hesitated. Then he raised his head.

"Uh, all right, kids," he said with unconvincing heartiness. "Maybe we'd better—uh—maybe you'd better fall in."

The boys snapped briskly into line. A moment before they had been a ragged, awkward group. Now they were two rigid, soldierly columns. Johnny's mouth opened in astonishment. Then he swung on his heel and began to walk down the path toward the ferry. He did not turn his head to either side or look back.

"Come on, come on," Fuller said irritably. "What's the matter with you kids? Start walking, will you? It's getting late."

But the boys waited until Johnny had gone about ten yards before the two silent columns moved forward. They walked in perfect formation. Carefully, as though by agreement, they matched their pace to his. They were very precise about this. They did not seem to want to close the large gap that now separated them.

I Knew What I Was Doing

They thought they were tossing me around like an adagio dancer. But as long as I knew what *I* was doing, I figured they could think what they wanted. It sounds dangerous, but it isn't. All you have to do is learn how to fall.

I didn't realize he was going into an act until he followed me into the models' dressing room as though he had been watching for me, and said: "I wanted to tell you about tonight."

I didn't like the way he said it.

"What about tonight?"

"I'm sorry, Myra," he said, "but we'll have to call off the date for tonight. Mr. Weiss just told me he's taking me along when he goes out with the spring line. We're leaving tonight." He should have given himself the benefit of another rehearsal. He was running his speeches together. "You know how those things are, Myra. A guy doesn't want to be a shipping clerk all his life. I been pestering Weiss for months he should take me along when he goes on the road. Now I got the chance, I can't turn him down. See, Myra?"

"Of course," I said. If he expected me to act sore, he was crazy. You miss too many tricks that way. "I know how those things are."

"If only I'd known before," he said, "I'd've told you. Or we could've gone out last night or something. But Mr. Weiss only told me this morning."

There was no question about it. One or two extra rehearsals would never have hurt him.

"That's all right, Jack," I said, smiling a little and letting the disappointment come through just enough for him to see it. "I wouldn't want you to pass up your big chance just on account of a date."

"I knew you'd understand, Myra," he said. That's what I like in a person, confidence. "It's funny, though," he said, shaking his head, "how those things work out." He didn't know how funny it was. "Here I been looking forward to this date for a week now and then *this* has to come up."

Sure, just like I was looking forward to going to the dentist.

"We'll make it some other time, then," I said.

"You bet," he said quickly, "some other time," and went out.

I drew the curtain between the dressing room and the showroom and took off my smock. Then I began to dress carefully. I put on the new brassiere I'd bought when I went out to lunch, and I slipped into the dress I'd had one of the operators in the back press for me. I took my time with the make-up too. Everything had to be just so. I gave myself a good shot of eye-shadow and a sweet coat of lipstick. I straightened the seams in my stockings and pulled the hat far over one eye. I couldn't make up my mind for a minute about the coat, but then I decided to carry it on my arm. What's the sense of investing eighty-nine cents on a new uplift if you're going to hide your figure under a coat? One more look in the mirror, and everything was set.

I walked around through the back to the front entrance to the showroom and pushed the door in quickly.

Weiss and Jack both turned around to face me.

"Hello, Jack," I said.

He gave an imitation of a deaf mute pretending to be tongue-tied.

"Well, I'll try once more," I said. "*Hello*, Jack."

"What are you doing here, Myra?" he said.

"I'm playing ping-pong," I said. "What do you *think* I'm doing? We've got a date, haven't we?"

"But didn't I tell you it was—?"

"Listen," I broke in, "is this Thursday, or isn't it? And is it a quarter to seven, or am I cockeyed?" He kept opening his mouth to say something, but I wouldn't let him. I was looking and talking in his direction, but I wasn't saying a word to him. The party I was really addressing was a gentleman by the name of Weiss. And if Mr. Weiss had the brains and the eyesight of the average dress salesman he'd get the drift before long. "And does that mean you and I have a date, or doesn't it?"

"But *Myra*, I *told* you—"

"Wait a minute. Wait a minute. Wait a minute." Mr. Rudolph Weiss tuning in. "What's going on here, anyway?"

I turned to face him, as though I hadn't seen him before.

"Oh, hello, Mr. Weiss," I said, smiling. "I didn't see you before."

"Lady," he said with a grin, "I wouldn't miss *you* like that." I didn't mean he should. "How'd you know my name? And what's yours?" He turned to Jack. "Say, why don't you give a guy a knock-down to your girl friends?"

No question about it. There was nothing wrong with his eyesight.

"Ah, quit kidding, Mr. Weiss," Jack said. "You know her. It's Myra. Miss Gross, our model."

"What?"

He came over and looked under the hat.

"Well, I'll be a so and so," he said, holding my arm.

I'll bet he could, too.

He stood off and looked me over. I could tell from where his eyes stopped that the eighty-nine cents was a good investment.

"Well, I'll be a such and such," he said.

Who should know better than he?

"I swear I'd never've recognized you with all the fancy clothes on," he said. He slipped his arm around my waist. "Without that smock you're always wearing, and in these clothes—saaay, you know, you're a knockout!"

It's nice to be told.

"Thanks," I said, sounding a little peeved. "A lot of good that's going to do me tonight."

"But Myra," Jack said, "I told you about Mr. Weiss and me going out on the road tonight. I told you we'd—"

I'll say this for him. He couldn't have been coming in better with his lines now if I'd've rehearsed him myself.

"That makes everything just dandy, doesn't it?" I said. "I get all dressed up, and then you—"

"I'll tell you what," Weiss said, holding up his hand. "This is really all my fault. I mean, I should've told him a little earlier, given him a couple of days' notice, or something. But since I didn't, and since this is all sort of my fault, I'll tell you what." He wasn't so bad, either. "*You*"—pointing to Jack—"you finish packing the samples. Then, when you're finished, you take the cases down to Penn Station and check them. Me and Miss Gross—Myra, here—" he put his arm around me again. Did I say his eyes were weak? Pardon me. He was blind.—"We'll go out to dinner. How's that? Will that square things up?"

"Oh, Mr. Weiss," I said, "it certainly will!"

"But, Mr. Weiss," Jack said, "what about the train? We gotta make the—"

"Forget it," Weiss said, winking at me. "We'll make a morning train."

II

I was plucking my eyebrows when Weiss came into the dressing room.

"Be with you in a minute, Rudy," I said, talking into the mirror. "Sit down for a while. You look all worn out."

Weiss did, too. But a chair wasn't what he needed.

"Thanks, Myra," he said. "I can't. I'm in a hurry."

What he needed was four square yards of toweling to wipe the sweat off his forehead.

"Warm, isn't it?" I said, still talking to the mirror. I had to hand it to myself. The arm I was working the tweezers with didn't even quiver. Just an old campaigner. "It's hot as hell for April."

"Yeah," he said, rubbing his face with his hand. "I'll tell you, Myra—"

"Don't bother," I said sweetly. "Let *me* tell *you*."

He stared at me with his mouth open.

"What?"

I pulled the smock up around my shoulders.

"Pardon the bare back," I said. "I didn't realize myself how warm it was."

He started again.

"I wanted to tell you—"

"I know," I said, squinting at myself as I worked. "You wanted to tell me the date for lunch is off. Right?"

His mouth opened a little wider. I figured one more notch and I'd be able to see what he had for breakfast.

"How did you know what I—?"

I shook the tweezers clean and started on the other eye.

"I guess I'm just psychic," I said. "But don't let me steal your stuff, Rudy. You go ahead and tell it to me all over again, just like I didn't know a thing."

He closed his mouth.

"I'm not kidding, Myra," he said.

I could take his word for that, all right.

"It's just that D. C. asked me to go to lunch with him," he said. "He wants to talk over the summer line. What could I do? He's the boss, Myra. You know that."

It was nice of him to tip me off.

"We'll make it for some other time. Maybe tomorrow. Or the day after. Okay?"

It was getting a little boring. Didn't they have enough brains to think up a new exit speech?

"Of course, Rudy," I said. "I know how those things are."

Come to think of it, I could use a new exit line myself.

"I'll have to run along, then, Myra. D. C.'s waiting for me," he said. "Be good."

"Don't worry," I said. "I'm getting better and better."

When I was dressed, I passed the switchboard quickly, as though I were in a hurry.

"Hey, Myra!"

I stopped and turned.

"For God's sakes," said Flo, "let's take a look at you."

I struck a pose and turned around two or three times.

"Boy," she said, "you're an eyeful, all right. Where'd you find all the clothes?"

"Find nothing," I said, "I *earned* them."

She grinned. "Tell a girl how, will you?"

Maybe I would. But I wasn't quite ready to publish yet. The system was still in its infancy. I might even want to get it patented. Who could tell?

"I can't stop now," I said. "I'm in a hurry. I have a luncheon engagement."

That's what I call progress. Two months before I had dates for lunch. Now I had luncheon engagements.

The restaurant was only a few blocks away. I walked in and looked around. D. C. sat facing the door, talking to Weiss who had his back to me. I walked over and tapped Weiss on the shoulder. He looked up and almost fell out of his chair.

"Myra!"

"Nice of you to remember me," I said, smiling.

"Didn't I tell you—?"

"Maybe you did," I said, looking around, "but I don't seem to recall. I never think well when I'm standing up. Can't you arrange for a chair for me?"

The waiter shoved one under me and I sat down.

"Myra, *please*," Weiss said. His face was red and he kept looking at D. C. "I told you I had an important—"

"Really," I said, "I don't understand you, Rudy. You go and make a luncheon appointment with me, and then, when I keep it, not only do you forget to even offer me a chair, but you get all excited and start making speeches and—"

"Pardon me, Miss, but don't I know you from someplace?" I turned to face D. C., who had put his hand on my arm and was smiling at me. "There's something familiar about you."

There was life in the old girl yet. That made two times I was remembered in as many minutes.

"There's something familiar about *you*, Mr. Cantor," I said, turning on the dazzling smile.

"Saaay," he said, "how'd you know my name?"

"Intuition," I said archly. I mean I leered at him a little and acted coy. That's archly, isn't it?

"No kidding, though," he said, "where've I seen you before?"

"Well," I said, "we've never been formally introduced, but we've met *dozens* of times."

"Yeah? Where?"

"Guess," I said. Right. Archly again. It wasn't really as bad as it sounds. They all fall for it, from shipping clerks up.

"I'm sorry about this, Mr. Cantor," Weiss said, turning to him. "I told her—"

"For God's sakes," Cantor said, "will you stop talking so much, and tell me who she is?"

That left jab shook dear old Rudy up a little. But it cleared his head, too.

"What, are you kidding me, Mr. Cantor?" he said. "That's Miss Gross. Myra Gross, one of our models."

"What?"

It was easy to keep smiling while he stared at me. All I had to do was look at Rudy and think what a dead ringer he was at that moment for Jack, the shipping clerk. The hard part was to keep from laughing out loud.

"Well, what the hell do you know?" Cantor said slowly, his eyes popping.

"Shall we consider Mr. Weiss' words a formal introduction?" I said, smiling sweetly, and reaching out my hand.

"You bet," he said, taking my hand and holding it.

I felt so good I could've reached over and kissed Weiss. Calling your shots and making them is the greatest sport in the world.

"The thing that gets me," he said, shaking his head, "is how in the showroom I never even gave you a tumble. And here—" he shook his head again.

"Maybe it's the clothes," I said.

"Maybe you're right," he said. Maybe I was. "Where'd you find them all of a sudden?"

I began to feel more at home. They all spoke the same language.

"They're a gift," I said, "from a former admirer." Accent on the former.

"I admire his taste," he said.

"I said *former*," I said, grinning at him.

"Glad to hear it," he said, grinning back.

I tugged gently at the hand he was still holding.

"Mind if I borrow this back for a minute?" I said. "I'd like to powder my nose."

His face got red and he laughed. "Oh, sure, sure," he said. "But remember, it's only a loan."

We both laughed. But Rudy didn't laugh. Rudy looked like the doctor had called him back and told him he'd made a mistake; that he had cancer after all.

"I'm sorry as hell about this interruption, D. C.," he said, screwing up his face. "I didn't mean to break up our conference like this."

Come on, D. C., use your right; he's wide open.

"I don't know what you're sorry for," Cantor said. "This is just what I've been needing. I've been working too hard lately." He turned to me. "We're going to make a real celebration out of this. You know," he said, taking my hand again, "I haven't felt so good in weeks."

Good old D. C. I knew he'd come through.

"But, Mr. Cantor," Weiss cried. "How about what we were talking about? What about the summer line?"

"You're right," Cantor said, shaking his head seriously, but winking at me. "We mustn't forget the summer line. After all, business is business. I'll tell you what," he said brightly. Weiss stopped scowling. "You're not in the mood anyway, Weiss. You go back to the place." Weiss started scowling again. "The piece-goods salesmen and the trimming people are all coming in this afternoon. They'll ask for me. You tell them I'm sick or something, and *you* see them. Anything you think is okay. You place the order." He winked at me again. "And tomorrow, or maybe even tonight, when I come back, I'll look everything over and give it the final okay."

Weiss opened his mouth, then closed it and got up. The waiter came over quickly.

"Is anything wrong, sir?"

"Not a thing," Cantor answered for him. "Everything's perfect. The gentleman's been called away suddenly, that's all." Well, Weiss had nothing to complain about. At least he was being called a gentleman. "The lady and I are lunching alone."

"Yes, sir," the waiter said.

I didn't have anything to complain about, either. Things were starting off swell. Here I was being called a lady.

III

Cantor stuck his smiling face in from the showroom.

"You feel all right, kid?" he asked.

I twisted around on the couch to face him and smiled back.

"Of course, Dave," I said. "Why?"

He certainly had me guessing. According to my calculations he should have been rehearsing his exit speech for weeks already. But he wasn't. Instead, he seemed to become more interested every day.

"I didn't want you to be all tired out for tonight," he said. "That's all."

I couldn't make up my mind whether I liked it or not. At least with the other heels you knew where you stood.

"Oh, you don't have to worry," I said. "Since you moved this couch in here for me, I haven't been tired a minute."

"That's fine," he said. "Think you can go through the line just once more?"

"Of course," I said, sitting up.

He watched me comb my hair.

"If it was an ordinary buyer, Myra," he apologized, "I wouldn't bother you."

This tenderness baloney was beginning to get me. What was he driving at, anyway?

"Don't be silly, Dave," I said. "Who's the buyer?"

"It's Bob Roberts."

Well! That was different. I shook my hair down and parted it again, more carefully.

"You mean of Liggett-Lustgarten?" I said.

"Yeah," he said. "He's leaving for Chicago tonight, and he wants to see the line once more before he goes." That was a *new* name for me. "After the big order he placed yesterday, I couldn't turn him down. Otherwise I'd never bother you, Myra."

Bother my eye. This was going to be a pleasure.

"Don't be silly, Dave," I said again, smiling at him. "I wouldn't let you down with one of your best customers, would I?"

"Good girl," he said, patting my cheek.

He started me off by calling me a lady, and now I was a good girl. Where the hell was this thing going?

"Okay, then, scram," I said, pushing him playfully. "Let's get started."

"Okay," he said, turning in the doorway to blow me a kiss. "Run it off the regular way. Sports, street wear, Sunday afternoon, and finish off with the evening gowns. Okay?"

"Right," I said, blowing the kiss back at him. He was making a regular sissy out of me.

Cantor and Roberts were the only ones in the showroom when I came out wearing the first dress.

"*That's* the number I came back to see," Roberts said, grinning.

I grinned back.

"It's one of the best in our line," Cantor said. "You'll never go wrong on *that* number, Bob."

"That's just what *I* thought," Roberts said, winking at me.

I pretended I didn't see.

"Look at the lines on it, will you?" Cantor said. He got up and stood behind me, tracing the sweep of the dress. "Just look at it."

Judging by his face, Roberts didn't need the advice.

"I'm looking, Dave," he said, "I'm looking."

With Cantor behind me I figured it was safe to risk the return wink. Roberts' face spread out like an accordion.

"You got *some* number there, Dave," he said.

"Take my advice, Bob, and order a few more. For a number like this, you don't even need salesmen. It'll walk right out of your store by itself."

"Okay," Roberts said. "Send me another half-dozen of them."

He got more enthusiastic with each dress I modeled. When I went in to change for the evening gowns, I decided to leave off the brassiere. Not that I was worried. I knew my own strength. Roberts was poured from the same mold as Jack and Weiss and Cantor. Just a grade or two higher, that's all. I knew where I stood. But I wanted to make sure.

"How's this one?" Cantor said when I came in.

"Wonderful," Roberts said, shaking his head and kissing his fingertips toward me. "Marvelous!"

Well, I guess I could publish any day now that I wanted to. The system was perfect.

"How about another half-dozen of these, Bob?" Cantor said.

"Send me a dozen," Roberts said.

I turned to go.

"Hey, wait a minute!" Roberts said, getting up from behind the showroom table. "Where you running?"

I looked surprised.

"Why, I'm going to change, Mr. Roberts."

"So what's the hurry? C'mere a minute. I want to tell you something." He walked over and put his arm around my waist. I guess there's something about the dress business that ruins everybody's eyes. "You know, I owe you an apology."

"For what?" I said.

"Why, for making you go through the whole line again, and all that," he said.

"Oh, Mr. Roberts, you don't have to apologize for a thing like *that*," I said. "I get paid for it."

"Well, I want to apologize," he said.

"Well, in that case," I said, laughing, "I guess I'll have to accept your apology."

"Good," he said, laughing with me, and patting my back. Funny how they all seemed to have gone to the same school. "And you know how I usually apologize to a pretty girl like you?"

"How?"

"I take her out to dinner and to the theater and show her a good time. What do you say?"

"Well, I—"

That was the only weak point in the system. It wouldn't hurt it at all if I learned how to blush prettily.

"Come on, now," he said, "you said you accept my apology."

"But I—"

So I *couldn't* blush, so what? You can't have everything.

"No buts. What do you say?"

"All right," I said.

"But Myra!" David Cantor, my boss and current boy friend, talking. "We have a—"

"Oh, gee, that's right," I said scowling and snapping my fingers. "I forgot all about it."

Sure, like Admiral Byrd forgot his fur coat.

"What's the matter now?" Roberts asked.

"Gee, I'm sorry, Mr. Roberts," I said. "But Mr. Cantor and I have a date for tonight—"

Roberts turned to Cantor and leered.

"Why, Dave! You little devil, you! A confirmed bachelor like you," he said, "going out with a beautiful girl like this?" I guess he must've stood pretty high in his class. "Nothing doing, Dave," he said, shaking his finger at him. "I wouldn't dare trust you alone. I'll tell you what. We'll all go out together. The three of us." He turned back to me. "What do you say?"

"Well, I don't know," I said slowly, looking pointedly at Cantor.

"Oh, come on, Dave," Roberts said. "It's my last night in town, after a busy buying trip like this." He accented the word buying. "You wouldn't want to interfere with my having a good time, would you?"

This guy was the slickest yet.

"Of course not, Bob," Cantor said quickly, grinning like he had a toothache. "Sure. We'll all go out together and have a good time."

"It's a date," Roberts said, putting his other arm around me.

I bet I could have done it just as easy with the brassiere on.

IV

By the time we hit the night club, Cantor was so sore he wasn't even talking. But I couldn't be bothered. I was giving my undivided attention to Mr. Robert Roberts, head buyer for Liggett-Lustgarten of Chicago, Illinois.

"You know, Dave," Roberts said when we were seated, "you don't look well at all. You really ought to go home."

"No, that's all right, Bob," he said. "I feel swell."

"Well, you don't look it," Roberts said. "What you need is a little solitude," he said with a loud laugh, and turned to me. "What do you say we dance, Myra?"

"Okay," I said, getting up.

It's wonderful how you don't even need a vocabulary with these guys.

"You know," he said as we danced, "I feel like hell having to leave tonight."

"Why?" I asked.

"Why do you think, why?" he said. "I'm just beginning to enjoy myself, that's why."

"If I liked a town as much as you seem to like this one," I said, "I'd stay a while."

"You would?"

"I most certainly would," I said, smiling up at him.

"Lady," he said, "you tempt me."

When we got back to the table Roberts said to Cantor, "You know, Dave, you know what I feel like doing?"

"What, Bob?"

"I feel like staying in town another week and taking this fascinating young lady around a bit. How's that for an idea?"

"But Bob," Cantor said quickly, "you've got to get back to Chicago!"

Roberts put on a long face.

"You're right," he said.

Cantor began to look a little better.

Suddenly Roberts smacked the table hard. "The hell with Chicago," he said. "Chicago won't run away. It'll wait another week." Now Cantor had the long face. "You wait here," Roberts said, getting up.

"Where you going?" Cantor asked.

"I'm going to put through a long distance call," he said. "I'm staying in town another week."

He walked away and left us alone.

Cantor put his arm across the table and took my hand. "Listen, Myra," he said earnestly, "I don't want you to think I'm a killjoy, or anything like that."

Well, here it comes, I thought. It was a little past due, but even late it would be a relief. I braced myself for the shock. Although I didn't really have to. I'd gotten to the point where it wasn't a shock any more.

"I like to see you have a good time and all that," he said, "but what's the matter, Myra, don't you like me any more?"

I sat up a little. What the hell was this, anyway? Wasn't he getting his lines twisted?

"Of course I like you, Dave," I said. "What ever gave you *that* idea?"

"Gee, I don't know," he said sheepishly. "I guess when a guy's in love he gets crazy ideas."

Love? Oh, my God!

"Maybe it's my own fault," he said. "I guess I should've told you long ago. But I don't know, Myra, it's kind of hard to say those things. I guess when a guy reaches my age and he hasn't used the words before, they get a little rusty."

For a few seconds, I was groggy.

"That's why I've been acting like such a mope all evening," he said. "I couldn't stand it to see you laughing and dancing with him. I kept thinking what a dope I was not to have spoken to you before. What do you say, Myra?" he said quickly, leaning forward. "What do you say we get married?"

I knew I was looking in his direction, but I swear I didn't see him. My mind was jumping around so quickly that it was all I could do to keep track of it. No wonder he hadn't come through with the exit speech. No wonder he'd had me guessing all these weeks. *He wanted to marry me!*

"What do you say, Myra?" he said.

All of a sudden I felt sore. Who did he think he was, anyway? What did I work myself up from heels like Jack and Weiss for? What did I work out the system for, getting it down to the point where it couldn't miss? So I should bury myself by marrying a dumb dress manufacturer and let the whole thing go to waste?

"Look, Myra," he said, putting his hand in his breast pocket and pulling out a paper. "I went down and got the marriage license to-day. What do you say?"

Across the dance floor I saw Roberts coming toward us, threading his way in and out among the dancers. On his face he had a grin a mile wide. One thing was sure, Chicago wouldn't be seeing *him* for at least another week.

"What do you say, Myra?" Cantor said, holding out the paper to me. "Look, here's the marriage license."

I shook myself a little to clear my head. It had been a narrow escape. But I'd made it. I wasn't worrying. I'd tested my strength, and I knew just where I stood. As long as the world was full of guys like Robert Roberts, I wasn't stopping until I reached the top. What the hell did I want with a dope like Dave Cantor?

"Forget it, Dave," I said, just as Roberts reached the table, grinning. "You can keep it," I said, pushing the marriage license away from me. "Paste it in your hat," I said.

Invicta!

It was not going to be easy. That much was certain. Nor was it necessarily going to be free from unpleasantness. That was something about which Miss Isabel Cranston was even more certain. The extent of her knowledge did not cheer her. She was an old campaigner. She understood clearly the advantage that lay in total ignorance of the odds to be faced.

Just the same, the knowledge that it was not going to be easy, the certainty that the evening stretching ahead might be strewn with unpleasant moments, her complete awareness of the odds arrayed against her neither deterred nor upset Miss Cranston. Like King Henry at Agincourt, Miss Cranston placed her trust, not in numbers, but in the stoutness of her heart and the justice of her cause. Being a modest person, she did not herself realize how worthy she was of that trust.

"Beg pardon, ma'am," a voice said. "That was the dinner gong."

Miss Cranston turned in the deck chair. She might have looked funny to most men. The trained observer, however, the person gifted with an eye for seeing beneath the surface, would have seen at once in Miss Cranston what was there in admirable abundance: the toughness of moral fiber that had cleared a wilderness, the strength of character that had opened a continent. With exaggerated reluctance she brought her glance from the enormous segment of the Atlantic Ocean on which the sinking sun was spreading a filigree of crimson and green. She looked up. It was one of the three stewards, the nice one with the gold tooth that showed when he smiled. The tooth was in full view now.

"Yes, I know," Miss Cranston said, smiling back at him. "Thank you so much."

She spoke with an airy grace that was a bit startling in a person with her pleasant but round and somewhat plain face. Miss Cranston knew this too, because she knew a good deal more about herself than most people do. She knew something else, however. Miss Cranston knew that there were times when airy grace, even though a trifle unsuited to a person with her reasonably good but undeniably substantial figure, could be a formidable weapon. She had seen it work for others. Miss Paige of Baltimore, for example. With only one evening left, one short evening out of sixteen long days, Miss Cranston could no longer afford to disregard any weapon, however unsuitable. She had tried most of the others.

"I thought maybe you didn't hear it," the steward said again. "I mean," he added with sudden discomfort as though, if he had recognized her before she turned around, he would not have bothered to stop, "I was just passing by and everybody else went down to dress right after the first gong, so I sort of thought maybe you missed it, ma'am."

"No, I heard it," Miss Cranston said. "It's so nice and cool, though, and the sunset is so lovely, I just couldn't tear myself away."

"Well, you don't want to be late for the captain's dinner." The gold tooth disappeared as the steward backed away awkwardly. Miss Cranston, who had only been testing the weapon, wondered if it might not be better to save her experiments with airy grace until the evening was well advanced or at least until after sundown. Another steward had once said to her, "All kinds of things go on, ma'am, you know."

Miss Cranston knew. There were few subjects on which she was so well informed as she was about life on a cruise ship. The knowledge had been gained at considerable expense and acquired over a long period of time. Miss Cranston preferred not to think about time or birthdays. It was the kind of thinking that did you no good. The past, counting the almosts and reliving the ifs, never helped. It was the future that mattered.

Miss Cranston, who was beginning to feel a trifle chilled in slacks and a halter, shivered slightly. The future, until her next vacation rolled around a year from now, consisted of approximately seven hours. She was not very happy about wasting three quarters of one of those precious hours lying out on deck, becoming cold and pretending to be enraptured by the sunset. There was no alternative, however.

She had decided that tonight it was important not to go down to her cabin to dress for dinner until she was certain her cabin mate, Miss Marilyn Paige of Baltimore, was dressed and out of it. Miss Cranston had been on enough cruises to know that the decision was a sensible one. She wanted no witness to her preparations. And she wanted no companion when she walked into the dining salon. She had watched Miss Paige dress for dinner often enough to know that, on this night, the girl from Baltimore would not be finished and out of their cabin before quarter to eight.

Her wrist watch now showed half past seven. She would probably catch her death but it couldn't be helped. She knew what she was doing. A heavy and obviously masculine step sounded on the deck behind her. Miss Cranston, like an old fire horse responding to the bell, turned. Her eager smile, which was actually more attractive than most men thought, faltered.

"Oh," she said. "Hello."

The lack of warmth in her voice troubled her. In Miss Cranston's heart, which was as large and kind as it was stout, there was no room for dislike. The lack of warmth in her voice did not trouble Mr. Harvey Murdoch of Pittsburgh. It was quite obvious that the large man in the white dinner coat was well on his way to the state of alcoholic stupefaction which, for sixteen days, he had managed to achieve with monotonous regularity by the time the bingo game started at nine-thirty.

"For Pete's sake," Mr. Murdoch said with amazement. "What are you doing, still out on deck in that getup? Didn't you hear the gong?"

Miss Cranston hesitated. Not so much because she could not bring herself to employ again the small and purely tactical untruth about the sunset. Miss Cranston hesitated because she was always disturbed when she found herself faced by a member of the opposite sex in whom she could see no possibilities at all. In Miss Cranston's eyes the opposite sex possessed few such members. It was a commentary on Mr. Murdoch that Miss Cranston, whose standards in these matters had been eroded by the years to a point where they could no longer be called high, had never been able to think of him with hope.

One reason for this, of course, was the disillusionment of experience. Miss Cranston had been on too many cruises. There were always two or three Mr. Murdochs on every passenger list. Miss Cranston knew the type. In her private lexicon they were known as pack wolves: the philanderers who lacked the nerve to do battle on their own, but traveled in groups, or at least in teams, like Mr. Murdoch and his friend from Albany, Mr. Bacon, protecting each other against their victims, who, silly young creatures that they were, always seemed eager to enter the fray alone.

There was another and more compelling reason, however, for Miss Cranston's inability to think optimistically of Mr. Murdoch. It had nothing to do with her age and experience. And it was too bad because, in all respects save one, Mr. Murdoch of Pittsburgh was the most eligible possibility Miss Cranston had encountered on her last four cruises. Mr. Murdoch was not young, which automatically eliminated the whole body of tiresome jokes about cradle snatching, but he was not old, either: a comfortable fifty. He was a widower. And, to judge by the way he spent money in the bar, he was plentifully supplied with worldly goods. Unfortunately, in spite of these great advantages, there was that one far greater disadvantage: Mr. Murdoch himself.

In Miss Cranston's eyes, which were infinitely more charitable than most, he was not a nice person. This unfortunate but insurmountable fact, which meant quite clearly that, in the eyes of the rest of the world or at least the rest of the passengers, Mr. Murdoch was an outright boor, seemed to be known to everybody on board except Mr. Murdoch himself and his cabin mate, Mr. Bacon.

"I'm just enjoying the sunset," Miss Cranston said. She didn't like to be impolite but there was something about Mr. Murdoch's beefy face that troubled her. For a moment Miss Cranston, who feared almost nothing, was afraid of him. She put as much coldness into her voice as a person with her natural warmth and friendliness could muster. "It's so lovely," she said, "it seemed a shame to rush down and dress just because tonight is the captain's dinner."

"It's not a shame to everybody else on this bucket," Mr. Murdoch said. He seemed to find, in his own boisterous words, some secret touchstone of overwhelming wit. Mr. Murdoch slapped his thigh with a hamlike hand and roared with laughter. Miss Cranston winced. She liked people to be soft-spoken, to have manners, to act like ladies and gentlemen. "You want to get going," Mr. Murdoch bellowed hilariously. "This is the last chance you'll get to do any hunting on this cruise."

The fact that the remark was true did not diminish its impact. On the contrary. For a moment Miss Cranston lay helpless in the deck chair. She could feel her cheeks grow hot and her heart turn leaden as she stared, through a slowly forming film of tears, at her tormentor. How could one person be so cruel to another? Had she ever done anything, in sixteen days, to hurt Mr. Murdoch? When other passengers had remarked that in his cups Mr. Murdoch was a revolting spectacle, had she not defended him? "He probably has troubles, poor man, like everybody else," Miss Cranston had murmured to passengers who had not of course bothered to listen. A trace of bitterness, so rare in a person of her sunny disposition that Miss Cranston scarcely recognized the emotion, washed through her mind.

What was the use? You practically starved yourself, hoarding pennies all year. You worked nights and even Sundays, to make up for the two extra days you would need away from the office in order to stretch a two-week vacation to the dimensions of a sixteen-day cruise. You forced yourself to the indignity of borrowing from other and younger girls in the office bits of equipment—a white patent leather purse, a pair of red suède wedgees, a black sequin snood— that you could not quite work into your budget. You came aboard with the paraphernalia and the high hopes that had taken a year to accumulate. You did your best, against formidable odds, for sixteen days. The men, like all men, did not appreciate your best and the girls, like all girls, showed no mercy. Nevertheless, you neither whimpered nor revealed a trace of disappointment. Undaunted, you gathered yourself for one final attempt, and what happened? Somebody you had never injured, somebody whom you had actually tried to help, came along and struck you down, wantonly, cruelly, at a moment when you needed every ounce of your waning confidence.

The word, stabbing its way through Miss Cranston's unusual dejection, brought her up short. It acted on her in much the same way that straight bourbon acted on Mr. Harvey Murdoch. It stopped the downward flow of her bitter, self-pitying thoughts. Confidence was something about which Miss Cranston knew a good deal. She sat up in the deck chair. The movement seemed to release those inner springs of strength that had nourished her through many cruises, many captains' dinners, many encounters with calloused pack wolves like Mr. Murdoch of Pittsburgh.

Miss Cranston, of Greenwich Village and the bookkeeping department of The Knickerbocker Box & Lumber Co., Inc., rose to her full five feet two inches. With all the dignity of a seasoned soldier who has remembered, in a moment of shattering crisis, his strength and his duty, she stared at her tormentor.

"At least," Miss Cranston said and the calm serenity of her manner gave to her face a touch of something that nature, more heartless than Miss Cranston, had denied her: a touch of beauty. "At least," she said with quiet scorn, "I do my hunting by myself!"

Miss Cranston turned and strode from the deck. Inside, on the companionway, she stopped and glanced at her watch. Seven thirty-five. She was ten minutes earlier than she intended to be. Nevertheless, still buoyed by the wave of confidence that had enabled her to vanquish Mr. Murdoch, she was certain that it was safe for her to return to her room.

It was a mess, of course, as it always was after Miss Paige finished getting dressed, but it was empty. Miss Cranston, closing the door behind her, smiled happily. The chill she had suffered by lying out on the deck, even the distasteful encounter with Mr. Murdoch, had been well worth it. The first step in her last campaign on board this ship had gone according to schedule. It was a good omen. Perhaps, after all these cruises, after all these years, this was going to be her night at last.

Unaware that she was humming the refrain of a song that had been popular when most of the other girls on board were still wrangling with their mothers about using lipstick, Miss Cranston slipped

out of her slacks and began to dress. She moved quickly and surely,
without hesitation. She knew exactly what she was going to wear
because she had worked it all out in advance, long before the ship
sailed from New York. What was a trifle amazing, in the shambles
Miss Paige had left behind her, was the fact that Miss Cranston knew
exactly where each item of apparel was located. It is possible, as some
cynics maintain, that the years do not bring wisdom but Miss Cranston was walking proof of the fact that they did bring an understanding of the value of neatness. The less time you had, the more
important it became to waste less of it in hunting for nylons and
bobby pins.

When she was all dressed, except for the sequin snood, Miss Cranston paused to look at her watch. It lacked five minutes of eight.
Miss Cranston permitted herself a small smile of anticipatory triumph. She would be entering the dining-room at eight o'clock, a
half hour after the eager and inexperienced novices, a quarter hour
after the chronic laggards, a full ten minutes after the most intrepid
of those who would delay deliberately to make an impressive entrance.

Still smiling and holding the sequin snood poised over her head,
Miss Cranston stared into the mirror over the washstand, turning this
way and that, examining, from as many angles as she could, what
the crowded dining salon would see when, far too late to be overlooked, she would make her entrance. What she saw would not have
attracted a second glance from those somber dark-faced sullen little
men who sit down in front at theatrical opening nights on the pre-
text, perhaps even in the hope, of discovering some bit of new talent for the insatiable appetite of Hollywood. Miss Cranston's standards were less demanding. She gave herself several glances. And she
approved of what she saw.

The long dress, which she had kept hidden all during the trip, was
well worth the three weeks' salary she had spent on it. The snug
waist enhanced that quite good feature of her figure, and the flaring
skirt concealed the features that were, at best, merely adequate.
The neck line was cut low enough to attract attention but not so
low that it might elicit comment. And the color, a pale and slightly
off-shade blue, brought out so perfectly all the gleaming intensity of
her really remarkable blue eyes that it gave the observer at least a

fighting chance to overlook the unfortunate fact that the jaw beneath all that surprising loveliness would have been more appropriate on an up-and-coming welterweight.

Miss Cranston, bringing the sequin snood carefully down on her hair, gave her reflection a final nod of satisfaction. It would do. It might not work, but it would do. If there were any men on board who, after sixteen days, had not yet made any sort of commitment or were unhappy about the commitments they had made, this carefully delayed entrance in this carefully chosen outfit would give them their chance. And hers.

As chances went, it was a long one, because Miss Cranston had a fairly accurate idea about the commitments of every passenger on board, but she was not afraid of long chances. In fact she had learned that at her age long chances were her best bets.

Miss Cranston's fingers, nimbly anchoring the snood in her hair with bobby pins, faltered. Quickly, her heart leaping with sudden fear for plans endangered, she turned to face the scratching sounds at the door. Before she could move, Miss Marilyn Paige of Baltimore, resplendent in black tulle and gleaming silver, stood in the doorway.

"Oh," Miss Paige said in surprise. "I didn't know you were here. I thought you—"

Her voice petered out. The door slammed shut behind her. She was a pretty girl and a friendly one, with a pleasant voice and an attractive manner, and Miss Cranston wished her well. But Miss Marilyn Paige was the last person in the world Miss Cranston wanted to see at this moment. In fact Miss Marilyn Paige of Baltimore was the last person in the world Miss Cranston would have chosen as a cabin mate. The choice had not been hers to make, however. Those things were in the lap of the gods. More accurately they were in the control of pursers, a breed of men who did not seem to realize how unfair it was to place a girl like Miss Cranston in the same cabin with a girl like Miss Paige. It was not that Miss Cranston disliked Miss Paige or was jealous of her. Dislike and jealousy were emotions for which Miss Cranston had no time. It was merely that the years had washed away any possible areas of communication between herself and a girl like Miss Paige. It was like sharing a cabin with a yardstick that showed to the world at a glance your own shortcomings. The contrast was too great and too obvious. Miss Marilyn Paige did not need black tulle and gleaming silver. She could have done without her pleasant voice and her attractive manner. Miss Marilyn Paige did not even need her generous endowment of beauty. She had something far better. The dew was still on her. She was twenty.

"I thought," she said with the thoughtlessness of youth, "I thought you were already in the dining-room."

"I fell asleep on deck," Miss Cranston said cautiously. "I didn't hear the dressing gong."

She turned back to the mirror. Working more slowly, trying to stretch the task as long as possible, she pretended a complete absorption in the fastenings of the black sequin snood. Out of the corner of her eye, however, she watched Miss Paige hurry across the cabin and begin to hunt furiously through the tangled contents of one of her several suitcases. In spite of her preoccupation with this new and urgent problem of delaying her preparations until Miss Paige left the cabin, Miss Cranston's experience of many cruises suggested that Miss Paige had probably had a spat with that nice young Mr. Cartwell, the medical student from Chicago with whom Miss Paige had spent practically every moment of her time since they had met during the first evening of the cruise. This was too bad, because Miss Cranston had thought they made a very handsome couple and, even though she and Miss Paige had moved in separate orbits all during the cruise and the younger girl had not confided in her, Miss Cranston had assumed that something permanent was going to come of the Paige-Cartwell relationship. Even as she felt her sympathies going out to the younger girl, Miss Cranston felt the stirrings of irritation. This was no time for her to be worrying about Miss Paige. She had her own problems. Resolutely she stared into the mirror and worked on the sequin snood.

"Thank goodness," Miss Paige said. "I was afraid for a minute that I'd lost it." She turned and extended her hand, holding out the object she had found in her suitcase. "My fountain pen," she said. "I forgot to take it down to dinner with me. They've got the menu pasted in a special little souvenir book, with a ribbon on top, and the passenger list printed in it, and a few pages in the back for autographs. Everybody is signing everybody else's book and I wanted my pen."

"I know," Miss Cranston said. "They always do that at the captain's dinner."

Miss Paige, moving toward the door, stopped and turned back. She stared at Miss Cranston for a long moment, as though she were seeing her for the first time. Miss Paige, chewing her lower lip, seemed to be trying to make up her mind about something. When she spoke, there was no doubt about the awkwardness of the decision she had reached.

"Coming down?" she said.

"Why," Miss Cranston said, feeling trapped. "Why," she said again, trying to control her voice, "I'm not quite finished." If she were a person given to quick anger she would have been in a rage at the moment. She felt she would have had a right to be. It was infuriating that the regal entrance on which she had been staking everything for this last night should be endangered because Miss Paige, after a silly spat with her Mr. Cartwell, had run out of the dinning-room and now wanted somebody to accompany her on the way back. "You run along," Miss Cranston said firmly. "I'll still be some time."

Miss Paige hesitated again. Apparently she was reconsidering the decision she had reached a moment before. In a flash of comprehension that left her almost stunned with shock, it occurred to Miss Cranston that perhaps Miss Paige was hesitating now, not because she had quarreled with her Mr. Cartwell and she wanted company, but because she was feeling sorry for Miss Cranston. If there was anything Miss Cranston detested more than pack wolves like Mr. Murdoch, it was sympathy. The notion that another girl, especially a younger girl like Miss Paige, was feeling sorry for her left Miss Cranston weak with terror. She didn't want sympathy. All she wanted was a fighting chance.

"That's all right," Miss Paige said. "I don't mind waiting." Before Miss Cranston could reply, the younger girl had come back across the cabin. "Here," Miss Paige said, "let me do that for you." She took the bobby pins from Miss Cranston's fingers and with three swift movements she finished anchoring the snood in Miss Cranston's hair. "Come on." She seized Miss Cranston's hand and smiled. "You look wonderful," she said. "Let's get down before all the fun is over."

Feeling so miserable that she could not summon up the words of a reply, Miss Cranston caught up her small rhinestone bag and her flowing silk handkerchief as the younger girl pulled her to the door. They hurried along the corridor, down the companionway, and paused finally on the threshold of the dining salon. The ordinarily colorless room was, in the phrase Miss Cranston would have employed if she had been capable of speech at the moment, a riot.

Colored streamers and Japanese lanterns had been strung across the ceiling. Toy horns and whistles were being tooted furiously by the enthusiastic diners. Each of the thirty large round tables had its quota of flowers, gay flags and noisemakers. Every passenger wore a comic crepe paper hat. Balloons were being inflated and tossed around. At the captain's table the master of the vessel, looking ruddy and fit in his white uniform and gold braid, was puncturing them industriously with a lighted cigarette as they floated by. The sound of popping balloons rose above the steady roar of laughter and hum of voices.

"Isn't it fun?" Miss Paige said with delight. "Come on."

Before Miss Cranston could protest or protect herself, the younger girl reached down, recaptured her hand and drew her into the room. The indignity of being led forward like that, as though she were a timid child, was almost too much for Miss Cranston. She flushed scarlet and stumbled on. Several boisterous young men looked up and waved their hands and yelled, "Hi, Baltimore!" Miss Paige raised her free hand and called back, "Hi, Kansas!" or "Hi, Memphis!" Nobody shouted, "Hi, Greenwich Village!" Miss Cranston didn't expect it. Her entrance was ruined.

In the center of the crowded noisy room she stopped and freed her hand with a sharp tug. This was the last time, she told herself, that she would allow her carefully laid plans to be upset by a momentary kindness. Miss Paige's quarrel with her Mr. Cartwell was her own affair. She had no right to use her cabin mate, to whom she had scarcely spoken a dozen words during the entire cruise, to cover her ignominious return to the dining salon. Miss Paige would have to learn, as Miss Cranston had herself learned, that it was not fair to count on others to pull you out of difficulties in which you had become enmeshed by your own foolishness.

"Well," Miss Paige said through her very young smile. "Have fun at your table."

"Thanks," Miss Cranston said coldly. "You too."

She crossed the room and paused behind the vacant chair at her table. The waiter pulled out the chair. Mr. Lindley, the lawyer from Washington, turned to her.

"Oh, hello," he said. "Sort of late, eh?"

"A little," Miss Cranston said with a smile. "I'm afraid I dozed off in my deck chair and didn't hear the gong when—"

But Mr. Lindley was not listening. He had turned back to Miss Norbert, the blonde who said she was a legal stenographer from Boston. A balloon exploded in Miss Cranston's ear. She jumped slightly. Mr. Cunliffe, the insurance broker from London, smiled apologetically as he brushed a piece of balloon from her arm.

"Sorry," he said. "Good fun, what?"

"Yes," Miss Cranston said. "It's—"

But she was talking to Mr. Cunliffe's right shoulder. Mr. Cunliffe was talking to Miss Durant, the redhead from Pelham Manor who had started eating kippers for breakfast as soon as she discovered that Mr. Cunliffe's accent was genuine. Miss Cranston turned her smiling glance down on her souvenir menu. Several moments went by before enough of the film of tears had cleared from her eyes so that she could read the choice of entrees.

By nine o'clock when the captain signaled the end of this phase of the evening's festivities by rising from his table, Miss Cranston had recovered sufficiently to face the next problem. It was not a large one. In fact, since she knew the status of every one of these people with whom she had shared three meals a day for sixteen days, Miss Cranston knew it was not a particularly important problem, either. She knew that her own table was barren ground. Still, she was a fighter. Even barren ground could serve to cover an orderly retreat. If she could manage to leave the dining salon with an escort just once, particularly tonight, she would consider as canceled the large debt the table owed her.

As the chairs started to scrape, Miss Cranston cast her quick experienced glance to right and left. Both Mr. Lindley and Mr. Cunliffe, busily snubbing out their cigarettes, were momentarily defenseless. Their partners, Miss Norbert and Miss Durant, had scurried across to get the captain's autograph before he escaped from the room. All Miss Cranston had to do was loop her arm through that of Mr.

Lindley or Mr. Cunliffe and, before her victim could recover from
the surprise, start leading him toward the door. Once they were out
on deck, she would be just as pleased as he would be to allow him
to escape.

Miss Cranston tried hastily to decide between the two. She had
just about made up her mind that she would choose Mr. Lindley, not
because she found him more attractive than Mr. Cunliffe, but because Mr. Lindley's Miss Norbert had been ruder to her than Mr.
Cunliffe's Miss Durant, when a hand fell heavily on her shoulder.
Miss Cranston leaped nervously and turned.

"May I have the honor," Mr. Harvey Murdoch of Pittsburgh said
with a leer, "of escorting you to the bingo game?"

It was obvious that he considered the request a tremendous joke.
It was even more obvious, from the grins on the surrounding faces,
that others shared his opinion. For a moment, as she stared up into
the heavy face, the temptation was almost too much for Miss Cranston. But only for a moment. Her sense of dignity came forward to
save her. The distinction between defeat and disgrace may not be
apparent to some people. It was crystal-clear to Miss Cranston. She
had suffered many defeats. She would never submit to disgrace.
With some regret, it is true, but without any hesitation she rose
from her chair and stared coldly into the grinning countenance of
Mr. Harvey Murdoch of Pittsburgh.

"I'm terribly sorry," Miss Cranston said. She picked up her purse,
her handkerchief and her souvenir menu, and swept past him. "I
have another engagement."

Her purposeful gait did not falter until she reached the sheltering
shadow of a lifeboat on the starboard deck. Here she paused to allow
her quivering nerves to calm down and to consider her next move.
Two choices were open to her. There would be dancing in the
salon, and in fifteen minutes bingo would start in the smoking
lounge. Quickly, Miss Cranston weighed the relative merits and de-
merits.

Bingo would cost her at least a dollar. There were never less than
four games at a quarter each and, once you had a seat, you couldn't
very well walk out before the games were over. But there was no
denying the fact that it was the sort of simple-minded game to which
unattached males were addicted.

The dancing in the salon presented a different problem. The only couples who would be dancing so soon after dinner would be the ones who were known in Miss Cranston's cruise dictionary as "solids": Mr. Cunliffe and his Miss Durant, Mr. Lindley and his Miss Norbert, Mr. Cartwell and his Miss Paige. It was the sort of setting that usually provided very poor hunting. On the other hand, since it was the solids who quarreled most unexpectedly, it was also the sort of setting in which a man, blinded for sixteen days by a relationship that had just exploded, might very well begin to see the charms he had hitherto missed in another girl. A girl like Miss Cranston, for example. She had known it to happen. Not to herself, of course, but to other girls, on other cruises.

"Hello, there."

Turning quickly in the shadow of the lifeboat, she found herself facing Mr. Cartwell of Chicago.

"Why, hello," she said, somewhat embarrassed. Miss Cranston didn't know Mr. Cartwell very well. The gap in their ages had kept them apart during the entire cruise. Besides, every moment of Mr. Cartwell's time had been devoted to Miss Paige. Still, he was a terribly nice boy, one of the nicest Miss Cranston had ever seen on any cruise. If only she had been a dozen years younger, or even six or seven—Miss Cranston shook her head, as though to fling away the foolish thought. Nine-thirty on the last night of a sixteen-day cruise was no time for daydreaming. There was work to be done. Miss Cranston said, kindly enough, but not so kindly that the shy youngster could possibly mistake her meaning, "What are you doing out here alone at this time of night?"

Even in the shadow of the lifeboat she could see his handsome face flush darker.

"Why," Mr. Cartwell said, "I was looking for you."

"For me?"

"I wanted to ask you something," Mr. Cartwell said uncomfortably. "You haven't seen Marilyn, have you? Miss Paige, I mean?"

Miss Cranston felt a wave of relief. She had been right. It had been a lovers' quarrel, not sympathy for her cabin mate, that had prompted Miss Paige to accompany her into the dining-room. Her spirits soared at once, as though a vague doubt about her own ability, which had been shackling her capacities to think and act, had been removed. Also, the last vestiges of her resentment against Miss Paige, for having ruined her carefully planned entrance, evaporated.

"I haven't seen her since eight o'clock," Miss Cranston said. "We came in to dinner together." She hesitated and then very quietly she said, "What's the matter? Have a fight?"

Mr. Cartwell's face grew a shade darker.

"Sort of," he said awkwardly. "It was my fault. I'm trying to find her to tell her I didn't mean—" He turned and looked down the deck as though trying, with the intensity of his remorse and the strength of his desire, to pierce the darkness and the bulkheads and find where, on the large and crowded vessel, Miss Paige was hiding from him. "I guess I'll run into her in a little while," he said as though he were talking to himself and then he seemed to become newly aware of Miss Cranston's presence. "It sort of leaves me at a loose end for a while." Mr. Cartwell smiled shyly. "I feel sort of silly, standing out here. Would you like to go in and dance?"

Miss Cranston smiled back at him. It was always pleasant to know that you had been right about someone. There was no doubt about it. He was a nice boy. And Miss Paige was a nice girl even though—and Miss Cranston felt a small pang in her heart for the foolishness of the very young—it was obvious that neither one of them was being very bright.

"Let me give you a piece of advice," Miss Cranston said and she had to pause for a moment because there was a small lump in her throat. "The quickest way to find her is not to go around asking other girls to dance." She touched his sleeve lightly. "Thanks for the invitation but I'm afraid I have an engagement to play bingo in the smoking lounge."

The large room was crowded. Miss Cranston stood in the doorway and surveyed the scene. Each table had five chairs. The tables that were not completely filled held two couples. The odds were heavy that most of those couples had sat down together. There was always the small chance, however, that in at least one or two instances the arrangement was accidental. By plumping herself into one of the vacant chairs, Miss Cranston would make the lineup at that table three girls to two men, and she didn't see how anybody could expect better odds than that. Certainly she didn't.

The trouble was that she might choose a table at which both couples were solids, in which case she would be out of the running for the duration of the session. You couldn't change seats in the middle of a bingo game.

Miss Cranston had just about decided to make her choice on the basis of color, to select the table at which no other girl was wearing blue, when her roving eye stopped on a table to the right of the door. She could scarcely believe her eyes or, as her heart leaped with hope, her luck.

The table had two vacant chairs. Two men and a girl, their backs to the door, occupied the other three chairs. The girl was talking animatedly to one of the men. The second man, if the back of his head could be taken for a reliable guide, was either thoroughly bored by, or disinterested in, the conversation of his neighbors. Miss Cranston did not waste many seconds in thought or hesitation. She swept across the room, hauled out one of the two empty chairs and sat down.

"May I?" she said brightly. "I was just—"

Her words stopped but her mouth remained open with astonishment. Not because she felt she should have recognized Miss Paige, even from the back, by the black tulle and gleaming silver. Miss Cranston's astonishment was caused by the fact that the recipient of Miss Paige's animated confidences was Mr. Bacon of Albany. It was true that Mr. Bacon was not nearly so irritating a person as his cabin mate, Mr. Murdoch of Pittsburgh. Mr. Bacon was a good deal younger, for one thing; and if you wanted to be fair about it, something Miss Cranston found it impossible not to be, Mr. Bacon had a certain amount of rudimentary charm. Nevertheless, after sixteen days it should have been plain, even to a guileless youngster like Miss Paige, that Mr. Bacon was a member of that most loathsome of cruise ship species, the pack wolves.

"Why, hello," Miss Paige said with genuine delight. "What a nice surprise."

"It got too hot to dance in the salon any more," Miss Cranston said. "I thought I'd come in here to play a game and cool off."

"So did we," Mr. Bacon said maliciously. "I didn't see you in the salon."

"Maybe you were too busy to look," Miss Cranston said in her iciest tone. She may have been afraid of a lumbering drunk like Mr. Murdoch of Pittsburgh, but she knew how to handle the junior member of any team of pack wolves. Miss Cranston stared through Mr. Bacon and smiled at Miss Paige. "I just ran into somebody out on deck who is looking for you," she said. "I think he has something interesting to tell you."

Miss Paige's pretty face colored quickly.

"If it's all that interesting," she said with a toss of her lovely but, in Miss Cranston's opinion, brainless young head, "I imagine he can write me a letter about it."

"That's what I always say," Mr. Bacon said heartily and he clapped Miss Paige on the back in a manner that Miss Cranston found distinctly offensive. "Always make them put it in writing," Mr. Bacon boomed.

Miss Paige laughed a trifle nervously and Miss Cranston, with a mental shrug, turned away. She wasn't here to chaperon young fools of twenty. The evening was getting on, and she had work to do. Miss Cranston turned on the other man at the table the full strength of her smile.

"I hope you weren't saving this chair for somebody," she said, opening her rhinestone bag and fishing for her change purse. "I think bingo is so much fun if you just choose a place at random, without—"

"No, no, not at all," the man said and Miss Cranston, wondering why she had not noticed him during the preceding sixteen days, wondered also why he had that far-away look in his eyes. "That chair isn't—" The far-away look disappeared. A happy smile took its place. "Serena!" the man said, jumping up. "I thought you got lost."

He helped Serena into the vacant chair on his left and gave her a bingo card.

"After I got my fountain pen," Serena explained breathlessly, "I found it was dry, so I had to go down to the purser's office to get some ink and he had a lot of people with him and they all insisted on signing my menu. I thought I'd never get away, but gosh—" She paused, in a sort of ecstasy of remembered pleasure. "It's been such a wonderful trip, I don't want to miss anybody."

Miss Cranston's shoulders sagged just the faintest bit. As the eager Serena started passing her souvenir menu and fountain pen around the table, Miss Cranston saw, out of the corner of her eye, that Mr. Bacon's attention was not completely absorbed by the lovely Miss Paige. The junior member of Mr. Murdoch's team of pack wolves was watching Miss Cranston, too, with a malicious smile. She could tell that Mr. Bacon knew, as Miss Cranston herself knew, that for her the bingo session was another defeat. She wondered dully if it had been such a wise move, after all, to turn down young Mr. Cartwell's invitation to dance. At least in the salon she would not be immobilized, as she was here, for a full hour.

Miss Cranston paid her quarters mechanically as each game started and, as they were called, she covered the numbers on her card with kernels of corn from the bowl in the center of the table; but her heart was not in it. For that matter, neither was her mind. Miss Cranston's mind was on the three phases of the evening that still lay ahead of her: the amateur entertainment, the midnight costume contest, and the one o'clock dance.

She wondered, with a certain amount of surprise, why the prospect did not excite her. It always had. There was no reason why it shouldn't this time. Miss Cranston roused herself, almost as though she were nudging a friend who had dozed off at a sermon. Why, the best and most hopeful part of the evening still lay ahead. What was the matter with her? Was it possible that she was beginning to run down? After all these years, all these cruises, all these campaigns, was she beginning to lose her wind? What sort of nonsense was this, anyway? Her head went back. Her spine straightened. She pushed herself up in the chair. Just because the first part of the evening had yielded no results, she told herself severely, that didn't mean she had to act as though the world had come to an end. She would stop this silly—

The fierce little pep talk slithered from her mind. Miss Cranston's eyes beheld a sight that froze her with horror. Coming across the room, heading directly for her, was the grinning, malevolent, inebriated countenance of Mr. Harvey Murdoch of Pittsburgh. For a long moment, as though she were already stunned by the impact of the blow that had not yet fallen, she could not believe what she was seeing. Then her mind, taught by experience to believe anything— no matter how outrageous—of a pack wolf, leaped in a spasm of warning. There was some connection, there had to be, between Mr.

Murdoch's mocking attempt to escort her from the dining salon after dinner and his descent on her now. It was probably some complicated practical joke by which he had decided to pay her back for the cutting truth she had hurled at him before dinner. Miss Cranston could not imagine what Mr. Harvey Murdoch intended to do to her. She knew only with terrifying urgency that she shouldn't wait to find out.

"Excuse me," Miss Cranston said, rising hastily. "I'm afraid I must leave." Even in her desperation she was aware that, of the four people bent busily over their bingo cards, only Mr. Bacon seemed to appreciate what was happening. In fact, Mr. Bacon seemed to be enjoying it. Miss Cranston gasped, "I have another engagement."

Mr. Murdoch saw his quarry move toward the door. He emitted a little yelp and changed his course. A roar of laughter rose from the bingo players. Miss Cranston, her face so hot that it hurt, side-stepped and managed to stumble through the door into the cool of the night. She didn't pause to gulp the fresh air for which her panting lungs hungered. She kept right on going, up the deck, down the companionway, along the corridor and into her cabin. Without a thought for the flaring skirt that had cost three weeks' salary, heedless of the fragile sequin snood that had been grudgingly entrusted to her only after so many vows of tender care, Miss Cranston flung herself on her bunk, face down.

It has been recorded that Alexander wept when he learned there were no more worlds to conquer. Perhaps he did. And perhaps Miss Cranston, lying on her face in a bunk on a cruise ship off Sandy Hook, was doing the same. Certainly the suspicious moisture that dampened her pillow could have been identified as tears. And yet the word seems somehow inadequate.

Not because Miss Cranston's warm and eager soul had never lusted for a world. Not because her long and ardent quest had always been of such simple and harmless dimensions. The word seems inadequate because it is possible that there are no words to describe the brutal shattering of a will, the wanton destruction of a human being's valor, the ruthless quenching of an inner fire.

The struggle against insuperable odds is one thing. Miss Cranston had never shrunk from it. Man's inhumanity to man, and woman, is something else again. Miss Cranston, who had learned so much in her annual pilgrimages across blue water, had at last learned that, too.

She did not know how long she had been lying there when she heard the timid tap on the cabin door. She raised her tear-stained face from the sodden pillow.

"Yes?" she called in a dazed voice. "Who is it?"

"Marilyn?"

She recognized the nice, and now quite worried, tones of young Mr. Cartwell of Chicago.

"No, she's not here," Miss Cranston called wearily. "Try the smoking lounge. She was in there, playing bingo, a few minutes ago."

"A few minutes ago?" Mr. Cartwell sounded startled. "Why, the bingo was over at ten-thirty."

Miss Cranston sat up on her bunk. "What time is it now?" she called frantically.

"Almost two o'clock," Mr. Cartwell said through the cabin door. "Ten minutes of."

Miss Cranston, glancing hastily at her watch, saw with horror that he was right. Before she quite realized where she was and why she was there, her mind was already recording the lamentable fact that she had missed the amateur entertainment, the midnight costume contest and, in all probability, the one o'clock dance on the forward deck. By the time she realized why she had missed them, Miss Cranston's irritation with herself was far stronger than her recollections of the stunned misery to which Mr. Murdoch's drunken humors had reduced her. Like a good soldier who awakes to find that he has dozed at his post, all her senses and energies seemed to become alerted at once. They strained, not backward, with remorse for her defection, but forward, to repair the damage done. Miss Cranston, who had so much less time for everything than younger girls, had no time for remorse. Not at two o'clock in the morning on the last night of a sixteen-day cruise.

"I'll be up on deck in a minute," she called briskly to Mr. Cartwell. She ran across to the basin and started to pat cold water on her face. "With two of us looking for her, we ought to find her," she called. She dried her face hastily, found her compact and began swiftly to repair the ravages of a despair that seemed already so utterly preposterous that she could almost believe it had happened to another person. "Where will you be," she asked, fluffing out the skirt of her dress, "if I run into her first?"

"How about the lounge?" Mr. Cartwell's voice came from behind the closed door. "That all right?"

"Fine," Miss Cranston said, rearranging nimbly the anchoring bobby pins of her sequin snood. "If I locate that Marilyn of yours, I'll get her to the lounge if I have to carry her piggyback."

"Thanks a lot." There was a pause. Then Mr. Cartwell's young and troubled voice said, "You know something, Miss Cranston?"

"What?"

"You're a peach."

"Go on now," she called tartly. "And stop acting silly."

Some peach, she thought irritably as she gave herself a rapid final glance in the mirror. After all these years, after all her experiences with the insect life of cruise ships, to allow herself to be driven from the most promising scenes of a last night by a pack wolf like that Mr. Murdoch of Pittsburgh! Honestly, it was enough to make a girl lose faith in herself. Miss Cranston seized her rhinestone purse and her flowing handkerchief. Still tugging the flaring skirt into better alignment, she trotted out of the cabin. Recalling, as she sped back along the corridor, the mood in which she had last covered this route, Miss Cranston blushed with shame for her weakness.

At the rail below the bridge she paused for breath and looked down on the forward deck. Four or five floodlights were still on, but the music had stopped and there were no couples on the dance floor. The upward climb of Miss Cranston's spirits stopped abruptly. She was too late. It was all over. The festivities were finished. And so, for another year, were her chances.

Dejectedly, forgetting to keep her shoulders back and the flowing handkerchief from trailing at her feet, she turned and walked aft. Moving along the deck in the moonlight with dragging steps, she tried, as she had always tried in the past on similar occasions, to think. Not of the defeat, but of the lessons to be learned from it, of the pieces of knowledge that could be dredged up out of the defeat and added to her already ample store for future use, for the next

year, the next cruise, the next captain's dinner, for the victory she
had never doubted would one day come.

But she could dredge up no pieces of knowledge. Perhaps at last
she had learned it all. Perhaps for her there would be no more lessons. Perhaps, in succumbing to the terror of Mr. Murdoch's threatened mockery, she had succumbed to something from which there
was no recovery. Perhaps for her there would never be a victory.

"Hey, Miss Cranston!"

She leaped nervously and turned. She was standing in the doorway of the salon. Fifteen or twenty couples were sitting about, having a nightcap. In their midst, holding aloft a highball and his souvenir menu, was Mr. Harvey Murdoch of Pittsburgh. As she stared at
the beefy face she saw, without looking at them directly, the spreading expectant grins of the people in the room. Again she almost wept
with anguish. Why couldn't he leave her alone? Hadn't he done
enough?

"Where you been hiding?" Mr. Murdoch bellowed. "I been looking
for you all evening." He winked at his delighted audience. "I've got
everybody's autograph in my book except the one I want. You can't
do this to Harvey Murdoch," he shouted, advancing toward her.
"Come on, now, Miss Cranston. Make this wonderful cruise perfect
for Harvey Murdoch. You got to write in my book."

For a moment, as the sea of grins became a rippling wave of
smiles and started to break into the roaring surf of laughter, Miss
Cranston wanted to turn and run. The instinct, common enough
to most people but still foreign even to the shattered Miss Cranston, struck her with the force of a physical blow. It was as though,
for the first time since she had fled from the bingo game, she had
been granted a clear glimpse of herself, of the depths to which she
had sunk. The sight was shocking. She reacted to it as only the old
campaigner can be counted upon to react under stress.

The cruelty of the laughter stabbed and bit, searing its way down
into regions of her heart that had never before been plumbed, touching off something Miss Cranston had never before felt for another
human being. Up through the layers of weariness and rejection, out
of the leaden mantles of rebuff and defeat, it surged forth: a seething flame of anger, but anger channeled, anger under control, anger
for this middle-aged pack wolf who had hounded her all night, al-

most as though it were a deliberate plan: on deck before dinner, in the dining salon after dinner, at the bingo game, and now here before this laughing audience.

Miss Cranston's shoulders went back. The trailing handkerchief came up. Miss Cranston of Greenwich Village would show Mr. Harvey Murdoch of Pittsburgh a thing or two about practical jokes. She would show him what it meant to bait innocent people, to make someone a public laughingstock.

"Why, of course," Miss Cranston said with airy grace, employing at last the weapon she had decided before dinner to save until later in the evening. "I'll be delighted to write something in your book, Mr. Murdoch." She advanced calmly into the salon. "What would you like me to write?"

Mr. Murdoch seemed to realize that he had apparently underestimated his victim, that his crude humor was about to backfire. He cast an uncertain glance at the people around him. The surf of laughter had retreated into a wave of smiles. The wave gave every indication of being about to recede further to a sea of uneasy grins.

"Why, I'd like you to write something I'll never forget," Mr. Harvey Murdoch said. The words seemed to restore his confidence. "That's right," he cried. "I want you to write something you won't want Harvey Murdoch ever to forget."

"Let me think, now," Miss Cranston said, still airily, still gracefully, but enunciating so clearly that she could be heard by everybody in the now silent room. She put a forefinger to her cheek, dimpling it prettily, and she seemed to lose herself for a moment in deep thought. "I know," she trilled. "I've just thought of something I won't want you ever to forget." She turned to the man nearest her. It was Mr. Cunliffe of London. She said pleasantly, "May I borrow your pen?"

"Of course," Mr. Cunliffe said. He plucked it hastily from his pocket. As he handed it over, a look of grudging admiration began to take shape on his face. "There you are."

"Thank you," Miss Cranston said, as Mr. Murdoch held out to her his souvenir menu.

"Remember, now," Mr. Murdoch chortled. "It's got to be something you don't want me ever to forget."

"Oh, I'll remember," Miss Cranston said lightly. "The question is, will you remember?"

Leaning down, resting the booklet on Mr. Cunliffe's table, so that he and his neighbors could see clearly what she was doing, Miss Cranston wrote in the clear marching script that had for so many years helped make her an important member of the bookkeeping department of the Knickerbocker Box & Lumber Co., Inc.: "Isabel Cranston, 32 O'Duffy Street, New York, N. Y., Mohawk 4-8076."

She straightened up. As she recapped the fountain pen and returned it to Mr. Cunliffe she could see the grudging admiration on his face change to a frank stare of awe. He murmured something to his neighbor. The murmur spread. A whisper of amusement slid through the room, mounted and crashed into a roar of laughter. They had been willing to see her as the butt of a jokester. Now it was evident what she thought of their jokester—a cheap masher, a collector of telephone numbers.

This time Miss Cranston did not mind the laughter. This time she welcomed it. She closed the souvenir menu and slipped it behind the handkerchief in the outer breast pocket of Mr. Murdoch's dinner jacket. She did it with a gesture of graceful triumph. The room was laughing at Mr. Murdoch.

"You sure you won't want me to forget what you wrote, now?" he said uneasily.

"That's entirely up to you," Miss Cranston said coolly. "You'll never miss out if you get a long-enough list."

The laughter roared out again. Mr. Murdoch winced and looked foolish. Miss Cranston sent her triumphant glance around the room, hunting for Mr. Murdoch's partner, Mr. Bacon of Albany, who had grinned at her so maliciously at the bingo game. Miss Cranston, flushed with triumph, wanted to see if Mr. Bacon was grinning now. Her glance faltered. Mr. Murdoch sensed apparently that something had changed.

"What's the matter?" Mr. Murdoch said and laughed. "Want to change your mind about what you wrote?"

"Change my mind?" Miss Cranston said. "Oh, no." She didn't want to change her mind. She wanted desperately to get it to work again. Mr. Bacon of Albany was not in the salon. Neither was Miss Marilyn Paige of Baltimore. Their absence had reminded Miss Cran-

ston of her promise to young Mr. Cartwell of Chicago. He was still
waiting for her in the lounge, under the impression that she was
hunting for Miss Paige. "Of course not," Miss Cranston said, trying
to think quickly, trying to assemble a number of pieces of the evening
that she instinctively felt belonged together. "Why should I want to
change my mind?"

"I don't know," Mr. Harvey Murdoch said and he staggered as a
spasm of laughter shook his large frame. "From the way you been
running away from me all evening, I thought maybe you didn't like
me."

"How silly!" Miss Cranston exclaimed. It was worse than silly. It
was unforgivably stupid. The pieces had fallen into place, had
become a pattern so clear and obvious that she was amazed to realize she had not seen it earlier.

Her moment of suspicion, when Mr. Murdoch had started to de-
scend on her at the bingo game, that there was some connection
between his impending assault and his earlier lumbering attempts to
escort her from the dinner table, had been justified. This request
for her to write something in his souvenir menu was part of the same
plan. With her long and intimate knowledge of the habits of pack
wolves, how could she possibly have overlooked the connection? Of
course it was a plan. Mr. Murdoch had obviously been detailed to
keep her occupied and out of the way so that his partner, Mr. Bacon,
could have a free hand with her cabin mate, Miss Paige. The silly
fool! For a moment Miss Cranston didn't know whether she had intended the epithet for herself or for Miss Paige. She felt that they
both deserved it. Miss Cranston's smile became dazzling. "How
could you possibly have thought that, Mr. Murdoch?" she said, slipping her arm through his. "Why, of course I like you."

She regretted, more than anything she had ever regretted in her
life, the seething anger of a few minutes ago. It was an emotion she
had always distrusted. Now she knew she had always been right. If
she had not succumbed to anger she would not have forgotten her
promise to Mr. Cartwell; she would have noticed at once the absence of Mr. Bacon; she would have understood immediately the
danger that threatened the silly Miss Paige; she would not have lost
precious minutes. Miss Cranston reached out and plucked the sleeve
of a passing steward. He stopped and turned. It was the one she

had always thought was nice, the one with the gold tooth that showed when he smiled. Miss Cranston said, "Would you get us two highballs, please? And could you bring them out on deck for us?"

"You bet," the steward answered. The gold tooth was in full view now. "Right away, ma'am."

"Thank you," Miss Cranston said. "Come along, Mr. Murdoch," she said in clear bell-like tones. "Let's have a nightcap out on deck, and I'll tell you just how wrong you are in thinking I don't like you."

He was a heavy man and the amount of liquor he had consumed had not made him more manageable, but Miss Cranston was not slender, either. Besides, she was in a hurry. If she were to avert the disaster her stupidity had prevented her from seeing until now, she would have to work fast. If indeed she was not already too late. A murmur of laughter followed her as she dragged Mr. Harvey Murdoch out on deck. Miss Cranston did not hear it. Her mind was making a swift calculation, adding minutes and subtracting them. How long had she been gone from her cabin? She could only hope. And act swiftly. Mr. Murdoch sagged against the rail.

"Say," he said. "You know something? You're nicer than I thought. I guess I owe you an apology for—for, well, you know. I didn't mean anything. I was just trying to, to—" He shook his head, as though to free it of the fumes that impeded the formation of a slow, lumbering and apparently important thought. "Funny thing about these cruises," Mr. Harvey Murdoch said thickly. "You rush around so fast, raising Cain for sixteen days, sometimes you miss the best—I mean," he made a determined effort to bring Miss Cranston into focus, "I never really looked at—"

Miss Cranston turned to the approaching steward.

"Would you do me a favor, please?"

"You bet, ma'am."

"We don't really want the drinks," Miss Cranston said. "I ordered them just to get Mr. Murdoch out of the salon. He's had more than enough. What he needs is sleep. Would you take him down to his cabin?"

The gold tooth flashed in the moonlight. "You bet, ma'am," the steward said.

Miss Cranston smiled. She was never wrong about people. He *was* the nicest of the stewards. He set down the small tray and relieved her of the large swaying body.

"Hey!" Mr. Murdoch called, his voice a wavering receding protest. "I want to talk to you," he mumbled. "I been trying to tell you something. What I mean is, what I'm trying to say, I mean—"

"I know what you mean," Miss Cranston called back across her shoulder. It was too bad about Mr. Murdoch. Perhaps what he needed after all was a little shock treatment. It seemed to take effect. She added, "If you still remember, you might try telling me in the morning before the ship docks."

She sped up the deck, down the companionway, along the passage and into her corridor. Her heart was pounding with fear as she turned the knob on the door of her cabin. It was not locked! She pushed open the door and snapped on the light. The cabin was empty! Almost sagging with relief, Miss Cranston closed the door behind her and tried to dismiss her last fragments of doubt. Her calculations had to be right. She couldn't be wrong. She knew too much about last nights of cruises, about the innocence of young girls like Miss Marilyn Paige, about the techniques of pack wolves. She couldn't possibly be wrong. And yet—

Miss Cranston turned. Outside, coming down the corridor, were the unmistakable sounds of the age-old struggle. Her heart leaped with gratitude. Her calculations had been right. Her instincts had been correct. A girl like Miss Paige, silly though she was, would not go to a man's cabin. The man, if he had any experience, would understand that and try instead to maneuver a girl like Miss Paige to her own cabin. Swiftly, almost savagely, Miss Cranston removed the anchoring bobby pins from the sequin snood. The fragile web came free with a sickening rip. Miss Cranston didn't care. When the door opened, her hair was tumbled loosely on her shoulders and she was holding a toothbrush.

"Oh, hello," she said brightly to Mr. Bacon of Albany and to Miss Marilyn Paige of Baltimore. "I was just about to turn in. Have fun?"

The gasp of relief with which Miss Marilyn Paige freed her hand from Mr. Bacon's clutch and stumbled into the room was a trifle pitiful but also highly satisfactory to hear. It told Miss Cranston what she wanted to know. She was not too late.

"Oh yes, it was—it was very nice," Miss Paige stammered. She turned to face Mr. Bacon in the doorway, then stepped back behind Miss Cranston. Speaking across the protective barrier of the older girl's shoulder, Miss Marilyn Paige said with surprising firmness, since her voice was quivering, "Thank you very much, Mr. Bacon, and good night."

Mr. Bacon did not answer. It was possible that he would be incapable of speech for some time. He looked, as he glared at Miss Cranston, somewhat like a visiting big-league hitter who has been struck out in an exhibition game by the pitcher of the local high school team. Miss Cranston patted Miss Paige's hand reassuringly and walked to the door.

"I think you heard my cabin mate," said Miss Cranston. "She said good night." Miss Cranston raised her hand like a cavalryman drawing his saber and she pointed the toothbrush at Mr. Bacon's rumpled dinner jacket. "Before you go, let me give you a bit of advice you might be able to use on future cruises," she said. "Next time, stick to girls your own age," Miss Cranston said, emphasizing her point with a thrust of the toothbrush. "And next time, when you pick a partner to cover up for you," the toothbrush sank into Mr. Bacon's midriff, "make sure it's someone who can stay on his feet."

She slammed the door in Mr. Bacon's furious face. For a moment she stood there, waiting. Then, as she heard his heavy, angry, frustrated steps retreating up the corridor, Miss Cranston turned to face Miss Marilyn Paige of Baltimore. The young girl, no longer resplendent because her black tulle and gleaming silver were mussed beyond splendor, nevertheless seemed lovelier than ever. The disheveled look helped. Even the tears made their subtle, if unreasonable, contribution. Miss Cranston was not surprised. You didn't need much when the dew was still on you.

Before Miss Cranston could prevent her, the young girl was in her arms and the hot tears were ruining the shoulder straps of the gown that had cost three weeks' salary. Miss Cranston sighed.

"Oh, I'm so ashamed and I don't know how I'll ever be able to thank you," Miss Paige sobbed. "I was so stupid and he was so awful. I thought he was nice at first when he came up and asked me to play bingo with him after dinner, but he isn't nice at all. You can't believe how awful he is. He—"

"I can believe it and there's nothing to be ashamed of and you don't have to thank me," Miss Cranston said softly, patting the heaving shoulder. "We all do stupid things. The only thing that matters is to remember, to learn from experience and try not to do them again." She tugged Miss Paige's hands from her neck. "Now," Miss Cranston said. "I know you're tired and I know you want to get to bed but there's one more thing you have to do tonight."

"I couldn't," Miss Paige sobbed. "I'm too worn out. I'll pack in the morning."

"We'll both pack in the morning," Miss Cranston said. "Right now you have to go up to the lounge. Somebody is waiting for you there. He's been there a long time. I wouldn't make him wait much longer."

Disbelief, joy, doubt and hope chased one another in a wild scramble across Miss Paige's lovely tear-stained face. Joy won. It always did, at twenty.

"Oh," Miss Paige said and then, pulling open the door, she said the word again, as though after careful thought she had decided that the single syllable was the highest and most subtle point ever attained by man in his long struggle to express his complex feelings in words. Miss Cranston, whose own eyes were filming, was not at all sure that Miss Paige wasn't right. "Oh," the young girl said once more and then she paused. "Gee," she said, with the astonishment of discovery, "I've never met anybody as nice as you."

"Yes, you have," Miss Cranston said. "He's up in the lounge right now."

Miss Paige smiled her wonderful smile and then her face clouded. "Gosh," she said. "These cruises." She shook her head, as though trying to straighten out the tangled scraps of a thought that, because it was so new, was somewhat unmanageable. "They're funny things," Miss Paige said. "You're so busy for sixteen days, you sort of miss some of the nicest people. I wish," she said and her mind worked for another moment at the thought that had baffled Mr. Murdoch up on deck a few minutes ago. "I wish we'd spent more time together. Now that I think of it," she said, not because she was unkind or even thoughtless, but because she was twenty and the sense of responsibility to others was still new to her, "you haven't had a very good time, have you?"

"Oh, I don't know," Miss Cranston said as her fingers probed for the damage in the borrowed sequin snood. She was not computing how many lunches she would have to forego during the coming weeks in order to replace the piece of borrowed finery. Miss Cranston was remembering what, in her moment of angry retaliation, she had written in Mr. Murdoch's souvenir menu. Perhaps, when she had defended him, when during the past sixteen days she had murmured to other passengers that Mr. Murdoch probably had troubles, poor man, like everybody else, perhaps she had been more than merely kind. Remembering what he had tried to tell her so incoherently on the deck a few minutes ago, Miss Cranston was suddenly convinced she had been right. All Mr. Murdoch of Pittsburgh needed was some help, and Miss Cranston of Greenwich Village did not mean the kind of help he and Mr. Bacon of Albany had been giving each other for sixteen days. "Don't you worry about me," Miss Cranston said cheerfully. She smiled at Miss Marilyn Paige of Baltimore. "I can't complain."

Even if Mr. Murdoch would not remember to tell her, in the morning before the ship docked, what he had tried to tell her a few minutes ago on deck, she was pretty sure he would remember to tell her, and probably say it better, in a letter from Pittsburgh. That souvenir menu was safely tucked in his pocket and nobody, not even Mr. Harvey Murdoch, could fail to make out her clear legible handwriting. "I've had a perfectly wonderful time," Miss Cranston said, feeling a surge of her old confidence and, more important, a delicious tremor of something completely new, something she had never before experienced but for which she had waited so long: the imminence of victory. "You go along and find your nice Mr. Cartwell and stop worrying about me," Miss Isabel Cranston said happily. "I'll get by."

I Thought About This Girl

I thought about this girl quite a lot. We all did—my mother, my father, my brothers, all of us. It seemed silly to let ourselves be upset by a girl who worked for us, but we couldn't help it. She worried us. All we knew was that for a long time she was happy with us, and then suddenly she wasn't.

She said nothing, of course, right up to the end. She was too considerate and friendly and kind to say anything, but we could tell. We could tell by the way she stood behind the counter in our little bakery, by the way she served a customer. She used to laugh all the time and keep the whole store bright with her energy and her smile and her pleasant voice. People spoke about it. It was such a pleasure to be served by her, they said.

"The smartest thing I ever did," my father would say with a smile as he watched her. "Hiring that girl was the smartest thing I ever did."

It wasn't that way very long, though. Not that we had any fault to find. She still came in early. She still worked hard. She still was polite and friendly and quick, but it wasn't the same. She didn't laugh any more. She stood very quietly when it wasn't busy and looked out of the window. She was worried about something.

At first we thought it would pass away, but it didn't. It got worse and worse. We did the obvious thing, of course. We asked her what was wrong.

"Nothing," she said at once, smiling quickly. "Nothing is wrong."

We asked her many times, but we still got the same answer, and knew it wasn't true.

It annoyed my mother.

"Why should we be bothered like this?" she asked sharply. "We've treated her like a daughter. Why should she be unhappy? Anyway, we didn't need her to start with."

And, of course, we didn't. We had always managed pretty well in the store. We were seldom overworked, because it is only a small bakeshop, though business is brisk and profitable. It happened very simply. A woman, a very good customer of ours, came in one day and told us about her—a poor girl from Poland whose parents were still on the other side and who had no one here to take care of her except an old aunt, herself far from wealthy. Wouldn't it be wonderful, this customer said to my mother, if it were possible to find some sort of job for the girl, something to help her support herself and make her less of a burden to her aunt? My mother was sympathetic and interested at once—she is always like that—and the woman went on to wonder casually if we mightn't be able to find a place for this girl in our own shop. Poor Mother was too far gone in compassion to realize that she had been trapped, and said quickly that we certainly could; she would talk to my father.

At first, of course, we laughed. There was scarcely enough work in the shop to keep all of us busy. It seemed ridiculous to hire anybody else.

"We'll be waiting on each other," my father said.

In the end, however, Mother brought us around. We can afford it, she said, and think how nice it would be to have a young girl's face in the store, how nice for the customers. Her arguments weren't very impressive, but Father seldom denies Mother anything she wants, so he said all right, let's take a look at her. And then, of course, as soon as we saw her, we were lost. She was so fresh and cheerful and bright, with her round face and her ready smile and her yellow hair.

"My God," my father said, "she looks like she was made for a bakery."

He pinched his chin between his thumb and forefinger and said well, maybe now he'd be able to have a little time to himself. There was a book on elementary chemistry that he'd been nibbling at cautiously for almost thirty years, ever since he came to America. Now, he said, he might get a chance to read it. There were also a lot of things my mother had always wanted to do. There were dishes she had yearned to make but had never dared try. Now she'd have time to experiment a little.

"You'll be able to cook," my father roared. "After thirty years you'll finally be able to cook."

It was a boisterous and happy occasion. The girl had done that for us.

After she had been with us a short while, however, we began to notice that my father hadn't made much progress with his chemistry and that there were no startling innovations at my mother's table. We knew the reason, of course. The habits of thirty years are not easily broken, and they were spending as much time as ever in the shop. But nobody seemed to mind. It was pleasant just to watch this girl with her bouncing energy and her happy laugh. Often my father would cock his head admiringly and repeat, "Smartest thing I ever did, hiring that girl."

Then suddenly he didn't say it any more. He still thought the world of her. We all did, but he was just as worried as the rest of us. What was wrong? Why was she no longer happy?

Before we could find an answer, and before our vague irritation could turn to anger, however, she came to us. She said she was leaving.

It was typical of her to wait until we were all together before she told us. She could have told my father or my mother or any one of us, but she knew how we all felt about her. It was hard for her to say it to all of us at the same time. She picked the harder way, because it seemed to her to be the right way.

"Leaving?" we asked, startled.

"Yes," she said quietly, dropping her eyes from ours. "I must leave."

Apparently it was something she had been wanting to tell us for a long time, something she had been afraid to tell us.

"But why?" we asked. "Why are you leaving?"

She didn't answer. She just shook her head and bit her lip.

"Aren't you happy here?" we asked.

"I am very happy here," she said.

"Don't we pay you enough?" we asked. "Do you want more?"
She shook her head quickly.

"No," she said, "you pay me enough."

We didn't want to make her cry, but somehow we couldn't stop asking questions.

"You have another job, maybe? A better one?"
She shook her head again.

"No, I have no other job."

"But you *need* a job, don't you?"

"Yes," she said, "I need a job."

"Then why?"

She didn't want to tell us, but we liked her too well not to insist on knowing.

"You can tell us, Mary," my mother said kindly. "We are your friends. You can tell us."

She looked up at us. She seemed confused and beaten, but she saw she would have to tell us.

"My mother," she began almost inaudibly, "my mother wrote me a letter from Poland—"

She stopped to blink away the tears, and then began again.

"My mother wrote me it isn't right," she said softly, brokenly. "She says it isn't right to—it isn't right to work for Jews."

She kept her puzzled, tearful glance upon us for another moment. Then she turned and walked away slowly, her shoulders shaking with her sobs.

Joust

For some reason, perhaps because of the congestion of people and houses, Fourth Street between Avenue D and Lewis was either bitterly cold or stiflingly hot. Spring and autumn were unknown on the block. One day in June, or so it seemed, the sun would suddenly become unbearable, the heat intense, breathing difficult. Then winter was over for Fourth Street and the older boys were free to go swimming from the dock.

The water was the only practical escape from the heat of Fourth Street. Trips to Coney Island involved too much time and preparation and were always in the nature of an event. The East River was a commonplace. You grew up with it and accepted it, like school and the inevitability of occasional illness.

Every boy on the block knew how to swim and used the river regularly. Periodically some parent would get a first clear glimpse of the oily filth in the water and forbid his offspring to swim from the Fourth Street dock. Such injunctions, however, always proved temporary and were regarded by the rest of the block as an unwarranted display of a finicky and undesirable trait known as being "high tone."

As a matter of fact, most parents on the block, not being swimmers themselves, were rather proud of their sons' prowess in the water. Mrs. Gordon, for instance, whose most prominent characteristics were her incredible obesity, her candy stand on the Lewis Street corner, and her son Mozzick, was particularly outspoken.

Mozzick was the block's champion swimmer, but his mother had never seen him in action because she was so fat that the task of shifting her bulk from the candy stand to the dock in the hot sun was beyond her.

"That's how life is," she said philosophically. "You raise them up, you slave, you suffer, and then, when they're old enough already they should do something you can be proud of, so then you can't see them do it! You gotta be fat! It's a lucky thing he isn't a singer. Otherwise, with the luck I got, I'd probably all of a sudden get deaf!"

Nor was Mozzick's ability as a swimmer overrated. He was not only the undisputed champion of Fourth Street, but he had successfully vanquished pretenders from other blocks who had come in summers past to wrest the title from him. Fifth Streeters in particular couldn't stand his supremacy. They were practically all Litvaks, while we on Fourth Street were almost exclusively Galician, and the traditional rivalry between the two had been carried over from Middle Europe to America and was kept alive from generation to generation.

Once, in fact, the Litvaks made such a concerted drive for Mozzick's crown that the entire neighborhood was in an uproar for weeks.

The Fifth Streeters' campaign was a subtle one. They didn't come forward with their customary annual challenge, which would have been followed by Fourth Street's customary acceptance and should have ended in Fifth Street's customary defeat. They started rumors of a mysterious swimming marvel who had been discovered in their midst and they made certain that these stories seeped into Fourth Street. When the time came for their annual challenge, in its stead Fourth Street received a set of new rumors, to the effect that the mysterious swimmer was being carefully groomed and wasn't quite ready for public appearance. And finally there were the tales of the unknown's astonishing physique: shadowy phrases, which defied substantiation, about his strange background, his appearance, his ability.

Many people on Fourth Street were upset by the vague yet persistent stories, but Mrs. Gordon was laughingly indignant at the mere thought of anyone's questioning her son's supremacy.

"What has that Litvak got?" she demanded of Fourth Street in

general and of her customer at the moment in particular. "Four
hands? A dozen feet? Maybe he's got a steam engine in his behind,
it makes him swim faster? Don't listen to those dopes from Fifth
Street."

The rest of the block shared her convictions, but not her placidity.
It was difficult for a street of Galicians to listen to the smug assump-
tion of Litvaks that they could win whenever they chose and only
refrained from so doing because they weren't quite in the mood for
it yet. So difficult was it, in fact, that Fourth Street, somewhat incredibly, finally broke down and challenged Fifth Street to produce
its swimming marvel and enter him in a race with Mozzick Gordon.

The offer was accepted and the cleverness of the Fifth Street Litvaks became apparent at once. As possessor of the champion,
Fourth Street should have received the invitation. But instead of
waiting patiently it had lost its head and issued the summons. The
result was that Fifth Street, having been challenged, had the right to
state terms and conditions. The race, they said firmly, would be
from the Fourth Street dock across the East River to Brooklyn and
back; no pause on the Brooklyn side for rest; both swimmers to be
accompanied by rowboats. Galicians are traditionally too proud
to protest, especially to Litvaks, and the terms were agreed to. But
Fourth Street knew it had been tricked and dealt a blow.

It was a fact well known that Mozzick Gordon could move
through dirty water quickly. His endurance was an unknown quan-
tity. And the distance that Fifth Street had insisted upon, to Brooklyn and back, made two things perfectly plain: endurance, not
speed, would be the deciding factor in the race, and Fifth Street
was especially confident of its candidate's staying powers.

There was a good deal of comment on Fourth Street about the
stupidity of certain unnamed people in permitting themselves to be
trapped in such fashion, and on the day of the race there were probably only three people on the block who felt utterly confident that
Fourth Street would retain its East Side swimming supremacy. They
were Mrs. Gordon, her son Mozzick, and Srul Honig, whose father was
a professional gambler and ran a poker game in their fifth-floor apartment on Fourth Street. Srul was taking bets on the contest, basing
his confidence on some mysterious version of what he called the
"lawvaverages."

On the day decided on for the race a large crowd assembled on the dock and spread over onto the huge, flat coal barges that were moored alongside. Srul Honig moved through it quickly, jotting down bets and loudly giving his opinion of the outcome. A small knot of Fifth Streeters was gathered at one side, completely surrounding and hiding from view their contestant. A similar group of Fourth Streeters surrounded Mozzick Gordon at the other side of the dock. Somebody blew a whistle and the noises on the dock stopped. The Fourth Street group parted and Mozzick Gordon stepped jauntily to the edge of the dock. He wore a pair of trunks and a wide grin, and he bounced up and down on his toes as he waited.

Then the Fifth Street group parted and three people stepped out. Two were fully dressed and between them walked a grotesque-looking young man of uncertain age. A murmur of amazement crossed the dock quickly. He was short and thin and stooped. He had only one arm and his face bore the blank, childish look of the mental defective. The two men brought him to the edge of the dock. Mozzick, a few feet away, stared at them with his mouth open. Before he could speak, however, the whistle blew again.

"Ready?" the starter called.

Mozzick nodded, crouching on the edge of the dock.

"Ready," said one of the men with the Fifth Street swimmer.

There was the crack of a gun. Mozzick dived gracefully outward. The two Fifth Streeters seized their man firmly and pushed him off the dock. He fell without a cry and struck the water with a loud slap. Everybody craned to see him as he rose to the surface and began to move. The helplessness he had displayed on the dock was suddenly gone. He glided through the water smoothly and evenly, lying on one side so that only his one arm was visible as it rose and fell to pull him forward. There was grace in the rhythmic rise and fall of his single arm and there must have been power, too, because Mozzick did not appear to be increasing the lead he had gained by his dive. The two rowboats pulled out after them and the crowd on the dock settled itself for a long wait.

As the bobbing heads and the accompanying rowboats grew smaller many people left the dock. It was estimated that the swimmers would not be back for several hours. A few small groups, consisting of those who had placed bets on the event and those whose allegiance to one or the other of the contestants was deeper than the discomfort of the hot sun, lay about on the coal barges, shielding their eyes, listening to the slap of the water and the creaking of the ropes as the barges strained at their moorings.

Gradually, as the hours went by, people began to drift back onto the dock, until it was almost dangerously crowded.

"There's one of them!"

Everybody followed a pointing finger. A rowboat was coming toward the dock, growing larger with each pull of the oars.

"There's the other one, too!"

The second rowboat seemed just slightly behind the first one, a little to one side. It was hard to tell how much space separated them. And it was still impossible to identify the swimmers.

"Who's in the lead?"

"Can't tell yet!"

But soon they were close enough for the crowd to see that one of them rolled from side to side as he swam, while the other glided evenly, swinging one arm in a tireless circular motion, and that the latter was in the lead.

"Fifth Street's ahead!"

And he was, by quite a distance. The Litvaks cheered wildly, but nobody even bothered to urge Mozzick on. He was too far behind and he seemed too tired for a spurt. The Galicians watched glumly while the Fifth Streeters began to call instructions to their swimmer.

"Over here, dope! There's a ladder here!"

They were pointing to a ladder that was nailed to the end of the dock. But he paid no attention to them. He continued his easy, powerful strokes without raising his head from the water, heading straight for a huge coal barge which was moored loosely to the dock, so that it swung to and fro, bumping against the dock with soft, deadly force at regular intervals.

"Head him off!" the Fifth Streeters cried to the men in the rowboat. "Steer him around to the ladder!"

The men in the rowboat, who had stopped rowing as their swimmer neared the dock, suddenly realized that he was about to enter the narrow strip of water which had just opened between the barge and the dock. One of them bent to the oars while the other began to scream. "Over to the left! Stay out of there! Get over to the ladder!"

The swimmer did not change his course or seem to hear the shouting.

"He don't understand anything!" the Fifth Streeters on the dock cried. "All he knows is how to swim! Hurry up! Grab him!"

But there was too much distance between the rowboat and the swimmer. Before they could reach him, he had glided into the dangerous opening. The screaming and the shouting stopped, suddenly. A long line of heads peered over the edge of the coal barge at the swimmer, below, watching in terrified silence. Every face twisted with the same tense thought. It was a long barge, but he was swimming strongly, rapidly. He might get through.

The barge completed its outward swing and was brought up with a shudder as it reached the end of its ropes. It hung hesitant for a moment and then began its backward swing. The space of water narrowed slowly, inexorably. He was two-thirds of the way along its side when one man on the barge pulled back his head and turned away quickly. Everybody did the same.

There was a single, weird scream, and then the barge touched the dock gently and began to swing away again.

The Kinnehórrah

Every family in our block had a reputation of sorts. The Fabians were authorities on citizenship papers and remittances to Europe, because Mr. Fabian was secretary of a lodge. The Lessings (even the children), on the strength of their father's drugstore, gave out medical advice. But we—our family—we were weather prophets.

There was really nothing extraordinary about our ability to foretell the weather, just as there was nothing very unusual about the extent of Mr. Fabian's knowledge about citizenship papers. There were probably a score of people on the block who could have given you as good advice about either. But the people of our block were funny. When they wanted advice, whether they intended to take it or not, they wanted it from a source that was commonly conceded to be authoritative.

Perhaps it doesn't sound so very important. But it was, really. Take, for instance, the problem of a trip to Coney Island. What with the walk to Essex and Delancey for the subway, the changing at Canal Street, and the ride itself—nearly an hour—it was a good two-hour trip from where we lived on Sixth Street and Avenue D. And then the food that had to be made ready, and the bundles of bathing suits and sweaters and blankets that had to be wrapped and tied. Naturally, it wasn't very pleasant to complete all these preparations, or, worse yet, actually start out, and then have it all go to waste because of rain.

Mother was the real authority, and to her we owed our reputation. She had a set of corns that were known from Sixth to Houston Street. And when she squinted at the star-dotted sky of a summer evening and said, "The weather will be bad tomorrow; my corns," you could be sure of at least two things: the people on the stoop who had sought her advice would cancel their contemplated trip to Coney Island or Fort George, and it would rain or be cold the next day.

Our house was a large, five-story tenement, with six tenants on each floor. We lived on the third floor, and were on borrowing terms with all the neighbors on our floor, but the Liebeskinds were our special friends. There were three left in the family: Mr. and Mrs. Liebeskind, and their daughter Ester. Two sons and another daughter were married and had children of their own. Ester was the youngest, twenty-eight. The old people were well past sixty, very religious, and beginning to worry about Ester.

One day Mrs. Pincus came in for a kernel of garlic and told Mother, suppressed excitement in her voice, that she thought Ester Liebeskind was "going steady." Twice the week before she had seen her leave the house with the same boy. On Avenue D, every unmarried man is a "boy," and even spinsters of forty are "girls."

Mother went right in to Mrs. Liebeskind to verify the good news. I tagged along.

"*Shah, shah,*" the old lady beamed. "Who is it that can say? Perhaps there will be yet something from it." And she gave me a big *Eierküchel,* still warm from the oven, because it was Friday.

In a week the whole tenement was buzzing with the news. A new marriage was in the making.

When he started to eat supper regularly at the Liebeskinds', everybody knew it was definite. And one night Ester brought him in and introduced him to us. His name was Tenner, Irving Tenner, and he worked in the post office. Soon he was a frequent visitor to our apartment, coming and going almost as readily as the Liebeskinds themselves. We became such friends that Mother was asked to help with the preparations for the engagement party, and for a solid week before the event she lived in the kitchen, baking and cooking, and stacking the buffet and table in our front room with sponge cake and honey cake and prune tarts and stuffed sides of veal and fish in sauces at once sweet and sour and cabbage leaves rolled with chopped meat and rice.

The wedding was set for the third week in April, right after Passover. It was to be a "couple supper" at Lenox Assembly Rooms, which meant that only two adults from each family that received an invitation could attend. Mother and Father, naturally, were invited. There were to be no children at the wedding—there never were any children at couple suppers—but since there were no small boys in either of the two families, I was chosen as page boy.

The very first day after the Second Days of Passover, about a week before the wedding, a small crowd of us—Ester and Irving, the old people, Father and Mother and I—went out to rent tuxedos and evening gowns.

We went to Benny Bauer's place on Houston Street for the tuxedos. We didn't have much trouble there, except for the difficulty of getting a collar small enough to go with the special page-boy's tuxedo that I was to wear. Then we went to Madame Jennie's store, on Clinton Street, for the women's stuff. Mr. Liebeskind decided to go home, and Father and Irving went with him.

I was sitting on a pile of boxes near the window, watching the lights of the Palestine Theater across the street. Madame Jennie, fat and overflowing, was taking down dresses and hanging them up. They were all bright green and orange and yellow, without sleeves.

I heard Mother's voice. "What color wrap you going to get, Ester?"

"What does she need a wrap?" Mrs. Liebeskind said. "It's spring. It's April. It's after Passover."

Madame Jennie kept puffing around.

This time Mother was speaking in a very low voice. I could hardly hear her. "I think you ought to get a wrap, Ester. I'm afraid you'll be cold in that thin dress. Without sleeves yet."

Mrs. Liebeskind must have been listening carefully. "What's the matter with you?" she snapped. "Are you trying to make her spend money? For what black year does one need a wrap in such weather? Don't talk it into her."

The night before the wedding, we were all in the Liebeskind apartment. Father was sitting at the kitchen table, drinking beer from a bottle and telling about weddings he remembered in Europe. Mr. Liebeskind's married daughter was trying to get her father to trim his beard, but he kept shouting over and over again that he wouldn't do it, "he should so live!" I was sitting on the washtub, eating matzoths from a box left over from Passover. Mother was squatting at Ester's feet, putting a tuck in her gown. Natie, one of Ester's nephews, banged in. He'd just come from Irving's house, and Irving wanted to know if he could come over. Mr. Liebeskind yelled that he couldn't. It was unorthodox. Natie banged out. I leaned over to get another matzoth.

"What will you wear over your dress?" Mother was asking Ester.

"Nothing," Ester said. "Mamma says I don't need anything."

Mother took a couple of stitches in the dress. Ester stood up very straight, so the tuck would be even all the way around. "You ought to get a wrap," Mother said. "I think the weather is going to be bad tomorrow. My corns hurt."

The old lady must have heard, because she spoke angrily. "Don't be a fool. Wish nothing upon us. You and your corns! It's after Passover now! It's spring! What's the matter with you?"

About four o'clock the next day we began to dress. At five-thirty Natie yelled up from the street to ask if we were ready. The cars, he said, were waiting.

Mother looked out of the window and said to Father, "You know, it feels chilly. I'm going to take my coat. My corns hurt."

A howl of laughter greeted us when we came downstairs. Mother was the only one who was wearing a coat.

"Why don't you get a pair of ear muffs?" Mr. Liebeskind cried, tugging at his beard as he laughed. Mother smiled, but said nothing.

We climbed into one of the cars, and the small procession rode very slowly down the few short blocks to Lenox Assembly Rooms. I missed the dancing that preceded the wedding ceremony, because Mother took me into a small room just off the large dance hall to dress me in the tuxedo. All I could hear was the band playing "Yes! We Have No Bananas" over and over again.

When we came out, finally, the dancing had stopped and the big hall was set for the ceremony. At the far end, under a blue canopy held up by four men, stood Ester and Irving and the rabbi. He held a small black book in his hands. Stretching away to the rear of the hall, where I stood, was the assembly of guests. They stood about uncomfortably in two groups, one on either side of the room, forming a long lane down the middle. Somebody handed me a white satin pillow, with four large tassels hanging from the corners and a gold wedding ring sewed lightly to the top. They adjusted my hands and arms so that I was holding it out in front of me, palms up, like a tray, and gave me a gentle shove.

I walked down the aisle slowly, the way I had been taught, and on both sides I could hear loud whispers. "Look on him. Isn't he cute? So sweet."

When I got to the end, the rabbi reached down and tore the ring easily from the top of the cushion. I walked back. There was a slight explosion. I knew what it was because Father had once explained it to me. Irving had stamped on a wineglass. It was part of the ceremony.

Mother took me into the small room again and helped me to change out of my tuxedo. By the time we came out, everybody was going downstairs for the meal.

We sat at the next table but one from the bride and the groom. There were seven people at our table. I sat directly facing Ester.

When the waiter brought in the second plate of stuffed derma, he said, "You know, it's snowing outside."

"Go away!" an old man at our table said. "Who you fooling? After Passover? Snow? Go away!"

"On my honest word!" the waiter insisted. "Go give a look, I should live so, it's snowing."

Father reached for the derma. "It could be," he said. "I remember once when I was a boy in Europe it happened."

Mother said, "It is as though I would have known. I felt it in the feet all day yesterday. My corns. It is yet a good thing I wore a coat."

The whole dining room was buzzing with excitement. Snow in April! After Passover! It was unheard-of.

After a few more courses, the waiter came around with a plate for the tips. "Better make quick," he said. "It looks like the snow is going to stop soon."

But it didn't. It snowed for nearly an hour. Everybody was talking about it. We left about one o'clock. The snow had stopped, but we took a taxi because Mother was the only one who had a coat, and it was chilly in the street.

A couple of mornings later I learned the news. Ester had caught a cold the night of the wedding. The next day she became feverish and Irving took her home from their new apartment, back to the Liebeskinds. They called the doctor. He said it was the grippe.

As soon as Mother heard about it, she rushed across the hall to see if she could be of any help. But Mrs. Liebeskind would not let her into the apartment.

"We don't need any help," she said angrily, standing in the doorway.

"Isn't there something I can do?" Mother asked anxiously.

"Nothing," the old lady said, and slammed the door.

Nor would she, during the week that followed, accept Mother's repeated offers of assistance. After Ester's illness developed into pneumonia, Mrs. Liebeskind would not even open her door when someone knocked. And by the time Ester died, less than two weeks after her wedding, we had not seen or spoken to the Liebeskinds for days.

I asked Mother if I could go to the funeral, but she said no. I had to content myself with watching from our front-room window.

Starting from the stoop, a line of almost ten cars stretched down the block. The first one was a hearse. The drivers, in long black alpaca coats, stood leaning against one of the cars, a small group, smoking cigarettes and chatting. Once in a while a rattle of laughter came up from them. A crowd dotted both sidewalks, and two or three old men with long, white beards made their way along the block, from group to group, rattling their *pushkes* brazenly for alms.

There was a lull in the pattern of noises. A white pine casket issued from the doorway immediately beneath me. The two men in front were straining it above their heads, trying to keep it on a level with the rear. The stoop was a steep one. From where I was watching, the casket seemed to be coming out without support in the back, like a pennant floating in a slow breeze.

The drivers stamped out their cigarettes and climbed into the cars. The hearse was opened, the casket shoved in, the doors slammed shut.

The pallbearers and relatives were stowing themselves in the cars.

I saw Irving come down the stoop, supporting Mrs. Liebeskind. Since the night of the wedding she seemed to have become a little more stooped, a little more shrunken. He led her to the first car behind the hearse and settled her in the rear. It was an open touring car, with the top down.

Suddenly she caught sight of Mother, standing near the stoop. She sprang up, almost falling out of the car. Irving grabbed at her. She began to scream and flail her arms.

"You did it! You! You! You murderer! You couldn't bear to see her happy! You wished it on her! You gave her a kinnehórrah! You killed her! You—"

Her voice cracked. Irving succeeded in pulling her down. He put his hand over her mouth and signaled to the driver. The cortege started.

A week later we moved.

Let Me Explain You Something

He was short and fat and bald. His face seemed to have been polished to a high lustre, and when he talked his features worked so violently that at times his eyes were almost completely hidden by rolls of flesh. Twice a month, every second Monday, he arrived at the office, one hand holding his soiled derby to the opposite shoulder, like an officer in civilian dress saluting the flag, the long, narrow cardboard box under his arm resting a bit on his paunch.

The girl at the switchboard had strict instructions not to let him in, but I could always tell when he had arrived by the commotion in the outer office. There was no back door through which I could escape, and he knew that if he waited long enough I would eventually see him. In the beginning I used to try to outwait him. But his patience was inexhaustible. So as soon as I heard his voice, I hurried out to try to get rid of him as quickly as possible.

"Hul*lo*, my friend," he shouted as soon as he saw me, advancing with his hand outstretched, carrying the box with him, and smiling. "How *are* you? How's business? How—?"

"Look, Mr. Prensky," I said, "I'm very busy now. And, anyway, I don't need any ties. Why don't you—?"

He stopped short with a gesture of amazement.

"Ties I'm trying to sell you? Who said something about ties? I can't come visit a couple my friends without they should think all the time I'm trying to sell them ties? Listen, let me explain you something."

He put the box down on a chair and seized my lapel with his free hand, still holding on to the derby with the other.

"Business I wish by you should be so good, a million dollars you should make every week. Orders you should get by the thousanders so many, fifty letter carriers they should have to use extra for you alone special in the post office. But God forbid, you should get sick tomorrow, what good all the business and all the millioners is gonna do you? You should have a couple good *friends* better, than all the money in the whole world, first *then* you're better off."

I started to say, "I'm very busy, Mr. Prensky, and—" but he shook me into silence.

"Wait, wait. Let me explain you something. I'm walking past the building, just like this. I look up, I see the number, I say to myself I got a friend of mine in this building. Y'understand, I'm in a hurry. I got business to tend to, but I say to myself: What's business? A friend is a friend, but what's business? All the business in the whole world, it isn't worth a *nickel* compared next to a good friend. So I come up like this, just to say hello, how are you. And right away you think I'm trying to sell you ties."

"I'm sorry," I said, beginning to feel uncomfortable. "But I don't wear those ties anyway, and I don't want you to waste your time—"

"*Sure*," he exclaimed, jerking me violently by the lapel for emphasis. "I *know* you don't wear these ties. But who's trying to sell you ties? Listen, let me explain you something. I got a wife, she should live a hundred and twenty years; when I married her thirty years ago she went around so high class you would think, hoo-hah, she was a governor's daughter at *least*. But I said to myself, it's better it should be like that, than a dope who don't know nothing. When I took her to the theayter the second balcony wasn't good enough. It hadda be the dress circle. Came to get something to eat, a cafeteria she wouldn't even look on. Hadda be at least the chink's, with a waiter. But I figured, all right, the more it costs, the better you get. So now I'm married thirty years, what do you think I got? Not even a son I haven't got. A daughter, she should live a hundred and twenty years, I got. And like her mother she is, to the minute. What do you think she's doing now?"

I shook my head and tried to break away, but he held me more tightly and even dropped his hat to seize my other lapel.

"Wait, just let me explain you something. She's already more than twenty-seven years, and my wife she keeps on telling me all the time she's worried Frances is gonna be an old maid, she's not gonna get a feller, she don't go out with boy friends enough. For my part, I'm not worried. I'm not saying I'm such a college professor, but I'm not such a dope neither. I figure like this, if her mother, she should live a hundred and twenty years, she could find a sucker like me, then Frances got nothing to worry. And what do you think? Just like I said, not long after, she comes home with a feller, they're engaged, go make them a wedding. All right, I said, why not, I'll make you a wedding. So I hire a hall, I made a couple sopper, I rent a full dress, I buy schnapps, I hire a band. So it's good, no? But not by my wife. She goes around all day with a face long like a horse. What's the matter, I say, the hall is no good, the meat is got worms, the full dress got a hole in the pants? What's the matter? Everything is all right, she says, excepting the band. What's the matter with the band, I say. Well, she says, Frances got a friend, she got married not long before to a certified accountant, and everything was the same except in the band. Why shouldn't Frances have also eight pieces in the band, just like her friend, instead only six, especially Frances is marrying a lawyer better yet than a certified accountant?"

He stopped for a moment and released me long enough to wipe his mouth with the back of his hand, but then he seized my coat again.

"A lawyer he is! Everything is called a lawyer! Such a lawyer like he is, all my worst enemies should be! Who is he, who? A little snot-nose, he just finished school, he didn't even take yet the bar exam, go make him a wedding, he's gotta have a band with eight pieces. Six isn't good enough for him. Eight pieces it's gotta be! But what can you do! You got a wife and a daughter, they should live a hundred and twenty years, they got tastes like they was a regular Mrs. Vanderbilt. Not enough I gotta make a wedding, I gotta hire yet two extra pieces for the band."

Here he paused dramatically and stepped away from me, his arms outstretched.

"So what I'm telling you all this for? Why I'm taking up all your time, you a busy man like you? Let me explain you. A wife is like a tie. You think you pay more, you get better quality. Maybe you do. I don't say no. But you get more headaches, too. A high class wife, she wants for her daughter expensive weddings, with eight-piece bands. A high class tie, you gotta watch, no gravy should fall on it, no soup should spill on it. But I got here"—he darted to the box and had it open under my nose in a single movement—"a selection ties. A number one, costs only fifty-five cents apiece, special price to my friends, looks just like a regular high class—"

I bought three.

A Lodging for the Night

"Is that far out?" Lieutenant Driscoll said, reading the address from the canvas-backed pocket notebook that had his initials burned into the small leather square saddle-stitched to the cover. His mother had sent it to him from Mark Cross for Christmas in 1942 when he was still in OCS at Fort Sill. "Twenty-three sixteen Forty-first Street Northwest?"

"Not too far," the taxi driver said without turning. "It's in the third zone. Place called Glover Park."

Driscoll looked at the rate schedule pasted to the window near his ear, suddenly surprised and not quite pleased by a twinge of loneliness, a loneliness he must have been feeling for some time without knowing it, and he read the numbers backward: third zone, single passenger rate, seventy cents; group passenger rate, forty cents.

"Well, take it easy," Driscoll said, not meaning it, feeling the slow, mounting excitement begin to wash away the loneliness, feeling it in spite of the knowledge, buried deep down in his mind where he could keep it separate and under control, that he was not entitled to the excitement, this excitement that he nevertheless wanted, wanted very badly, to feel. "But not too easy," Driscoll said. "I promised I'd be there about ten."

He put his feet up on the Val-Pak, doing it self-consciously, even though there was nobody to watch him, doing it as an exercise in self-control, telling himself to take it easy, and he humped his back into a comfortable spot in the lumpy, scuffed leather upholstery.

He slipped the canvas-backed notebook into his right-hand breast pocket, under the Presidential Citation, and his fingers, reflecting the churning in his stomach, slipped once or twice as he slid the button through the buttonhole and clicked the two snap fasteners, at the pointed ends of the pocket flap, into place.

"It's twenty to ten now, and it's about a fifteen-twenty-minute ride," the taxi driver said. "You'll make it."

"I made it," Driscoll said, watching the lights on Pennsylvania Avenue shoot by, and he hoped the implication of his remark was not lost on the taxi driver. "Is that the White House?"

"No, that's State," the taxi driver said. "We passed the White House a block back. You getting out?"

"I'm out," Lieutenant Driscoll said. "Tomorrow, when I get to New York where my mother's been keeping my clothes, you can call me mister."

Tomorrow was the time, not now, he told himself, but he didn't really believe it, and he grinned at himself in the darkness. Tomorrow was the time, but this was the way he felt now, and it wasn't his fault. He had been told to do it, he had been urged, and he was doing what he had been told. If the feeling that was mounting in him was part of doing what he had been urged, that wasn't his fault. Driscoll relaxed and allowed the sense of anticipation to encircle him, and take him, and carry him forward twenty minutes, to Glover Park, whatever that was.

"Okay, mister," the taxi driver said. "Where were you when they quit?"

"In a C-54 out of Guam heading for Pearl," Driscoll said. "Where were you?"

"In this cab at Fourteenth and G, and I didn't move for three hours," the driver said. "The city went nuts. That's the Carlton, over there up ahead, where Anthony Eden and all them diplomats stay when they come."

"The sort of white and tan one?" Driscoll said to be polite. "With the lights?"

"No, that's the Statler," the driver said. "This side of the street, the dark gray one. What happened then?"

"The pilot dipped his wings a couple of times," Driscoll said, wishing the taxi driver would shut up. Driscoll didn't want to talk.

He wanted to be alone with his anticipation, to roll it around on his tongue like good liquor. "That woke up the guys who were sleeping and then everybody brought out the bottle he was saving. Damnedest plane ride I ever had, but we made it," Driscoll said and then, as though he were repeating the tag line of a joke or the refrain of a song that had captured his fancy, he said, "I made it."

"Well, good luck, Lieutenant," the taxi driver said and, as though the song had become infectious but there was another line that he preferred, the taxi driver added, "I mean mister."

"Thanks," Driscoll said. "You, too."

He lit a cigarette and tried to put the match into the nickel ash tray set in the back of the front seat, but now he was so nervous that he missed, and then, when he tried again, he found that the thing was jammed, so Driscoll dropped the match on the floor. They'd be putting new cabs on the street soon, with snap ash trays that worked, and he'd be riding in them, night after night, whenever he wanted to, feeling again this slow, mounting, wonderful tension that was part of going to pick up a strange girl, a new girl, a girl he had never seen. Driscoll dropped his feet from the Val-Pak and sat up on the flaking seat. He was getting his taxi rides mixed up. He had no right to that tension. Not on this ride.

Driscoll moved all the way over to the side of the cab and stretched the leg out straight on the seat to ease the slight, almost delicious, pain in his knee, and then he looked around quickly in the semi-darkness, moving his head back and forth several times, very fast, before he realized what was wrong. There was no meter. Driscoll grinned and looked out the window. In all the taxi rides he had taken in his mind by day and in his dreams at night during the past two years, there had always been a meter. Well, this wasn't his city. Not yet. And this wasn't that kind of taxi ride, either. Not yet. The clustered lights had disappeared and now the cab was rolling up a wide, dim thoroughfare with tall trees and large, imposing stone houses on both sides, mansions set back from the street in landscaped grounds and guarded by gates, and the street lights were widely spaced.

"Massachusetts Avenue," the taxi driver said without turning. "That's the British Embassy on your right. All the big ones are along here."

Driscoll didn't answer, although he continued to look out the window. The anticipation to which he was not entitled had given way to a more practical consideration. He was suddenly worried about the Val-Pak. Probably it would have been better if he had gone to the hotel first. Not that he was afraid he would lose the room. They had said, on the phone from the airport, that they would hold the room for him no matter how late he came in. Driscoll was worried because now the taxi was beyond Massachusetts Avenue, obviously beyond the heart of the city, riding through quiet tree-shaded streets of small, neat, nest-like houses that reminded him of Scarsdale and Bronxville, streets so quiet that he could hear the low tearing hum of the taxi's tires, and it occurred to Driscoll that on streets like these at ten in the evening, a reasonable hour downtown but clearly quite late out here, a Val-Pak might look funny, even a Val-Pak accompanied by a man who had just stepped out of a plane. Driscoll snapped the cigarette out the window and he saw it shatter on the pavement in a shower of tiny sparks as the taxi turned a corner and stopped in the middle of a block of two-story frame houses that stretched from corner to corner. They were all alike, with party walls and mansard roofs and small scraps of lawn that led into each other, like the houses themselves, and narrow flagstone walks running from the sidewalk to the doors on which the metal house numbers were nailed at an angle, all slanting up toward the identical wrought-iron mail boxes.

"Twenty-three sixteen?" Driscoll said.

"I thought you said twenty-three twenty-six," the taxi driver said. He started the motor again and pulled up five doors and stopped in front of the only house on the street that showed a light. "Twenty-three sixteen," he said.

Driscoll got out and swung the Val-Pak to the sidewalk and looked up and down the silent street as he put his hand into his pocket. "What do you do for transportation around here?" he said and then, when he saw the look on the taxi driver's face, "I mean around about midnight?"

"Not much chance of getting a cab," the driver said, taking the dollar bill and pressing the plunger of the coin machine tied to the side of his steering wheel shaft three times. "They don't cruise out here that late, but there's a bus stop around the corner, around that

one, there, on the far side. It runs twice an hour on the half hour
till one in the morning. You take that D-2 bus and it'll get
you downtown, pretty near any place you want to go, or some place
where you can get a cab, anyway."

"Thanks," Driscoll said. "That's all right."

"Thank you, Lieutenant," the driver said and he nodded as he
slid the three dimes back into the coin machine. "I mean mister,"
the driver said.

The taxi rolled off down the street and around the corner, and
Driscoll picked up the Val-Pak and started up the flagstone walk
toward the door with the numbers 2316 nailed to it. The door
opened and a girl, in a flowered dirndl and a white blouse with a
V-neck and flat-heeled saddle shoes, came down the walk.

"You're Herb," she said, laughing as she shook his free hand and,
without any sign of surprise, reached for the Val-Pak. "Hello," she
said. "Let me help you with that."

"No, that's all right," Driscoll said, swinging it out of her reach.
"You're Betsy. Hello." She made another try for the Val-Pak, but he
held it away, and she laughed again and went on ahead and held
the door for him. Driscoll dumped the Val-Pak next to the umbrella
stand and she closed the door. "Sorry to mess up your place with a
thing like this," he said. "But I thought if I went to the hotel first
and left it and started washing up and all that, why, it might be
too late to come out, and then I wouldn't have another chance, because I've got a seat on the nine o'clock train to New York tomorrow
morning, and I promised Roger I'd stop by to say hello on my way
through. Whew," Driscoll said. "How's that for an explanation?"

"One of the nicest I ever heard," Betsy Parker said. "And you can
see for yourself that it's impossible to mess up this place any worse
than it is. I've been trying to do a frantic tidying job since you called,
but it was too much, so I just gave up and left it as is. Do you mind?"

"Not at all," Driscoll said. "It looks swell."

"Why don't you give me your hat, and what will you drink?"
Betsy Parker said. "I've got blended whiskey and that's all, but I have
tons of that. One of our girls got married last week and we sneaked
three bottles from under the noses of the very drunken guests."

"I am the world's champion devotee of blended whiskey, whatever that is," Driscoll said, and he handed her his hat. "I will take

two inches, with the same amount of plain water, and a lump of ice if you have it. Who's the lucky girl?"

"You wouldn't know her," Betsy Parker said, putting his hat on the keyboard of the upright piano, next to a blue bowl the bottom of which was covered with the stale dust of pretzel sticks eaten long ago. "She's one we got after I stopped writing Roger about the inmates of this asylum. There were just too many to keep track of. Can I get you a hassock or a chair for your leg? Roger wrote—"

"Your brother Roger is one of the sweetest guys currently in the Pacific Ocean," Driscoll said, sitting down on the couch. "But he is the greatest little worrier between here and Nagasaki, especially about his friends. There is nothing wrong with my leg that two inches of blended whiskey, plus the same amount of water, plus a lump of ice, will not cure. If there is ice?"

"There is plenty of ice," Betsy Parker said. "Now you just wait. I won't be a second, and I want to hear everything."

She went out through an archway that led into what looked like a dining alcove and she disappeared to the left, presumably into the kitchen, and Driscoll looked around the room. It was not very large, although it ran the entire width of the house, and Betsy Parker had spoken no less than the truth. The room was not very neat. The fireplace was choked by stacks of newspapers that may have been waiting for the salvage collector, but somehow did not look it, and bits of potato chips and salted soy beans were imbedded in the multi-colored rag rug. Somebody had started to paint a mural across the front of the upright piano, but had stopped in the middle of a tree with pink branches. The dust covers on the chairs were wrinkled and some of the seams had parted. There were two Chinese prints on the wall above the couch, and half a dozen tarnished brass candlesticks on the mantelpiece over the fireplace. None of the ash trays matched and most of them were chipped and all of them were full. A dozen or more wedding invitations were pasted in a line all around the woodwork of the archway that led to the dining alcove. Driscoll counted eighteen of them. A large wardrobe trunk, slightly open, stood in the center of the room. Betsy Parker came back with the drinks in two glasses of different size that had obviously once been jelly jars.

"Thanks," Driscoll said. They toasted Roger in the Pacific

and drank, and she sat down at his feet on the hassock he had spurned, and Driscoll, reflecting that you certainly could not tell from the appearance of a friend what his sister would look like, was suddenly very glad he had come. Betsy Parker was a damned pretty girl. "What's that?" Driscoll said, pointing to the trunk. "You going somewhere?"

"No, that's Elsa's," Betsy Parker said. "One of the inmates. She's going to Canada for a couple of weeks and she went to the drug store around the corner to get some Kleenex before she locks it."

"Oh," Driscoll said. "She coming back soon?"

"In a few minutes, probably," Betsy Parker said. "But then she has to run. She's taking the midnight to New York, and the express people are calling for the trunk in the morning."

"Canada?" Driscoll said.

"Elsa's Austrian," Betsy Parker said. "She has some sort of relatives up there who escaped in 1938, I think, and got as far as Montreal, but they haven't been able to get their entry visas into this country yet. Elsa's got sixteen days of annual leave coming to her from FCC where she's a research analyst, so she's going up to see them for a while. She was a year behind me at Bennington. Now about Roger."

Driscoll told her about Roger, who was fine, and Driscoll said Roger should be coming home soon, which was a lie because Roger did not have nearly enough points, but excusable because she was Roger's sister. Then Betsy Parker asked where he had been when the Japs quit, so he told her about the crazy plane trip, and then she wanted to know about his leg, so Driscoll told her about the piece of flak and his knee and the wonderfully troublesome water that kept accumulating under the cartilage, not enough to bother him but enough to get him out, and Driscoll kissed his finger tips and tapped the knee reverently and they both laughed.

"Now about you," Driscoll said, and he pointed to the string of wedding invitations pasted around the archway that led to the dining room. "Begin with those things," he said.

"Let's have another one of these before I start on me," Betsy Parker said. "Same?"

"Same," Driscoll said, handing her his glass. "But maybe three inches this time and two lumps of ice and a little less water. If you have a little less water?"

"I have tons of less water," Betsy Parker said. "Now, don't you move."

She came back with the drinks, and she sat down on the hassock, and she explained that the wedding invitations were from all the girls who had lived in the house and been married out of it since Betsy had rented the place in the summer of 1942, when she came down, after graduating from Bennington, to work for the Office of Censorship. The rent was sixty-five a month, unfurnished, and there were three bedrooms upstairs, two doubles and a single, so they could sleep five, although there had been times when six girls had lived in the house all at once, the sixth sleeping on the couch Driscoll was sitting on at this very moment. It had been pretty hectic at times, especially since there was only one bathroom and that was upstairs, but Betsy Parker had kept the lease in her own name and she'd been pretty careful about the girls she chose to live in the house, so there had never been any real trouble and most of the time it had been fun, in spite of the problems of communal cooking and shopping and dividing up the dusting and dish washing, although in a way that had been the most fun of all. That was all finished now, of course, because the war was over and the sort of girls that Betsy Parker wanted to have in her house were all leaving Washington, although she herself liked the city and she had switched over to Agriculture when the Office of Censorship folded after V-J Day and she intended to stay on indefinitely, although she'd probably have to give up the house and find a small apartment somewhere, much as she loathed apartments with all their stupid formality, because she and Elsa were the only two left and, when Elsa went off to Canada in a few minutes, Betsy would be all alone in the place. Driscoll took a long swallow and, for a moment, he felt slightly troubled about sitting so high up and looking down on a girl at his feet in a low-cut V-neck blouse who was Roger's sister, so he took another swallow and asked about the furniture.

"Yours is empty," Betsy Parker said, and she finished her own drink. "I'll make a couple of fresh ones before I go into *that*. A little more less water this time?"

"Well, maybe not so much less water," Driscoll said, wondering why they were drinking so fast. "I've got a nine o'clock train to catch in the morning, and I've still got to get to my hotel with that Val-Pak."

While she was out in the kitchen, he looked around for another place to sit, a place not so high up, but the only thing in the room that met this particular specification was the hassock, and Betsy Parker was back with the fresh drinks before he could decide to do anything about that.

"The furniture was the most wonderful part of it," she said, dropping onto the hassock and folding her legs under her skirt. "We just made it a rule that before a girl could come and live in the house she had to donate one piece of furniture, second-hand or new, it didn't matter, and she couldn't take it away with her when she left. I started with this couch and two frying pans and now look at the place."

Driscoll turned to look and the leg, which had gone slightly stiff, didn't move with him, so he slid halfway off the couch before he could catch himself, and his drink spilled.

"Oh, say, look," he said, feeling foolish as he hiked himself back up on the couch. "I'm sorry."

"Don't give it a thought," Betsy Parker said. "I've got tons of the stuff. Let me replace what you lost."

"No, thanks, this will do," Driscoll said, holding the glass away from her. "I mean the mess."

"On *this* rug?" Betsy Parker said. "In *this* house? Look at that piano. The girl who was painting that little number got married eight months ago, when she was halfway into the tree, and it's been that way ever since, and you're worrying about a little spilled blended whiskey. My, my, you fliers. Here, let me freshen that."

She captured the glass and went out with it, and Driscoll, relaxing quite suddenly and completely on the couch, said what the hell to himself.

"I just had an idea," Betsy Parker said when she came back, and he could see from the color of her glass that she had freshened her own drink, too. "It's almost eleven now, and I think it's foolish for you to go all the way across the city to a hotel at this hour. The house is empty and there are two extra bedrooms, so why don't you stay the night here, and you can go direct to the train in the morning, when I go to work."

"Oh, hell, now, wait a minute," Driscoll said. "I couldn't do that."

Betsy Parker laughed and handed him his refilled glass.

"Now, don't tell me we're getting modest," she said, sitting down on the hassock and looking at him across the rim of her glass as she took a long sip. "A great big warrior like you." Betsy Parker nudged his shoe playfully. "If it will make you feel any better, it's happened here dozens of times and my reputation on this street hasn't suffered one bit," she said. "All these girls we've married out of here, their men came in from all over when they were courting, in all kinds of uniforms, and we always put them up on the couch or in one of the spare bedrooms, when there was a spare."

Driscoll took another long swallow, half wishing he were not, and looked down at Betsy Parker. Then he said what the hell to himself again and he grinned at her. He certainly had got his taxi rides mixed up. He started to say what the hell to himself once more, realized he must look quite foolish, and he made an effort to control his slackly grinning face. There was a knock on the front door and he turned to look.

"Come in, Elsa," Betsy Parker said. "The door's not locked."

A girl in a dark suit came in and stopped just inside the door, clutching a large square parcel wrapped in tan glazed paper.

"Oh," she said, and Driscoll could detect the slight accent even in the single syllable. "I am so sorry."

"There's nothing to be sorry about," Betsy Parker said. "This is a friend of my brother's. Lieutenant Driscoll, Elsa Miehler."

"Hello," Driscoll said, and he started to get up but Betsy Parker put her hand on his knee and pressed him back. "Sorry to butt in on you this way when you're packing," he said.

"You are not butting in," Elsa Miehler said with a smile. "My aunt said in her letter they still cannot obtain face tissue in Canada and I thought it would be nice to bring her some. I must hurry to catch the eleven o'clock bus."

She went to the trunk and dropped to one knee and started poking the glazed paper parcel into it. Driscoll made an effort and slid off the couch and stood up.

"This famous bathroom," he said. "May I?"

"Upstairs," Betsy Parker said. "First door on your left at the top of the landing."

Driscoll excused himself and went through the archway and up the stairs and into the first door on the left at the top of the landing. It was easily the most crowded bathroom he had ever seen, and when he realized, with considerable surprise, that he had brought his glass with him, he had several moments of indecision about where to put it. He looked around. There were seven towel racks nailed to different parts of the wall and, over each rack, was pasted a humorous cartoon with a hand-lettered legend that said, "This is Elsa's towel" and "This is Betsy's towel" and so on, through a list of names that were new to Driscoll. He decided, finally, to set the glass in the middle of the bathtub and, when he reached for it later, his hand misjudged the distance and he struck the glass with his fingers. It fell with a clatter but did not break and Driscoll, whose breathing was quite heavy now, was glad the drink was gone. When he came back downstairs Betsy Parker was lying on the couch, supporting her drink on her chest, and her saddle shoes were on the floor. The trunk was locked and Elsa Miehler was gone.

"I thought something happened to you," Betsy Parker said, getting up. "Now it's my turn. While I'm upstairs, I might as well get you a pillow and some blankets. Unless you'd rather sleep in one of the spare bedrooms upstairs?"

"No, thanks," Driscoll said. "The couch will be fine."

"You're perfectly safe," Betsy Parker said, and she laughed quite suddenly. "I hope," she said.

"Well, suit yourself," Driscoll said, and he laughed, too. "Wherever you'd rather have me. What happened to Miss Miehler?"

"She had to catch that bus to Union Station," Betsy Parker said. "She asked me to say goodbye to you."

"Thanks," Driscoll said. "Seemed like quite a nice girl. If you hadn't told me, I don't think I would have taken her for a refugee."

"You would if you had to live with her," Betsy Parker said. "But thank God that's over."

"Thank God what's over?" Driscoll said.

"I'm not going to take her back when she comes back from Canada," Betsy Parker said.

"Why not?" Driscoll said. "I thought you were friends?"

"Oh, we're friends all right," Betsy Parker said. "But she's just too difficult to live with. She's always locking closets and doors and looking under things, and she insists on having bread with every meal, and she makes me show her all the food bills, and she adds them up seventeen times, as though I were cheating her or something. She's just too damned terrified and European, I guess, if you know what I mean."

"Does she know this?" Driscoll said, not quite understanding why he was feeling slightly dizzy but certain that the blended whiskey, taken too rapidly, had a lot to do with it. "That you're not going to take her back?"

"No, but I'll write to her tomorrow in Canada," Betsy Parker said. "Fix yourself a drink while I turn down your bed and go to the little girls' room. And here, make one for me, too, while you're at it. Yes?"

Driscoll took her glass and she smiled at him across her shoulder as she went out through the archway and up the stairs, making surprisingly heavy sounds for a girl with a good figure in bare feet. Driscoll stood there for a long moment, looking around quickly at the tarnished brass candlesticks and the Chinese prints and the fireplace stuffed with newspapers, like a man hunting desperately for a likely place in which to be sick. Then he went swiftly to the piano and picked up his hat and put Betsy Parker's glass down on the keyboard, next to the blue bowl powdered with the stale dust of pretzel sticks eaten long ago. He glanced at his wrist watch. It was twenty minutes after eleven.

Driscoll put on his hat and picked up the Val-Pak and he went out, closing the door softly behind him, aware that even in the eyes of his friend Roger he was doing a foolish thing. The knee was beginning to hurt a little as he cut diagonally across the narrow lawns that ran into each other, disregarding the flagstone walks, and headed for the corner around which the taxi driver had said he could pick up, twice an hour on the half hour, the D-2 bus that would get him downtown, pretty near any place he wanted to go or someplace where he could get a cab, anyway. This was not his city, after all. Not yet.

Marriage Broker

The fact that there was not a single old maid on all of Fourth Street, from Avenue D to the East River, could be attributed almost directly to Mr. Tannenbaum.

On our block, when a girl reached her sixteenth birthday, her mother gave a sweet-sixteen party and allowed her to put up her hair. After seventeen, she was permitted to go with boys and stay out late. If she wasn't married by the time she was nineteen, her mother took her to Tannenbaum, the marriage broker, and made her sit in his parlor at least three nights a week with the other girls. This last resort invariably proved successful.

Mr. Tannenbaum's reputation as a marriage broker was so excellent that he even attracted clients from other blocks. From as far south as Houston Street and as far north as Eighth Street, the difficult cases, the girls who were homely and who had small dowries, were brought to him. And it was a matter of pride with the people of the block, as well as with Tannenbaum, that none of them remained in his parlor very long. Some way or other, nobody knew how—certainly no other marriage broker on the East Side seemed to have a similar talent—he managed to marry them off. Among a people that looks upon spinsterhood as the least desirable of states, this was no mean accomplishment.

As a result, Tannenbaum was quite a personage. No other man on the block, for instance, could have avoided ridicule while wearing clothes like the ones Tannenbaum wore. Nobody knew what hap-

pened on those daily expeditions when the marriage broker, resplendent in a frock coat, wing collar, huge, wide-brimmed black
hat, and silver-headed cane, fared forth to, as he put it, "see about
some boys." But the people of the block judged by results. And if
Mr. Tannenbaum chose to dress as he did when he went husband-
hunting, nobody on the block, nobody with a sister or daughter of
marriageable age, would be foolhardy enough to incur his displeas-
ure by laughing at him. Indeed, it never occurred to anybody on the
block to treat the marriage broker with anything but deference. He
was looked up to, and respected; he was placed in charge of the
block's collective activities, its entertainments and charitable drives;
and, with the exception of a short period during the year following
the war, not a single word of criticism was ever heard against him.

But that year, right after the war, something was wrong at Tannenbaum's. The girls sat and sat. Every morning Tannenbaum de-
parted, swinging his silver-headed cane jauntily, but nothing happened. Some of the puzzled mothers insisted that the girls sit in
his parlor four nights a week, instead of three.

"Why not?" Tannenbaum agreed, with a generous shrug. "So it'll
cost me a little extra electric, so what?"

This did not seem to help. The girls continued to sit, but there
were no weddings. Tannenbaum did not seem to be disturbed by
the almost complete cessation of activity in his business. He continued to crowd his already overflowing parlor with the "difficult
cases" that were brought to him from other blocks; he continued
to push, with a patriotic fervor that had not diminished with the
armistice, the sale of Liberty bonds on the block; he continued to
supervise the preparations for the block party that the people of
the block were planning for their returned soldiers.

The worried mothers assembled on the bench in front of Gordon's candy store and talked it over. What was wrong? Why were
there so few matches that year? Why was this year different from
all the others?

The theories advanced were many and varied, but in the final
analysis the causes of complaint against Tannenbaum were two: one,
he was hurting the chances of the girls on the block by jamming his
parlor with the ugly ducklings of other blocks, and, two, he was
diluting his talents with his other activities at a time when he should

have been applying them in all their concentrated strength to the increasingly urgent task of finding husbands for the girls who had been entrusted to him.

Nobody, of course, had the intrepidity baldly to present a complaint, necessarily tinged with criticism, to the great man, but gradually, by innuendo, the marriage broker was made aware of the general dissatisfaction with his lack of success that year and the popular conception of the two causes for it.

Bluntly, if good-humoredly, Tannenbaum dismissed the notion that his preoccupation with the sale of Liberty bonds and the coming block party had anything to do with the paucity of marriages that year. The war, he said, had made young men lose their taste for domesticity. And then, too, times were bad. Young men hesitated. Maybe if the dowry was a little bigger, another couple hundred dollars, you know, maybe *then*. And as far as the presence in his parlor of the girls from other blocks was concerned—nonsense! He had been a marriage broker too long to consider any case hopeless. And with times so bad, he wasn't throwing away any chance, however remote, of earning a commission.

Another month went by, and still no results. None to speak of, that is. There *were* two or three matches, but not very good ones. Mrs. Heimowitz's daughter married a cloaks operator who was learning to be a cutter, and Mrs. Margaretten's oldest daughter married a young man who had a pickle stand on Fifth Street. But there were no grocers, no dentists, no butchers, not even a post-office clerk!

There was no denying the gravity of the situation. If the girls were not married off this year, what chance would they have next year, with new girls coming in, younger ones? Indeed, things were becoming so serious that the mothers actually began to speak in whispers about the possibility of taking their daughters away from Tannenbaum. Rumors began to circulate of the existence of a marriage broker on Columbia Street, between Stanton and Rivington, who had married off six girls in one week, a record of which even the peerless Tannenbaum might well have been proud.

But there was nothing in the way he continued to wear his rakishly cocked hat, or in the way he continued to swing his silver-headed cane, to indicate that he was concerned by, or, for that matter, even aware of, the practically blasphemous censure that his

reputation was being subjected to. He continued blandly to direct
the electricians in the stringing of colored lights from roof to roof,
and the carpenters in the construction of the bandstand and barriers that would be needed for the block party, for all the world as
though his career were not at stake.

How seriously or permanently Tannenbaum's standing on the block
would have been affected by the wave of criticism will always remain conjectural. Because just when the feeling against him was
at its peak, and the angry mothers appeared on the verge of doing
what seems, in retrospect, almost inconceivable, namely, breaking
into open rebellion and taking their daughters away from him, the
entire problem was solved by the block party. It was run off on its
scheduled date, but to many people it seemed to arrive rather
breathlessly just in time to avert an unfortunate crisis in the relationship between the block and Mr. Tannenbaum.

Under the marriage broker's direction the entire block had been
overhung with colored lanterns and oddly shaped strings of electric
lights. Flags had been raised and bunting tacked to everything in
sight. Across the two entrances to the block, one at Avenue D and
another at Lewis Street, wooden fences, with gates in the center,
had been erected. And in the middle of the block a platform had
been raised.

The night of the party was clear and cool. Shortly after supper,
the people began to come out of their houses and the band made
its appearance on the wooden platform. Two boys were stationed
at each gate to collect ten cents from every stranger who wanted
to enter the block and dance to the strains of "Tip-Top Tipperary
Mary" that came from the band on the platform. A discerning observer might have noted two things: the surprising number of shy,
neatly dressed young men among the strangers who thought it
worth a dime to enter the block, and the absence of Mr. Tannenbaum.

Before long the street was quite crowded with dancing, laughing,
shouting couples. The confetti had given out, but every now and
then the breeze raised clouds of it, together with the dust of the
gutter, and sent it whirling over the dancers. Nobody seemed to
mind. An infectious gaiety was in the air, and soon all barriers were
down.

At ten o'clock, when the jollity was at its height, Tannenbaum's front door opened suddenly and the marriage broker led the entire group of girls from his parlor out onto his stoop. There were at least fifteen of them. He surveyed the lively scene before him for a few moments, and then, slowly but firmly, he eased his charges down the stoop and into the crowd, which fell back to make room for the closely packed squad of girls.

He led them down the block slowly, then turned and began to lead them back again. Soon the novelty of the regimented group in the midst of the lively crowd wore off, and the dancers began to circle the group, laughing at the girls and heckling Tannenbaum. But the marriage broker smiled good-naturedly and continued to keep his squadron in motion. Gradually this was becoming a more difficult task. The excitement of the music and the laughter was having its effect on the girls. They were smiling openly at the visitors from other blocks, many of whom, similarly influenced by the gaiety, were walking along with the group, talking to the girls and joking with them. The ranks were spreading out, taking up more room as they went up and down the block, with the danger that strangers would be swept into the gaps and the group would lose its identity. Tannenbaum circled about, like a collie tending a flock of sheep, driving stragglers into line and warding off the attacks of the strangers. His conduct seemed puzzling, in view of his by now obvious purpose in bringing the girls out.

But soon it could be seen that there was method in the marriage broker's tactics. He was driving off the undesirables, the irresponsible young men, the returned soldiers in whose honor the block party was being given. Eligible young men, those shy, carefully dressed and combed strangers, were not being driven off, but, rather, led on, coaxed forward. Tannenbaum circled faster and faster, losing a good deal of his composure, but nothing of his dignity.

Suddenly one of the girls broke away and paired off with one of the neat strangers. A cheer went up from the crowd as Tannenbaum gave the couple his sanction, in the form of a hasty pat on the back, and they disappeared into the crowd. The marriage broker turned back to his charges. Soon another of the imported young men found a girl to his liking. Again the cheer from the laughing crowd, again the approving pat on the back from the marriage broker.

After a little more than an hour, six or seven of the girls had disappeared into the crowd with officially approved young men. For another short period Tannenbaum continued to shepherd his flock up and down the street, but the intoxication of the music had begun to wear off. The shyness of the eligible visitors had returned and they were no longer stepping forward to claim the marriage broker's girls. Tannenbaum was quick to sense the change, and suddenly, without a visible shift in pace, he herded the remaining girls up to his door and into his parlor.

The marriage broker and his girls had been the high point of the evening, and with the disappearance of this attraction, the block party began to die down. Soon the music stopped, the crowd dispersed, and the lights were put out.

But the event was one not easily to be forgotten. The mothers who had criticized Tannenbaum most severely for his laxness were now most lavish with their praise and their reassertions of confidence in him. For there could be no doubt that the presence of those shy young men at the block party had been no accident. It was now clear that Tannenbaum's morning expeditions during the past months "to see about some boys" had only *appeared* fruitless.

The mating system on the block was fundamentally an efficient one. Or perhaps times got better—or dowries larger. Or perhaps the block party had done something to make young men lose that distaste for domesticity that Tannenbaum had blamed on the war. At any rate, the block party broke the spell of matrimonial inactivity. And not only were the seven matches that had started at the block party brought successfully to the altar, but before long all the girls who had participated in the famous march under the lanterns and confetti were married off, and new ones moved into their chairs in Tannenbaum's parlor.

The marriage broker returned once more to the high esteem from which, for all the criticism, he had never quite fallen. Not a whisper of reproof was ever again heard against him. Nor did Tannenbaum ever indicate resentment at the fact that for a time he had not been accorded the homage and respect which were his due. In fact, only once did he even refer to the brilliant coup by which he had recaptured the waning confidence of the block.

"*Anybody,*" he was heard to say disdainfully, "can rent a parlor on Columbia Street and marry off six or seven girls in a *week*. But" —here a note of pride entered his voice and the silver-headed cane twirled more jauntily than ever—"no man can call himself a marriage broker until he has married off seven girls in one *night!*"

Monsoon

The first two days out of Aden, when the passengers complained to one another of the heat, they did it with polite, good-humored smiles. Not to mention the heat at all in the Arabian Sea in August would have been ostentatious, even in those late summer days in 1939, when the clouds of war were so close they were almost visible in the burning, mirrored skies, and subjects for conversation were not difficult to find. On the third day, when the thermometer in the bar went up above the hundred mark and stayed there, the smiles disappeared. Nobody mentioned the heat all of that third day. Everybody talked about the monsoon, which, according to Mr. Madgwick, was due to strike the vessel along about the middle of the next day, the fourth out of Aden and a full week, perhaps even eight or nine days, before the *Baroda* would reach Colombo.

Mr. Madgwick was a small, compact, middle-aged Englishman with a full beard which was shaved around his lips, so his face looked like a fur coat from which a round hole had been gouged, revealing a pink section of the wearer's skin. He was a rubber broker in Singapore, where he lived with his mother, a tiny, fragile, friendly old lady who was stone-deaf. Her son had taken her to England for a gallstone operation, which had been successful, and now they were on their way back to Malaya.

During the first two days out of Aden, Mr. Madgwick had been just another passenger, more odd-looking than most because of the peculiar gap in his otherwise impressive beard. On the third day, how-

348

ever, when the monsoon replaced the heat as a subject of conversation, Mr. Madgwick became the centre of a good deal of attention. He knew a lot about the East. He had lived in the Malay Peninsula for almost thirty years, and he was pleasant and modest while imparting his knowledge to others, especially to the six American passengers, who made no secret of the fact that they had always thought a monsoon was a sudden, violent, and dangerous storm quite capable of breaking a vessel of the *Baroda's* size in two.

"It isn't that at all," said Mr. Madgwick, with a kind smile. "You're thinking of a typhoon, which is a horse of a different color, as the fellow says." Mr. Madgwick had a precise way of wrapping his pink, almost girlish lips around every word he uttered, pronouncing each one with equal clarity and giving each syllable its proper weight, so he seemed to be bestowing on his listeners, in addition to information, a small unobtrusive lesson in elocution. "A monsoon is a wind and nothing more, a wind that blows part of the year from one direction and part from the opposite direction. The monsoon we are heading into, for example, blows across the Indian Ocean from the southwest from the latter part of May to the middle of September, and from the northeast from about the middle of October to the middle of December. Coming from the southwest, since this is August, it will strike us thus." He arranged an ash tray and a half-dozen matches in a pattern on the black marble top of the bar table. "Assuming the ash tray is our ship and these matches are the wind—here." He moved the matches across the table until they touched the ash tray. "You see? A slow, steady, monotonous wind and nothing more. The ship will roll a bit, and I daresay we'll all be jolly uncomfortable for a while until we get used to it, but you needn't worry, really. I've been in it a dozen times or more and so has my mother, and I know. It won't do any of us a tuppence-worth of harm, as the fellow says."

Toward the end of the third day, when Mr. Madgwick's popularity and his authority had been established, he explained about his beard. His mother's deafness had made it necessary for her to learn how to read lips. She was wonderful at it, he said, and could understand almost anyone, except certain cinema stars who specialized in rapid, lipless patter, but Mr. Madgwick's beard had proved a definite obstacle to their conversation. He hadn't wanted to shave it all off, because he had grown fond of it, so he had compromised by shaving only his mustache and a small area under his lower lip. It looked odd, he knew, but he had become accustomed to it and, he added with a twinkle in his eye, he was afraid he was starting something of a fashion in Singapore. He had noticed two Dutch planters with similar beards in a club on Pasir Panjang Road before he left, and he was willing to wager a five-pound note against a sixpenny bit that there would be at least a dozen more like it by the time he got back.

The air of quiet authority in Mr. Madgwick's voice and manner when he spoke of the East led the other passengers to consult him about an anxiety almost as pressing as the monsoon: the two Chinese who were also passengers on board the *Baroda*—should they be treated as social equals or should they be ignored?

If there had been a group of younger people among the passengers, the question would not have come up. But there were no young people. Even the six Americans were middle-aged. It was an uncomfortable problem to face, especially in the heat of the Arabian Sea in August, and several of the more stuffy English passengers announced that they were going to write to the line's head office in London at the first opportunity. It wasn't that they objected to having Chinese on board, but they did think it was a bloody outrage for the company to saddle the white passengers with the problem of how to treat them. After all, the two Chinese were traveling first class. Luckily, in this particular case, the two Chinese were sensible and, after Mr. Madgwick's authoritative assurance that it was perfectly all right, the problem had disappeared by the end of the third day out of Aden.

Every morning the two Chinese came up on deck together just as the Lascars were finishing their scrubbing, a full hour before any of the other passengers, including the six energetic Americans, were awake. The two Chinese, wearing expensive flannel slacks, silk sports shirts, and complicated leather sandals, would begin pacing the deck for exercise. They would take two of the large, juicy oranges that the Goanese stewards left for morning walkers in a basket near the companionway leading to the bridge. As they circled the vessel side by side, walking firmly but delicately, as though they were anxious not to disturb the other passengers, who were still asleep below them, they would peel their oranges, picking the strings fastidiously from each segment, and fling the skin and seeds overboard on the lee side so that the wind, of which there was as yet very little, would not carry the refuse back to the deck.

At first glance they looked alike, but only because they were both Chinese. Actually they were very dissimilar. Mr. Ton was tall and thin, with deep hollows under his high cheekbones, and his eyes, which were devoid of lashes, were mere slits. Mr. Wiu was short and plump. Both had strong, black, shiny hair clipped close at the temple. It was impossible to tell their ages, but they looked young— somewhere around thirty or thirty-five.

By the time they had walked a mile and a half, checking the distance against the sign on the capstan just under the bridge, near the basket of oranges, the other passengers would begin to come up on deck for their constitutionals before breakfast. Mr. Ton and Mr. Wiu would move closer to the wall, so that the white men and women could have the more desirable right of way against the rail. When they passed the two Chinese, they would smile and say good morning, and Mr. Ton and Mr. Wiu, grinning delightedly and showing their strong, white, handsome teeth, would nod their heads and say good morning in reply. The other passengers never stopped to chat and never slowed or quickened their pace to catch up with the two Chinese so they all could walk side by side. Mr. Ton and Mr. Wiu always walked alone, clearly by their own choice, the other passengers were able to say with relief and with complete accuracy.

In the dining room Mr. Ton and Mr. Wiu sat together at one of the small tables for two against the wall. There were eight of these small tables, but the other seven were unoccupied, mainly because the few wisps of air that were caught by the tin scoops stuck in the portholes above these tables passed right over them and benefited only those people who sat at the large tables in the centre of the hot dining room. Mr. Madgwick, who sat with his mother and the six Americans at a centre table, assured the other passengers that this was perfectly all right. The Chinese were more accustomed to heat than white people, he said, and besides they preferred to be alone. This was undoubtedly true, people agreed. Mr. Ton and Mr. Wiu obviously had a good time. They ate together, with beautiful table manners, and watched the other diners with small, restrained smiles of pleasure.

After breakfast they sat side by side in deck chairs, reading. They would glance up every now and then from their books to nod politely to a passenger who, in passing them, had nodded first. After tiffin, which the six Americans stopped calling lunch on the second day, Mr. Ton and Mr. Wiu would disappear belowdecks for a nap. At three o'clock they would come up, fresh and clean, looking highly polished in more immaculate slacks and more elaborate sports shirts. They would walk slowly and carefully across the games deck, stopping behind the ping-pong table, the deck-tennis court, or the shuffle board square to watch a game for several minutes before moving on. Occasionally, when a ball or a quoit went out of bounds, Mr. Wiu would retrieve it quickly and, in response to the short smile or nod or word of thanks from the middle-aged player, both Chinese would smile delightedly and bow with pleasure.

They always entered the bar together and they always took the narrow couch which stood under the thermometer, and seated only two. In this way they could be in the room with the other passengers without creating a situation. Everybody in the bar had the feeling that Mr. Ton and Mr. Wiu were not being ostracized and at the same time everybody was relieved of the danger of having consciously to avoid sitting down with them. It was considered a bit of luck that the bar had this fortunate piece of furniture.

At night, when there was dancing on the upper deck, the two Chinese would appear together, impeccably dressed in white mess jackets, and stand against the rail, smiling with appreciation as their eyes watched the sedate dancers. They always retired just before the dancing broke up, so that nobody would be embarrassed by the necessity for not including them in the groups that were going off to have a nightcap. All in all, it was very well done, and more than one passenger said, somewhat pompously, perhaps, that Mr. Ton and Mr. Wiu deserved a good deal of credit for the discreet and sensible manner in which they were handling a situation that could very easily have been unpleasant.

In the middle of the fourth day, the monsoon struck the *Baroda*, as Mr. Madgwick had predicted, and, precisely as he had said, nobody was much the worse for it. The ship rolled a little more, and two of the six Americans didn't eat as much dinner as usual, but that was about all. By morning of the sixth day everybody was accustomed to it.

That afternoon, just before tea, the ship took a deep roll. A marble table in the bar broke loose from its fastenings, slithered across the polished floor, and struck the couch on which the two Chinese were sitting. Mr. Wiu's legs were caught between the table and the couch and his ankle was broken.

Mr. Wiu was terribly embarrassed by the excitement this accident caused. He smiled at the circle of sympathetic passengers, his watery, protruding eyes filling with tears of gratitude and remorse, while the doctor examined him. Finally the doctor straightened up and said it was nothing serious. A simple fracture. The bone had not been completely severed. He would put the ankle into splints and Mr. Wiu would have to remain in bed for the rest of the trip. Nothing to worry about. His ankle would be as good as new two weeks after he landed at Colombo. Mr. Ton smiled and nodded his thanks to the other passengers for their kindness and sympathy to Mr. Wiu as he and the doctor and three stewards carried the helpless, apologetic little man out of the bar and down to his cabin.

Neither Mr. Ton nor Mr. Wiu showed up on deck for the rest of the trip.

The first night after the accident several passengers asked the doctor how the injured Chinese was feeling, and he said irritably that he'd told them once there was nothing seriously wrong with Mr. Wiu's ankle. He had bound it in splints, the Chinese was in bed resting comfortably, and there was Mr. Ton to take care of his wants, which, they should have known by this time, were simple and few. Within forty-eight hours everybody had forgotten all about the two Chinese.

On the fourth day after the accident, Mr. Madgwick took two of the Americans, whose names were Gerard and Winter, down to B Deck. He wanted to show them the engine room, which he knew intimately, this being his sixth voyage on the *Baroda*. They were walking forward, through a section of the vessel that was unoccupied because there were so few passengers on this trip, toward the companionway that led down into the bowels of the ship, when

they heard a faint cry. They stopped and stared at one another. The
cry was repeated, feeble, croaking.

"It's back this way," Gerard said. "One of these cabins on the
right."

The three men turned and retraced their steps. Once more the
sound came. The three men stopped, turned again, and ran back
to Cabin 709, which they had just passed. Mr. Madgwick twisted the
knob and pushed the door open. The three men stopped short in
the doorway.

Mr. Wiu was lying half on his bed and half on the floor, clutching
the side of the bunk and trying weakly to raise himself. Both his legs
stuck out straight and stiff behind him. His pajamas and the sheets
of his bed were soiled. The odor in the room was dreadful. On a
table beside the bunk, Mr. Wiu's water bottle was lying on its side,
empty. A fruit basket was on the floor, also empty, in the middle of
a small pile of curling orange skins and yellowing apple cores. Beside the bed were the splintered remains of a cup and teapot from
the tray that had slipped from the table. Mr. Wiu's lips were parched
and cracked, and there were little blobs of dried black saliva in the
corners. His tongue, dry and thick and heavily coated, stuck far out
of his mouth, as though the effort of calling for help had exhausted
his control over it and he lacked the strength to pull it back into his
head.

"Holy smoke!" Winter said in astonishment. "The poor guy's dying of thirst!"

They rushed into the room. Mr. Madgwick stripped the soiled,
foul-smelling sheets from the bed and flung them into a corner of
the cabin. The two Americans lifted Mr. Wiu gently onto the bed.
His legs still stuck out stiffly, like the tines of a carving fork. Mr.
Madgwick seized the water bottle, filled it from the tap at the other
side of the room, and brought it to the bed. He wet Mr. Wiu's lips,
poured a few drops on his tongue, and then lifted his head gently
into drinking position. The water revived Mr. Wiu at once. He
clutched at the bottle, but Mr. Madgwick held it firmly and would
allow him only a little at a time.

"It looks like nobody's been near this room since he broke his leg
four days ago," Gerard said excitedly. "Where the hell is that side-
kick of his, Mr. Ton?"

Winter stepped out into the corridor. "Mr. Ton!" he called. "Mr. Ton! Hey, Mr. Ton!" There was no answer. Winter came back into the room and bent over Mr. Wiu.

"Where's Mr. Ton?" he asked. The fat little Chinese shook his head weakly.

"These cabins are all unoccupied at this end," said Mr. Madgwick. "The ship is terribly understaffed at this season, and those lazy Goanese will only do so much." He looked down at Mr. Wiu. "Where's your friend? Where's Mr. Ton?" Mr. Wiu's puffy eyelids flicked up and down over his protruding eyes. He licked his lips slowly with his bloated tongue. "He can't talk," said Mr. Madgwick. "One of you chaps run up and fetch the doctor, will you? We'll find Mr. Ton later."

The two Americans hurried out. At the companionway they parted. Gerard went off to find the doctor, and Winter went forward to the purser's office and told him what they had discovered.

"We couldn't find Mr. Ton anywhere," Winter said, talking rapidly. "He wasn't in their cabin, and even though I yelled my head off in the corridor, he didn't show up. Nobody showed up. Not even a steward. That part of the ship seems deserted. Do you know where we can find him? Nobody's seen Mr. Ton since four days ago, when Mr. Wiu's leg was broken."

"You might try his cabin," the purser said.

"I just told you we were in there," Mr. Winter said impatiently. "He wasn't anywhere around. We yelled for him and—oh." Mr. Winter looked at the purser in surprise. "You mean they're not—?"

"No, of course not. Mr. Wiu is in 709 on B Deck. And Mr. Ton is in—let me see." The purser flipped the pages of a loose-leaf notebook. "Mr. Ton is in 550 on A Deck."

"Oh, I see," Mr. Winter said. "I thought they were both—we all thought they were—I mean, because of the way they were always together, coming up on deck together and going down together, we all thought—"

He stopped talking, as though he could not find words to express the simple thought that had never occurred to him or to any of the other passengers.

"We'd better take a look at the injured one and then have a go at finding his friend," the purser said briskly. "Come along."

On the way down to B Deck, the purser told Winter that Mr. Ton was a research chemist who had recently completed some work in the States at Johns Hopkins and was now on his way to a post in Shanghai. Mr. Wiu was an insurance agent who had been visiting the central office of his firm in London and was now returning to his own office and home in Hong Kong. When the purser and Winter reached Mr. Wiu's cabin, they found the doctor in the middle of a crowd of excited, puzzled, indignant passengers. The purser pushed his way through to the bed on which Mr. Wiu was lying comfortably, his round, fat face creased in a smile of apology for this new disturbance he had created.

"He's all right," the doctor said to the purser. "He can't talk yet, but he will in a short while. I've given him some broth and some water. It's my fault, I suppose," he said, scowling. "I should have looked in on him, but it's been so beastly hot and it seemed such a minor injury. You see what happened." He turned to the passengers, as though he were seeking justification for his neglect. "In addition to his broken ankle, he apparently received a severe blow at the base of the spine when the table flung him against the back of the couch. Must have caused a hemorrhage in the spinal canal. The bleeding brings pressure to bear on the nerves leading to the legs and causes paralysis. Temporary, of course. Lasts several weeks, perhaps. What's known technically as paraplegia." He seemed to take comfort in the sound of the word. "Very rare, you know. There are no immediate symptoms. It occurs twelve to twenty-four hours after the blow. I never dreamed it might happen in this case. Very rare. Very rare indeed." The passengers nodded and looked at Mr. Wiu on the bed. The doctor turned to the purser. "I had no way of knowing, you see. Besides, I assumed his friend was taking care of him and would let me know if anything was wrong. Damned rotten, deserting his pal like this without letting anybody know. The poor beggar might have been done in if Mr. Madgwick hadn't happened along. Where the devil *is* Ton, anyway? Nobody seems to have seen him since—"

The purser was pushing his way through the crowd to the door. Mr. Madgwick, plucking nervously at his beard, followed. They reached the corridor and hurried up the companionway to A Deck. In front of Cabin 550 they stopped and the purser tapped on the door.

"Yes?" Mr. Ton's voice said. "Come in."

As the purser pushed open the door, Winter and Gerard and perhaps a dozen more excited passengers came hurrying down the corridor and crowded in behind them. Mr. Ton was sitting at his writing table, wearing a silk dressing gown, looking very clean and bright as he ate lunch from a tray and read a book that was propped up on a tumbler of water. He folded his napkin neatly, dropped it on the tray, and stood up to face the crowd in the doorway. Before the purser could speak, Mr. Madgwick pushed forward.

"Look here," he said petulantly, tumbling his words out with indiscriminate haste, not at all like a man accustomed to precise diction. "We've just found your friend Mr. Wiu in a terrible state. Nobody's been near him since he broke his ankle. He hasn't had food or water for almost four days. The poor man might have died."

"I am so sorry," Mr. Ton said politely. "That is too bad. But I fail to see how that is my responsibility, which I assume you think it is from the tone of your voice."

The passengers behind Mr. Madgwick gasped.

"You fail to see how— But he's a friend of yours! The two of you are—"

"A friend of mine?" Mr. Ton raised one eyebrow disdainfully. "That stupid, fat, ignorant insurance salesman? I never set eyes on him before I boarded this ship."

For the first time since the *Baroda* had left Aden, Mr. Madgwick was at a loss. He scratched his beard perplexedly and looked behind him at the purser, at the Americans, at the other passengers. Nobody seemed to know what to do or say. Mr. Madgwick turned back to the Chinese, and his full, red, almost girlish lips parted and closed several times, quickly, as he hunted for words.

"If you don't mind," Mr. Ton said with a small, icy, polite bow of dismissal, "I should very much like to finish my lunch."

Movable Feast

"Perhaps I can explain it this way," Miss Holcomb said, keeping one eye on her wristwatch. "Let me give you an example, children. Let's take Washington's Birthday. That always comes on February twenty-second. It has to, because that's the day the father of our country was born. Washington's Birthday is always on February twenty-second. It never changes. It can't. Do we understand that?"

She looked anxiously down into the faces of the forty little boys. It was the last day of school before the Christmas vacation, and in a corner to the right of Miss Holcomb's desk was a Christmas tree. The forty little faces looked back up at Miss Holcomb. Some of them were fat and some were thin. Some were dark and some were pale. Some looked as though they belonged at the scarred, once honey-colored desks, and some looked as outrageously misplaced as they would have been on a silver platter in a performance of "Salome." Yet in one way all the little faces in Miss Holcomb's 1A class looked curiously alike. It was quite clear that they didn't understand what was going on. Miss Holcomb turned quickly to look at David Sternshus, the boy who had asked the question. Usually she felt in him a depth of understanding and sympathy, inarticulate but definite, for what she was trying to do. But now the lean, wide-eyed face of little David Sternshus looked exactly like the thirty-nine others in the classroom.

"Good," Miss Holcomb said without conviction. Her glance strayed for a moment to the windows, plastered with silver stars and prancing reindeer and small, fat cut-outs of Santa Claus. Through the glass she could see the city snow, piled in dirty mounds along the curbs of Houston Street. "Let's take—well, let's take Labor Day. Labor Day doesn't come on a particular date. It comes the first Monday in September. Now, if the month of September begins on Monday, why then Labor Day comes on September first. But if the month of September begins on any other day, let's say on a Thursday, then Labor Day that year comes on—let me see now, Thursday is the first, Friday the second, Saturday the third, Sunday the fourth —Labor Day that year comes on September fifth. Because that year September fifth is the first Monday in September. Is that clear, children?"

She stole another look at David Sternshus. The little boy's face had not changed.

"That's not the way it is with Christmas," Miss Holcomb said. "Christmas Day is like Washington's Birthday. It always comes on December twenty-fifth. Do you understand that, children?"

Most of the really bad waterfront tenements have now given way to a beautiful and somewhat implausible East River drive, and no cold-water flat, however small or mean or poor, is without a TV set or a daily newspaper. But in those days, shortly before the first World War, when Miss Holcomb passed her examinations and received her certificate and was assigned to teach the first grade at P.S. 188, on New York's lower East Side, there were no radios and the only newspapers that were sold in the vicinity of Houston Street were read from right to left. The Lewis Street streetcars that ran in front of the school were still drawn by horses, and the East Side world Miss Holcomb came down to every day from Morningside Heights was far removed from the world she was used to.

That was what had excited Miss Holcomb about her job. It was her first job and she was young—twenty-three—and she wanted desperately to do good things for the underprivileged. She felt there was so much she could bring into the narrow, drab lives of these six-year-old sons of Polish and Austrian and Russian immigrants. She disliked the older members of the faculty—callous, middle-aged women who had been teaching children like these for fifteen and twenty years and called them kids. The older teachers had tried to tell her about the necessity for a calm, reasonable, even cautious approach to minds that were at once infantile and aged, fragile and tough. Miss Holcomb attributed these warnings to the jealousy these older teachers must feel toward her, the youngest teacher in the school, and refused to be discouraged by what they said. But she had to admit that she had not accomplished as much as she had hoped to. Four months was such a short time, yet at least in little David Sternshus her efforts had been crowned with some success. He had learned from her the right words for asking to leave the room. He drank his milk at recess without gulping noises. He even whipped off his cap when he met her on the street. Miss Holcomb had high hopes for little David Sternshus and, through him, for the rest of her 1A class, for her future as a teacher.

Miss Holcomb's young man, whose name was Alfred Orcutt, approved of her zeal. They were going to be married as soon as he finished his internship at Bellevue and set himself up in practice. He listened with interest to her tales of life below Fourteenth Street and at first he had shared her indignation when, the second week in December, she came home with the amazing information that she was the only teacher in the first grade who planned to give her children a Christmas party.

"When I mentioned it at lunch in the teachers' rest room today," she said, "they told me to forget it. They said it had been done before several times and the children hadn't appreciated it. Can you imagine that, Alfred? Can you imagine children of six not appreciating a Christmas party? They're lying to me."

"I guess they are," Alfred Orcutt said. "But I don't see why they should. Come to think of it, if you gave the children a Christmas party, you'd have to pay for it yourself, wouldn't you?"

"Of course," Miss Holcomb said impatiently. "But you don't think I'd let that stop me, do you? After all, it's just a few dollars for candy and favors and decorations, things like that, but to those poor children it would mean—" She waved her delicate, manicured hand to indicate the entrance of loveliness, sunshine, and joy into lives now darkened by the absence of all three.

Miss Holcomb and Alfred Orcutt made a list of things needed for a Christmas party, and they shopped in the evenings, when he could steal an hour or two from his duties at the hospital. During the day,

Miss Holcomb had the children paste decorations on the classroom windows and copy Christmas scenes out of picture books onto the rear blackboard with colored chalk. The party was to be held in the classroom the last day of school, right after lunch, from one o'clock to the three-o'clock dismissal bell. Alfred had got permission at the hospital for time off and was to drop in at P.S. 188 about two o'clock. He would have a hired Santa Claus suit with him and the plan was that he would appear in the classroom while the festivities were at their height and distribute the stuffed gauze stockings under the Christmas tree.

The day before the party, Miss Holcomb had a feeling that all was not well. She didn't know why. She just felt it in her bones. But in the late afternoon, snow began to fall and her spirits soared again. It would be a white Christmas on Houston and Lewis Streets. The following morning, as Miss Holcomb approached the school, she saw that snow on Lewis Street was not quite the same as snow on Morningside Heights. Once she entered the gaily decorated classroom, however, she forgot about the dirty-gray mounds outside.

All morning she found it difficult to keep her mind on the arithmetic and spelling lessons she was giving her children. She was thinking of the moment when Alfred would come in dressed as Santa Claus.

A small Christmas tree stood in the corner to the right of her desk, and it was all twinkly with slivers of tinfoil and bright balls of red and blue and yellow glass. Under the tree were forty red gauze stockings, stuffed with cookies, raisins, nuts, and inexpensive gifts, such as whistles, toy soldiers, pencil boxes, and mechanical tops. On Miss Holcomb's desk stood the purchase that had given her and Alfred Orcutt the most pleasure—a huge box of bright little hard candies, each with a tiny Christmas scene or a colored design all the way through the sugar, so that the pictures would not disappear until the candy itself disappeared. It was the sort of candy that Miss Holcomb and her young man remembered having at Christmas parties all through their childhood.

During her lunch hour, Miss Holcomb scarcely spoke to the teachers in the faculty rest room. At one o'clock, when the forty little boys streamed back into the classroom, she met them with a happy smile and fingered the sprig of holly she had tucked into her hair.

They took their seats sedately and looked up at her. Miss Holcomb's heart skipped a beat. It occurred to her suddenly that she didn't know how to begin a Christmas party like this.

She looked desperately around the room. She couldn't start by distributing the stockings under the tree. That was reserved for Alfred. She couldn't begin by asking the boys to come up and take scoops of candy out of the large wooden box on her desk. That was too abrupt. Her discomfort was not helped by the growing realization that there was more curiosity, more bewilderment, on the faces of the children than anticipation. Miss Holcomb took one look at David Sternshus, her favorite and her barometer, and at once she was convinced she knew what was wrong. Why hadn't she thought of it before?

In all the excitement of preparing for the party she had neglected to tell these children the significance of the various preparations. They had to be explained to these children in the same way that they had had to be explained to her and to Alfred Orcutt when *they* were children. Miss Holcomb glanced at her wristwatch. It was a quarter after one. She had three-quarters of an hour before Alfred would arrive. Smiling brightly, she launched into a history of the Yuletide celebration.

As the minute hand of her watch passed the one-thirty mark and began to crawl toward two o'clock, she became aware of the stillness in the room. None of the little boys had moved. Miss Holcomb stumbled over a word or two, managed to finish her sentence, and looked at her pupils.

"Are there any questions, children?" she asked. "Is there anything you want to know before we begin our party?" Not a sound came from the forty boys. Miss Holcomb's heart seemed to drop out of her body. What was wrong with these children? The watch on her wrist said quarter of two. If only Alfred would be early. If only he would come bursting in through the door now. Miss Holcomb turned to her favorite pupil. "Is there something you don't understand, David?"

The little boy moved uncomfortably in his seat. He tried to lower his eyes, but couldn't. He stared back at the beautiful, clean, rich, puzzling young woman from uptown. She wanted him to do something. He didn't know what it was. Then her voice came to him, louder this time. He took the words apart and put them together again so they made sense.

"Why is it Christmas now?" little David Sternshus asked. "Why does it come this week?"

When Miss Holcomb had finished her explanation, it was seven minutes after two, and still no sign of Alfred Orcutt.

"That's why Christmas Day always comes on December twenty-fifth," she said. "Because it doesn't move, like Labor Day. It's always the same day, like Washington's Birthday. Is that clear, children? Now, do we all know why Christmas always comes on—"

The door burst open. Miss Holcomb hurried to meet the tall young man with a badly pasted-on white beard and a bulging red flannel coat.

"Alfred! I thought you were never—" she whispered.

"Sorry to be late, darling," he said out of the corner of his mouth. "Got stuck." And then, in a loud, booming voice more false than his beard, "Let's see what Santa Claus has for all these good boys. Let's see what old Santa brought in his pack. Ah, here we are. A present for every little boy."

Miss Holcomb, smiling and nervous with happiness, called the boys up by name, one at a time. Alfred Orcutt adjusted his awkward disguise and handed out the red gauze stockings under the Christmas tree. As the pile of stuffed stockings grew smaller, Miss Holcomb's nervousness disappeared. When all the boys were seated behind their desks again, the Santa Claus and Miss Holcomb turned to face the classroom. They beamed happily on the forty little boys and, at that moment, they seemed to realize that the forty little boys were not beaming back at them. The dismissal bell rang. Forty pairs of small feet began to shuffle under the desks. Miss Holcomb glanced at her wristwatch. It was three o'clock.

"The candy!" she said. "We've forgotten the candy!" She hurried to her desk and picked up the tin scoop from the box. "The party isn't over yet, children. There's a scoop of candy here for everyone. Alfred, the paper bags, please!"

From out in the hallway came the sound of children hurrying by on their way home. Their voices poured in through the open transom above the door.

"Here we are," Alfred Orcutt said, opening a paper bag. Miss Holcomb poured a scoopful of the little hard candies into it and he twisted the top of the bag closed. "Come on, boys," he said. "One at a time."

He held the bag out to the boy behind the first desk in the first row. The boy didn't reach for it. Alfred Orcutt shook the bag and held it out again, a trifle further. The boy remained motionless.

"Come along, Abraham," Miss Holcomb said. "Take the candy from Santa Claus." The boy didn't move. "Abraham! I'm talking to you!"

Alfred Orcutt touched Miss Holcomb's arm. She looked at him and he shook his head. Then he turned with a smile to the second little boy in the row.

"Here we are, son," he said heartily. "A bag of nice candy from Santa Claus."

The second little boy didn't reach for the bag. Alfred Orcutt bit his lip and got a mouthful of false beard with it. The sounds of feet and voices in the hallway grew louder. Now the sounds were coming in from the street, too, but Miss Holcomb's classroom was quiet. The young intern shrugged helplessly. The expression on Miss Holcomb's face changed to anger. She snatched the bag of candy from Alfred's hand and stalked down the aisle between the desks until she reached the seat of her favorite pupil.

"I don't know what's got into the other children," she said. "Here, David. Take this. It's perfectly all right. It's another present. There's a bag for everybody."

The little boy looked up at her. His small body bent back in the seat, stiffly, as though he were trying to escape from her. He shook his head.

"Will you stop this nonsense?" Miss Holcomb snapped. "Take this!"

"Look," Alfred Orcutt said uncomfortably. "Maybe they don't want—"

The door opened. Miss Holcomb whirled around. In the doorway stood a group of the older teachers. Boys streaming by on their way home stopped to gather behind the teachers. Soon there was a large group in the doorway. They all stared into the room.

"Oh," one of the teachers said. "We were just wondering how the party was going. We thought we'd drop in and—"

The forty boys in Miss Holcomb's class rose halfway in their seats, their faces puckered with relief.

"Close that door!" Miss Holcomb said. "Sit down! All of you!" The little boys sank back in their seats. "Nobody is going to leave this room!" She rushed to the door. "Get out! All of you! Get *out!*" She pushed the teachers and the staring boys out into the hallway and slammed the door shut. Then she turned back to the class, her hands clasped on the doorknob behind her. "Nobody is leaving this room until I find out what's wrong."

Alfred Orcutt snatched off his false beard, flung it aside, and came toward her. "Listen," he said. "They just don't want it, darling. Let them—"

She shook her head. "I don't care what they want or don't want. I've gone to all this trouble. I've spent good money to give them a party. They've been difficult all day. Now they won't take the candy. It's good candy. It's Christmas candy. It's the kind of candy I had at Christmas parties when I was a little girl in school. I want to know why they won't take it." She strode down the aisle again until she reached David Sternshus. She held the paper bag out to him. "Are you going to take this, David, or aren't you?" The boy didn't answer.

"Listen, darling," Alfred Orcutt said. "Don't—"

"Keep quiet!" Miss Holcomb said to him. "David, I'm talking to you! Why won't you take this candy?"

The little boy's lips began to quiver. He didn't hear Miss Holcomb's words. Fright was blocking everything out. All he could see was the bag of bright, hard candies. The same sort of candies he and the other boys had been tricked into taking the year before at the party in the kindergarten class, the party that had been called by the same name, the party that had come at the same time of year, when there was snow on the ground. His brain froze with terror. The temptress from uptown was holding out a paper bag filled with sweet little pellets of treachery, bits of bright hardness that would crawl into the holes in his teeth, into the cavities that a dentist could have fixed for him and for the other boys if the father of David Sternshus and the fathers of the other boys had been in America long enough to have learned about dentists or could afford to send their children to one. In the small boy's fevered mind was stamped only the blinding horror, the pain of last year's toothache.

"Answer me!" Miss Holcomb said. "Why won't you take the candy?"

The door opened. Everybody turned. The school janitor, white-haired and bent, wearing brown overalls and carrying a broom, stared into the room.

"Excuse me," he said in surprise. "Didn't know anybody was still here. Everybody's gone home."

"Get out!" Miss Holcomb screamed. "Get out of here! I don't want—"

She stopped. David Sternshus had slipped out of his seat, stumbled against her, and was running down the aisle. Before Miss Holcomb could recapture her balance, the other boys had leaped up. The janitor gaped and moved hastily out of the way. The forty little boys poured past him, out of the classroom and into the hallway. Their feet pounded down the corridor toward the exit. The janitor blinked stupidly, scratched his head, and dragged his broom out into the hallway after him. Very gently he pulled the door shut on the classroom.

Alfred Orcutt slipped out of his Santa Claus suit. "Listen, darling. Don't let it—"

Miss Holcomb's rigid body folded. She dropped into one of the little seats and stared around the silent room, at the colored chalk pictures on the rear blackboard, at the scarred desks, on which were lying forty stuffed red gauze stockings, at the Christmas tree up front, at the decorated windows, in which were framed the mounds of dirty snow on Houston Street. She ran her hand through her hair. The sprig of holly tumbled to the floor. Her clenched fist pounded the desk noiselessly.

"Those kids," she said. "Those horrible kids."

My Father Sits
in the Dark

My father has a peculiar habit. He is fond of sitting in the dark, alone. Sometimes I come home very late. The house is dark. I let myself in quietly because I do not want to disturb my mother. She is a light sleeper. I tiptoe into my room and undress in the dark. I go to the kitchen for a drink of water. My bare feet make no noise. I step into the room and almost trip over my father. He is sitting in a kitchen chair, in his pajamas, smoking his pipe.

"Hello, Pop," I say.

"Hello, son."

"Why don't you go to bed, Pa?"

"I will," he says.

But he remains there. Long after I am asleep I feel sure that he is still sitting there, smoking.

Many times I am reading in my room. I hear my mother get the house ready for the night. I hear my kid brother go to bed. I hear my sister come in. I hear her do things with jars and combs until she, too, is quiet. I know she has gone to sleep. In a little while I hear my mother say good night to my father. I continue to read. Soon I become thirsty. (I drink a lot of water.) I go to the kitchen for a drink. Again I almost stumble across my father. Many times it startles me. I forget about him. And there he is—smoking, sitting, thinking.

"Why don't you go to bed, Pop?"

"I will, son."

But he doesn't. He just sits there and smokes and thinks. It worries me. I can't understand it. What can he be thinking about? Once I asked him.

"What are you thinking about, Pa?"

"Nothing," he said.

Once I left him there and went to bed. I awoke several hours later. I was thirsty. I went to the kitchen. There he was. His pipe was out. But he sat there, staring into a corner of the kitchen. After a moment I became accustomed to the darkness. I took my drink. He still sat and stared. His eyes did not blink. I thought he was not even aware of me. I was afraid.

"Why don't you go to bed, Pop?"

"I will, son," he said. "Don't wait up for me."

"But," I said, "you've been sitting here for hours. What's wrong? What are you thinking about?"

"Nothing, son," he said. "Nothing. It's just restful. That's all."

The way he said it was convincing. He did not seem worried. His voice was even and pleasant. It always is. But I could not understand it. How could it be restful to sit alone in an uncomfortable chair far into the night, in darkness?

What can it be?

I review all the possibilities. It can't be money. I know that. We haven't much, but when he is worried about money he makes no secret of it. It can't be his health. He is not reticent about that either. It can't be the health of anyone in the family. We are a bit short on money, but we are long on health. (Knock wood, my mother would say.) What can it be? I am afraid I do not know. But that does not stop me from worrying.

Maybe he is thinking of his brothers in the old country. Or of his mother and two step-mothers. Or of his father. But they are all dead. And he would not brood about them like that. I say brood, but it is not really true. He does not brood. He does not even seem to be thinking. He looks too peaceful, too, well not contented, just too peaceful, to be brooding. Perhaps it is as he says. Perhaps it is restful. But it does not seem possible. It worries me.

If I only knew what he thinks about. If I only knew that he thinks at all. I might not be able to help him. He might not even need help. It may be as he says. It may be restful. But at least I would not worry about it.

Why does he just sit there, in the dark? Is his mind failing? No, it can't be. He is only fifty-three. And he is just as keen-witted as ever. In fact, he is the same in every respect. He still likes beet soup. He still reads the second section of the *Times* first. He still wears wing collars. He still believes that Debs could have saved the country and that T.R. was a tool of the moneyed interests. He is the same in every way. He does not even look older than he did five years ago. Everybody remarks about that. Well-preserved, they say. But he sits in the dark, alone, smoking, staring straight ahead of him, unblinking, into the small hours of the night.

If it is as he says, if it is restful, I will let it go at that. But suppose it is not. Suppose it is something I cannot fathom. Perhaps he needs help. Why doesn't he speak? Why doesn't he frown or laugh or cry? Why doesn't he do something? Why does he just sit there?

Finally I become angry. Maybe it is just my unsatisfied curiosity. Maybe I *am* a bit worried. Anyway, I become angry.

"Is something wrong, Pop?"

"Nothing, son. Nothing at all."

But this time I am determined not to be put off. I am angry.

"Then why do you sit here all alone, thinking, till late?"

"It's restful, son. I like it."

I am getting nowhere. Tomorrow he will be sitting there again. I will be puzzled. I will be worried. I will not stop now. I am angry.

"Well, what do you *think* about, Pa? Why do you just sit here? What's worrying you? What do you think about?"

"Nothing's worrying me, son. I'm all right. It's just restful. That's all. Go to bed, son."

My anger has left me. But the feeling of worry is still there. I must get an answer. It seems so silly. Why doesn't he tell me? I have a funny feeling that unless I get an answer I will go crazy. I am insistent.

"But what do you *think* about, Pa? What is it?"

"Nothing, son. Just things in general. Nothing special. Just things."

I can get no answer.

It is very late. The street is quiet and the house is dark. I climb the steps softly, skipping the ones that creak. I let myself in with my key and tiptoe into my room. I remove my clothes and remember that I am thirsty. In my bare feet I walk to the kitchen. Before I reach it I know he is there.

I can see the deeper darkness of his hunched shape. He is sitting in the same chair, his elbows on his knees, his cold pipe in his teeth, his unblinking eyes staring straight ahead. He does not seem to know I am there. He did not hear me come in. I stand quietly in the doorway and watch him.

Everything is quiet, but the night is full of little sounds. As I stand there motionless I begin to notice them. The ticking of the alarm clock on the icebox. The low hum of an automobile passing many blocks away. The swish of papers moved along the street by the breeze. A whispering rise and fall of sound, like low breathing. It is strangely pleasant.

The dryness in my throat reminds me. I step briskly into the kitchen.

"Hello, Pop," I say.

"Hello, son," he says. His voice is low and dream-like. He does not change his position or shift his gaze.

I cannot find the faucet. The dim shadow of light that comes through the window from the street lamp only makes the room seem darker. I reach for the short chain in the center of the room. I snap on the light.

He straightens up with a jerk, as though he has been struck. "What's the matter, Pop?" I ask.

"Nothing," he says sharply. "Only put out the light."

"What's the matter with the light?" I say. "What's wrong?"

"Nothing," he says. "I don't like the light."

I snap the light off. I drink my water slowly. I must take it easy, I say to myself. I must get to the bottom of this.

"Why don't you go to bed? Why do you sit here so late in the dark?"

"It's nice," he says. "I can't get used to lights. We didn't have lights when I was a boy in Europe."

My heart skips a beat and I catch my breath happily. I begin to think I understand. I remember the stories of his boyhood in Austria. I see the wide-beamed *kretchma*, with my grandfather behind the bar. It is late, the customers are gone, and he is dozing. I see the bed of glowing coals, the last of the roaring fire. The room is already dark, and growing darker. I see a small boy, crouched on a pile of twigs at one side of the huge fireplace, his starry gaze fixed on the dull remains of the dead flames. The boy is my father.

I remember the pleasure of those few moments while I stood quietly in the doorway watching him.

"You mean there's nothing wrong? You just sit in the dark because you like it, Pop?" I find it hard to keep my voice from rising in a happy shout.

"Sure," he says. "I can't think with the light on."

I set my glass down and turn to go back to my room. "Good night, Pop," I say.

"Good night," he says.

Then I remember. I turn back. "What do you think about, Pop?" I ask.

His voice seems to come from far away. It is quiet and even again. "Nothing," he says softly. "Nothing special."

The Neat Mexicans

The wide asphalt square behind the Pershing Building was marked off by painted white lines into numbered parking spaces, all slanting away from the narrow grassy island that ran down the middle of the square, and all reserved for division chiefs and bureau heads: CAF 14s and above, sixty-five hundred a year or better. This was the side of the building that Crossett liked, not only because it faced the river and on clear days you could see the Potomac from the fifth-floor Conference Room, but also because it was quiet. For Crossett this was the one place in the city where, even in the morning when the car pools from Chevy Chase and Alexandria and Silver Spring were unloading, you could sit and think for a few minutes.

Crossett was not a division chief or a bureau head, but he was a CAF 15: economist and planner, senior grade. Even in Washington they had enough sense to realize that you couldn't do much economic planning if you were running a bureau or were saddled with responsibility for the work of a division staff. All Crossett had asked for, back in 1941 when he was invited to take a leave of absence from Harvard and come down for the duration, was a room with an outside window and a secretary who didn't chew gum. They had given him both and then, after V-E Day, when things eased up a little, they had thrown in the parking space. Crossett had no complaints and that, he told himself as he swung his 1936 Chevrolet into number 168, was the trouble.

He cut the wheel sharply and leaned out of the window to look, breathing hard because the lunch had been a dandy and two martinis at twelve-thirty were getting to be heavy going for a man of fifty who seldom drank at noon and hated exercise. The Chevrolet's left front wheel was well over the line, a foot or more into parking space number 167, and Crossett grunted as he put the car into reverse and backed out for a new try. One martini would have been enough.

"Hey!" somebody yelled. "Watch out!"

Crossett kicked the brake and turned to look. A shiny pale blue Oldsmobile, a 1941 or 1942 model, was circling away from the back of the Chevrolet in a wary arc. A young army officer with a thin black mustache was at the wheel.

"Sorry," Crossett called.

"To hell with being sorry," the officer said. "Just try being careful."

The Oldsmobile shot off down the square, toward the public parking lot at the end, before Crossett could rap back a reply, and he treated the Chevvy a little roughly as he parked it properly. He switched off the ignition and flipped the keys back into the worn leather pouch with the snap fastener and shoved the pouch into his pocket. He sat back, his right arm resting on the steering wheel, the heel of his hand pumping delicately up and down on the broken horn button and, even though he knew he was late, Crossett took advantage of the one place in the city where you could sit and think. He knew he wasn't thinking well because the offer, made across a corner table in the Hay-Adams dining room, was still so fresh and new and exciting that it looked larger in any calculation he was likely to make, with two martinis not quite dead inside him, than it had a right to look. Just the same it was damned pleasant, and Crossett figured the war effort and his role in it had both reached a stage where he could afford to let the Planning Committee wait a few minutes.

Until two hours before, at exactly twelve-thirty when he walked into the Hay-Adams to meet the president of the Ohio college whose name he would probably learn to pronounce some day, Crossett had been in as good a position as several thousand other men in Washington who had answered the call just before December 7,

1941, when things were beginning to cook, or after Pearl Harbor, when they were boiling. He had an assistant professorship waiting for him in Cambridge any time he was ready to go back and take it. Now, two hours later, he was in a far better position than most. All he had to do was call the room number at the Raleigh that was written down neatly in the small looseleaf notebook he carried in the outer breast pocket of his coat, behind the folded handkerchief, or, if he preferred to take the month he had been given in which to make his decision, all he had to do was write to the unpronounceable address on the same page of the same notebook, and he was a dean, not at Harvard, true, but at twice the salary Harvard had been and would be paying him. That was all there was to it, but, as he got out of the car and closed the door without slamming it because the hinge was loose, Crossett knew he was kidding himself. There was a hell of a lot more to it. There was what Crossett called his trouble.

He crossed the square and went into the Pershing Building through the back entrance. The guard in the swivel chair near the revolving door looked up from his copy of the *Times-Herald*, recognized Crossett, and nodded. Crossett nodded back, and walked down the black and gray marble hallway to the elevator, and punched the gold button. The elevator came and the handsome, stout Negro woman, in the neat blue uniform with PB embroidered in silver over her left pocket, smiled and pressed the number five button without waiting for Crossett to call his floor. She smiled again when he got out on the fifth floor, and Crossett knew there wouldn't be anything like this in Ohio, dean or no dean.

"You're late," Miss Gough said as he walked into his office. "They started at two-thirty sharp, when Captain Iverson arrived."

"They'll wait," Crossett said, crossing to the door of his own room. "I got stuck."

Miss Gough shook her head at him with a half smile, as though he were a little boy, and it occurred to Crossett that one of the advantages of Ohio would be that there would be no Miss Gough. He closed the door behind him and went into his private washroom. There were only three offices with private washrooms on the fifth floor of the Pershing Building and, as he dried his hands on the small towel with the initials PB stamped in blue in one corner, it seemed to Crossett that here was his trouble in a nutshell: Miss Gough and the private washroom.

If he had not insisted on a room with an outside window before he came down from Harvard in 1941, he would not have drawn one of the three private washrooms, they would have thought of him as just another professor and, after the shooting war was over, they would have let him go quietly, the way they were letting other professors go. Instead, they had looked around, noticed the private washroom, decided anyone who rated one of them was obviously too important to be let go, and he had been saddled with reconversion. Anybody who knew the score knew that the shooting war had been a picnic by comparison with the mess of reconversion, and Crossett knew the score.

If he had not insisted on a secretary who didn't chew gum, he might have drawn any one of the hundreds of nice little girls, from Arkansas or New Hampshire or Kentucky, who wagged their jaws while they typed and pasted picture postcards from vacationing friends on the wall over their desks and let their bosses alone. But Crossett had insisted on a non-gum chewer and he had drawn Miss Gough, who had gone to Smith and spelled beautifully and wore tailored suits and was so damned efficient and devoted to her job that she would cut her own lunch hour, and hang on to a phone for ten minutes, while he was paged at the Hay-Adams, to remind him that he was due at a two-thirty meeting of the Planning Committee. A man with a desk in one of the crowded offices down the hall and a girl with nothing more on her mind than tomorrow's blind date could pack up when the shooting war was over and go back to whatever he had been doing before Pearl Harbor or take an attractive, better offer. A man with a private washroom and Miss Gough had a conscience. Crossett rinsed his mouth and he was drinking a glass of water when Miss Gough came in.

"They just called from the Conference Room to ask if you were back," she said. "It's two-forty, Mr. Crossett. Is that cold enough? I could get you a glass from the cooler?"

"No, this is all right," Crossett said. It wasn't cold enough but all at once, with the alcohol dying inside him, he was so sick of Washington and the war effort and reconversion and Miss Gough's bright devotion, that he could scarcely swallow. Why couldn't they let him alone? He had done his job. Four years were enough. Why couldn't they get along with the bright young men, with this Captain Iverson and his prize-winning plans and the scores of others like him? Crossett put the glass down on the edge of the black marble basin, came out into the office, and kicked the washroom door shut. "What's on the agenda?" he said.

"Final approval of the master memorandum for the President," Miss Gough said. "And the preamble you wrote. That's all."

"All right, I'll go in now," Crossett said. "Oh, say, look. The left front door of my car is going to fall off any minute unless I do something about that hinge. Do you think you could?"

"Why didn't you tell me?" Miss Gough said. "Of course I can. I know the man at the filling station on Wisconsin and Q. He'll do anything for me. You go on ahead to the meeting, Mr. Crossett. I'll call him right away."

"Thanks," Crossett said and went out, wishing he hadn't asked her, yet knowing it was the only way the car would ever be fixed. He went down the hall to the conference room and turned the knob quietly, but not quietly enough. The Director was at the head of the long table, reading from the thick memorandum, and he stopped to look across his glasses at the door. He smiled at Crossett and nodded and waited while Crossett came into the room and closed the door. Crossett started for his usual chair, halfway down the table, facing the window, and then he saw that it was occupied by a man in uniform. Crossett went around the table, to the other side, and he slipped into the vacant chair facing his regular seat, his back to the window. The Director resumed reading and Crossett looked around.

All the deputies were there, as well as the liaison boys from FEA and WPB and WMC and Crossett remembered, now that he was here, how important the meeting was and how much he had wanted to be on time. His head ached slightly and his mouth felt furry, the way it always did in the afternoon if he drank at lunch, and now he really regretted that second martini. His glance came down the long table and stopped on the man in uniform, the man in Crossett's chair, and Crossett sat up straighter.

The man had two silver bars on his shoulder, and his face was dark and thin, and there was a narrow, black, very new mustache, so narrow and so new that it looked as though it had been drawn on with an eyebrow pencil, running in a straight line across the middle of the wide space between his nose and his upper lip. Crossett knew very little about medicine but he was willing to bet, from the shape of the young man's head, that Captain Iverson had suffered from rickets or some other disease of malnutrition when he was a boy. Crossett turned and looked out the window, down the long double line of cars parked along the grassy island, to the public parking lot at the end, and there it was, the shiny pale blue Oldsmobile, the 1941 or 1942 model. It was parked arrogantly, facing Seventh Street, taking up more room than one car was entitled to, but ready for getting away without turning. Crossett swung back and looked at Captain Iverson with interest.

A month before, Iverson had won the fifteen-thousand-dollar first prize in a national contest, sponsored by a breakfast food company, for the best manuscript plan on the problems of the postwar world. The newspapers, in which his picture had appeared in the news columns as well as in full-page advertisements paid for by the breakfast food company, had said he was twenty-seven years old. He looked older, though, with his gaunt face and his thick black hair falling forward over his eyes. Crossett wondered how he had found the time, while on active duty, to prepare a book-length manuscript on such a subject. Crossett examined Captain Iverson's uniform. There were no campaign or area ribbons over his left pocket and, on the shoulder of his left sleeve, he wore the red, white, and blue patch of the Service Forces. That, Crossett said to himself, explained that. After four years in the nation's capital, much of that time spent at meetings in the Pentagon and Navy buildings, it was Crossett's belief that, if Tolstoy had served at a desk in the Service Forces in Washington, he could have written *War and Peace* without turning down a single cocktail invitation.

Crossett had not read the prize-winning plan, nobody but the contest judges had read it yet because the rumor around town in agency circles was that no trade publisher was interested, but the Director of Crossett's outfit had been impressed by the newspaper accounts, and he had asked the army to allow Captain Iverson to sit in on the meetings of the agency's Planning Committee. This was Captain Iverson's first visit, and it looked as though he was not im-

pressed, but Crossett had seen too many men look like that at too
many meetings to feel that his appearance was conclusive. The
young captain sat slouched down in Crossett's chair, his thin little
body hunched over, his lips twisted in what might not have been a
contemptuous sneer, his eyes half closed, and his nervous fingers
played with a beautiful gold fountain pen, obviously purchased quite
recently, like the pale blue 1941 or 1942 Oldsmobile, out of the
prize money.

"We've all read copies of the memorandum itself prior to this
meeting," the Director said. "And before you arrived, we found that
we're all in substantial agreement on the main points, so there's
not much to be gained by rehashing the document itself here." Crossett realized with a start that the Director was talking to him, and
he swung his glance down the table. "The plan itself, then, with all
our main recommendations, goes to the President's desk as is. Is
that correct, gentlemen?" Everybody nodded and Crossett noticed
that the Director's glance remained on Captain Iverson. Everybody,
including Crossett, turned and looked at the young man. He pursed
his lips and, after a pause that seemed to Crossett just a little too
long even for a much older man, Captain Iverson nodded grudgingly,
without straightening in the chair. "Very well," the Director said.
"The only thing about which there seems to be some disagreement,
then, is the preamble you wrote, Crossett."

"The preamble?" Crossett said. "Why?"

"The point has been raised that it is, well—" The Director hesitated. "That it is needlessly belligerent, shall we say," the Director
said. "I don't say that I agree with the objection, Crossett, but it has
been raised, and I think we ought to get it settled at this meeting.
The memorandum must go to the printer tomorrow."

"Would you read it aloud, sir?" Crossett said.

"I just did," the Director said. "Weren't you listening?"

"It didn't sound belligerent when I wrote it," Crossett said, evad-
ing the question. "I didn't intend it to be belligerent. I don't know
what that word means in this connection. I'd like to hear it read
again and see where there's anything in it that anybody can object
to."

The Director cleared his throat and started to read again. He didn't
read particularly well, but it seemed to Crossett that you couldn't

read that sort of thing badly. Half of it was direct quotation from Roosevelt's speeches. The rest was practically a restatement of President Truman's affirmation, in his first address to Congress, of his administration's objectives. The artless words and phrases, about education, work for all, a decent standard of living, came through the Director's bad reading voice with all the old simplicity and power. The Director finished and looked up. Crossett looked around the table. Nobody met his glance. He turned back to the Director. Their eyes met and then the Director looked away quickly. He cleared his throat.

"Captain Iverson?" the Director said.

"It's pointless," Captain Iverson said, talking to his gold fountain pen. "I think it will do more harm than good."

"Why?" Crossett said, leaning forward slightly, talking directly across the table at the younger man. "How can it do harm?"

"The President presents it to Congress," Captain Iverson said, still addressing the gorgeous fountain pen. "They're fed up with that Utopia stuff. It'll get their backs up."

"I don't think it's our job to worry about the backs of Congress," Crossett said. "Those few paragraphs, that's what this agency was created for. That's the whole point of the document itself. Let's do our job, and let's let the President worry about getting it through Congress."

"It's not practical," Captain Iverson said. "It's like looking for a neat Mexican. There ain't no such animal." Half the people around the table laughed, and Captain Iverson's eyelids lifted for a moment as his lips and his mustache twisted a little more to the left in what was apparently a modest smile. "I say nuts to the high-flown words and the fancy preambles," he said, his attention fixed once more on the gold fountain pen. "There's too much of that around. Let's show the President and Congress that we're not a bunch of long-haired dreamers," Captain Iverson said. "Let's show them we're as good businessmen as they are," he said. "That way we don't get their backs up, and we've got a chance to really sell a program."

Crossett opened his mouth, but the words wouldn't come, and he closed his lips without speaking. It was just as well. They would have been the wrong words. He leaned back in the chair, which was exactly like the chair in which he always sat at these meetings, but this one didn't feel comfortable or right because his back was to the window and he couldn't see the Potomac, and he realized that it wasn't the martinis at all. It was the accumulation, the four years, that was all. He had been at it too long. Crossett remembered a phrase the sportswriters used about a pitcher who began to walk too many men and allowed too many hits: he had lost the zip on his fast one.

"I'll tell you what," the Director said, gathering the loose pages and jogging them into an even pile on the glass top. "I'll think this over and make the decision myself before I send the memorandum to the printer. Thank you, gentlemen."

The chairs scraped and the men broke up into small groups as they moved toward the door. The WPB man, who was on loan from Yale, fell in beside Crossett and said something humorous about the reconversion job the universities would have to do on themselves but, before Crossett could reply, one of the deputies pulled the WPB man aside and, as he went through the door, Crossett found himself next to Captain Iverson. Crossett was surprised by how short the younger man was. He had seemed taller behind the wheel of the Oldsmobile.

"Quite seriously," Crossett said. "What was your real objection to the preamble?"

Captain Iverson looked up and, as his lips twisted, he glanced quickly to his right and then to his left, as though to see if anybody was listening. Half a dozen men were.

"All that stuff about milk for babies, hell," Captain Iverson said through his thin smile. "I don't want everybody to be the same size."

Crossett was off balance when he hit him, so he recoiled with the impact and his own shoulder hit the marble wall, spoiling his view. But he must have connected in a good place because, when he turned around, all he could see, sticking out from the group of excited executives bending over the younger man, was a pair of brown strap shoes and six or seven inches of cuffless pinks. Captain Iverson was out cold. Cold enough, anyway. Crossett stepped on something, saw it was the gold fountain pen, and he paused just long enough to kick the damned thing back toward the jabbering group. Then he walked on down the hall to his own office and went in.

"I talked to my man at the filling station on Wisconsin and Q," Miss Gough said. "He said if you drive by there tonight on your way home he thinks he'll be able to fix that door for you, but you'd better not work late tonight because he closes at seven. What's all that excitement out in the hall?"

"A top executive just resigned," Crossett said. He crossed the room and opened the door of his private office. "Get me the Raleigh, will you, Miss Gough?" he said across his shoulder.

Crossett closed the door and sat down at his desk, still breathing irregularly, and he pulled the small looseleaf leather notebook from behind the folded handkerchief in his outer breast pocket. He flipped it to the page with the room number on it, and he set the open book flat in the middle of the green blotter, and he waited for his breathing to become regular again. When the phone rang Crossett was sucking his knuckles. They burned slightly.

"I've got the Raleigh," Miss Gough said. "Who did you want there, Mr. Crossett?"

"Just put me on," Crossett said and she did and then, as he read off the room number to the girl at the Raleigh switchboard, he remembered another phone call. Crossett had made that one almost four years ago, from the faculty lounge, between classes, to the man at the Copley-Plaza who had come up to Boston from Washington for a few days and had taken Crossett out and fed him two martinis before lunch.

"Five oh nine is busy," the girl at the Raleigh switchboard said. "Will you wait, sir?"

"Yes, I'll wait," Crossett said and he waited, for the man from Ohio who two hours before had pointed the way out that Crossett had just taken with his bruised knuckles, and he waited also for the suddenly remembered feeling that was four years old but still as fresh and hard and exciting as it had been then, that day in the faculty lounge, when martinis before lunch did not die until late afternoon, when he was forty-six.

"Here's five oh nine now, sir," the girl at the Raleigh switchboard said. "Thanks for waiting."

There was a click at the other end and Crossett looked around the room quickly, in a sudden panic of regret, not for the private wash-room, or the guard in the swivel chair at the back door, or the stout woman in the gilded elevator who knew his floor without asking, or even for parking place number 168, but for something else, for the endless foolish meetings, and for the few quiet minutes every morning while the car pools from Chevy Chase and Alexandria were unload-ing, and even for Miss Gough's relentless efficiency, for something he had been part of for four years. He would never have that again. Not in Ohio.

"Hello," Crossett said in a tired voice, and he turned with the phone to look out the window. It was a clear day and you could see the Potomac.

Off Season

"There's not a square inch of khaki in sight, he's got pretty much a whole quarter-mile of beach all to himself, and he's right in front of us." The middle-aged man spoke with his eyes closed. He lay back in the deck chair, completely relaxed, his face tipped up to the afternoon sunlight. "He's not going to get contaminated in the next forty-five minutes. Guaranteed."

"Go ahead, make it sound as though I'm unpatriotic, a subversive agent or something, and you are at least George Washington. It's upsetting to children to see badly wounded soldiers. That's all." The woman in the silver-fox cape, who lay in another deck chair beside her husband, had twisted herself up under the steamer rug and was peering anxiously across the beach though her green-rimmed harlequin-shaped sun glasses. A boy, about ten or eleven years old, was kneeling in the broad shadow of the Steel Pier a few hundred yards away. "I happen to be worried because he's so close to the pier, not about soldiers. It's damp and cold there in the shadows. What's he doing? Can you see?"

"Digging sand," the man said without opening his eyes, which were shaded from the sun by the brim of his gray fedora. His well-cut double-breasted overcoat was bunched up around his shoulders, so that the American Legion pin in the left lapel was just under his ear. He wriggled his feet lazily under the plaid steamer rug. "Or piling it up. Whatever boys do with sand. And it's no more upsetting to children than it is to the soldiers themselves. Relax."

"I want him to stay out in the sun," the woman said. "He'll catch cold in all that damp." She sat up. "Richard!" she called. "Richard!" The boy raised his head and squinted toward the deck chairs. "Play out in the sun, dear! It's damp there by the pier!" The boy stood up, shuffled out of the shadows, stood about awkwardly in the sunlight for several moments and then knelt down again. The woman settled back, rearranged her steamer rug and looked around. "This is the first sunny day we've had since we came," she said. "You'd think they'd be doing more business with these chairs."

"They don't count on making much during the off season," her husband said. Between the boardwalk, which was almost deserted, and the beach, the concessionnaire had set up a semicircular windbreak, five or six feet high, made of canvas squares stretched between posts driven into the sand. Inside the windbreak about a hundred deck chairs were lined up side by side to face the afternoon sun. It was not a very good day, in spite of the sun. The wind was cold and strong and it seeped through the vents in the canvas. The woman in the silver-fox cape and her husband were the only two customers. The concessionnaire, a little old man with a deeply tanned face, sat huddled in a parka on the last chair near the boardwalk, reading a racing form folded into small squares to keep it from flapping in the wind. "When the season really starts, late June, July, he makes it back," the man in the double-breasted overcoat said. "Whatever he picks up now is gravy. And wounded soldiers don't come down here to rent deck chairs at two bits an hour. They have their own at the hotels the Army took over for them."

The woman lit a cigarette and tossed the match to the left where, some distance away, the surf rolled in, drumming steadily. To the right, above the boardwalk, loomed the huge hotels and, below them, the hot dog stands and custard parlors and shooting galleries, most of them shuttered because there was so little trade. Ahead, high over the Steel Pier that stuck out into the sea and beside which the boy played in the sand, the tremendous clock on the whisky billboard, with the manufacturer's name spelled out around the face instead of numbers, showed ten minutes after three.

"Forty more minutes," the woman said. "We sat down ten to three."

"You don't have to keep track," the man said. "He comes and tells you when your hour is up and asks for another quarter. Relax."

The uneven tramp of feet and the low murmur of many voices came across the sand from the boardwalk. The woman turned quickly to look. A squad of soldiers in fatigues was moving along, close to the rail. There were about sixteen of them in a double column, with a sergeant at one side. Even though they kept formation, they moved raggedly and slowly, because some limped, two or three walked with canes, and one man at the end hobbled along on a single crutch. They laughed and joked as they went and even shoved each other now and then, but never hard enough to throw a man off balance or to break the formation.

The woman in the deck chair shot a quick, worried glance at her son playing in the sand. The boy had stopped to watch the soldiers. She looked toward her husband and opened her mouth to say something, but he looked past her, squinting against the sunlight, and she brought her lips together without speaking.

As the soldiers passed the deck chair concession, a girl went by on the boardwalk, going in the other direction. The soldiers whistled. The girl smiled with nervous embarrassment and walked more quickly. The sergeant, grinning widely, snapped an order. The soldiers laughed and moved on up the boardwalk, out of sight from the canvas windbreak on the beach. The woman in the deck chair threw away her cigarette and scowled as she settled back.

"It's quite different from when we used to go to the Haddon Hall, isn't it?" she said after a few moments. "With their own private sun deck. Remember?"

"Listen, we're in the best hotel still open to civilians, even if it doesn't have a private sun deck, and we're doing fine," her husband said, speaking up to the sun with his eyes closed, his voice flat, as though he were reciting a poem he had learned long ago in school just to see if he could remember the words. "For a week it won't kill us. The Army needed the Haddon Hall and the other hotels for hospitals and things. There's a war on. Men get hurt."

"Look, he's back there in the damp again." The woman sat up. "Richard!" she called. "Richard, play out in the sun, dear!" The boy came out of the shadow of the Steel Pier and started walking about in the sunlight, in small aimless circles. His mother watched him for a while, supporting herself on one elbow, then dropped back into the deck chair, pulled the silver-fox cape close around her throat, lit another cigarette and looked at her husband. "Are you falling asleep?"

"If I do," he said to the sky, "remind me to send it in to Ripley."

The woman raised the cigarette to her lips, stopped, and held it in mid-air. From the boardwalk, behind the windbreak, came the sound of many feet shuffling out of step and the murmur of voices. She twisted in the chair and turned to look. The squad of soldiers was coming back. Now they were carrying baseballs and bats and medicine balls. They passed the windbreak and, when they came abreast of the wide open space between the deck chairs and the Steel Pier, the sergeant barked an order. The soldiers broke ranks and started coming down the wooden steps to the beach. The woman dropped her cigarette and began to get up. Her husband put his hand on her arm. She fell back into the chair.

"They're convalescents," he said in his flat voice. "They're out for a little exercise. They won't bite him. Relax."

The boy stopped digging in the sand and stood up to watch. The soldiers broke into groups of two and three. They began to bat out fungoes, pitch to each other and toss the medicine balls around. The exercise was not very violent. Because of their injuries they couldn't bat very well. They pitched by tossing the baseballs underhand and all they did with the medicine balls was roll them about on the sand. A soldier with a cane hobbled toward a baseball that had been tossed to him. He didn't get to it fast enough. The ball hit the sand and rolled away into the shadows of the pier. The boy ran forward, picked up the ball and threw it back. The soldier yelled his thanks.

"Let's go back to the hotel," the woman said, getting up. "It's time for his bath. Richard!" she called. "We're going back to the——"

"There's plenty of time," her husband said. He pulled her down gently into her deck chair and nodded to the clock on the whisky advertisement. "It's three-thirty. We have twenty minutes." He turned to face the beach. The small boy was coming toward the windbreak, looking shyly across his shoulder at the playing soldiers.

"Go ahead, Dick," his father called, waving him back. "We have plenty of time."

The boy stopped, grinned quickly and turned. The soldier with the crutch was standing at one side, away from the others, resting his weight on the crutch, bouncing a baseball up and down in his hand and rolling a bat back and forth lazily on the sand with his good foot. He saw the boy and called something to him. The boy nodded eagerly. The soldier picked up the bat, balanced himself carefully on the crutch, tossed the ball into the air and, swinging the bat with one hand, popped out a weak grounder. The small boy fielded it neatly. He drew back his arm to return the ball and then, apparently realizing the soldier with the crutch couldn't catch it, the boy returned the ball by rolling it on the sand. The soldier laughed, scooped it up easily and batted out another one. The boy laughed, too, fielded the ball and returned it the same way.

"He'll be late for his bath," the woman said, scraping lipstick rapidly from her lower lip with her upper teeth. "That means he'll be late for his supper and he won't sleep. I'm not going to let——"

"He won't be late for anything," the man said without turning his head, keeping his eyes on his son and the soldier. "Let him alone."

The woman's lips disappeared into a thin line. She sat up in the deck chair as though it were a bench and her face grew red in places where there wasn't any rouge. She kept swinging her head from the boy and the soldier to the clock over the pier. Her husband lay back in his chair and watched. There was a small smile of pleasure around his lips. The boy's happy laughter and the soldier's cheerful shouts rolled across the sand more often than the baseball.

"Here comes a fast one, now," the soldier yelled. "Hang onto it, son."

"All right," the boy yelled back. "Smack it out."

The soldier took a swing that almost threw him off his crutch. He connected. The ball flew low and hard, hit the sand and went bouncing along in short, fast hops. The small boy moved into position, put out his hands and crouched down for the catch. His mother was looking at the clock over the pier. The minute hand jumped to the letter L, which stood for the numeral ten.

"The hour is over," she said, getting up. "It's ten to four." She turned and called, "Richard!"

The boy jumped nervously. He swung his head around to face his mother. The ball missed his outstretched hands and hit him in the belly. He dropped to the sand, clutching his middle.

"Richard!" his mother screamed. She kicked off the steamer rug and ran toward him. "Richard!"

Her husband was right behind her when she reached the boy. The soldier with the crutch was hobbling rapidly toward them. The other soldiers had turned to look and a few of them came over, one by one.

"Oh, I knew it, I knew it, I knew it," the woman cried. "I told you not to let him——"

"Shut up," her husband said. He pushed her aside and helped the boy to his feet. "You all right, Dick?"

"Yes," the boy gasped. "I—I think so." He rubbed his middle and grinned weakly. "Just knocked the breath out of me," he said more slowly. "I'm—I think I'm all right."

"I'm awful sorry, ma'am," the soldier with the crutch said. "I didn't mean to——"

"It's quite all right," the woman said stiffly. She took the boy's hand. "Come along, Richard."

The soldiers watched her take the boy across the sand toward the wooden steps that led up to the boardwalk. Then they moved off as they had come, one by one, slowly, until only the soldier with the crutch remained.

"I'm sorry, sir," he said uncomfortably. "I didn't mean to hurt him."

"You didn't hurt him," the man said. "And it wasn't your fault. He's all right." He dipped down, picked up the baseball and smiled. "No point in spoiling your afternoon," he said. "Would you like to bat out a few to me?"

The soldier looked at the middle-aged man. His eyes took in the expensive overcoat, the gray fedora, stopped for a moment on the American Legion pin, and came to rest on the strong, fleshly, well-barbered face.

"Thanks a lot, sir," he said, his voice awkward, his forehead creased with embarrassment. "That's very nice of you, but——"

He glanced desperately behind him at the other soldiers, as though looking for help, but they were all busy. "I mean, you'd get your clothes all dirty, and——" The middle-aged man straightened up slightly, as though someone had made a remark about his posture. "No, I don't mean that, sir," the soldier said hastily. "What I mean is——" The sergeant behind him barked an order. "I mean," the soldier said with a quick, nervous smile of relief, "our time is up. Have to go back now." He snatched the baseball from the man's hand and, as he hobbled away to join his comrades, called back over his shoulder, "Thanks just the same."

The middle-aged man waited on the sand until the soldiers had picked up their equipment, climbed to the boardwalk, fallen in and shuffled away. Then he walked toward the concessionnaire.

Old Clothes for Poland

The moment Louis put his hand on the doorknob he remembered that his father had been asking him to do something all week. He hesitated a moment, trying to recall what it was, but he couldn't.

"What's the matter, Lou?" Barney asked, behind him.

"Oh, nothing. I just tried to remember something. Come on in."

There was a light in the kitchen at the other end of the flat. He closed the door softly, hoping his father was not at home.

"Who's dere?" It was his mother's voice, uneven and high, raised in a shout. "Who's dere?" she called again.

"It's O.K., Ma. It's me," Louis yelled.

"Is dat you, Loy?" Her voice sank lower as she came from the kitchen toward her son's room.

"Yeah, Ma. It's me. Me and a friend."

She stood in the doorway of his room, wiping her hands on a dish towel and watching him take off his coat. He turned around and saw her.

"Hello, Ma," he said. "This is a friend of mine, Barney."

"Hello," she said. "You're hungry, Loy?"

"Nah, I don't know. Maybe I could eat something if you got it ready. I'm in a hurry, Ma. I've got to go away."

"Your friend wants something maybe?" she asked.

Louis looked at Barney, who shook his head and smiled.

"Nah, Ma, he doesn't want anything. Just give me something. Anything you got."

"*Nu*, all right," she said, "come in da kitchen. Oll give you eat," and she walked away from the door, down the flat to the kitchen.

"I'll be back in a couple of minutes, Barney. There's a *Ballyhoo* there or something, if you want it. I just want to take a bite."

"I don't want to read, Lou," Barney said. "I'll come in and watch you." He stood up and came toward the door, but Louis pushed him playfully back into his chair.

"Nah, you stay here, Barney. I'll be back in a couple of minutes. I just want to grab a bite," he said, and walked to the kitchen, rolling up his shirtsleeves as he went.

He stepped out of the darkness of the front room into the bright light of the kitchen and saw his father quietly reading the paper in one corner.

"Hello, Pop," he said, trying to remember what his father had wanted him to do.

His father looked over the edge of his paper and said, "Hello, *Leballe*."

Louis sat quietly at the table, hoping his father would continue to read. His mother set a plate of hot soup before him.

"What's that, Ma?"

"It's soup," she said. "Go ahead, eat. It's good. Come on."

"Ah, gee, Ma. You know I don't like soup. Haven't you got something else?"

"Sure I got. But fuyst eat da soup up. Go 'head. It's a good soup. Come on, Loy. Be a good *boychick*," she said.

"Ah, gee, Ma," he said, and took up his spoon.

His father folded his paper and watched him as he ate. When the plate was empty, he put the paper aside and folded his arms.

"Loy, ven you gonna write me dat list, hah?" His voice was mild and pleasant.

Louis suddenly remembered what his father had wanted.

"Gee whiz, Pop, I forgot all about it. I'll do it tomorrow. O.K.?"

"But Loy, I *need* it f' t'morra."

"Ah, gee, Pop. I'm in a hurry now. I got a friend waiting for me in my room. I'll do it tomorrow sure thing." He stood up, talking rapidly.

"But Loy, I gotta take it t' the consul t'morra in da morning."

Louis stood there, hesitating, his face creased perplexedly. "Ah, gee, Pop," he said. "I'm in a hurry now."

His father stood up too. "But Loy, I esked you to do it a whole week. An' I need it for the consul in the morning. How long it'll take you? A coupla minutes?" His voice was a coaxing sing-song.

His mother turned around from the gas range with another dish in her hand. "Where you going? Ain' you eatin' no more?"

"Ah, no, Ma. I'm not hungry. I'm in a hurry."

His father was speaking again. "How long it'll take you? A coupla minutes? Put it in da typerider an' in a coupla minutes y're through."

"Go 'head, Loy," his mother said. "Papa needs it for in da morning. It'll oney take a few minutes. Go 'head. Papa needs it."

"Ah, gee. O.K., Pa. Come on. Let's hurry up. Nah, I don't want any more, Ma. I'm not hungry. O.K., Pa, come on." He hurried out of the kitchen, his father close behind him.

Barney was sitting on the bed, turning the pages of a magazine. He looked up and smiled tentatively, as though expecting to be introduced. But Louis strode over to his desk and sat down without speaking. He whipped off the cover from his typewriter and inserted a sheet of paper.

"Come *on*, Pop. I'm in a hurry," he said, clapping his hands impatiently.

The old man eased himself into a chair and began to fumble with a packet of papers he drew from his pocket.

"Come *on*, Pop," Louis said.

His father handed him a sheet of printed paper and said, "Read it over, Loy, an' oll bring in the bundle in here so you c'n mark everything down right."

"Don't you know what's in the bundle without bringing it in here?"

"Yeah, I know, but da list is gotta be puyfick, Loy. Oll bring in da bundle."

Louis stood up. "Wait a minute, Pa. I'll go in the other room with you."

His father stopped him with his hand. "No, no, you got da typerider here. Oll bring in da bundle," he said and hastened out.

Louis looked around at Barney. He had stopped reading and was watching him. He started to grin, but Louis looked past him, at the wall, for a few seconds, pretending he hadn't seen, and then turned back to his desk.

His father came in, puffing, with a large cheesecloth sugar sack in his arms. He inverted it in the middle of the room and tumbled out a pile of many-colored, crumpled garments. A strong smell of camphor filled the room. Louis kept his eyes on the typewriter.

"*Nu,* Loy, you ready?"

"Yeah, Pop, come on."

"Did you read over da paper?"

"Yeah. Yeah. Come *on,* will you, Pa?"

"What does it say?"

"It says you gotta make a list of everything in the bundle. Come on, *will* you?"

The old man fumbled with the clothes and brought up a green dress. "All right, Loy, mark down. One—," he hesitated, kneading the dress in his hands. "What would you call dis?" He held it aloft, shaking out the folds.

"For cryin' out loud, Pa, it's a dress, isn't it? Like this we'll never get through. One dress," Louis said savagely, accompanying his words with heavy strokes on the keyboard.

"I'da mean dat, Loy," his father said. "I mean what kind dress it is. It says in da printed paper no silk, un' no fur, un' no— Give a look on da paper, Loy."

"I *know* what it says, Pa," Louis said. "I read it. No silk and no fur and no new stuff. That's all. Now come on." He turned back to his typewriter.

The old man shook the dress and held it at arm's length, his head cocked sideways and his eyes narrowed appraisingly. "All right," he said. "Mark down. One cotton dress. No, wait. Say—" He turned to Barney and waved the dress toward him. "What would you call dis, cotton or wool?" Barney reached out and felt it.

"Gee whiz, Pa, let him alone. What's the difference? Cotton or wool. Let him alone. One—old—used—cotton—dress," Louis said, pronouncing each word carefully as he tapped it out on the typewriter.

His father dropped the green dress and picked up another one. "Dat's a good way to say it, Loy. One old used cotton—yeah, dat's good. You see," he said, turning to Barney, "the Polish consul won't let you send nuttin' what ain' old or made from silk or fur because it's supposed to be for oney poor people who ain' got no money—"

"Come on, Pop," Louis broke in. "He doesn't want to hear that. Come on. I'm in a hurry."

There were not many articles in the bundle. Two or three dresses, a suit, sweater, and several pairs of shoes. The listing was soon over.

Louis took the paper from the machine, covered it, and began to dress hurriedly. His father knelt on the floor, stuffing the old clothes into the white sack and talking to Barney, who still sat on the bed, smiling and attentive.

"It's for my brudder an' his wife an' children in Poland. They're very poor people, an' it's gettin' near winter. The Polish gover'mint don't let send no more den twenny-tree pounds, or I'd sen' dem more. An' it's gotta be ol' cloes oney, or dey—"

"Gee whiz, Pop, what are you telling him all that for? He's not interested in all that," Louis said, drawing the knot of his tie snug at the throat.

"—open it up an' keep it demselves," the old man continued, uninterrupted. "B'lieve me, I wish times was better an' I had da money. I would sen' dem better money den ol' cloes. It's so hard to make a livin' dere in da ol' country. You ought t' see da letters he writes me. You could cry sometimes jus' readin' it. The children ain' even got no shoes to wear, an' his wife—"

"Come on, Barney," Louis said, reaching for his coat. "So long, Pop."

The old man stood up suddenly and clapped his hand to his head. "*Oy, wehs mir*. Loy, wait! I forgot. Da *Swiadectwo ubostwa*. Wait!" He began to fumble in his breast pocket.

"The *what?*" Louis asked, turning back.

"The *Swiadectwo ubostwa*. Wait. Oll show you. You gotta fill it out for the consul. It's a paper." He held his coat wide with one hand and poked with the other, his head bent inward. He talked disjointedly, hurriedly, and seemed to be addressing the coat. "It says they're poor an' need the cloes. You gotta have it."

"Ah, hell, Pop, I'm in a hurry now. I'll do it tomorrow," Louis said.

"No, no, Loy. Wait!" His father's voice rose excitedly. "Dey won't let me send da bundle without it. It's gettin' winter soon. Please, Loy. Just anudder minute. Ah, here I god it." He waved a folded paper.

"Ah, gee, Pop," Louis said. "I'm in a hurry."

"Aw go ahead, Lou," Barney said, behind him. "We've got loads of time."

Louis shrugged, waving his head slowly from side to side, and came back into the room. He took off his coat and threw it on a chair. "O.K., Pop. Let's see it. Come on," he said, uncovering his typewriter.

"Here," his father said, handing him a much creased yellow paper.

Louis peered at the strange print. "This isn't English, Pop. What do you want me to do?"

"I know, Loy," the old man said. "It's *Poylish*. Jus' write on da boddim my name 'n' address an' on da top dis here." He pointed to the return address on a foreign-looking envelope, square and mauve-colored. He peered at it, hunched over, tracing the irregular script with a forefinger. "*Potok gorny. Vol—osh—o—no—wa,*" he said slowly, spelling out each syllable. "Yeah. Yeah. Dat's it. Voloshonowa. Dat's like here da city, y'know. Den write Poland. Yeah, Loy. Dat's right." He turned to Barney, who was again sitting on the bed, bouncing himself up and down gently.

The old man's voice was apologetic. "See, dis is like we call here in America a—a," he pursed his lips and described a circle in the air with his hand, hunting for the correct word, "a—like a c'tificate of poorness. Y'know what I mean?"

There was a sharp whirring sound as Lois tore the paper from his machine. "How sh'd he know what you mean? Why don't you let him alone, Pop? Here," he slapped the paper onto the desk and struggled with his coat. "I hope you're all through with this damn crap. Come on, Barney."

His father held the door open for them. "Denks very much, Loy. Y're a good boy. God'll give you a *mitzvah* for dis. Hev a nice time, *boyiss*. They'll be happy when dey get da warm t'ings for da winter—"

His voice sank lower as they went down the stairs until finally it was quiet. They paused for a moment in the hall downstairs to turn up their coat collars.

"I'm sorry about this, Barney," Louis said. "The old man's got a lot of nutzy ideas. You know how it is. I don't think we're very late, though."

"That's O.K.," Barney said. "Forget it."

Pennants Must Have Breezes

Papa has been a Socialist ever since I can remember. I can remember back when he was not even a citizen. We lived on Fourth Street, near Lewis, at that time. The Socialist headquarters for the Sixth Assembly District were on Seventh Street and Avenue C. That was before they tore the building down and built the Public National Bank there.

I must have been about six at the time, maybe seven. I did not know the difference between citizens and non-citizens. Every Friday night, for weeks before election, Papa would take me to meetings on street corners, or in Lenox Assembly Rooms, or Hennington Hall on Second Street, or at the "Club." That's what they called the Socialist headquarters.

Of course I didn't know what the speakers were talking about, but I learned that if they were speaking from a small step-ladder platform, and not from the back of a truck, and to a smaller crowd, they were Socialists. If there was a big crowd, and they had electric lights connected to the back of a truck from a nearby building, then it was either a Democratic or a Republican meeting. It did not matter which. Then you yelled Baloney or gave the Bronx cheer. You never stopped to listen.

Every year, before election, Papa took me up to the Club and I got a big canvas sign and some cardboard posters and a box of tin buttons that said Workers Of The World Unite. I tied the sign to the fire escape and stuck the posters in the windows. Of course, the posters did not do much good, because we only had two windows to the front, and we lived on the third floor, so you couldn't read what they said from the street. But the canvas sign was legible all right.

Then I would stick a row of tin buttons all around the outside of my cap and down the lapels of my coat. I was supposed to give the buttons out, but all the kids on the block played for them, so I did the same. Papa once saw me spinning underlegs for buttons and he said, "That's not what you're supposed to do with the buttons. You're supposed to give them out." I told him that I usually lost, anyway, so they got distributed just the same.

One day I was razzing Artie Pincus because his father voted for the Democrats. His big brother Natie came along, so I tried to show I knew something. I remembered something I heard William Kaplan say a couple of nights before at a meeting, and I said his father was a cog in the capitalist machine. Natie, we called him Sweatnose because that's where he perspired, got sore. He said, "What the hell are you talking about? Your old man ain't even a citizen."

I didn't know what that meant so I backed out of the argument. At night, I asked Papa what a citizen was. He said it was a grease ball who had passed certain tests and then was permitted to vote on Election Day. I asked him if he was a citizen. He said not yet, but he would be one next year.

And sure enough, next year he was. Mama too. I knew because before election the Democrat captain, Millstein, came up with another man and they sat around for about a half hour trying to talk Papa into voting for them. I thought Papa would get sore, or put up an argument or something. But he didn't. He just listened to everything they said and even seemed to agree with them. Then, when they got up to go, the captain took out a cigar and gave it to Papa and said, "Well, good night. I hope to see you again, and we'll be expecting your vote on Election Day."

When they were gone, Papa said to Mama, "I'll vote for him. Like hell I will. The dirty *gonuvim*. The dirty Tammany *Hallnick*."

At first I used to be puzzled by the fact that no Socialists ever won the election. I asked Papa about it. He said that was because the Socialists were too honest to bribe the people to vote for them, like the Republicans and the Democrats did. I asked what was the good of running, then, if you never won. Papa said it was for the principle

of the thing. He said that some day enough people would vote for the
Socialists to elect them. Then the reins of government would be in
the hands of the proletariat. They would govern themselves in accordance with their own wishes, not those of the capitalists, and the
world would be a much better place to live in.

I didn't think it was such a bad place at the time. And I was getting tired of having the other guys, like Artie Pincus, laughing at me
after election for sticking up for the losing side.

Papa seemed to be used to it, though. In fact, I don't ever remember
when he seemed confident before election that any Socialist
would win. Only once, but that was many years later.

One winter I heard Papa talking to old man Granat, who owned the
sweater store, trying to get him to vote Socialist. Granat finally said
that this year he would vote a Socialist ticket. And Papa said that it
looked like Pankoff had a good chance. I had heard him say things
like that so many times, that I didn't pay any attention, thinking
that he was just trying to convince Granat that his vote would not be
wasted.

Election night I went up to the Club with Papa to watch the returns. Usually, this was a pretty quiet affair. Most of the noise was
made at the Republican Club on Third Street or the Democratic
Club on Seventh. At the Club one man sat at the telephone, it was
usually Joe Bakerman, and called off the figures he got over the wire
to another fellow who marked them on a blackboard. During the
rest of the year, the board was used for lectures and, in between,
for games of tick-tack-toe.

I was pitching paper balls with Sunny Weingart at the big picture of Karl Marx that hung on the wall. The idea was to see who
could land more balls on the ledge of the heavy gold frame. I don't
exactly remember, but I think Sunny was leading. Suddenly we
heard somebody say, "Jesus Christ, look at this, will you?" Everybody
ran over to the blackboard. I couldn't see anthing, but everybody
was saying "Pankoff's leading" or "Pankoff's elected" or something
like that.

There was a lot of noise and Sunny's old man made him go
home, so we quit playing. After a while Papa came over and told me
to go home and tell Mama he'd be home late.

Pankoff was elected to the municipal court bench for a term of ten years. Nobody ever knew how it happened. In all of those ten years, I never heard of another Socialist being elected to any office in the city. But Papa still remained a Socialist.

And as my sister Lena grew older, she began to spend her time at the Club too. Mama objected, but couldn't do anything about it. Gradually, I stopped going to the Club with Papa, and by the time Pankoff was running for re-election, I hadn't been there in more than four years. I really don't know why. Unless it was the feeling I had that somehow or other I would have a great deal of money some day, and that I could not have it and be a Socialist at the same time.

Well, anyway, the year that Pankoff ran for re-election, ten years after I pitched paper balls at Karl Marx' picture with Sunny Weingart, was the first year that Lena really worked in an election. She helped with the campaigning before election, and on Election Day she stayed at the Club to answer the telephone. Everybody was pretty confident that Pankoff would be re-elected. Even the Democrats and the Republicans said so. In fact, they had offered him their indorsement, and, when he refused it, they put up very weak candidates against him. Morris Umansky voiced the general opinion when he said it was in the bag.

I slept late on Election Day. I got up about ten o'clock and Mama gave me some breakfast. I asked where Papa and Lena were. She said that Papa was a watcher and Lena was already at the Club. Mama and Papa had gotten up early and voted about seven o'clock. After breakfast I went over to Chink Levine's house. When I passed the school on Seventh Street, I could see a couple of Democrats handing out cigars on the steps. About twenty or thirty feet away, down the block, was a big white cardboard sign. On it was printed in blue letters No Electioneering Between This Point And The Polls.

Chink's mother gave us some lamb chops and potatoes, and we went out to the Palisades for a little hike. We got back about six o'clock. When I came into the house, Papa and Lena were eating supper. Papa was saying, "Well, it looks like we'll have at least one good judge on the bench for another ten years." Lena said, "If the people who vote for Pankoff would vote for the other Socialists, we'd win the whole election." Mama said something sarcastic. I don't remember what it was.

After supper they got their hats and coats and asked me to come along with them to the Club to get the returns. "No," I said, "I've got homework. I'll stay home with Mama."

Mama went to bed about half past ten, and about eleven I was getting ready to follow her. Suddenly there was a crash on the door like somebody had fallen against it hard. I opened it and Lena nearly fell in. She was crying like hell and her hat was on all cockeyed. I grabbed her in time to save her from falling, and put her into a chair. She put her head down on the kitchen table and continued to cry. I was afraid she would wake Mama, so I tried to keep her quiet. But she kept right on crying and wouldn't answer any of my questions. Sure enough, Mama came running out in a few minutes and got all excited when she saw Lena. We both tried to get her to talk, but all she could do was cry. Mama got a glass of water and made her drink it. In a few seconds she was quieted down a bit.

"What's the matter, Lenalle," asked Mama.

Lena tried to control herself and then she stammered out, "P-Pan-Pankoff l-lost."

I yelled, "Jesus Christ, is that any reason to scare the life out of us?"

Mama got sore too. She called Lena a dope and a fool and a lot of other things. Then she stamped off to bed and kept talking from the bedroom for nearly an hour. She said it served Lena right for being such a fool to spend her time at the Club. And she said wait until she got hold of Papa, she'd tell him a couple of things for getting his daughter to waste her time on a hopeless cause and nearly get sick in the bargain. It sounded good the way she said it in Yiddish.

Lena finally went to bed. I didn't feel sleepy any more, so I tried to read, but I couldn't put my mind on the printed pages. I had a peculiar and uncomfortable feeling. As if there was something to be done, but I couldn't remember what it was.

I thought of what Lena had said. Pankoff lost. So what? For over ten years now, I had heard similar announcements on the night of Election Day. First I had not reacted at all. The fun of the campaign had wiped out the bitterness of defeat. Then I had been angry, but after several years I had become used to it. And for the last four years I had not even been to the Club. By rights, I kept telling myself, it should not have made any difference to me, one way or the other. But inwardly I had to confess that, for all my outward indifference, I had really wanted Pankoff to win.

Suddenly I realized that he was the one link that had kept me, at heart, interested in the Party. Every day, for ten years, I had been unconsciously aware of the fact that hundreds of people, lawyers, policemen, politicians, ordinary men and women, addressed a Socialist as Your Honor! The dignity and confidence of a minority had rested upon him. And now that too was gone.

For the briefest flash I understood what a hold a thing like that could have on a person. If it could affect me, at heart a capitalist and a disinterested party, that way, I began to appreciate how Lena must have felt. She had worked with all her heart, banked upon at least this seemingly sure thing.

And how about Papa? All the years of his life that I could remember distinctly, he had worked for the Party. He too must have been sustained by the actuality of Pankoff's position on the bench. Very probably he had looked upon Pankoff's election as the first step, the beginning of the end of capitalism. I could see him expecting the Party to make rapid strides during the ten years of Pankoff's term. The years had slipped by, but he had been able to reassure himself with the fact that Pankoff, a Socialist, was on the bench.

How sharply this night's news must have brought home to him the apparent uselessness of those ten years of work. And how about Pankoff himself? And his wife? And Bardsley, and Clossons, and Bakerman, and Kaplan, and the countless others to whom this defeat must have come with the finality of a death knell.

The brilliant stroke, the blast that was to start the avalanche had turned out to be a dud, had fizzled and died. A feeling of worry, almost fright, came over me.

I decided to sit up and wait for Papa.

Philadelphia Express

The waiting room of the midtown bus terminal was lined with benches, on which perhaps a hundred people were sitting. They all looked tired and they all had some sort of luggage—cheap suitcases, parcels wrapped in paper, battered hatboxes—resting on their laps or on the benches beside them or on the floor between their feet. Above the archway leading to the asphalt platform was a large electric clock. The clock showed twenty-five minutes after midnight. Two middle-aged men and two girls hurried in together from the street, glanced around, and stopped short.

"Well, what the hell you know?" the short, solid man said. "Damn thing's not even here yet."

"That's buses." The tall, sharp man's voice rasped. "Train says it leaves ten-twenty, it leaves ten-twenty. Leaves twelve-thirty, leaves twelve-thirty. These damn buses. Even on a Sunday night, end of a weekend, you can't depend on them."

The two girls laughed, exactly the same way, a moment too late, as though they had been reminded to do so by a sharp nudge. Then, both at the same time, they noticed that the two men were not laughing. The men looked annoyed. The girls stopped their laughter, brought it up short, as abruptly as they had started it. They exchanged a worried glance, dropped their eyes guiltily, and raised them at once to look with feigned interest past the two men into the waiting room.

It was a large, square room with a high ceiling and a great many lights. All the lights were turned on, yet they did almost nothing to dispel the atmosphere of thick, brownish gloom. The left wall was broken by a line of ticket windows. The wall at the right had two doors, on each of which was a dignified brass sign. One sign said "Ladies" and the other said "Gentlemen." In the wall at the far end of the room was a huge, wide, arched doorway that led out to the asphalt platform, empty now, on which the buses stopped to unload and pick up passengers.

"Gee, Charlie," said the girl in red. "What do we do now?"

Her voice sounded like a musical saw, whining and weak and delicately metallic. It brought the head of the short, solid man around in an arc until he was looking at her across his shoulder. He had no hair on the top of his head. His scalp was the same color as his fleshy face, a leathery, sun-tanned brown that looked unhealthy. His lips seemed too large for his mouth. They moved around too much when he talked. The coat of his single-breasted, wrinkled seersucker suit was open, making him look more slovenly than he actually was. The end of his long, washable blue-and-white tie was tucked into the belt of his trousers.

"What do you *think* we do?" he said. "We wait."

"I only meant—" the girl in red said. "I only asked—"

"Sure, Flo," the tall, sharp man said kindly. "Charlie only meant we're on time, your bus is late, what the hell, there's nothing else to do. *Nat*urally we wait. What else?"

The kindness in his voice petered out gradually with each word until, when he reached the last one, his voice sounded exactly the way Charlie's had. In appearance he was entirely different from Charlie. He was much taller and much thinner and much neater. His head was thatched with thick black hair and the stripes of his seersucker suit were wider. He wasn't sunburned. Yet somehow, at first glance, the men gave the odd impression that they looked exactly alike. A second glance showed why. It was almost as though they were imitating one another—in the expressions on their faces, the sound of their voices, and their attitude toward the two girls.

"Sure. Herbie's right," Charlie said. "That's all I meant." Some instinct of chivalry, buried deep under layers and years of neglect and misuse, fought through to the surface of his lumpy, perspiring

face. He forced a smile that showed his bad teeth. He even patted the
girl's arm awkwardly. "Don't be sore, Flo."

Flo laughed nervously, again a moment too late. The girl in yellow laughed, too.

"I'm not sore," Flo said. "I'm never sore. Am I ever sore, Iris? Am
I?"

"Crazy," Iris said. "Flo sore?" She laughed harder, without mirth
and with unconvincing nonchalance. "Flo's *never* sore. All the years
I know her, I never saw Flo sore. You ever, Herbie?"

The tall, sharp man was setting his wristwatch by the electric
clock over the archway. He glanced up and pushed in the watch stem
with a faint click. "What?" he said. "Oh. Nah. Flo's never sore. Nobody's sore. What's with these damn buses?" He spoke directly to
Charlie, as though the girls had disappeared. "What do we do?"

"Wait here," Charlie said. "You just wait, all of you." He stepped
between the girls, across their two tiny suitcases, and strode toward
the ticket windows. His was the only movement in the large, hot,
tired room. All the people on the benches, the people who had been
idly watching the two middle-aged men and the two girls, turned
their heads as their glances followed Charlie. When he came back
to the group near the doorway, all the heads turned again.

"That Philadelphia Express, it's plenty late," he said. "Guy there
says the twelve-thirty, it won't be in before one, maybe a quarter
after. Anyhow, I bought the tickets." He sounded angry, trapped.

"Oh, Christ," Herbie said. "These damn buses."

"Gee whiz," Flo said in her weak, whining, metallic voice. "That
means Iris and me, we won't get home before maybe four in the
morning. Maybe even later."

The two men scowled at one another. The girls watched them
anxiously. Charlie's oversized lips worked impatiently.

"Well, the hell with it," he said finally. "We're stuck. Might as
well have a drink."

The girls brightened at once and dipped down to pick up the
suitcases, which were so small they looked like boxes of candy to
which handles had been attached.

"No, wait," Herbie said. "I'll tell you what." The bright looks vanished from the faces of the girls. They straightened up, holding the
tiny bags in front of them. "We better see about parking the car

first," Herbie went on. He smiled at the girls with exaggerated enthusiasm. "So we won't get a ticket, see?"

"That's right," Charlie said. He grinned. "We'll just go out and make sure the car is parked O.K. So we don't get a ticket. You girls sit down and wait. We be right back. All right?"

"Better give Flo and Iris the tickets," Herbie said as he took their arms and started herding the girls toward a vacant bench. "So's just in case the bus comes while we're parking the car, the girls won't be left flat and—"

"Aah, gee," Flo said. "You gonna—"

"No, no, no," Charlie said hastily. "Hell, no. Nothing like that. No, I'll hold the tickets." He scowled at Herbie and shook his head —a short, quick nod of warning. Then, with a smile, to the girls he said, "Don't you worry. We won't run out on you. We're not that kind of guy. We be right back. In a couple minutes, soon's we get the car parked right. Then we'll have a drink before the bus comes and slip you girls a piece of change. One last drink. Just a couple minutes."

The girls sat down on the bench. The two middle-aged men grinned, waved, turned sharply, and strode out of the waiting room into the street. The girls watched them with lips parted slightly, with doubt in their eyes. The moment the men crossed the threshold and disappeared, the girls turned toward each other. The doubt in their eyes was replaced with quick anger. Their thin, pinched, heavily made-up faces creased into scowls.

"Listen," Flo said. "You think they—?"

"No," Iris said. "Don't be crazy."

"Them bastids," Flo said bitterly. "They try that, I'll—"

"Sh-h-h." Iris made a small motion with her head toward the people on the benches all around them. She spoke out of the corner of her mouth. "You got to expect that once in a while, kid. There's all kinds."

Flo bit her lip. Both girls straightened up. They sat very erect, keeping their backs primly from touching the bench. The tiny suitcases rested on their laps. They kept their knees together, their hands folded on the suitcases, and watched the big red second hand sweep smoothly around and around the face of the large clock on the wall. A terrible awkwardness, a frightening discomfort, had suddenly settled down on them. They were absolutely motionless, yet the eyes of all the tired people waiting for buses were turned on them with almost murderous concentration.

The two girls in their red and yellow dresses, sitting stiffly erect, seemed to shrink slightly, as though from an accusation unspoken but clear, familiar yet dreaded. They were all right so long as there was constant motion, so long as there were no gaps like this one, oases of silence and inactivity with nothing to do or say or drink to help drown out the condemnation of respectable eyes. All their brassy gaiety was gone. In these few moments of silence their only buffer against terror had been stripped away.

The door marked "Ladies" groaned open and a fat woman came out. The small sound caused the girls to jump. The people on the benches turned their heads to watch the fat woman walk self-consciously to a bench. Flo fumbled for her purse. She couldn't get it open.

"Gimme a cigarette," she said. "Huh?"

"Sure." Iris struggled with her purse. "Here."

She held the match for Flo and then brought the flame to the end of her own cigarette. The fat woman sat down. All the heads in the room swung back. Iris's hand jumped nervously. The people on the benches stared at them. The two girls sat up straight, their eyes on the clock's circling second hand, their faces set in hard little lines of unconvincing bravado, minute ridges of tiredness and misery. The freshly lighted cigarettes burned disregarded in their hands, which were folded on the tiny suitcases on their laps.

A huge Negro in dirty brown overalls came into the waiting room through the door marked "Gentlemen." He was carrying a pail and a large broom. He sprinkled water on the littered, dusty floor and began lazily to sweep up the cigarette stubs and matches and chewing-gum wrappers. All the heads in the room turned to watch him. The two girls hastily stole puffs from their cigarettes. By the time the heads turned back to them, they were again sitting primly erect. Worriedly, they watched the clock. It was now a few minutes after one o'clock. The only sound in the room was the soft scratching of the Negro's broom across the concrete floor.

All at once the silence was shattered by the noise of a bus roaring to a halt on the asphalt platform outside. A low hum of conversation and movement spread across the waiting room. The tired people started to get up, began to gather their bundles and hatboxes and suitcases. Flo and Iris looked at each other with quick, confused dismay. They stood up halfway, sat down again, turned nervously toward the row of ticket windows, swung around to look out through the archway. Across the front of the huge bus was an electric sign that said "Philadelphia Express."

"What do we do?" Flo said. "They got the tickets."

"Them bastids," Iris said. "I guess I better buy us a couple new ones. Otherwise we'll miss this bus and—" She stopped, and then, quickly, she stood up and laughed with relief. "Here they are!"

Charlie and Herbie strode toward the two girls. Both men looked flushed. The end of Charlie's long, blue-and-white washable tie had pulled loose from the belt of his trousers and was swirling around in front of his large, solid belly. Herbie didn't look quite so sharp and neat any more. Their eyes took in the bus outside, the people walking toward and climbing into it. They saw that the moment of departure had finally arrived, definitely and irrevocably. There would be no more postponements. The men started to grin. They walked faster toward the girls.

"Here we are," Charlie said boisterously. The smell of brandy was strong on his breath. "Had a little trouble getting the car started, but we got it parked all right. Got back just in time. See the bus is here. Come on, girls."

He fumbled in the pocket of his seersucker suit for the tickets and reached for the two tiny suitcases.

"No, wait," Herbie said grandly. Now that they were finally getting rid of these girls neither one of them could seem to control his exuberance. "We do this in style." He snapped his fingers in the air. "Porter!" he called. "Porter!"

The people walking out to the bus were attracted by this disturbance. They turned and looked back. The girls blushed. Iris reached up and pulled down Herbie's arm.

"Gee, don't," she said. "We don't need no porter. We'll miss the bus."

"Say, what do you think we are?" Herbie said. "A couple of pikers? We're sending you girls back in style. Right, Charlie?"

"Sure," Charlie said. "No small-time stuff for us."

"Porter!" Herbie bellowed. "Porter!" The people on the asphalt platform outside and the people still in the waiting room stared at the two men and the two girls. Nobody answered Herbie's imperious call. "Wait a second," he said. "I'll get a porter." The girls tried to stop him, but he shook them off and ran over to the ticket windows. "Say, buddy," he said pompously to the man behind the grille, "you got a porter around here to carry some bags?"

The man looked out at Herbie. Then he looked across Herbie's shoulder at Charlie and the two girls. It was the look of a man who had seen situations like this before and had contempt for the actors in it. His glance came back to Herbie, and he nodded toward the large Negro who was sweeping the floor.

"That's him," he said. "The only porter around here."

Herbie turned and hurried across the room. "Here," he said as he shoved a coin into the Negro's hand. "Take these bags out to the bus, will you?"

The Negro stared with astonishment at the money in his hand, at the two tiny suitcases, then back at the money. A slow, silly grin spread across his face. "Sure thing, boss," he said. "Sure thing."

He dropped his broom and picked up the two bags. He did it with one hand. The bags were so small and so light that they did not even pull his arm down straight. He strode out through the archway to the bus, grinning widely, as though he had been let in on some tremendous private joke.

Charlie took Flo's arm and Herbie seized Iris's. The two men, smiling, propelled the girls, in the wake of the Negro, across the waiting room and out toward the bus. The people on the asphalt platform smiled. The two girls hung their heads just a trifle and tried to smile, too. They couldn't quite do it. Their lips twitched and their cheeks bunched into little, thin hills, but they were not smiling. They took small, quick, mincing steps, trying to keep up with the bouncing strides of the exuberant men. The girls kept their eyes on the ground. Their faces and necks were flushed. When they reached the bus it was almost full. The Negro went ahead of them.

"Take care of them bags, boy!" Herbie called after him. "I want you to treat them like they was your own."

"Yes, suh." The Negro laughed. Everybody in the bus watched while he put the bags on two empty seats and walked back to the door. He stepped out onto the asphalt, grinning, and touched his hand to his cap. "All safe, suh."

Herbie helped the two girls up the step into the bus. Charlie leaned in and handed the tickets to the driver.

"That's a couple of great girls you got there," he said cheerfully and loudly. "You take good care of them."

A few people in the bus laughed. Most of them just stared. The driver took the tickets, but he did not speak. He looked at the two men the way the man behind the grille of the ticket window had looked at them. Iris and Flo blushed a deeper red. Their lips quivered. They ducked their heads to walk down the narrow aisle toward their seats. Charlie stepped up to follow them.

"Just be for a second," he explained grandly to the driver. "Want to make sure these two girls are comfortable. A couple of great girls like these, don't want them to be—"

Flo swung around and said "Oh," a small, compressed gasp of exasperation, a whimper of anger she couldn't seem to control. Her thin, badly made-up face contracted sharply, as though with a pain that had suddenly become too much to bear. All the little tired creases stood out near the corners of her mouth. Iris turned quickly and put out her hand warningly. She was too late. Flo beat her fists against Charlie's chest.

"Get out!" she gasped. "Get out, get out, get *out!*" Her voice no longer sounded like a musical saw. All the whine and all the weakness were gone. It was desperate with accumulated suffering, with hatred too long suppressed. "Get out!" she panted, hammering at Charlie's chest. "Get out!"

The short, solid man tumbled out of the bus. He fell against Herbie. They grabbed each other and staggered about for a few seconds until they recaptured their balance. Both men stared into the bus with astonishment. Then Charlie let out a bellow of anger and started for the door. The driver closed it in his face. He hit the starter, gunned his motor, and the bus began to roll.

Flo turned to Iris and looked at her guiltily, then caught her breath in a sob. "I don't care," she said desperately. "I don't care. I don't care if we never get another party in New York again." Her voice rose higher. "I don't care. I don't care."

Iris bit her lip and stole a glance at the people around them.

"Sure," she said as she guided Flo down the aisle of the swaying bus toward their seats. "Sure, kid. It's all right."

"I don't care about the money," Flo cried. "I don't care. I couldn't stand any more. A whole weekend they—they were—two whole days." Her voice broke. "It was too—they—" Then the tears came. "I don't care about the money," she wailed brokenly. "I don't care. I don't care. I don't *care!*"

"Sure," Iris said. "I know."

The Pleasure of the President

Locke didn't want to go but his wife Susan insisted. Locke didn't want to go because he was lazy, and he admitted it, and Sunday afternoon, the only time in the long week when he could forget the Legal Division of the Department of the Interior and lie around the apartment in his pajamas reading the New York papers and indulging his laziness, was no time to go steaming halfway across Washington with a yowling baby to spend several tedious hours with Joe Stockwell, who was inclined to be a little stuffy even on his day off because he was with State, and his wife Hilda, who made a career of reminding people who did not live in Georgetown that she did and it was the only place *to* live, and listen to *their* yowling baby. End of breathless sentence.

If he had to listen to bawling infants, Locke figured one at a time was enough, and he preferred that one to be his own, and if Susan was warming up for her regular weekly routine about how he wouldn't be so lazy and tired Sunday afternoons if he didn't spend his weekday evenings running around town with half the chippies in Washington when he said he was at the Interior Building, working late, she could put on her act just as effectively in the apartment for him as in Georgetown for a larger audience.

But Susan wanted to go because she was cooped up all week with the baby in two small rooms and a bath on Connecticut Avenue, so that even a trip across town on Sunday was an event, and besides, the Pruitts were going to be there and she hadn't seen Ruth and Larry Pruitt for weeks, and Dick Locke knew he liked Ruth and Larry, whether he was willing to admit it or not, and if he wasn't running around with half the tramps in Washington when he told her he was working late, why wasn't he at his office in the Interior Building to answer the telephone when she called him at night, so they were damn well going. "End of *my* breathless sentence," Susan said.

"Okay," Locke said, dropping the *Times'* The News of the Week in Review and yawning himself off the couch. "But if the kid yells, you're the one goes upstairs to shut him up, and if you tear off any witty cracks about how much more attention I'm paying to Ruth Pruitt's legs than to my chicken salad, or whatever the Stockwells will be feeding their guests today, don't expect a beautifully typed affidavit of denial till we get home. I will be stiff."

"No doubt, dear," his wife said.

The baby was fine all the way across town and didn't even cry when they reached S Street and Locke started to swear. Cars were parked solidly down both curbs, and Locke had to leave the Ford at the foot of the block, practically on T Street, and walk back. A dozen or so small Negro children were playing baseball in the middle of the street, and, as Locke came toward Susan, waiting with the baby in front of the Stockwells' house, the boy at bat hit a low fast grounder out of bounds. Locke fielded the ball neatly from the sidewalk and tossed it back, and the kids all yelled and cheered, and Locke stopped swearing and forgot that he had not wanted to come.

"Pretty good for an Interior lawyer," Joe Stockwell said with a grin as he pulled the door open for them. The front door of the Stockwell house had a large, curtained, diamond-shaped window in it, and it was Susan Locke's belief, which her husband shared, although he wouldn't give Susan the satisfaction of admitting it, that the Stockwells spent all their time at home, crouched behind the curtain, watching to see who went in and out of the Undersecretary's house down the street. "We're so glad you could come," Joe Stockwell said, holding the beaded silver cocktail shaker away from his blue velvet smoking jacket, keeping the door open with his hip, and shaking hands formally. "Come in, won't you? Dick? Susan? Little fella?"

He tickled the baby's chin and closed the door and took the cocktail shaker in both hands.

"Nothing to it," Locke said, sailing his hat across the room because he knew it would annoy Stockwell. "You should have seen me in my prime, meaning about a month or two after V-J Day, when the Dodgers were after me to quit Washington and go into left field for them. Nice to see you, Joe. Written any good treaties lately? We the first? Those martinis?"

"Why, yes," Stockwell said, looking worried all the way from the center part in his neat black hair to the cleft in his stubby, square chin. "I mean yes, they're martinis and yes, the Pruitts haven't come yet. I can make something else, if you'd rather?"

"I wouldn't have anything else," Locke said. "Just that if they're martinis, that's enough shaking or they'll become malteds. Hilda all right?"

"Swell, yes, she's upstairs with Timmy," Stockwell said, and he stopped shaking. "I always forget you're a stirrer, not a shaker. You can make the next batch. Susan, why don't you leave your things here, in the closet, and take the baby upstairs?"

"Fine," Susan said. "Thanks. Dick, my coat?"

Locke took the coat from his wife's shoulders and Stockwell walked across the room to retrieve Locke's hat, smoothing away the dent the brim had made in the sofa pillow. Then he hung the hat and the coat, over the handles of the vacuum cleaner and the dust mop, in the tiny crowded closet with the slanting roof under the stairs. Susan went upstairs with the baby and Stockwell, still carrying the cocktail shaker, went into the kitchen for the glasses, leaving Locke alone in the ridiculous living room of the ridiculous house.

Locke had the same Civil Service rating as Joe Stockwell and, as a matter of fact, because of the In Grade raise he had received a couple of months after V-J Day, Locke's government salary was five hundred dollars a year greater than Joe Stockwell's but, all through the war and since, Stockwell had continued to receive a substantial income from his junior partnership in the New York law firm he had left in 1942 to come to the State Department for the duration plus one year that he had promised to stay in Washington. Locke didn't have any income from the small practice he had turned over to a friend when he went down to Washington, but he was five years younger than Stockwell and he knew he would get back his

practice when he finished his reconversion assignment for the Department of the Interior and returned to New York, so he wasn't
really jealous of Stockwell, but Locke did envy him and Hilda their
house, even though Locke didn't like it. The house was too damned
expensive, and too damned cute, and living across the street and
four doors up from the Undersecretary didn't mean a damned thing
in Locke's young life. But the two small rooms and a bath and no
maid on Connecticut Avenue were murder for Susan and the baby,
especially in the summer, and every time Susan acidly wanted to
know what sort of legal business he had been transacting for the
Secretary of the Interior over cocktails in the Shoreham bar with
that frowsy-looking redhead when one of Susan's friends or neighbors happened to drop in and see them, there was a whole lathe-
and-fiberboard apartment house full of flopping ears to hear his reply. A house, even a cute one, would have made this protracted
interlude in Washington at least bearable. The doorbell rang.

"That must be the Pruitts," Stockwell called from the kitchen.
"Would you, Dick?"

Locke went to the door and it was the Pruitts, Larry and Ruth
and the baby, plus a tall, rangy blonde with good shoulders and an
excellent figure and a pretty mouth and the sort of wise, laughing
look that Locke found a little unsettling but definitely attractive.

"You're late but welcome," Locke said. "The host is in the kitchen
with the martinis, and the hostess is upstairs with her baby, and
Susan is upstairs with our baby, and if the Pruitts know what is good
for them Ruth will get the hell upstairs with the Pruitt baby before
the trouble starts. Who is your handsome friend?"

"This is my sister, Mrs. Benson," Ruth Pruitt said. "She's staying
with us for a few days and don't you get fresh with her, Dick
Locke, because she has a husky Military Government major husband
who is running half, or maybe it's three-quarters, of the American
zone in Germany, and he taught her how to punch before he left.
Oh, dear, he's done it again. Larry, the diapers, please?"

Larry gave her the diapers and she went upstairs.

"I'm very pleased to meet you, Mrs. Benson," Locke said. "How
about letting me take everybody's things? It's a pretty tricky closet
but I've been practicing and I think I've got the hang of it."

"You can call me Ilka," Mrs. Benson said, laughing as she gave

Locke her coat and he took Larry Pruitt's hat. "Ruth and Larry told me all about you."

"Yes, sir," Larry Pruitt said. "The wolf of the Department of the Interior. Hello, Joe."

Joe Stockwell came in with the glasses and the cocktail shaker on a silver tray, and Larry introduced him to Mrs. Benson while Locke poured the drinks.

"To the brave major occupying Germany," Locke said. "And to his beautiful wife on S Street."

They all laughed and drank, and Mrs. Benson looked brightly around the room.

"Gosh," she said. "This is cute."

That is the word, all right, Locke thought, grinning to himself as he felt the first long swallow begin to take hold. The house was little more than a two-story box, with a living room and a Pullman kitchen on the ground floor, and two small bedrooms and a bathroom upstairs, and so little closet space that Joe's expensive clothes were kept on an improvised rack behind a waterproof curtain in one corner of the tiny bathroom, but it was in Georgetown, on a fashionable street, and the Stockwells were delighted to pay a hundred and eighty a month for it, unfurnished. Not that Hilda Stockwell would take a furnished house under any circumstances, even across the street, or almost across the street, from the Undersecretary. Hilda had been an interior decorator after leaving Vassar and before she married Joe, and she had done a job on this house. The rear half of the living room was almost completely filled by a Steinway grand, even though neither Hilda nor Joe played, so that you had to walk sideways, with your hands over your head, when you went from the front of the room to the kitchen or to the scrap of back yard that Hilda called the garden; the walls were painted pale blue and hung with gaudy Navaho rugs; and every square inch of horizontal surface in the room, with the exception of the chairs and the sofa, was covered with pottery or hand-woven baskets. It wasn't like anything else in Washington, certainly not like the rambling, roomy, sixty-dollar-a-month clapboard job the Pruitts had in Arlington, but it was cute, all right.

"I'm so glad you like it," Joe Stockwell said. "Hilda did it herself."

The three wives came down in a group, congratulating themselves

on the surprising but welcome peace that reigned upstairs, and Ruth
Pruitt introduced her sister to Hilda Stockwell and Susan Locke while
Larry Pruitt poured drinks for them. Larry, who had taken his Ph.D.
in political science at the University of Wisconsin before he came to
the Postwar Planning Board of the Department of Agriculture,
poured cocktails as though they were beer and you had to watch
out for collars, but Locke liked him. Larry Pruitt made forty-six hundred a year and he had nothing to look forward to but an instructor-
ship at Wisconsin, but he was a solid citizen with a brain from here
to here and he wouldn't be found dead in a blue velvet smoking
jacket on Sunday afternoon, or any other time, for that matter, and
he was full of delightful surprises, like this knockout blonde sister-in-
law, for example.

"But I can't get over it," Mrs. Benson said to Hilda Stockwell. "It's
so, so, so un-*Wash*ington, if you know what I mean. It's so cute."

Hilda beamed, meaning that her thin, bloodless, refined face
looked less pained than usual, and the kids upstairs started to cry,
all three of them.

"We're off," Locke said, finishing his drink. "On a clear day, Mrs.
Benson, you can hear them all the way out at Aberdeen Proving
Grounds. Okay, girls, go to it. Mr. Locke will be in the kitchen,
making a new batch, stirred not shaken."

"Oh, let me go," Mrs. Benson pleaded. "Please. I think they're so
cute and wonderful."

Locke saw his wife's eyebrows go up slightly, and he would have
groaned inwardly if he had not had at least one drink under his
belt, because he knew he was going to get a caustic earful from Susan about Mrs. Ilka Benson when they got home, but the girls took
Mrs. Benson along with them and Locke squeezed past the piano,
holding the cocktail shaker aloft, and went into the kitchen. When
he came back into the living room, Joe Stockwell was standing in
front of the fake fireplace, looking down on Larry Pruitt in the zebra-
striped chair, and telling the younger man why he thought the lib-
erals were all wrong in their criticism of Frankfurter's dissenting
opinion in the Bridges case. The three wives were sitting on the
couch, all in a row, swapping nuggets of misinformation about the
polio epidemic and checking up on Dr. Grossveldt, the pediatrician

they all used, by comparing notes on the last visits they had paid to his office with their babies.

"What's happened to the soldier's wife?" Locke said. "Glasses, everybody."

"She's upstairs with the children," Hilda Stockwell said. "Just a short one for me, Dick. Thanks. Apparently she's wonderful with them. The moment she came in, they stopped crying, didn't they?"

"They shut up right away," Ruth Pruitt said. "She's crazy about babies. Mother used to leave us all in her care. Not yet, Dick. I'll nurse this one for a while."

"Well, we can't let her do sentry duty on a dry palate," Locke said, filling two glasses on the tray. "I'll take her drink up to her."

"I told her you would," Susan said sweetly. "And you're to call her Ilka."

"Woo-woo," Locke said, picking up the glasses and speaking across his shoulder. "Square me with my wife, Ruthie, will you? This is strictly a Gunga Din act. Honest."

Upstairs, the Stockwell baby was asleep in his crib in the small bedroom and, eighteen inches from the door, across the preposterous hallway, the two other babies were asleep on Hilda and Joe's double bed, which almost filled the larger bedroom. Mrs. Benson sat in the chintz-covered rocking chair near the window, her long, handsome legs crossed, and she was smiling brightly. She put her finger to her lips and took the drink he held out. Locke looked at the sleeping children on the bed, and then he turned to look through the open door at the crib in the other bedroom, and he shook his head admiringly.

"That's the first time *that's* ever happened," he said. "You must have had a lot of practice. How many of these things of your own have you got?"

"None yet," Mrs. Benson said, batting her long eyelashes across the rim of her glass. "But I can't wait to begin."

"What's holding you up?" Locke said. "It'll ruin that wonderful figure, but they tell me it's worth it."

Mrs. Benson giggled noiselessly and almost spilled her drink. "I've been married nineteen months, next Thursday," she said, cupping the glass in both hands. "And my husband's been overseas eighteen months and eleven days, almost twelve." She looked at her wristwatch. "It's six o'clock. In two and a half hours, at eight twenty-five to be exact, he'll have been overseas eighteen months and twelve days. That's what's holding me up."

"Hell," Locke said, wishing he had not asked her, because now his mouth felt dry and uncomfortable, the way it always felt when he found himself at the beginning of something he did not want to begin and, after it was begun, he would not finish. What she had told him was probably true, he had no reason to doubt the facts, but she sounded phony, and the trouble with Dick Locke was that he had an instinct for these phonies, an instinct that he never acted upon but that got him into trouble with his wife Susan just the same. "Why doesn't he come on home?" Locke said. "It's all over. Duration plus six. What's he want to hang around a place like Germany for, with a babe, sorry, girl like you waiting for him? How's that drink?"

"Wonderful," Mrs. Benson said, taking a good long swallow. "Did you ever read one of those commissions? Duration plus six *or* the pleasure of the President. That can mean anything. Occupation for God knows how long. How about another one of these?"

"You bet," Locke said, taking her glass quickly and wishing he were not the only person in the house who knew, God knows how he knew those things, but he always did, that Ruth Pruitt's sister, who was wonderful with children, was also a pushover. "It's the stirring that does it," he said. "Shaking kills them. You hold the fort. I won't be but a minute."

When Locke came down into the living room with the glasses, the three wives and Larry Pruitt were standing in the open doorway, wearing their hats and coats, and Joe Stockwell was pulling his crushed Tyrolean number from the snarl of broomsticks and mop handles in the silly closet.

"Hey," Locke said. "What goes on?"

"We're going over to the Orient on Wisconsin to bring back the supper," Joe Stockwell said. "Chow mein and eggs Foo Young and that sort of thing. They put it up very nicely in containers, you know. We won't be long, Dick."

"All of you?" Locke said. "For God's sake?"

"It takes two or three to carry it all," Hilda Stockwell said. "We're getting lobster Cantonese and pork fried rice, too, and we're all out of cigarettes. They always have name brands there late Sunday afternoon. If we all go we can get two packs each. We won't be gone more than twenty minutes, will we, Joseph?"

"A half hour at the most," Joe Stockwell said, smoothing the hat into shape. "You and Mrs. Benson have another drink while we're gone."

"Aah, now, look," Locke said, feeling foolish and a little frightened and resenting it.

"Don't be a pig and see that Ilka gets one, too," Susan said, far too sweetly, even for Susan. "We don't have to warn you about not waking the babies," she said. "You both seem to be doing so beautifully."

Then they were gone and Locke could hear them, through the diamond-shaped window in the front door, chattering as they piled into Joe Stockwell's huge Buick. Locke went to the kitchen, forgetting to raise his arms when he passed the piano, and he took a nasty crack on his elbow. He mixed the drinks angrily, without quite knowing what he was angry about, and he made them good and stiff, four and a half to one. He went upstairs with two clean glasses and the shaker. The kids were still sleeping soundly and he could tell, from the extra brightness with which Mrs. Benson smiled at him, or perhaps he couldn't tell at all, that she knew they were alone in the house.

"They went to get the supper," Locke said, handing her a glass. "Chinese stuff, over on Wisconsin, and they're going to get on the line for cigarettes. Better take it easy on these. They're spiked."

"I'll try," Mrs. Benson said, and she laughed. "But that's the way I love them. I'm a very weak character," she said, giggling.

There didn't seem to be much to say after that, and there was no place for him to sit, so they drank too fast, and Locke was beginning to feel really foolish, because he could see Mrs. Benson's bright expectancy changing under the influence of gin to puzzled surprise at the way he was carefully keeping his distance, and then to mounting resentment, and he didn't really blame her, because he had gone through all the motions, he had led her to expect that he was going to finish what he had seemed to be starting, even though he wasn't really starting anything; but the pushovers never knew that, they had no way of knowing that Dick Locke was merely flexing his muscles, until it was too late, and when it was too late, and they did know, they were sore, justifiably sore because, even though he had not meant to trick them, that was precisely what he always did, and precisely what he had done now. His feet were beginning to hurt when there was a loud crash downstairs. They both jumped and then the children started to cry, all three of them at once, and Locke saw that Mrs. Benson had spilled part of her drink down the front of her dress.

"It's those damned kids playing baseball," Locke said with quick relief. "Be back in a minute."

He bumped the banister twice going down the stairs, and he stopped short at the bottom. The Stockwells would have a little trouble with drafts for a while, but their view of the Undersecretary's guests was highly improved. The pane was gone, except for a few jagged pieces of glass around the edge of the diamond-shaped window, and the baseball was caught in the sagging curtain as though it were in the net of a lacrosse stick. Locke reached in behind the curtain gingerly and pulled out the ball. He opened the door and walked out onto the front step. The fresh air felt good on his face. The Negro boys were gathered in a frightened group across the street, huddling together as though for protection and staring wide-eyed at the door.

"That's the end of the ball game," Locke called, swept by a wave of exhilaration for his own generosity and kindness and for the narrowness of his escape, and he tossed the ball to them underhand. "You kids better beat it before Mr. Stockwell comes back."

One of the boys caught the ball and they all remained there for another moment, staring at Locke on the front step, before they broke and ran silently down the block, toward T Street. Locke went back into the house and closed the door and, as he started up the stairs, he became aware of the babies crying. He could tell best by his own baby's voice, but it was in the sounds the Pruitt baby and Timmy Stockwell were making, too. They were crying badly. Locke took the rest of the stairs two at a time and his elbow, still sore from the bump against the piano, took another crack as he hit the doorway.

"Hey!" Locke said. "Hey, for Christ's sake!"

Mrs. Benson did not look up. She had clearly passed beyond the stage where all the world seemed cute to her. She was standing over the double bed, shoving and tugging his son and the Pruitt baby with her long lacquered fingers, hauling the infants back and forth savagely, her face contorted by liquor and disappointment and stupidity into a sort of fierce, irritated loathing because the father of one of them had tricked her into revealing herself, and because they would not stop yelling. The harder the babies screamed, the harder she jerked them back and forth. Locke grabbed her shoulder and pulled her away and pushed her back toward the rocking chair, and Mrs. Benson fell into it with a dull plop, loosing one of her shoes, and her long, handsome legs sprawled very unprettily.

"Pleasure of the President my eye," Locke said, panting and wishing he were not so drunk and realizing that she was even drunker than he was. "The poor bastard probably doesn't *want* to come back," Locke said. "And if I were in his shoes I'd stay in Germany, or wherever the hell they'll let him stay, I'd stay there forever."

He turned toward the screaming babies on the bed and the screaming baby in the crib in the other room, but Mrs. Benson shoved herself up out of the rocking chair and grabbed him and hauled him around.

"You're a dandy little guesser, aren't you?" Mrs. Benson said, and she slapped his face so hard that his ears rang. "That's for being such a smart little guesser," she said, "you son of a bitch."

Locke blinked and felt his face, which was beginning to sting, and he looked down foolishly at his hand. He was still holding the empty glass. He started to set it down, but there was no place to set it, and he saw that the front of his coat was wet, where he had spilled his own drink, and suddenly there was so much to explain, the broken window and his soiled coat, her soiled dress and the welts on his face, the screaming babies who could never be quieted in time even if they had both been sober, and the years of suspected infidelities of which he was not guilty, so hopelessly too much to explain, even to a level-headed wife who did not really believe the things she suspected, or to a mild-mannered friend who taught political science at Wisconsin and liked him, that Locke dropped the cocktail glass. It shattered noiselessly on the black and red and white Navaho rug.

"Shut up," Locke said loudly, above the noise of the screaming babies, keenly aware of the helpless terror in his own voice, and he slapped Mrs. Ilka Benson across her pretty mouth, hard. "Shut up, you," he said.

Portrait of a Gentleman

I had a few clean shirts in the dresser, but I didn't put one on. I didn't shave either, the way I usually did just before I went to meet her. This business of shaving twice a day is hell on my face, anyway.

Then, when it was time to go, I sat down and smoked a cigarette. I wanted to be a few minutes late.

It wasn't even ten after eight when I came around the corner, but she was already tapping the sidewalk with her toe and looking up and down the block anxiously. I didn't change the serious look on my face, but inside I had to laugh a little to myself. I had her down pat, all right.

"Gee whiz, Tom," she said, smiling and putting her arm through mine, "you had me worried. You're *never* late." She was telling me!

She was still too happy at seeing me to notice the shirt and the shave, but that didn't worry me. I was building this up slowly. When the time came, she'd remember the little things all at once. She was quick on the uptake.

"Hungry?" I asked.

"I'm starved," she said.

When we came to the restaurant I didn't stop.

"Aren't we going in?" she asked, surprised.

"Let's try a new place tonight," I said, walking her past the door. I had the new place all picked out. It wasn't so terrible, but it was a little cheaper than the one we usually went to. She didn't say anything, but I knew it was registering.

Later, in the movies, I put my arm around her, but I didn't hold her tight. I just let my arm lie along the back of the seat, resting against her shoulder a little. Take my word for it, she didn't enjoy the picture.

When we got out I yawned and said, "How about a little snack? I'm hungry again."

"All right," she said.

This time I took her to a nice place. The groundwork was all laid, so I figured I might as well eat something decent. She didn't talk much, and I wasn't exactly making speeches, either.

When the waiter brought the check I took out my wallet and held it so she couldn't see the ten and the five inside. I pulled out two singles and put them on top of the check in the little tray.

"Keep the change," I said to the waiter.

"You didn't have to tip him so much," she said.

"I know," I said. "But I wanted to make my exit like a gentleman. Swan song and all that sort of stuff. You know."

"What are you talking about, Tom?" she said, and her brow began to wrinkle up. This was the point where all the little things I'd dropped along the way began to come back to her. The shirt, the shave, my being late, the cheaper restaurant, my arm in the movies. Everything. She was no rummy. She knew me too long.

I tapped the wallet and bent it to show how thin it was.

"Those were my last two bucks," I said quietly. "I lost my job over a month ago."

"Tom!"

At least she still remembered my name.

"Why didn't you tell me?" she cried.

"I thought I'd be able to get something else right away," I said. "I didn't want to break up all our plans if I could help it."

"Oh, Tom, you didn't have to do that. You could have told me."

Sure I could have. But I hadn't.

"Well," I said with a shrug, "I didn't want to break up everything all at once. I thought I'd be able to get something."

"But you didn't?"

I shook my head. "Nope," I said. "Not a thing."

I kept my eyes on the tablecloth, but I could feel her looking at me. "What's going to happen, Tom?" she asked.

I shrugged, but I didn't look up. I kept pushing the salt shaker around in little circles. "I guess the wedding is off, Stella," I said. "For the time being, anyway."

She didn't say anything, so I added: "I'm going away."

That brought her out of it.

"Where?" she asked quickly. "Why?"

"I've got a brother in Chicago," I said. (Yeah, and my old man owns General Motors.) "He might be able to do something for me."

"But why do you have to go away?" she cried.

If she was going to bawl, she could have my handkerchief.

"I'm broke," I said. "Flat. That's why."

"But Tom, I've got something in the bank. I could let you—"

"Forget it, Stella," I said. "Thanks. But forget it."

After a time she said, "When are you going?"

"Tonight," I said.

"Tonight?" she cried. She was getting to be pretty good at it. "But why? Why so soon?"

I guess I didn't make myself clear.

"I'm broke," I said again. "Flat. I'm two weeks behind in my rent. I just got my suitcase out before the landlady grabbed it. It's checked down in Grand Central."

"But Tom, I could let you have—"

"That's all right, Stella," I said. "But forget it." I was getting pretty good at it myself.

She tore little pieces of bread from a slice and kneaded them into tiny balls. When she had nine of them, all stretched out in a straight line, she said in a very low voice, "Why can't we get married anyway, Tom?"

Now, that was a fair question. And I could have answered it, too, in a short little essay of some fifty or sixty pages. But I had writer's cramp just then.

"I'm sorry, Stella," I said. It was getting to be a regular whispering campaign. "But if I can't support a wife, I don't get married."

"Oh, Tom, don't be so foolish!"

Foolish? Well, maybe. But I knew a better word. Smart.

"I'm sorry, Stella," I said. "But that's how I feel about it."

She had one more arrow in her quiver, whether she knew it or not. And I was willing to take the short end of any odds that she would find it within two minutes, flat.

When the tiny dough balls numbered nineteen, she picked them all up and crushed them together in her fist. "You still love me, don't you, Tom?" she said, without looking at me.

I would have won the bet easy, hands down.

"Why should you doubt it, Stella?" I said. "Have I said or done anything to—?"

"You still love me, don't you, Tom?" she repeated.

"Of course I do," I said.

We were both quiet for a few minutes, but I didn't worry about it. I figured it was her move. When she spoke, finally, her voice was so low I could hardly hear her. But I managed, all right.

"Why don't you get your suitcase and bring it up to my room," she said, squeezing the lump of dough flat on the tablecloth. "You can stay with me until you get something."

Now she was talking.

"Well, I don't know, Stella," I said.

"There's nothing wrong in that, is there?" she said, trying to keep her voice level. "When you get something, we can be married. I don't want you to go away, Tom. It's silly that a thing like losing your job should break up everything for us."

"Well, I don't know," I said.

"I'm not asking you to marry me, Tom," she said quickly, looking up at me. "I understand about your pride and things like that. I don't blame you. But there's nothing wrong in this, is there? As long as we love each other. When you get a job again, we can get married. I don't want you to go away, Tom."

"Well—" I said.

She leaned across the table toward me.

"If you love me, Tom," she said, "you'll—"

"Okay, Stella," I said taking her hand. "Okay."

II

As soon as I heard the door open downstairs I folded the dope sheet and put it in my back pocket. Then I walked into the bathroom to drop the cigarette into the bowl and came out again for a quick look around. There was no hurry. Stella walked very slowly.

When I went out onto the landing to meet her, I could tell almost exactly the step she'd be standing on when I reached her. And I knew, too, exactly what she'd say and what I'd say and what we'd both do for the next five minutes.

First we kissed, then she handed me the packages she was carrying, then she asked anxiously, "Any luck?"

I shook my head and said, "Nope."

For a second she looked disappointed, then she brightened up and said, "Well, maybe tomorrow."

That was my cue to smile gamely, like I had three smashed ribs and a slightly dented collarbone but was going in to die for dear old Rutgers anyway. So I said: "Sure, kid. Maybe tomorrow."

After that it was all right to climb the rest of the stairs and go into the room.

I didn't say anything while she was preparing the meal. But it didn't make any difference then, because she was too busy over the little gas range. When she began to set the dishes on the bridge table, though, I didn't bring the two chairs over. I continued to sit near the window, looking out into the street.

"Food's ready, Tom," she said sharply, and I looked up, surprised, like I'd been lost in thought.

"Oh—! Oh, all right," I said, and brought the chairs over as absent-mindedly as I could.

I was good and hungry, but I kept staring past the plate as she set the dishes before me, and I didn't reach for the spoon or the fork until she reminded me. Finally she said: "What in the world's the matter with you, Tom? You look—"

"Who, *me?*" I said, smiling suddenly and very brightly, to make sure it looked faked. "I'm okay. I'm swell."

"Yeah, you're swell!" she said. "You look like your dog died or something. What's the matter, Tom?"

"Nothing, Stella. Everything's okay."

"Come on, Tom, what's the matter? You can tell me."

"Honest, Stella. I mean it. Everything's okay. What ever gave you the idea—?"

"Listen, Tom," she said, putting her hand on my arm, "you don't have to hide anything from me. I know when you've got something on your mind. What's the matter?"

I gave a pretty good imitation of a guy breaking down. Maybe I should have been an actor.

"Well, it's really nothing," I said, biting my lip. "I mean, it's not—"

"You don't have to keep anything from me, Tom. You know that."

I put my hands on the table and began to examine them like it was the first time in my life I was seeing them.

"I almost had a job today," I said quietly.

"You mean it, Tom?" she said quickly, smiling happily. "You mean it?"

"Almost," I repeated.

"Oh!" she said, sinking back against the hard upright of the chair. "What happened?"

"Well, I—"

"What happened, Tom?"

"They said I was—I was too—too shabby."

"Oh, Tom!"

Oh, Tom, my eye! I wasn't interested in sympathy.

"They said I fitted in perfect. They as much as told me if I'd've been wearing a decent suit and a pair of shoes without holes in them, I would've been in."

"Gee, that's too bad, Tom."

"That makes the third time," I said shaking my head at the table-cloth, and bending down to inspect a particularly interesting knuckle on my right hand.

"The third time?"

"Yeah. The same thing happened before. Remember the one I told you about, the importing house? About three-four weeks ago? You remember."

"Yeah. Yeah. So?"

"Well," I said, "I met one of the guys from the place later. He said he heard the employment manager say that if only I'd've been a little more decently dressed, if only I'd've been, well, you know, if only that, I would've had the job. It happened another time, too. This makes the third time."

We were both quiet for a while, and then she said, "What are we going to do, Tom?"

I didn't answer. For two reasons. First, because as far as I was concerned the question was rhetorical. She knew damn well what we were going to do. And second, where did she get this we stuff? Who did she think she was, Lindbergh?

"I'd have to take it out of the bank," she said finally, scowling a little, and rubbing her lip. "And, gee, I hate to do that. There isn't much there, Tom, and I haven't been able to put in anything these last few weeks, you know, since we, since you—"

"Since *I* moved in. Right? Isn't that what you mean?"

"Now, please, Tom," she said quickly. "Don't—"

"But that's what you mean, isn't it?" I said again. Tough guy. You know. "Well, whose idea was it, anyway, that's what I want to know? Did *I* suggest it? Did *I* ask you to—?"

"Tom, *please!*" she said, getting up and coming around the table to my side. "Let's not start a fight. I didn't mean anything. I only meant it's, well, *you* know—"

She put her hand on my shoulder, but I was still giving my undivided attention to my knuckles.

"How much would it be, Tom?" she asked finally.

I didn't answer.

She pushed my shoulder gently, playfully. "Come on, Tom. How much would it be?" Her voice was wheedling. "Don't be a baby, Tom. How much would it be?"

"I don't know," I said finally.

"Well, then, guess. How much, Tom?"

I shrugged. "About forty, fifty, maybe," I said.

She straightened up a little. "So *much?*"

"Well, it's a suit and shoes and maybe a hat or something, isn't it? Hell, you can't buy junk."

"All right, Tom," she said quietly. "I'll take the money out of the bank tomorrow."

I reached up and pulled her down onto my lap and kissed her.

III

Right after the door opened downstairs I knew something was wrong. She didn't come up the stairs slowly. She almost ran. I just had time to douse the cigarette and stand up when the door banged open.

"Stella!" I said. "What's the matter?"

Her hat was on cockeyed and her coat was open. She wasn't carrying any packages and she swayed back and forth a little in the doorway. She had the kind of dopey look on her squash that made my palm itch to slap it off.

"What happened?" I said sharply.

"I—I—" she began, and I went forward to meet her. She collapsed on my shoulder and then the floodgates opened. As I guided her to a chair I congratulated myself on the fact that I was wearing the old suit. The tears she was shedding would have made a wreck out of the new one.

"Okay, kid," I kept saying soothingly, "okay," and stroked her shoulder. I wondered what the hell was the matter, but I knew she wouldn't be able to talk until she spilled enough tears to float a couple of battleships. That baby could certainly cry.

After a while she quieted down and I said, "What happened, Stella?"

"I—I lost my job," she said. Well, at least I'd gotten the suit and the shoes and the hat in time. "I l-lost my j-job," she said, and started off again.

What I felt like doing was wrapping a chair around her neck, but I continued to stroke her shoulder. Finally she straightened up and began to dry her eyes.

"Things've been getting worse and worse there," she said, still shaking a little. "They've been letting people go for a long time already. But I didn't think—I mean, I didn't think they'd—"

"That's how those things are," I said. My idea of a snappy comeback.

"But what are we going to do, Tom?" she said.

Well, I didn't know what *we* were going to do. But I had a general idea of what at least one of us was going to do.

"Hell, between the two of us we ought to be able to land something," I said. "One of us ought to be able to get something before long. How do we stand?"

She shook her head.

"Bad as that?" I said.

She nodded. "I haven't been able to put anything in the bank these last few weeks," she said. "And now most of that's gone, too. Oh, Tom," she said, holding me tight and beginning to cry again, "what's going to happen? What'll we do?"

"Don't worry," I said, remembering to kiss her. "One of us is sure to find something."

IV

When the alarm clock rang, I hopped out of bed and shut it off. Then I came back to wake her, but she was staring up at me, without blinking.

"Come on, kid," I said, pushing her a little. "Don't take it to heart like that. People've lost jobs before. Come on, snap out of it. We're both going out to look. I got a hunch today we'll find something."

She didn't move, so I pulled back the covers sharply and said: "Come on, Stella, let's not waste time. You have to get out early if you want to get something. The best jobs don't stand around waiting."

"Tom," she said, without moving. "Suppose we don't get something? Then what?"

"Who says we won't get something?" I said. "Didn't I just tell you I had a hunch? Come on, Stella, let's eat."

"But suppose we don't, Tom? What's going to happen to us?"

With all my other troubles, she had to start a gab fest.

"What's the sense of worrying about that now?" I said. "We've got time to worry about that later. First, let's try to get something. We'll get something, don't worry. Why shouldn't we?"

"You know it's not so easy, Tom," she said quietly. "You don't have to treat me like a kid. It's more than two months already since you've been trying to get something for yourself. Things aren't any better now than they were then. What chance've we got now that we didn't have before?"

If she didn't stop soon, I'd gag her.

"Aw, come on, Stella," I said, bending down to kiss her. "Don't look at things that way. If you look at things that way you're licked before you start. Come on," I said briskly, kissing her again. "What do you say?"

"Okay," she said, smiling suddenly, and hugged me to her.

Before we left the room, she took a dollar out of her purse and slipped it into my pocket. "Let's try to make it last, huh, Tom?" she said.

"Sure," I said with a smile, and patted her cheek.

We walked to the corner together.

"Remember," I said, looking her straight in the eye, like they do in the movies, "keep your chin up. Okay?"

"Okay," she said, and I kissed her, right on the street.

What the hell, kisses don't cost anything.

"I'll see you tonight," I said. "Good luck."

"Good luck, Tom," she said, and turned uptown. I went downtown.

For a while I just walked. I didn't bother going in any place. I'd learned two months before what I was up against. No more ten-carat heels were going to tell me sorry, nothing right now, suppose you leave your name and address. I wasn't even thinking about that. I was thinking about something else. I knew what I was going to do, but I couldn't make up my mind exactly how I was going to do it. There were two ways. One was a pushover, and I could do it immediately, but there was no fun doing it that way. It was too easy. There was no satisfaction. All right, I said to myself finally, I might as well give her a run for her money.

When I made up my mind about that I found I was hungry. I looked at my watch. It wasn't quite twelve. That meant I had about six hours, which was plenty of time. I bought a pack of cigarettes, and had a bite to eat, and then went into a cheap movie. I came out about three o'clock and went back to the room.

I took out the suitcase from under the bed and dusted it off. Then I began to pack. First I was going to leave the old suit and shoes in the closet, but then I put them in. I figured you never can tell. I was glad she'd just taken my shirts out of the laundry the day before. I hate like hell to pack dirty shirts into a suitcase. From the bathroom I took the tube of toothpaste, but I left the bottle of mouthwash. The glass might break in the suitcase and dirty up everything. And anyway, there wasn't very much left in the bottle. I took a last look around. I had everything. I strapped the suitcase and set it near the door.

I looked through my wallet. I still had the ten and the five and the change from the dollar she'd given me in the morning. Everything was all right.

By this time I was hungry again. I took in the stuff from the window sill and fried myself a couple of eggs. I drank the milk and put the dishes in the sink. Then I pulled out the dope sheet and a pencil, put my pack of cigarettes where I could reach it, and settled myself to wait.

V

I heard the hall door open downstairs, but I didn't get up out of my chair. I waited until it slammed shut and the footsteps began to come up the stairs. Then I lit a cigarette and put my feet on the radiator.

Half-way up, the footsteps stopped. But I didn't let that bother me. I just drew on my cigarette. I was through with that business of walking half-way down to meet her.

After a few seconds the footsteps resumed. Then the doorknob turned and the door opened. But still I didn't move. I just sat there.

"Hello, Tom," she said, trying to make her voice sound tired. It was an old gag, but she could have saved herself the bother. It just wasn't working today, that's all.

I looked up, like I hadn't heard her until she spoke.

"Oh, hello, Stella."

She was carrying a couple of paper bags, but I didn't get up to take them from her. I was through with that bull, too. It wouldn't kill her if she carried them over to the table herself. I'd give her a written guarantee on that, if she wanted it.

She put the bags on the table and started to take off her coat. "I brought some bread and some potatoes," she said. "We've still got the eggs and the butter and some milk out on the window sill." That's what *she* thought. "That ought to be enough, don't you think?"

"To tell you the truth," I said, "I haven't been thinking so good lately. You better not count on my opinion."

She looked at me in surprise and opened her mouth to say something, then closed it. That was a break, anyway.

She finished taking off her coat and put it on the bed with her hat. Then she came back to the table and began to play around with the bags.

I couldn't make up my mind whether to wait until after we ate or not. But then I remembered about the milk and the butter and the eggs. And anyway, I wasn't hungry. I got up and reached for my coat on the nail in back of the door.

"What are you doing?" she asked quickly.

"Maybe I'm wrong," I said, poking my arms into the sleeves, "but it looks to me like I'm putting on my coat."

"Where are you going?"

Cross-examination, eh? Well, they couldn't scare me. I had an alibi.

"I'm going out to get my face lifted," I said, tossing the cigarette to the floor and stepping on it.

Her eyes dropped to my feet, to watch me grind out the cigarette, and she noticed the suitcase.

"Tom," she said in a quick, scared voice. "Tom, you're not coming back!"

What a brain!

"Oh, I wouldn't say that," I said. "There you go again, jumping at conclusions. You ought to cut it out. It's bad for your figure."

I put my hat on and adjusted it in the mirror. I'm funny that way about my hat. I don't like to have it look like I went to bed without taking it off.

"Tom!" she cried in the same scared voice. "You're not coming back!"

Now, didn't I hear that some place before?

"Tom, you're not coming back!" she said again.

"Listen, Stella," I said, "you better turn that record over."

She came over quickly and grabbed me by the arm.

"Tom!" she almost screamed. Once more and I'd change my name to Clarence. "Tom, what's the matter? Why are you going away?"

"The service here is getting lousy," I said, holding her off with one hand and reaching for the suitcase with the other. "Two days in a row, now, the soup's been served cold."

Send Four Men to Hanoi

There was more to the cable than the first sentence, of course, to make it stick in Reardon's mind, much more. For one thing, it was quite long. It covered two and a half of the blue flimsies used for all incoming cables in the offices of the Halstead-Schick Petroleum Corporation throughout the world. For another, it was the first cable in God knows how long to be received from China in the company's main offices, on lower Broadway. The first cable, that is, to come through from China on Halstead-Schick's private wires since the Japs had taken Hong Kong, and, therefore, clearly an event; the first indication, so to speak—for Halstead-Schick, anyway—that the war was over, really over. And, finally, the cable came to the message center, on the fifth floor, from the code room, on the sixth floor, marked "CHINA FOR CARPENTER ONLY REPEAT CARPENTER ONLY." Reardon, who had been chief of the Halstead-Schick message center for eleven of the twenty-eight years that he had worked in the huge oil company's New York offices, had learned one thing during those years: anything marked "FOR CARPENTER ONLY" had to be watched carefully or there was bound to be trouble.

S. B. Carpenter, to whom Reardon referred in private as Sour Ball, was Far Eastern manager for Halstead-Schick and, in Reardon's eyes and archaic language, a thoroughgoing scoundrel—and Reardon had proof.

A couple of months before the war, Carpenter had replaced his private secretary, a middle-aged widow named Hanson who was supporting three children and an invalid sister. Mrs. Hanson had been with the company for twenty-two years and had served as Carpenter's secretary since the big reorganization in 1933, but Carpenter had got rid of her just like that, without giving her a chance to defend herself, because he claimed she had caused him to miss an important luncheon date with the company's Batavia representative, who had been in town for two busy days on his way back to Java after a visit to the company's fields in Oklahoma and Texas. Mrs. Hanson swore, and Reardon believed her, that she had entered the engagement on Carpenter's calendar exactly as he had told her to when he put up his phone after talking to the Batavia man at his hotel.

None of the other employees had cared to take sides in the matter, but Reardon was sure that there were the usual number of toadies who accepted Carpenter's explanation that Mrs. Hanson was a sickly old woman and so harried by private worries that she had long ago ceased to function usefully and efficiently in the office and should have been retired on a pension years before. He was certain, too, that they had swallowed this barefaced lie merely because Sour Ball was a power in Halstead-Schick. Reardon, who had never even talked with Mrs. Hanson before, had gone to see the weeping woman at the time and had taken her to lunch in the basement cafeteria of the Halstead-Schick Building, where everybody could see them together. And that night he had tracked the Batavia man from his hotel to La Guardia airport and managed to have a short talk with him before he boarded his plane.

The next morning, instead of allowing one of the ten routing clerks who worked under him in the message center to make the regular nine-thirty delivery to Sour Ball's office on the twenty-second floor, Reardon had delivered Carpenter's cable to the Far Eastern manager's office himself. He had got by the executive's new secretary with the curt announcement that he was carrying confidential cables that had to be delivered in person, and then, without wasting time on preliminary explanations that would have given Carpenter an opportunity to prepare himself for the onslaught, Reardon had confronted Sour Ball with the Batavia representative's statement that he had arranged on the phone to lunch with the Far Eastern manager on Tuesday, the day for which Mrs. Hanson had made the entry on Carpenter's desk diary, and not Wednesday, the day Carpenter for some reason had assumed he was to lunch with the man from Java.

Reardon still remembered with grim satisfaction the look of astonishment on the Far Eastern manager's face when Reardon presented his evidence. It was a cheerful, friendly, attractive face. The casual observer would have said it belonged to a man who liked children and was sentimental about birthdays and wedding anniversaries. Reardon was not a casual observer. Faces did not fool him, and Carpenter's look of astonishment had disappeared quickly. The middle-aged, well-groomed executive had leaned forward across his large, carved desk, his face now expressionless, and said, "Let me get this straight." His voice, calm and even on the surface, hummed with almost apoplectic incredulity. "You went all the way out to La Guardia last night after work just to find that out?"

"I did," Reardon had answered firmly.

"May I ask why?"

"To see justice done."

"What is Mrs. Hanson to you?"

"A fellow-employee," Reardon had said, staring straight back at Carpenter; the tricks of intimidation used by bullies in positions of power were old stuff to Reardon. "A fellow-employee who has received a raw deal."

"Nothing more? Just a fellow-employee?"

"Just a fellow-employee. That's enough for me."

"I see," Carpenter had said politely. "May I tell you what I consider enough for me, Mr.—? I'm sorry, I've forgotten your name."

"Reardon," Reardon had said evenly, watching his voice with care, avoiding the trap men like Carpenter always set with their own fabricated calm, hoping the false restraint will trip you into the fatal error of losing your temper. "Employee of this company for twenty-three years. Chief, message center, fifth floor, for the past six years."

"That would seem to be long enough for you to know that we do not deal unjustly with our employees," Carpenter had replied with a mildness that Reardon knew was insincere. "Your desire to see justice done does you credit, Mr. Reardon, but I'm afraid it is misplaced in this case. I did not fire Mrs. Hanson, as you put it, because she made me miss an important luncheon engagement. That was merely coincidental. I have been troubled by Mrs. Hanson's—how shall I put it?—by her deterioration, shall we say?—for a long time. The poor woman is too old and has too many private troubles to function efficiently in an office. She has not been fired. She has been retired on a fairly decent pension that should enable her to live in comfort for the rest of her days." Carpenter had paused and looked faintly troubled. "There is one further point," he'd said. "I assume from the assurance with which you burst in on me, Mr. Reardon, that there are some top executives in this company who take instructions from the chief of the message center on how to run their offices. This is something of a surprise to me. My statement that I am not one of those executives may come as a surprise to you, Mr. Reardon. I must ask you to note that the matter of who I want for my secretary is one that I must decide for myself. May I suggest that we'll both be much happier if you go back to your message center and tend to your own knitting, and allow me to tend to mine? Do I make myself clear?"

"Perfectly," Reardon had said. "Would you mind making just as clear what you intend to do about the information I have just given you?"

"Why, I intend to forget it," Carpenter had answered with a friendly smile. "And I would suggest that you do the same."

"The difference in our positions makes it necessary for me to take note of your threats, but I'm afraid I must decline to take your advice," Reardon had said, and then had turned and walked from the office, outwardly composed but inwardly quivering with the fierce and pleasurable excitement generated by the neatly phrased retort the Far Eastern manager had made it possible for him to utter as a parting shot. In Reardon's lonely undertakings, these windfalls came only rarely and for that reason were doubly welcome, but there was always the danger that the selfish process of enjoying them would deflect you from action. Reardon had gone back to his own office, and, even though he made it a point never to do these things on company time, he'd violated his strict code of conduct and had written a letter to the Batavia representative, asking that gentleman if he would be good enough to commit to writing the information he had given Reardon at La Guardia airport the night before. In view of the fact that the matter was urgent, and because there were opposing forces at work that could only be described as unscrupulous, Reardon had requested that the reply be sent to his home in the self-addressed air-mail envelope he was enclosing with his letter.

The reply, which arrived six weeks later, was couched in the nervous, frightened, equivocal phrases that Reardon had come to accept as commonplace from cowardly underlings, fearful of losing their jobs. The man in Batavia wanted to know what information he had given Reardon, and who Reardon was, and what did he want the information for, and just what was this all about, anyway? The tone of the letter, the obvious backsliding from the clear and forthright statement the man had made at the airport, reminded Reardon grimly of the *bordereau* in the Dreyfus case. The pattern of injustice was always the same.

Reardon had spent all of the next Sunday in his apartment on Bank Street, where he lived alone, composing a long, carefully worded second letter, which was shrewdly designed to allay his correspondent's fears, to elicit the written corroboration of Carpenter's duplicity, and to make the man at the other side of the world feel that he, like Reardon, was embracing a cause that was far more important than any minor embarrassment he might suffer from helping a wronged fellow-worker. It was a good letter. Before it could reach Batavia, however, the Japs had attacked Pearl Harbor, and Halstead-Schick's representative, along with hundreds of other Americans and Europeans in Java, had disappeared. Then Sour Ball Carpenter was granted a leave of absence to accept a majority in the army and left his desk on the twenty-second floor of the Halstead-Schick Building to serve with the OSS in the Far East for the duration. Reardon had lost track of Mrs. Hanson.

Several times during the war the unfortunate woman had crossed Reardon's mind and he had wondered what had become of her, but other and more pressing matters intervened. To begin with, there was the constant battle with the administrative office, on the third floor, which expected the message center to continue making six mail deliveries a day to every office in the twenty-seven-story building, not counting special trips with cables and memoranda marked "RUSH," or for personal attention, even though eight of

Reardon's ten routing clerks had been drafted and all the personnel office could provide as replacements were young girls, most of them not particularly bright and all of them untrained. And there was the fight with the ration board that had issued to Reardon a defective book, from which a whole page of red points and two sugar coupons were missing, and then when he had asked to have his book changed, the board had been so dilatory that he was forced to conclude that its members were accusing him by implication of having used the missing coupons to augment his meat and sugar supply. That mess had dragged along for almost four months and brought on a recurrence of the migraine headaches from which Reardon had been relatively free since shortly after his fiftieth birthday, in 1939, when he had successfully carried his struggle for a refund right up to the president of the department store from which he had bought an Alpacuna overcoat for $65.95 two days before the store featured the same coat, in full-page advertisements in every morning paper in town, at $54.50.

Several months after V-J Day, Carpenter had obtained his release from the army and returned to his desk on the twenty-second floor of the Halstead-Schick Building, but even though Reardon had been watching all communications from the Far East with great care and interest, he had seen nothing to indicate that the company's Batavia representative had been found. Reardon had to admit to himself with some regret that the Mrs. Hanson affair, now almost five years old, was a dead issue. This was a pity. If the war had not come along, the Mrs. Hanson matter would have been a beauty, an open-and-shut case, one of the simplest he had ever undertaken. Sour Ball Carpenter, however, was very much alive, and even though the end of the war had returned to their old jobs enough of Reardon's experienced routing clerks to enable him to put the message center back on its feet, he had intensified rather than relaxed his vigilance since the Far Eastern manager had resumed his old duties.

Therefore, even if the cable had not had the striking opening sentence that in itself was enough to make it stick in Reardon's mind, and even if it had not been the first cable to come through from China on Halstead-Schick's private wires since the Japs took Hong Kong, the mere fact that it was marked by the code room

"CHINA FOR CARPENTER ONLY REPEAT CARPENTER ONLY" would have been enough to put him on the alert.

One morning, shortly before eleven, as he came back into his office from a visit to the infirmary, on the twenty-seventh floor, where Miss Klauber, the company nurse, had given him a small dose of the barbiturate that sometimes helped his headaches, Reardon noticed Bill Kain, the message-center log clerk, talking on the telephone and, with his free hand, turning the pages of his cable log-book. There was something about the faint flutter of nervousness in Bill's usually slow, drawling voice that caused Reardon to stop in the middle of the office and turn and cross over to Bill's desk.

"What's the matter?" Reardon said.

"What?" Bill said, and then, recognizing Reardon, his face froze and he shook his head quickly. "Nothing much," he said, and, into the phone, "The sixteenth. That's right. . . . No, the *six*teenth. That's exactly three weeks ago. A Thursday. . . . That's what it says here in my log, Miss Sheppard. The sixteenth. Thursday." The mention of Miss Sheppard's name brought all of Reardon's faintly alerted senses into a sudden, sharply focussed knot of awareness that caused his slowly receding headache to throb back to new life. His eyelids flicked, and this thin shoulders straightened just a trifle in the gray alpaca office coat. Miss Sheppard was Carpenter's new secretary, the second girl that the fussy and demanding Far Eastern manager had hired since he came back. "Well, you check, Miss Sheppard," Bill Kain said. "And call me back." He hung up the phone, and seeing that Reardon was still beside him, he said, "Those dumb clucks on twenty-two. Boy!"

"What's wrong?" Reardon said.

"Some damn cable three weeks ago," Bill said. "The first one from China since the war."

"For Carpenter, yes," Reardon said. "What about it?"

"His secretary says he just got an airmail from China mentioning the cable, and Carpenter doesn't know what cable. She called to check and I told her we logged it in on the sixteenth and delivered it right away."

"That's right," Reardon said. "We did. I remember it clearly."

"Boy!" Bill Kain said. "Some of these new secretaries—they must have got them out of the Pentagon or something."

"Don't you worry about it," Reardon said. "If she calls back, switch the call to me."

"I can take care of it," Bill said. "It's part of my job. Besides, one thing I learned in the army—I know how to handle these rear-echelon babes."

"No, I'd rather take care of this myself," Reardon said sharply as he picked up the logbook. Since Bill and some of the other clerks had come back, Reardon had noticed a slight truculence, an air of resentment on their part when they were dealing with him directly. Reardon supposed this was inevitable and he tried to be understanding and not hold it against them, but their belligerence, as though they felt that in the three years while they were away they had become too important for their menial jobs and he had grown old and weak and incompetent, was a constant source of unpleasantness. Reardon was fifty-seven years old, but aside from his headaches, he knew he was in much better physical and mental shape than any of these immature youngsters, with all their smoking and drinking and helling around all night and endless babble about experiences under fire. "I'll just take this back to my desk," Reardon said. "If she calls, you have it switched to me."

He went to his desk at the far side of the office, near the window from which you could see a sliver of City Hall Park, and sat down. He placed the open logbook on the desk and leaned back in his swivel chair, and as the familiar excitement, the slowly mounting anticipation that was almost orgiastic, began to churn in his stomach and spiral upward, spreading the delicious warm anger to all parts of his body, he looked down on the I.R.T. kiosk on the corner and, very delicately, stroked a throbbing vein in his temple. The phone rang.

"Yes?" Reardon said. "No, this is Mr. Reardon. I asked Mr. Kain to have your call switched to me. What seems to be the difficulty?"

"Oh, gee, I don't know," said Miss Sheppard. "There's some darned cable Mr. Carpenter is supposed to have received from China three weeks ago—a pretty long one, this letter says. This letter he received today that mentions the cable, I mean."

"Mr. Kain has filled me in on the facts," Reardon said. "I repeat, Miss Sheppard, what seems to be the difficulty?"

"Well, Mr. Carpenter says he never saw the darned thing," Miss Sheppard said. "He doesn't know anything about it."

"Do you know anything about it?" Reardon said.

"What?" Miss Sheppard said, and then, "Say, listen, if I did, what do you think I'm calling for?"

"I haven't the remotest idea," Reardon said, putting an edge into his voice. "The records of the message center indicate that the cable in question was delivered to Mr. Carpenter's office at ten forty-five on Thursday, the sixteenth. The responsibility of the message center ends there."

Reardon hung up and, still stroking his temple, waited. At noon, when the first shift of routing clerks went to lunch, Bill Kain came over and asked if there was anything Mr. Reardon wanted of him before he went out to eat. Reardon curtly said no, thanks, not a thing, and then, as the young man was turning away, Reardon said, well, wait a moment, if Bill didn't mind, would he bring along a sandwich and a bottle of milk when he came back, tuna or ham on rye —it didn't matter, anything at all. An hour later, when Bill Kain came back with Reardon's lunch, the phone had not rung. Reardon ate the sandwich and drank the milk at his desk. When the second shift came back from lunch, at two o'clock, the phone on Reardon's desk was still silent. Reardon waited another hour. Nothing happened. At three o'clock he stood up, took the logbook, and walked over to Bill Kain's desk.

"You'd better hold onto this," Reardon said, putting down the book. "If Carpenter's office calls about that cable, you don't know any more about it. Say I'm handling it and I'll call back. I'm going upstairs for a while."

"You bet," Bill Kain said. "Headache bad again?"

"What?" Reardon said, and then, "No, but I think I can use half a teaspoon of bicarb to settle that liverwurst on rye you brought me. I won't be long."

It was ten minutes to four when Reardon came back. He knew what Bill Kain was going to say before the log clerk opened his mouth.

"Carpenter's office called about twenty minutes ago," Bill Kain said. "Three-thirty. He wants to see you right away. About that cable."

"Did he ask for me by name?" Reardon said.

"Well, it was that Sheppard babe did the calling," Bill said. "I told her I didn't now any more about the damn thing than I'd already told her and you'd call her back, the way you said. She got off the phone for a minute—I guess she was passing that on to His Nibs —then she came back on the wire and said O.K., would I tell you to come up to twenty-two when I saw you."

"Let me have the logbook," Reardon said. "If I get stuck, I'd like you to stand by till I come back."

"Well, I've got a date for right after quitting time," Bill Kain said, and then, after a moment of rather obvious debate with himself, he said, "You don't expect to be up there *that* long, do you?"

"You never can tell with the Carpenter type," Reardon said. "I'll try not to make you late for your date."

Reardon took the elevator to the twenty-second floor and went through the door at the end of the corridor into the outer office of the Far Eastern manager's suite.

"I'm Reardon, message center," he said to the dark-haired girl who looked at him inquiringly across her typewriter. "Mr. Carpenter wanted to see me."

"Oh, yes." Miss Sheppard's face cleared. "Did you find it?"

"I believe it was Mr. Carpenter who wanted to see me."

Miss Sheppard's face looked blank for a moment, and then, blushing, she stood up and came out from behind her desk. With a short, puzzled backward glance at Reardon, she opened the door into Carpenter's office.

"Mr. Carpenter," she said, "Mr. Reardon is here."

"Who?" the executive said.

"Mr. Reardon," Miss Sheppard said. "From the message center. About that cable."

"Oh," Carpenter said. "Yes. Send him in." Miss Sheppard held the door for Reardon to pass her, and the Far Eastern manager said, "You, too, please." Miss Sheppard nodded and came in, and the door swung shut behind her and Reardon. "I'm sorry to cause you all this trouble and drag you all the way up here," Carpenter said with a smile of apology, "but there's been a small snafu somewhere along the line."

"The efficiency of the message center has never been questioned during the eleven years that I have served as its chief," Reardon said. "Any business you have to transact with my unit, Mr. Carpenter, will be made considerably simpler if you limit yourself to the facts and refrain from unnecessary and unjustified slurs on the people who work for me."

Miss Sheppard, just behind Reardon, made a small, sucking noise, and the Far Eastern manager blinked quickly, like a man who has come unexpectedly around a street corner into a gust of whirling cinders.

"I received an air-mail letter from China this morning," Carpenter said, forcing his cheerful voice, word by word, into a flat, strained monotone. "It refers to a long cable that was sent to me three weeks ago. I never saw that cable."

"That's too bad," Reardon said. "The message center delivered it to your office."

"How do you know?" Carpenter said gently. "I haven't even told you what cable I'm referring to."

"I know the cable you mean," Reardon said. "I remember it clearly."

"You do?" Carpenter said. "How?"

"Very simple," Reardon said. "First, the cable was a long one. It covered two and a half sheets of flimsy. I keep an eye on the cable files myself and I always remember the long ones. Second, the cable had a very unusual opening line and my mind automatically records things like that. Third, it was the first one to come through from China on our private wires since Hong Kong fell, an event that even a man with a poor memory is not likely to forget. Fourth, and most important, Mr. Carpenter, it came from the code room marked for your special attention, and I have always made it a point"— Reardon allowed his voice to drop just a trifle—"to pay particular attention to anything marked for your special attention."

There was a long, almost completely silent pause, during which Miss Sheppard nervously chewed the end of her pencil. Then Carpenter said, "Say, I remember you. You're the man who came steaming in here one day before the war. About that Mrs. Hanson? You followed our Batavia man to La Guardia? Isn't that right?" Carpenter's voice rose, as though he was pleased with this feat of his memory. "You followed him after work. Isn't that right?"

"That's right," Reardon said. "I fail to see, however, what all this has to do with this cable."

"Reardon, that's your name," Carpenter said. "I remember the whole thing now. My goodness," he said, shoving his arms straight out in front of him and putting his hands on the desk, palms down, "so you're still around." The Far Eastern manager shook his head slowly from side to side with an odd expression of amazed gratitude, as though he were contemplating some astounding phenomenon that, under ordinary circumstances, would be revealed only to more deserving men. "As a matter of fact," he said finally, "it has nothing to do with this cable. I'm sorry that you've decided, for some mysterious reason of your own, to make an issue of a fairly routine and unimportant matter. Having made that decision, however, you leave me no recourse but to talk bluntly. Mr. Reardon, your job is to see to it that cables marked for my attention get to me, not to follow people to La Guardia or talk to people who catch you falling down on the job."

"I've done my job," Reardon said. "That cable got to you."

"I say it didn't," Carpenter said. "Now I want to say something to you that is intended in all sincerity and for your own sake, Reardon. I want you to listen to me."

"I'm afraid I'll have to ask you to listen to me first," Reardon said. "You say the cable didn't reach you, but I say it did. I happen to be able to prove my statement." Reardon stepped forward and dropped the logbook on the desk. The canvas binding made a dull thump as it hit the glass top of the desk. With two short contemptuous movements, Reardon flipped the book open and spun it around in front of Carpenter. "We make it a practice in the messenger center to log all cables as they come back from the code room, not only by their serial numbers but, to ensure accuracy of identification, by their opening lines. Here." Reardon's finger poked at the open page. "There's the serial number and there's the opening line: 'Send four men to Hanoi.' Logged in at ten-forty A.M., on Thursday, the sixteenth, three weeks ago today. In the handwriting of my cable-log clerk, Bill Kain. Here." Reardon's finger moved to the next column. "There's the time, ten forty-five, when the cable was delivered to your office. Here." Reardon's finger jabbed at the last column.

"There's the initial of the person who accepted the cable for you, in her own handwriting."

Carpenter looked down at the logbook, then up at Reardon, and his lips worked back and forth several times, as if he had bitten into something distasteful.

"Whose initial is that?" he said.

"Miss Barth," Reardon said, "who was your secretary until two weeks ago, when you fired her and hired Miss Sheppard."

"I see," Carpenter said. "Miss Sheppard." The girl behind Reardon made the sucking noise again and came forward in a frightened jump. "Miss Sheppard," Carpenter said, "was that cable among the papers Miss Barth turned over to you before she left?"

"I don't think so," Miss Sheppard said uncomfortably. "I mean I don't remember. I never saw the thing. Honestly."

"Thank you," Carpenter said. He turned back to Reardon. "The fact remains that the cable is not here. As for the initial, I have only your unsupported word for it that it *is* Miss Barth's. Now let's—"

"I'm not accustomed to having my word questioned," Reardon said. "And I'm sure that Miss Barth will be willing to testify."

"Testify, eh?" Carpenter said. "I see." He pushed himself slowly away from the desk. "You know," he said, "I feel very sorry for you, Mr. Reardon." He turned and said, "Miss Sheppard."

"Yes, sir," Miss Sheppard said.

"Will you be good enough to ask this—this—this gentleman to leave us alone?" Carpenter said. "We've got some work to do."

"Yes, sir," Miss Sheppard said.

She put the chewed end of her pencil back into her mouth and looked uncertainly at Reardon. He leaned over, flipped the logbook shut, picked it up, and walked out. He went directly down to the personnel office and got Miss Barth's home phone number from the records. He called her home, and her mother gave him the phone number of her new job, and his next call reached her there just as she was about to leave. Miss Barth remembered the whole thing clearly. It had seemed so odd at the time, she said, the unusual opening line, the first cable from China in several years, all that. Reardon thanked her and hung up.

When he entered the message center, Bill Kain got up from his desk and came across the room.

"Everything all right?" Bill asked. "You were up there so long, I was getting worried."

"Was it that long?" Reardon said. "Yes, everything's fine. I hope I didn't make you late for your date."

"Heck, no," Bill Kain said. "It's not five-thirty."

When Reardon put his key in the lock of his apartment door, he was surprised to find he had the evening papers under his arm. He did not remember buying them. The apartment—two rooms and a bath, facing an attractive little garden behind Bank Street—looked even neater than usual. On the kitchen table his supper—cold lamb and salad with the dressing mixed and waiting in a small glass that had once been a jelly jar—had been laid out by his part-time maid.

He ate the food, washed and dried the few dishes, and settled down to read the papers, but the headache that had been drumming dully in his temple since he walked out of Carpenter's office seemed to kick at the side of his head, as though it were trying to force its way out into the open. There was no point in further delay. He went to the bathroom. He swallowed two tablets from the bottle Miss Klauber had given him, and closed his eyes to wait for the barbiturate to take effect. When he opened them, the throbbing in his temple was dulled as though the pain had been wrapped in cotton batting. He was ready.

He went to his desk, uncapped his fountain pen, and pulled a foolscap pad from the drawer. "Sumner Halstead, Esq.," he wrote. "President, The Halstead-Schick Petroleum Corporation. Sir . . ." As his pen moved across the page the pain in his head began to mount again, but he did not feel it. The phone rang, but he paid no attention to it. He was completely absorbed. It was an absorption that went deeper than pleasure. In the composition of such letters there was for Reardon a whole world of secret excitement, the gratification of drawing together, sometimes from a great distance, the pieces of a puzzle that had baffled others, the surge of power that came from bringing to the bar of justice a scoundrel who felt he was safe from detection or punishment.

Reardon raised his head. The doorbell was ringing. He shoved out his breath in a gasp of anger, tried to close his mind against the interruption, and bent back to his task. The doorbell continued to ring. Reardon pushed himself away from the desk and staggered across the room and pulled the door open.

"Boy!" Bill Kain said. "I sure am glad to see you."

"What the hell are you doing here?" Reardon said harshly. "What do you want?"

"He's a friendly guy, isn't he?" said a girl who was holding Bill Kain's arm.

Reardon turned abruptly to look at her. The girl giggled nervously and stepped back, as though she had been slapped. Her hat, a small cluster of green canvas flowers, was askew in her blond hair.

"We been calling you from Keeney's around the corner," Bill said. "We been calling and calling. We thought you were sick or something."

"You're drunk," Reardon said impatiently. "What do you want?"

"Who's drunk?" the girl said. She tugged Bill Kain's arm. "Let's go back to Keeney's," she said.

Reardon started to close the door, but Bill Kain caught it with his toe. "Wait a minute," he said. "Right after you left, just about five-thirty, Carpenter called from upstairs. Not that Sheppard. Carpenter called, himself. He wanted to talk to you."

Reardon became aware of the pain in his head. He tried to grip the door with his other hand and saw that he was still holding the fountain pen.

"What did he want?" he said. "Why did he call?"

"He wanted to apologize to you," Bill Kain said. "He said he was sorry he lost his temper when you were up there in his office, because you were right. Sheppard found that damned cable from China. After you left, Carpenter made her look all over the joint. She'd shoved it in with a lot of other papers in her desk and forgot about it. Carpenter said he wanted you to know and to apologize for everything." Bill Kain stopped, and his face, animated by liquor and the excitement of revelation, seemed to contract. "I tried to call you at home before I left the office, but I guess you hadn't reached here, yet, because there wasn't any answer," he said. "I was telling Alice, here—I was telling her about it while we were eating over at Keeney's—all about the fuss Carpenter's office made, I mean, and she said it was a shame, you were probably worrying about it and I ought to call you again. We called you three times from Keeney's, but there was no answer, and Alice said maybe you were sick or something." Bill paused once more, as though he were waiting for Reardon to deny this, but Reardon merely stared at the younger man and listened to the hammer strokes in his head that were blinding him. "We looked up your address in the phone book," Bill Kain said. "You're just a couple of blocks from Keeney's so Alice said let's go over and see if anything is wrong."

He stopped again. Nobody spoke. The girl made an ineffectual attempt to straighten the cluster of green canvas flowers in her hair, and then tugged Bill's arm. "If you ask me, I think he's the one that's drunk," she said. "We come all the way over here to give him some good news, so he won't have to keep worrying, wait to hear it till the morning. We come all the way over here to see maybe he's dead, you'd think he'd say come on in, or offer us a drink, at least say thanks. Some boss you got! Come on, let's go back to Keeney's," she concluded, pulling Bill toward the stairs.

"Anyway, that's what Carpenter said," Bill Kain said, speaking across his shoulder as the girl dragged him away. "He wanted to apologize to you."

Reardon drew a deep breath and slammed the door shut. He leaned his forehead against the cool, varnished wood. The girl's voice came up the stairs.

"Some boss you got," she said. "The cheap—"

Her voice died away. Reardon pushed himself from the door and groped his way back across the room to his desk. He sat down with a thump, as though he had misjudged the distance to the chair, and put the fountain pen beside the foolscap pad. His eyes blurred with anger and disappointment as he tore from the pad the neatly written pages addressed to Sumner Halstead, Esq., President, The Halstead-Shick Petroleum Corporation, but he did not stop. He was not a weak man. The pain in his head made it difficult for him to see, and his rage at having been cheated shook his thin body so hard that his fingers slipped and fumbled, but he managed to find a clip and fasten the pages and put them carefully into the lower drawer and lock it. Nothing was ever really wasted. There would be another time.

Shoe-Shine

The car was a good one, very new and expensive-looking, but it was small. It was too small to have a chauffeur, much too small for a chauffeur in such an elaborate uniform. He looked odd on the front seat in his military cap with its stiff gleaming visor and his trim black coat with the row of buttons that ran all the way up the left side of his chest to the shoulder. He belonged in a bigger car, something long and heavy, with a speaking apparatus and discreet silver mountings; not in this flashy little roadster.

What made the whole thing look silly was the young man who sat beside the chauffeur. He had very broad shoulders, with humps of muscle on his back and arms that showed through the perfect fit of his expensive tweed coat. He was deeply tanned and his long, lean jaw stuck out a trifle too much, enough to give his pleasant, handsome face more than ordinary strength and assurance. His dark brown felt hat, with the snap brim and the little colored feather in the ribbon, was pushed back slightly on his head with careless rakishness, and his blond hair was closely cropped at the sideburns.

He looked like a football or crew man from a middle-western university, with a family that hadn't worried about money for three generations, who was constantly being photographed for the rotogravures and reported engaged alternately to debutantes and night club singers. Between the husky young man and the impeccably liveried chauffeur there was so much obvious competence on the front seat of the tiny roadster that it was a ridiculous sight to watch the chauffeur's difficulties as he tried to park.

There was plenty of room in front of the office building for the small roadster. But the chauffeur was apparently accustomed to a heavier car. He kept twisting the wheel too sharply and his touch on the gas was too heavy. The little roadster responded jerkily. Twice he scraped the brand new tires against the curb and had to back out and try again. The young man beside him didn't say a word. He watched the chauffeur's efforts with a small, delighted grin. Finally, the car came into the open space at a fairly good angle. The front wheel went up onto the sidewalk. The chauffeur swore under his breath but twisted the steering wheel and kept the car moving forward slowly until the front wheel slipped off into the gutter. Then he pulled the emergency brake and turned off the ignition.

"You're getting pretty good," the young man said. "You ought to get into that soap box derby, if you could make the age limit."

"You made that crack yesterday," the chauffeur said. "Why don't they give me a bicycle to drive next?"

He got out of the car and walked around the back until he came up on the sidewalk on the other side. The young man looked at the open space in front of the roadster and twisted in his seat to look at the open space behind.

"Look, Hull," he said. "Somebody else may want to get in here. There's room for another car. If you pull her up just a little?"

"Nuts," the chauffeur said. "Parking this peanut stand is wearing me out. I won't be long. I'll just leave the package and come right down. Anybody wants to park here they can wait a minute."

"I'll tell them what you said. Quote you verbatim?"

"How about laying off the sarcastic stuff for a little while," the chauffeur said. "Gimme the package." The young man handed him a small box wrapped in white tissue paper and tied with a narrow green ribbon. The chauffeur turned to walk across the sidewalk into the building, then stopped and looked back. "Want something to read till I come down? Get you a paper, Dick?"

"Thanks, no," Dick said, and he grinned. "I'll just look at the girls' legs for a few minutes while I'm waiting."

"Now, listen, Dick. Your mother said you—"

"Oh, go on, Hull, hurry up," Dick said, and his grin spread out wider. "Before somebody else tries to park in here or you get a ticket or something. Go on, hurry up."

The chauffeur squeezed his lips together until they disappeared. He gave the young man in the car a long, baffled look, then turned and walked into the office building. Dick looked casually up and down the sunny street. He whistled an experimental bar or two from a song, tried another, a third, found one that he liked and swung into it softly. Very few people went by. No girls at all. After a few moments of looking at the people and whistling, Dick pulled a nail file from his pocket and went to work. He did all of his left hand and then started on his right. He was digging at the cuticle of his right thumb when an automobile honked loudly behind him. He looked up and turned on the seat. Two young men had driven up in a sedan and stopped a few feet behind the roadster. The driver leaned out on his window and pointed to the small space against the curb between Dick's roadster and the car behind.

"Say, bud," he called. "You mind pulling up a few feet so we can get in there?"

"Well," Dick said. "I'm afraid you'll—" He looked toward the office building. The revolving door was motionless. He swung his head back to the sedan behind him. "Would you mind waiting just a minute? My chauffeur will—"

The driver of the sedan waved his hand.

"Your car," he called. "Move it up a couple of feet, will you?"

"In a minute," Dick called back. "My chauffeur is—"

The young man beside the driver of the sedan stuck his head out of the other window.

"Hey, pal," he called. "Move that peewee up a few feet." Dick hesitated and gave the office building another quick glance. The young man beside the driver of the sedan leaned further out of his window. "Hey, handsome, you're not deaf, are you?" he bellowed. "I said goose that little pushcart up a ways so we can get in behind you."

Two old ladies were walking by. They turned at the sound of the yelling to look at the two cars. Dick flushed dark red under his tan and his strong jaw moved forward a fraction of an inch. The little muscles on the side of his face twitched as his teeth bit together. He pulled his hat down over his eyes and turned his back on the sedan. He folded his arms on his chest and stared straight ahead. The two old ladies walked on.

"Hey, Joe College," the driver of the sedan called. Dick didn't answer or turn his head. "Hey, quarterback!" Dick didn't move. The driver of the sedan stepped on the gas and brought his car alongside the roadster. "What's the matter, handsome? Can't you hear? We asked you to move your little pony cart up a few feet so we can park behind you."

"I heard you," Dick said. "So did half the people over there in Central Park. Why don't you invest in a megaphone?"

The driver of the sedan stared in astonishment. He turned to look at his friend on the seat beside him.

"What goes on here?" the driver said. "Am I crazy?"

"No, you're all right," his friend said. "We just happened to draw a wack here. Or maybe he's a wise guy." He leaned out of his window toward Dick. "Look, quarterback, save all that for when you get back to your playmates in college. My friend and I, we're very busy men and we don't want any trouble. We haven't got time for trouble. We just want to park. You gonna move that toy dingus of yours up a few feet so we can get in, or aren't you?"

"No, I'm not," Dick said and he grinned at the two young men in the sedan. "Anything you two gentlemen want to do about it?"

The driver of the sedan seemed to explode. He rose angrily in his seat and leaned across his friend toward the window nearest the roadster.

"Listen to that twirp talk," he snarled. "Just listen to him! Isn't bad enough he's got to hog the parking space, but he gets tough, too! Listen, college boy, I'll bend that straight nose of yours for you if you—"

"Take it easy," his friend said, pushing him back into his seat. "We'll bend his nose later. First I wanna find out what makes this guy such a wise guy. We're busy, but we're not too busy for that." He leaned out of the window toward Dick. "You're not gonna run away for a few minutes, are you?" he asked with elaborate politeness. "Just for a few minutes?"

"I don't see any reason to," Dick said. "What's on your mind?"

"I just wanna talk to you," the young man said very slowly and distinctly. "You're a type that all of a sudden I'm fascinated by. We'll just get rid of the car first."

"I'll be waiting right here," Dick said. "If you can find your way back, that is."

The driver of the sedan rose angrily in his seat again. But his friend pushed him back. He motioned forward with his hand and the driver started the car. It moved down the block until it reached an empty space against the curb near the corner. A moment later the two young men appeared on the sidewalk. They reached into their car and pulled out a couple of large leather folios with zipper fasteners along the top, the kind that salesmen and lawyers carry. They tucked them under their arms and came walking up the block toward the roadster. Dick watched them approach calmly. He swung his small, sneering smile over to one corner of his mouth, pushed his hat up a bit further on his tanned forehead, and tipped his head slightly to one side and backward until it rested against the roadster's expensive leather upholstery. He seemed to enjoy watching the approach of the young men in the same way that he had enjoyed watching Hull, the chauffeur, maneuver the roadster into position.

When the young men stopped on the sidewalk Dick could see that they were not as young as they had looked in the sedan. The driver was on the fat side and his friend, who had sat beside him on the front seat, would have done well to stay away from bread and potatoes. They were neatly dressed, but their shirts had been worn for at least two days already, and while they didn't need shaves very badly, they had definitely not used razors that morning. Also, they were not lawyers because the leather folders under their arms bulged in funny places, as though they contained salesmen's samples of some mechanical device for stopping falling hair or dicing onions without causing tears. On each of the leather folios there was a small set of gold initials in the upper right hand corner. The driver's folio said L.D. and the other one said M.G.G. Dick pulled a package of cigarettes from his pocket and lit one. He inhaled deeply and blew the smoke out at the two salesmen as he shoved the pack back into the pocket of his tweed coat.

"Yes?" he said with his delicate grin. "You gentlemen said something about wanting to talk?"

"Not me," L.D. said as he moved forward. "You can talk if you want to, but me, I'm just going to slug the head off this sunburned baloney."

"No, no, just a second," M.G.G. said, stopping him. "Before we smear this thing off the map, I want to find out something. I'm like a student of psychology all of a sudden. I want to know why when you ask a guy a simple little thing like he should move up a few feet so's you should be able to park, he has to get snotty."

"Why don't you try asking it?" Dick said, and he blew more smoke at them. "Or is the language too much for you?"

"Say, listen," L.D. said, "I've had enough. I'm gonna knock this guy's—"

"Just one second," M.G.G. said, stopping him again. He turned back to the roadster. "All right, fullback, tell me. What makes you so clever, such a stinking genius all of a sudden, such a wow with your trap?"

"You really want to know?" Dick asked.

"I'm standing on pins and needles," M.G.G. said. "Both of us."

"It's very simple," Dick said. "I don't like you. Not just you. Collectively you. Both of you." He cocked his head to one side and examined them coolly. There was so much insolence on his face that L.D. squirmed and clenched his fist. But M.G.G. held him back with his hand. "First of all, I don't like you because you drive a sedan. I don't like sedans. Then because you're both fat. I don't like fat people. Then because you could use a shave, and I hate people who could use a shave. Not to mention the fact that you don't change your shirts often enough. That sufficient? Or shall I go on?"

"By all means," M.G.G. said, but his face was tightening up and there were white patches on his cheeks. "Don't let me stop you."

"You couldn't," Dick said. "But to go on. I also don't like you because you're obviously salesmen. I think salesmen stink. Especially salesmen of some sort of gadget that still looks like a gadget even when you hide it in those portfolios. Incidentally, just in passing, I hate all gadgets, too. What else? Oh, yes. Also because you talk too loud and because you don't say please when you want a favor, such as a little more room for parking. Enough?"

"More than enough," M.G.G. said. He took the folio from under his arm and held it out to his friend. "Here, you hold this for a minute. I have a small murder to commit."

"Oh, no," L.D. said, pushing the folio away. "You hold mine. I'm gonna knock Joe College's razor-edged tongue down his throat. Then I'm gonna kick his beautiful white teeth right down after it. Here, hold this."

"When you two boys get it settled," Dick drawled, "let me know. Or would you prefer that I take you both on at once?"

The two salesmen glared at the husky young man in the small roadster. "Both on at once," L.D. said finally. "Both on at once. By God, I'm telling you, I'm going to tear this snotty little heel into small—"

"Get up out of that car," M.G.G. said. "Come on, get up on the sidewalk and—"

"I don't feel like wasting too much energy on you two bums," Dick said, and he blew smoke into M.G.G.'s face. "Suppose you get me out on the sidewalk first?"

Both salesmen moved forward at once. But just then a boy of twelve or thirteen, with a shoe-shine box slung across his shoulder, stepped between them. He had come along the street unobserved and he didn't seem to realize that the three men were about to start a fight.

"Shine, mister?" he said to Dick. "Shine 'em up? Good shine?"

Dick shook his head and brushed him aside with his hand. He was smiling coolly across the boy's head at the two salesmen.

"Whaddaya say, mister?" the boy persisted. "Shine 'em up good? Make 'em like new?"

"No," Dick said, his eyes still on the salesmen. "No shine."

"Aah, come on, mister. Giviz a show. Shine 'em up good. Whaddaya say?"

L.D. reached down and grabbed the boy's shoulder.

"Come on, beat it," he snapped. "We got some work to do on this handsome—"

"Just a minute," Dick said suddenly. He looked from the bootblack to the two salesmen and back to the bootblack. Then he tossed away his cigarette. "Okay, son," he said slowly, and the small smile on his face twisted all the way over to one side. "I think I will have a shine, at that."

The boy grinned and started to swing the shoe-shine box from his shoulder. Dick reached over, pushed the catch on the door, and shoved it open. As the door swung out slowly, the boy moved forward. Then he stopped and he let out a small, stifled gasp. His little face, with the smudges of shoe polish across the cheeks, grew white. The husky young man in the expensive roadster had no legs. They were amputated above the knees.

"Gee," the boy said, "I—I—"

He grabbed his box and turned and ran. Dick started to laugh. He did it with his whole body, shaking up and down on the roadster seat, his head thrown back, roaring out the sounds loudly. He laughed so hard that tears came to his eyes. The two salesmen stared at him for a long, astonished moment. All the belligerence and anger went out of their faces until only shocked disbelief remained. Then that disappeared, too, and the horror that had come so suddenly to the little shoe-shine boy came to them. They looked at each other, dropped their eyes, and turned to walk away in silence. The office building's revolving door whirred and Hull, the chauffeur, came out. He stopped short when he saw the young man in the car laughing. His experienced eyes moved quickly to take in the roadster's open door, the two salesmen slinking down the block, the small bootblack running hard and looking back over his shoulder. Then the chauffeur's glance returned to the roadster. His lips grew thin as he strode across the sidewalk.

"Damn it," he said, "I can't leave you alone for a minute, can I?"

The Third Alphabet

The room that housed the typists' pool was at the foot of the long corridor, on what was considered the least desirable end of the building, the south end, facing Pennsylvania Avenue and Eleventh Street Northwest. The building was shaped like a flatiron at that end, so that the room was almost completely surrounded by traffic noises and, because there were tall, wide windows on both sides, the sun poured in all day. This was not really an inconvenience, because the sun helped keep the room warm in winter, and the building was air-cooled in the summer.

When the agency was created, two weeks after Pearl Harbor, and it took over the entire second floor from the overflow staff of one of the old-line agencies whose new marble and sandstone structure on the Mall had just been completed, the Space Committee had assigned the room to the typists' pool because it was so oddly shaped that there was no way of cutting it up sensibly into smaller offices, no matter how the partitions were arranged. Besides, even though half the girls used noiseless machines, the other half pounded away on vintage L. C. Smiths and Remingtons and Underwoods, anything at all that could be dug up and put into some sort of working order, and when all the typewriters were going the racket could be heard forty feet down the corridor. It made sense to keep the typists at the south end, as far away from the executive offices, at the north end, as possible.

Miss Keating, coming out of her office near the north end, four

doors from the mahogany arch that led to the executive offices,
looked up from the memorandum in her hand. Something had
plucked at her mind. After a moment she dropped her eyes back to
the half sheet of pale blue paper with the name of the agency printed
across the top in a rich, darker blue ink. Miss Keating went through
the arch, reading as she walked, turned left, and stopped in front
of a door on which was lettered "Office of the Associate Director."
Miss Keating finished reading, opened the door without knocking,
went in, and put the sheet of pale blue paper in the middle of the
desk that almost filled the small room.

"Be with you in a minute," a girl called from the inner office.
"Who is it?"

"Miss Keating," Miss Keating said. "Don't bother. Mr. Jowett
wanted the lower echelon personnel estimate for the budget hearings." The memorandum would have reached Mr. Jowett just as
quickly if she had put it into the box on the desk in her own room.
The inter-office messenger system, which was one of Miss Keating's
responsibilities, was fast and efficient. When Miss Keating was dealing with something she considered important to herself, however,
she did not trust it even to a system she had herself created. "I'm
leaving it on your desk," she said. From the pile of letters at one side
of the desk Miss Keating took a paperweight, a round thick piece
of magnifying glass with a picture of the Lincoln Memorial pasted to
the flat bottom, and put it on the memorandum she had just
brought in. "There's no rush," she said.

"Mr. Jowett is out to lunch," his secretary called from the inner
office. "Just leave it on my desk."

Miss Keating went out and returned to her own room. It was not
large, perhaps twice as big as Mr. Jowett's secretary's room, but it had
a thermos water jug on a small table behind the desk, a nontipping
smoking stand next to the visitors' chair, and the desk itself had a
glass top. Miss Keating opened her black suède purse with the lucite
ball on the thong of the zipper, took out her large silver compact,
and made a few small adjustments to her face. She was a tall, cool,
pretty girl with a long, pointed chin and very black hair parted in the
middle and wound into two severe buns at the base of her skull.
Miss Keating, who was twenty-eight, looked a year or two past thirty

and would probably look exactly the same age for another six or seven years. She had that kind of face.

Miss Keating snapped the compact shut, plucked a loose hair from the shoulder of her good, neat, well-cut, single-button black suit, adjusted the collar of her pin-tucked white silk blouse, slipped the purse up under her arm, and looked at her wristwatch. It was twelve-thirty. The heavy silver bracelet, which matched her heavy silver earrings, both purchased during her summer in Mexico after she graduated from Wellesley, tinkled dully as Miss Keating walked out of her room and down the long corridor to the south end of the building.

As she put her hand on the knob and pushed in the door of the room that housed the typists' pool, Miss Keating knew what it was that had plucked at her mind a few minutes earlier. The clatter of typewriters that could usually be heard forty feet down the corridor was missing. A dozen girls looked up when Miss Keating came in. They were standing around the desk of Nancy Hull, the little girl from Vermont with the cute figure and the round face. A box from the Statler Flower Shoppe, in which a corsage of gardenias lay in a bed of crinkled green wax paper, stood on Nancy's typewriter and an open box of candy sat on her desk calendar. Nancy was holding a smaller box, about two inches square, and her lips were pursed in a small circle of awed delight. All the girls looked up at Miss Keating in the doorway and then stepped back a little, as though to clear a path between her and Nancy.

"Hello," Miss Keating said with a smile. "It's twelve-thirty, Nancy. Ready?"

"Yes, I'm ready," Nancy said. "Look, Miss Keating. The girls gave them to me. Aren't they pretty?"

Miss Keating came forward and took the box from Nancy and looked at the silver earrings in their small square nest of white cotton.

"Yes, they are," Miss Keating said, and she handed the box back. "They're lovely."

"They're just the most beautiful things I ever had," Nancy said. "And look, flowers, too, and a box of candy. Honestly, I'm so, gosh, I don't know what to say." Nancy smiled at the girls around her and they smiled back happily, but none of them spoke. "Would you like a piece of candy, Miss Keating?" Nancy said, picking up the box from the desk calendar. "They're delicious."

"Thanks, Nancy, not before lunch, I don't think," Miss Keating said. "Perhaps later. Hadn't we better go along?"

"Oh, yes," Nancy said, and she giggled. "I'm so excited, honestly, I don't know if I'm coming or going." She put the cover on the box of earrings and she put the box into her purse, a large white bag made of imitation leather that matched the belt around the waist of her flowered organdy dress and her white high-heeled shoes. "'Bye, now," she said to the girls. "I'll see you later. Meantime, thanks a million again."

The girls murmured in a happy group, but none of them said anything distinguishable, and Miss Keating and Nancy Hull went out.

"They're so sweet, honestly, Miss Keating," Nancy said as they walked down the corridor. "It makes me feel terrible to be leaving."

"Why don't you reconsider, then?" Miss Keating said. "And stay?" Nancy looked startled, as though a completely revolutionary idea for which she was wholly unprepared had been tossed into her mind, and her shoulder bumped the jamb of the doorway into which she was turning, the doorway that led to the hall that led to the cafeteria. Miss Keating took Nancy's elbow and pulled her back gently into the corridor. "No," Miss Keating said. "We're eating upstairs."

"Upstairs?" Nancy said and then, when she understood, she said, "Oh, upstairs."

They walked on to the elevator and Nancy stood there quietly, playing with the snap fastener of her white imitation leather purse, while Miss Keating pressed the button. Neither of them spoke. The elevator came and they stepped in and Miss Keating said, "Five, please," and they got out on the fifth floor. Here Miss Keating went on ahead and Nancy followed a foot or two behind. The executives' dining room was not crowded, because the rush didn't start until one, but half the tables were taken.

"Two today," Miss Keating said to the white-haired woman with the armful of menus who was standing near the cashier's desk. "A side table if you have it, please?"

The woman nodded and gave Nancy a short glance before she led the way across the room. Everybody in the room looked up and several men smiled and nodded to Miss Keating, who smiled and nodded back. Aside from the white-haired woman, Miss Keating and Nancy were the only girls in the room. They sat down at a wall table, facing each other, and Nancy didn't know what to do with her bag until she saw Miss Keating put her black suède purse on the table, leaning it against the wall next to the sugar bowl. Nancy did the same, and she waited until Miss Keating took the folded paper napkin from the plate in front of her and opened it and spread it on her lap, before she picked up her own napkin. The white-haired woman handed Miss Keating a mimeographed menu and then gave one to Nancy.

"I thought I'd be able to put my hands on a leg of lamb for to-day, but no luck," the white-haired woman said, speaking to Miss Keating. "The meat loaf is good, though, and we have real hot fudge to go with the chocolate ice cream."

"I'll have the apricot salad," Miss Keating said, handing back the menu. "And a hot fudge sundae. No beverage. You, Nancy?"

"I'll have the same," Nancy said. "With a glass of milk?"

"Wouldn't you rather have the meat loaf?" Miss Keating said. "It's so hard to get these days?"

"No, I'll have the salad," Nancy said. "And a glass of milk, please?"

The white-haired woman wrote the order, took back the mimeographed menus, and went away. Nancy looked around the room quickly, as though memorizing her surroundings for the future, and she saw the white-haired woman give their order slips to a Negro waiter before she brought her glance back to the maple table top in front of her.

"I was quite serious," Miss Keating said. "Why don't you reconsider and stay?"

"Gosh, I'd like to," Nancy said. "But I just can't, Miss Keating."

"Why?" Miss Keating said with a smile. "Someone you're interested in back home in Vermont?"

Nancy looked up, as though she had been punched, and then she started to blush. She shook her head quickly.

"Oh, no, Miss Keating," she said. "It's not that."

"What is it, then?" Miss Keating said. "You can tell me, Nancy."

"Gosh, there isn't anything to tell," Nancy said uncomfortably. "Honest, Miss Keating. It's just I feel I've got to get back home."

"I see," Miss Keating said, and she leaned back to let the waiter set down the salads. She waited until he went away before she leaned forward again. "How old are you, Nancy?"

"How old?" Nancy said. "Twenty-one," she said. "Last April."

"Twenty-one," Miss Keating said. "And how long have you been in Washington?"

"A little over ten months," Nancy said. "Be eleven months next week."

"Oh, then you worked for somebody else before you came with us?" Miss Keating said.

"I was with Agriculture for two months when I first came," Nancy said. "And then I switched to OSS for four months before I got this job."

"First time away from home?" Miss Keating said with a small, kind smile. Nancy nodded. "Where do you live here in Washington?"

"I've got a room in a house up on Holly Street, near Silver Spring," Nancy said. "They're very nice people; her two sons are in the army and she has the space."

"Holly Street," Miss Keating said. "That's all the way out in the third alphabet, isn't it?"

"Yes," Nancy said. "But it's not so bad, Miss Keating. I take the Georgia and Alaska bus down Sixteenth, and then I transfer to the Number Thirty trolley at Pennsylvania and Fifteenth. It's only about forty-five, fifty minutes. Sometimes less."

Miss Keating put down her fork, wiped a dab of cottage cheese and apricot delicately from the corner of her mouth with the paper napkin, and looked down at her heavy silver bracelet. She moved it back and forth on her wrist for several moments, chinking the thick links dully against each other, her wide, smooth forehead, from which the black hair was so neatly combed away, creased in thought. Finally, she looked up and leaned forward again.

"Look, Nancy," Miss Keating said. "I don't want you to think I'm prying into your personal affairs, but there is something I'd like to say to you and it has nothing to do with the office. I'm speaking of you, Nancy. You personally. You understand that, don't you?"

"Yes," Nancy said, because there was nothing else to say, and she stared across the table at the cool, tall, pretty girl wearing the sort of suit it had never occurred to Nancy Hull to buy, the girl playing with the sort of heavy silver bracelet Nancy Hull had never dreamed of wanting, and even though she didn't understand at all, Nancy nodded again. "Yes," she said. "I understand."

"I'm so glad you do, Nancy," Miss Keating said. "Because this is so important to you, so much more important than you can imagine at the moment, Nancy. This is the first time you've ever been away from home, the first time you've been out of Vermont, the first time you've been in a large, metropolitan city. I know how difficult it is, how much you can miss your home and how lonely you can be in a large, strange city, even when you work all day with a group of nice, friendly girls, and how strong the temptation is to pack up and leave and go back. That's just the thing you mustn't do, Nancy. Because if you do that you admit defeat, you admit to yourself that the big city, the outside world has beaten you. And once you take a beating like that, you never really recover. You never again have the nerve to take a second chance. You're stuck up there for the rest of your life, you're locked away forever in a prison of your own making, in Vermont or Minnesota or Arkansas or wherever it is. You must fight it, Nancy. You mustn't give in. You mustn't crawl back, beaten."

Miss Keating stopped and leaned back, and the younger girl with the round face, wearing the cheap organdy dress, stared down at the table as the waiter took away her half-eaten apricot salad and replaced it with a hot fudge sundae.

"Thank you, Miss Keating," she said in a low voice. "You're very nice to me and I think you're right in what you say, but I don't know, it isn't exactly that."

"Waiter, we get one glass of milk here," Miss Keating said. The waiter nodded and went away and Miss Keating said, "What is it, Nancy?"

"It's, oh, I don't know how to say it," Nancy said and then, to her own surprise, it seemed all right to say it. "I came here because my three brothers are in the army and I wanted to do something in the war effort and Miss Lauchlin, she's our high school principal in Battle Forks, she said they needed girls who could type and take shorthand in Washington, and my mother and father said it was right to go. But they didn't have much for me to do in Agriculture, I don't know why, so I switched to OSS, but it wasn't much better there, so I came here. I don't mean that I haven't been given enough to do here," Nancy said quickly. "It's just that when you're in the pool you don't feel you're working for anybody in particular, you just do whatever comes along and you take dictation from anybody that happens to need a stenographer that minute. What I mean is, you don't belong to anybody, you don't see your part of it piling up, sort of. You don't get the feeling you're helping with the war effort. It's just bits and pieces. But it's not only that," Nancy said, talking faster, rushing the words now, to get it all out before she was interrupted. "It's also I can't make out on my salary. I just can't, no matter how hard I try. Everything is so expensive here, by the time I pay my rent and buy my trolley pass and my lunches and suppers and my laundry and all those things, gosh, Miss Keating, there's nothing left. Last month I went to the dentist and I had to write my mother to send me the money to pay him. It makes a person feel terrible to do that, Miss Keating, write home for money when you're working and earning. I bought only three dresses in the whole ten months, nearly eleven, the whole eleven months I been here, and my mother and father, every month they have to send me something so I won't have to borrow from the other girls. That's not right, Miss Keating. They shouldn't be sending me money. I should be sending them something every month. That's the way it should be."

She stopped and looked up with a frightened little start, then she saw who it was and she leaned back to make room for the waiter. He set down the glass of milk and looked inquiringly at Miss Keating.

"That's all, thank you," Miss Keating said. "Nothing else."

The waiter took from his outer breast pocket the checks the white-haired woman had written. He added the figures, scribbled the totals, and put the checks on the table face down. Miss Keating pulled the two slips of paper toward her and tucked the corners under the edge of her purse.

"I'm glad you told me all this, Nancy," she said. "It's partly my fault that you haven't had an opportunity to tell me sooner, but that's how it is in Washington. You don't get to know a person until the day that person is leaving, when you take her to lunch for the first time to say goodbye." Miss Keating folded her long, slender fingers on the table and leaned forward. "If we could find you a place to live nearer the center of things, Nancy? Near Dupont Circle, for instance, where I live, and not all the way out there in the third alphabet? And if I talked to the administrative office about getting you upgraded, say to CAF 5, or even a six, perhaps? And if we could do something about not letting you grow so lonely, have lunch together once in a while, or something like that? I might even talk to Supply and get you a noiseless instead of that rattletrap old L. C. Smith? Nancy, if I could do all that, would you reconsider and—?" Miss Keating stopped, and the look of intense seriousness disappeared as her long, pointed chin tilted upward in a sudden, eager smile. "Hello, Mr. Jowett," she said. "I recommend the meat loaf. It's very good."

Nancy turned quickly. The Associate Director had stopped behind her chair.

"Thanks, I've just finished," Mr. Jowett said. "Sorry to bother you at lunch," he said across Nancy's head. "But I saw you on my way out and I thought I'd ask about that memorandum?"

"It's on your secretary's desk," Miss Keating said. "I left it there half an hour ago."

"I should have known better than to ask," Mr. Jowett said, laughing. "If the rest of my staff was as efficient as you are, I'd be the happiest bureaucrat in the war effort. We can't afford to lose any more of our stenographic help. If these kids keep on going home we'll have to close up shop. How does it look?"

"Not so bad," Miss Keating said, and her voice, suddenly edged with warning, went up slightly. "I think I can guarantee that your lower echelons won't be decimated."

Mr. Jowett's eyebrows went up, and he made a circle with his lips, and he looked down quickly at the top of Nancy's head, and then he winked across the younger girl at Miss Keating.

"Check," Mr. Jowett said. "Keep up the good work," he said, and he waved as he moved off toward the cashier's desk. "See you later," Mr. Jowett said.

Miss Keating followed him with her smile for a moment and then the smile disappeared as she brought her intense, serious glance back to Nancy and leaned forward again.

"If I did all those things, Nancy," she said. "Or tried, anyway? Would you reconsider and stay?" Nancy didn't answer. "For your own good?" Miss Keating said. "Will you not admit defeat and give yourself another chance?"

Nancy Hull's round little face was set so hard that, for the first time in her life, she looked older than her years and then, as she caught her lower lip in her teeth and bit hard, she looked young again. Young and something else, something new that was not part of her youth.

"Perhaps I could even get you out of that awful crowded room at the south end?" Miss Keating said. "And have you attached to one of the executives?"

Nancy reached across the table and took one of the two checks from under the edge of Miss Keating's purse and she looked at it. Salad twenty-three cents, sundae eighteen cents, milk six cents, total forty-seven cents. It was the right one. She'd had the milk.

"Oh, now, look," Miss Keating said, reaching out. "I'm taking that. I invited you."

"No," Nancy said, and she picked up her white imitation leather purse and she leaned back, as far as she could get, pressing the luncheon check against the purse so hard that she could feel the small box inside. "I'll pay my own," Nancy said.

"But how silly," Miss Keating said. "Let me have it, Nancy. You're my guest."

Nancy shook her head, trying not to think of the things she had said, trying to think it was only that she would never be able to wear the earrings in the little box because she would always remember that Miss Keating had been wearing a pair exactly like them when she had trapped Nancy into saying those things.

"I'll pay my own check," Nancy Hull said, getting up. "I'm not your guest."

The Tuxedos

Ever since the time, some ten years ago, when I worked for Mr. Brunschweig on Canal Street, I have been peculiarly sensitive to the half-hour of the day that comes between five-thirty and six o'clock in the late afternoon. Mr. Brunschweig was an excellent boss, as bosses go, except for one lamentable defect: he was a minute-pincher. He carried two large pocket watches and spent a good part of each day comparing them with each other and with the huge Seth Thomas on the wall. I am certain that he was a little terrified by the inexorableness of time and that his sensitivity to it was a direct result of the way he earned his living. Mr. Brunschweig rented tuxedos.

The tuxedo-renting business, as I knew it, was distinguished by two cardinal rules. First, the suits had to be made of the toughest and heaviest materials available. And second, it was necessary to deliver them as close to the moment of wearing as possible and even more imperative to pick them up as soon after they were taken off as the wearer would permit. Mr. Brunschweig's timing in this respect was so good and I was so nimble as a delivery boy that while many of his customers cursed him roundly for having delayed them in getting to a wedding, not one of them could say with honesty that he had worn a Brunschweig tuxedo to more than one affair for the price of a single renting.

My relations with Mr. Brunschweig were amicable if somewhat exhausting, but every day, as the hands of the clock crept around to half-past five, a definite tension would come into the atmosphere. My quitting time was six o'clock. As a general rule, Mr. Brunschweig arranged deliveries in such fashion that the last one carried me up to, or past, that hour. We had an understanding to the effect that if I took out a delivery at any time after five-thirty and could not get to my destination until six o'clock or a few minutes before, I did not have to return to the Canal Street store that night and was at liberty to go directly home. However, the possibility of his only employee departing for home five or ten minutes ahead of quitting time was so disturbing to Mr. Brunschweig that very often he would detain me in the store before I went out on my final delivery, talking about the weather or discussing the baseball scores, just to make sure that I could not possibly complete the delivery before six o'clock.

Strangely enough, I did not resent these obvious subterfuges, because I sensed that Mr. Brunschweig was a little ashamed of them. What I did resent was that unconsciously I was being forced into practices I didn't approve of to combat him.

For instance, I would instinctively stall on any delivery after five-fifteen to make certain that I would not get back to the store in time to make another delivery before quitting. Or I would rush through a four-o'clock delivery to make sure that there would be ample time for still another one before six o'clock. In either case it was very unsettling, and scarcely a day went by that I didn't have a struggle with my conscience or the clock.

There were times, of course, when my energy overcame my caution. One day, in an industrious mood, I returned from an uptown delivery at twenty minutes to six. It had been a long trip and I could have stretched it for another twenty minutes with ease, but I had temporarily forgotten Mr. Brunschweig's vice and I did not realize my mistake until I came into the store. He was boxing an unusually large order, and I could tell from his cheery greeting that this one would carry me well past six o'clock. I was about to dismiss the occurrence as simply another occasion on which I had been outmaneuvered by Mr. Brunschweig when I saw that he had stacked six boxes, one on top of the other.

"Is that *one* delivery?" I asked in amazement.

The average delivery weighed well over ten pounds and consisted of a tuxedo, a shirt, a tie, studs, and a pair of patent-leather pumps, packed neatly into a heavy cardboard box. Two or three of these boxes were a load. Six of them were an incredible amount.

"Yeah," he said cheerfully. "Italian wedding. It all goes to one family. I'll give you a help to the subway."

I should have been grateful to him for this offer, I suppose, since it was an unusual move, but all I could think of was the prospect of juggling sixty pounds of tuxedos through the subway in the rush hour.

"Where's it going?" I asked.

"Brooklyn," he said. "It's just over the bridge. Won't take you long."

The boxes weighed so much I could scarcely raise them from the floor.

"Here," he said. "You take the hats. I'll take the suits till we get to the train."

I hadn't even thought about top hats. They were not very heavy, but they were the most perishable items in Mr. Brunschweig's stock and consequently were always packed with great care in individual boxes.

"We gotta hurry," Mr. Brunschweig said, handing me a slip of paper with an address on it. "It's the bride's family and I promised them early. Name is Lasquadro."

He took the lashed tuxedo boxes and I took the pile of hatboxes, tied one on top of another so that they resembled a small steamship funnel. In the street we paused for a moment while he locked the store, and then we started off down Canal Street to the subway station.

The only satisfactory recollection I have of that evening is the brief memory of Mr. Brunschweig tottering along in front of me under the weight of six boxes of tuxedos and accessories. The rest was a nightmare. I remember being on the subway platform, between my two huge bundles, trying to get into train after train. I had to let seven or eight go by before I could wedge my way into one of them. Then I remember standing, perspiring and exhausted, outside the subway station in Brooklyn, looking at the two bundles and realizing that I could carry them no further. It had grown quite dark and I began to be worried, too, about being late with the delivery. Finally I worked out a plan. I dragged the tuxedos along the ground for a short distance, then went back for the hats, dragged them up to the tuxedos, and then repeated the process. It was an effective method but an extremely slow one. Though the address Mr. Brunschweig had given me was only three blocks from the Brooklyn subway station, it was almost twenty minutes later that I stopped, breathless, in front of the correct house number.

The street was deserted and dark; the house was a two-story brownstone affair and only the basement windows showed lights from behind drawn shades. As I wiped the perspiration from my face and tried to think of an excuse for being so late, I heard noises coming from the basement. Figures kept passing the windows quickly and the sounds of scuffling and angry voices reached me clearly. I was frightened and spent another precious minute trying to puzzle out a way of leaving my bundles without having to face the people inside the house.

Then, in a burst of nervous courage, I tumbled the bulky bundles down the steps that led to the basement door and knocked gently. There was no answer. The angry noises inside continued, and I knocked again. Still no answer. Then I discovered a push button on the wall beside the door, jabbed at it hastily, and a bell pealed shrilly somewhere inside the house. At once the door was pulled open and a small young man in shirtsleeves, with a tight, dark, scowling face, shot his head out and glared at me.

"What the hella *you* want?" he demanded harshly.

"The—the tuxedos," I said awkwardly. "I brought the tuxedos."

The young man turned his head and yelled at someone in the room behind him. "He brought the tuxedos! You hear that? He brought the tuxedos!"

He laughed unpleasantly and a man's voice replied from inside the room, "Tell him he knows what he can do with them!"

The young man in front of me reached for the door and started to slam it shut. The thought that I might have to drag those two bundles back to Canal Street that night was enough to make me forget my fright. I braced my shoulder against the door and held it open.

"I have to leave these here," I said quickly. "I have to—I have to get the receipt signed."

The little dark face glared at me and the hand on the door drew back threateningly. "Aah," he started to say, and then stopped. "O.K., O.K., come on. Bring 'em in and beat it."

He dragged the bundles in and the door swung shut behind me. As I began to fumble in my pocket for the receipt book, I stole a scared look at the scene in the room. It was a large, shabbily furnished living room, with a new radio in one corner, a huge potted rubber plant in another, and embroidered mottoes on the wall. A pretty, dark-haired girl in a white wedding gown was sitting at a table in the middle of the room. Five men, all in vests and shirtsleeves and all looking as if they must be brothers of the young man who had opened the door for me, were standing over her. One of the men held the girl and was twisting her arm behind her, and she was sobbing violently. A tiny old woman, with white hair in a knot at the back of her head and wearing a black alpaca apron, hovered on the outskirts of the group around the table, jabbering shrilly in Italian. The young man who had let me in joined his brothers. Nobody paid any attention to me.

"Come on," one of the men said, leaning over the girl. "What's his address? Give us that address!"

The girl shook her head and the man who was holding her arm gave it another twist. She screamed and dropped her head forward. Another man pushed his face down close to hers.

"Come on!" he yelled. "Give it to us. We're doing this for the family, ain't we? What's his address?"

The girl shook her head again; the little old lady chattered away. One of the brothers reached over and slapped the girl's face.

"Where was he when he called up?" he said. "Come on, tell us. We ain't gonna hurt him. We'll just murder the louse, that's all. Where was he?"

She didn't answer.

"Come on, you damn fool," the man who held her arm said. "Talk! You want him to go spreading it to the whole world he walked out on you an hour before the wedding?" He shook her angrily. "Where was he when he called up? Where does he live? We'll fix him so he won't talk. What's his address?"

The girl did not answer. He started to shake her again, then he saw me standing near the door. "Get that guy out of here," he said. The brother who had let me in came across the room in three steps and grabbed my shoulder. "Come on, kid," he said. "Beat it!"

I lifted my receipt book in front of his face. "The receipt," I said. "I must get my receipt signed. I can't leave the—" He snatched the book from me and fumbled in his vest pocket for a pencil. He couldn't find one. I held my own out to him and he scribbled his name in my receipt book.

"O.K., kid," he said sharply. "Outside!" and he shoved the receipt book and pencil at me. I took them and started toward the door. Suddenly the little old lady grabbed my arm and pulled me back.

"What the hellsa matter?" the young man asked angrily.

She gestured violently toward me and poured a stream of Italian at him.

"All right, all right," he said, and reached into his pocket, pulled out a coin, and tossed the tip to me. I caught it and turned toward the door again.

"Thanks," I said quickly. But before I could open the door the old lady was on me. She clawed at my hand until I opened it so she could see the coin. It was a quarter. She swung around to the young man and clutched his coat.

"What the hellsa matter now?" he cried. "I gave him the tip, didn't I?"

Again she started talking in Italian, pointing at the bundle of tuxedos and tapping off the boxes with her finger—one, two, three, four, five, six. She waved six fingers in his face and yelled at him. He bit his lip, dug into his pocket again, and slapped some more coins into my palm. At once the little old lady seized my hand again. Now there were two quarters, a dime, and a nickel in it. She counted them quickly, snatched up the nickel, and counted again. Sixty cents remained. Another glance at the tuxedos and another glance at the two quarters and dime in my hand. Six tuxedos. Sixty cents. She nodded sharply to herself. Now it was all right.

"Give us that address!" shouted one of the brothers. There was the sound of a slap and the girl screamed again. "Where was he when he called up?"

The little old lady pulled open the door, pushed me out roughly, and slammed it shut behind me.

Twice Blest

One day the people on Fourth Street woke up and found a spick living among them. He was a little bit of a man, dark and sleek-haired, and smiling and cringing. He moved into our house one night with his few sticks of furniture and his tiny wife, also dark and sleek-haired, and smiling and cringing. These diminutive Spaniards were out of place on our block. They didn't belong. It was a Jewish neighborhood, with an Italian barber, one or two Irish janitors, and a Chinese laundryman. Once in a while a Negro would pass through, sitting on top of a wagonload of coal coming from the dock. But, until this one settled among us, there were no spicks. He was a bus-boy in a Borough Hall cafeteria in Brooklyn, and he chose to live in our midst, far from the rest of his kind. The rent must have been the inducement. It was very low.

The boys of the block would wait until he showed up, hugging the building line as he came down the street, taking short steps, jerking his head from side to side, watching everything with a little scared smile. One of us would begin to follow. Soon there would be a crowd of us behind him. He would break into a run and we would chase him, throwing things at him, until he disappeared into the doorway of my house.

That summer we were getting ready to move. We moved every summer. It was easier to do that than to have the flat repainted. Everything was ready. The dishes were packed into barrels and the bedding was tied into bundles. That was all we were taking with us this time. For the new place, Mother had bought furniture and curtains and carpets and fixings. Everything new. We had the money, she said, so we might as well use it. Her theory was that if the banks should close suddenly, at least we would know that we had used the money well.

Everything new. But what about the old stuff? What about the furniture that had been with us all the years that I could remember —before I was born? It was old and big and funny-looking. But it was still solid and good. We couldn't take it along. And it was a shame to throw it out. So Mother decided to sell it.

Sell it to whom? The man who owned the moving van? He laughed when she asked him. Buy that old junk? For what? For firewood it was good, maybe. He could cut it up and take it away in pieces. But for furniture he should buy it? Go away!

The spick? Why not? Here, Mother decided, was a customer. And she sent me to fetch him.

They lived on the floor above us. I ran up and knocked on the door. It was Sunday, and he was home. He opened the door softly and looked out at me, fear in his eyes. Behind him I could see the scared face of his little wife, the large eyes frightened and staring, the red mouth open. They didn't speak. They just looked at me, afraid. Scared of a kid of twelve.

"Come on down," I said roughly, the way we always talked to him. "My mother wants to see you."

He nodded his head several times, saying, "Yes, yes, yes," and came out to follow me. She closed the door behind him, and from the look on her face I knew she would throw herself down somewhere, shivering with fright, and cry her eyes out until he came back.

He followed me downstairs.

"Here he is, Ma," I called, and my mother came out and took him by the arm and led him into the front room, where the furniture was.

"You want to buy some furniture cheap?" she asked. He did not answer. He just stood there, hunched over, his lips working, his fingers knitting, and, I swear, his knees trembling.

"Maybe he doesn't speak English, Ma," I said, but he nodded a little faster and rubbed his hands a little harder and said, "Me understand, lady. Me understand."

Mother explained about the furniture, going into detail about its various qualities. She smacked the sides to show how solid it was. She pulled out drawers to show its excellent condition. And all the while that she talked, he listened.

Then, still servile, still afraid, his head began to shake from side to side, negatively, and his smile became apologetic.

"Don't you want it?" Mother asked.

"No, lady," he said softly and sadly, pointing to the ceiling, indicating his wife in the tiny apartment above us. "She wants—like this—with a mirror—like this," and he made motions in the air, describing a piece of furniture.

"But this is good and solid," my mother said. "And you can have it cheap. Cheap. Understand? Cheap!"

Now the fear in his face was mixed with sorrow. He spoke slowly, still making the long, descriptive gestures. "With a—mirror—she wants."

And suddenly it dawned on me that he meant a dressing table. One of those trick arrangements with two sets of drawers, one on either side, and a mirror in the middle. She wanted one of those delicate, spindly things, and Mother was trying to force this huge ox of an affair, dating from the year one, upon him.

"I promise her—with a mirror. She wants—like this—with a mirror."

Mother didn't understand. To her, this massive creation was good. Good enough for spicks. Better than they were accustomed to. She couldn't understand his refusal. There was a mirror in this thing, too, wasn't there? Look!

But he only smiled that sickly smile of his and apologized with his hands, his arms, his eyes, his whole body. "With a mirror—like this—she wants."

Mother was exasperated. She offered it to him at any price he named. But he didn't want it. At her wits' end, she made him a gift of it. But still that cringing refusal.

"Don't you want it for nothing?" she cried, amazed and angry.

"No, lady," he said, his face creased with pain. "I promise her— like this—with a mirror—she wants."

He said it over and over, cowering fearfully from Mother's insistence. Suddenly I couldn't stand it any longer.

"Let him alone, Ma. He doesn't want it," I said, stepping between them. "Let him alone, Ma," I repeated, following him and covering his retreat to the door as he went out backward. I could feel the look of gratitude he turned upon me. But I could not bring myself to meet his eyes. I kept looking at the floor until the door opened and closed and I knew he was gone.

After that I never chased or threw things at a spick again.

The Waiting Game

Whenever I see a guidebook I am reminded of a remark I once heard a woman make about dictionaries. "They're all right if you know how to spell," she said bitterly. "But what good is one to me? I spent hours trying to find 'giraffe' under the letter j!"

According to our guidebook, *the Villa d'Este (16th cent.) on Lake Como is a former residence of Caroline of Brunswick, when she was Princess of Wales.*

"Who was Caroline of Brunswick?" my wife said.

I didn't know, and the lack of knowledge seemed curiously disconcerting. We had just arrived. Everything was exactly as our friends had told us it would be. In fact, it was better. The management had apparently mistaken us for honeymooners. They had given us a corner room on the second floor. Thus we had two views of the lake and the gaudy mountains that surround it. We also had two balconies between which we would have to choose when breakfast was served the next morning. At the moment it was late in the afternoon and my wife was unpacking while I tried to orient her, as well as myself, by reading aloud from the guidebook.

"What was she doing in Italy?" she asked.

"I don't know. The guidebook doesn't say."

"While I finish unpacking, why don't you go down to the desk and see if they've got any literature on her," my wife said. "It'll be time for cocktails soon, and I don't think I'll enjoy mine unless I know a little more about Caroline of Brunswick."

479

The chances of enlightening my wife from the store of knowledge possessed by the man at the desk were soon demonstrated to be slim.

"Caroline who?" he asked.

"Caroline of Brunswick," I said.

"I will look, *signore*." The man behind the desk turned to the registry index. "There is a Mrs. Caroline Brewster," he said. "Will she do?"

"No, of course not," I said. "I'm trying to—"

"Since when won't she do?"

I turned to face the person who had asked this. "Carrie!" I said.

I put out my hand, but Carrie Brewster had been living in Hollywood since 1939. Hollywood is a community in which only prize fighters shake hands. Carrie Brewster threw her arms around me and kissed me.

"Darling!" she said. "What are you doing here?"

"Celebrating my tenth wedding anniversary."

"Good heavens!" she said. "It's been a long time, hasn't it?"

"Sixteen years," I said.

"You were always good at dates." Carrie examined me through narrowed eyes, as though she were trying to guess my weight. "You've lost some more hair. But that's about all. How about me?"

"You've had your nose fixed."

A look of concern raced swiftly across her bold, handsome face. "Is it so very noticeable?"

"No, of course not," I said. "I read about it in the papers."

"What else have you read in the papers?"

"Nothing much," I said. "I'm a family man now. I don't have much time for reading the papers. What are you doing here?"

"Nick has been shooting a picture with Gaby Pagini in San Gimignano for the last six weeks. It's one of those costume affairs about the Borgias; she wears very little and he wears tights. They're finishing up around noon. I left early and drove up with the bags. Nick will be getting in around seven. We thought we'd spend a couple of weeks just resting up and loafing before we fly home." She turned and looked out at what the extraordinary sunset was doing to the lake and the mountains. "Isn't this absolute heaven?"

"That's why my wife and I came," I said.

"Why don't we have dinner together?" Caroline said. "We'd love to meet your wife."

"All right," I said.

"The bar at seven?"

"All right," I said.

I went back upstairs, wondering how best to explain to my wife not about Caroline of Brunswick, but Caroline Brewster. It was not going to be easy. Nick Brewster himself had never been able to explain her, not even in the early days of our friendship, when he had still been known to the world as Nat Brinker.

In those days, when neither of us was yet old enough to vote, he was an intense, sullen young man who used to play basketball in a gym to which I sometimes went for a workout. He had curly black hair and a tremendous number of muscles. We never spoke to each other beyond the few words necessary to keep the game under way. Then, one night after my shower, I found him getting dressed three lockers down from mine.

I nodded and uttered a casual greeting. It was as though some inner trigger of reserve had been tripped. By the time I was tying my necktie, he had explained to me why I was missing so many off shots, introduced himself as Nat Brinker, told me he was an actor, and asked what I was doing with the next half hour or so.

"I've got an eight-thirty class down at Washington Square every night," I said. "I usually get something to eat first."

"How about getting it at Steeger's? I'll have coffee with you," Nat Brinker said. "My girl's meeting me there at eight."

"Okay, but let's get going," I said. "I've got a little less than an hour."

Nat Brinker filled the time by telling me all about his girl. The phrase was his. What he actually told me could hardly have been considered "all about" anybody.

"Wait till you see her," Nat Brinker said as he peered anxiously toward the door. "Just wait till you see her."

But I couldn't wait. I had that class.

"I guess she's been held up somewhere," I said. "I'll be late."

"You coming to the gym tomorrow? I'll make another date with Carrie," Nat Brinker said. "You'll meet her tomorrow."

I didn't. Even though we waited in Steeger's for almost an hour before I had to leave to make my class.

After five or six of these sessions, during which the promised Carrie failed to make her appearance, I had learned a good deal about Nat Brinker. He was an orphan who had grown up in a tough neighborhood on Manhattan's West Side. But this short, muscular boy had come under the influence of the director of a settlement house who had a flair for amateur theatricals.

His unchanneled energies, which had been driving him toward juvenile delinquency, were suddenly poured in a single direction, and he began to live for that strange ambition: theatrical stardom.

Nat Brinker was not very bright. He was almost completely uneducated and it was impossible for him to read more than ten printed pages without suffering actual physical pain. But he had an extraordinary gift for mimicry, and he was powered by savage energy. In the theater these are frequently enough.

They were enough to carry Nat Brinker from the settlement house to fairly regular employment as a radio actor, and when I met him he had had three or four bit parts on Broadway.

When ambition appears in an essentially simple-minded person, there is almost nothing to baffle the imagination of the observer. Consequently I was not surprised to find Nat Brinker a bore, but what did surprise me was his relationship to the mysterious Carrie.

"Why does she make these dates with you," I asked, "if she has no intention of showing up?"

"No intention? You nuts or something? She'll get here, she'll get here," Nat Brinker said. "It's just she can't always control what happens."

"Why not?"

"She works on the registry desk over at Bellevue, but for Carrie that's only to buy groceries. It's like the way I do radio shows just to keep eating until I hit. What she wants to be, Carrie's big ambition, she's a painter."

"How good a painter is she?"

"How good?" Nat Brinker said. "She's terrific. Wait till you meet her."

About a week later my own girl invited me to a party over in Brooklyn that her parents were giving in honor of her brother. The girl her brother brought was tall and dark, with the sort of bold features that always draw a second glance.

The next night, when I was finishing dinner at Steeger's, Nat Brinker's sullen face brightened.

"Here she is!" he said. "Here comes my girl!" With a proud smile he introduced me to the girl with the bold features who had been at the party in Brooklyn.

"Hello," I said. "I think we've met."

"I don't think so," she said. I wondered if she was joking. She turned to Nat Brinker. "Waiting long?"

"Oh, no," he said happily. Not counting the seven preceding nights, we had been waiting almost an hour. "You sit down," he said. "I'll get you some coffee." He hurried away across the cafeteria to the steam tables.

"I don't know what the act is," I said, "but I don't think there are two girls in this town named Caroline Starr who look exactly alike. All I have to do is call—"

She laughed, and her laugh stayed with you, just as her features drew that second glance. Both made you a little uneasy.

"There isn't any act," she said. "It's just that Nat takes our friendship a lot more seriously than I do. He's a nice enough boy, and someday he might—" She shrugged. "I can't help it if he thinks I'm his girl."

"Are you?"

"Of course not."

"I see," I said. "Well, if you get any fun out of kidding him, I guess it's none of my business, but I think you ought not to let Nat go around telling people you're his girl."

"How can I stop him?"

"You talk English," I said. "And Nat understands quite a few words. Try telling him the half dozen that add up to the truth."

"Such as?"

"He's in love with you. He thinks you're his girl. If you're not, say so."

"It's not as easy as all that."

"Why not?"

"Nat's sort of simple-minded," she said. "I don't want to hurt his feelings."

"If you don't hurt his feelings now, all you'll do is hurt him really badly in the end. You can't let him go on like this, waiting for you night after night, while you're out with other men."

"Who says I can't?" she asked.

The confidence oozed out of me like air from a punctured balloon. I could feel my face flush. Carrie Starr watched me with a cool little smile.

"What do you get out of it?" I said. She didn't answer. "What do you *expect* to get out of it?" I said.

"Someday, when I think you're bright enough to understand," Caroline Starr said, "I may tell you."

Soon after I met her, Nat landed a part in a play that received fairly good notices. It ran for six weeks. During that time, I decided to leave law school and try for another career. My visits to the gym became less frequent, but when I did go, I played basketball with Nat Brinker. We still sat in Steeger's, drinking coffee and waiting for Carrie. And she still stood him up regularly.

I saw her around town, but the meetings were not especially cordial. Usually she was with somebody I didn't know, and, besides, I was bored with her and with Nat Brinker. Early in 1939, when I went abroad, it never occurred to me to look him up to say good-by.

About eight months later, in Sydney, Australia, I was asked to go to the movies with some people I had met in Singapore. They were eager to see a new American film that had rocketed to stardom an unknown actor named Nicholas Brewster.

Nicholas Brewster was none other than Nat Brinker. It was astonishing, but perfectly obvious, that he deserved the eminence he had achieved. His performance was magnificent. And there was absolutely no similarity between the Nat Brinker I had known and the Nicholas Brewster I had seen on the screen.

The man I had known was dull, sullen and not very bright. He was so lacking in perception that he had been unaware that the girl he thought was his girl was not even remotely that.

The actor I had just seen on the screen was vital and exciting. There was life in his every movement. There was intelligence in his grasp of the difficult role he played. When he talked, you listened. When he suffered, you suffered with him. He had that rare quality, the capacity to stir the heart.

"My word!" said the Australian girl sitting beside me. "That's quite a lad!" So he had sex appeal too.

A few weeks later, on my way back to New York, I paused for a brief visit with friends in Hollywood. Nick Brewster's name was in the forefront of most conversations. Even in that city of fantastic success stories, Nat Brinker's success story was more fantastic than most. I didn't mention to my friends or to anybody else the fact that, no more than a year ago, we had played basketball together. This reticence was not due to my disinclination to bask in reflected glory, even though I have always felt it is an illumination that makes most people look a bit sallow.

During my last months in New York I had dropped Nat Brinker because he had become a bore. I could hardly look him up now. But before I left Hollywood, I learned that I had misjudged Nat in another way too. Nick Brewster called me up.

"You big ape," he said with a touching mixture of eagerness and irritation. "Why didn't you let me know? From total strangers, by accident, I have to find out you been in town over a week?"

"Well, I—I've been busy."

"Busy? You talk to me about busy? You don't know what busy is until you get caught up in this town. Get a pencil and write down this address. You're coming to dinner tonight."

The house was in Bel-Air; it was a slightly implausible structure made of glass and sheet copper and redwood, built around a swimming pool and a butler. The butler started to tell me that Mr. Brewster would be down in a few minutes, but he never finished the sentence. At that moment Nick Brewster appeared with a basketball at the far side of the patio. He dribbled the ball fiercely across the flagstones, whooping as he went, circled me twice, leaped high in the air, dropped the ball into an olive tree, and enveloped me in a hug.

"You son of a gun!" he roared. "You look great!"

I told him he looked great too. But he didn't. Or perhaps I should say he didn't look the way I had expected him to look. I had expected him to look like Nick Brewster, the man on the screen who had affected me so. Instead, he looked like Nat Brinker, the man who had bored me in Steeger's. Apparently the transformation was purely professional.

"How about this!" he said, gesturing toward the pool and the sheet copper and the glass and the redwood. "Some dump, eh?"

I made the expected replies and accepted a drink from the butler.

"We'll have a few," Nick said. "While we wait for Carrie."

My reaction must have been reflected in my face, because he burst into laughter. "I guess you didn't know about Carrie and me," he said finally. "We got married the day after they sneaked my picture out in Glendale and the studio picked up my option."

All at once I felt I understood what it was that Carrie Starr had once said she might tell me someday when she thought I was bright enough to understand. "Congratulations," I said.

Nick and I had a few, and then we had a few more. But by ten thirty, when it was silly for either of us to keep up the pretense that we were not yet hungry, Nick and I went in to dinner alone.

"She'll get here in a little while," he said apologetically. "It's just she can't always control what happens."

"Why not?" I said.

"Carrie's working pretty hard at her painting. When she gets really going, she forgets all about time."

"Where does she do this painting?"

"She's got a studio up in the hills. Carrie doesn't want me to see any of her stuff until she's ready to show it."

When I left, at two in the morning, Carrie had not yet come home. The following day I went up to San Francisco to visit friends for a few days before going on to New York. Three days later the telephone woke me.

"Hello?"

"Come out of it, darling. You sound drugged. This is Carrie."

"Who?"

"How many Carries do you know?"

"Oh," I said, and I sat up in bed. "Where are you?"

"At the Mark Hopkins. We came up last night for the opening of Nick's new picture. What are you doing?"

"Trying to find my slippers."

"When you do, how about coming up to our suite for breakfast?"

"All right," I said.

It was not a happy occasion. The trouble was that all three of us tried hard to make it seem a reunion, and it's pretty difficult to re-unite what was never joined together.

Nick and I, for all the basketball we had played together and for all the hours we had spent at Steeger's waiting for Carrie, had never really been friends. And Carrie and I had never been more than acquaintances. They were so determined, however, to pretend otherwise that I could not deny them whatever satisfaction they found. All I got out of the meeting was that nothing much had changed.

Nat was obviously as madly in love with Carrie as he had ever been and, just as obviously, she was no closer than she had ever been to feeling for him anything even remotely resembling genuine affection. While all the rest of the world might know she actually cared nothing for him, Nick Brewster was as unaware of the deception as Nat Brinker had been.

Breakfast ended with both Brewsters insisting that I accompany them to Nick's opening that night. We arranged to meet at six.

When I arrived at the Brewster suite that evening, Nick was alone. "Where's Carrie?" I asked.

Nick's face looked as it had when we used to wait at Steeger's, and as it had when we dined together at his house. It was a look I would always associate with him, no matter how many times he changed his name or how many fortunes he acquired; it was the look of a bewildered puppy, cringing slightly but resigned to the inevitable blow, yet pitifully hoping that just this once it won't come.

"She'll be here in a little while," Nick said.

We had a quick drink, and then another one, and then I looked at my wristwatch.

"Maybe she figured we were supposed to meet at the restaurant," Nick said hesitantly. "Yeah," he added with more conviction. "That must be it. Let's get going. Carrie's waiting for us at the restaurant right now."

She wasn't, of course, and when we finished dinner Carrie was still missing.

"She'll be at the theater," Nick said. "She got stuck somewhere and saw she couldn't make it for dinner, so she went right ahead to the theater. You wait and see."

Everybody in San Francisco except Carrie seemed to be waiting in the lobby. At first, in the excitement of popping flash bulbs and screaming autograph hounds, I thought her absence would cause comment. However, I soon made a discovery that others have made before me: nobody, except perhaps the movie star's wife herself, ever notices the absence of a movie star's wife.

When we were finally inside the theater and the lights were dimmed, Nick leaned toward me. "Let's blow," he whispered. "Let's go pick up Carrie. She'll be at the hotel. You wait and see, she'll be there, waiting for us."

At midnight I put down my glass and stood up. "I've got a train to catch at seven-thirty in the morning."

"Stick around," he said. "You don't want to leave San Francisco without saying good-by to Carrie."

When I left Nick at three in the morning, Carrie had not yet arrived. Four and a half hours later I caught my train to New York.

In our room at the Villa d'Este on Lake Como, I said to my wife, "That was sixteen years ago, and in all that time I've never laid eyes on either one of them."

"Now really," my wife said. "Here we've been married ten years and you never told me you knew any movie stars."

"As I've been trying to explain, I never felt I really knew Nick Brewster or Carrie."

"That's because you never understood them. It seems simple enough to me," my wife said. "When they first met, he loved her but she didn't love him. All you saw back in those days was a not-very-bright basketball player. What she saw, maybe because she had an artist's eye, was a dynamic, exciting actor. But it didn't make her fall in love with him, and in the meantime she was fishing elsewhere. When Nick finally did come through . . ." My wife shrugged.

"There's one fact you've ignored," I said.

"What's that?"

"Once she landed him, she kept right on fishing elsewhere."

"But all she got, when she landed him, was money," my wife said. "What more did she want?"

"What he actually had—no matter how she treated him—from the moment he met her," my wife said: "the ability to inspire love."

"Then why didn't she love him?"

"Stop being silly," my wife said. "You can't decide to love some-one the way you can decide to marry someone. That's an accident. The people to whom it happens have nothing to do with it."

"Well, if you want to have anything to do with the Brewsters, let's get going," I said. "Carrie said to meet them in the bar at seven."

The bar was crowded, but no place is ever too crowded for cinema royalty. Carrie waved to us from a large corner table, at which the patrons jammed uncomfortably around the bar were staring with covetous irritation.

"Hi," I said as we reached her. "Where's Nick?"

"He must have been held up somewhere along the line," Carrie said. "You know these Italian roads." She turned and put out both her hands. "So this is your wife!"

The ensuing introductions went down smoothly enough, and so did the first cocktails. After that, everything went much more easily, and it was then that I realized, with some astonishment, that Carrie had been uneasy about meeting us. My wife and Carrie, however, got along beautifully, and this gave me an opportunity to examine Carrie at leisure. I saw how shrewd she had been to have her nose fixed. She had never been beautiful, and she was not really that now. But the operation had given her something she had never had before— a touch of softness.

At eight o'clock I said, "Look, I hate to break up this gab fest, but hadn't we better begin thinking about dinner?"

"Nick's probably upstairs dressing now," Carrie said. "I'll go see what's keeping him." She left us hurriedly.

"You know something?" my wife said. "I wonder if you couldn't have been wrong about her all these years?"

"In what way?"

"I expected her to be nasty. But you know"—my wife paused—"I don't get the feeling of nastiness at all."

I started to make a remark about the effects of plastic surgery on character, but I did not get very far with it. Carrie came back to the table. She looked troubled.

"Nick back yet?" I asked.

"No, not yet."

"How far away is San Gimignano?"

"I don't know," Carrie said, "but I drove it in seven hours."

"Maybe he didn't get away at noon," I said. "Why don't you call San Gimignano and ask what time he left?"

"I just did," Carrie said. "He left at eleven-thirty this morning."

"Oh," I said. "Now, listen, get that look off your face. If there had been an accident, or anything like that, they would have let you know."

Carrie laughed with a promptness that was unsettling. "Of course," she said. "He probably blew a tire, or something went wrong with the motor. Let's give him another half hour before we worry about dinner."

We gave him more than an hour, and by then my wife and Carrie had finished giving each other their autobiographies and my wife had filled Carrie in on the more endearing traits of our two young sons. By the time we were seated in the dining room, Carrie was well launched on a description of life on location in San Gimignano, where Gaby Pagini, who had been signed for the feminine lead by cable, had raised ceaseless hell because she was under the impression that she, and not Nick, was the star of the picture. At midnight I suggested that it was pointless to wait up any longer.

"Nick's been held up somewhere along the way. He's probably decided to spend the night on the road," I said.

"Of course," Carrie said. "Well, see you in the morning."

It was one of those mornings that never get into the travel circulars. When I woke up, both our views of Lake Como were hidden by a curtain of driving rain.

"Not only that," my wife said grimly. "We also have *two* balconies on which we can't have breakfast."

We had it in the dining room, wearing sweaters under our tweeds, and staring out glumly at the rain.

"I wonder . . ." my wife said when the coffee came.

"So do I," I said. "Think we ought to ring her room?"

"Let's wait a while and see," my wife suggested.

We waited until after breakfast. Then I asked the man at the desk if Mr. Nicholas Brewster had checked in during the night. He shook his head. "No, *signore*."

My wife and I stood aimlessly in the lobby, staring out of the French doors at the lake. With the rain pelting down on it, the water looked like stucco.

"If he's held up somewhere on the road," my wife said, "I don't see why he doesn't telephone, or send Carrie a wire."

"Did the guidebook say anything about what you're supposed to do at Lake Como when it rains?" I asked my wife.

"There's always cassino."

A number of other people had the same idea, but we managed to find a table in the cardroom. We played without enthusiasm. Carrie Brewster came in at eleven. She was wearing a yellow turtle-neck sweater. I thought her face looked drawn, but she gave us a bright, cheery smile. "Sunny Italy," she said. "Who's ahead?"

"He is," my wife said. "But he cheats. Any word from Nick?"

Carrie shook her head. There was something about the way she did it that touched a bell in my mind. But even though I listened hard, I couldn't quite catch the echo of memory.

"He'll be along by lunchtime," she said. "You wait and see. Any chance of my getting into this game?"

We played until one-thirty, but Nick did not show up. After lunch we decided to take naps.

"It's the only way to beat the weather," my wife said. "If you stare at it, the rain never lets up. But if you turn your back on it, go to sleep and show it you don't care, it stops."

This particular rain had apparently never heard of my wife's theory. When we woke up, at four-thirty, the rain was coming down so hard that it was no longer possible to see the mountains on the other side of the lake. The telephone rang while we were dressing. It was Carrie Brewster.

"This weather is beginning to get me down," she said. "How about a drink? Come along. I'm in two seventy-one."

Two seventy-one was a huge suite, but it was not necessary to inspect all the rooms to know there was only one person in it. The feeling of loneliness struck you in the face.

"I bribed the management into letting me have a fire," Carrie said. "So we're that much ahead of the game."

It was not until we had been sitting around the fire for almost an hour, watching in silence as the rain faded into the dusk, that I realized neither my wife nor I had asked about Nick. It was as though we had agreed, before going to a party, to avoid raising a subject painful to our host. And yet my wife and I had not made any such agreement.

At dinner, Carrie Brewster made a valiant effort to lift our spirits with slabs of Hollywood folklore. She knew how to tell a story, and she had a gift for hilarious detail and the explosive phrase. But the rain, and what the rain was doing to our thoughts about Nick, was too much for her. We sat there, listening to the splashing patter on the terrace, kneading bits of bread into gummy pellets, trying to laugh at her stories, and wishing we had not come to Italy.

On our way to the lounge for coffee, my wife nudged me fiercely and, after we were seated, I said: "Any word from Nick?"

Carrie stopped stirring her coffee, and the look that crossed her face touched another bell in my mind. But I could not bring the tantalizing memory into clear focus.

"He'll get here," she said. "He gets held up like this every once in a while."

When we got back to our room, after a couple of hours of cassino during which nobody's mind had been on the cards, my wife threw her bag on the dressing table with a gesture of finality.

"I can't stand much more of this," she said. "Let's get out of here tomorrow."

"All right," I said. "But what can't you stand? The rain or Carrie?"

"Both," my wife said. "I wouldn't mind the rain if I understood what's happening. Last night, when it looked as though Nick would be a little late, Carrie seemed annoyed and then upset. Today, when it's become obvious that he's more than just a little late, when any woman would be justified in having hysterics, she's suddenly acting as though nothing is wrong."

"Maybe nothing *is* wrong," I said.

"Oh, no?" my wife said. "Have you looked into her eyes?"

The next morning the rain was coming down harder than ever and I decided my wife was right. We would get out of here at once. I dressed and went downstairs to arrange for transportation.

The man at the desk was talking on the telephone, so I picked up a copy of the Paris *Herald* and glanced at the front page.

Staring out at me from the center of the page was the smiling face of Nick Brewster. He had his arm around the waist of a girl with a wicked, toothy smile. The caption under the picture read:

> *Nicholas Brewster, American screen star, and Gaby Pagini, the fiery queen of Rome's cinema, who have just arrived on the Riviera for a holiday, after completing a new film about Cesare Borgia.*

I turned and stopped. Carrie Brewster was standing there, refolding another copy of the Paris *Herald*.

"Hello," I said awkwardly. "I didn't know . . ."

"Neither did I," she said quietly. "Not until I saw this picture. This is yesterday's paper, you know." Carrie shrugged and then went on: "I should have suspected. She's a very sexy dish."

We went over to the windows that looked out on the lake.

"How long has it been going on?" I asked.

Carrie sighed. "Oh, I imagine this one has just started."

"You mean there have been others?"

"Yes," Carrie said. "Quite a few others."

"When did all this start?" I asked.

"About four years ago," Carrie said. "When someone is in love with you for as long as Nick was in love with me, you think they'll go right on being in love with you forever. Then one day you find out they're not in love with you any more." She uttered a short, dry laugh. "You go out and do a lot of silly things that you think will help. Like having your nose fixed." She shook her head. "It didn't help."

"Why didn't you divorce him?"

Carrie's lips twisted in a small grimace, and again it was the way it had been in the cardroom the day before and in the lounge over coffee last night: a bell in my mind had been touched. But this time the recollection came into clear focus. It was the same expression Nick Brewster used to have in Steeger's, the look he had the night we dined alone at his house in California, and the night we went to the *première* of his picture in San Francisco: the look of a bewildered puppy, cringing slightly but resigned to the inevitable blow, yet pitifully hoping that just this once it won't come.

"When I found out about it four years ago," Carrie said, "I couldn't divorce him. It was too late."

"Too late?"

"I was stuck," she said. "After twelve years of marriage, after fourteen years of not giving a damn about him, I suddenly found out I'd fallen in love with him."

In the long silence that followed, we stared out at the rain as though, in the dismal downpour, we could read the words that would break the awkward silence by which we were both trapped.

"My wife and I are going to try to get out of here today," I said finally. "We'll go anyplace to get away from this rain. Why not come along?"

"Thanks a lot," Carrie said. "But I'll just stay here and wait for Nick. It never takes very long. Two or three weeks, maybe a month. Sooner or later he shows up." She paused and cleared her throat. "The way I used to show up at Steeger's," she said, and then she added, "sooner or later."

"That doesn't sound very pleasant," I said.

"It isn't," Carrie said. "But you'd be surprised by what you can get used to, if you're in love." She paused. "Nick took it for fourteen years. Now it's my turn."

Where the Sun Never Sets

They never kidded him about the color of his tie or laughed good-naturedly at some trivial mistake he had made. They never asked him to buy a sweepstakes ticket or take a chance on one of the pickboards that somebody was always carrying around. When they went out to lunch, in groups of six and seven, they never asked him along.

It was something that a newcomer could not help noticing, especially since he seemed rather pleasant, and I tried to puzzle it out. I listened carefully when they talked about one another. But I never heard a word about him. I watched them closely as they moved about the large office. But they never stopped at his desk.

There was nothing definite, nothing you could put your finger on, nothing of which you could accuse him. Nobody ever spoke harshly about him. In fact, nobody ever spoke about him at all. To the rest of the staff he did not exist. Only when he was called to their attention did they take notice of him. And then their comments did little to explain their attitude.

When they asked me to join the baseball pool I glanced down the list of names to which they were adding mine.

"How about Sykes?" I asked casually. They had every name but his.

"Who, *him*?" The heads turned in his direction for a moment, as though they were seeing him for the first time. Then, with a slight twist of the lips and a tone heavy with sarcasm: "*That* Scotchman? A dollar a week would break his heart!"

That was all. For them the subject was closed. Thus they always disposed of him. A phrase or two, usually derogatory, and they were through. He wasn't worth more.

At any rate, I told myself, I had a clue. He was stingy. They didn't like misers. That was why they disliked him.

But soon I knew that this alone was not enough. I was sure of that. There was nothing about him that was offensive. His practice of economy was no different from my own. Nor was mine much different from the others. We were all on the same level. We all had the same income. None of us could afford to play the spendthrift, nor could any one of us have done it convincingly. We were all too much alike, at least outwardly. We all knew the little tricks and practiced them. We all wore colored shirts because they did not have to go to the laundry too often. We all knotted our ties higher up when they began to fray. We all ate in the Automat.

Then why this aversion for him? Why should they dislike him so? What was there about him that repelled them and at the same time attracted me? Their repugnance was clear even when they said and did nothing. It was plain in the way they unconsciously avoided him. It puzzled me. And the more puzzled I became, the higher my interest in him mounted. There was something about him, something elusive that I was trying to track down, that reminded me of myself. At times I would get a glimmer of it and I would feel, for a moment, that I knew what it was that set us both apart. But always it escaped me. Then I would redouble my efforts. I would watch him closely for hours, neglecting my work to stare across the large office at him.

But there was nothing in the figure bent busily over the desk that would explain my liking or their dislike. He seemed perfectly content to have them avoid him. Even while doing the most commonplace things, he seemed to exist in a world of his own. The things that occupied the others held no interest for him. He seemed to live by an inner fire.

Then, quite suddenly, the day I ran into him in the Automat, I found the answer.

He was alone at a small table and I was on top of him before I knew it.

"Do you mind if I sit here?" I asked awkwardly, angry with myself because I felt embarrassed. Why should *I* feel flustered, I asked myself. *He* was the outcast. *He* was the one to be embarrassed. But he wasn't.

"Of course not," he said quickly, with a pleasant smile, and helped clear a space on the table for my tray.

"These places certainly get crowded at this hour, don't they?" I said, trying to cover my confusion.

He looked about him, as though it were something he hadn't noticed before, and then nodded. "Yeah," he said, "I guess so."

We ate in silence for a time and I watched him. His attitude annoyed me. I realized that I had vaguely expected him to be grateful. He should have been thankful for my attention. He should have been respectful and eager. He should have watched my lips expectantly, hanging on every word I uttered, anxious to agree with me, to make himself pleasant, to show that he appreciated what I was doing for him.

But there was nothing in his face that could be mistaken for gratitude. He continued to lift food to his mouth as unconcernedly as before I had interrupted him. His self-possession was irritating. What right had he to sit there so calmly, taking my presence for granted? What right had he to accept me as his equal? My irritation was turning rapidly into anger.

As I watched him I could not help making comparisons. Nothing had happened. No words had passed between us. Yet I was angry and he was calm. The contrast was so striking that I forgot my anger—and all at once, I knew the answer. I knew why the others disliked him.

It seemed so simple and clear that I was surprised it had not occurred to me before. The answer had been waiting for me all the time. It was there before me now, in his face, in my anger, in our attitudes toward each other. No wonder the others hated him! He didn't need them, just as he did not seem to need me now.

If he had seemed hurt by their disregard of him, if he had tried to win their friendship, if he had suffered under their scorn—they would not have hated him. But because he *didn't* suffer, because he *didn't* try to win them, because *he* disregarded *them*, because they needed him, but he did not need them—that was why they hated him!

Of course, I said to myself. Look how I had begun to get angry with him! And I *liked* him! Then what could you expect from those others, those others who disliked him right from the start?

Then, suddenly, my enthusiasm fell from me. I had found the answer. But that's all it was—an answer. It was not a solution. I knew now why they hated him, but I knew, too, that this alone was not what had puzzled me.

I determined that this time I would clear the matter up.

"There's a good sale on shirts next door," I said, trying to sound casual. "Regular two dollar stuff for a dollar thirty-nine. You want to come in and look at them?"

He looked at me in surprise for a moment and then said in friendly fashion: "Sure, I'll go in with you."

He watched me hunt through the pile of shirts on the counter and said he thought the two I finally selected were very nice.

As I waited for my change, I said: "Why don't you get a couple of these, Sykes? They're a good buy at the price."

"I know they are," he said with a wistful smile. "I wish I could, but I can't afford it this week."

"I'll lend you the money," I said quickly. "It's a shame to let a thing like this go by."

"Thanks," he said with a grateful nod, and then shook his head. "I . . . I just can't afford it now. Thanks anyway."

My mind grasped eagerly at the straw. He couldn't afford it. Even if I should lend him the money, he said he couldn't afford it. He couldn't pay it back next week, or the week after, either. That meant his salary was budgeted in advance, that he had very little for himself. He probably had to turn most of it over to his family. No wonder they thought he was stingy. No wonder he couldn't waste his money on sweepstakes tickets or baseball pools. It wasn't his fault that he had an old mother to support. What right did they have to call him names, to dislike him?

From that day on I lost no opportunity to come to his defense. I went out of my way to stop at his desk, to run into him at lunch, to object when they spoke unkindly of him. They kidded me about it, but I didn't mind. I admired his fortitude, and the knowledge that I was the only one who knew his secret made it easy for me to withstand their jeers.

Our friendship, such as it was, grew stronger. We met in the Automat more often, we smiled when we met in the hall, occasionally he would even murmur an unintelligible greeting. But always the barrier of his reserve was between us. Even while chatting with apparent intimacy across the luncheon table, the far-away look remained in his eyes. And although he carried his end of the conversation quite well, I always had the disconcerting feeling that his mind was on other things.

It occurred to me that if I met him after office hours, if I saw him in different surroundings, I might understand him better. I suggested that we go to the theater some evening.

"No," he said regretfully, "I can't make it this week."

"How about next week, then?"

He shook his head.

"The week after?"

He smiled apologetically. "I'm afraid not," he said. "I can't afford it."

At once I was ashamed of my insistence. "I don't get much of a chance to go myself," I said with a hasty laugh. "Believe me, I know how close to the line you have to play, what with helping support a family and all."

He looked at me with astonishment. "A family?"

"Why, sure," I said helpfully. "I mean what you have to kick in to the family at home."

"I got no family," he said.

"Well," I said quickly, "I don't mean a *family* exactly. What I meant is, it's expensive enough just supporting your mother."

"My *mother*? I got no mother."

It was my turn to be astonished.

"You have no mother?"

He laughed good-naturedly and shook his head. "I've been an orphan since I was a kid. I haven't even got a second cousin. I'm all alone, thank God. Nobody goes around telling *me* what to do, or where to go or anything like that."

There was no mistaking the sincerity of his words. He really meant them. He was alone in the world and glad of it. But I had little time to devote to this new development. I was too dazed by his revelation that he had no mother even to realize that this was the first time he had ever spoken to me about himself.

The pattern of excuses and reasons I had built up had come tumbling down about my ears. He had no family. He had no mother. He was alone. Then what did he do with his money? Were the others right after all? Was he really a miser? Was he so stingy that he couldn't bear to spend a dollar a week for the baseball pool, or the few cents that a second-balcony theater ticket cost?

I tried, during the weeks that followed, to think up other excuses for him. But I couldn't. The disappointment had been too sudden and too complete. His attitude toward me had not changed. He was just as friendly, just as distant; just as pleasant, just as disinterested. But my own feelings had cooled appreciably.

Several weeks later he stopped me in the hall one day as I was going out to lunch.

"Hello," I said, surprised. It was the first time he had ever sought me out, and it was the first time I had ever seen him so nervous. His face was creased by a worried frown and he kept looking about him, from side to side, as though he were afraid of being overheard. For once the invisible film of detachment that stretched between him and the rest of the world was pierced.

"Listen," he said in a low voice, putting his hand on my arm, "you want to do me a favor? It's not much, just a little thing, but I . . ."

"Sure," I said. "But what's all the . . . ?"

He took my arm and steered me down the hall, away from the office entrance. "I'll tell you," he said hurriedly. "You doing anything tonight? I mean right after work?"

"Why, no, but . . . ?"

"Could you go some place with me for a little while? It won't take long. I want to get something and I don't want to go alone. It's not far from here. Could you go with me? It won't take long." His voice was pleading.

"Sure," I said heartily. "But why can't we go now? We've got a whole hour, and if it's not far from here . . . ?"

"No, I can't do it now," he said, shaking his head. "I don't want to do this on my lunch hour. I don't want to rush this. And anyway," he added, as though he were making things perfectly clear, "I've got to go to the bank now to get the money. What do you say?" he asked eagerly.

"O.K.," I said.

His face broke into a relieved smile. "Thanks," he said. "I'll wait for you right after work," and hurried away.

At five-thirty we left the office together. He offered no word of explanation, and my curiosity mounted as I tried to keep up with the pace he was setting. He moved along the streets quickly and surely, turning corners and crossing gutters without hesitation, as though he knew his destination so well, had, indeed, made the trip so often, that he could now do it without thought. There was a curious intensity about his face and the way he moved, with his head thrust forward a bit, his lips slightly parted and his chest heaving with suppressed excitement.

"What's all the hurry?" I asked after a few blocks.

"They may be closed," he answered without turning his head or slackening his pace. "I have to get there before they close."

In a few minutes we halted in front of an expensive-looking luggage shop. The windows were still lighted, but the handsomely-tailored men who moved about inside were obviously getting the place ready for closing.

Sykes peered through the glass for a moment, then turned to me.

"We still got time," he said, relieved, and then, falteringly, by way of explanation: "I was sort of . . . well, sort of a little scared to go in and buy it myself." He stopped and dropped his embarrassed eyes from mine. "I mean I thought . . . it sort of . . . well, it sort of looks better for *two* of us to come in, instead of one. I was a little afraid, I mean to, you know, to go in to buy it all by myself. But it won't take long," he added hastily. "Only a few minutes. That's all it'll take, then you . . ."

"That's all right," I said, "I'm in no hurry."

We went inside and a salesman came toward us, his head bent slightly to one side, a faint look of surprise on his face.

"You got a trunk," Sykes said at once. "It's called the Mercury De-Luxe. I've seen it in your window . . ."

"Certainly, sir," the salesman said. "Won't you step this way?"

"That's all right," Sykes said quickly. "I've seen it a few times already." He reached into his breast pocket and drew out a shabby wallet. "I want to buy it."

The salesman stared at him for a moment, and Sykes' face took on a worried look. "You got one in the house, haven't you?" he asked anxiously.

"Why, yes, sir," the salesman said, recovering himself.

"How much is it?"

"A hundred and twenty, sir. Plus two-forty tax makes a hundred and twenty-two forty."

"A hundred and *twenty*?" There was consternation in Sykes' voice. He stopped fumbling with the wallet and stared at the salesman. "I thought it was a hundred and fifteen? It's been a hundred and fifteen dollars for over a year. I know because I've watched the price. Why," he cried, "only last *week* it was a hundred and fifteen!"

"I know, sir," the salesman said with an apologetic smile, "but the manufacturer raised the price on us only three days ago. We can't help ourselves, sir."

"Gee," Sykes said in a disappointed tone, "I thought it was a hundred and fifteen. I brought just enough."

For a moment I thought he was going to cry.

"Here," I said, reaching into my pocket, "I'll lend you the difference."

His face lit up at once. "Oh, gee, thanks," he said gratefully.

"That's all right," I said, and really meant it. The feeling of relief that the last few minutes had given me was worth twice that amount. At last I knew the answer. Better than that. At last I knew the solution. At last I knew his secret. I knew what had made him seem so stingy. I knew what he had been saving for. And I knew, too, what it was that had drawn me to him. I, too, longed to travel, to sail across the seas to distant lands. I was glad now that I had not joined the others in their derision. I was glad that I had defended him. It was as though I had instinctively come to the aid of a brother or a sister. The lure of the horizon had made us kin.

The salesman had finished counting the money and took up his pencil.

"Where shall we send it, sir?" he asked.

"I want it delivered now," Sykes said. "I'll go along with it."

The salesman looked at him in astonishment. *"Now? Tonight?"*

"Yes, tonight."

"But it's too late, sir! Our delivery men are gone for the day. Our trucks are . . . Couldn't we send it around to you tomorrow, first thing in the morning? I'll tell our man to rush it over . . ."

"No," Sykes said firmly. "I must have it tonight."

The salesman stared helplessly, holding the money in front of him. "I'm afraid it's quite impossible, sir."

Sykes scowled at him for a time, then said: "I'll tell you what. We'll have to load it into a taxi. I must have it tonight."

The salesman looked relieved and hurried into the rear of the store for help. In a few minutes Sykes and I were driving uptown in a taxi with the trunk lashed carefully onto the running board.

He did not speak during the trip, and I asked no questions. We drew up, finally, before a brownstone rooming house on the West Side and helped the driver carry the trunk upstairs. After he left, Sykes excused himself and hurried out into the hall to wash. I sat down and looked around.

The room was a small one, an ordinary hall bedroom, drab and cheerless. It was cheaply furnished in the manner of thousands like it all over the city. There was nothing in the room that would have revealed the character of its occupant, nothing that would have set it apart from all the others, no spark of color, no picture on the walls, no litter of clothing or books or toilet articles. Nothing, save the gleaming, rich-looking trunk in the middle of the floor.

He must have everything packed and ready, I thought, although I wondered where it could all be.

In a few moments he was back, rubbing his freshly washed hands together, a happy smile on his face. He went to the trunk and opened it carefully, so that it stood in two sections, hinged in the middle, like an opened book standing on end. He squatted before it and played with the beautifully arranged compartments, pulling out drawers, lifting flaps, snapping catches into place.

"Look," he said, talking to me over his shoulder. "Here's how you hang your suits, with the pants here, like this, so they won't get creased." Or, "See this?" He slid out a leather folder. "That's for your ties. You can put in over a dozen, and they'll always be pressed." He turned to face me. "You know what this trunk'll hold?" he asked, his voice rich with enthusiasm. "You'll never believe it, but it's laid out so cleverly—an engineer designed it, a regular engineer —it's laid out so cleverly that these few square feet, just these few square feet here, they'll hold six suits, a dozen shirts, four hats, a topcoat, six pairs of shoes, ties, underwear, socks—anything at all that you want!" He slipped the leather folder into its groove and pressed the snap that fastened it.

"When are you leaving?" I asked.

He stared at me without comprehension. "Leaving? Where?"

"I mean, when are you going away? On your trip, I mean." I pointed to the trunk. "When are you *going?*"

He followed the direction of my hand and looked at the trunk. Then he said, "Oh!" and smiled wistfully and shook his head. "I'm not going away. I wish I could, but I can't afford it. Why," he said, "it took me over a year to save up enough for *this.*"

He patted the trunk affectionately and smiled at it. There was something in his face and the way his hands fondled the glistening leather and metal that made me feel ashamed to be watching. It was as though I had stumbled upon two lovers and was listening to their soft whispers and watching their caresses. His tenderness embarrassed me. I felt like an intruder.

I stood up and walked quietly toward the door. He did not notice me until the lock clicked when I turned the knob.

He looked up, as though he had been interrupted. "Oh," he said, and then seemed to remember me. "Thanks for all your trouble."

"That's all right," I said quickly, dropping my eyes from his.

As I started to close the door from the outside I saw him stroke the polished leather sides gently. His voice came to me through the narrowing crevice of the closing door.

"Boy," he was saying softly, his eyes alight, his head shaking slowly from side to side with admiration, "boy," he breathed, "with a trunk like this, with a trunk like this you could go *anyplace!*"

You and Yours

I know my trouble. I'm too much of a gentleman. Instead of thinking about myself, I spend my time worrying about what other people will think of what I do. Well, there's a limit even to that.

I picked up the receiver and spoke to the girl at the switchboard.

"Get my home," I said.

The phone rang.

"Yes?"

"Your home, Mr. Steers," the girl at the switchboard said.

A moment later I was speaking to the maid.

"Hello," I said. "This is Mr. Steers. Is Mrs. Steers in?"

"Why, yes, sir, but she's—"

"Get her for me, will you?"

"But, Mr. Steers, Mrs. Steers is in the drawing room, entertaining her—"

"Get her on the phone, will you?"

"Yes, sir."

I could hear the click as she put the phone down, and a few moments later it was picked up again.

"Hello," I said. "Who's this—Harriet?"

"Yes. What is it?"

Well, one thing was sure: Whatever it was she'd been entertaining in the drawing room, it hadn't helped thaw the icicles out of her voice.

"I've got something important to tell you," I said. "Get rid of that menagerie you've got in the drawing room. I'm coming right home."

"I'm very sorry, Benjamin," she said. "But I can't turn my friends out into the street just because you get a silly whim to come home in the middle of the day."

She was crazy; she didn't know how sorry she was going to be.

"Whim nothing," I said. "I've got something to talk to you about and I want to get it off my chest now. It's my house, anyway, isn't it?"

"You might try spending some time in it, then," she said coldly. "Perhaps if you did, you'd—"

"Well, I'm coming home to spend some time in it now. Those hyenas of yours won't freeze. They'll find some other place to push their bridge cards around for today. It won't kill them."

"Now, listen, Benjamin," she began in that low, steady voice of hers. "I'm telling you—"

"Oh, no, Harriet. You've got it wrong. Today *I'm* doing all the telling. I'm going to let you take a crack at a little listening for a change."

"Benjamin!"

"Try calling me Ben," I said. "It's easier to say when you're excited."

I hung up. As I reached for my hat I caught a glimpse of myself in the glass of a bookcase. I hadn't even started, and I was actually smiling already!

The house was quiet when I came in. I gave my hat to the maid and nodded toward the drawing room.

"Mrs. Steers in?" I asked.

"Yes, sir."

"What happened to the—what happened to her guests?"

"They left right after you called, sir."

I grinned to myself. I guess the new regime was in my voice, too.

"All right, Sophie," I said.

I walked to the door of the drawing room and stood there for a moment. She was in the big chair, near the window, looking out into the street. Her long chin and thin lips were set, and she sat without moving. The sun touched her hair a little and threw her whole head into outline. That was one thing you couldn't take away

from her, her appearance. She was good to look at, like a diamond.
But I was tired of jewelry.

"Hello, Harriet," I said, coming into the room.

She turned to face me, but did not speak.

"That's what I like," I said, "a good rousing reception."

"Hello, Benjamin," she said calmly.

I took the chair facing her and lit a cigarette. It was all I could do
to keep from laughing out loud like a kid. Boy, was I going to wash
that calm look right off her face!

"You know," I said, looking around the room, and leaning back
in my chair, "this isn't bad. I mean, sitting here like this, taking it
easy, and all. Not bad at all."

I was figuring there was no sense in rushing things.

"It's probably the novelty that makes it so appealing," she said.

Sarcasm, eh? Well, let her have her bit of fun. I'd knock all that out
of her with my little announcement soon enough.

"Either that," I said, "or the fact that it's not empty like this very
often."

Her lip curled a little.

"If you're referring to my guests—" she began.

"Let's keep the conversation on a higher plane."

"Monologue would be the more accurate word," she said.

Since when did she become such a bug on accuracy?

"You may be right at that. Fact is, Harriet, I feel a speech coming
on."

"Was that why you asked me to turn my guests out?"

If she knew what I knew, she wouldn't be so quick with the sneers.

"That was one reason," I said. "I didn't think you'd want an
audience for what I'm going to say."

She unclasped her hands in her lap and touched her hair for a
moment.

"I don't blame you," she said. "The introduction doesn't sound
very promising. You never were a very good speaker, Benjamin."

"Maybe. But I've improved a lot since you last heard me."

She shrugged.

"You might try coming to the point," she said.

Well, if she was in a hurry, she was in a hurry. I crushed out my
cigarette carefully.

"All right, I'll come to the point." I took a deep breath. "I've decided to call it quits, Harriet. I've had enough. I'm fed up. I'm walking out."

She smoothed the dress across her knees slowly and picked off a thread and looked at it for a moment before dropping it to one side. But her face didn't change.

What the hell was the matter with her?

"Maybe you didn't hear me," I said, leaning forward. "But I said I—"

"Oh, I heard you, Benjamin," she said calmly. "You said you were fed up. You said you were through. And you said you were tired, didn't you?"

What did she think she was, a comedienne?

"I said I—" I began.

"No, come to think of it, you didn't say you were tired," she continued. "That was the one word you left out, Benjamin. Perhaps it was just as well. Because I was just getting ready to use that word myself."

For a few moments I didn't move. Then I lit another cigarette slowly and watched her through my cupped hands as I held the match. She was looking directly at me, but there was no change of expression on her face. The cigarette tasted terrible. I crushed it out quickly.

"Well," I said finally, "I guess you can thank me for giving you the chance to use the word, then."

Her lip curled.

"If you take pleasure in such things," she said, "you're welcome to them."

What was going on here, anyway? I thought *I* was the one that was getting ready to walk out.

"Maybe we'd better not waste time discussing it," I said. "We've got more important things to talk about."

"It shouldn't take long. Unless I'm mistaken, Benjamin, you've probably given a good deal of thought to the details."

She was pretty good at these understatements.

"You don't have to worry," I said carefully. "You can have the divorce in any way you like. And you don't have to worry about the money angle, either. Regardless of your opinion of me—which doesn't matter any more, anyway—you won't have cause to—"

"You're wrong about my opinion of you," she said, "but you're right; it doesn't matter. It's just that I'm so sick of the whole thing, I've been so tired of the whole relationship for I don't know *how* many years, now, that I—"

I bit my lip and tried lighting another cigarette.

"You can skip the rest," I said sharply. "We'll get the details over as quickly as possible."

"The quicker the better," she said. "It'll be the first thing I've been thankful to you for in years."

I wondered what happened to men who slapped their wives good and hard just before they divorced them.

"Don't even mention it," I said sarcastically. "You can—"

The outer door slammed open and closed and footsteps came toward the drawing room quickly. Dick stopped in the doorway, holding his books, and stared at me in amazement.

"Why—why, hello, Dad," he said slowly. "What are you doing home now? Is—is anything the matter?"

I opened my mouth to say something, but she beat me to it.

"No, Dick," she said, "nothing's the matter. Your father and I are just talking over some important matters. Run along upstairs like a good boy, will you, dear?"

I looked at her quickly. The change in her voice was so sudden that I forgot the words on my lips. But her voice wasn't the only thing that changed. For the first time since I'd come home her face didn't look like it had a mud pack on that she was afraid to crack.

"Sure, Dick, run along," I said good and loud, with a smile. "Be a good scout."

He blinked at me for a moment in surprise, then looked quickly at her and went out.

I leaned back in my chair and lit a cigarette. This time it tasted fine. I inhaled deeply and got up.

"I think we were discussing something," she said. Her voice was low and even again.

I dusted my ashes elaborately and buttoned my coat carefully.

"Why, yes," I said, blowing smoke at the ceiling. "I think we *were* about to go into some unpleasant details. But why spoil the rest of the day? I think we'll let it ride for a while."

So she was good and tired of the whole relationship, eh? Well, she was going to be a whole lot more than just plain tired before I got through with her. I'd knock that North Pole look off her face for good even if I had to live with her another year. Now I knew how and where to hit.

"A few moments before," she said acidly, "you seemed to be in such a terrible rush to—"

"I know," I said. "But that was a few minutes ago. Right now I've got other things to do. What I think I'll do is go up and see Dick for a while."

II

As soon as I got back from lunch I rang for Miss Berry. One of the other girls came in.

"I rang for Miss Berry," I said sharply.

"I'm sorry, sir. Miss Berry isn't back yet. She—"

"All right, all right. Tell her I want to see her as soon as she comes in."

"Yes, Mr. Steers."

"Don't forget, now."

"No, sir."

She went out and I picked up the phone.

"Yes, Mr. Steers?" the switchboard operator said.

"Look this name up in the phone book," I said. "It's a school. R. H. McArdle School for Boys, or something like that. They're somewhere on the west side. I'm not sure of the street. But that's the right name, anyway. Look up the number and get them for me on the phone. Right away."

"Yes, sir."

I hung up. The door opened quickly and Miss Berry came in. I motioned her toward the desk as the phone rang.

"Yes?" I said into the mouthpiece.

"Did you say the *R. H.* McArdle School for Boys, Mr. Steers?" the switchboard operator asked.

"Yes," I said, "and where's the call, by the way? How long do I—?"

"I'm sorry, Mr. Steers, but there's no R. H. McArdle School in

the phone book. There's a *Thomas* McArdle School for Boys,
though, on West Seventy—"

"All right, all right. That's it. Use your head for a change, will you?
Get them right away." I slammed the receiver down and turned to
Miss Berry. "Did you get those tickets?"

"Yes, Mr. Steers," she said, putting them on the desk with the
change. "I'm sorry to be late, but they didn't have any at the stadium
and I had to go to an agency for them."

"That's all right," I said, picking them up.

The phone rang.

"Yes," I said.

"I've got the school on the wire, Mr. Steers."

"Put them on," I said, and then, nodding to Miss Berry, "All right,
Miss Berry. Thanks." She went out. I spoke into the phone again:
"Hello, McArdle School?"

"Yes, sir," the voice at the other end said.

"This is Mr. Steers talking, Benjamin Steers. My son Richard is a
member of your school and—"

"Oh, yes, Mr. Steers."

"Well, I'll tell you," I said, "I hate to interfere with your curriculum
or anything like that, but I wonder if you'd be good enough to in-
dulge me just this once."

"Why, certainly, Mr. Steers. Anything at all that we—"

"I'll tell you what I'd like to do. I'd like to come up there and
take my son out for the balance of the day. It's a rather important
engagement I want him to attend with me, and if—"

"Why, certainly, Mr. Steers."

"Then would you be good enough to call him out of class and
put him on this wire for me?"

"Certainly, Mr. Steers."

After a minute or so, I heard the receiver being picked up again.

"Hello," I said, "Dick?"

"Yes, Dad," he said in a small scared voice. "What's the—what's
the matter?"

I laughed to reassure him.

"I'll tell you why I called, son. How'd you like to go up and see
the world series game this afternoon?"

"The what?"

"The world series game," I said. "I've got a couple of swell box seats—"

I stopped. It didn't sound right. How the hell did you talk to twelve-year-old kids?

"But, Dad," he said finally. "I'm in—I mean, I'm in—I'm in school now."

"That's all right, son," I said heartily. "I just spoke to the principal. He said you could have the rest of the day off. What do you say?"

He still didn't answer. What a damn' fool I'd been not to have spent more of my time with him. Now I had to start from scratch.

"Sure, Dad," he said finally.

I grinned to myself. Who said I couldn't do it? I could almost see that mud-pack look on her face begin to slip already.

III

When I came into the dining room for breakfast she was already at the table.

"Good morning, Harriet."

"Good morning," she said.

I could feel her watching me as I poured my coffee.

"Have you decided on a date yet?" she asked finally.

I looked at her in surprise.

"Oh, yes," I said, as though I had just remembered. "Why, I'll tell you, Harriet, I've been so busy lately that I completely forgot about the divorce. But I'll be getting around to it one of these days. *You're* not in any terrific hurry about it, are you, Harriet?"

She touched her napkin to her lips.

"You know how I feel about it."

Sure I knew. But I knew something else that *she* didn't know. I knew how she was going to feel before very long.

"Well, if you can just bear up a little while longer, till I get things cleared up at the office, I'll see if I can't put you out of your misery."

The crack she was going to make next must have been a honey, but she didn't say it. Dick came into the room with a quiet "Good morning," and took his place at table guiltily.

"Really, Richard," she said gently, "you should try to be more prompt. I don't want you to bolt your food, and now you'll be late for school."

"I'm sorry, Mother."

"Oh, come, now, Harriet," I said in a cheerful tone, "don't blame the boy. It's my fault, really. I kept him up so late last night at the fights that I don't really blame him for oversleeping. It's not his fault at all." I turned to him. "How do you feel, Dick?"

He smiled at me.

"Swell, Dad."

"That's good," I said. "Take it easy there on the food. There's no rush. I'll drive you down to school myself. And if they get tough with you down at the school, why I'll come in and tell them a couple things."

We both laughed.

"How'd you like that fourth round?" I asked.

"You mean when he bounced off the ropes, Dad? Timmens, I mean? And he hit him with the left?"

"That's the one," I said.

He forgot his food and turned toward me excitedly.

"Gee, Dad, did you see the way his head snapped back when he landed with that left? Boy, I knew he was through then. He's a fighter, that Timmens, isn't he, Dad?"

"I'll say he is." I tapped the newspaper in front of me. "They're giving him a crack at the champ next."

"You mean it, Dad?"

"Sure, here, look." I pushed the paper toward him and he looked at the headlines quickly. "They're going to fight in Los Angeles, probably in a couple of months or so."

He looked up from the paper.

"Boy, Dad, I bet he knocks the champ out!"

"He ought to," I said.

She coughed at my elbow to attract attention and said, "Do you want some more coffee, Benjamin?"

"No," I said shortly, speaking over my shoulder in her direction. But I was laughing to myself. It looked like she was getting wise to the plan of attack.

I leaned over and slipped my arm across Dick's shoulders.

"How'd you like to go out west to see the fight, Dick?" I asked with a smile.

I could almost see the scared look begin to creep over her face, but I didn't look at her. I looked at the boy. He looked startled.

"You mean, way out—?" he began.

"Sure. We could make a nice slow trip of it, seeing the sights and all, and wind up in Los Angeles in time to see Timmens win the championship. Then, maybe, we could take a boat over to Honolulu or even China or something. Say," I said enthusiastically, for her benefit, "we could have a swell time, just the two of us. What do you say?"

"Gee!" he said, and looked at me with his mouth open.

"Don't be ridiculous, Benjamin!" she broke in sharply. "Don't put such silly ideas in the boy's head. He's got his school to think of. And —and—"

"And what?" I said, grinning at her.

"And besides, in a little while you won't—"

Oh, won't I?

"Don't worry about it, Harriet," I said casually. "Dick is bright enough to be able to afford a few months, or even a year, away from school. And, anyway, he'll probably learn more in a year on a trip like that than he could pick up in *any* school."

His excited voice rose again.

"Oh, *gee*, Dad, you *mean* it?"

I leaned over to pat his hand.

"Of course I do, son."

He hopped out of his chair and tugged at my arm.

"Come on, Dad," he said eagerly. "I want to get to school. I want to tell the fellows about it. Oh, boy, wait'll they hear this!"

I laughed and patted his head.

"Run along, son, and get your hat. I'll be with you in a minute."

As he left the dining room I turned toward her again. She was still sitting at the table, watching me with that expressionless handsome face of hers that she could set so you'd never even know she'd been hit.

"I'll try to get the date for that other thing we were talking about this morning set for some time before Dick and I go away," I said with just the faintest hint of a grin. "And then, of course, after the divorce, it won't really matter very much to you *where* we go, will it, Harriet?"

Her lips tightened the slightest bit, but she didn't say a word.

IV

"I don't think there's anything to be gained from prolonging this much further," the referee said, scowling slightly.

If he wanted that motion seconded, all he had to do was ask me.

He took off his glasses and rubbed the bridge of his nose with the tips of his thumb and forefinger. He looked across the desk at Harriet and then at me.

"If neither of you has, uh, had a change of heart," he said slowly, looking at her and then at me, "I mean, if both of you still want—"

His voice stopped and he looked at us inquiringly, moving his head from side to side. But nobody spoke. I was dying to get a good square look at her, but I wouldn't give her that much satisfaction. I stared straight ahead of me.

"All right," the referee said in a tired voice. "I suppose the only thing left to decide is the, uh, the custody of the child."

He picked up the papers in front of him, looked at them a moment, and put them down. He looked at the attorneys.

"I'll ask you gentlemen please to leave the room," he said. "Just for a few minutes. I want to talk to the boy alone; that is, in the presence of Mr. and Mrs. Steers only."

He picked up the phone on his desk and spoke into it as the lawyers went out. In a few moments the door opened and Dick came in. He looked scared.

"Come here, Richard," the referee said, smiling at him. He pulled a chair into position next to the desk and Dick took it, sitting up very straight.

"I want you to listen very carefully to what I say, Richard," he said kindly. "And I want you to *think* very carefully about something I'm going to ask you to decide for yourself. Will you do that for me, Richard?"

The old boy was all right. He had something on the ball. If I'd've known half as much about handling kids as he seemed to know, I wouldn't have had to kill so much time laying my groundwork.

"Yes, sir," Dick said in a low voice.

Well, at least she'd taught him to act like a gentleman.

"I suppose you know all about this by now," the referee said, leaning forward across his desk toward the boy and talking quietly. "But I want to repeat it so you'll know how important the thing is that I'm going to ask you to do." He cleared his throat and went on. "Your mother and father, Richard, have decided to separate. The reasons don't matter."

That's what *he* thought. I'd like to be around to ask *him* a couple of questions after he'd spent fifteen years in a locked room with the Statue of Liberty.

"The important thing, Richard, is that you can't be with both of them at the same time any more. You can only live with one. And I want you to help me decide, Richard, which one you'd rather be with—your mother or your father." He leaned back in his chair. "I leave it entirely up to you, Richard," he said.

That's just where I wanted him to leave it. I wasn't worried.

The boy looked at his hands and bent his head. His lower lip began to quiver. He caught it between his teeth and held it steady. I felt a little sorry for the kid, up there all alone. But I didn't have time to spend on sympathy. I was watching her at the other end of the table out of the corner of my eye. She was as steady and expressionless as ever. But I wasn't worrying. I knew what the kid was going to say, and she didn't. And I knew that when she heard it she was going to crack wide open. I'd been waiting for that moment for fifteen years. I wasn't going to risk missing it even if I had to turn around and stare right at her.

"Did you say something, Richard?" the referee asked.

"Yes, sir," the boy said in a low voice.

"Which one?" the referee asked.

I had my eyes glued on her face.

"My—my father," the boy whispered.

She stiffened in her chair and her lower lip began to jiggle. She caught it in her teeth, quickly, exactly the way the boy had done.

"Your *father?*" the referee said.

Why the hell not? Wasn't I as good as she was?

"Yes, sir," the boy said.

I leaned back in my chair. I knew in advance all that mother-love hooey wouldn't stand a chance when stacked up against a month of prize fights and hockey games and promised western trips.

"Very well, Richard," the referee said slowly, "if that's your choice."

I scowled hard to hide my grin. She was calm again, but I didn't care about that. I'd seen her a moment before, the way I'd wanted her. It hadn't been much, but at least I knew I'd done it.

V

I didn't know how long I'd been sitting like that, my nose to the glass, watching the cows and the trees and the patches of brown and green spin by. But I did know that it wasn't making me feel any better.

Suddenly I swung my chair toward the center of the car. His seat was empty. I looked around the car quickly; he wasn't there. I got up and grabbed the porter's arm as he went by.

"You haven't seen a boy—my son—you haven't seen him around, have you?" I asked. "He was just sitting across the—"

He looked at me in surprise.

"Ah think ah saw him goin' tow'd the observation platform, suh. Little while ago."

"Thanks," I said shortly and rushed past him.

I hurried through the train. I opened the door into the club car quickly and saw him sitting on the platform at the other end. I stopped short and the relief was so great that for a few seconds I couldn't breathe. Then my heart began to race crazily. He was leaning forward in his seat, with his chin and hands resting on the rail. I guess I wasn't the only one that had been counting the cows and the trees.

I paused to light a cigarette and inhale deeply. When I felt I was all right again I walked out onto the platform, and stood behind him for a moment. I wanted to touch him. I put my hand on his shoulder and squeezed it gently.

"Hello, son," I said. "I didn't know where you were. I was worried."

That was a *new* word for panic.

"Hello, Dad," he said. But he didn't look up. I knew why, too. He rubbed the back of his hand against his jacket to dry it.

If I'd had her anywhere within reach at that moment, I'd've wrung
her neck.

I sat down next to him and watched the track come shooting out
swiftly from under us and go pouring away into the distance.

"Nice view, isn't it, Dick?"

He nodded. That made two liars. The view was terrible.

Just the same I watched it for a while, hard, trying to figure out
where I stood. It was no good. But I knew that wringing her neck
wouldn't help. This was something that went down so deep that
nothing could help. All it could do from now on was hurt.

"This is really nothing, yet," I said. "It gets much nicer when
you hit—"

I didn't finish. I tossed the half-smoked cigarette away and started
to light another one, but didn't. Doing things like that wasn't going
to stop me from realizing what a complete fool I'd turned out to
be. What was I going to do, take my revenge on her out on the kid?

"You're not cold, are you, son?" I asked.

He shook his head quickly, but did not speak.

The funny part about it was that it wasn't her fault. Why couldn't
I have been satisfied to walk out quickly, the way I'd planned? Why
the hell did I have to spend a month trying to make her crack, and
end up by getting trapped by something I never even knew was in
me?

"Dick," I said, "I want to ask you a—" and stopped. What was
the use? His *words* weren't what counted. All I had to do was look
at him to see that. The only thing that mattered now was what was
best for him. And I knew the answer to that, too, damn her.

I put my arm across his shoulder and pulled him to me. He rested
his cheek against my coat and tried to control his sobs. I held him
tight against the rocking of the train and cursed her until the words
didn't mean anything any more. But it didn't help. She had me.

I got up suddenly and said, "Wait for me, Dick, will you? I'll be
right back."

"All right, Dad," he said.

I hurried through the train until I found a porter. I grabbed his arm
and he set down the suitcases he was carrying.

"Listen," I said. "How soon before we get to Chicago?"

"We're due there in less than a"—he looked at his watch—"fawty minutes, suh."

"What's the next train out of Chicago back to New York?" I said. "I mean, the nearest one after the time we arrive in Chicago?"

He stared at me.

"You mean you want to go back?"

"Yeah, yeah," I said. "Do you know, or don't you?"

He pulled out a batch of timetables, selected one, and hunted through it.

"There's one leaves, let's see, eight, nine, eleven, there's one leaves eleven minutes after this one arrives, suh, but I don't think—"

I didn't have time to listen to confessions.

"Never mind," I said quickly. "Just check on the time. Eleven minutes after this train hits Chicago there's one going back to New York. Right?"

He looked at the timetable again.

"That's right, suh. But—"

"Thanks," I said.

I gave him a coin and went back to the observation platform.

"I've got some bad news for you, Dick." I put my arm across his shoulder and held him close to me, so that he couldn't see my face as I talked. "I just got a telegram on the train. We'll have to call the trip off on account of business. I hate to do it, Dick, but it can't be helped. We're due in Chicago in about a half hour," I said. "There's a train leaving back for New York ten minutes later. I'm putting you on that train, Dick."

"Aren't you coming back too, Dad?" he asked in a small voice.

"No," I said. "I can't. That is," I added quickly, "not right now." Why should I let her think she won for good? Let it worry her for a while; let it hang over her. "I'll be coming back for you in a little while," I said. "Maybe in a month or so. As soon as I finish up my business here out west. Be sure and tell that to your mother, will you?"

"Yes, Dad."

"Tell her I had to send you back for the time being, for business reasons. But be sure to tell her I'm coming back for you."

I wondered what good it was doing me to lie about it.

"Yes, Dad."

It wasn't doing me any good.

"Don't forget to tell her," I repeated.

I held him in my arms all the rest of the way, but it didn't help. I couldn't think of a thing.

When the train reached the station I left him on the platform with the baggage.

"Wait right here for me," I said.

I hurried inside and bought his ticket. On the way back I passed a telegraph stand. I hesitated for a moment. But I figured the hell with her. She was getting enough as it was. Why should I give her the additional pleasure of the hours that she would be waiting for him, knowing he was on his way back? I hurried up to him.

"Here's your ticket, son," I said, putting it into his pocket, "and here's some money. Take a taxi right home as soon as you get to New York."

A porter picked up the bags and began to carry them to the train. I held Dick's hand and talked as we followed the porter.

"And don't forget to tell Mother what I told you," I said.

"I won't, Dad." He looked happier already. Well, at least I wasn't making a mistake from his angle. And that was all that counted now, no matter *what* she'd think.

We climbed the steps of the observation platform. I gave some money to a porter and told him to keep an eye on him.

"Yes, *suh*," the porter said with a grin.

"All aboard!" a conductor called.

I got off the platform. Suddenly he reached down and threw his arms around my neck. Well, at least it was something to know that it wasn't *only* the hockey games and the fights and the promises. He held me for a moment, tight. The train began to move. His arms slipped away from me.

"Goodby, son," I said, walking with the slow-moving train.

"Goodby, Dad," he said, rubbing his nose with the back of his hand quickly.

A month before I didn't even know I *had* a son. And now—

"Take care of yourself," I said, walking faster to keep up with the train, and raising my voice. "And don't forget. I'm coming back for you."

He smiled a little and said something, but I didn't hear him.

"Don't forget to tell her," I called, holding my hat as I trotted. "I'm coming back for you!"

Lord, how I hated that woman! The only thing she ever gave me that I could love she wouldn't let me keep.

"Don't forget to tell her!" I cried. I stopped running. I had reached the end of the platform. The train was moving away from me swiftly. I cupped my hands to my mouth and shouted. "Don't forget to tell her," I lied. "Tell her I'm coming back for you!"

ABOUT THE AUTHOR

JEROME WEIDMAN, novelist and short-story writer, was born in 1913 on New York's Lower East Side. At the age of twenty-four, he was studying law at New York University when his first novel, *I Can Get It for You Wholesale*, was published in 1937. He quit law school at once to devote all his time to writing, and has been doing so ever since, except during the war, when he served with the Office of War Information in this country and overseas. He has traveled extensively in America and the far corners of the world, from which he has brought back raw material for a dozen novels and approximately two hundred short stories, published in almost every magazine in the United States as well as in Canada, Europe, Australia and Asia. His books have been translated into eight languages. His first play, *Fiorello!*, written in collaboration with George Abbott, was awarded the 1959 Pulitzer Prize. His second play, *Tenderloin*, also written with George Abbott, is now running simultaneously on Broadway. MY FATHER SITS IN THE DARK, his eighteenth book, was finished in New York City, to which Mr. Weidman, his wife, and his two sons have returned after living in Westport, Connecticut, for a dozen years.